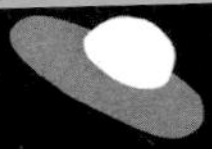

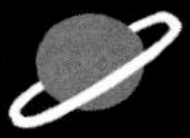

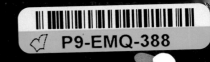

FOR LISA THOMSON,
MY BFF IN HIGH SCHOOL AND HAPPILY EVER AFTER

Graphic Universe™
A division of Lerner Publishing Group, Inc.
241 First Avenue North
Minneapolis, MN 55401 USA

For reading levels and more information, look up this title at www.lernerbooks.com.

Library of Congress Cataloging-in-Publication Data

Names: MariNaomi, author, illustrator.
Title: Losing the girl / by MariNaomi.
Description: Minneapolis : Graphic Universe, [2018] | Series: Life on Earth ;
    book 1 | Summary: As Blithedale searches for a missing girl, rumored to be
    abducted by aliens, a group of high school students experiences a series
    of romantic relationships and their effects on friendships.
Identifiers: LCCN 2017006225 (print) | LCCN 2017033504 (ebook) | ISBN
    9781512498578 (eb pdf) | ISBN 9781512449105 (lb : alk. paper)
Subjects: LCSH: Graphic novels. | CYAC: Graphic novels. | Dating (Social
    customs)—Fiction. | Friendship—Fiction. | Missing children—Fiction. | Alien
    abduction—Fiction.
Classification: LCC PZ7.7.M339 (ebook) | LCC PZ7.7.M339 Los 2018 (print) | DDC
    [Fic]—dc23

LC record available at https://lccn.loc.gov/2017006225

Manufactured in the United States of America
1-42842-26506-5/17/2017

LIFE ON EARTH · BOOK 1

LOSING THE GIRL

MARINAOMI

Graphic Universe™ · Minneapolis

PART ONE

Nigel Jones

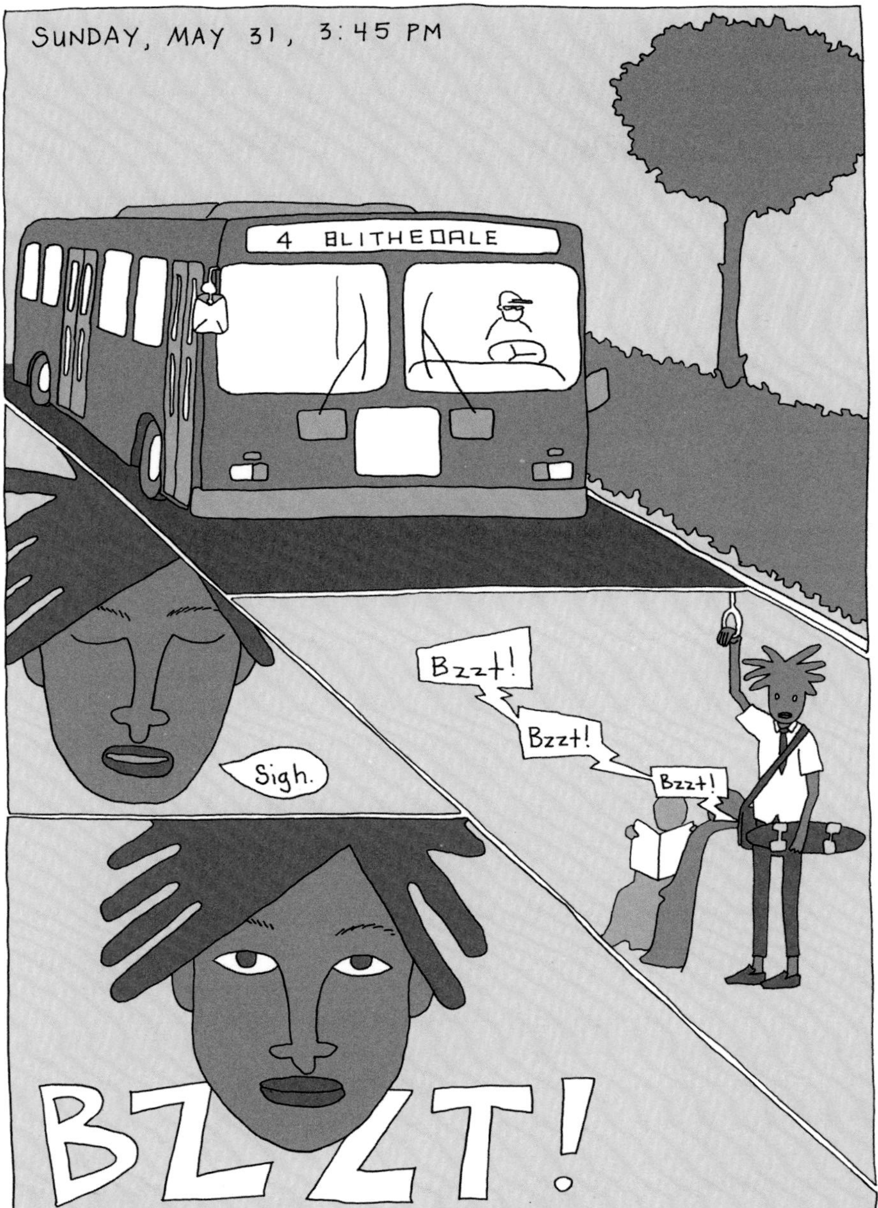
SUNDAY, MAY 31, 3:45 PM
4 BLITHEDALE
Sigh.
Bzzt!
Bzzt!
Bzzt!
BZZT!

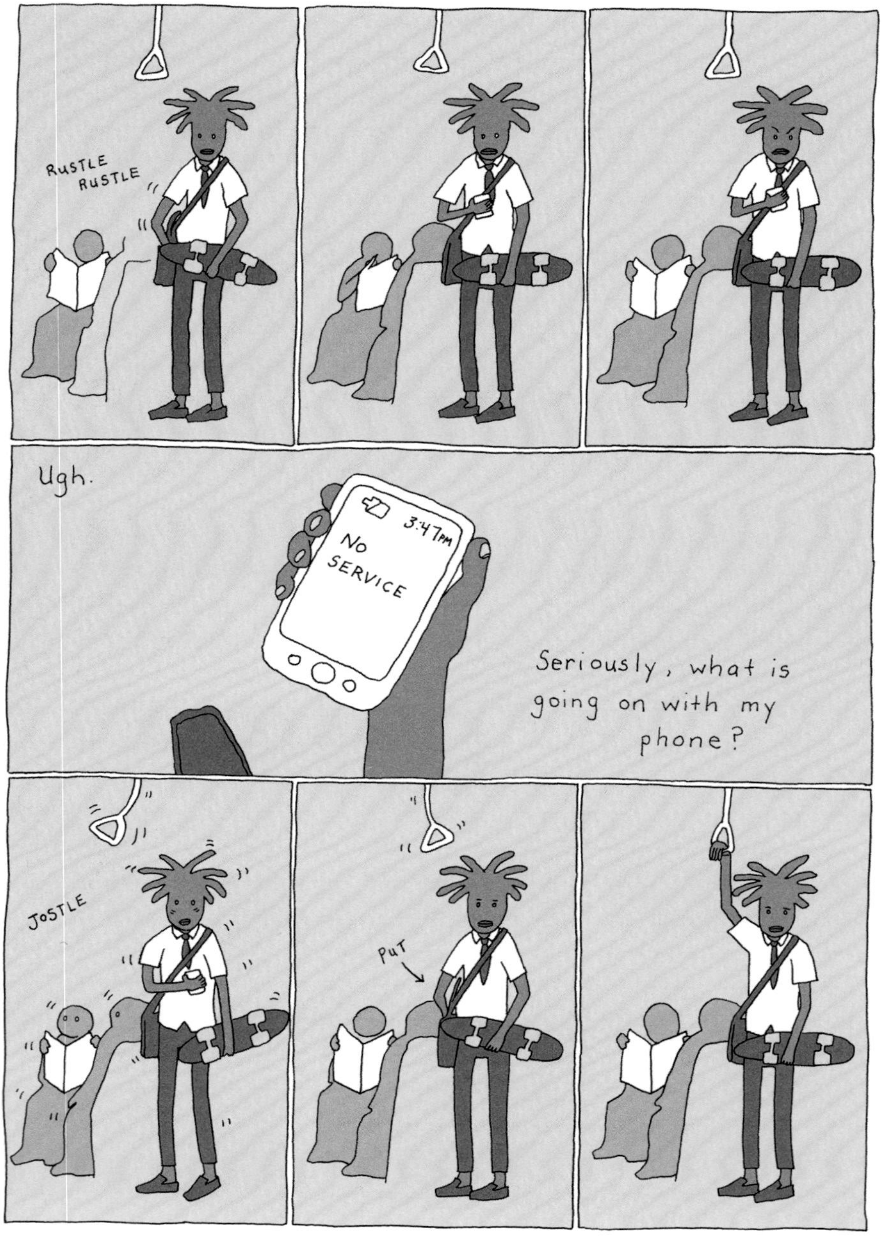
RUSTLE
RUSTLE
Ugh.
3:47PM
NO
SERVICE
Seriously, what is going on with my phone?
JOSTLE
PUT

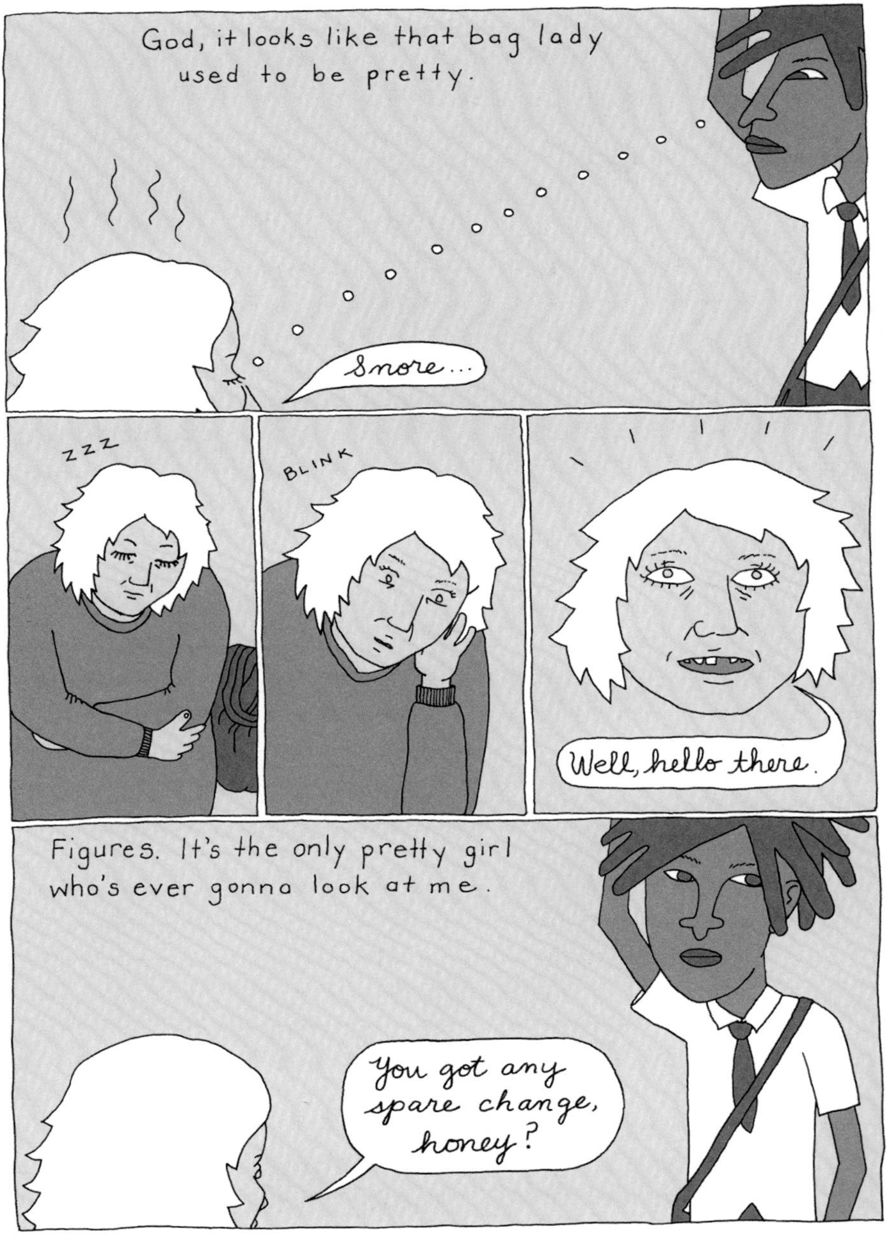
God, it looks like that bag lady used to be pretty.
Snore...
ZZZ
BLINK
Well, hello there.
Figures. It's the only pretty girl who's ever gonna look at me.
You got any spare change, honey?

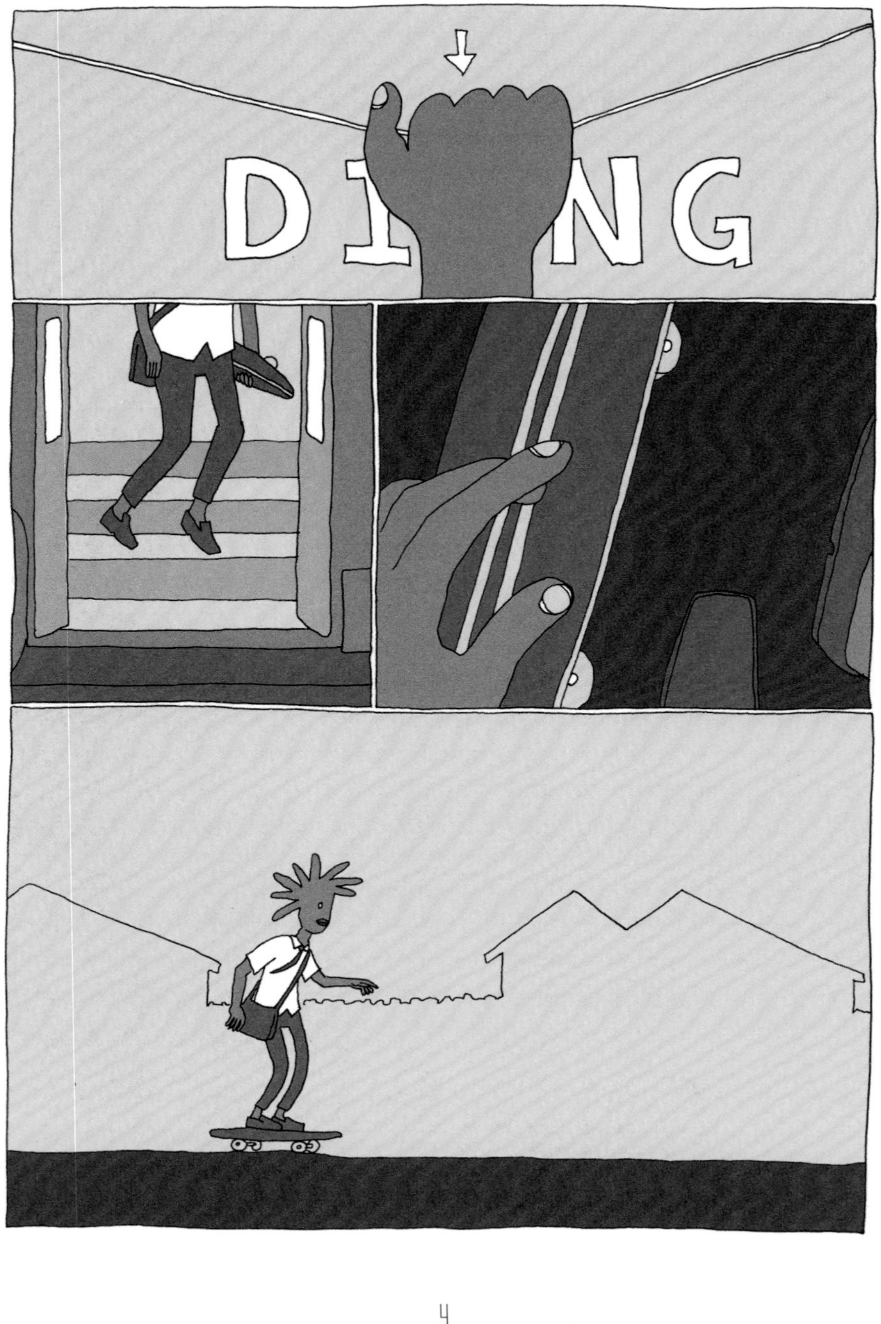
DI NG

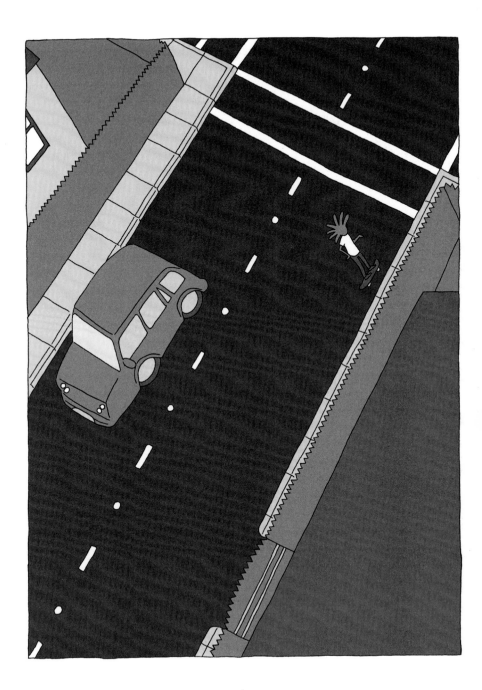

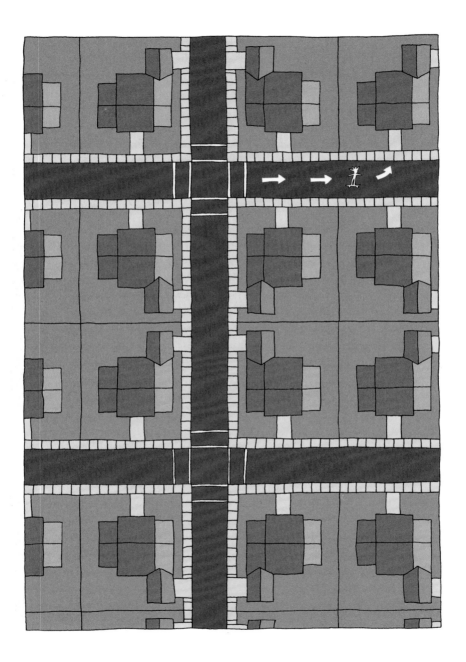

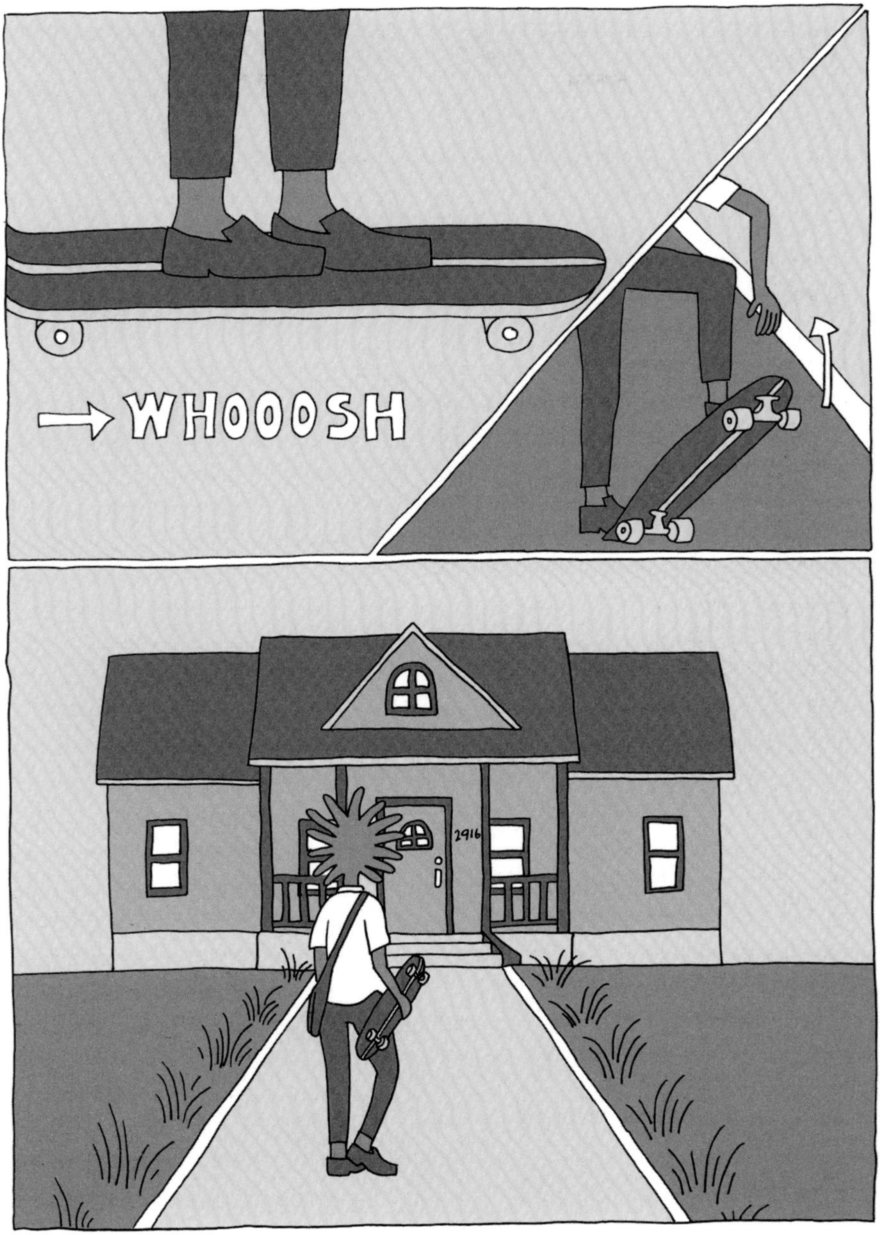
WHOOOSH
2916

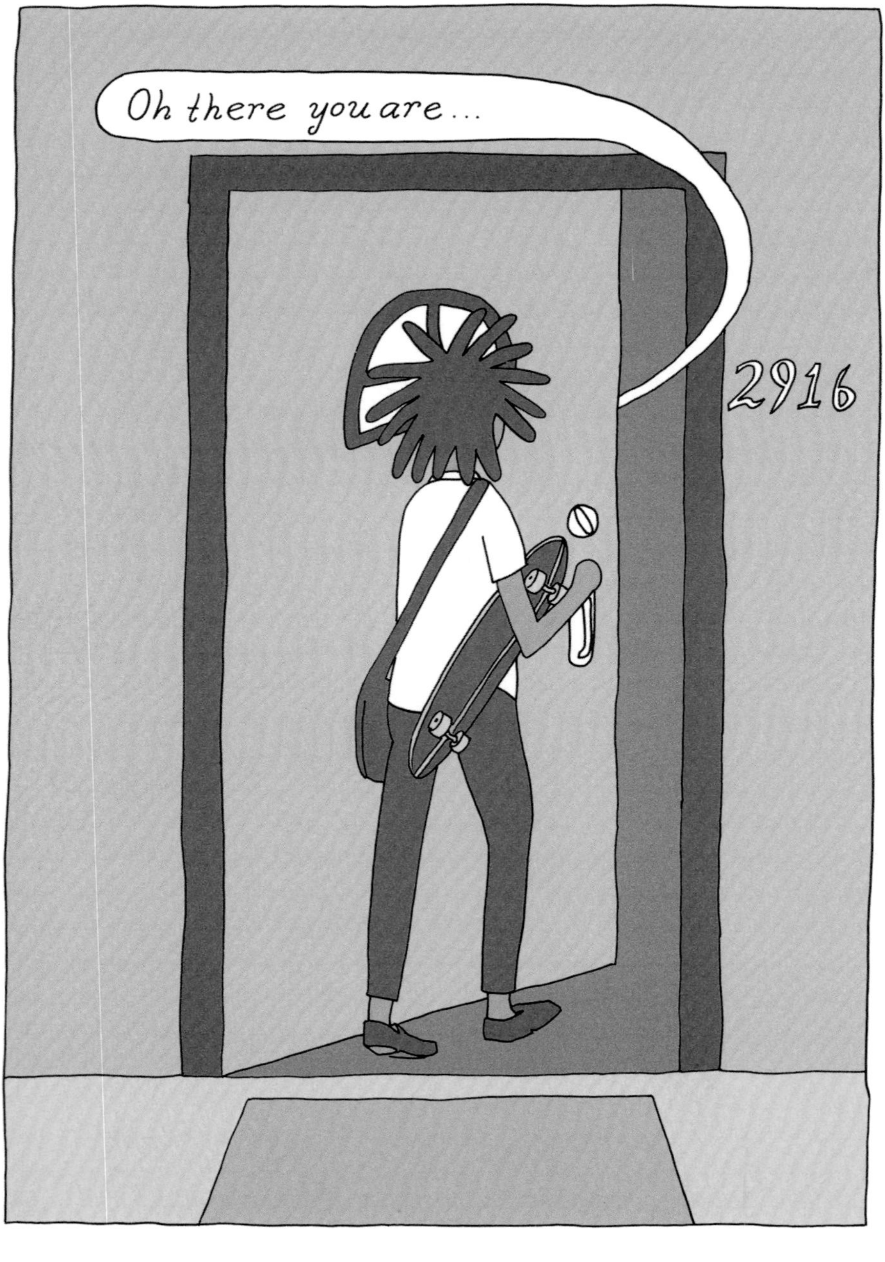
Oh there you are...
2916

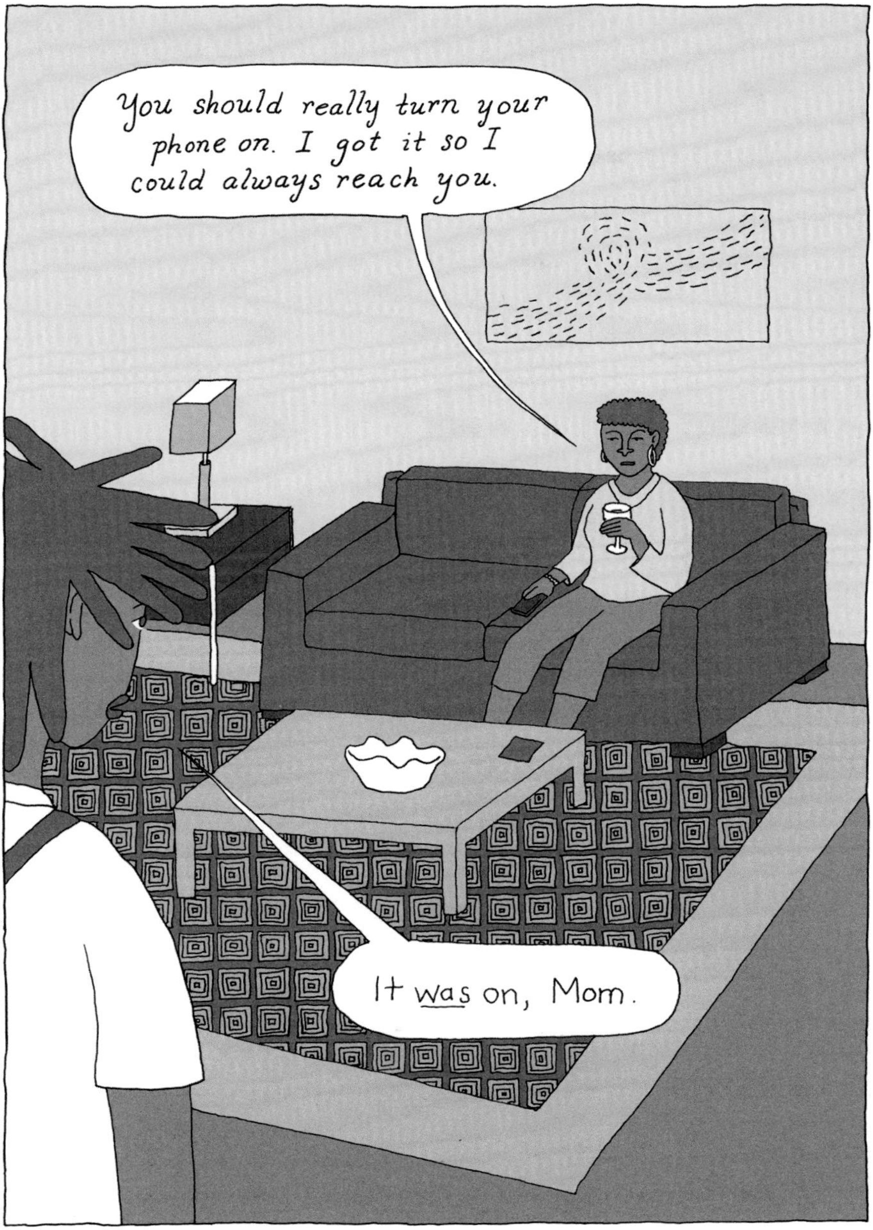
You should really turn your phone on. I got it so I could always reach you.
It was on, Mom.

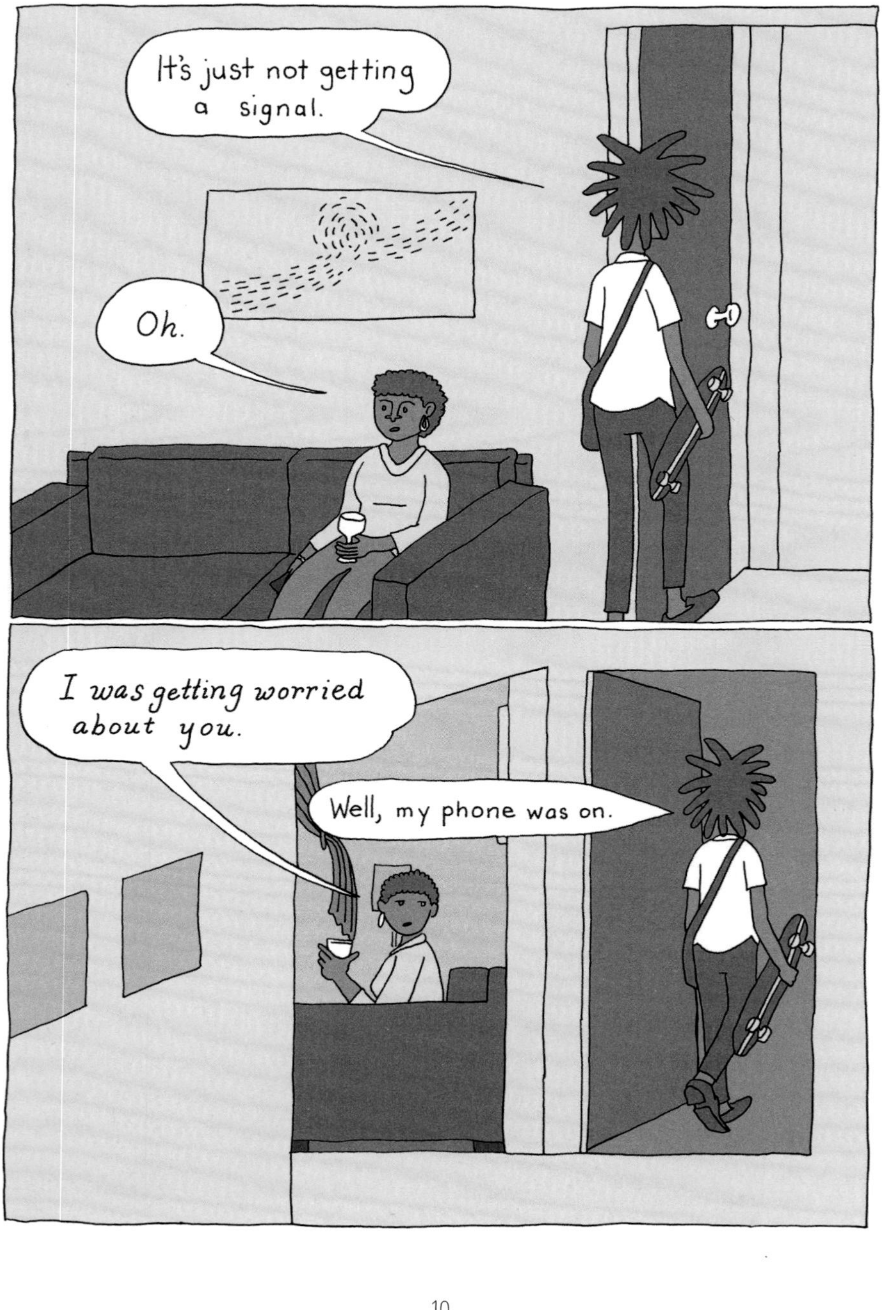
It's just not getting a signal.
Oh.
I was getting worried about you.
Well, my phone was on.

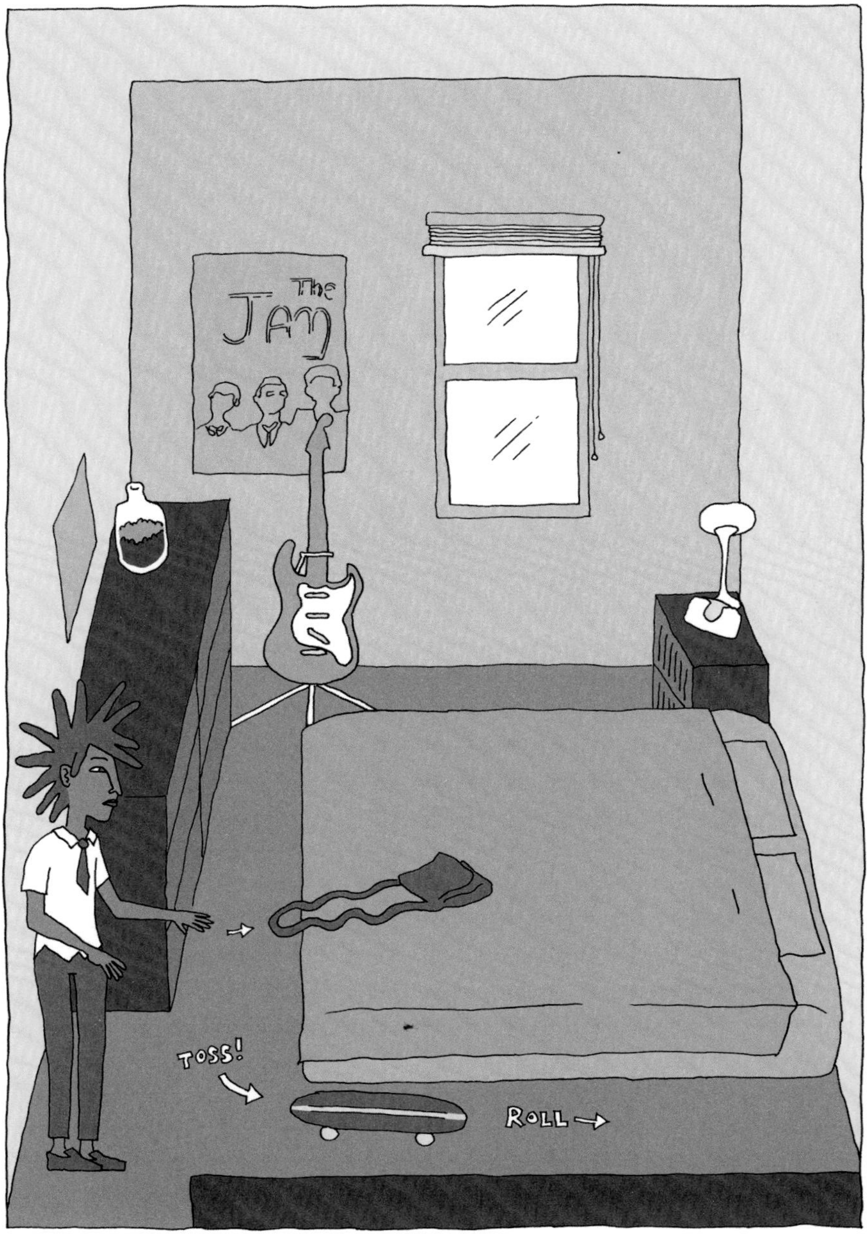
The JAM
TOSS!
ROLL →

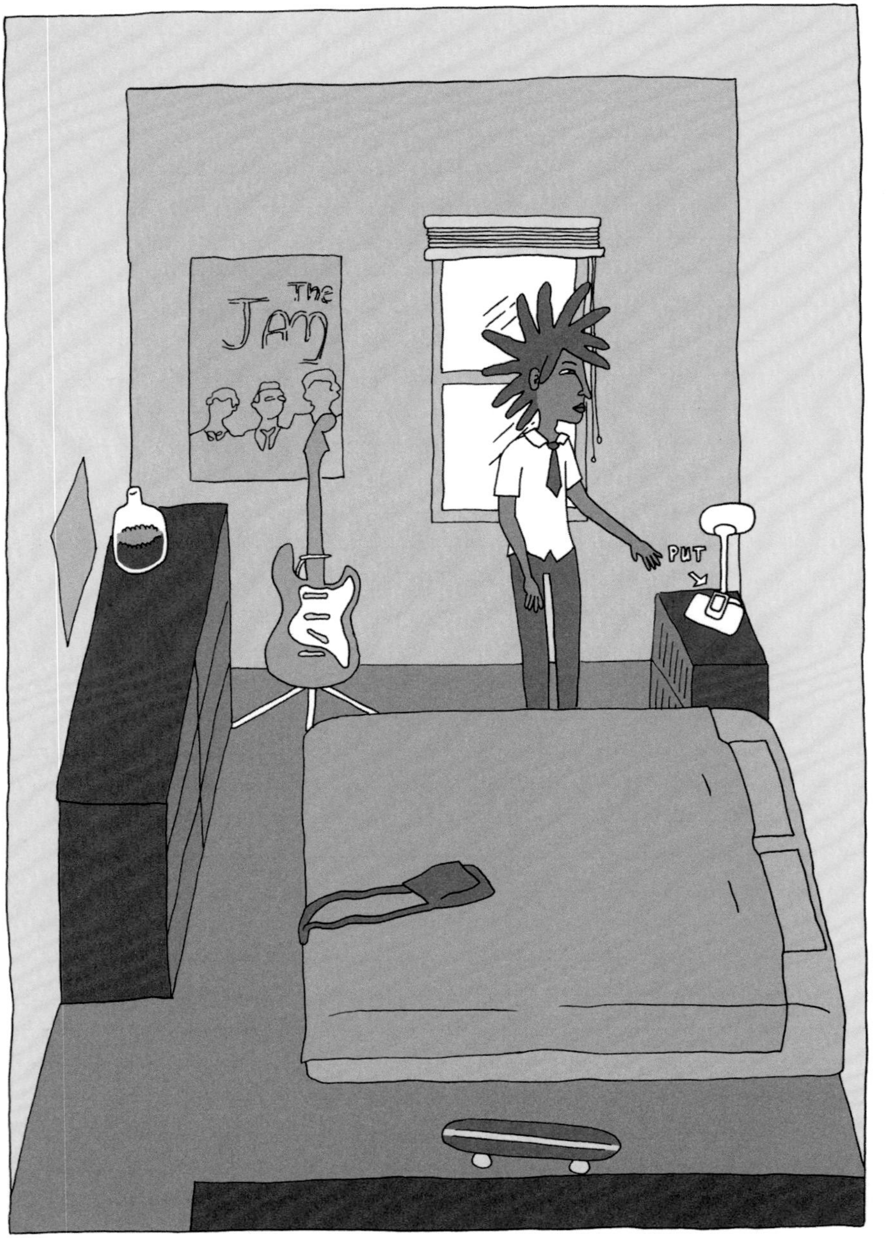
The JAM
PUT

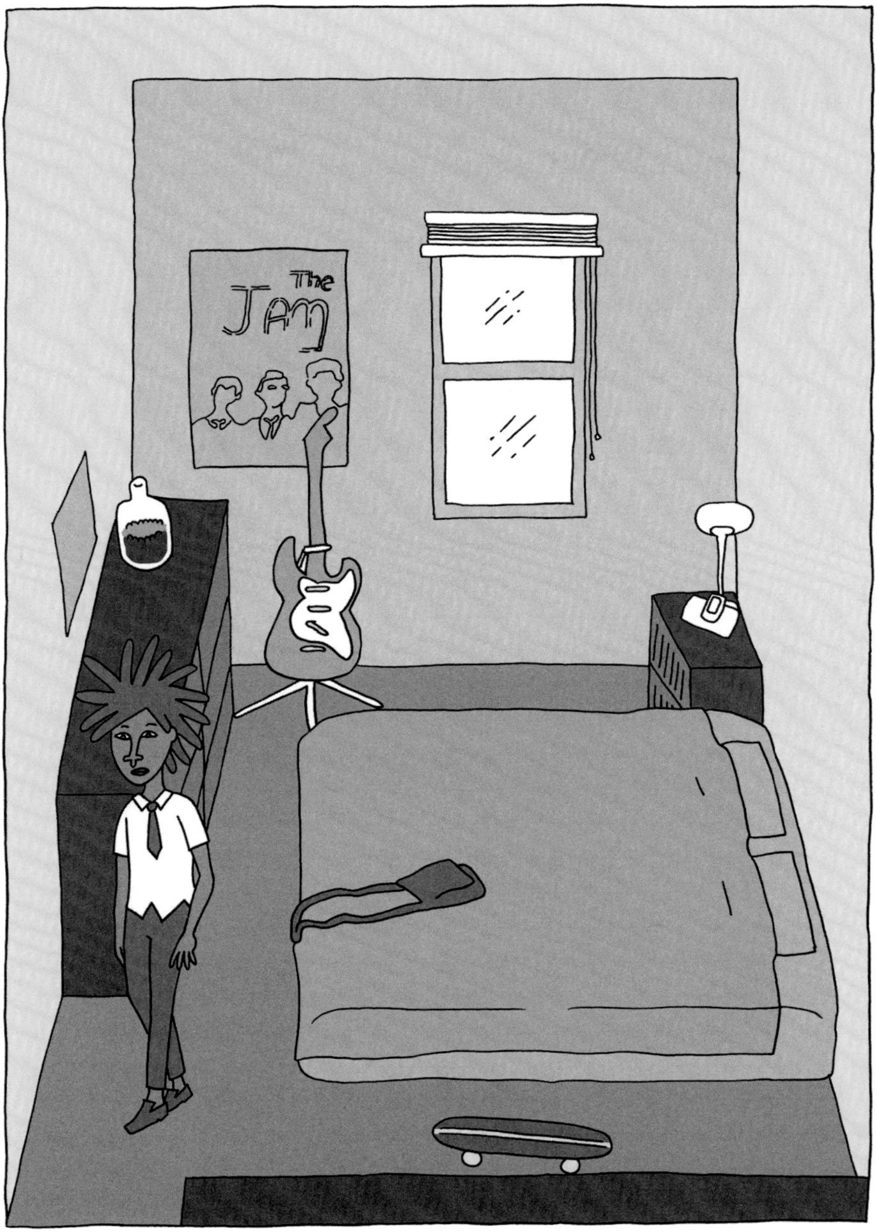
The
JAM

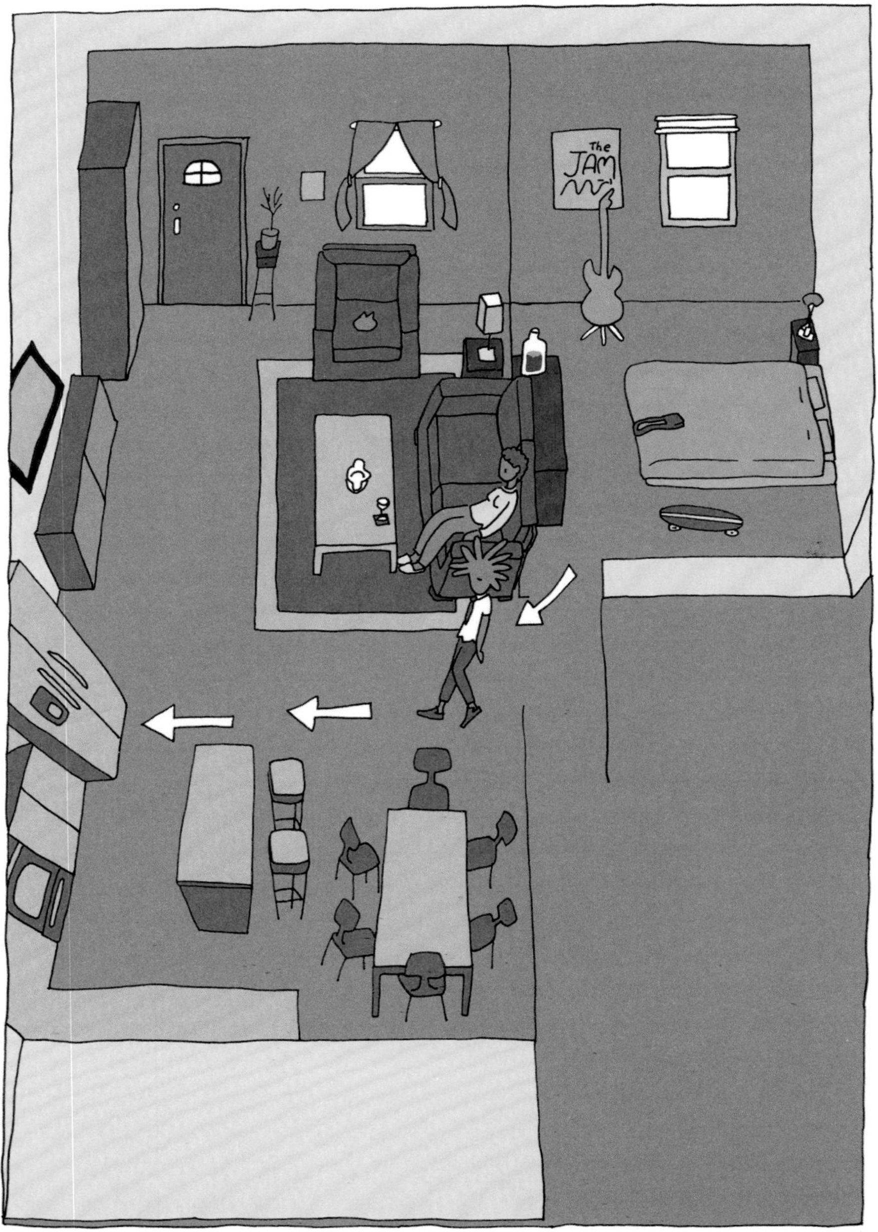
The JAM

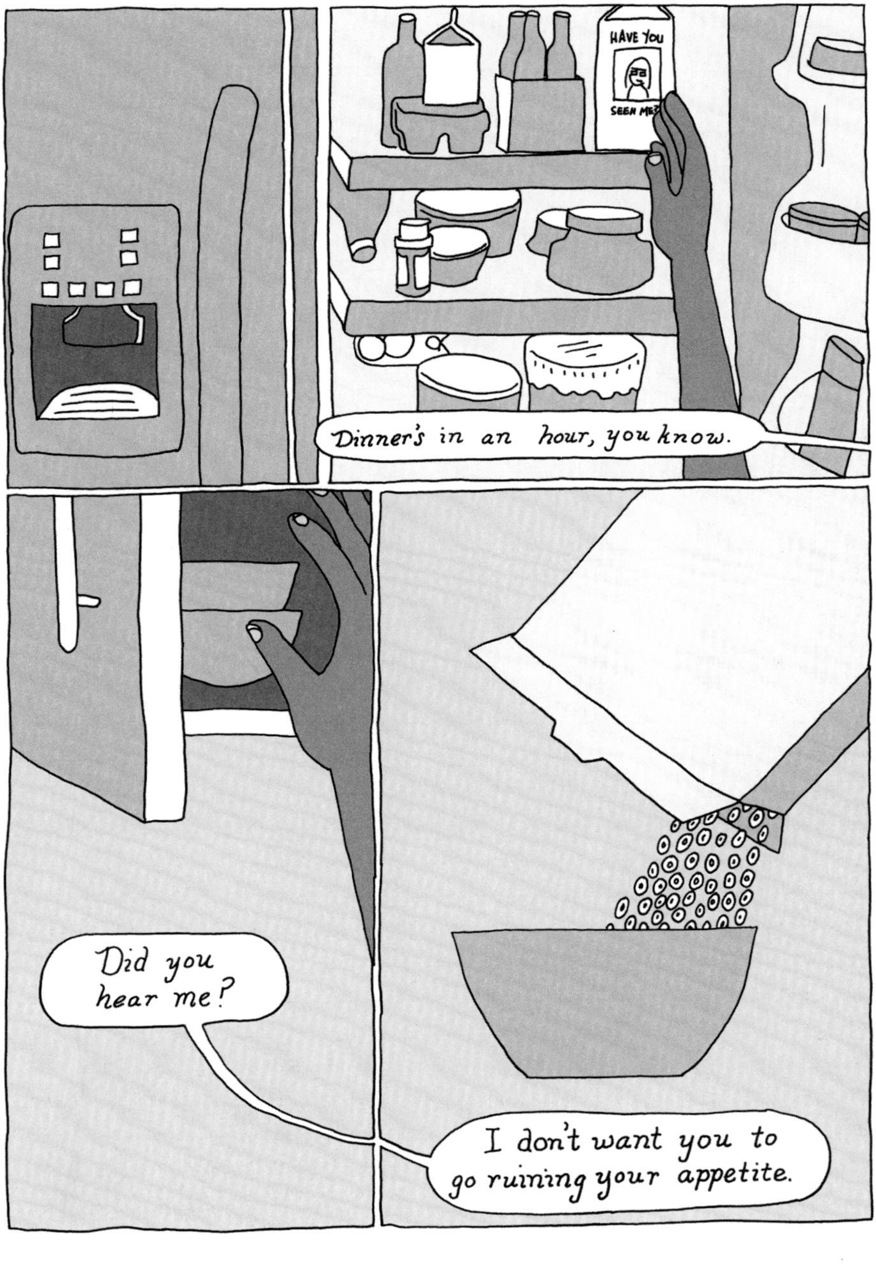
HAVE YOU
SEEN ME?
Dinner's in an hour, you know.
Did you hear me?
I don't want you to go ruining your appetite.

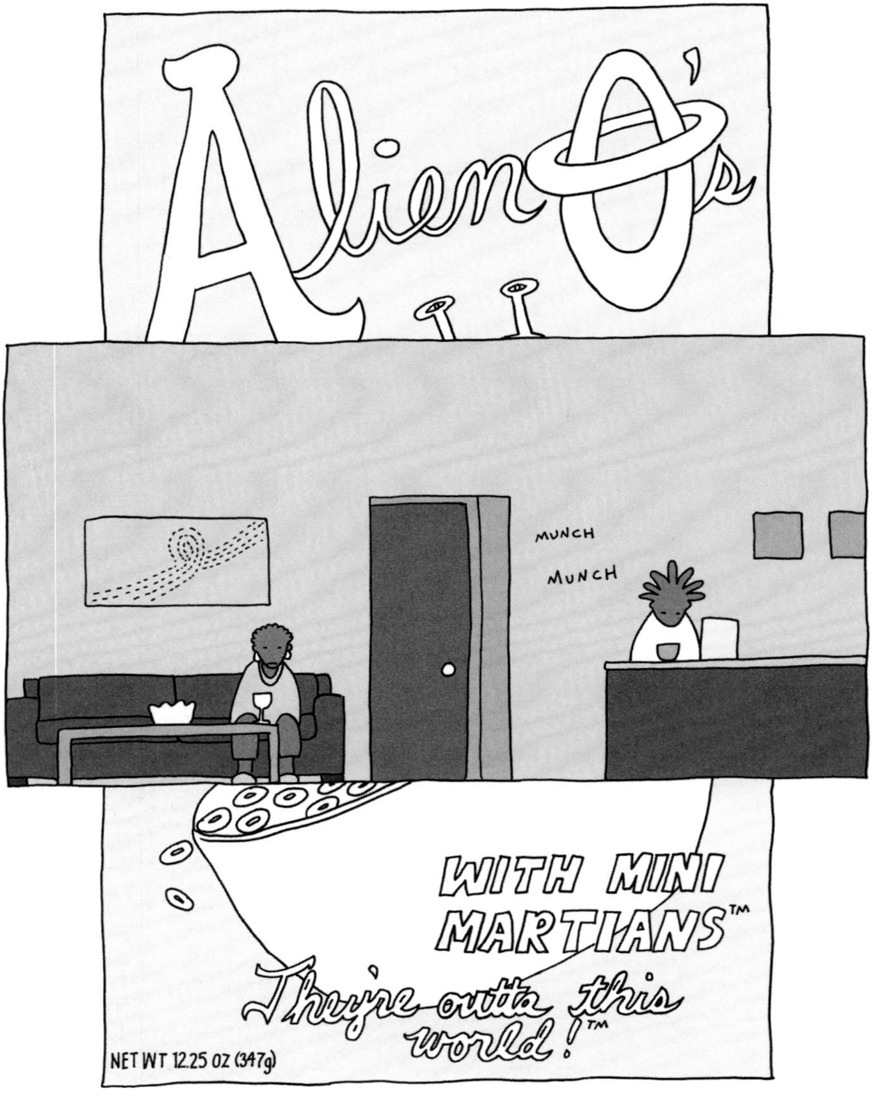

Alien O's
MUNCH
MUNCH
WITH MINI MARTIANS™
They're outta this world!™
NET WT 12.25 oz (347g)

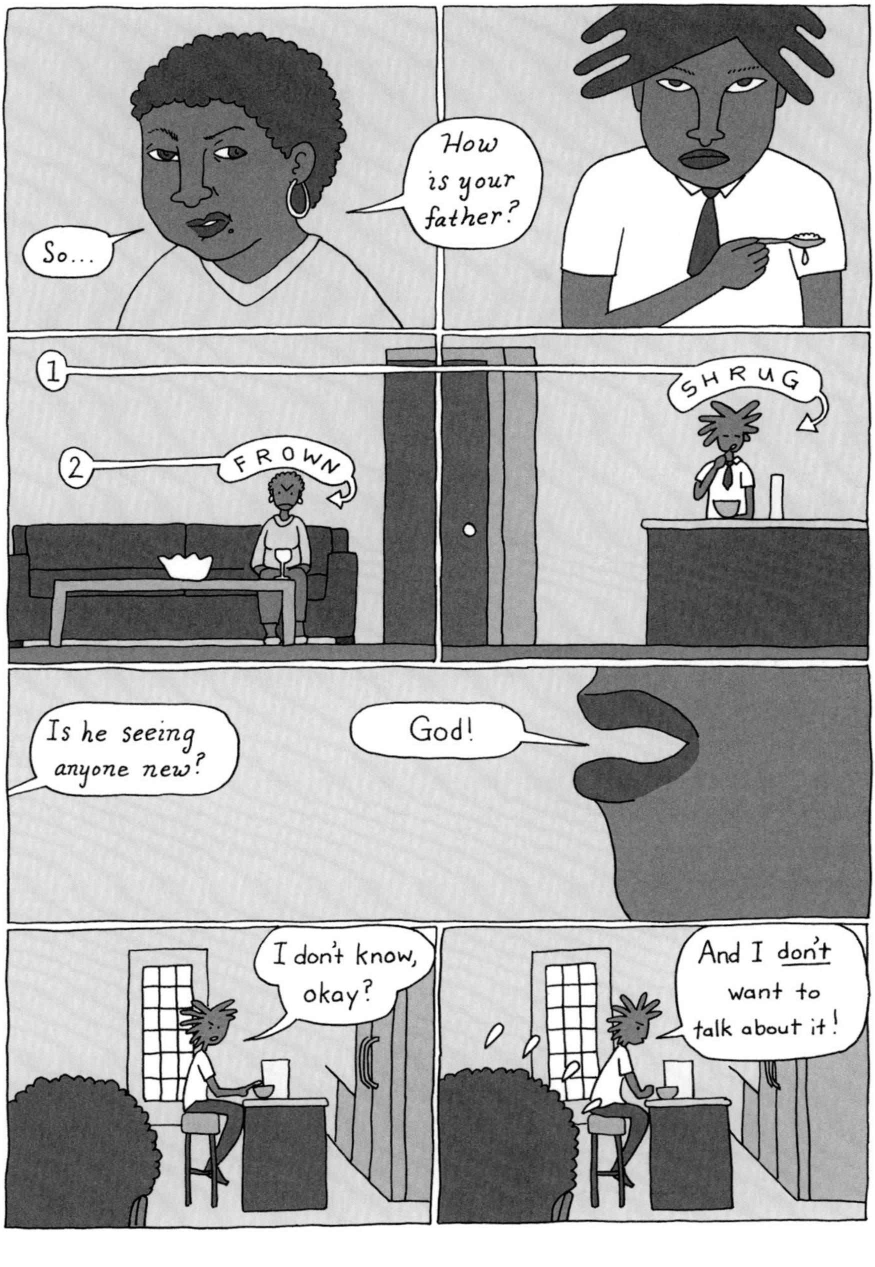
So...
How is your father?
1
SHRUG
2
FROWN
Is he seeing anyone new?
God!
I don't know, okay?
And I don't want to talk about it!

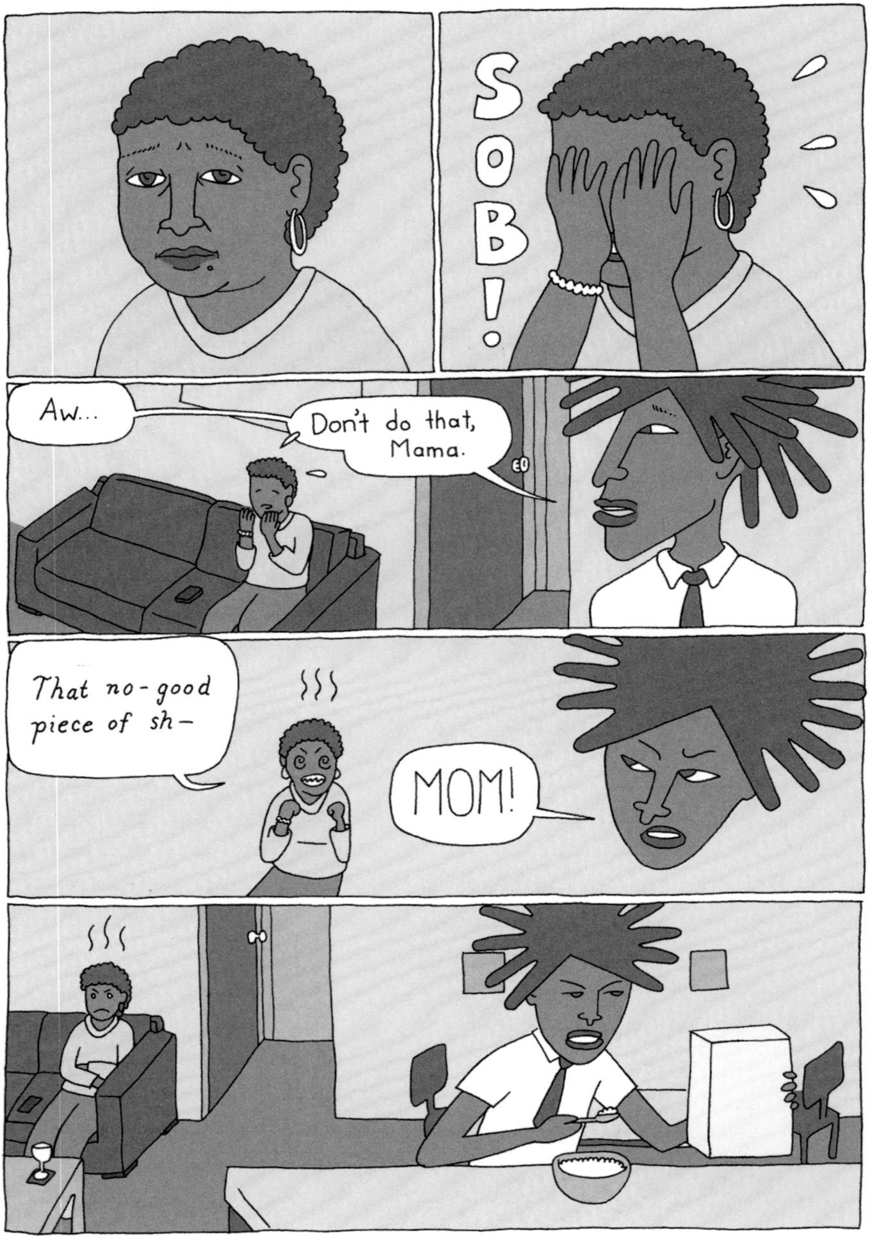
SOB!
Aw...
Don't do that, Mama.
That no-good piece of sh–
MOM!

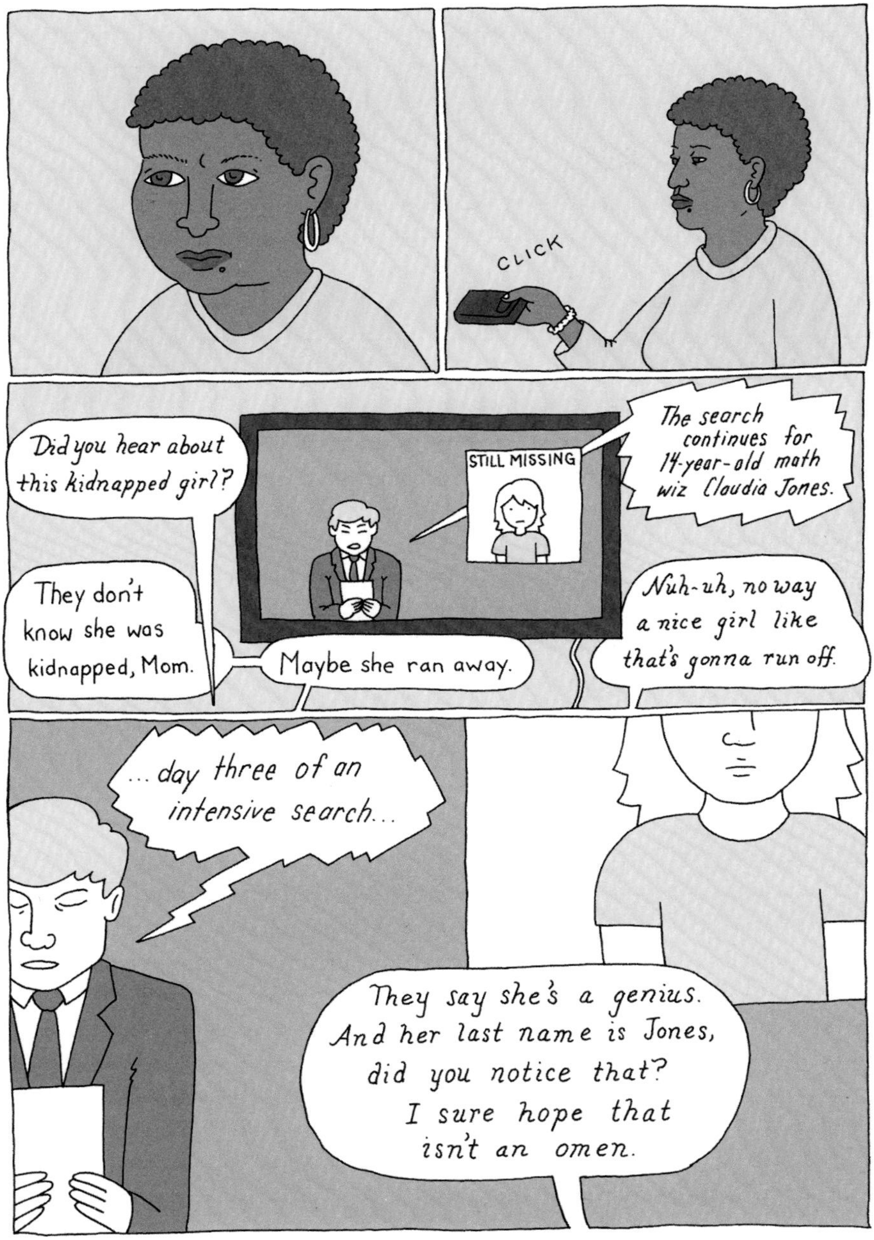
CLICK
Did you hear about this kidnapped girl?
STILL MISSING
The search continues for 14-year-old math wiz Claudia Jones.
They don't know she was kidnapped, Mom.
Maybe she ran away.
Nuh-uh, no way a nice girl like that's gonna run off.
...day three of an intensive search...
They say she's a genius. And her last name is Jones, did you notice that? I sure hope that isn't an omen.

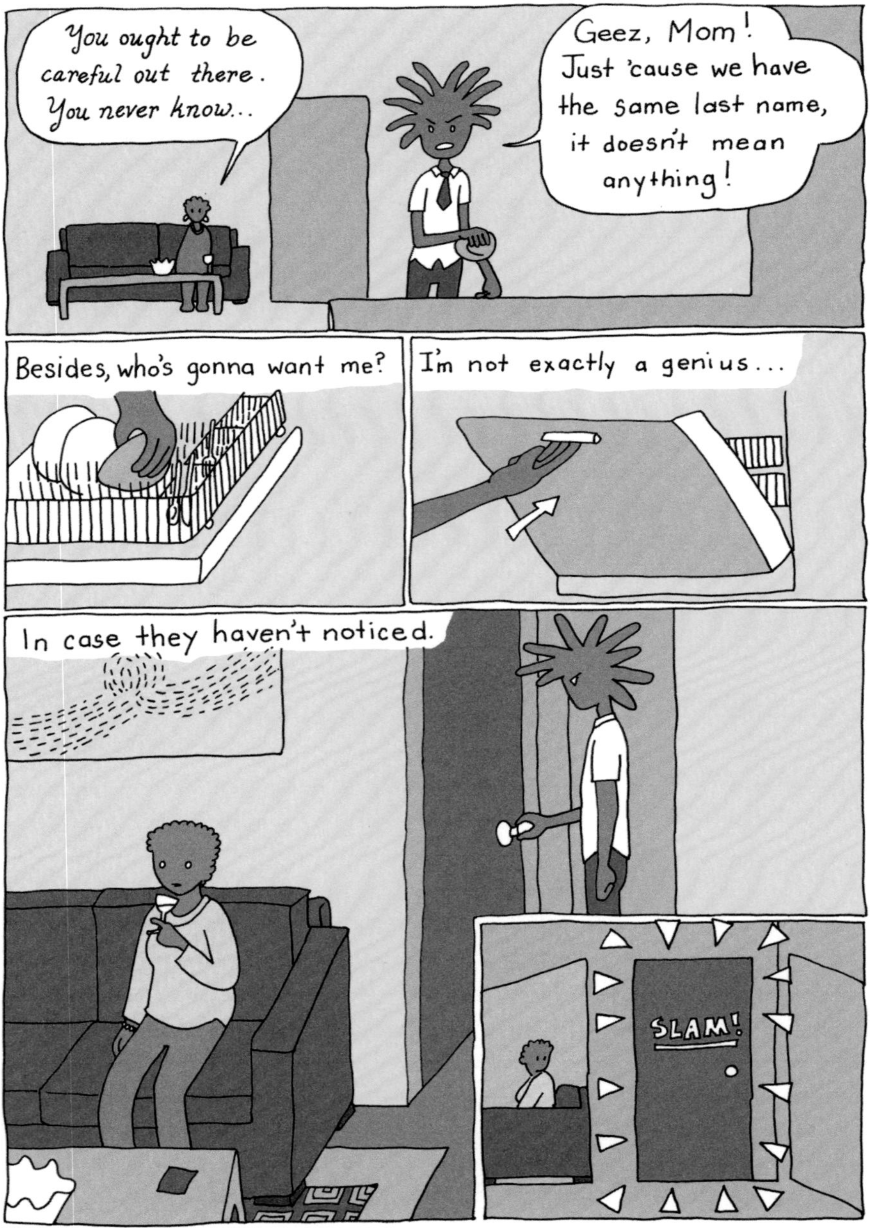
You ought to be careful out there. You never know...
Geez, Mom! Just 'cause we have the same last name, it doesn't mean anything!
Besides, who's gonna want me?
I'm not exactly a genius...
In case they haven't noticed.
SLAM!

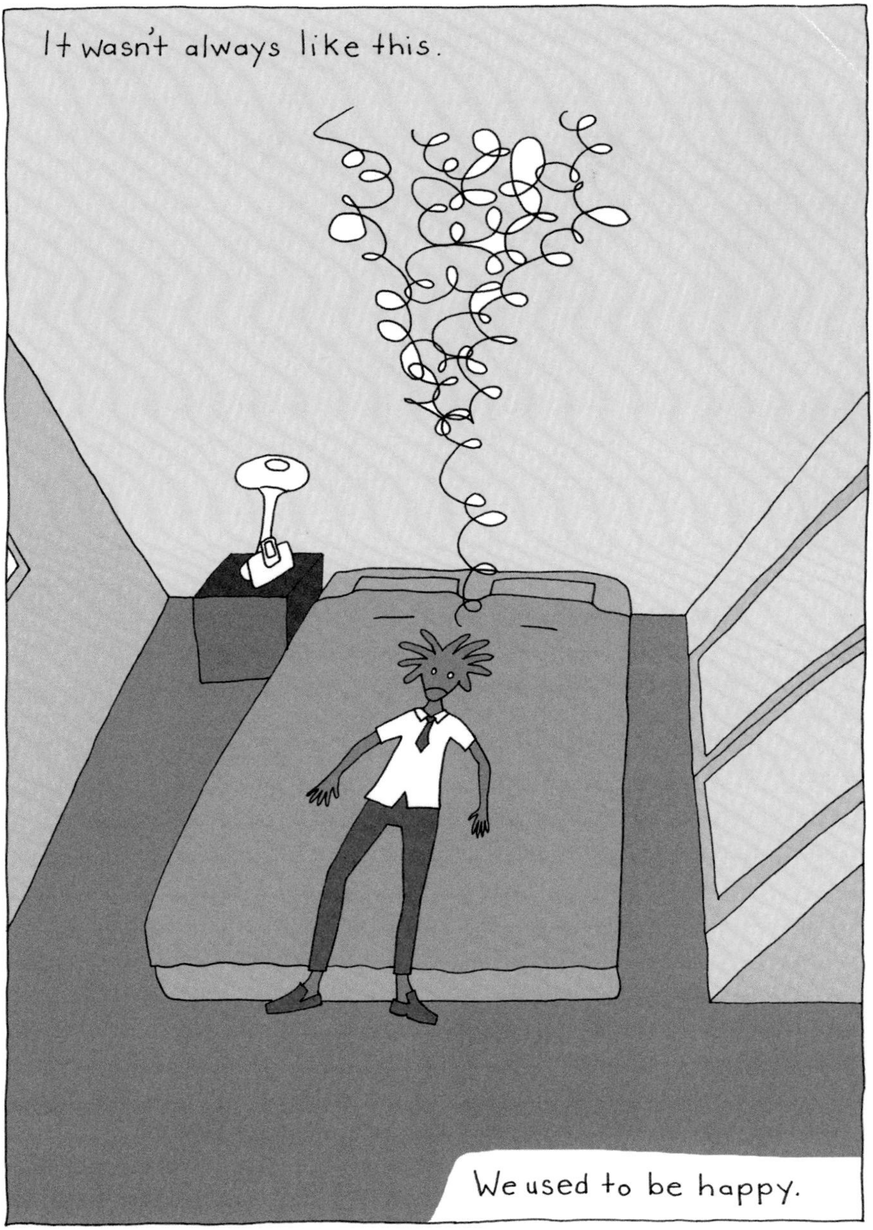
It wasn't always like this.
We used to be happy.

They were supposed to be together forever, but apparently all those movies and love songs lie.

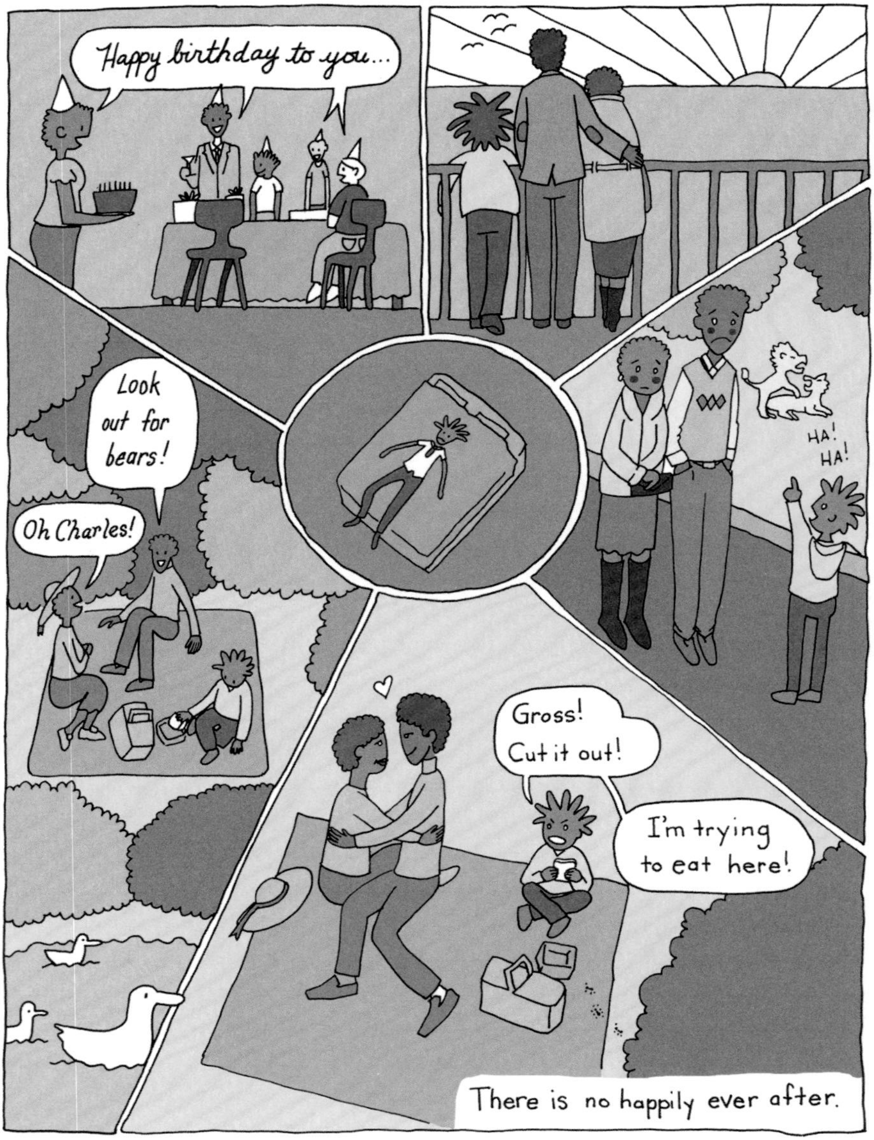

Happy birthday to you...
Look out for bears!
Oh Charles!
HA! HA!
Gross! Cut it out!
I'm trying to eat here!

There is no happily ever after.

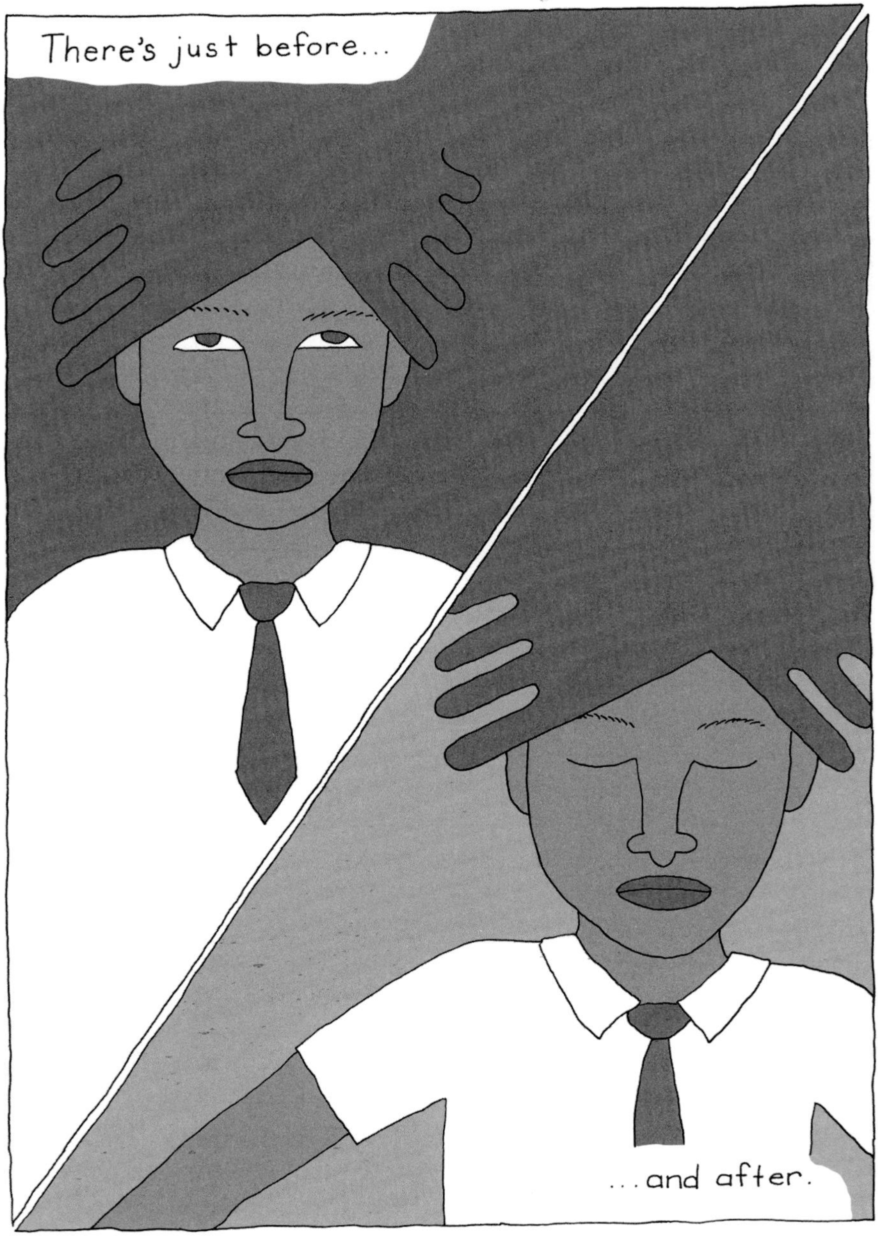
There's just before...
...and after.

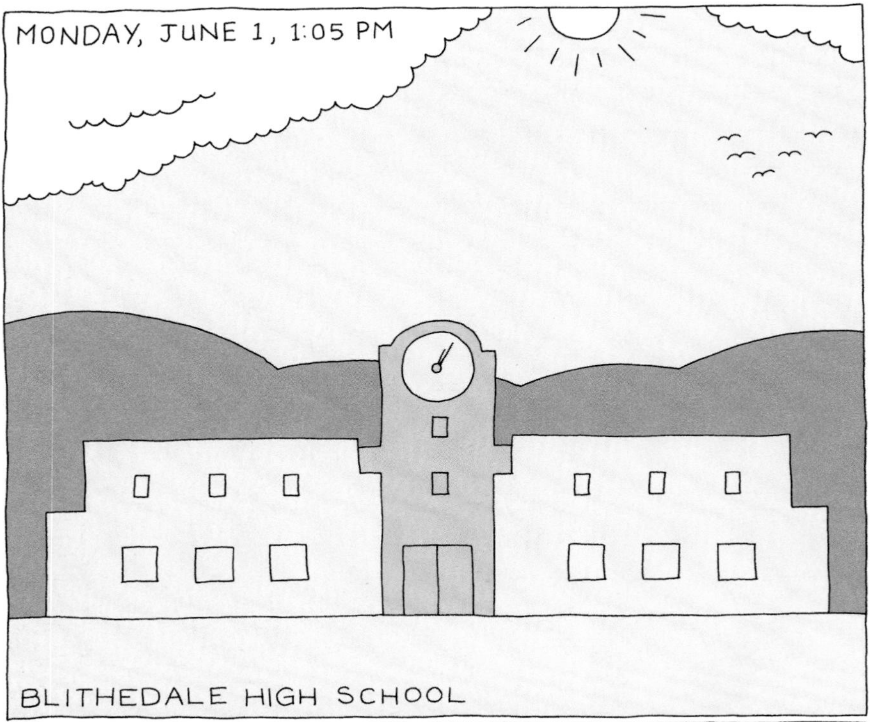
MONDAY, JUNE 1, 1:05 PM
BLITHEDALE HIGH SCHOOL

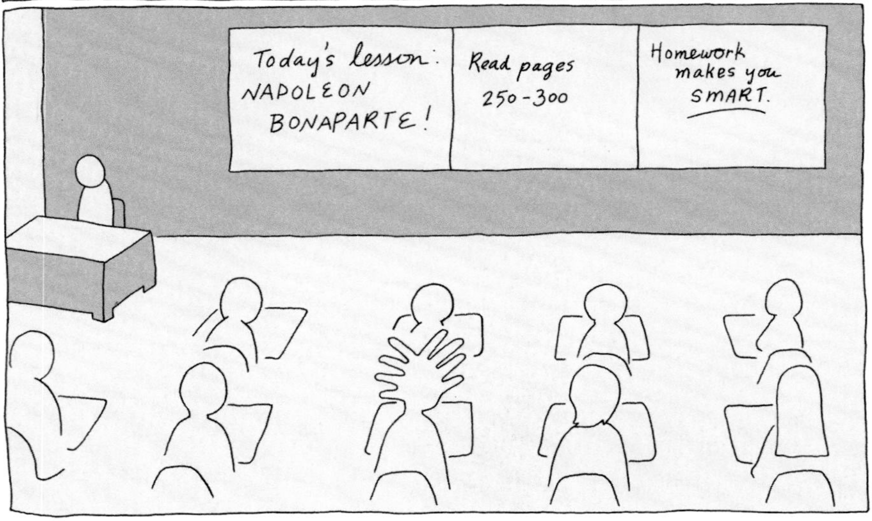
Today's lesson: NAPOLEON BONAPARTE!
Read pages 250-300
Homework makes you SMART.

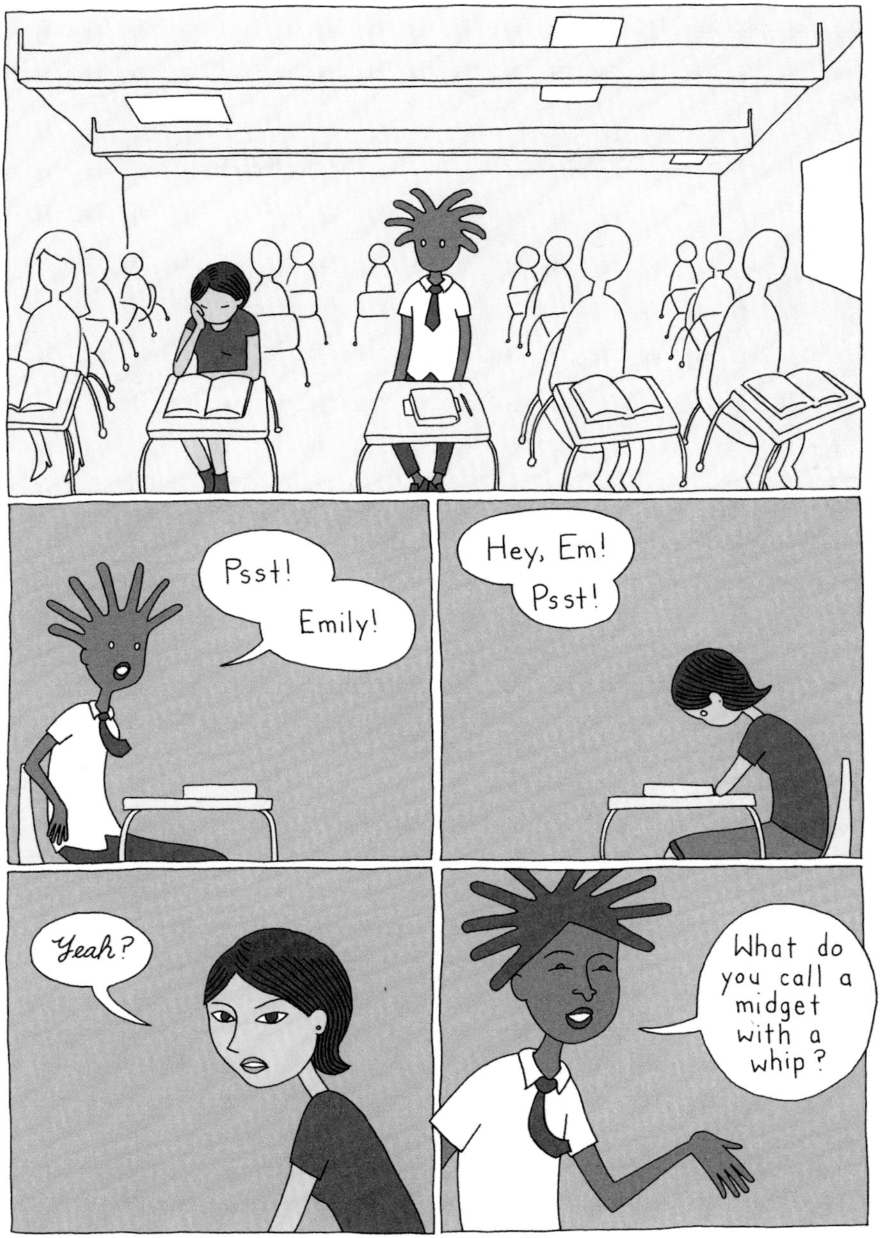
Psst!
Emily!
Hey, Em!
Psst!
Yeah?
What do you call a midget with a whip?

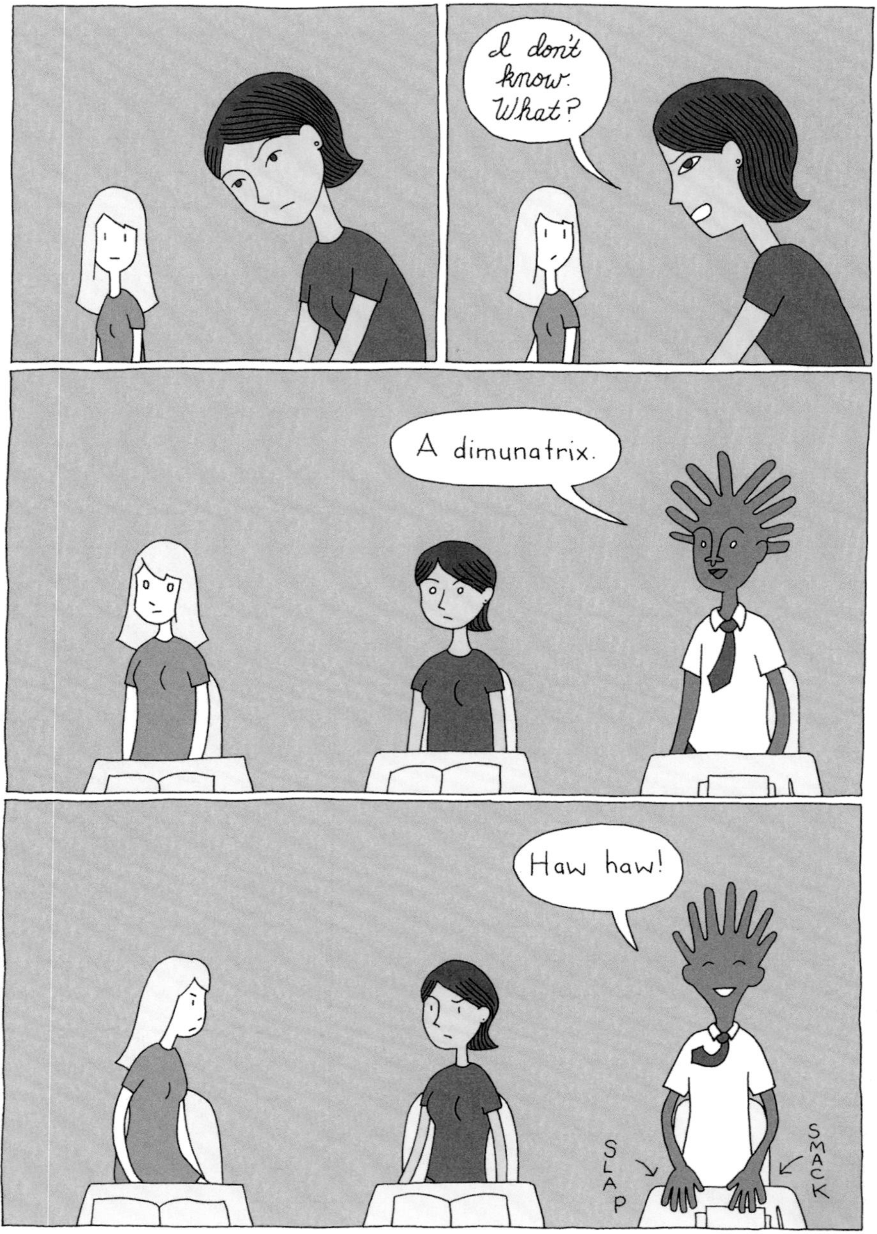
I don't know. What?
A dimunatrix.
Haw haw!
SLAP
SMACK

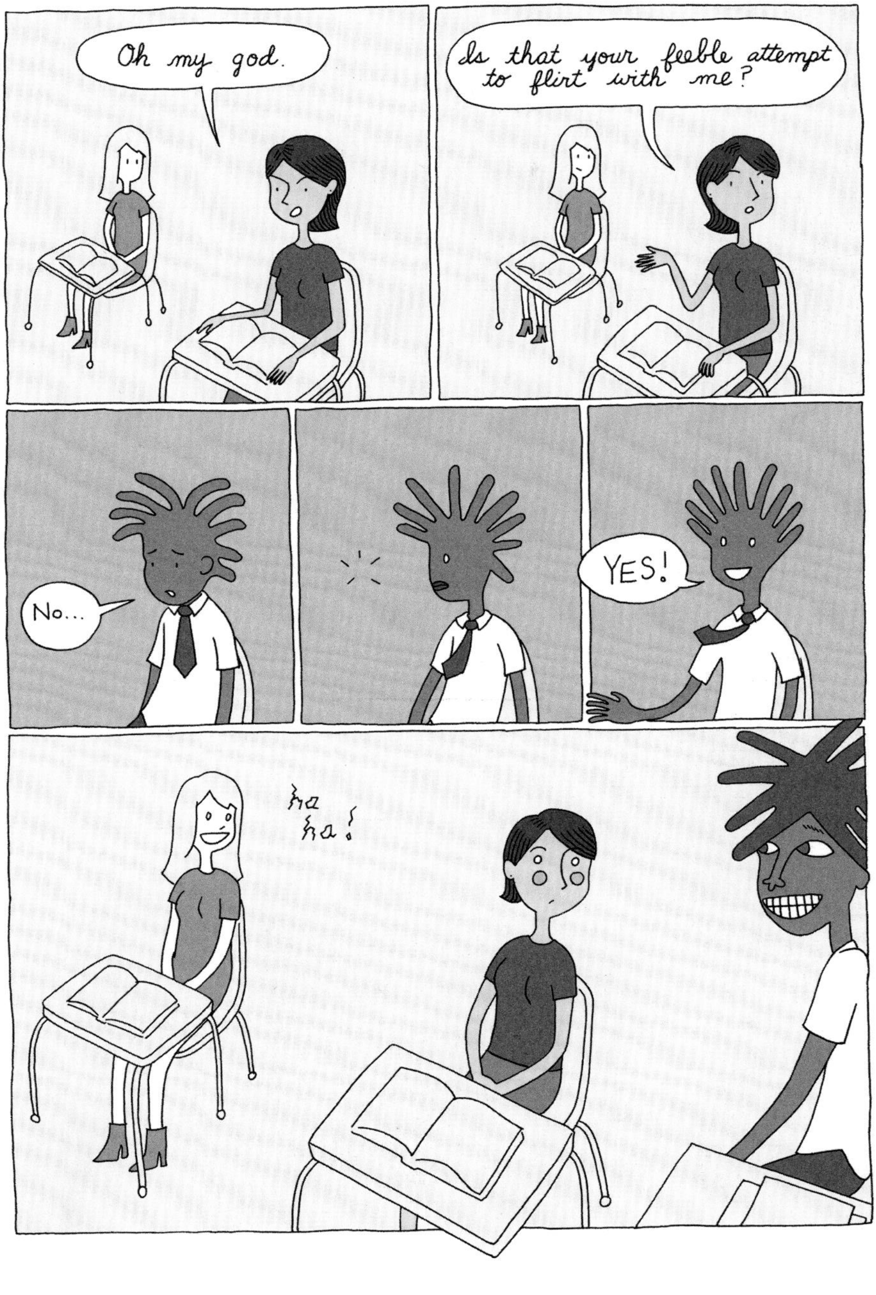
Oh my god.
Is that your feeble attempt to flirt with me?
No...
YES!
ha ha!

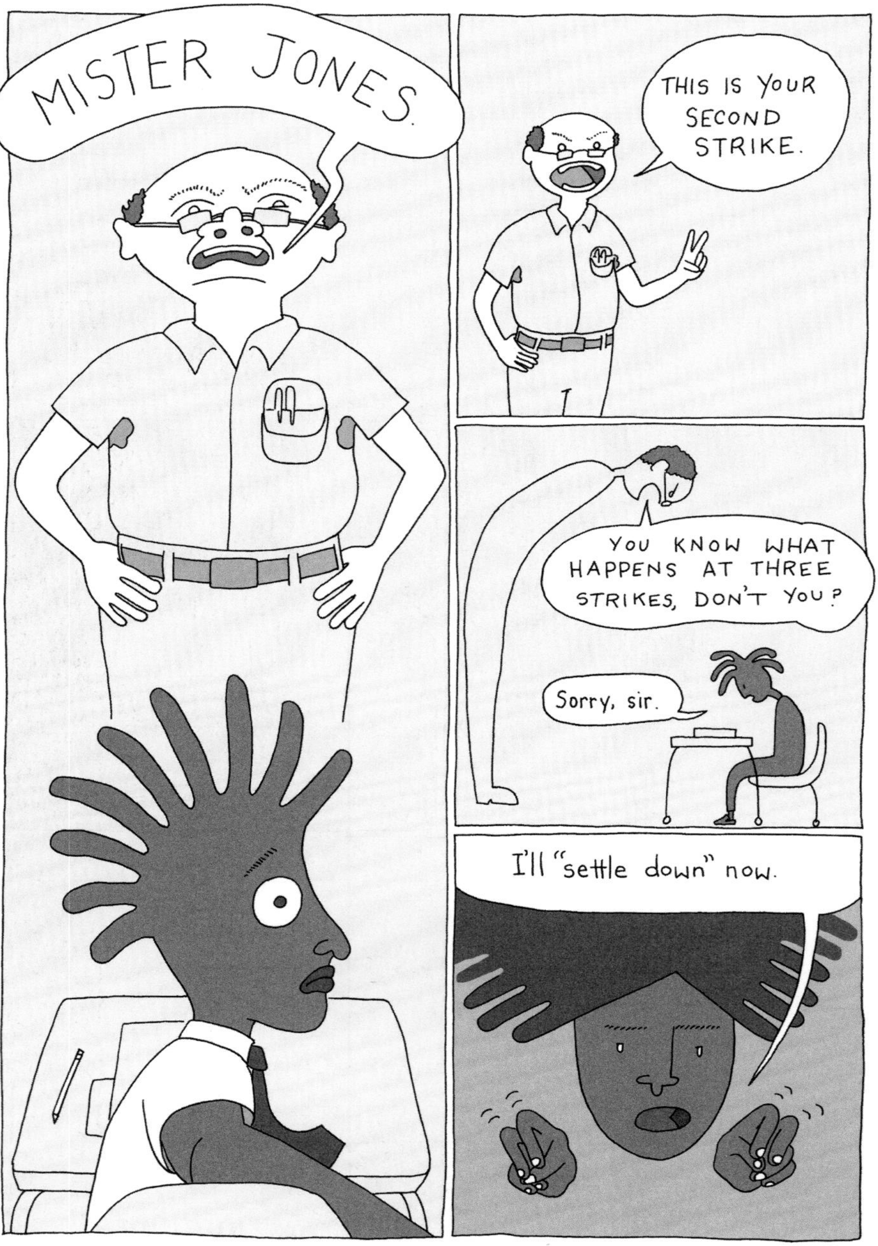
MISTER JONES.
THIS IS YOUR SECOND STRIKE.
YOU KNOW WHAT HAPPENS AT THREE STRIKES, DON'T YOU?
Sorry, sir.
I'll "settle down" now.

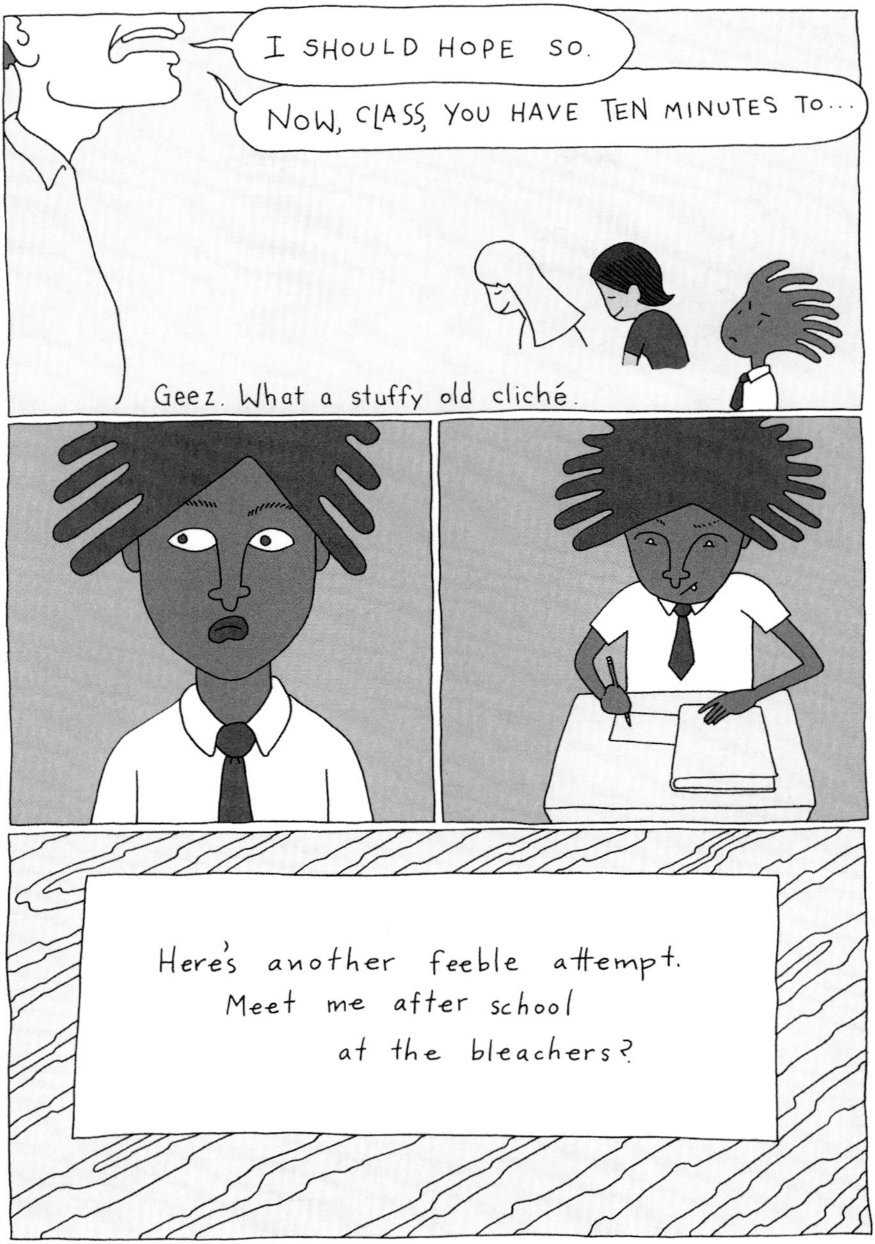
I SHOULD HOPE SO.
NOW, CLASS, YOU HAVE TEN MINUTES TO...
Geez. What a stuffy old cliché.
Here's another feeble attempt. Meet me after school at the bleachers?

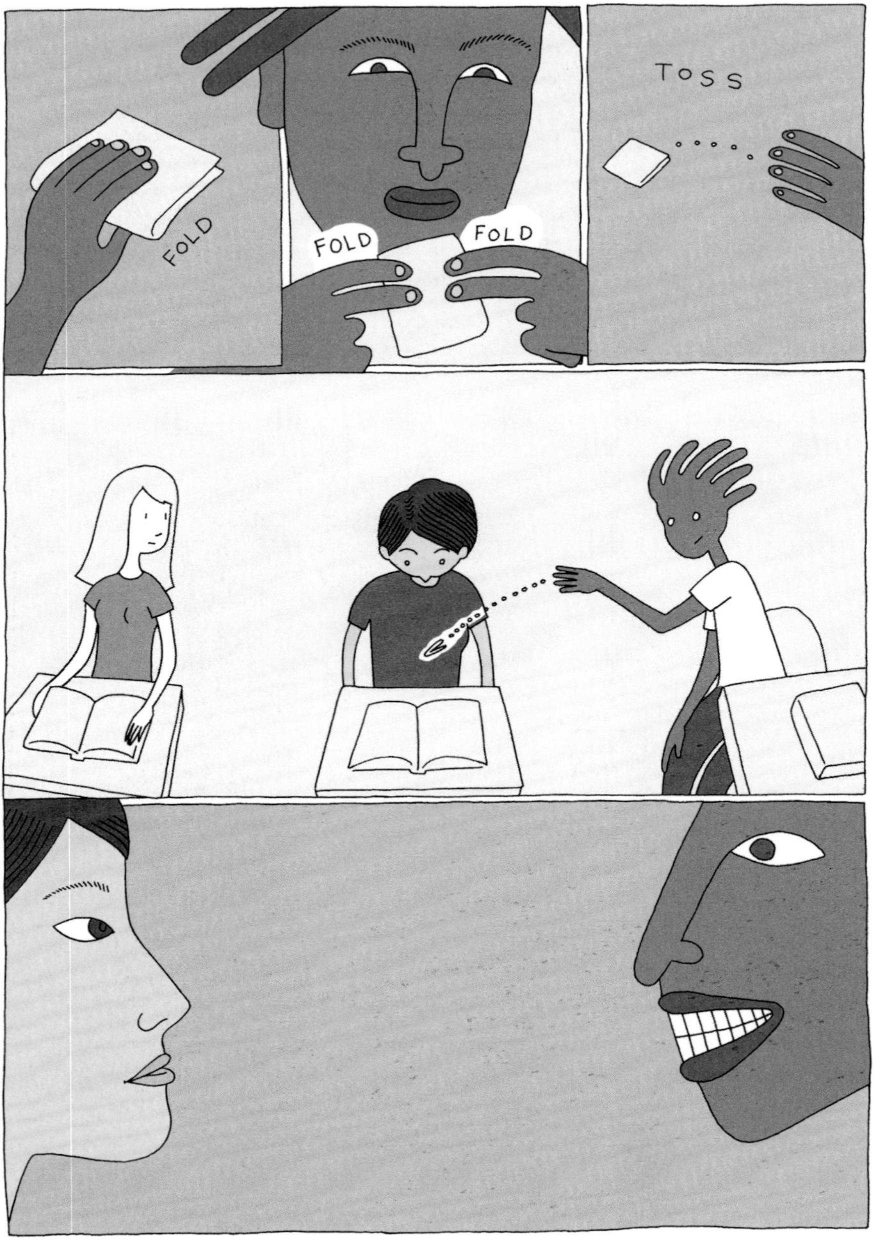
FOLD
FOLD
FOLD
TOSS

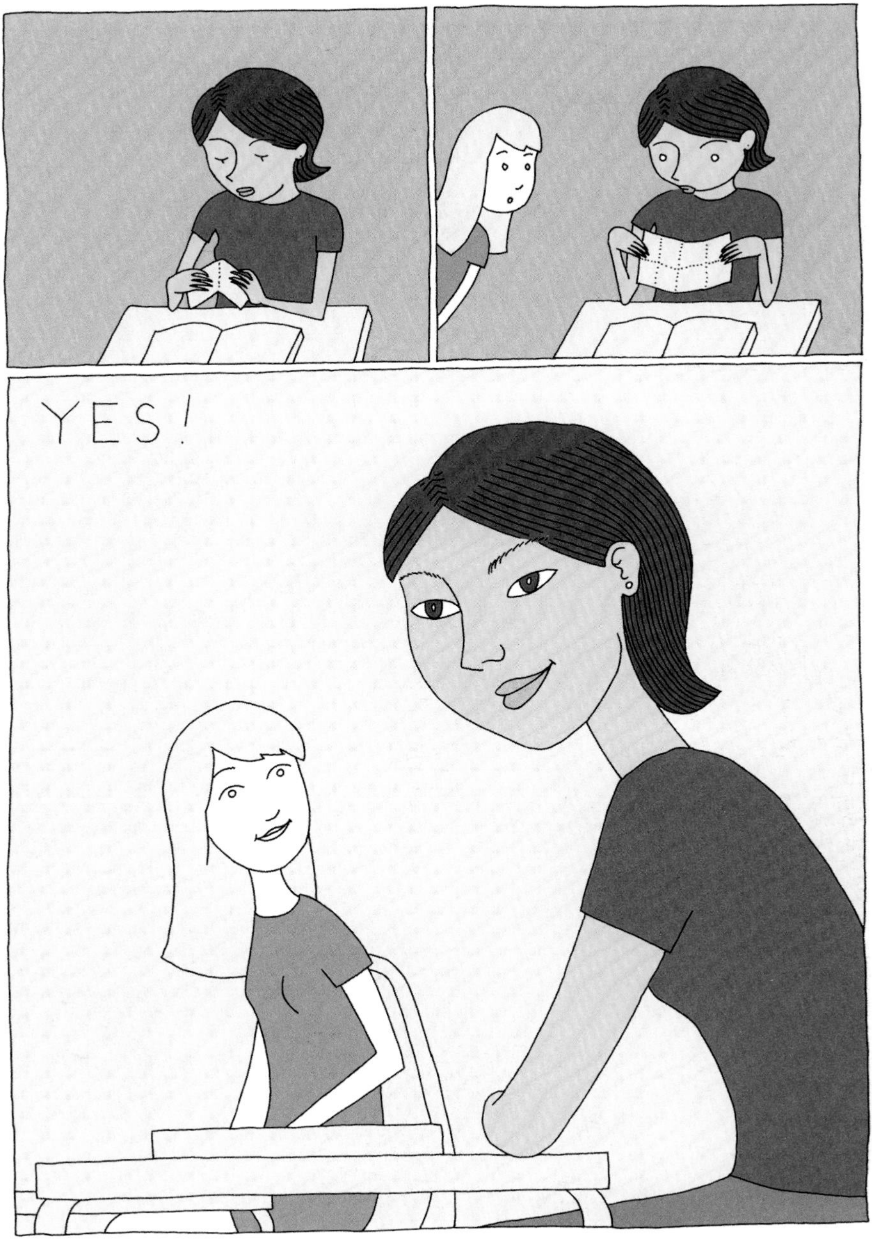
YES!

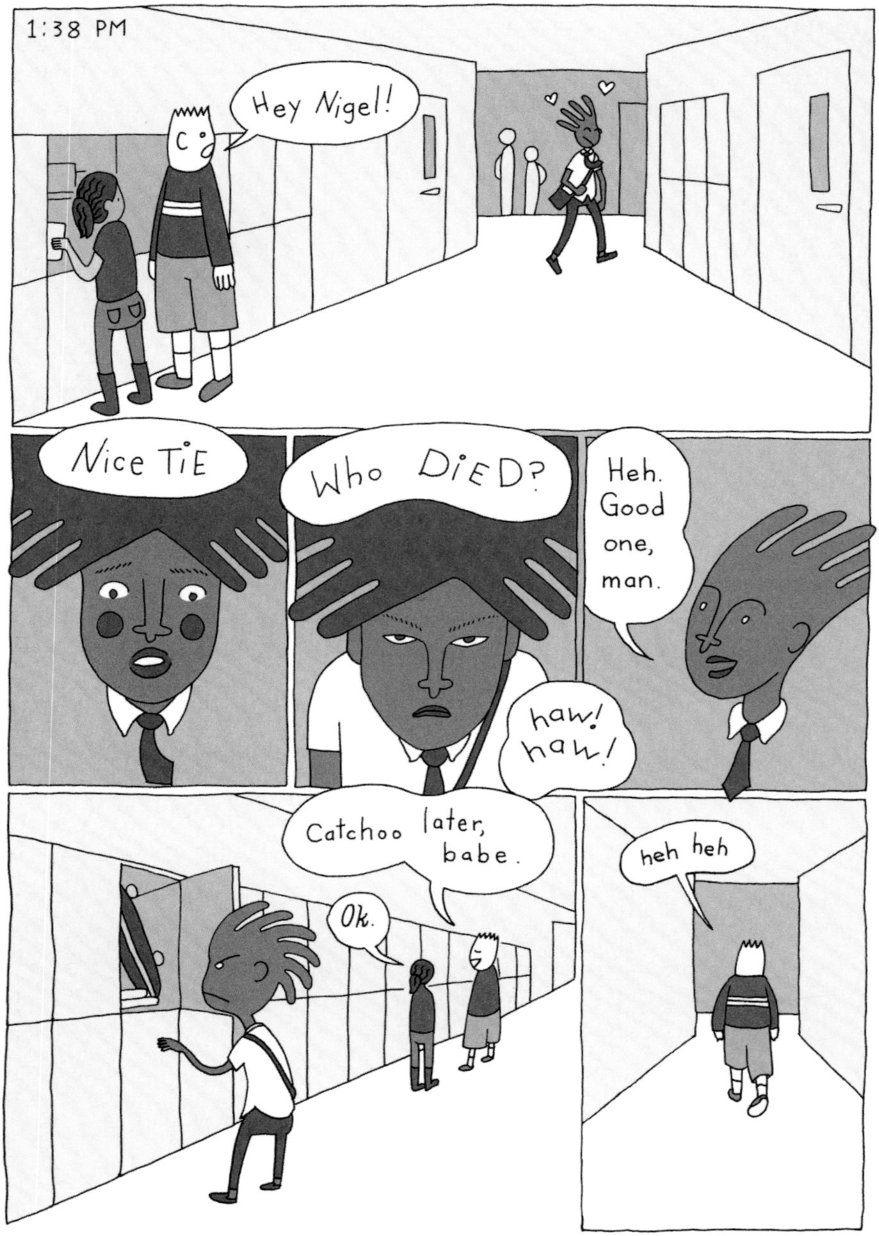
1:38 PM
Hey Nigel!
Nice TiE
Who DiED?
Heh. Good one, man.
haw! haw!
Catchoo later, babe.
Ok.
heh heh

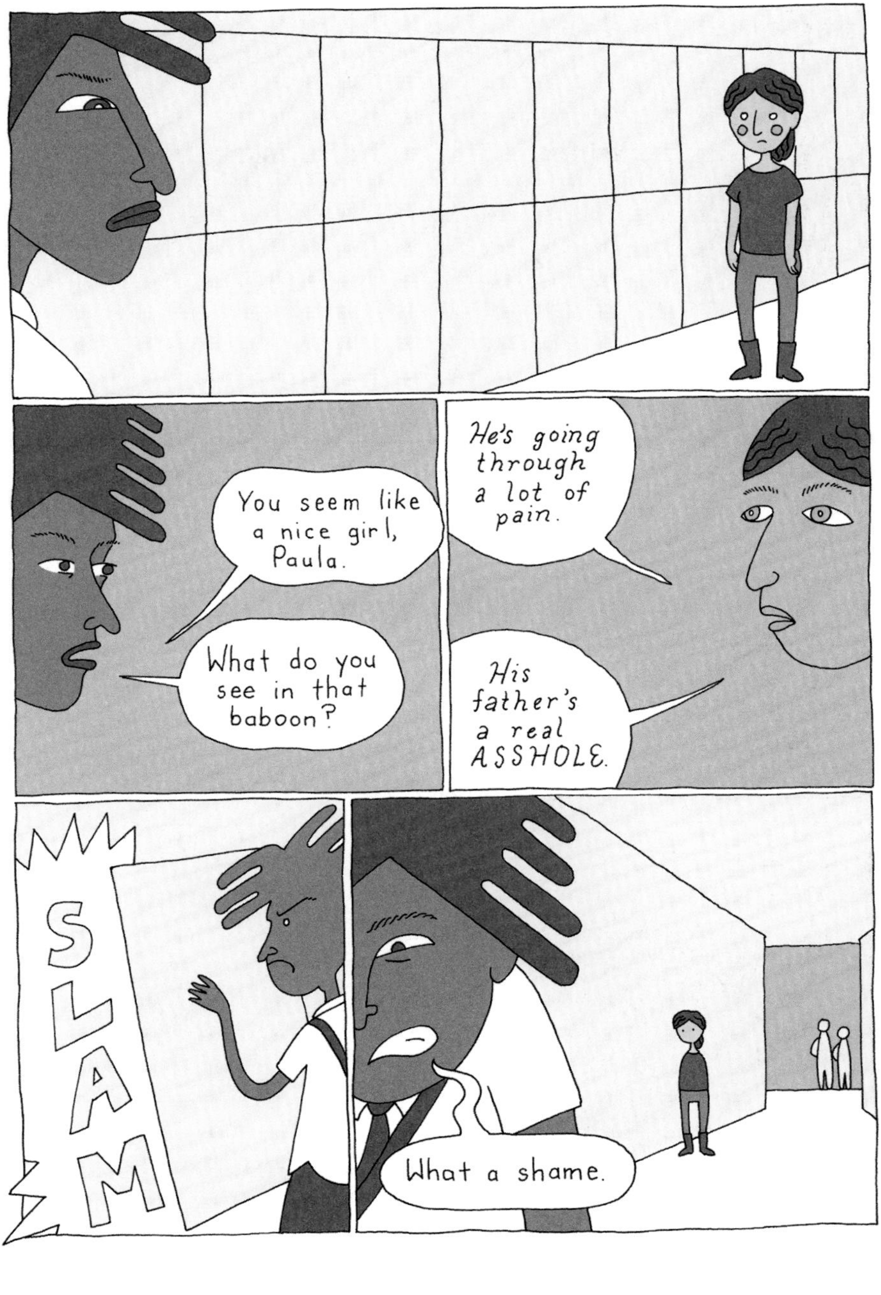
You seem like a nice girl, Paula.
What do you see in that baboon?
He's going through a lot of pain.
His father's a real ASSHOLE.
SLAM
What a shame.

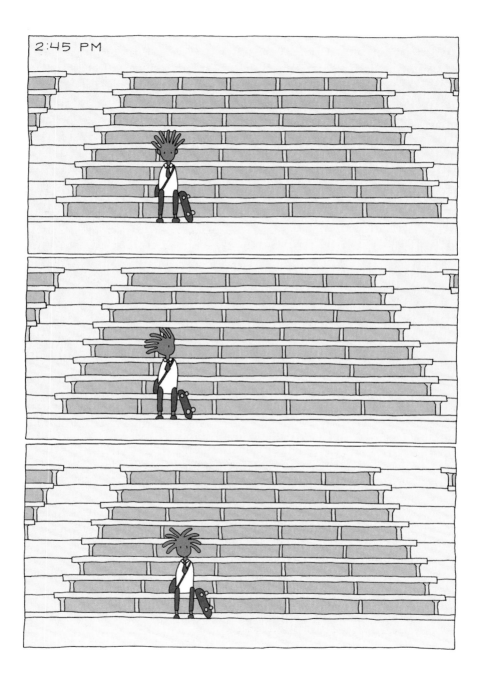

2:45 PM

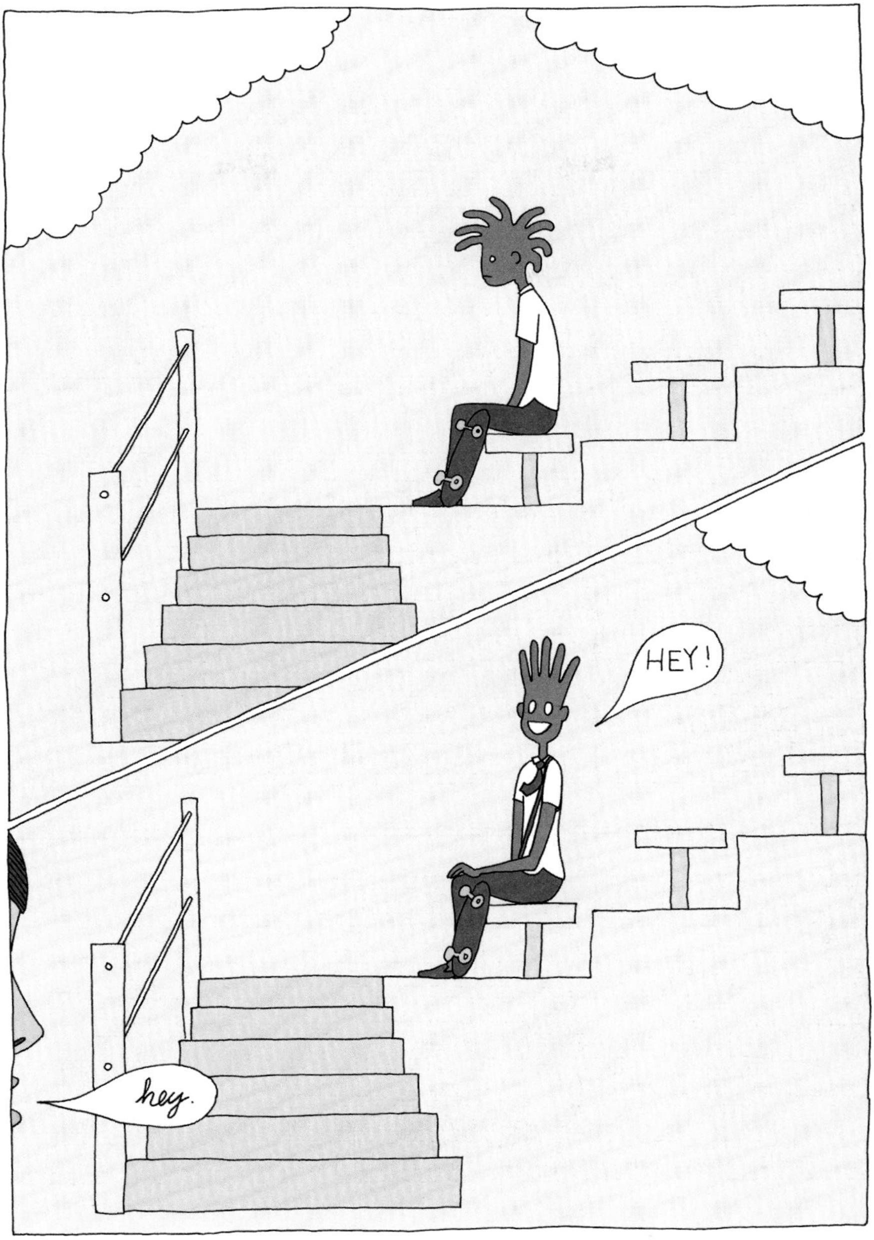
HEY!
hey.

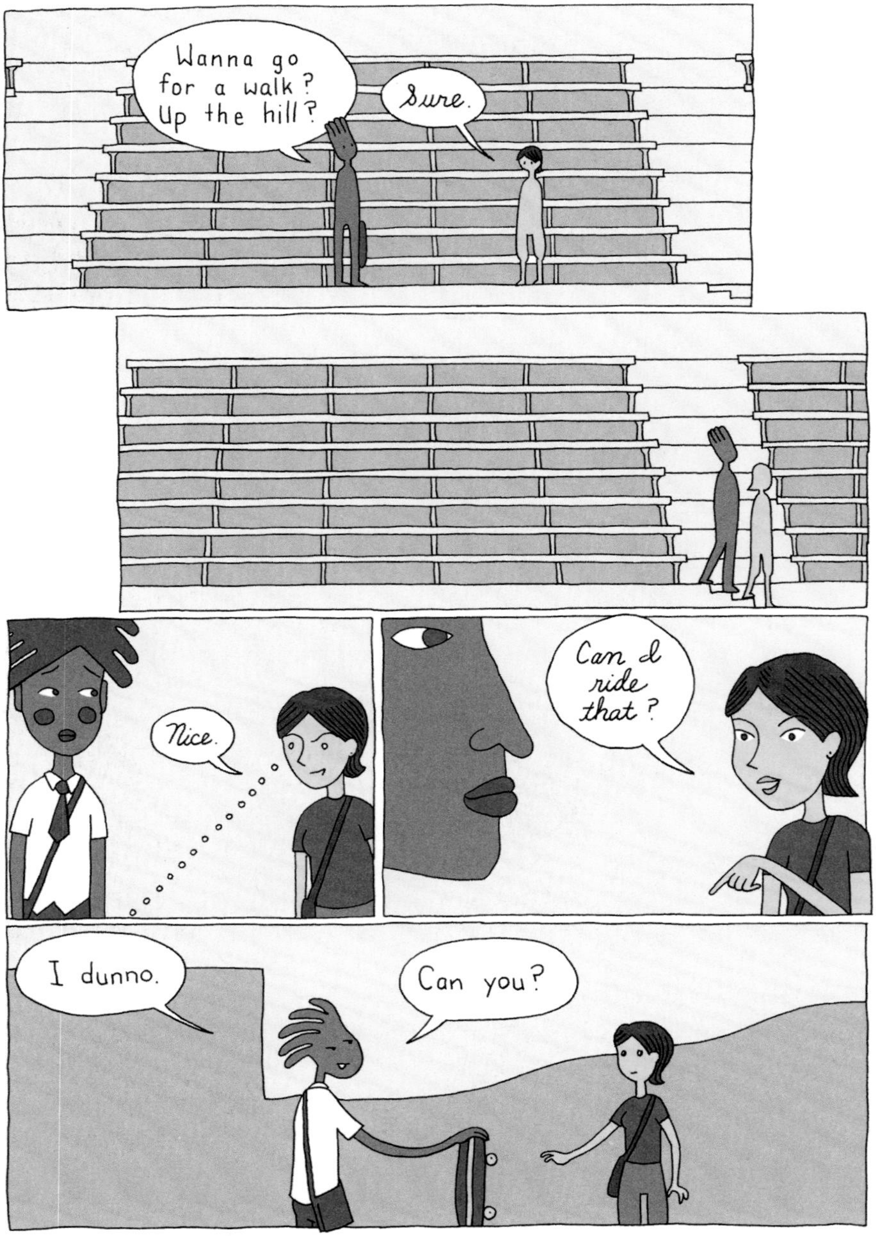
Wanna go for a walk? Up the hill?
Sure.
Nice.
Can I ride that?
I dunno.
Can you?

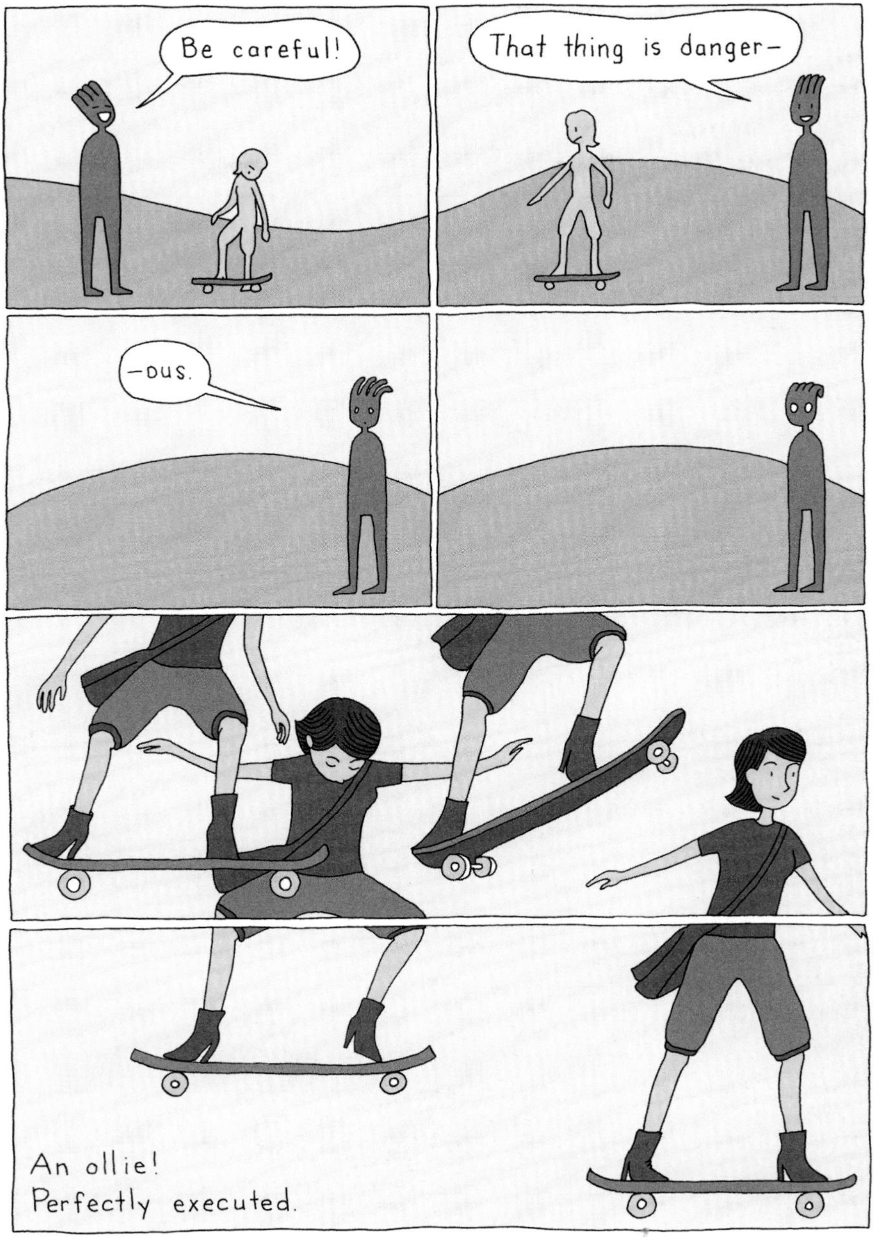
Be careful!
That thing is danger-
-ous.
An ollie!
Perfectly executed.

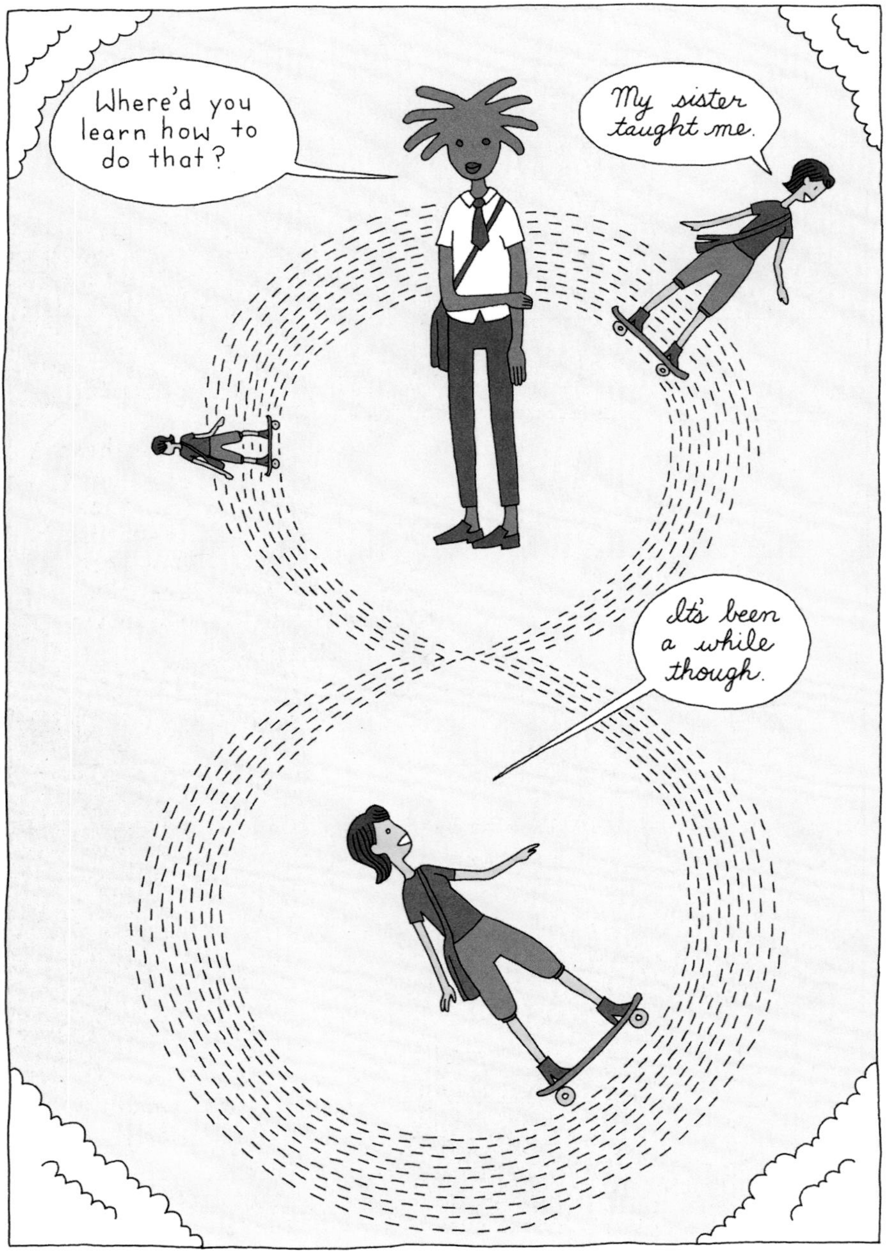
Where'd you learn how to do that?
My sister taught me.
It's been a while though.

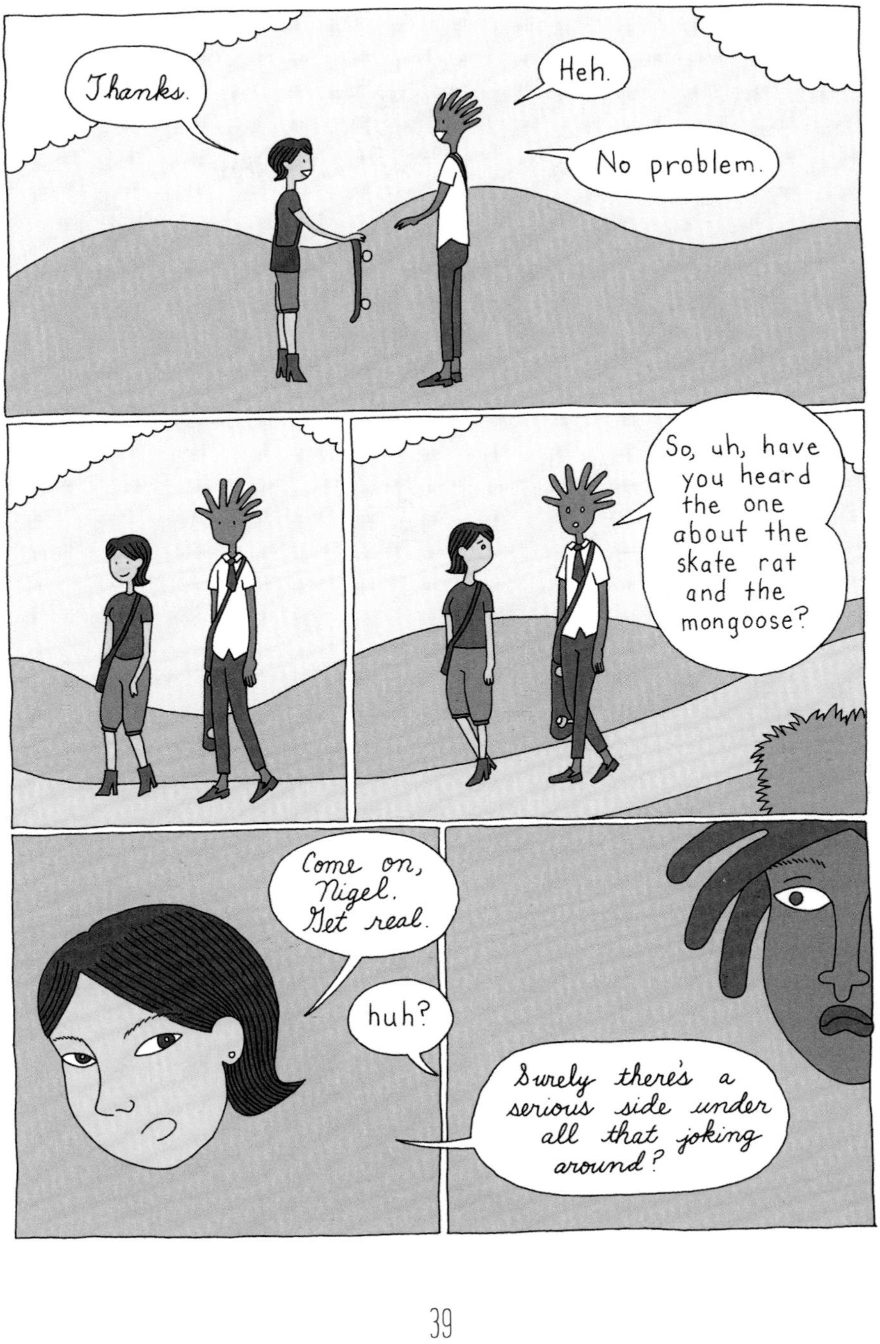
Thanks.
Heh.
No problem.
So, uh, have you heard the one about the skate rat and the mongoose?
Come on, Nigel. Get real.
huh?
Surely there's a serious side under all that joking around?

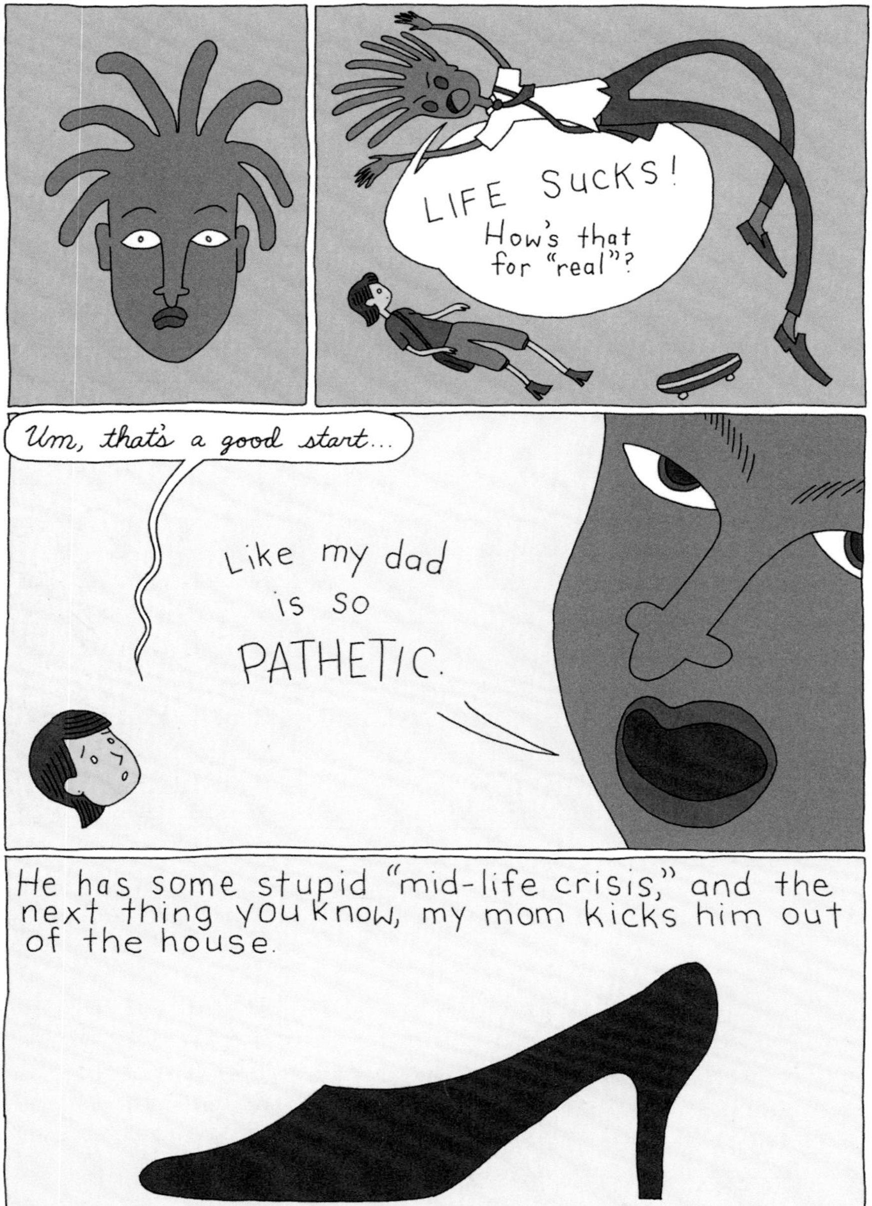
LIFE SUCKS!
How's that for "real"?
Um, that's a good start...
Like my dad is so PATHETIC.
He has some stupid "mid-life crisis," and the next thing you know, my mom kicks him out of the house.

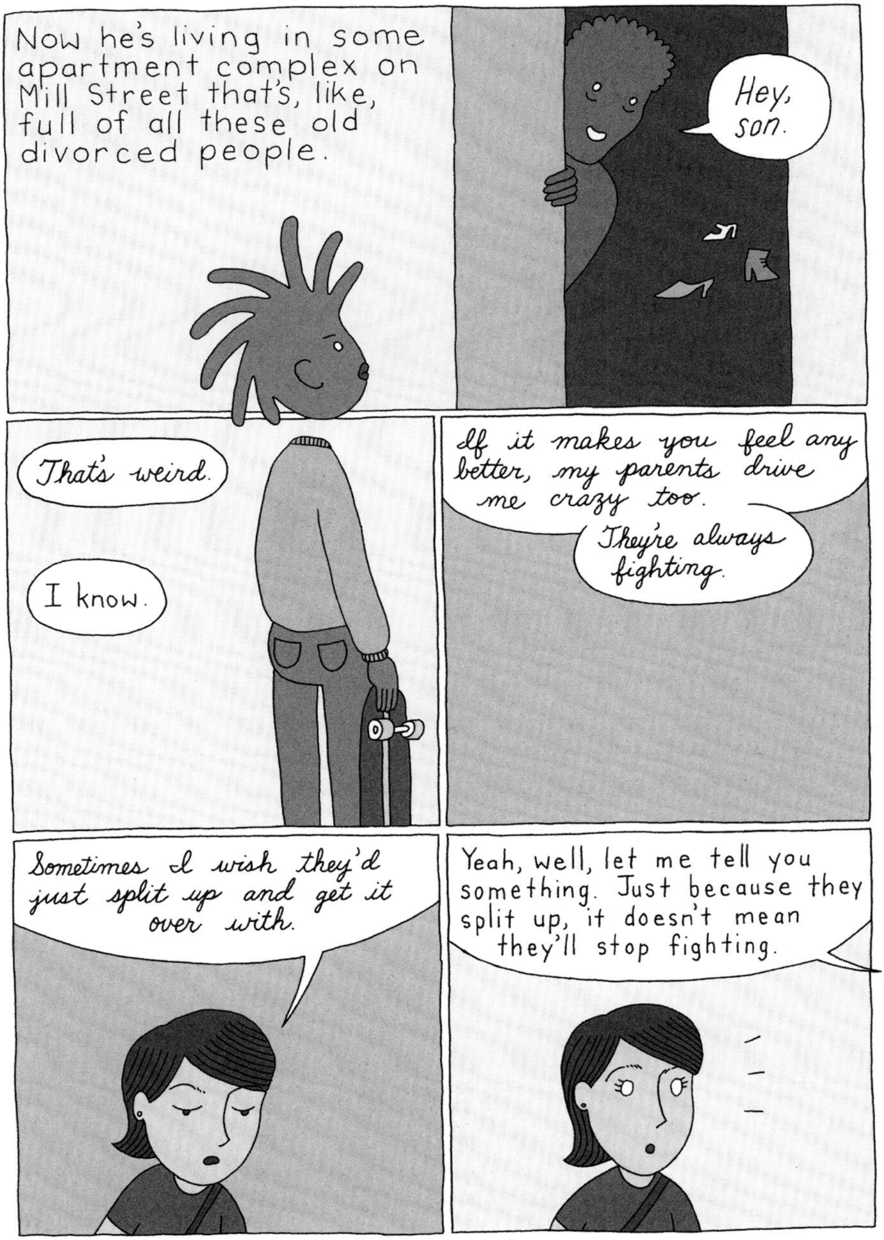
Now he's living in some apartment complex on Mill Street that's, like, full of all these old divorced people.
Hey, son.
That's weird.
I know.
If it makes you feel any better, my parents drive me crazy too.
They're always fighting.
Sometimes I wish they'd just split up and get it over with.
Yeah, well, let me tell you something. Just because they split up, it doesn't mean they'll stop fighting.

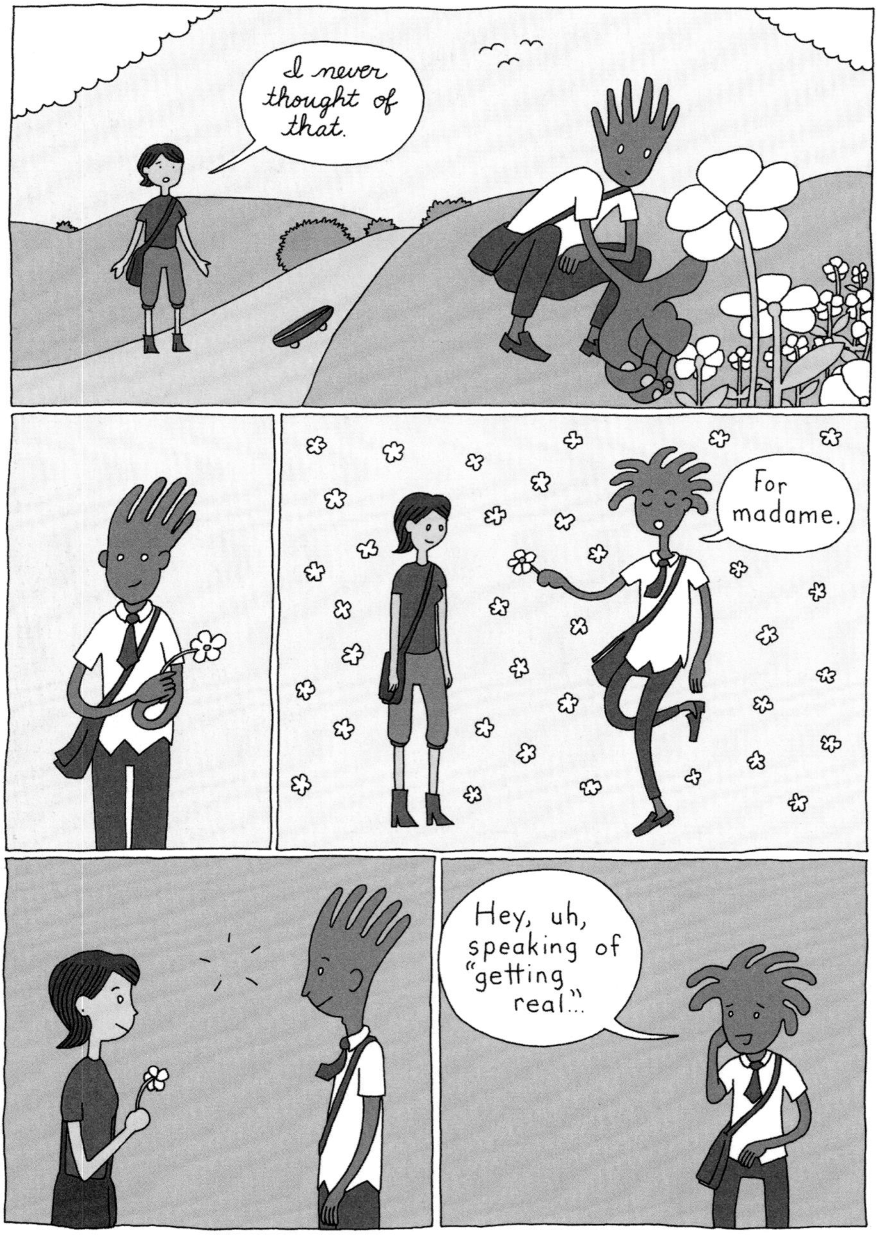
I never thought of that.
For madame.
Hey, uh, speaking of "getting real."..

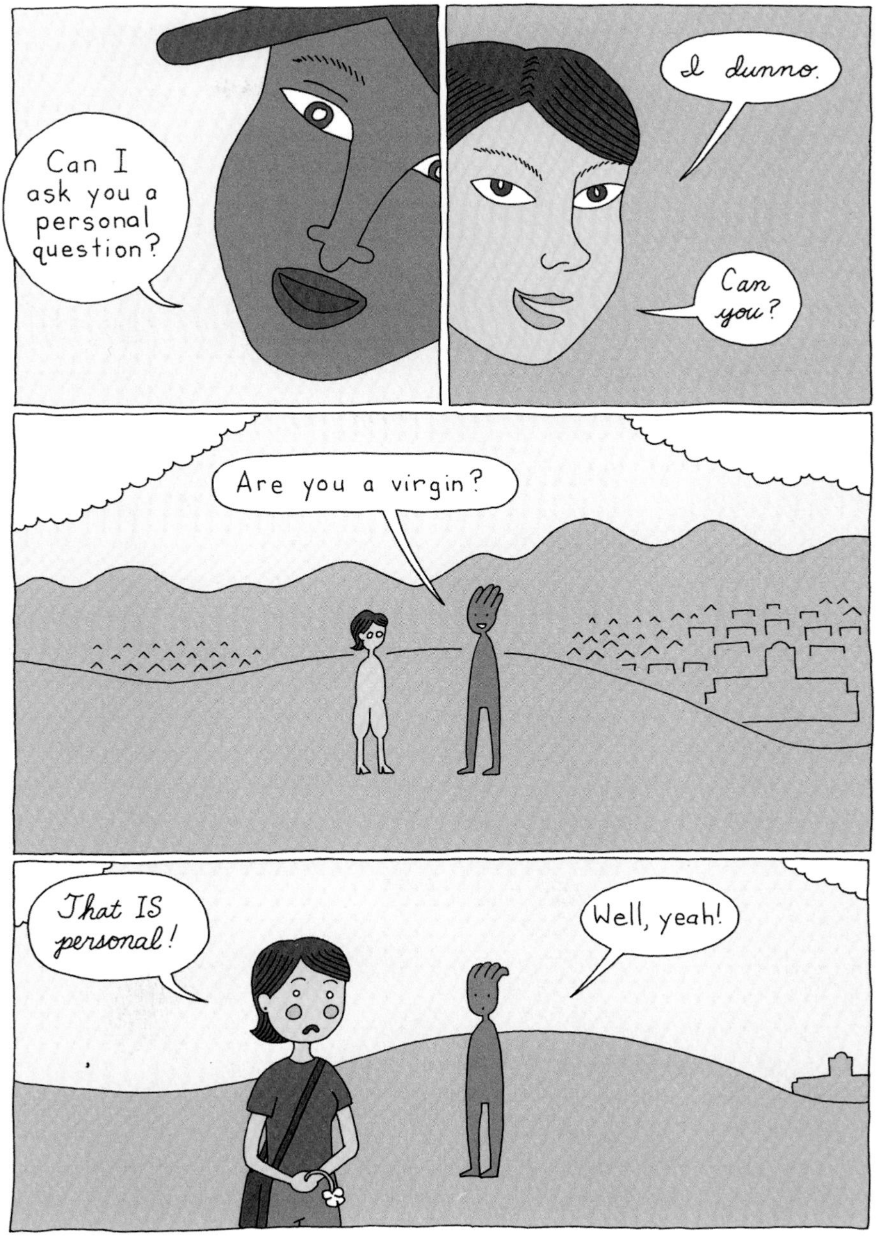
Can I ask you a personal question?
I dunno.
Can you?
Are you a virgin?
That IS personal!
Well, yeah!

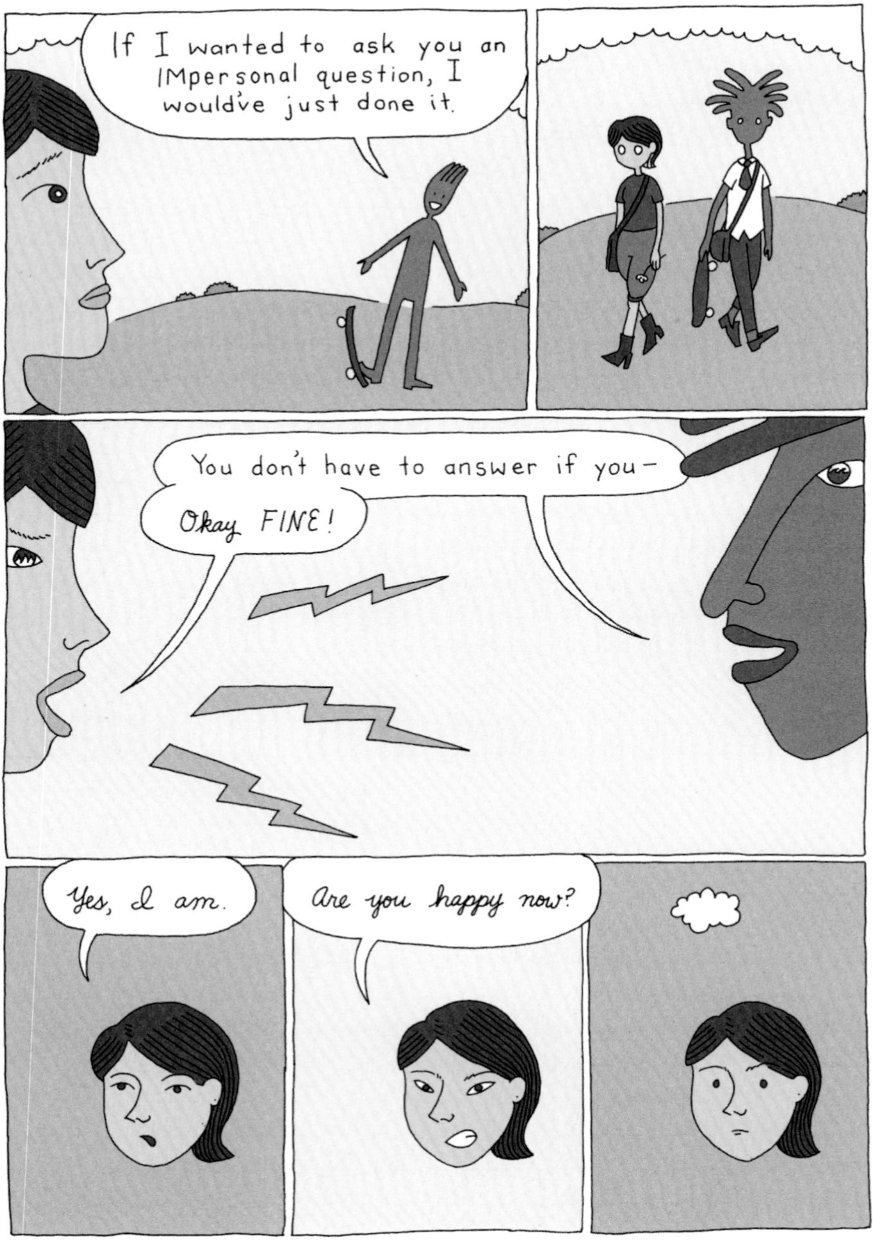
If I wanted to ask you an IMpersonal question, I would've just done it.
You don't have to answer if you-
Okay FINE!
Yes, I am.
Are you happy now?

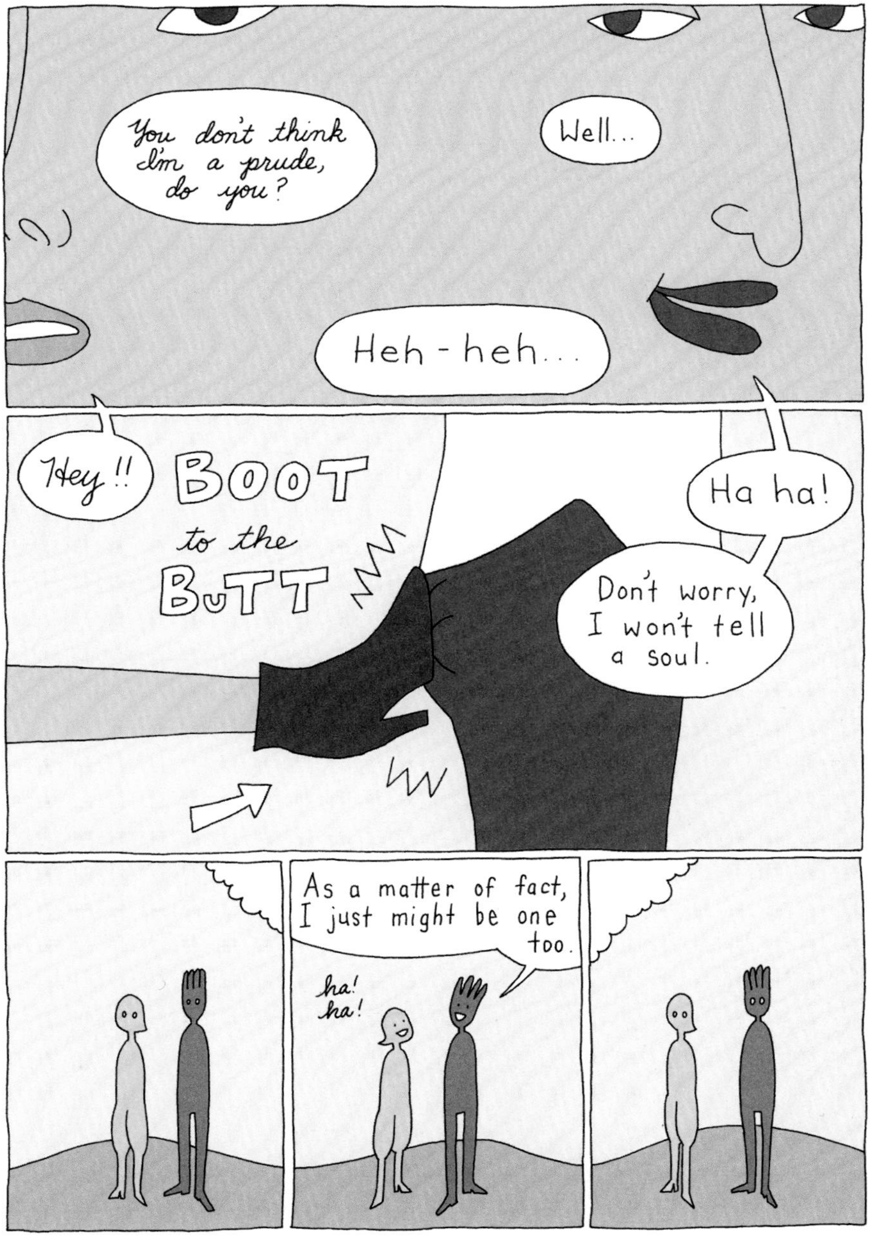
You don't think I'm a prude, do you?
Well...
Heh-heh...
Hey!!
BOOT to the BUTT
Ha ha!
Don't worry, I won't tell a soul.
As a matter of fact, I just might be one too.
ha! ha!

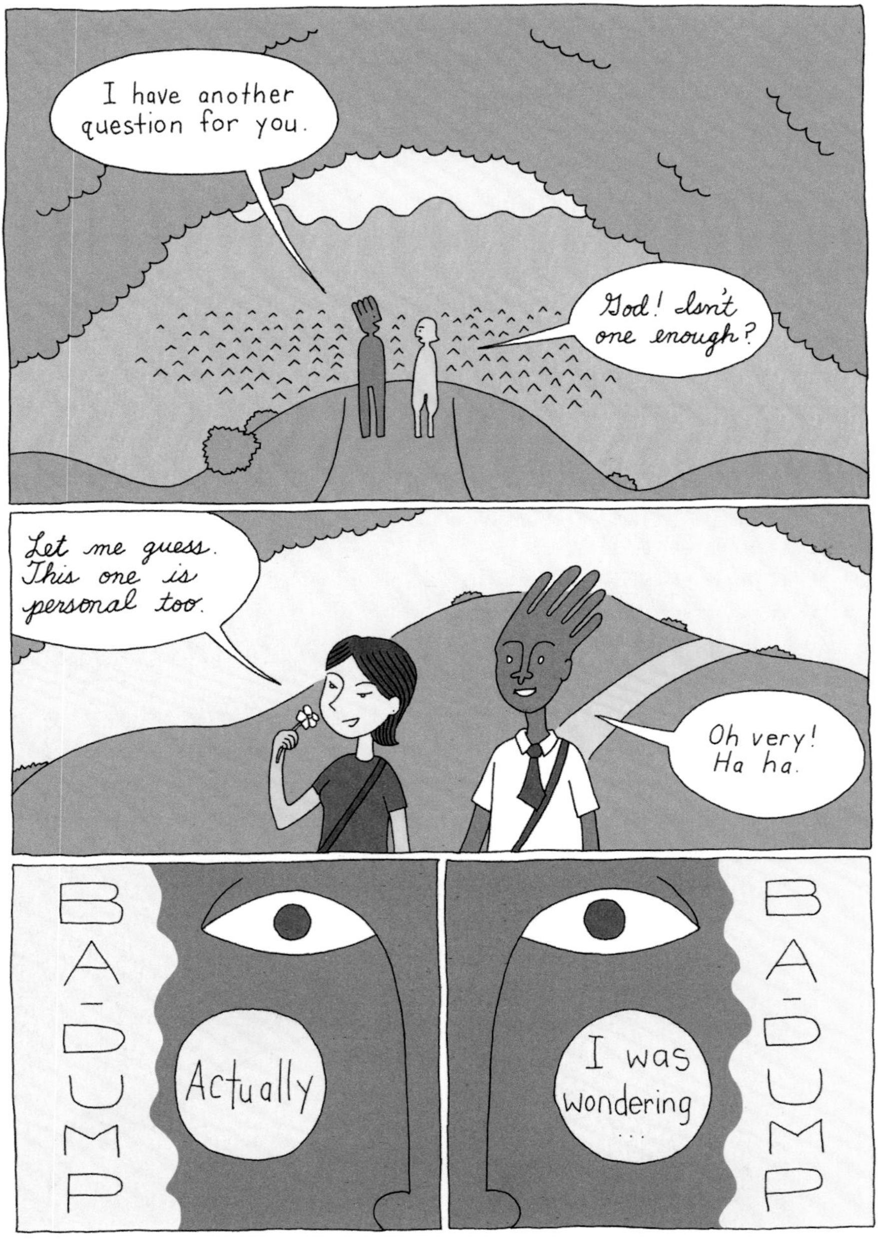
I have another question for you.
God! Isn't one enough?
Let me guess. This one is personal too.
Oh very! Ha ha.
BA-DUMP
Actually
I was wondering ...
BA-DUMP

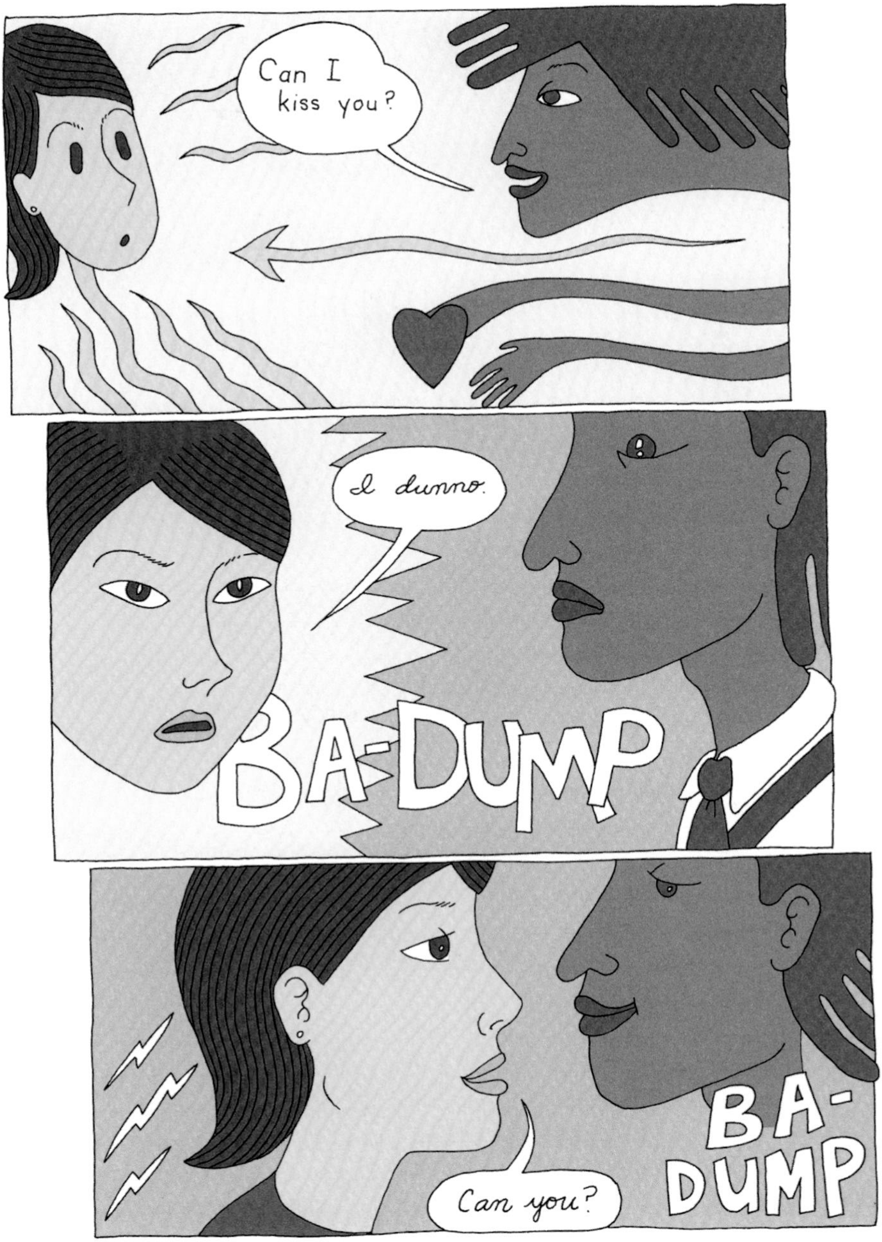
Can I kiss you?
I dunno.
BA-DUMP
Can you?
BA-DUMP

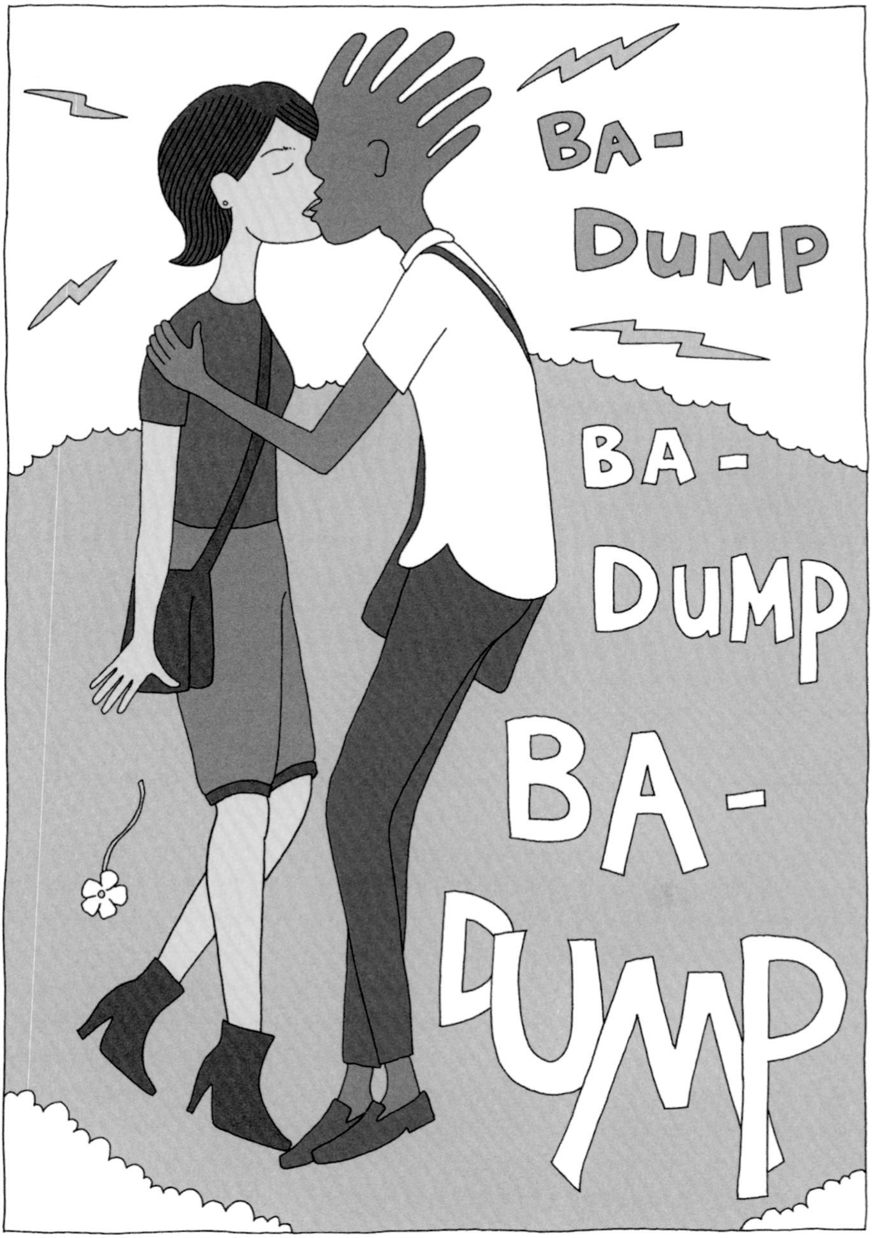
BA-
DUMP
BA-
DUMP
BA-
DUMP

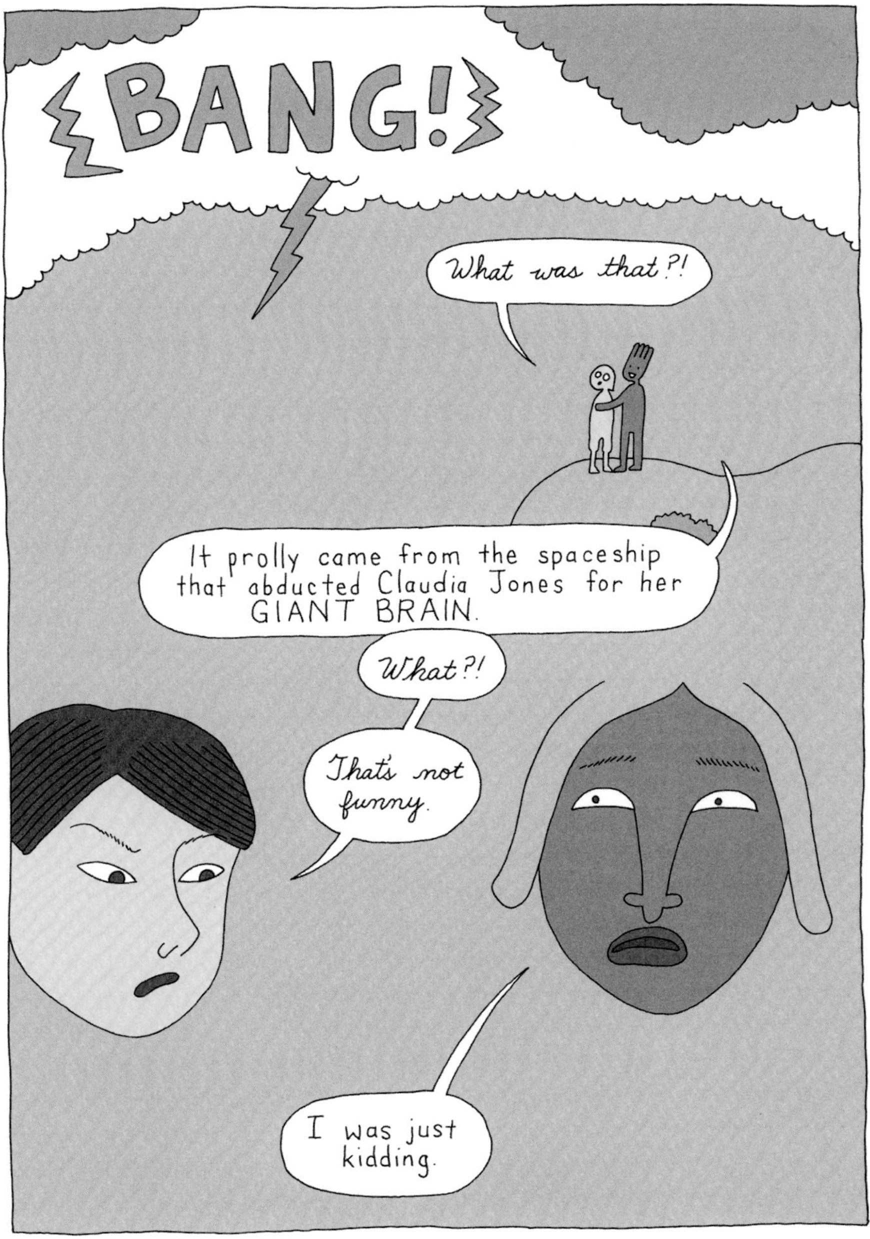
BANG!
What was that?!
It prolly came from the spaceship that abducted Claudia Jones for her GIANT BRAIN.
What?!
That's not funny.
I was just kidding.

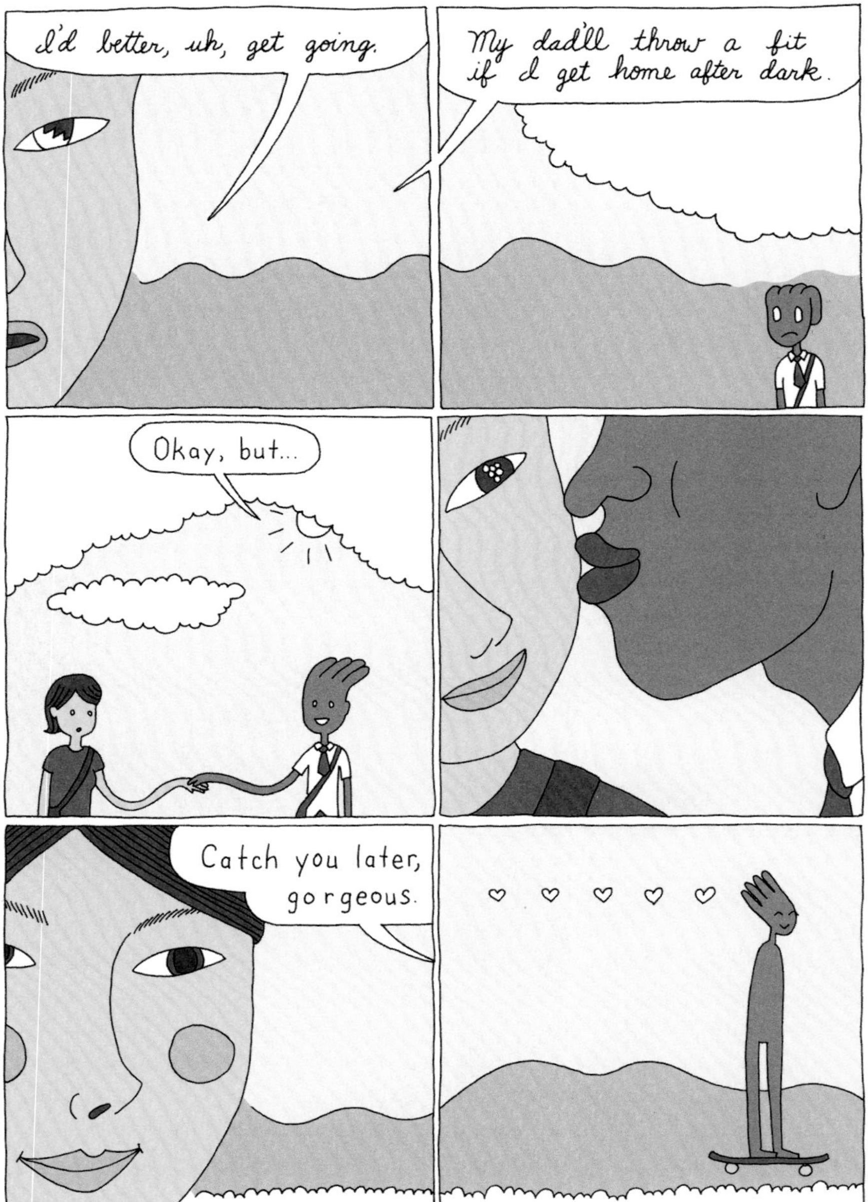
I'd better, uh, get going.
My dad'll throw a fit if I get home after dark.
Okay, but...
Catch you later, gorgeous.

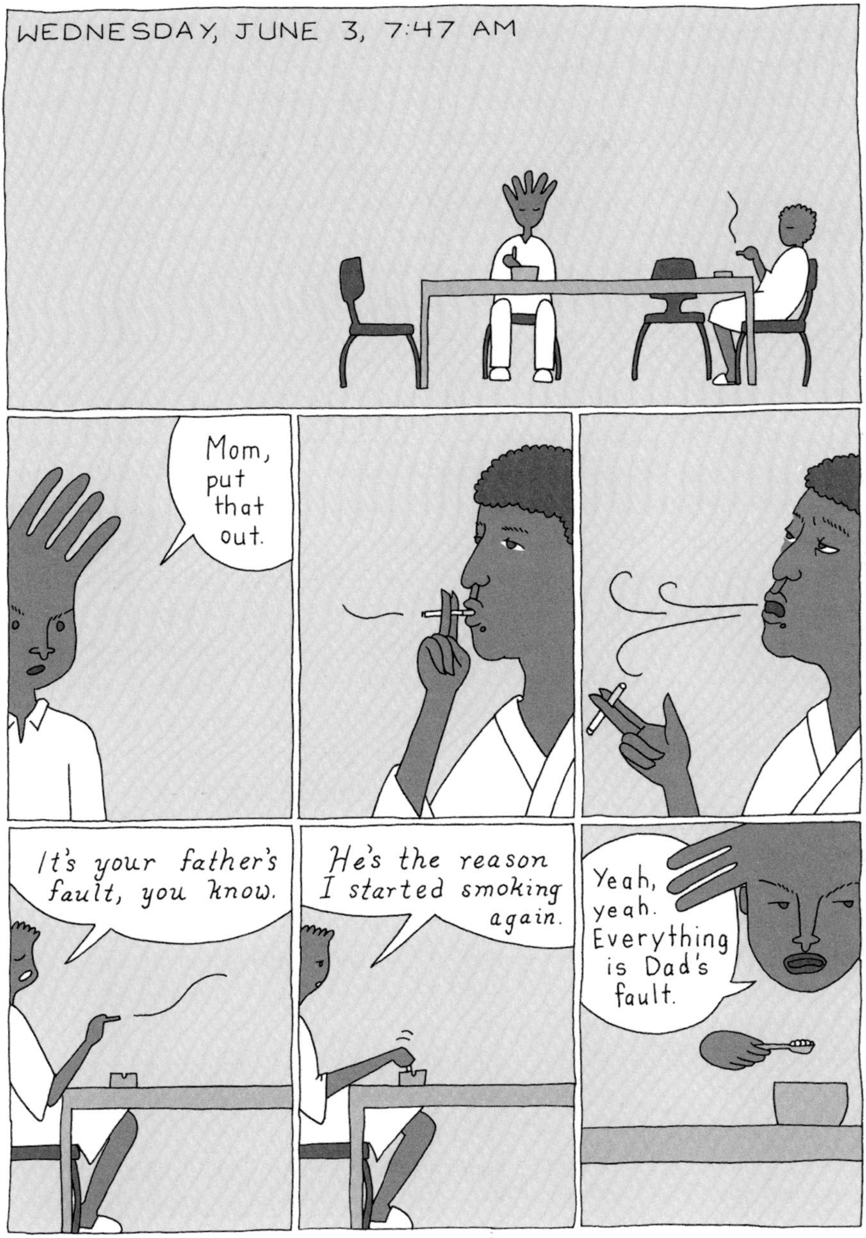
WEDNESDAY, JUNE 3, 7:47 AM
Mom, put that out.
It's your father's fault, you know.
He's the reason I started smoking again.
Yeah, yeah. Everything is Dad's fault.

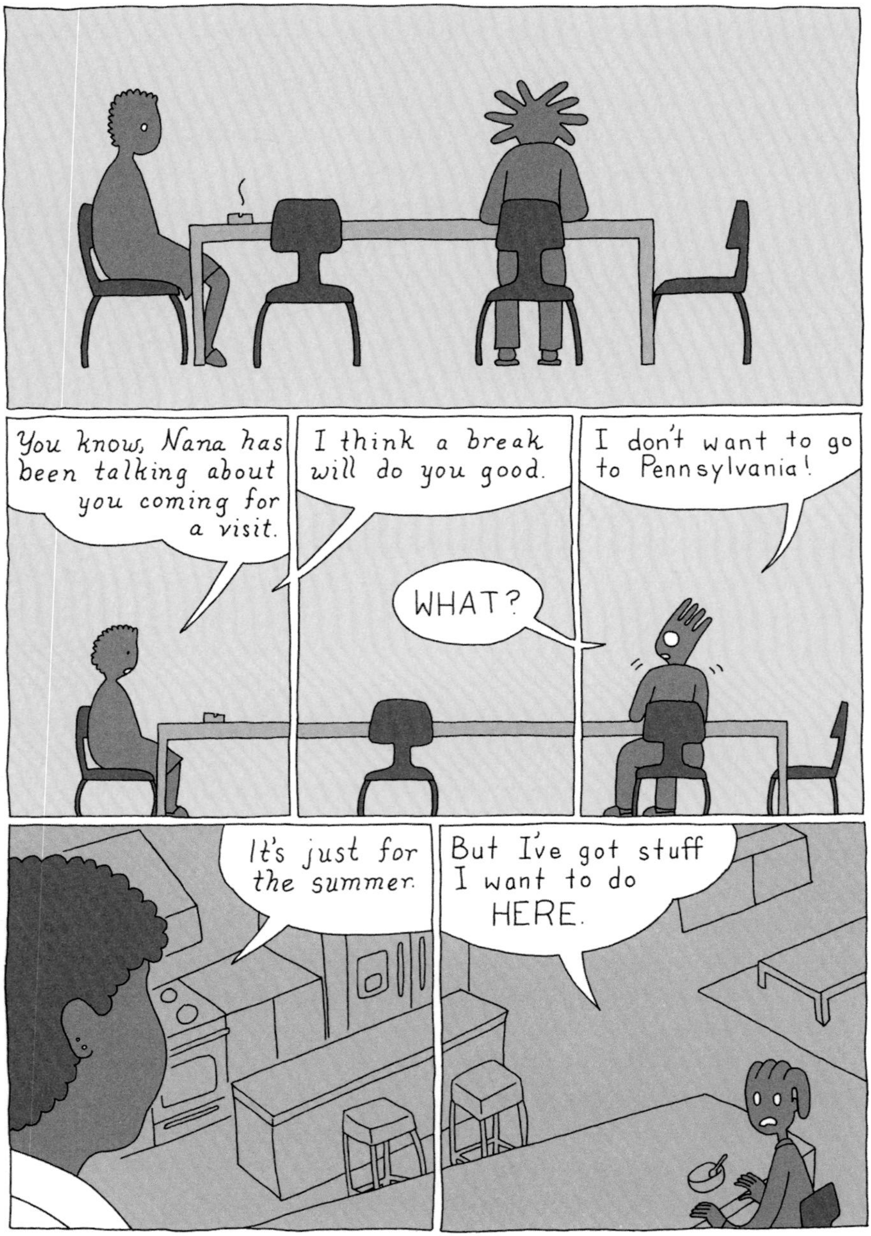
You know, Nana has been talking about you coming for a visit.
I think a break will do you good.
I don't want to go to Pennsylvania!
WHAT?
It's just for the summer.
But I've got stuff I want to do HERE.

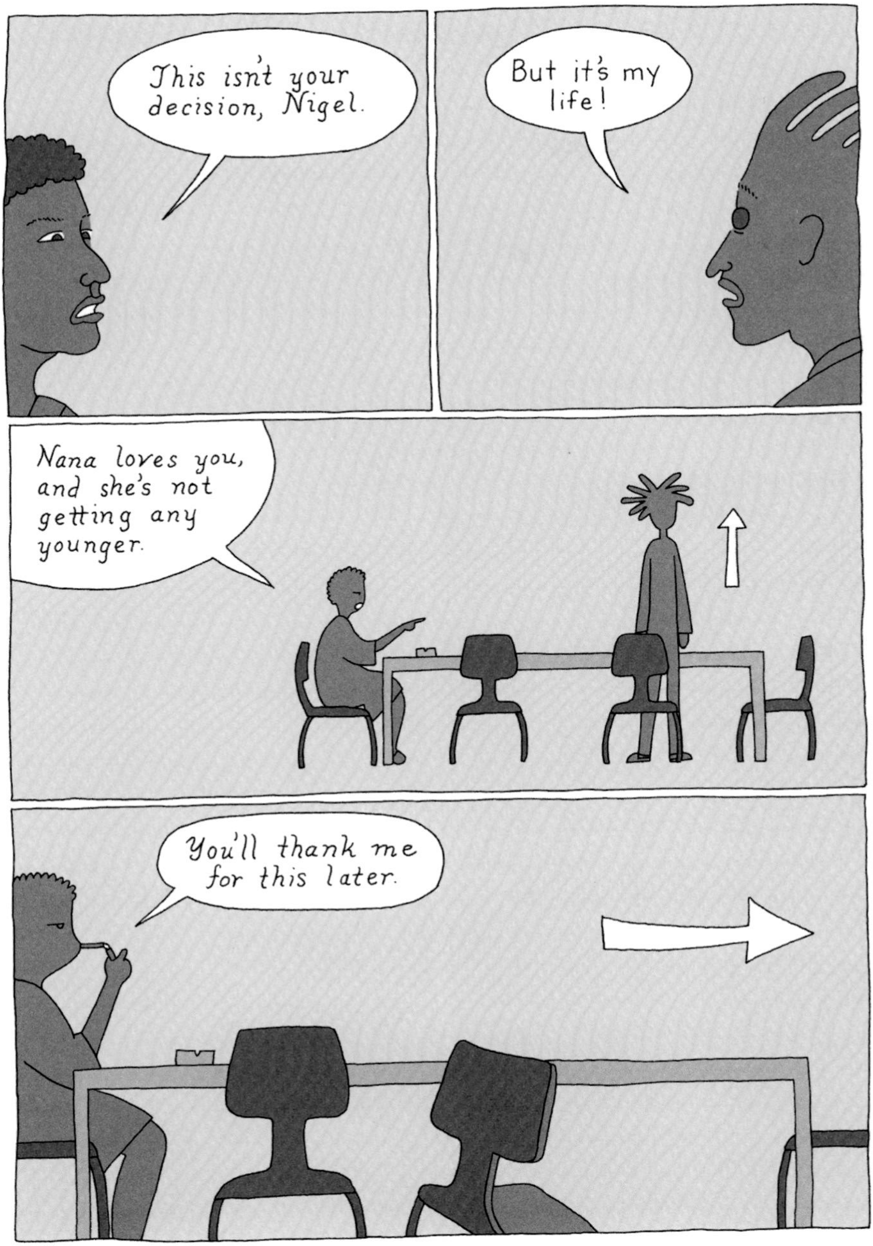
This isn't your decision, Nigel.
But it's my life!
Nana loves you, and she's not getting any younger.
You'll thank me for this later.

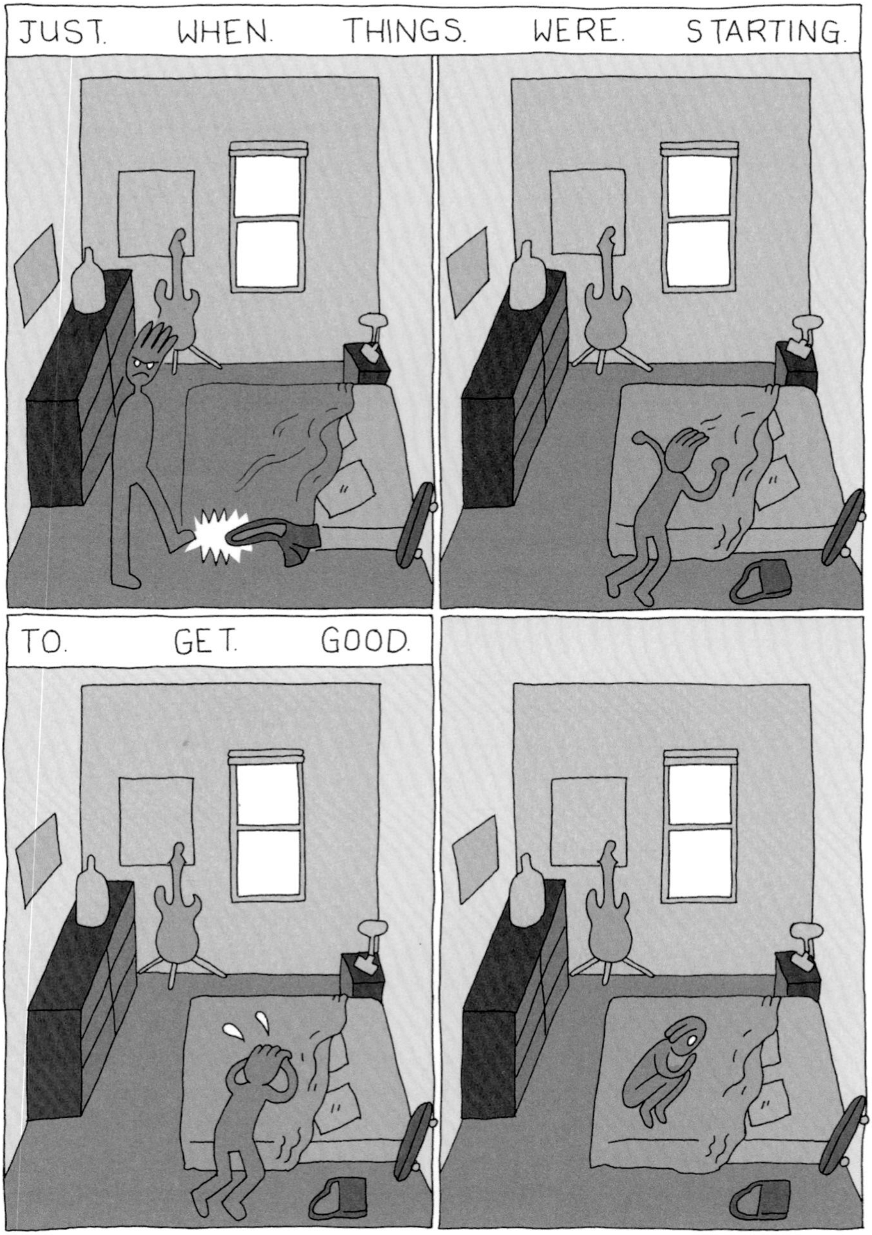
JUST. WHEN. THINGS. WERE. STARTING.
TO. GET. GOOD.

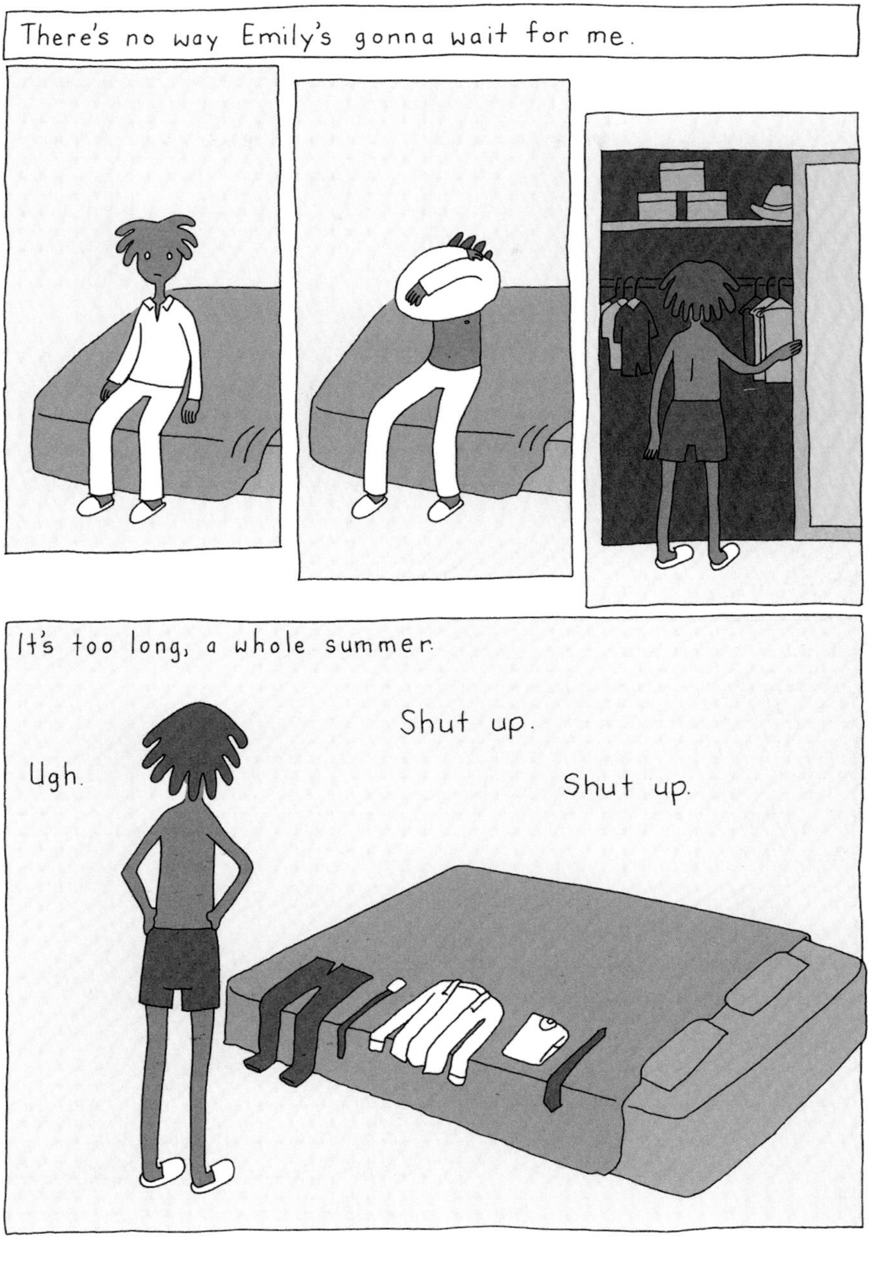
There's no way Emily's gonna wait for me.
It's too long, a whole summer.
Ugh.
Shut up.
Shut up.

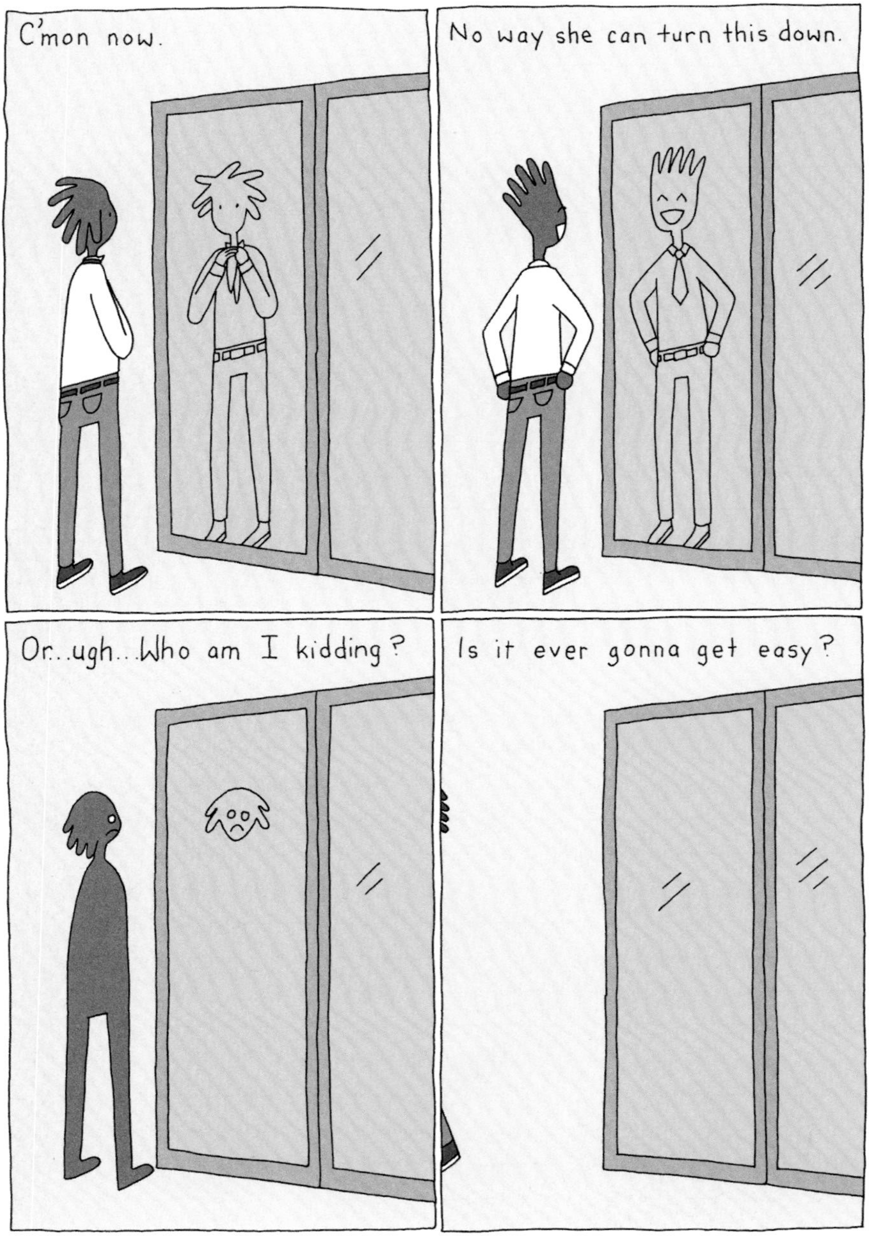
C'mon now.
No way she can turn this down.
Or...ugh...Who am I kidding?
Is it ever gonna get easy?

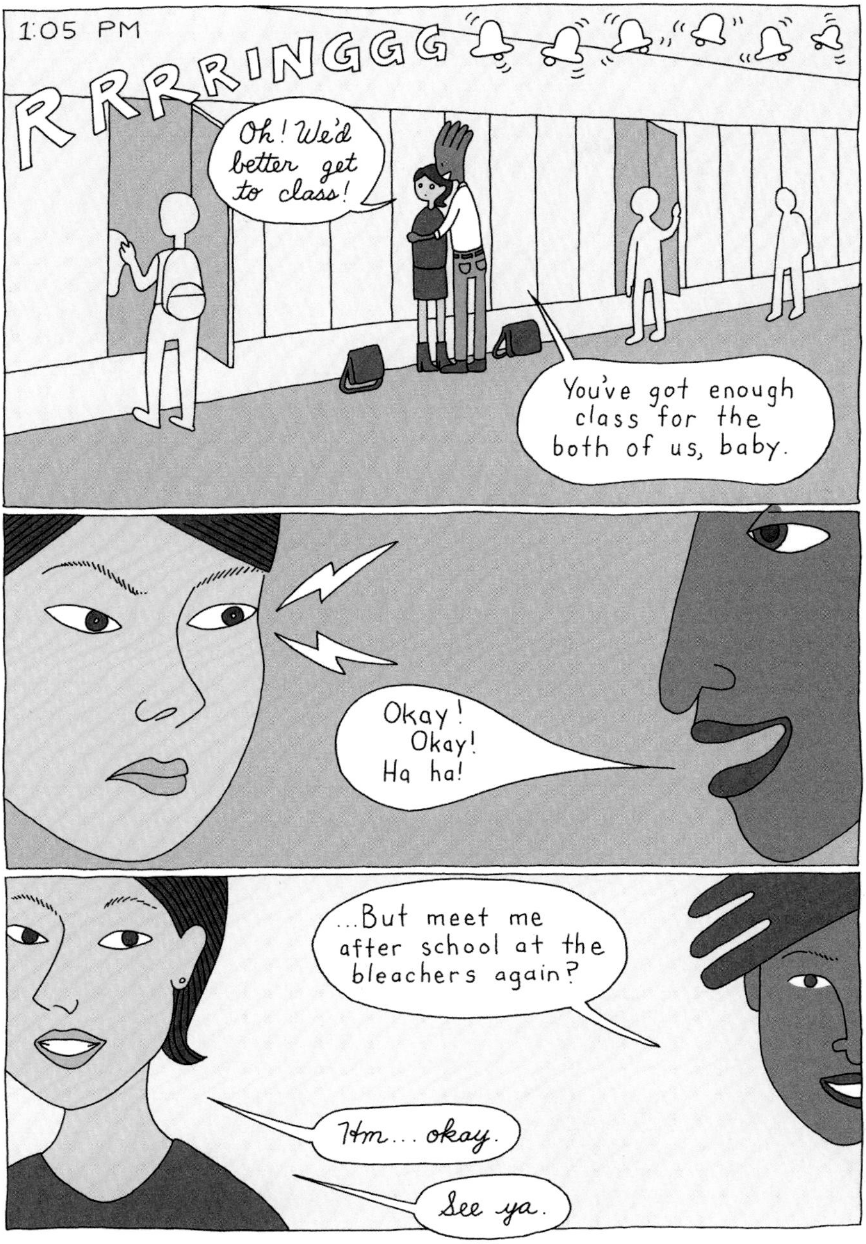

1:05 PM
RRRRINGGG
Oh! We'd better get to class!
You've got enough class for the both of us, baby.
Okay! Okay! Ha ha!
...But meet me after school at the bleachers again?
Hm... okay.
See ya.

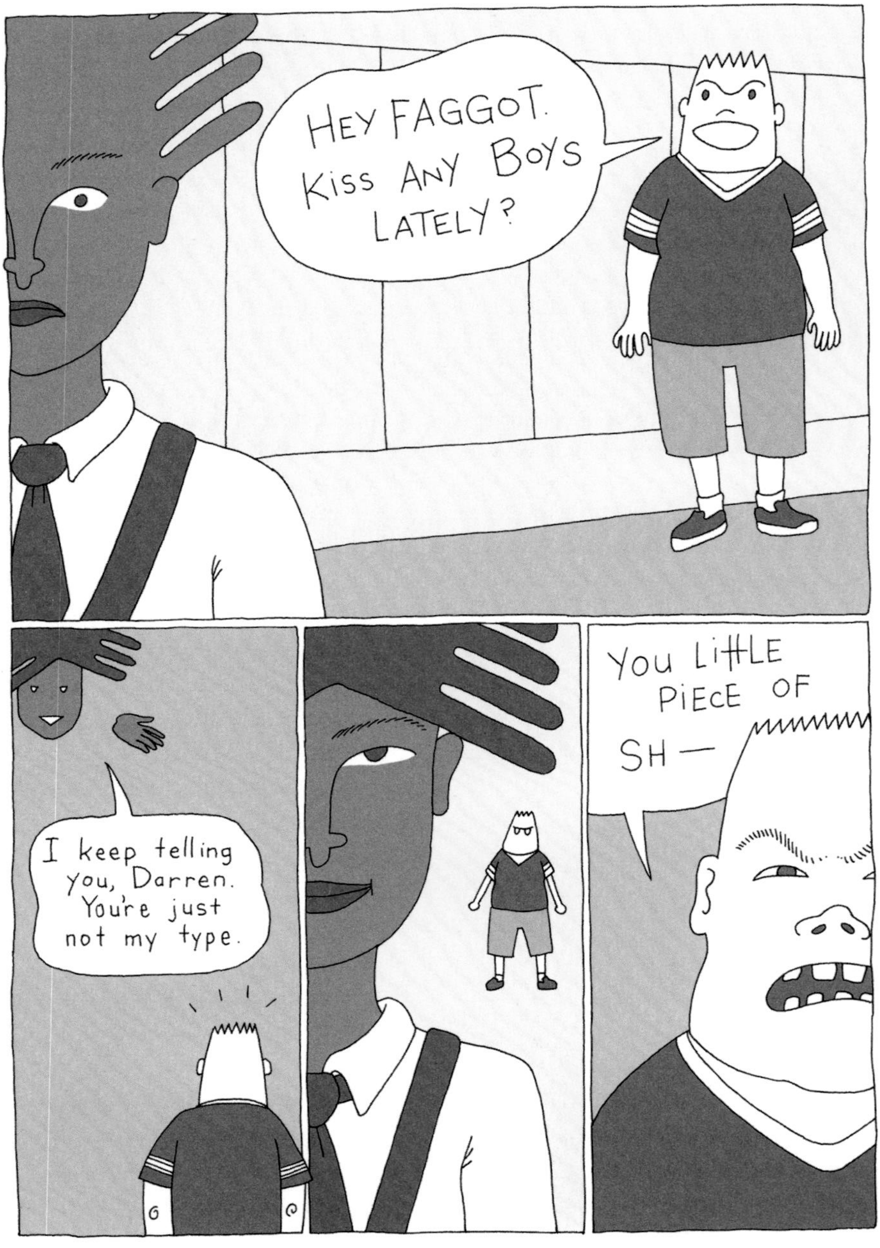
HEY FAGGOT. KISS ANY BOYS LATELY?
I keep telling you, Darren. You're just not my type.
YOU LITTLE PIECE OF SH—

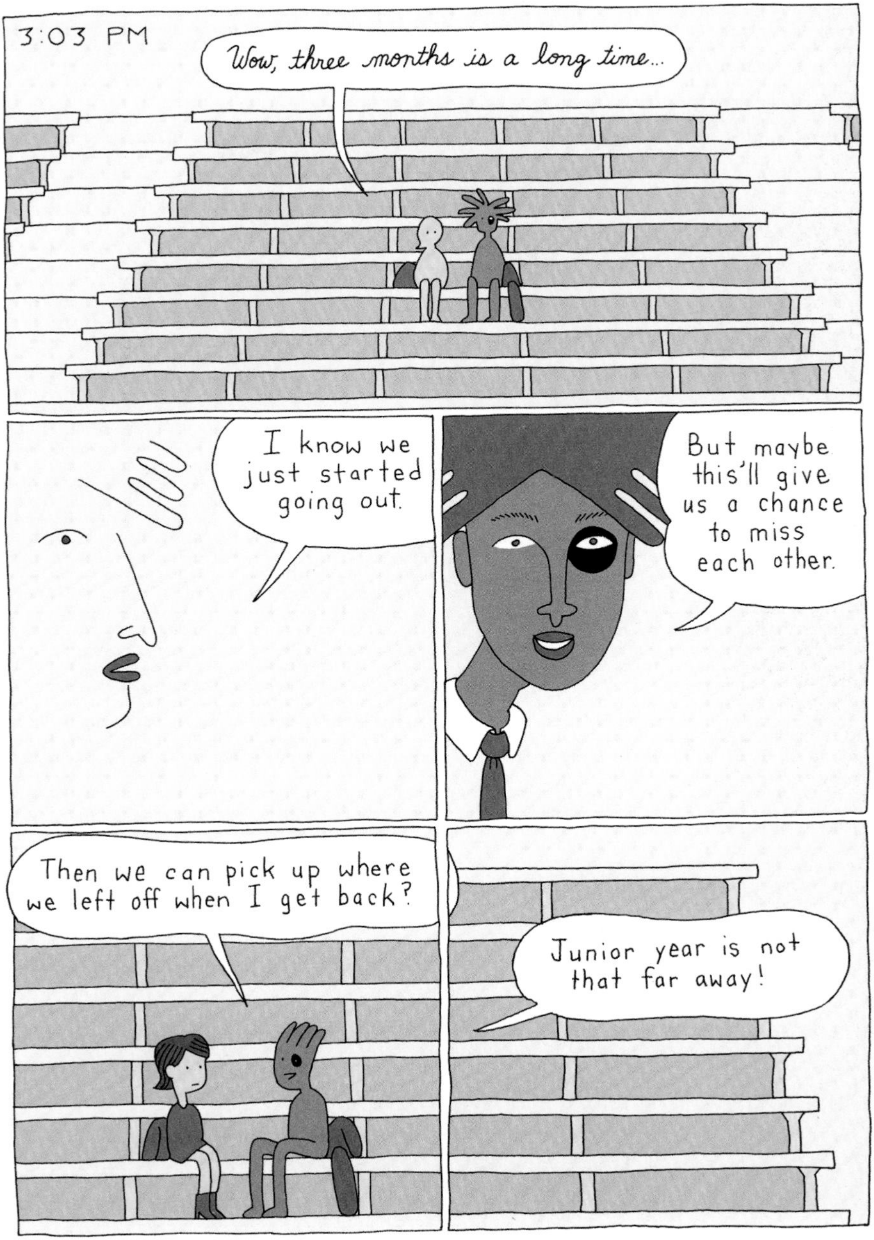
3:03 PM
Wow, three months is a long time...
I know we just started going out.
But maybe this'll give us a chance to miss each other.
Then we can pick up where we left off when I get back?
Junior year is not that far away!

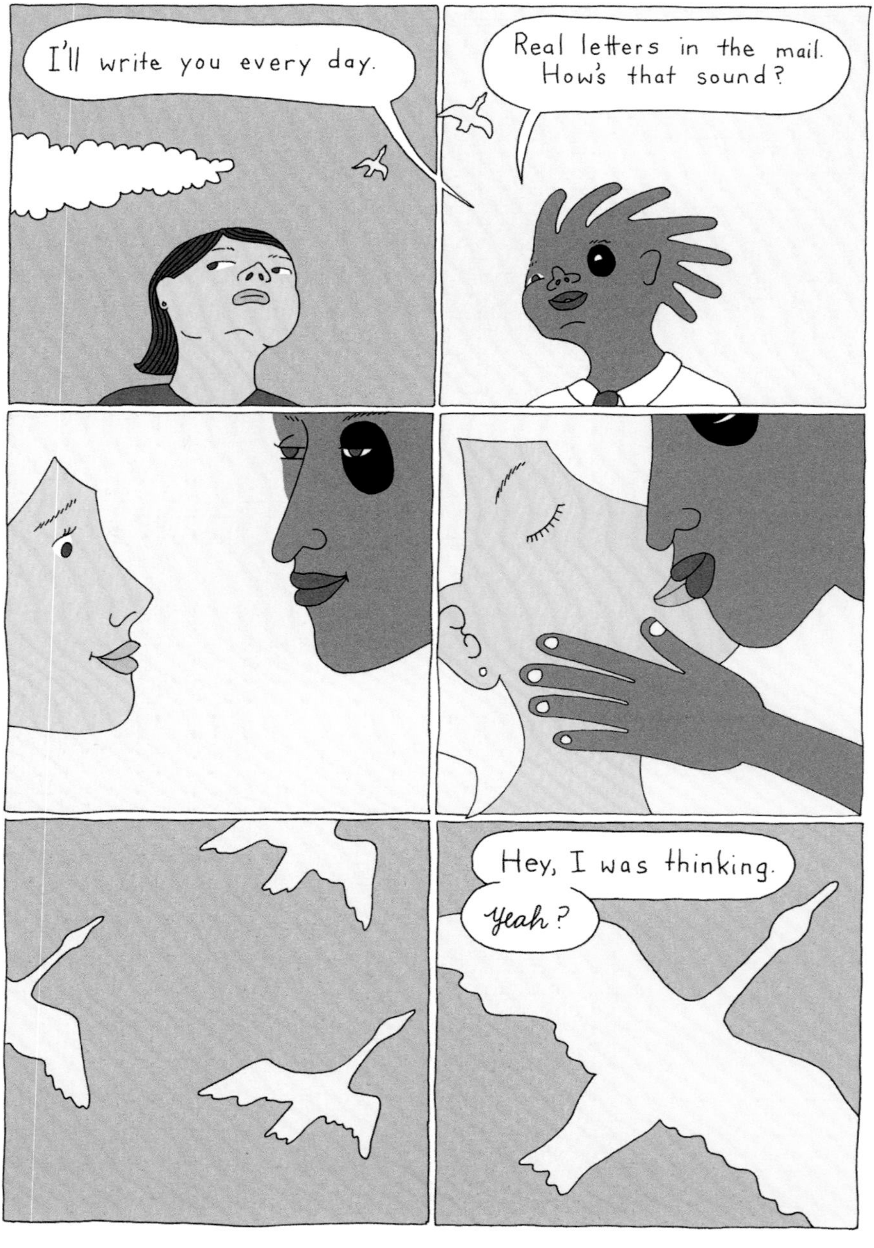
I'll write you every day.
Real letters in the mail. How's that sound?
Hey, I was thinking.
Yeah?

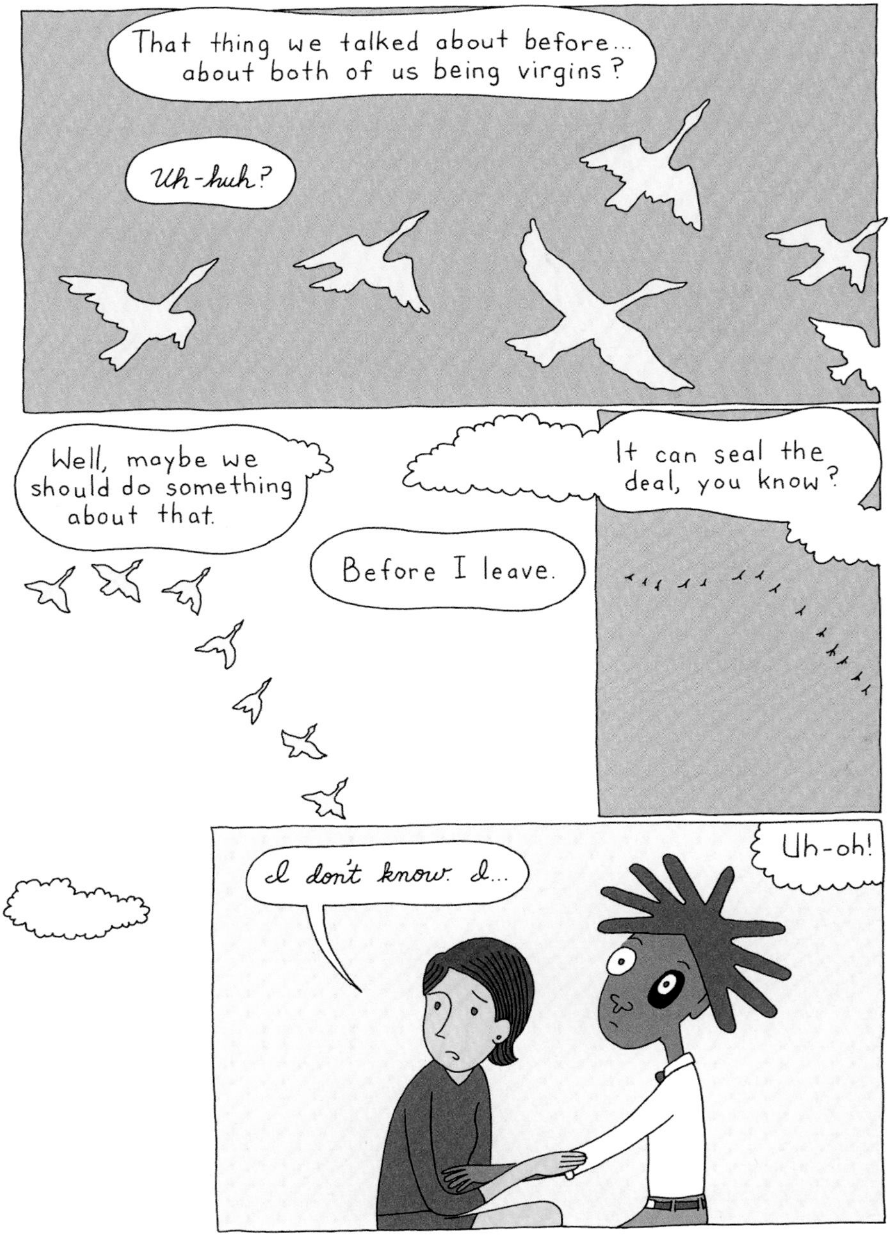
That thing we talked about before... about both of us being virgins?
Uh-huh?
Well, maybe we should do something about that.
Before I leave.
It can seal the deal, you know?
I don't know. I...
Uh-oh!

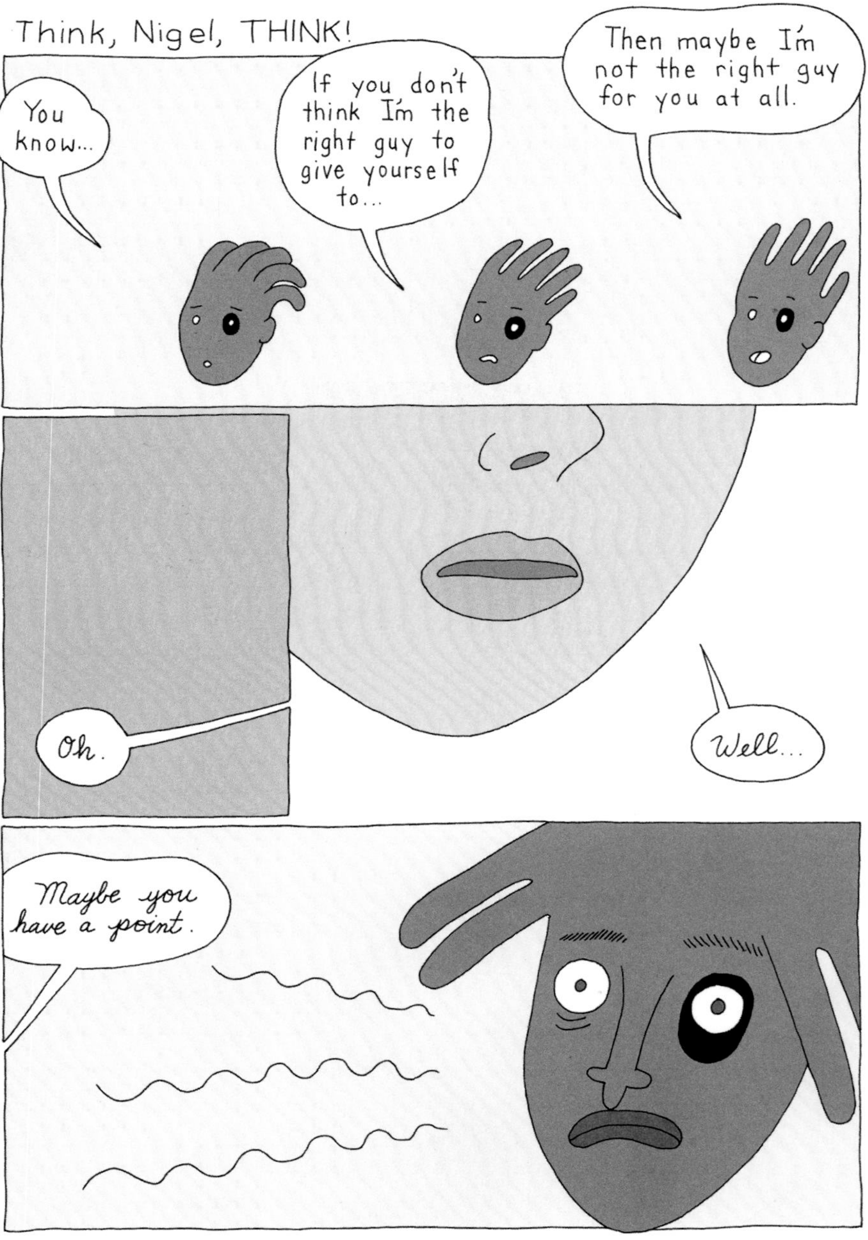
Think, Nigel, THINK!
You know...
If you don't think I'm the right guy to give yourself to...
Then maybe I'm not the right guy for you at all.
Oh.
Well...
Maybe you have a point.

PART TWO

Emily Hiroko Baker

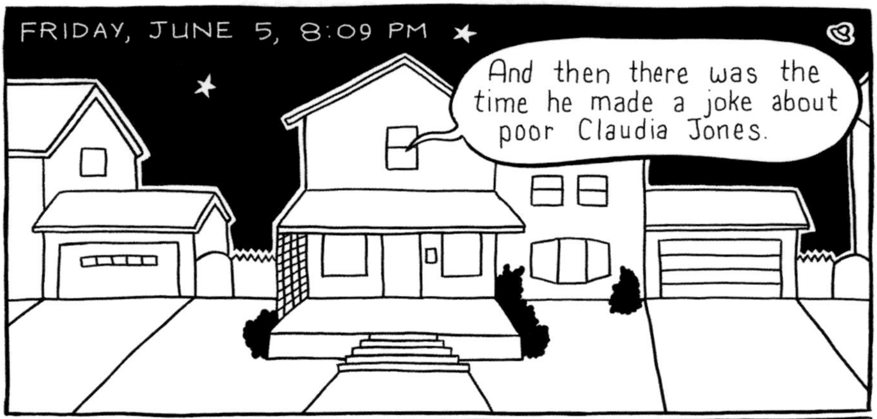
FRIDAY, JUNE 5, 8:09 PM
And then there was the time he made a joke about poor Claudia Jones.

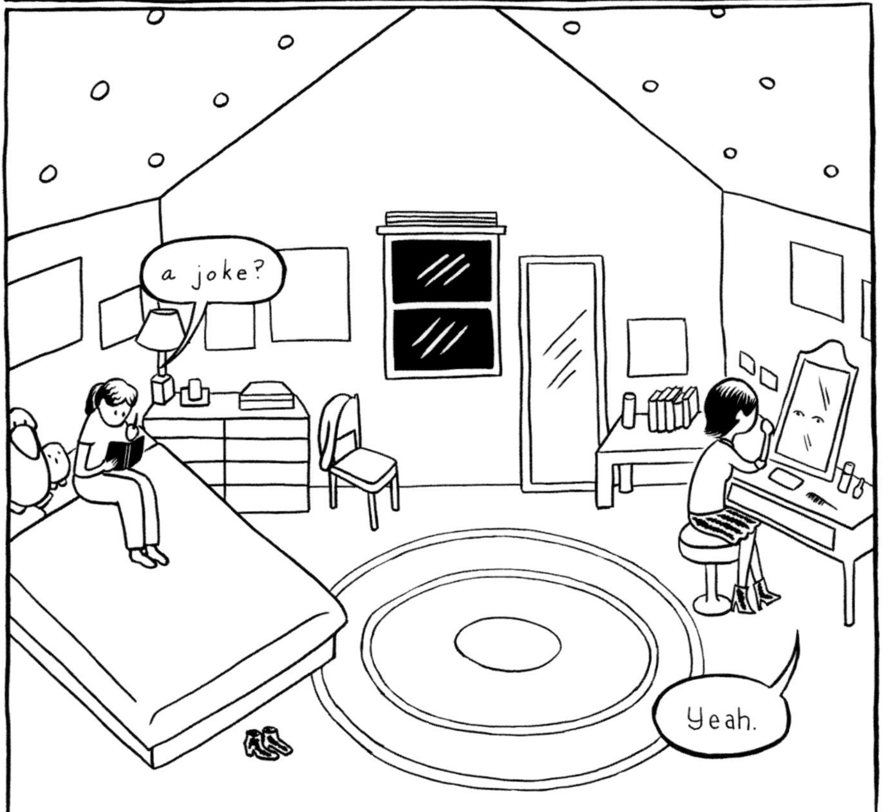
a joke?
Yeah.

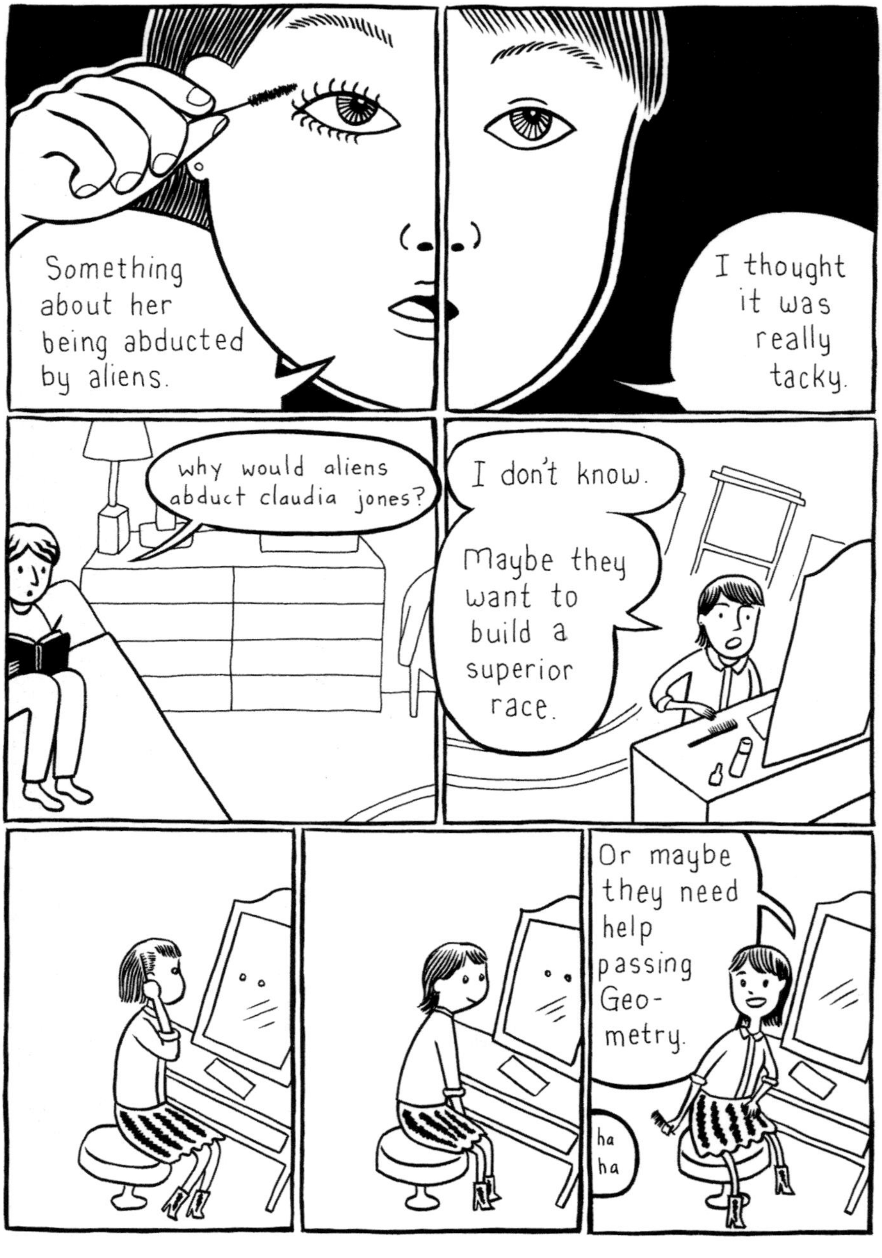

Something about her being abducted by aliens.
I thought it was really tacky.
why would aliens abduct claudia jones?
I don't know.
Maybe they want to build a superior race.
Or maybe they need help passing Geo-metry.
ha ha

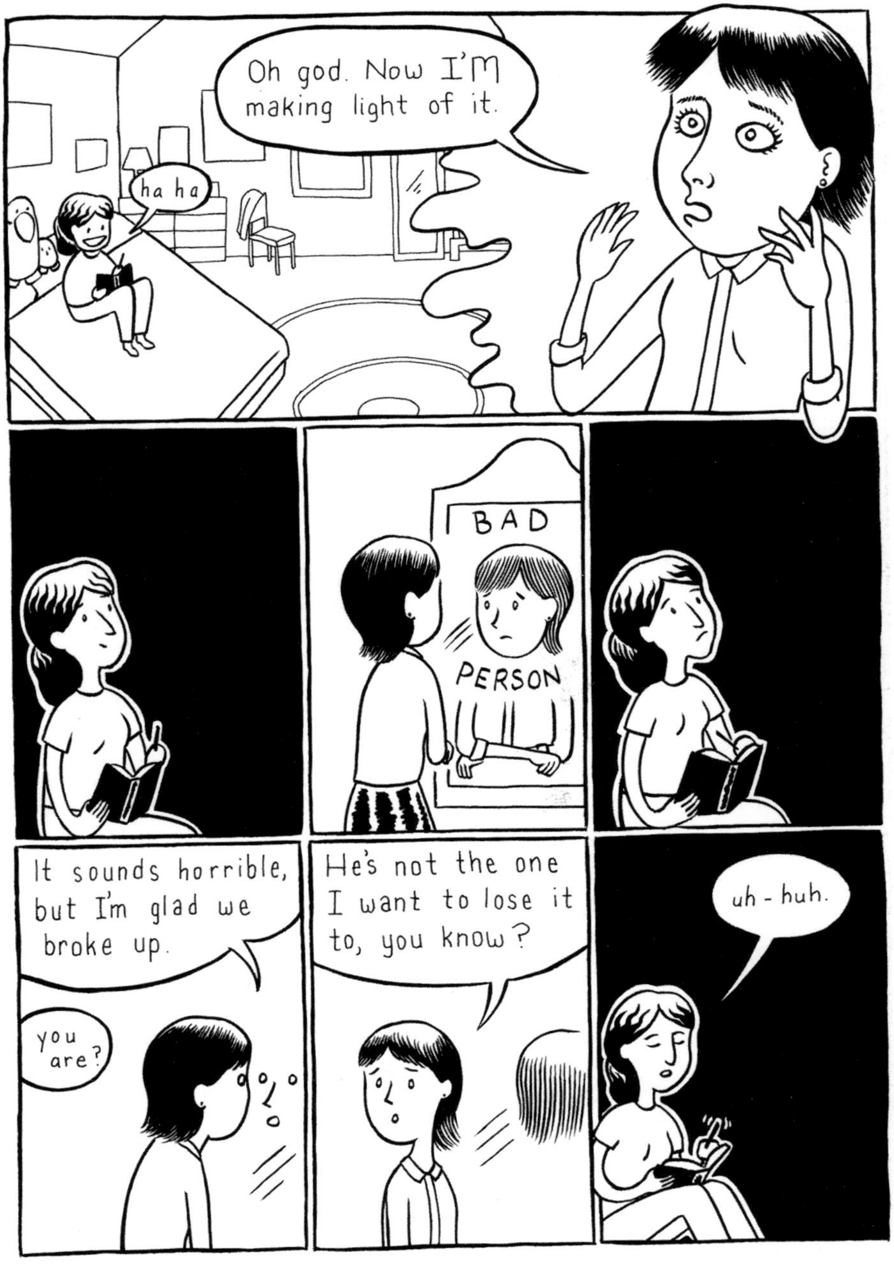
Oh god. Now I'M making light of it.
ha ha
BAD
PERSON
It sounds horrible, but I'm glad we broke up.
you are?
He's not the one I want to lose it to, you know?
uh-huh.

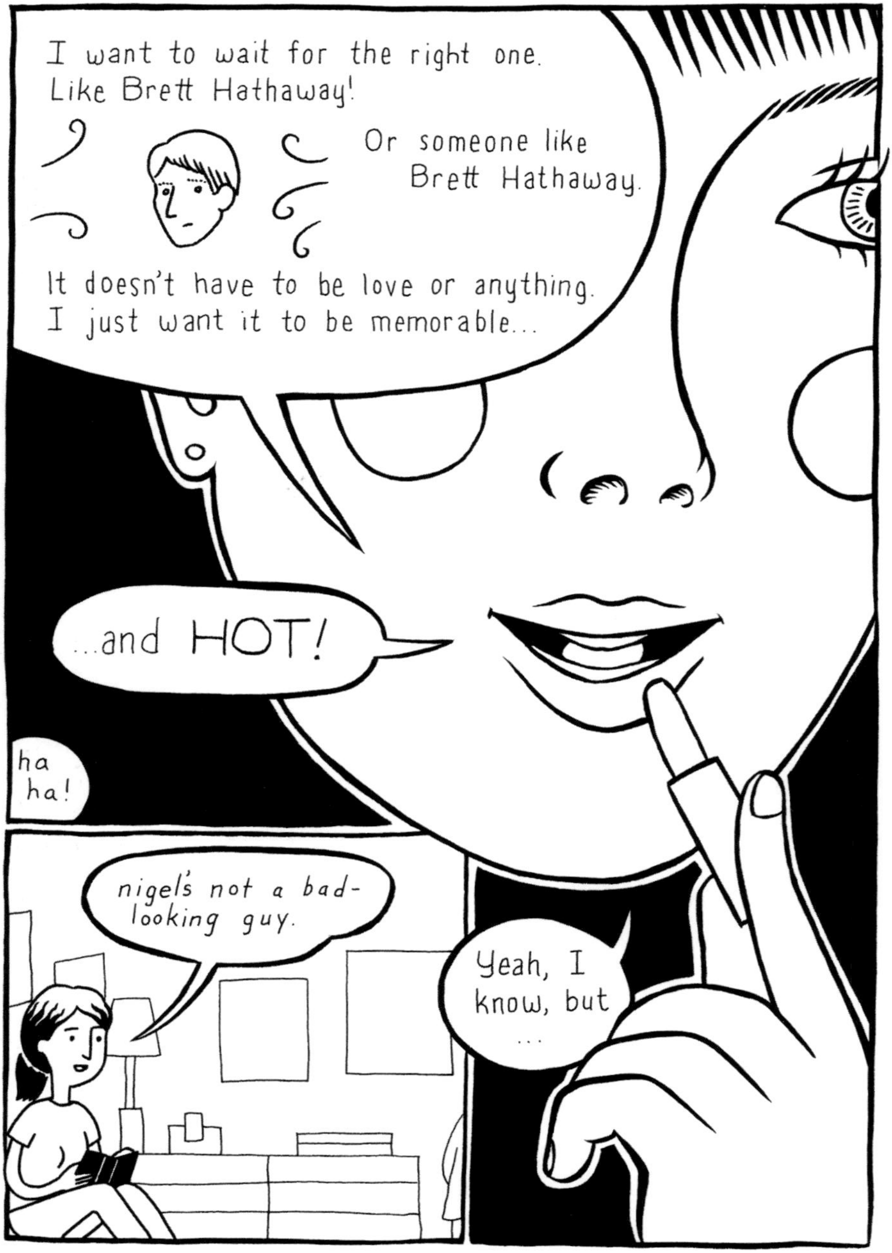
I want to wait for the right one. Like Brett Hathaway!
Or someone like Brett Hathaway.
It doesn't have to be love or anything. I just want it to be memorable...
...and HOT!
ha ha!
nigel's not a bad-looking guy.
Yeah, I know, but ...

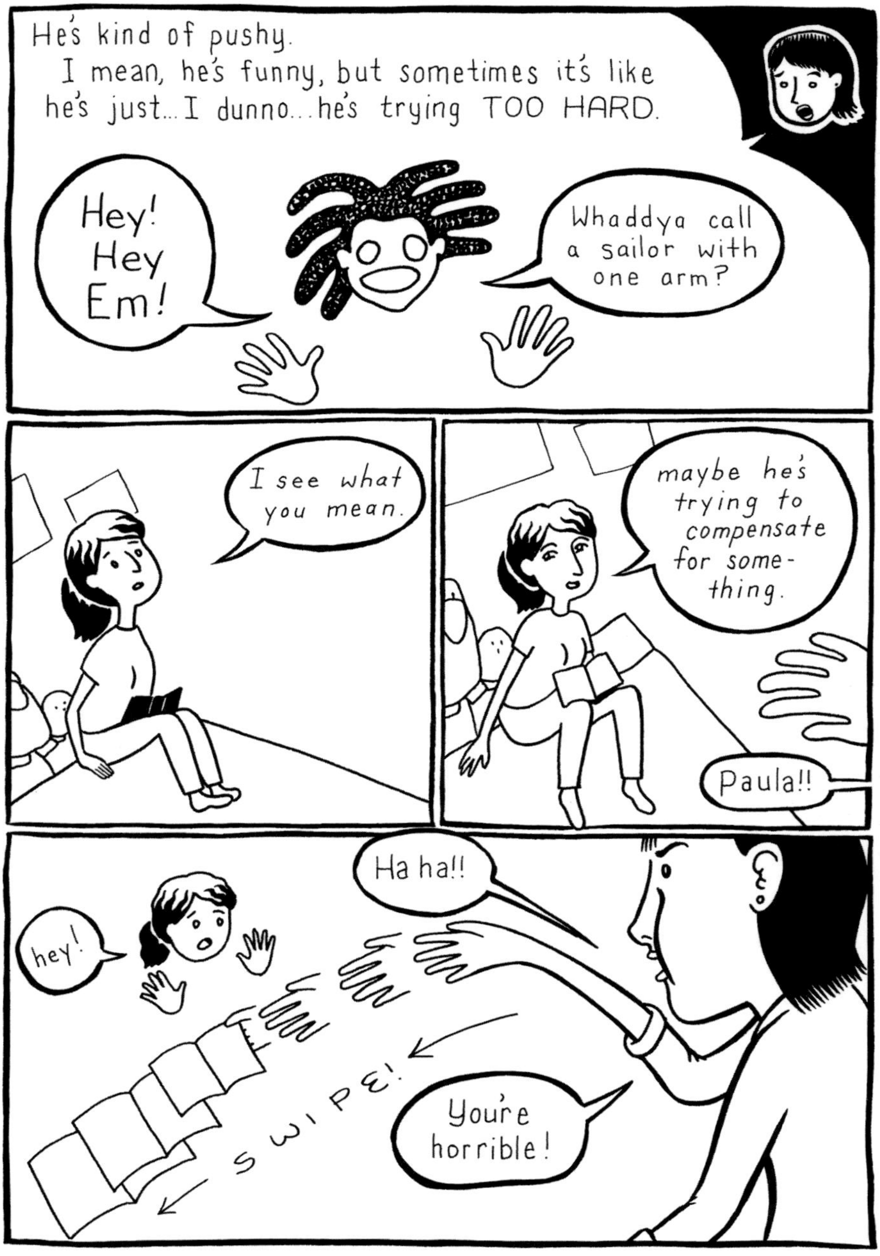
He's kind of pushy.
I mean, he's funny, but sometimes it's like he's just... I dunno... he's trying TOO HARD.
Hey! Hey Em!
Whaddya call a sailor with one arm?
I see what you mean.
maybe he's trying to compensate for some-thing.
Paula!!
Ha ha!!
hey!
SWIPE!
You're horrible!

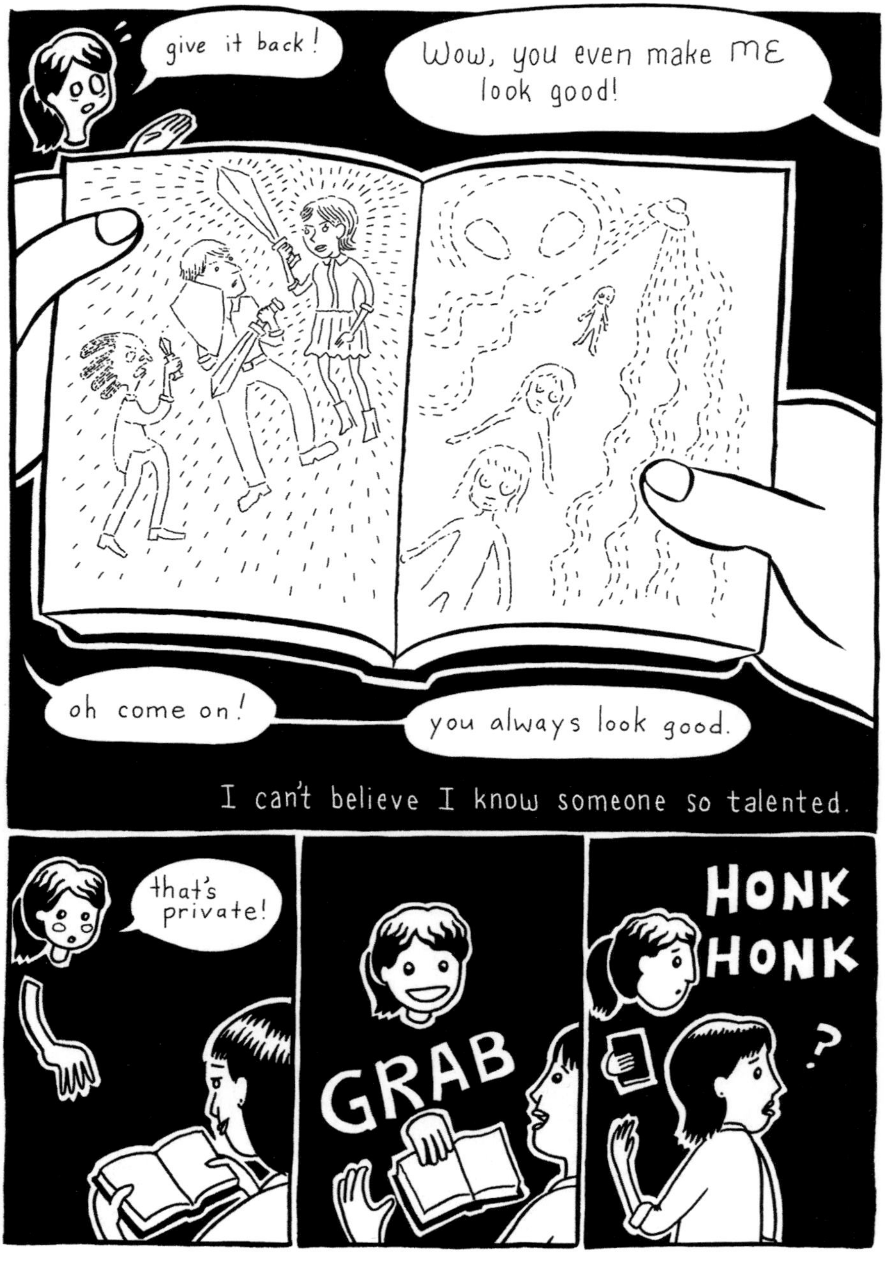
give it back!
Wow, you even make ME look good!
oh come on!
you always look good.
I can't believe I know someone so talented.
that's private!
GRAB
HONK HONK
?

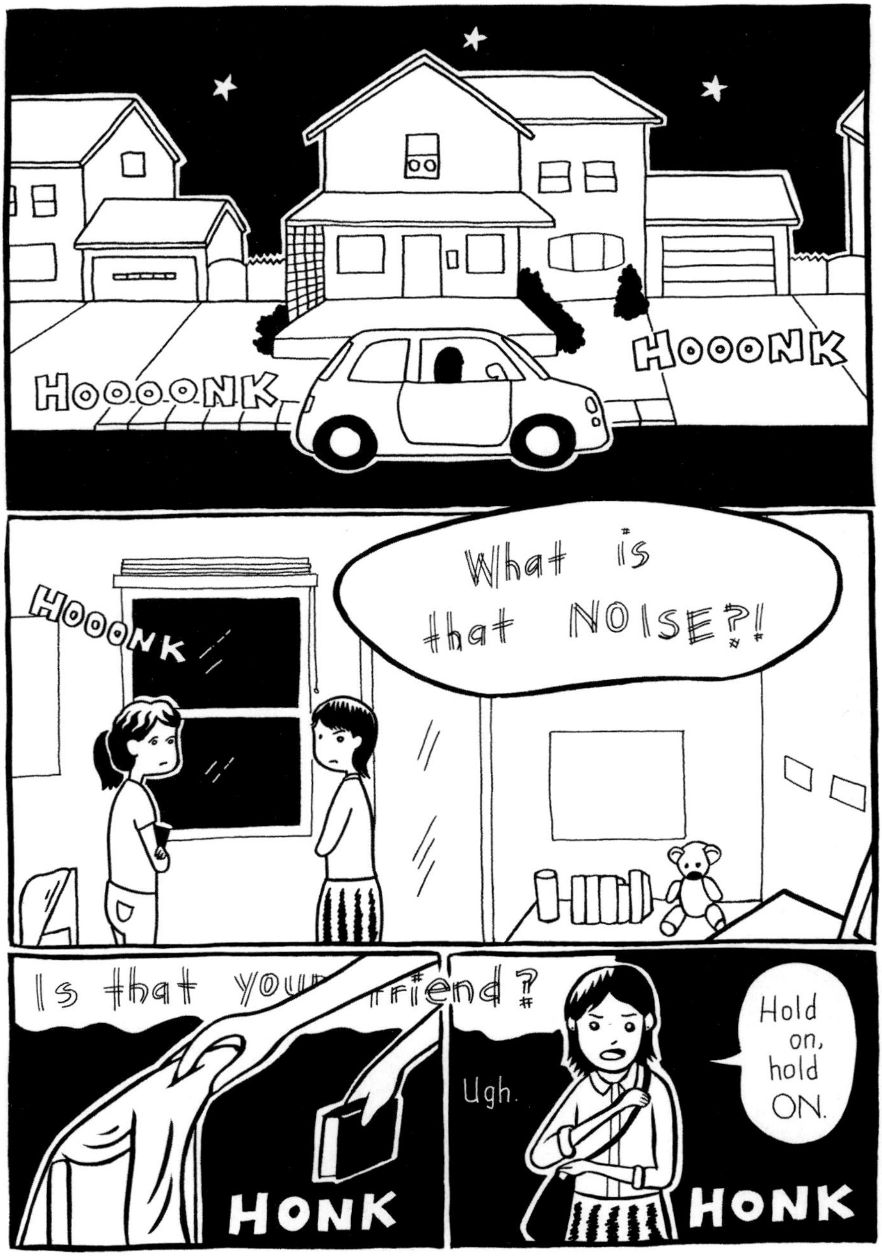
HOOOONK
HOOONK
HOOONK
What is that NOISE?!
Is that your friend?
HONK
Ugh.
Hold on, hold ON.
HONK

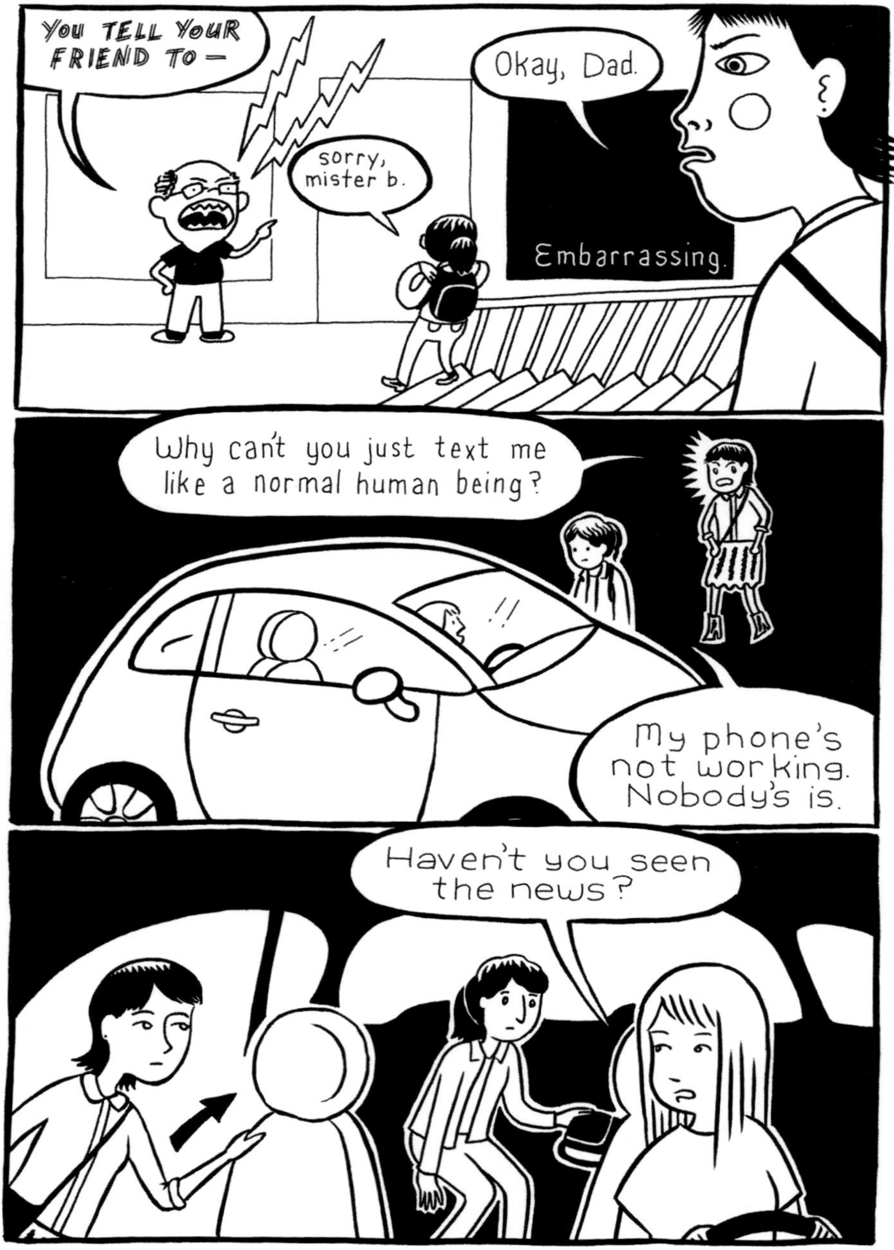
YOU TELL YOUR FRIEND TO—
sorry, mister b.
Okay, Dad.
Embarrassing.
Why can't you just text me like a normal human being?
My phone's not working. Nobody's is.
Haven't you seen the news?

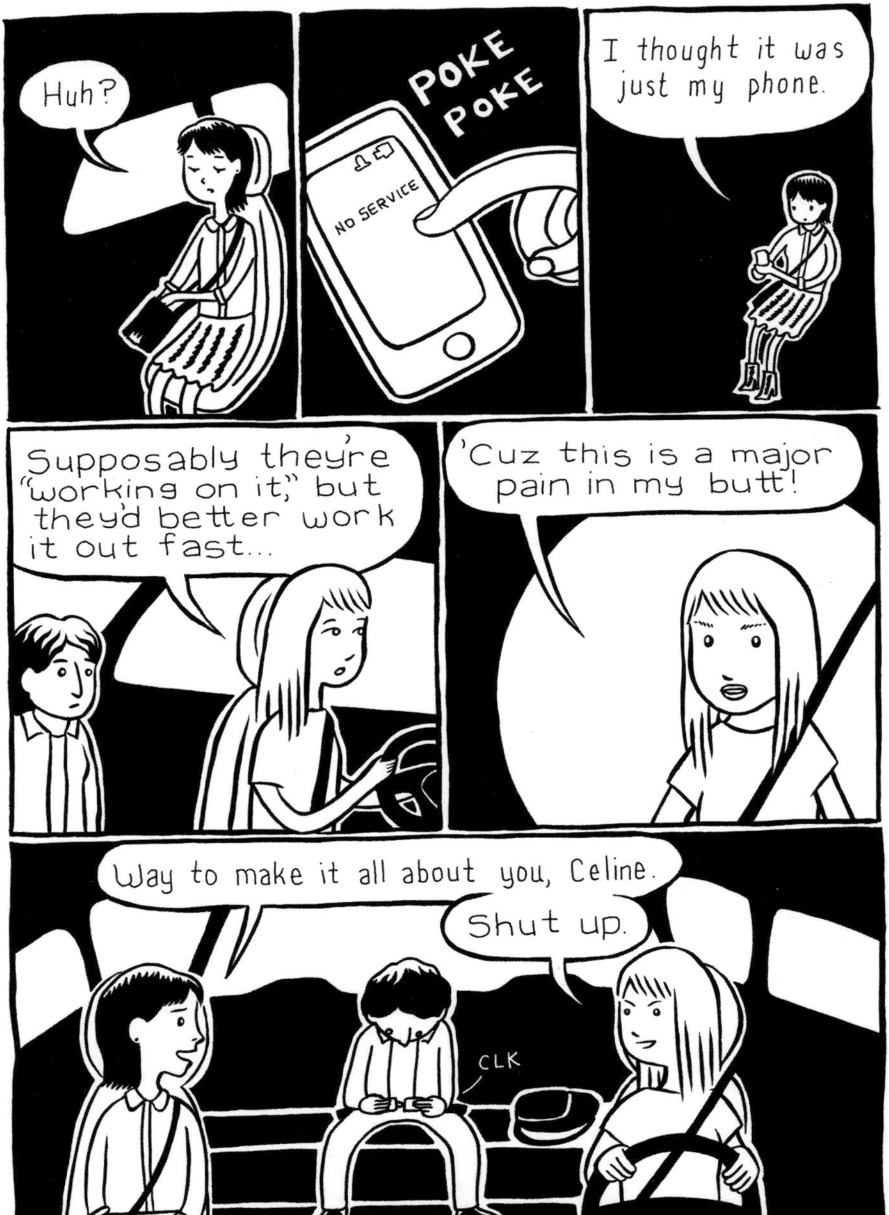
Huh?
POKE
POKE
NO SERVICE
I thought it was just my phone.
Supposably they're "working on it," but they'd better work it out fast...
'Cuz this is a major pain in my butt!
Way to make it all about you, Celine.
Shut up.
CLK

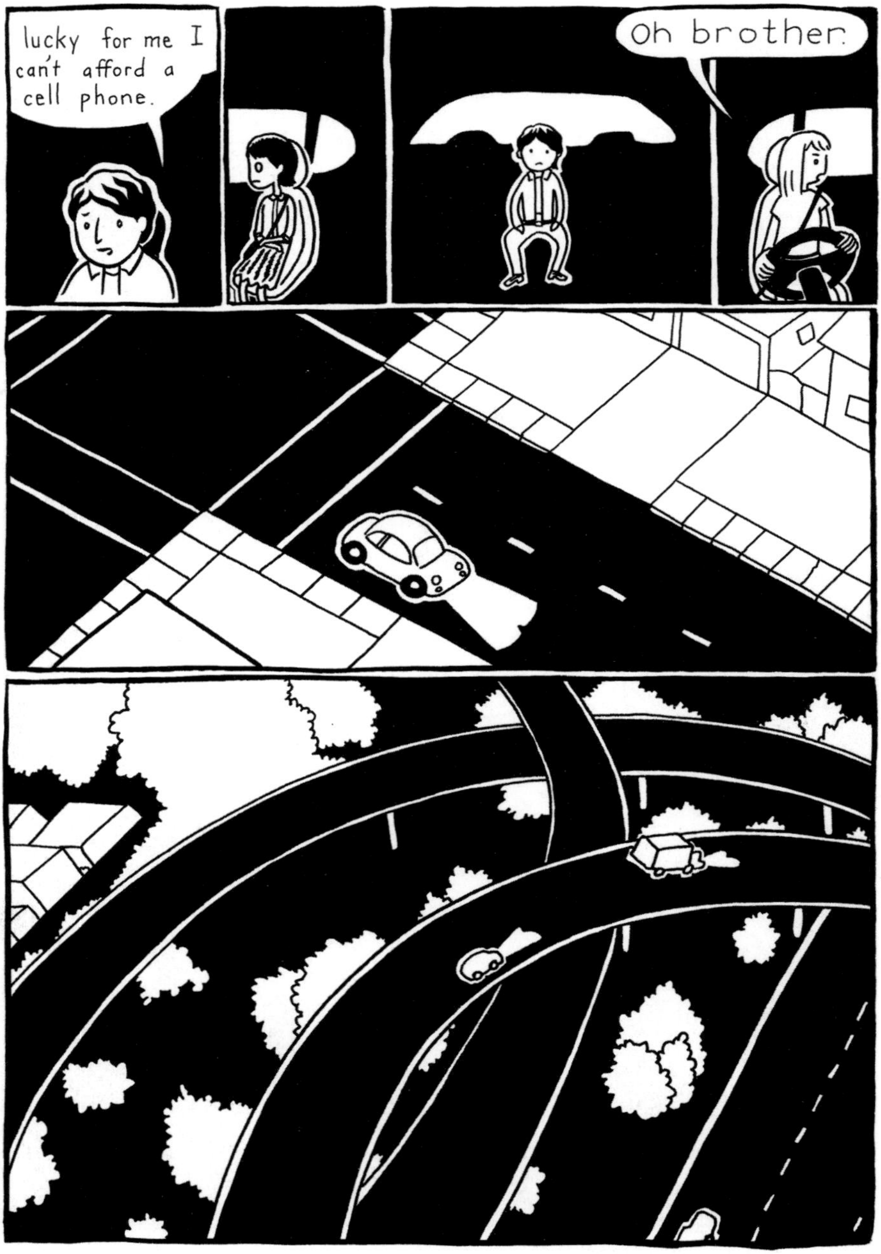
lucky for me I can't afford a cell phone.
Oh brother.

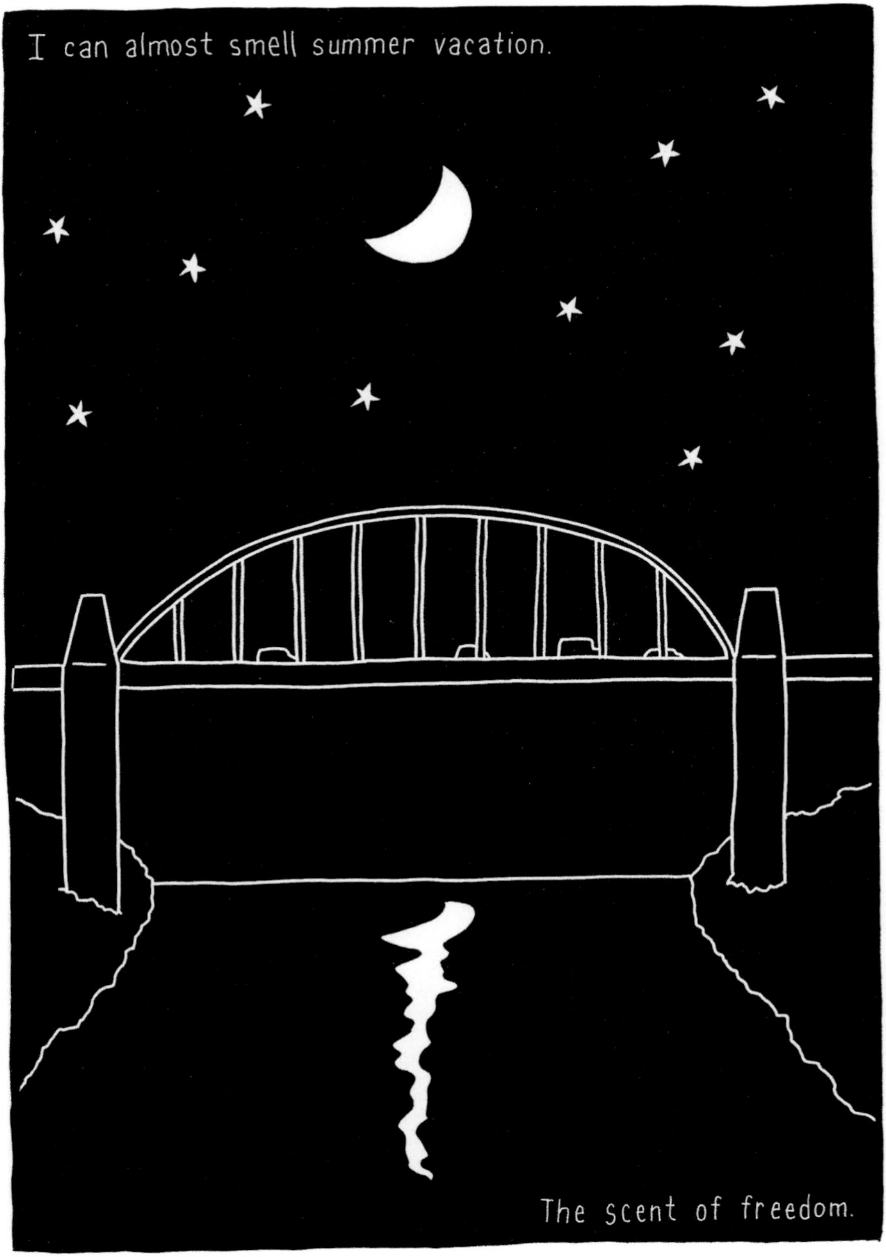
I can almost smell summer vacation.
The scent of freedom.

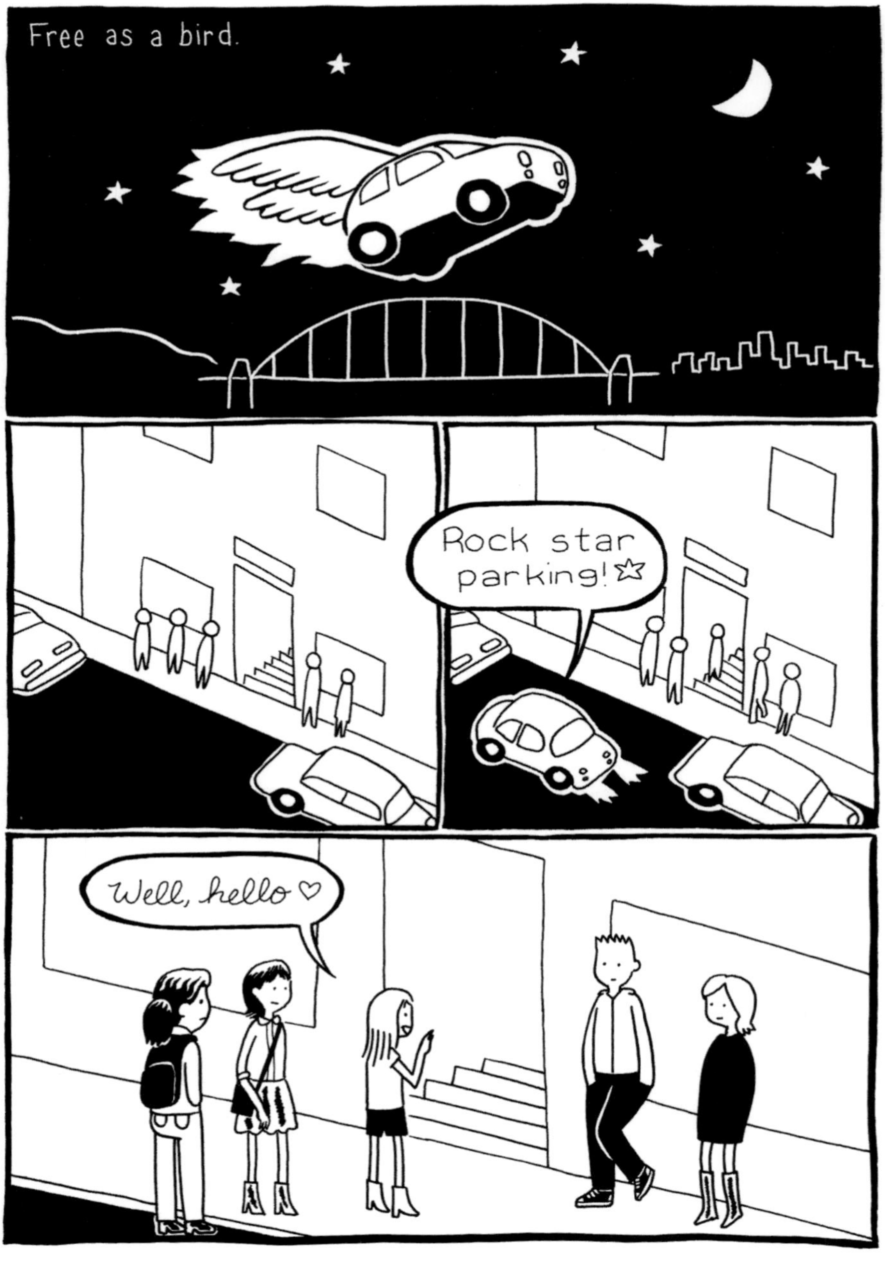
Free as a bird.
Rock star parking!
Well, hello

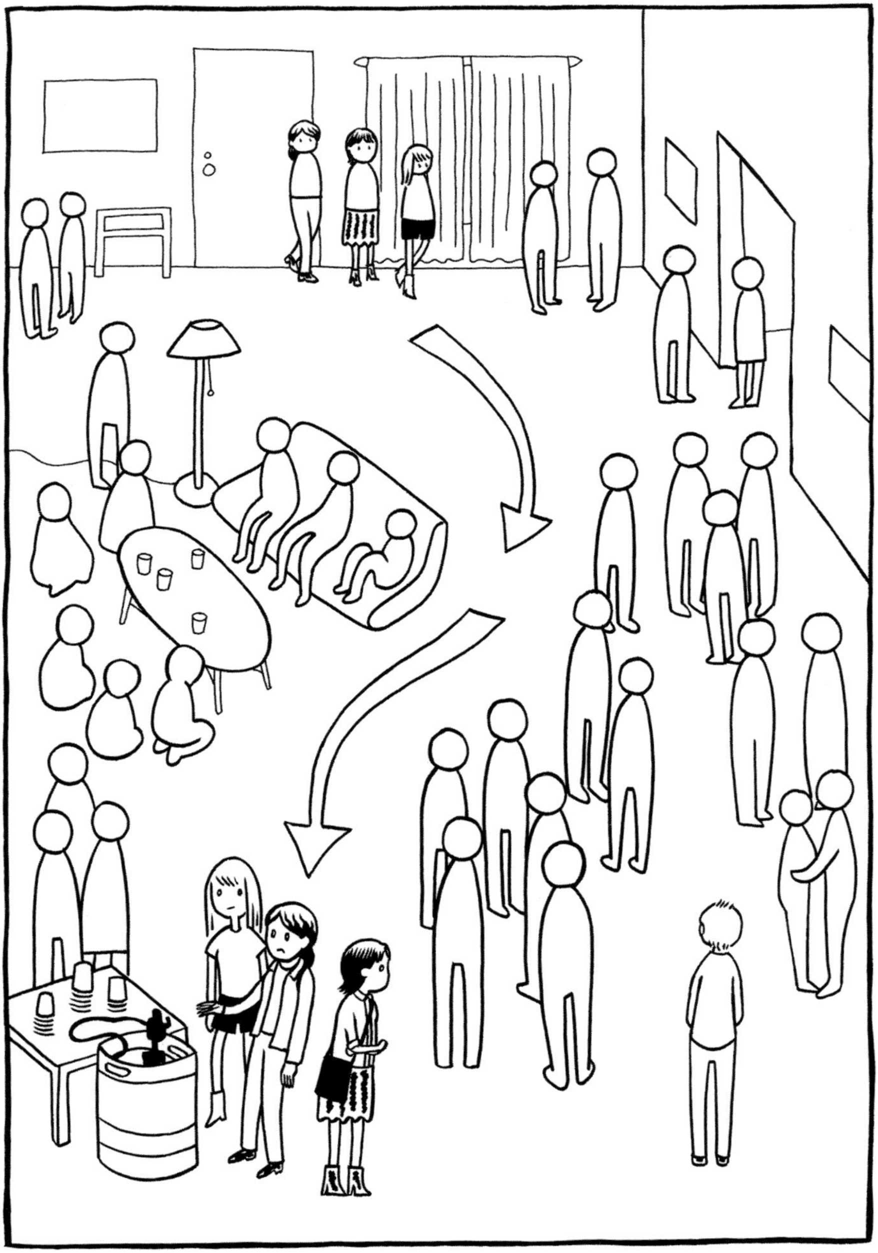

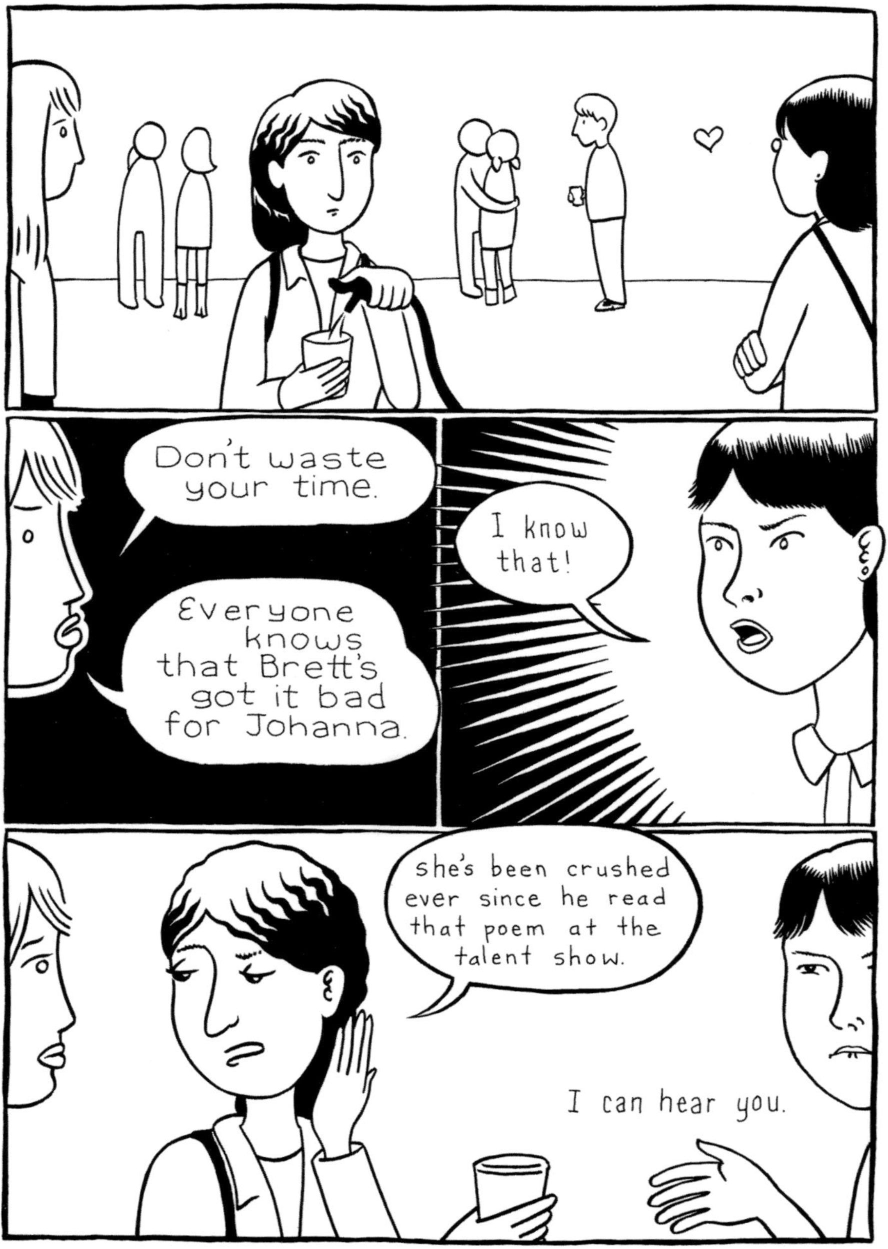
Don't waste your time.
Everyone knows that Brett's got it bad for Johanna.
I know that!
she's been crushed ever since he read that poem at the talent show.
I can hear you.

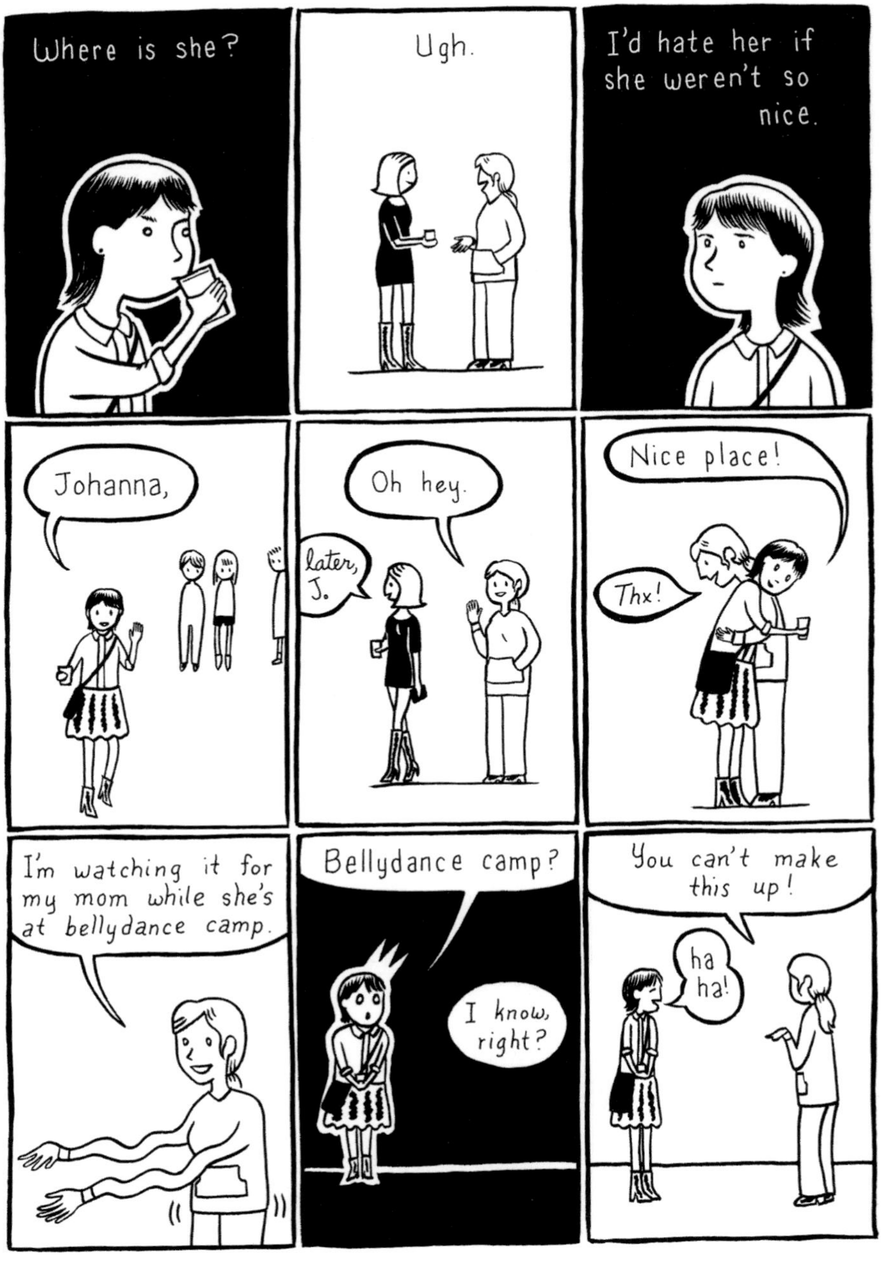
Where is she?
Ugh.
I'd hate her if she weren't so nice.
Johanna,
Oh hey.
later, J.
Nice place!
Thx!
I'm watching it for my mom while she's at bellydance camp.
Bellydance camp?
I know, right?
You can't make this up!
ha ha!

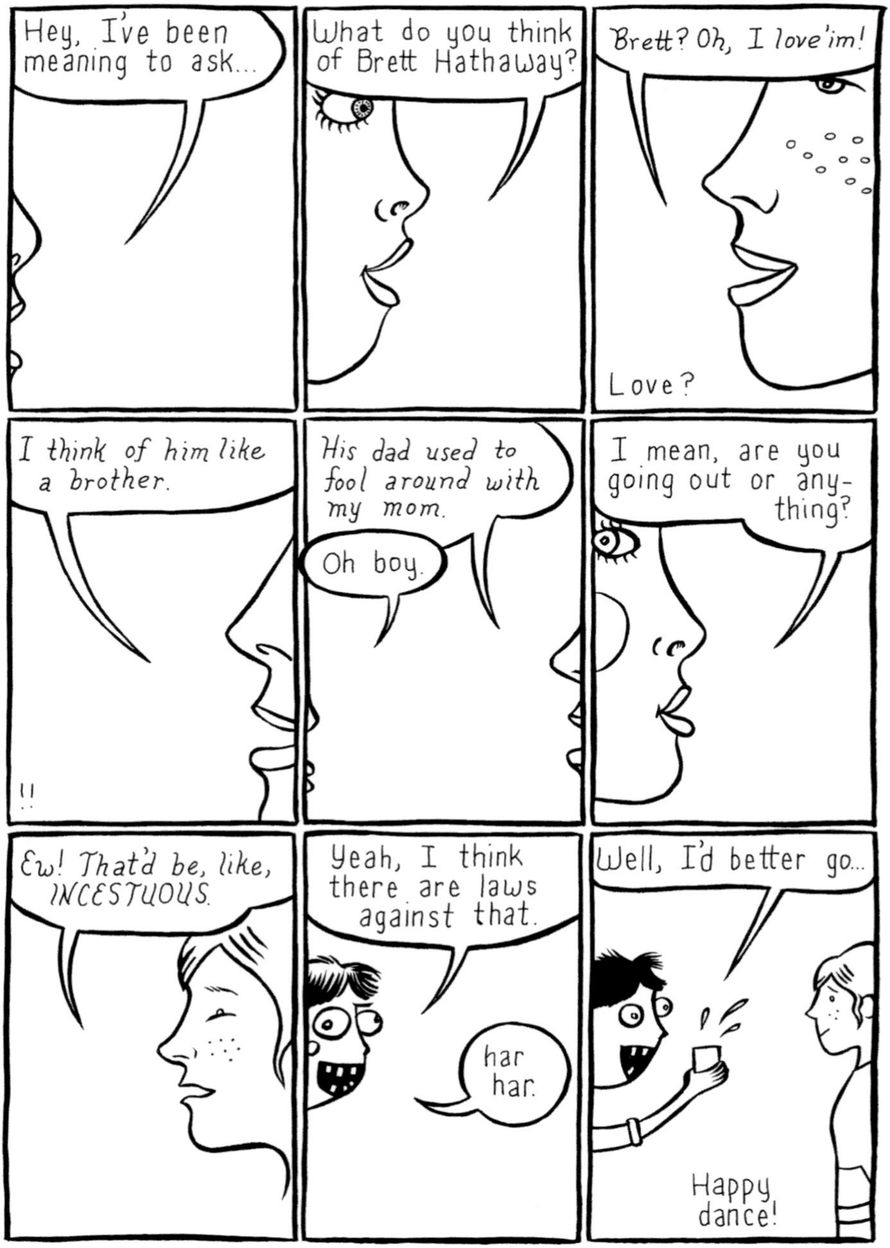
Hey, I've been meaning to ask...
What do you think of Brett Hathaway?
Brett? Oh, I love'im!
Love?
I think of him like a brother.
!!
His dad used to fool around with my mom.
Oh boy.
I mean, are you going out or anything?
Ew! That'd be, like, INCESTUOUS.
Yeah, I think there are laws against that.
har har.
Well, I'd better go...
Happy dance!

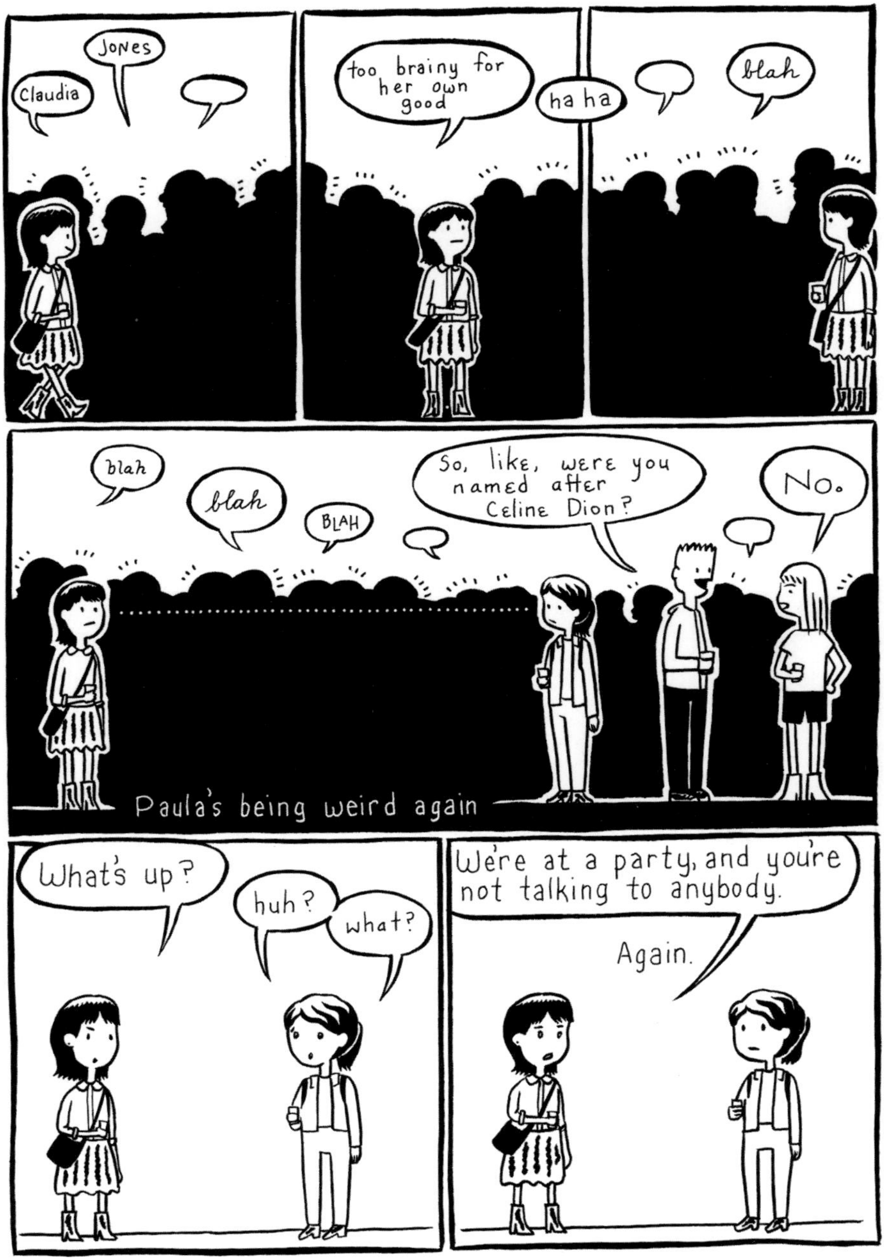

Claudia
JONES
too brainy for her own good
ha ha
blah
blah
blah
BLAH
So, like, were you named after Celine Dion?
No.
Paula's being weird again
What's up?
huh?
what?
We're at a party, and you're not talking to anybody.
Again.

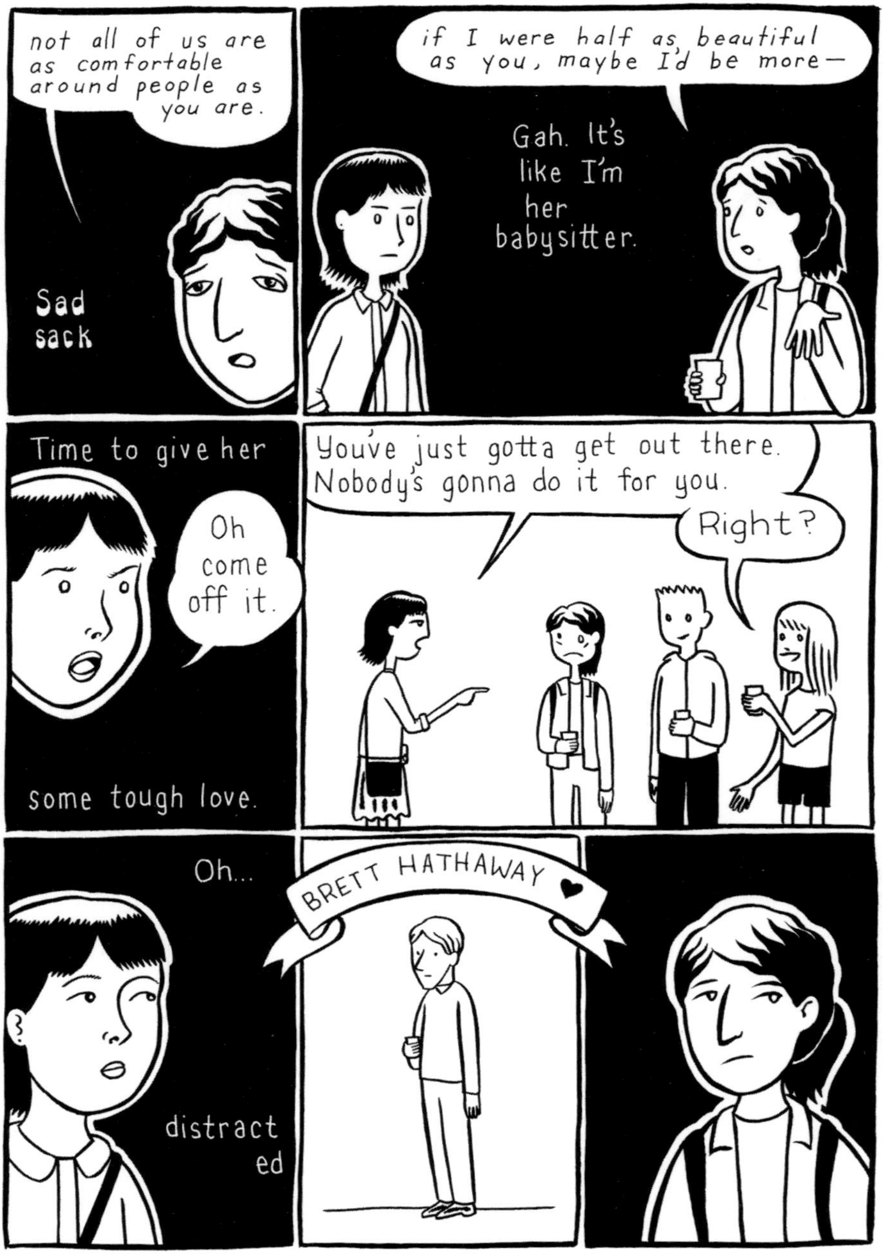

not all of us are as comfortable around people as you are.
Sad sack
if I were half as beautiful as you, maybe I'd be more—
Gah. It's like I'm her babysitter.
Time to give her
Oh come off it.
some tough love.
You've just gotta get out there. Nobody's gonna do it for you.
Right?
Oh...
distracted
BRETT HATHAWAY ♥

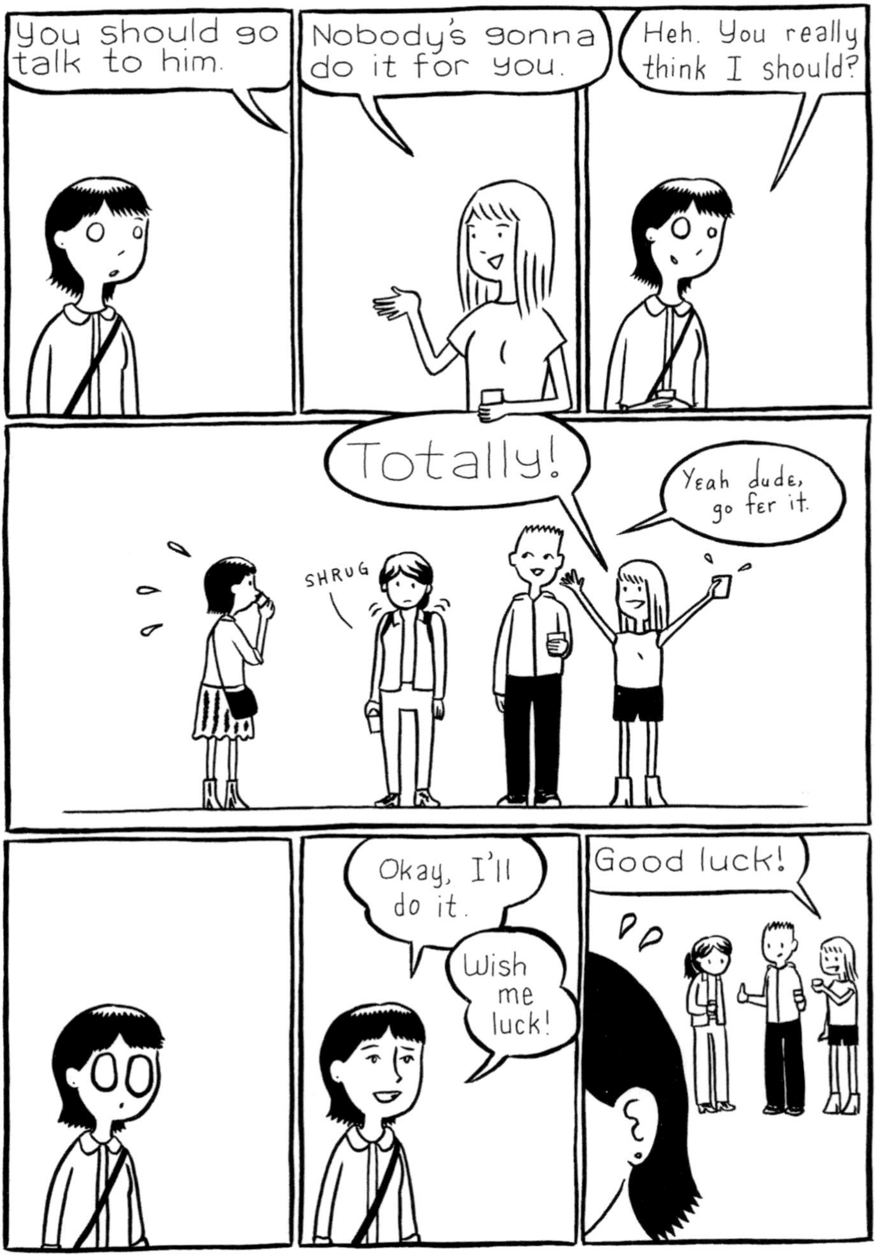
You should go talk to him.
Nobody's gonna do it for you.
Heh. You really think I should?
Totally!
Yeah dude, go fer it.
SHRUG
Okay, I'll do it.
Wish me luck!
Good luck!

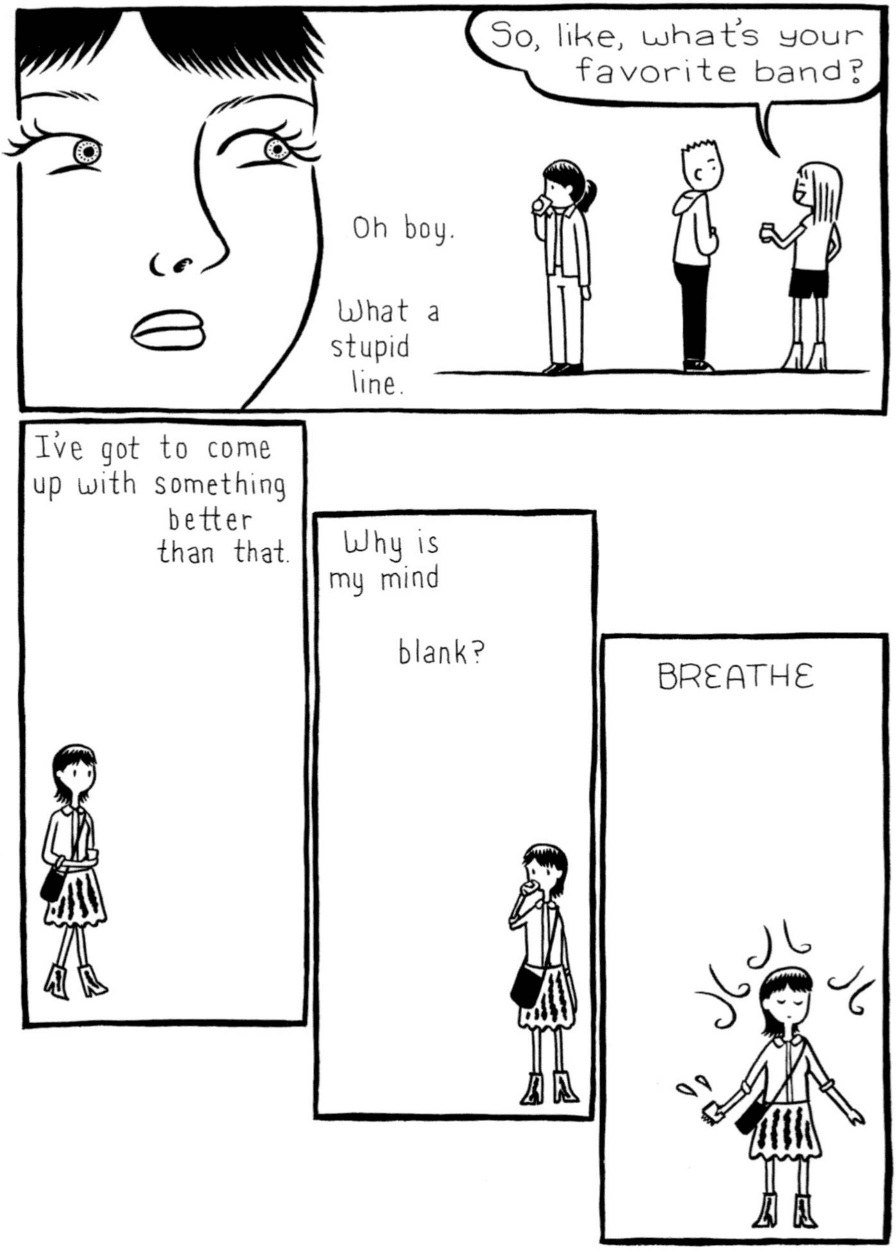
So, like, what's your favorite band?
Oh boy.
What a stupid line.
I've got to come up with something better than that.
Why is my mind
blank?
BREATHE

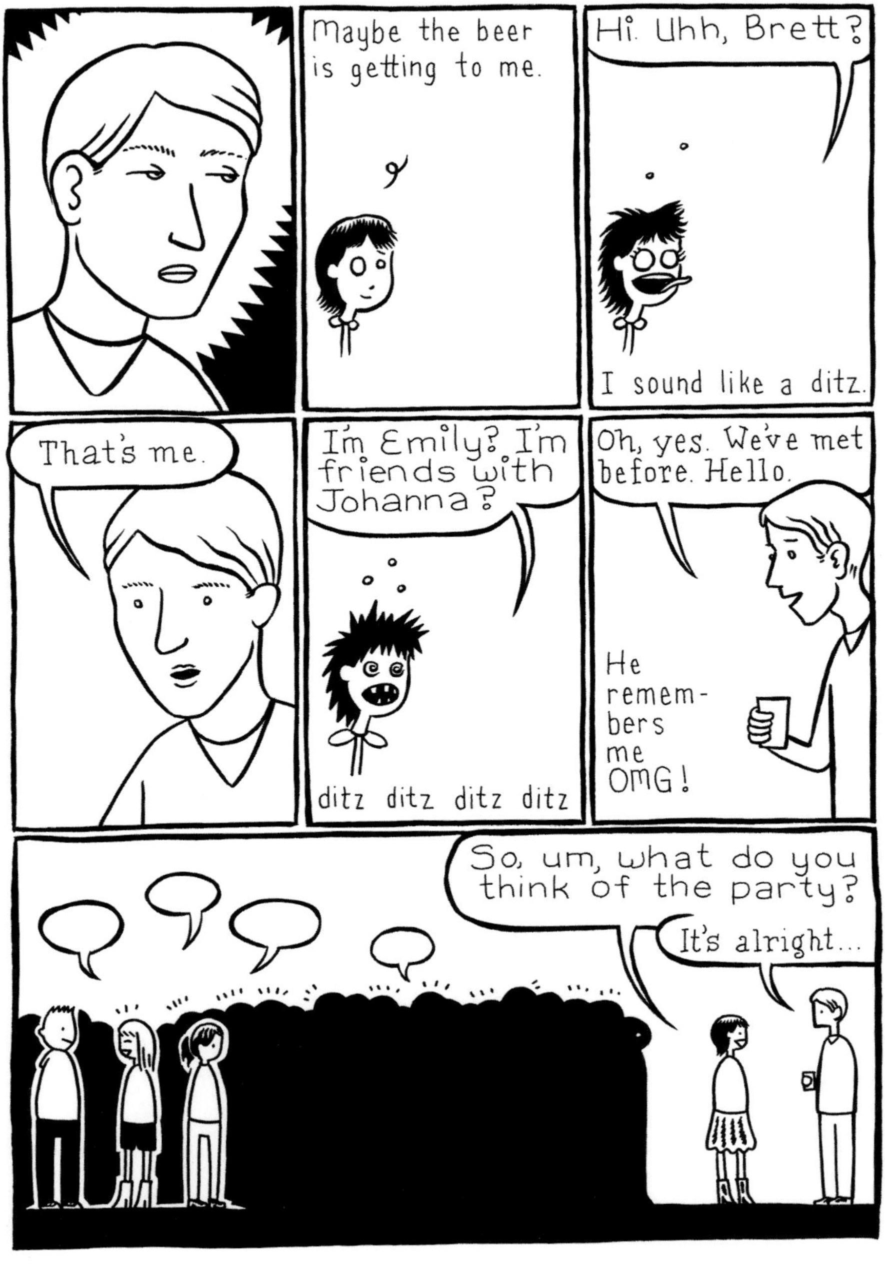
Maybe the beer is getting to me.
Hi. Uhh, Brett?
I sound like a ditz.
That's me.
I'm Emily? I'm friends with Johanna?
ditz ditz ditz ditz
Oh, yes. We've met before. Hello.
He remem-bers me OMG!
So, um, what do you think of the party?
It's alright...

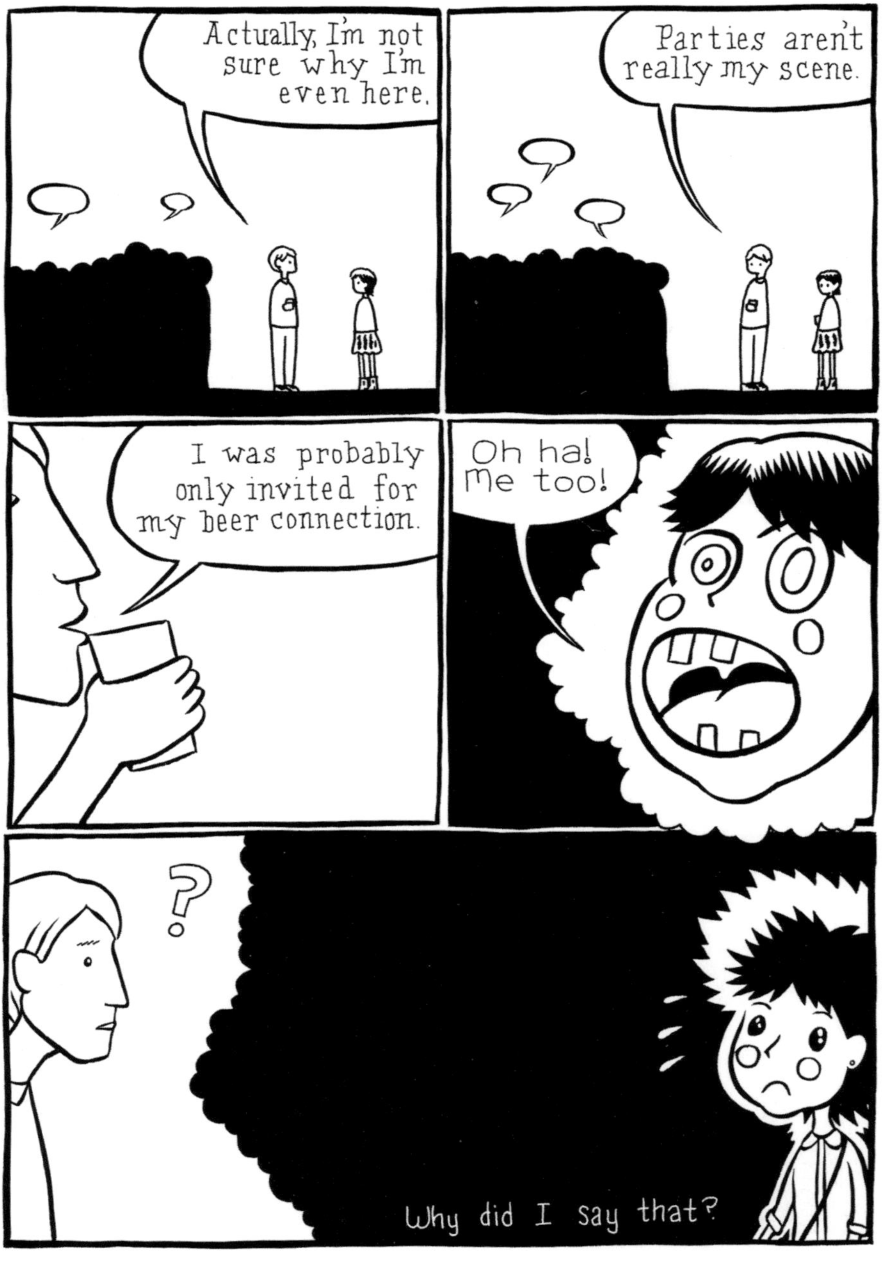
Actually, I'm not sure why I'm even here.
Parties aren't really my scene.
I was probably only invited for my beer connection.
Oh ha! Me too!
?
Why did I say that?

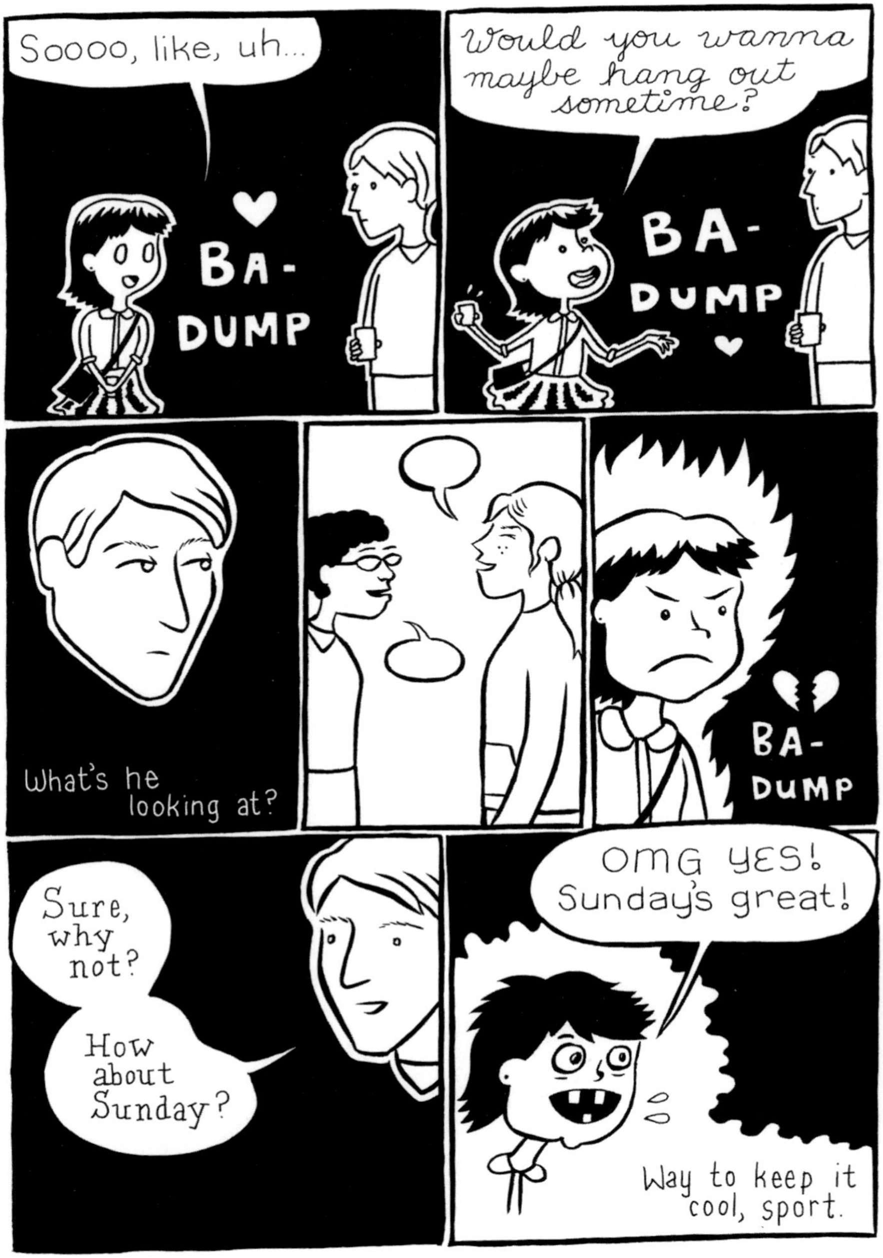

Soooo, like, uh...
BA-DUMP
Would you wanna maybe hang out sometime?
BA-DUMP
What's he looking at?
BA-DUMP
Sure, why not?
How about Sunday?
OMG YES! Sunday's great!
Way to keep it cool, sport.

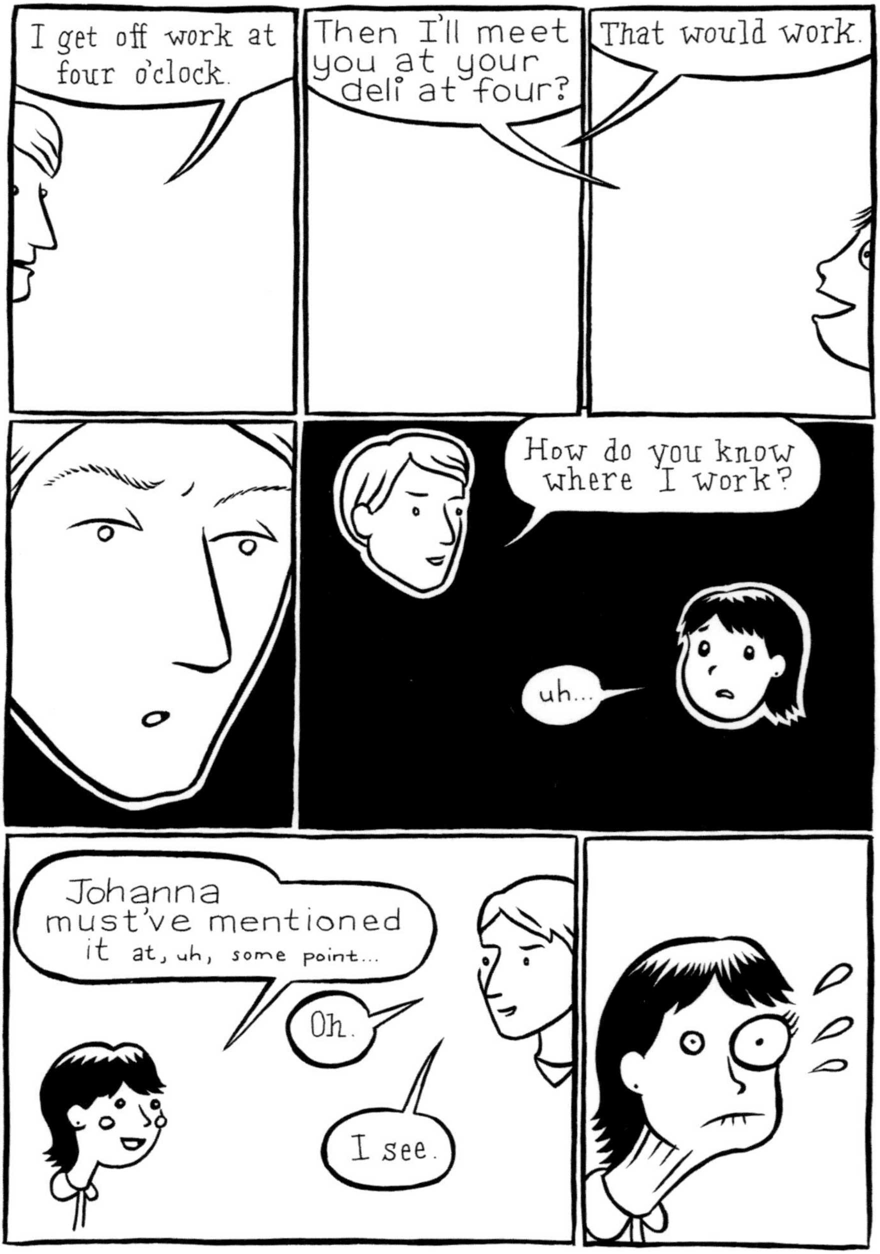
I get off work at four o'clock.
Then I'll meet you at your deli at four?
That would work.
How do you know where I work?
uh...
Johanna must've mentioned it at, uh, some point...
Oh.
I see.

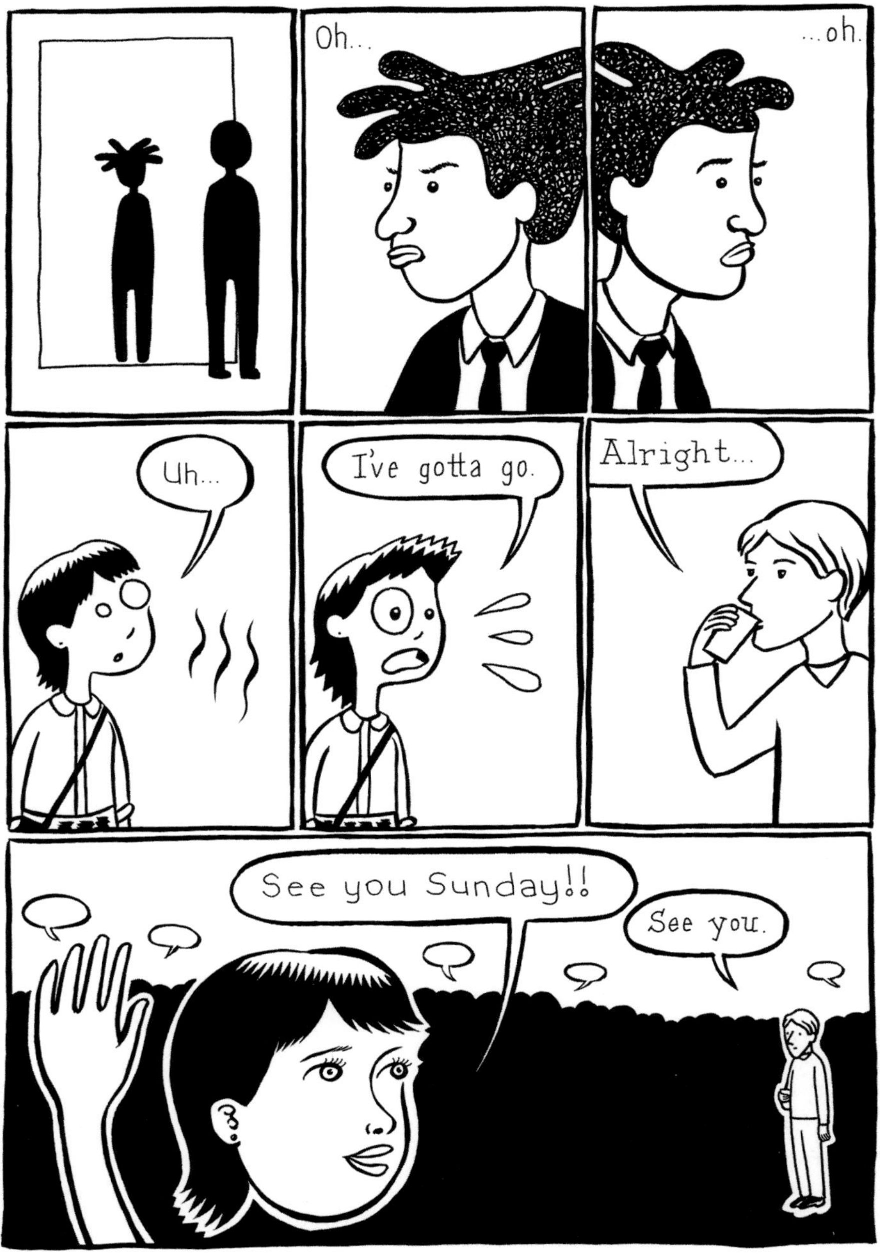
Oh...
...oh.
Uh...
I've gotta go.
Alright...
See you Sunday!!
See you.

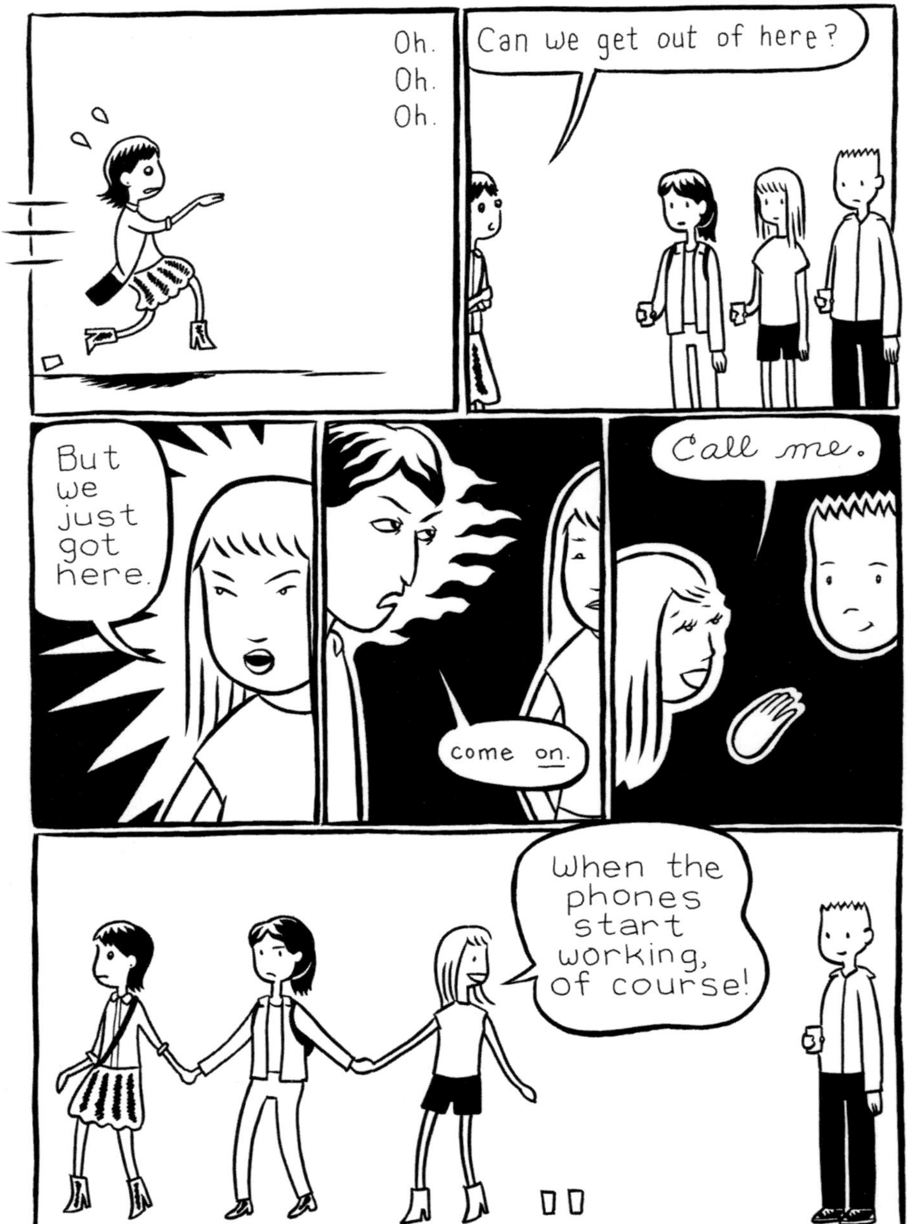
Oh.
Oh.
Oh.
Can we get out of here?
But we just got here.
come on.
Call me.
When the phones start working, of course!

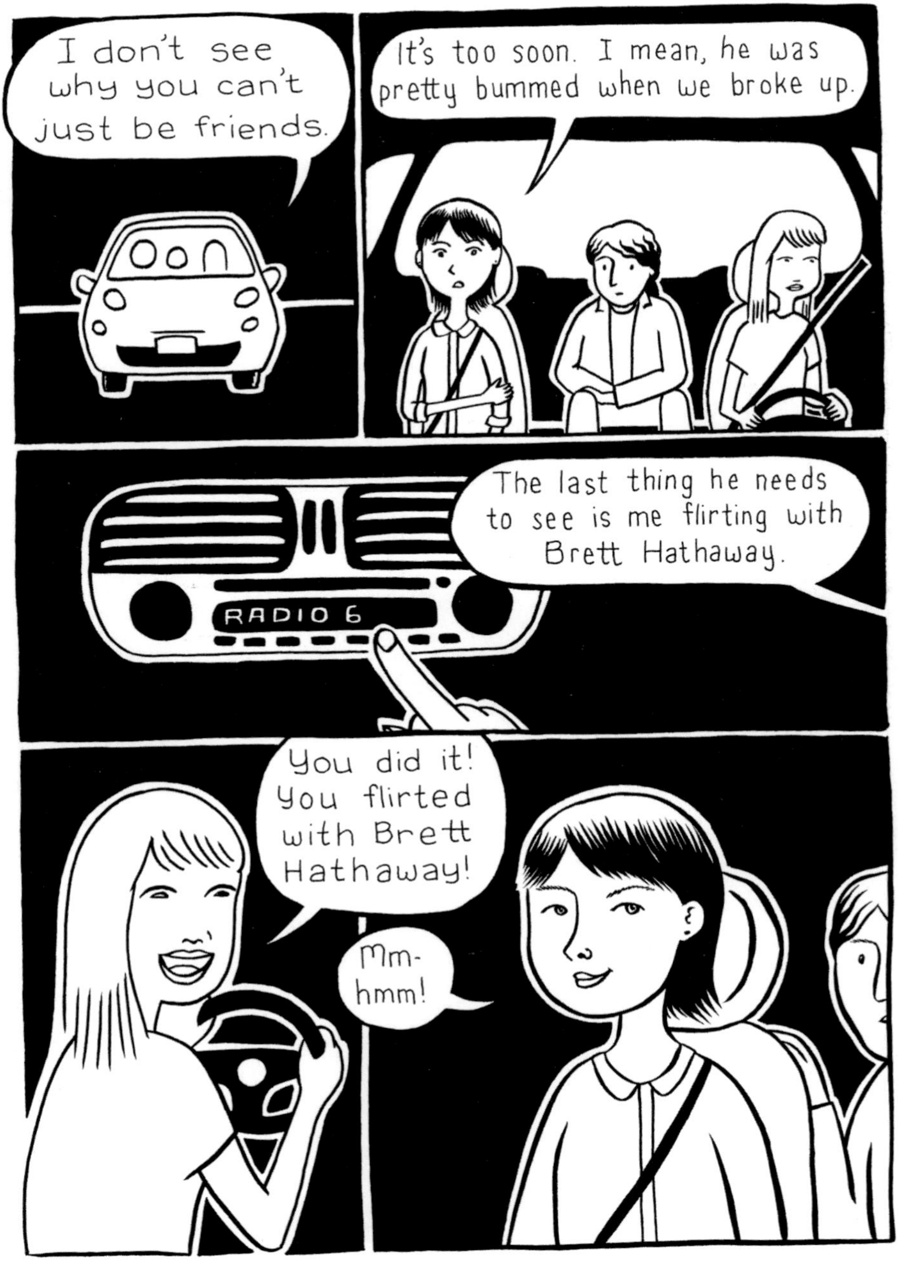
I don't see why you can't just be friends.
It's too soon. I mean, he was pretty bummed when we broke up.
The last thing he needs to see is me flirting with Brett Hathaway.
RADIO 6
You did it! You flirted with Brett Hathaway!
Mm-hmm!

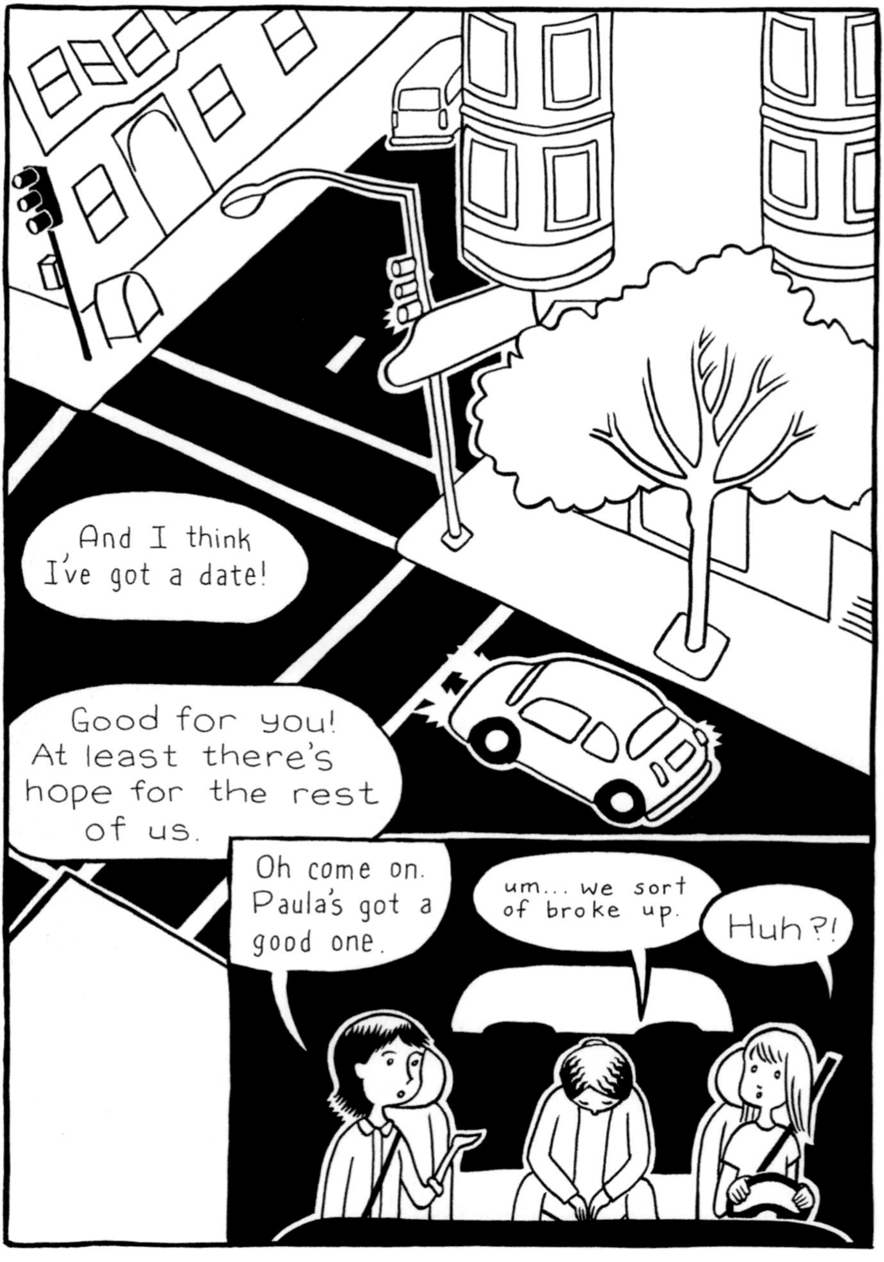
And I think I've got a date!
Good for you! At least there's hope for the rest of us.
Oh come on. Paula's got a good one.
um... we sort of broke up.
Huh?!

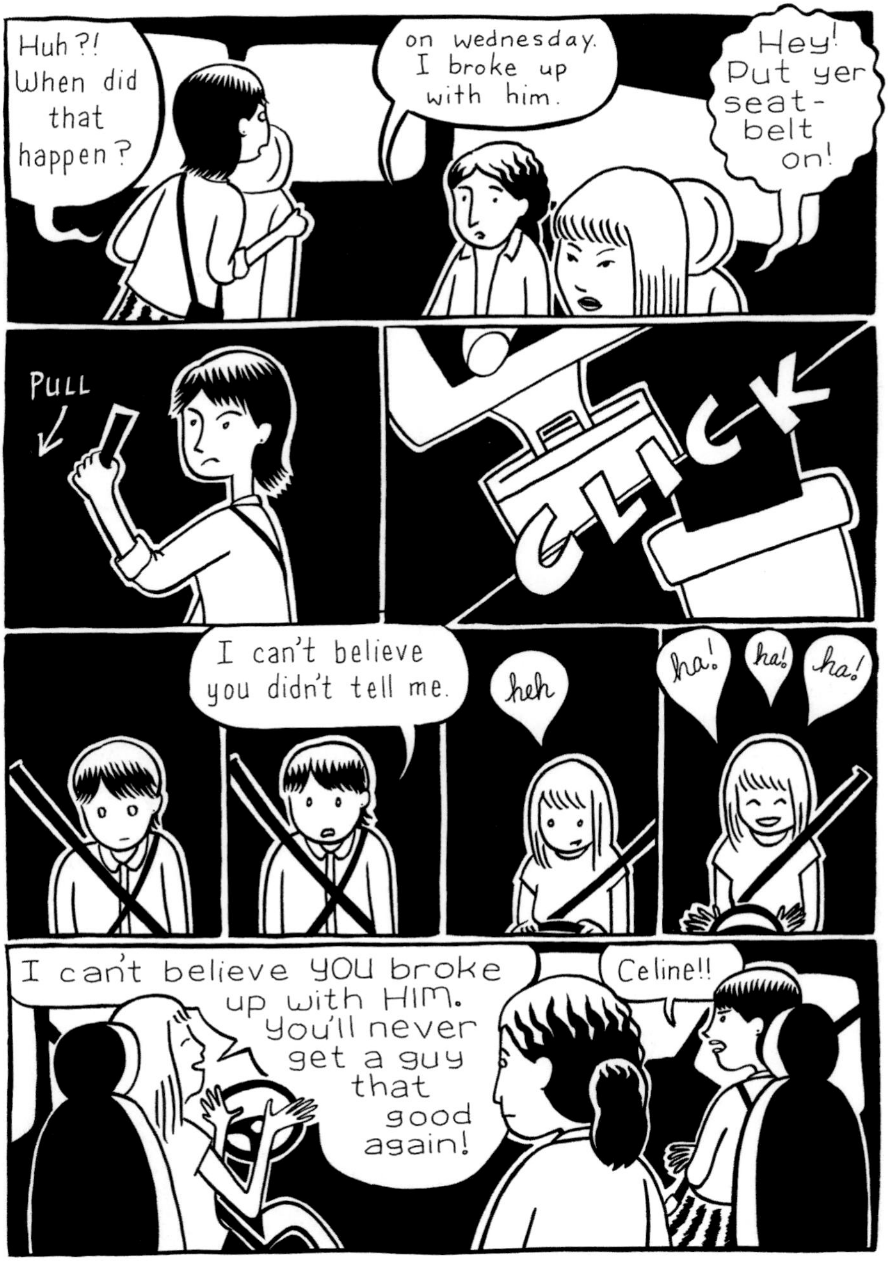
Huh?! When did that happen?
on wednesday. I broke up with him.
Hey! Put yer seat-belt on!
PULL
CLICK
I can't believe you didn't tell me.
heh
ha! ha! ha!
I can't believe YOU broke up with HIM. You'll never get a guy that good again!
Celine!!

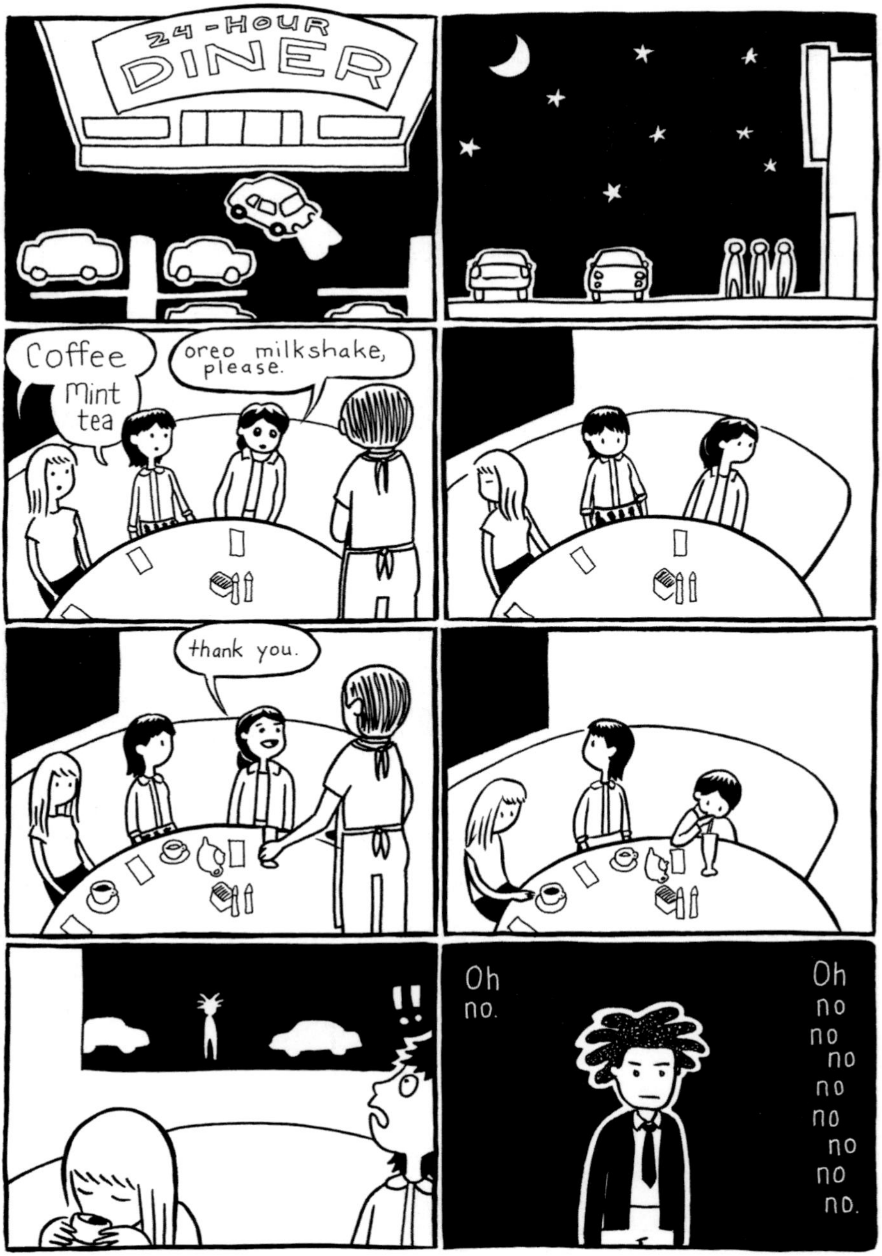
24-HOUR
DINER
Coffee
Mint tea
oreo milkshake, please.
thank you.
!!
Oh no.
Oh no no no no no no no no.

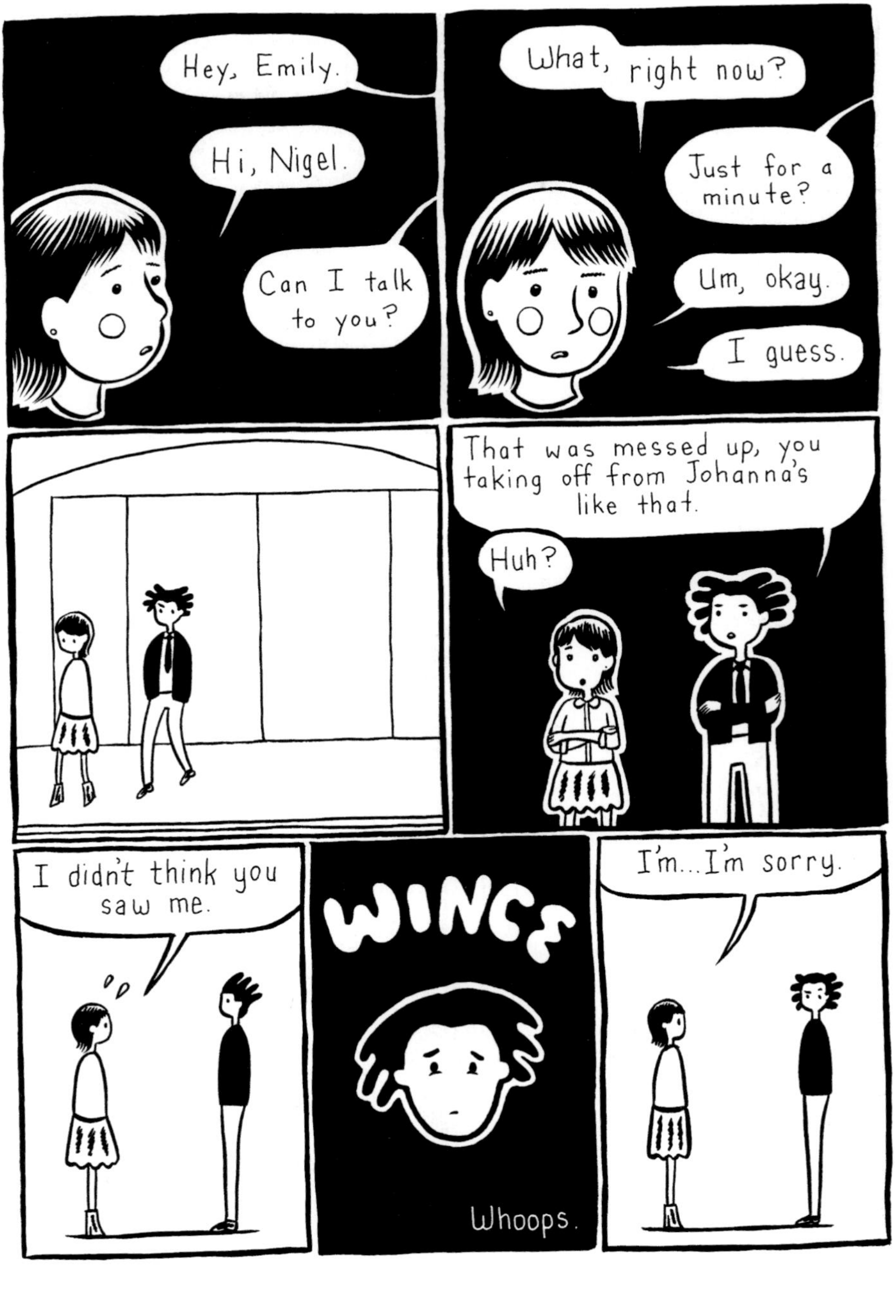
Hey, Emily.
Hi, Nigel.
Can I talk to you?
What, right now?
Just for a minute?
Um, okay.
I guess.
That was messed up, you taking off from Johanna's like that.
Huh?
I didn't think you saw me.
WINCE
Whoops.
I'm...I'm sorry.

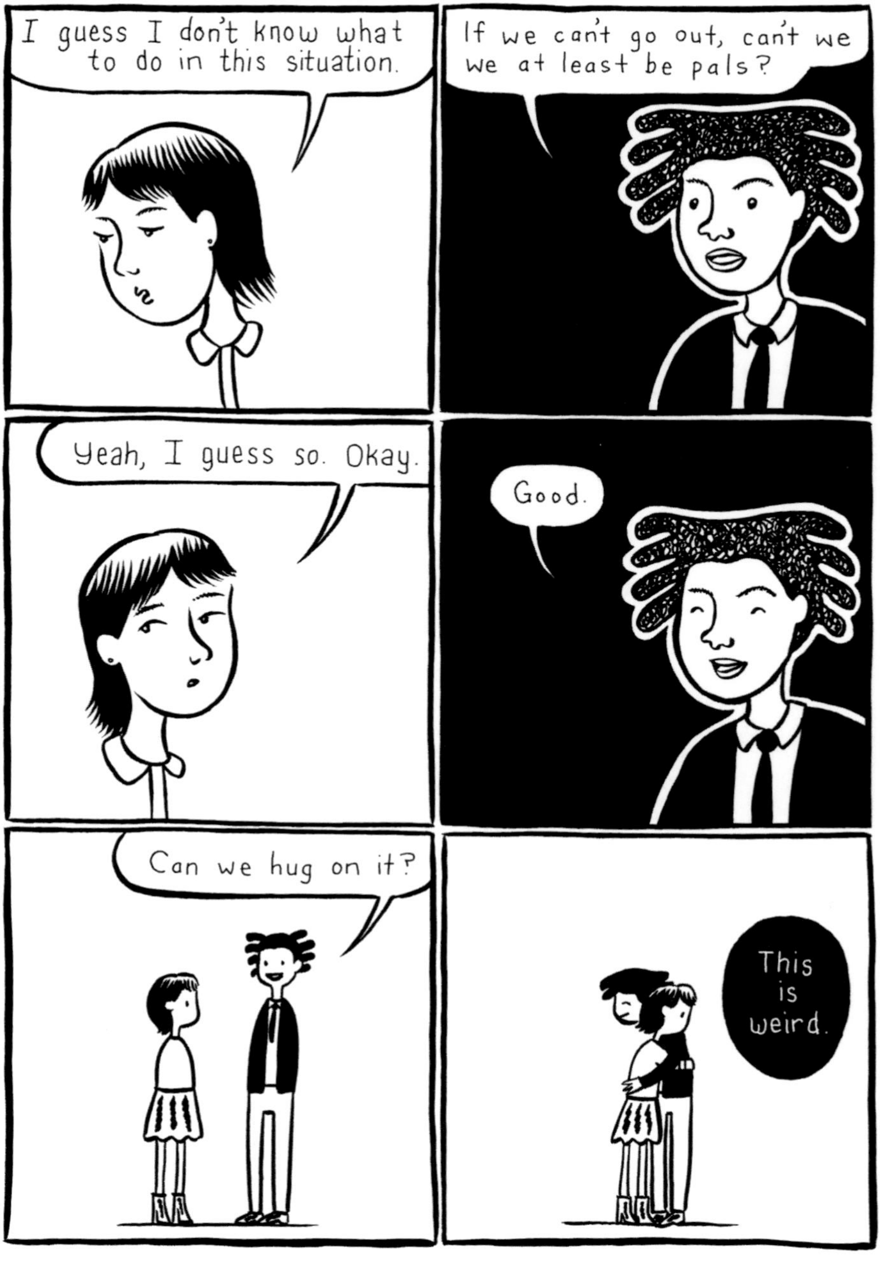
I guess I don't know what to do in this situation.
If we can't go out, can't we we at least be pals?
Yeah, I guess so. Okay.
Good.
Can we hug on it?
This is weird.

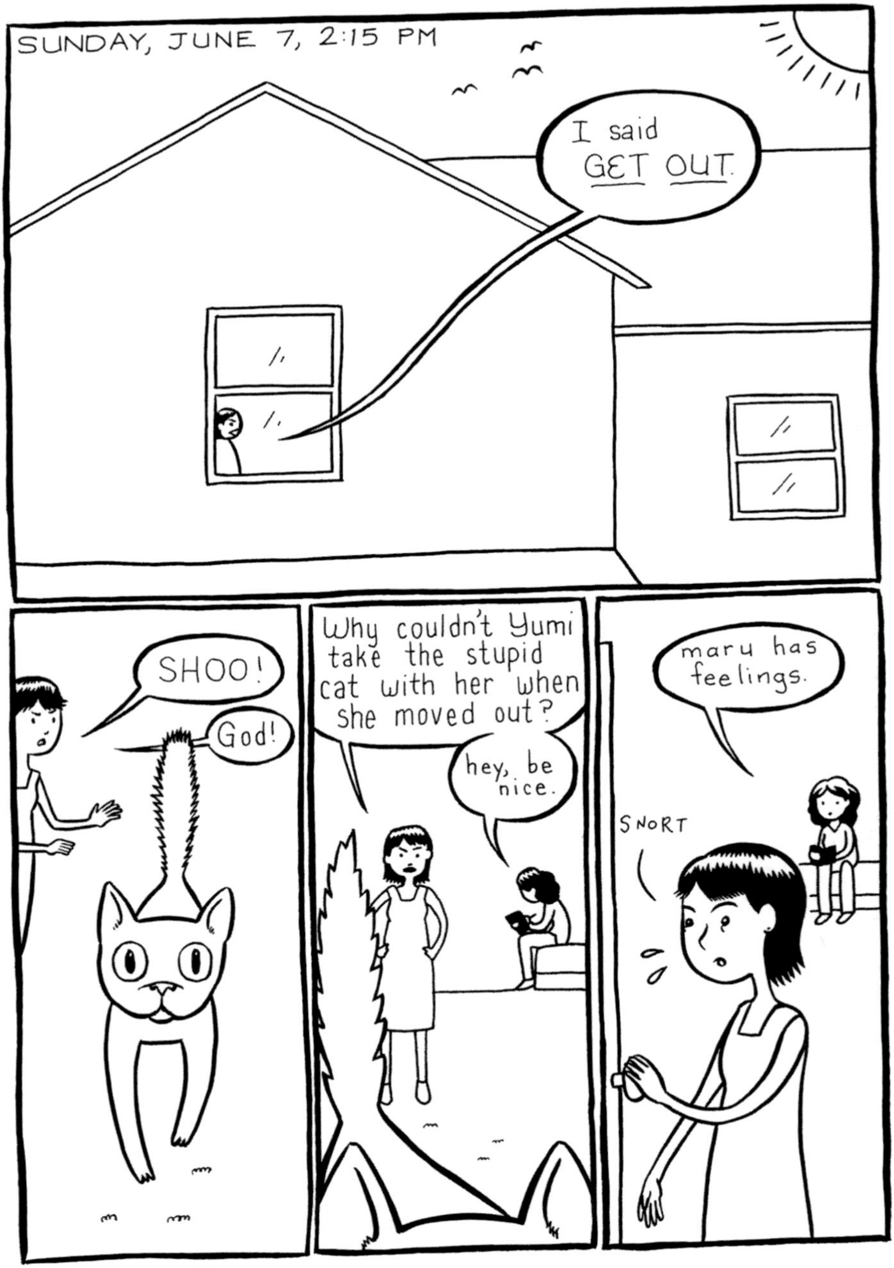
SUNDAY, JUNE 7, 2:15 PM
I said GET OUT.
SHOO!
God!
Why couldn't Yumi take the stupid cat with her when she moved out?
hey, be nice.
maru has feelings.
SNORT

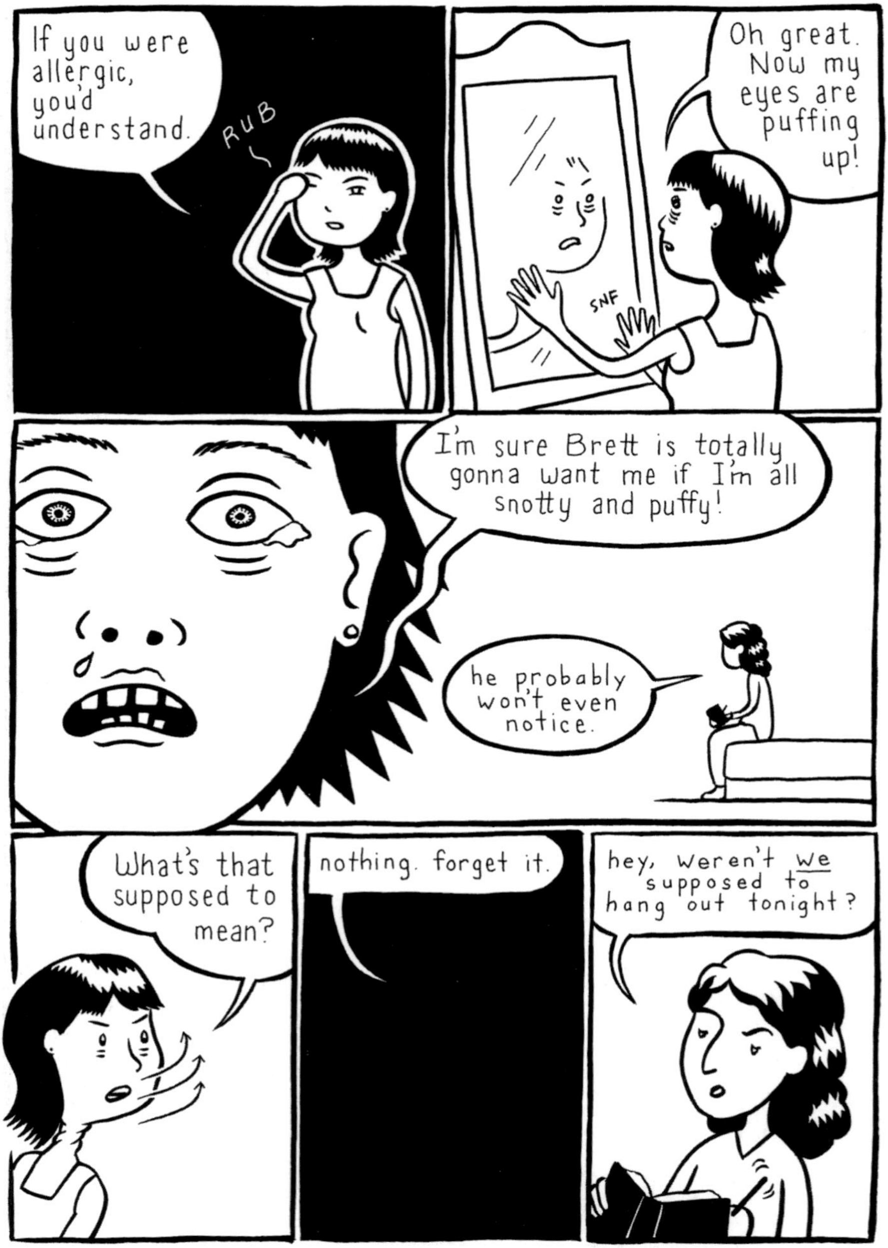
If you were allergic, you'd understand.
RUB
Oh great. Now my eyes are puffing up!
SNF
I'm sure Brett is totally gonna want me if I'm all snotty and puffy!
he probably won't even notice.
What's that supposed to mean?
nothing. forget it.
hey, weren't we supposed to hang out tonight?

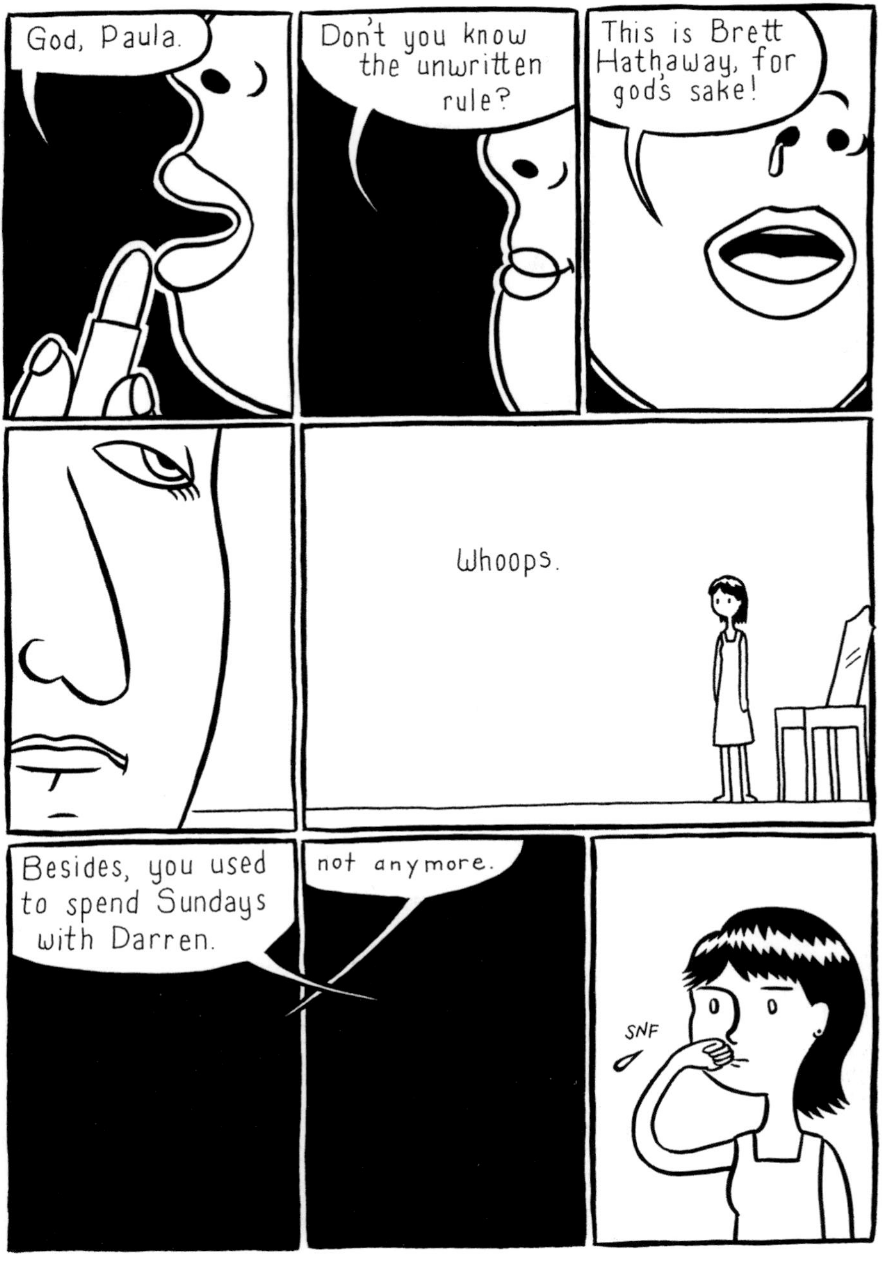
God, Paula.
Don't you know the unwritten rule?
This is Brett Hathaway, for god's sake!
Whoops.
Besides, you used to spend Sundays with Darren.
not anymore.
SNF

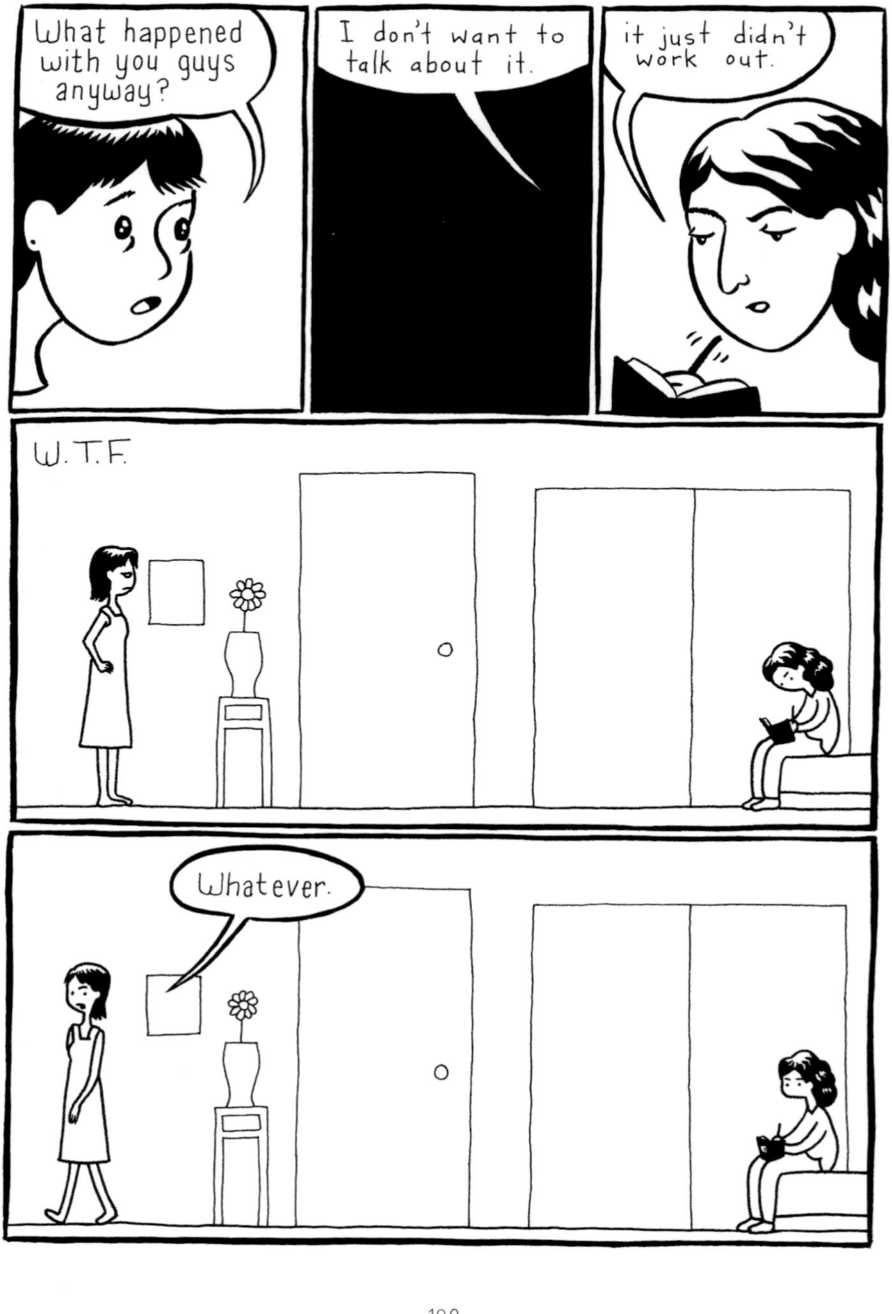
What happened with you guys anyway?
I don't want to talk about it.
it just didn't work out.
W.T.F.
Whatever.

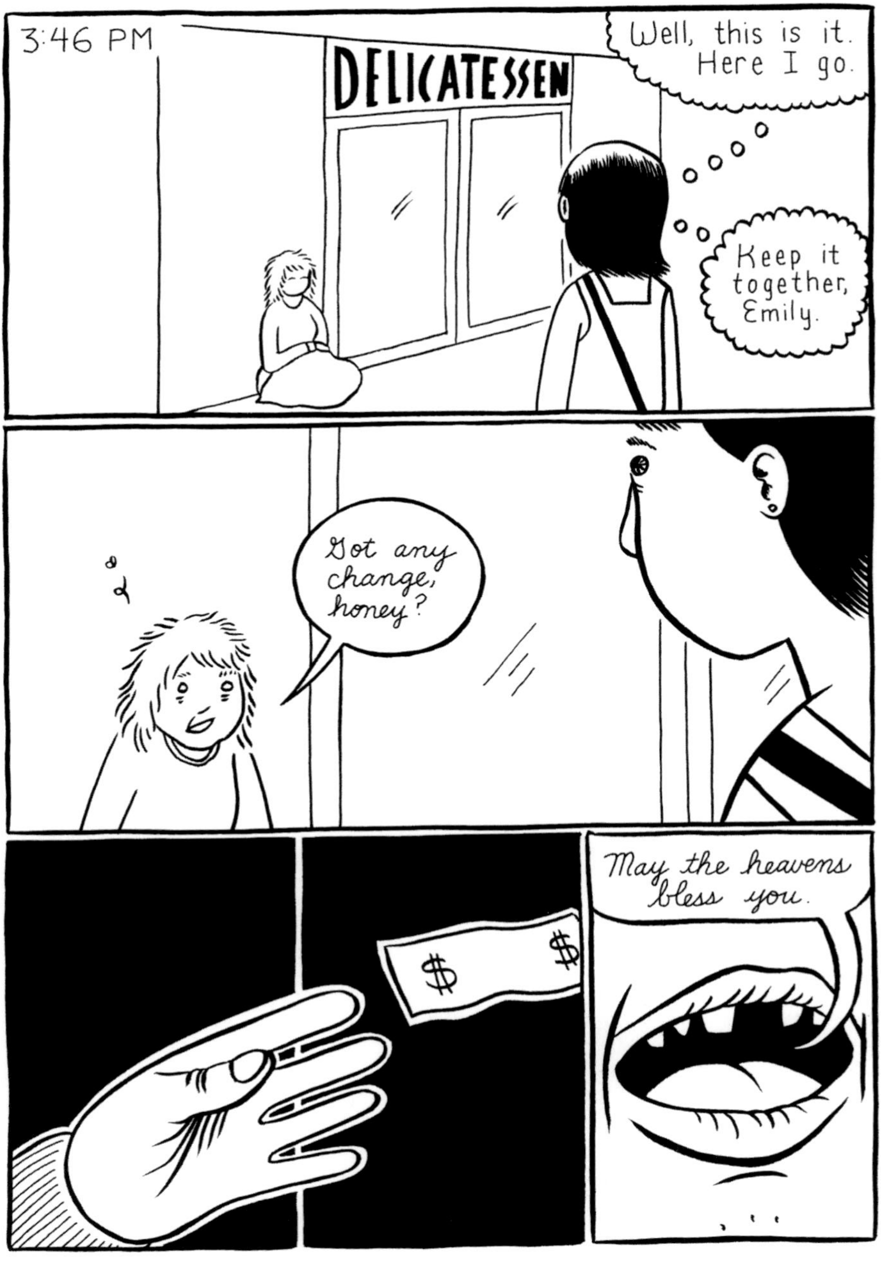
3:46 PM
DELICATESSEN
Well, this is it. Here I go.
Keep it together, Emily.
Got any change, honey?
May the heavens bless you.
. . .

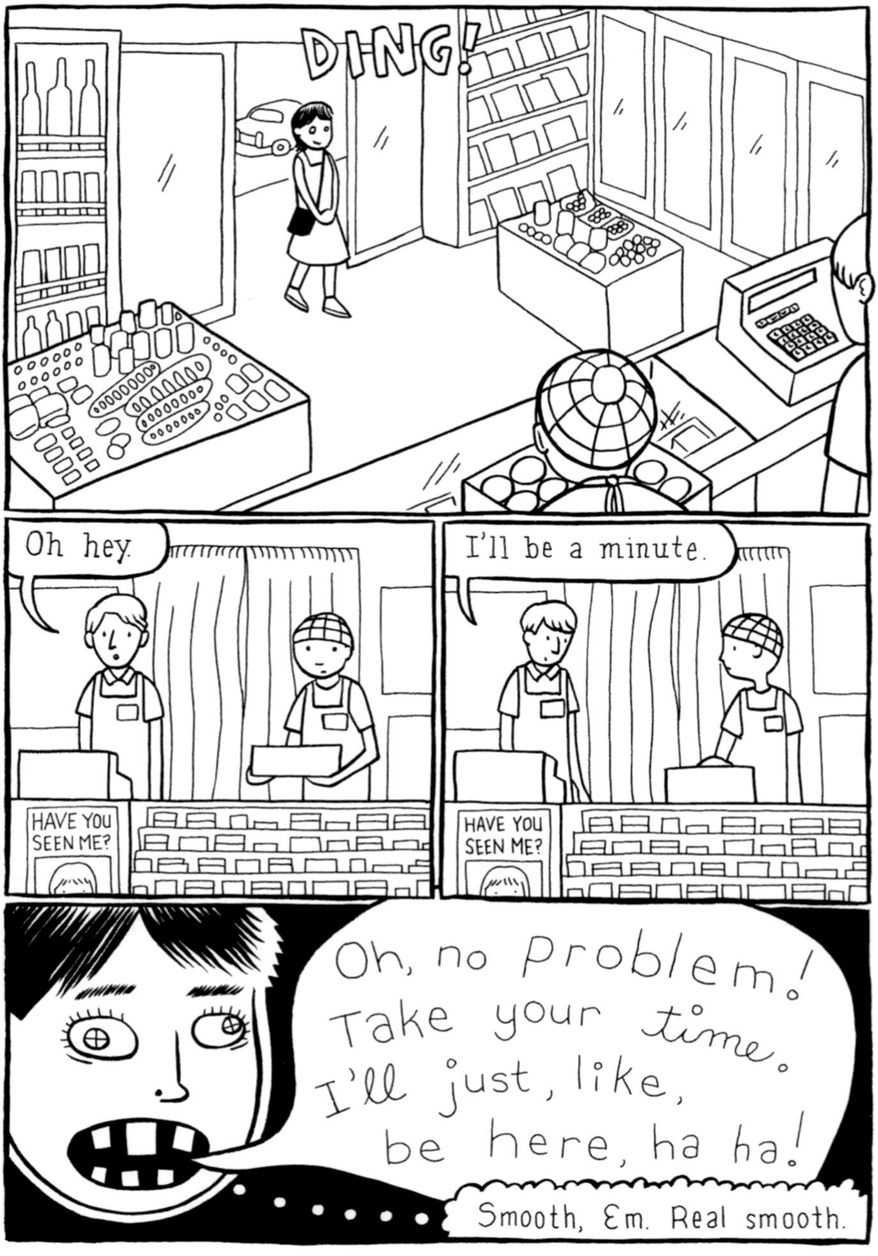
DING!
Oh hey.
I'll be a minute.
HAVE YOU SEEN ME?
HAVE YOU SEEN ME?
Oh, no problem! Take your time. I'll just, like, be here, ha ha!
Smooth, Em. Real smooth.

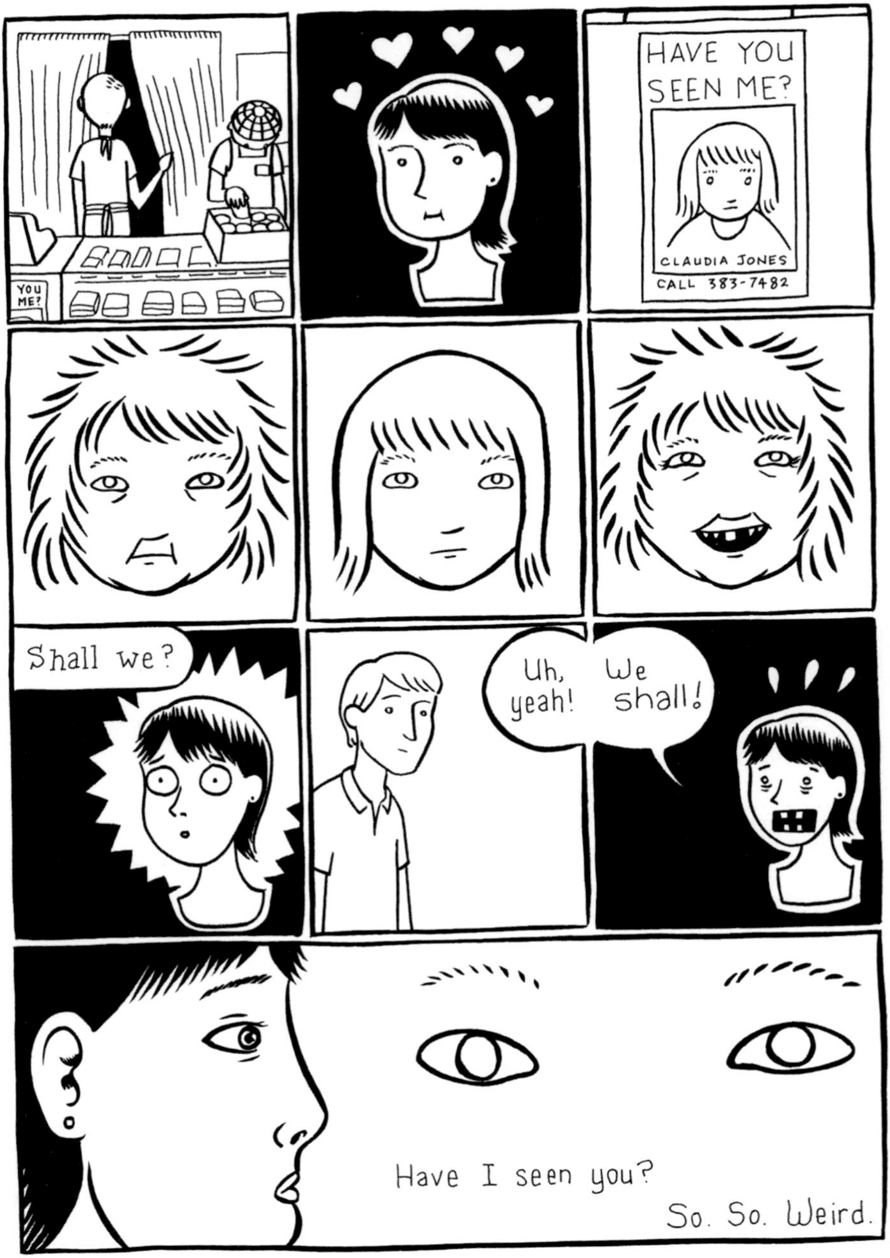
YOU ME?
HAVE YOU SEEN ME?
CLAUDIA JONES
CALL 383-7482
Shall we?
Uh, yeah!
We shall!
Have I seen you?
So. So. Weird.

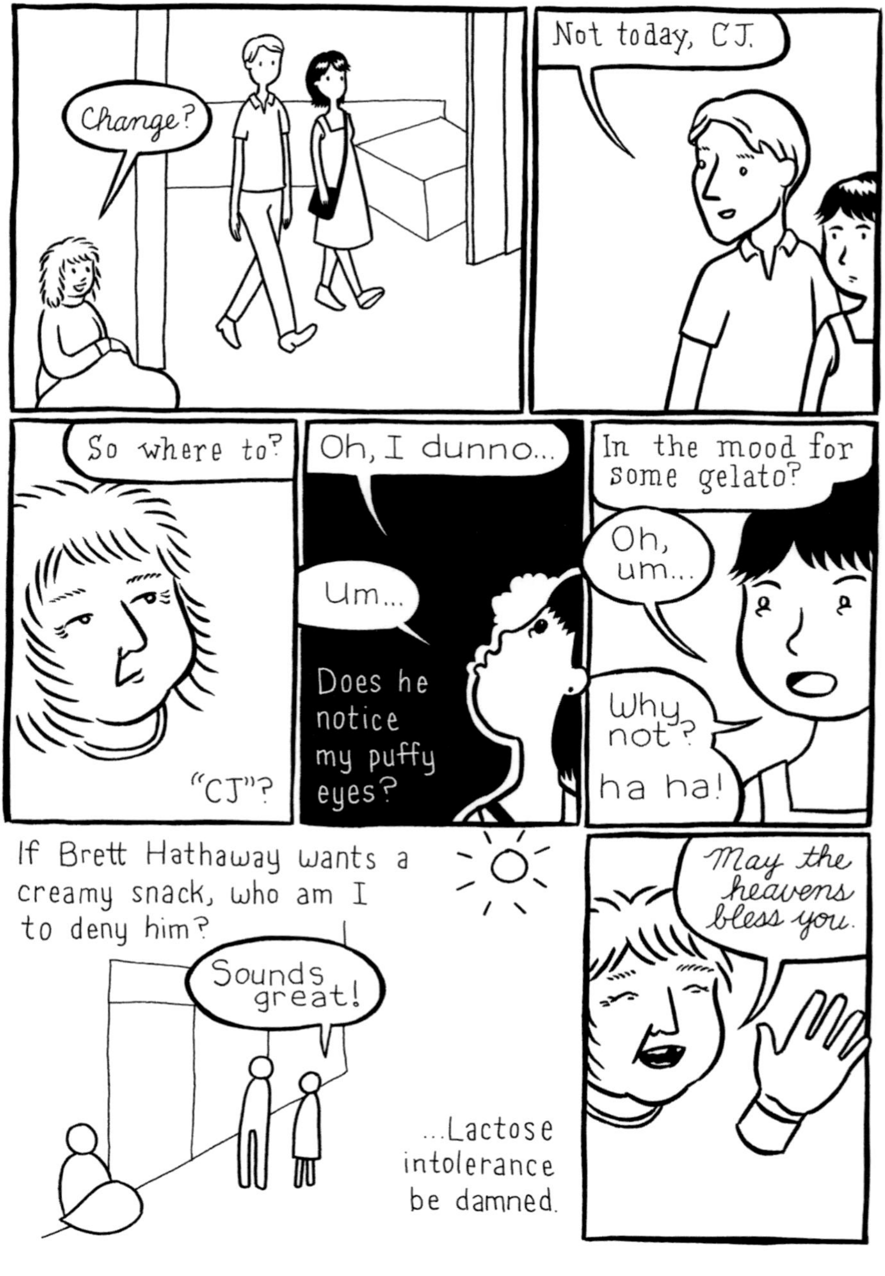

Change?
Not today, CJ.
So where to?
"CJ"?
Oh, I dunno...
Um...
Does he notice my puffy eyes?
In the mood for some gelato?
Oh, um...
Why not? ha ha!
If Brett Hathaway wants a creamy snack, who am I to deny him?
Sounds great!
...Lactose intolerance be damned.
May the heavens bless you.

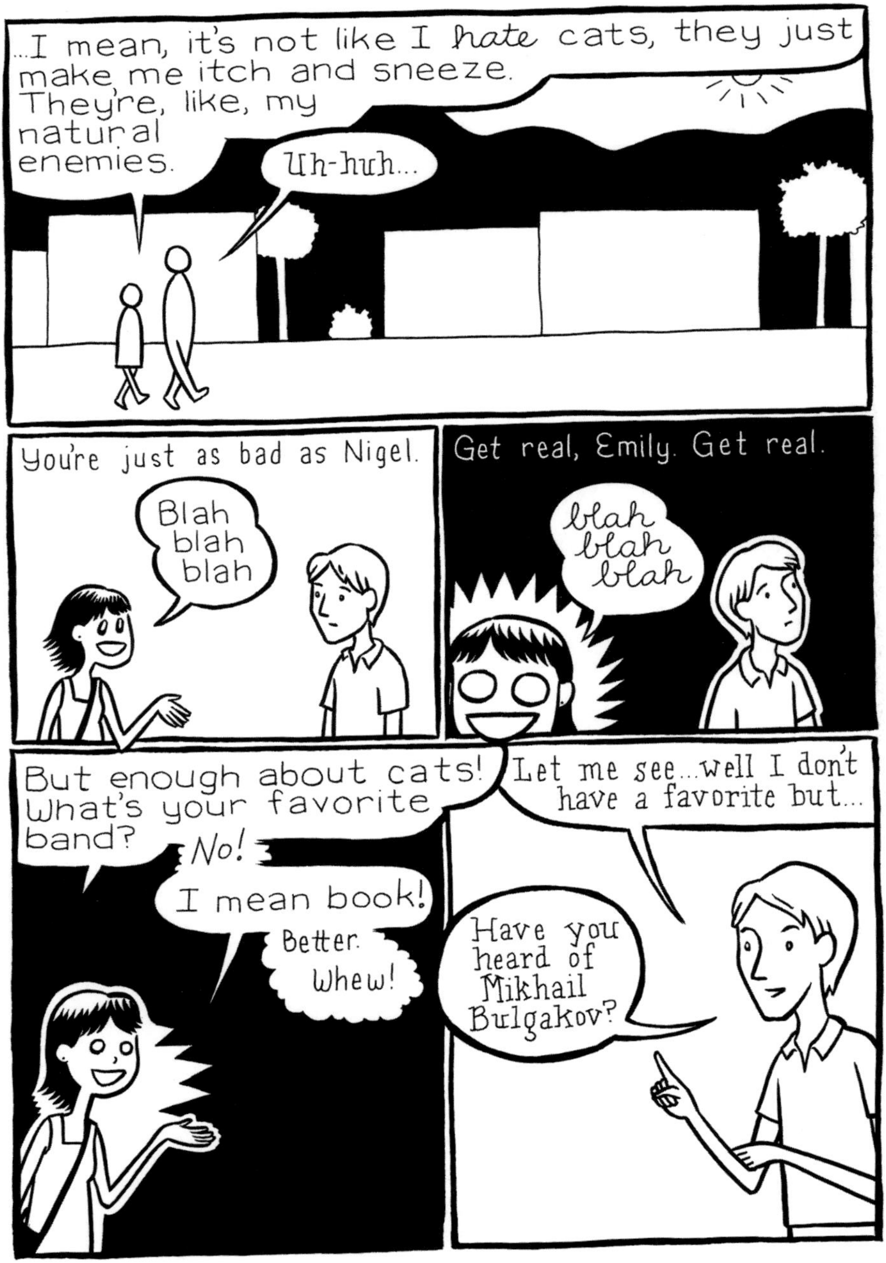
...I mean, it's not like I *hate* cats, they just make me itch and sneeze. They're, like, my natural enemies.
Uh-huh...
You're just as bad as Nigel.
Blah blah blah
Get real, Emily. Get real.
blah blah blah
But enough about cats! What's your favorite band?
No!
I mean book!
Better. Whew!
Let me see...well I don't have a favorite but...
Have you heard of Mikhail Bulgakov?

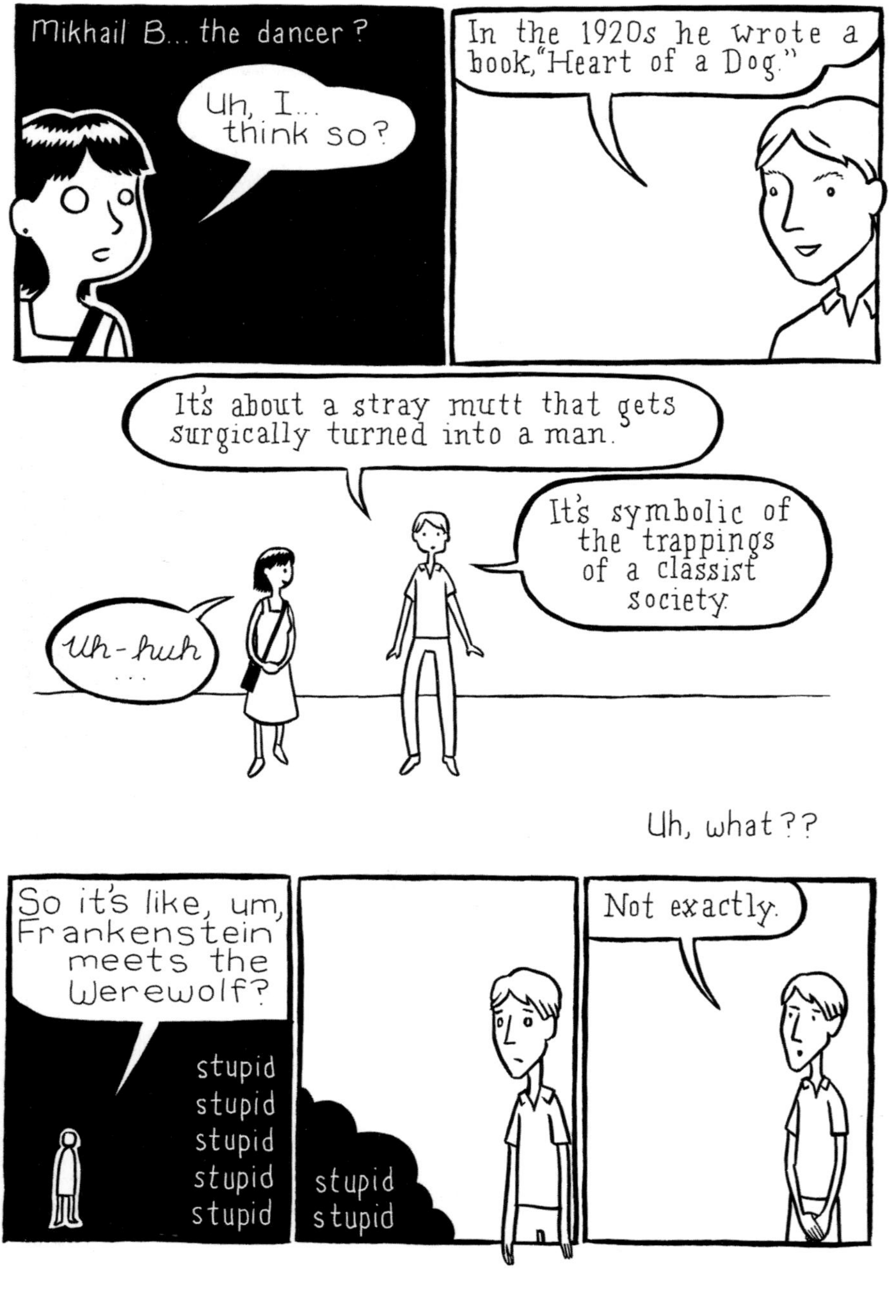
Mikhail B... the dancer?
Uh, I... think so?
In the 1920s he wrote a book, "Heart of a Dog."
It's about a stray mutt that gets surgically turned into a man.
It's symbolic of the trappings of a classist society.
Uh-huh ...
Uh, what??
So it's like, um, Frankenstein meets the Werewolf?
stupid stupid stupid stupid stupid
stupid stupid
Not exactly.

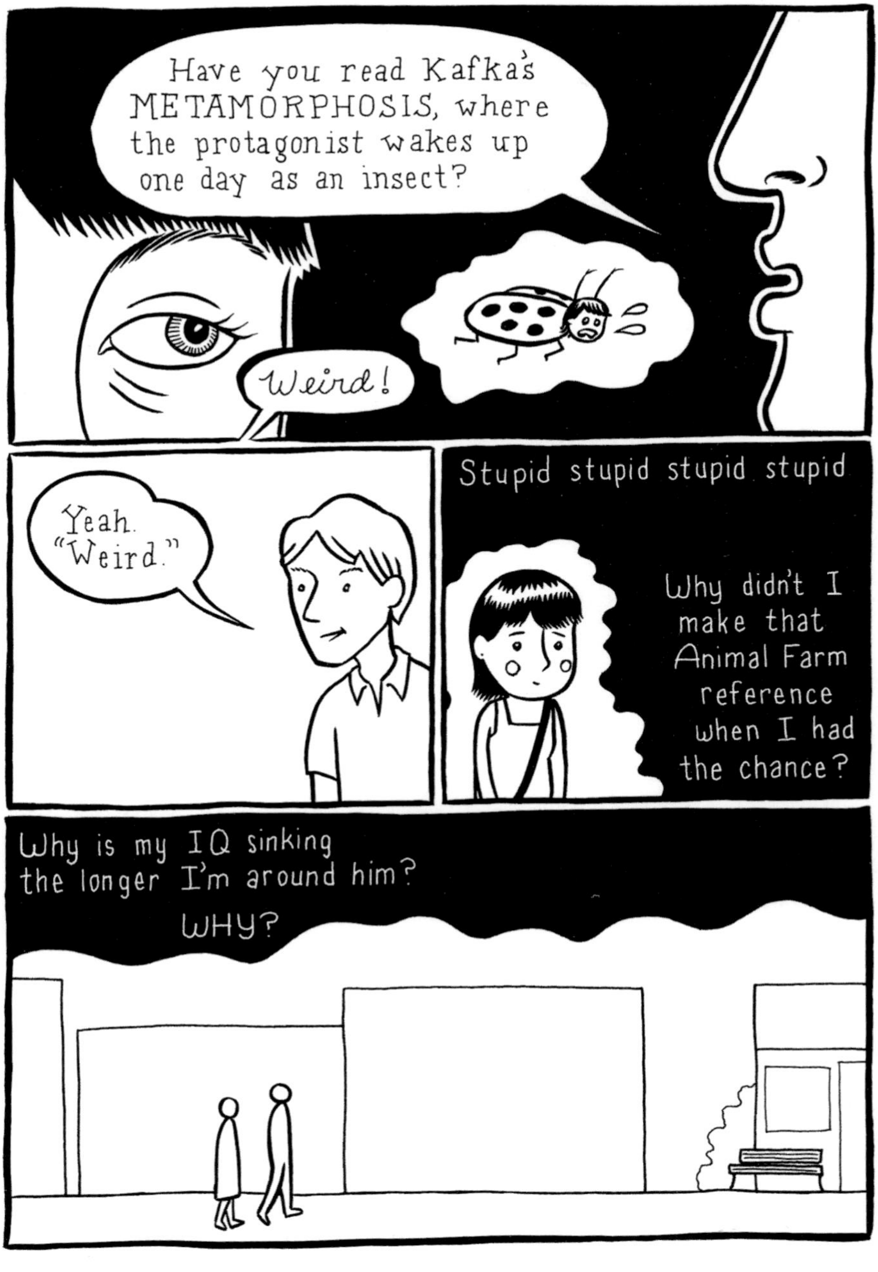

Have you read Kafka's METAMORPHOSIS, where the protagonist wakes up one day as an insect?
Weird!
Yeah. "Weird."
Stupid stupid stupid stupid
Why didn't I make that Animal Farm reference when I had the chance?
Why is my IQ sinking the longer I'm around him?
WHY?

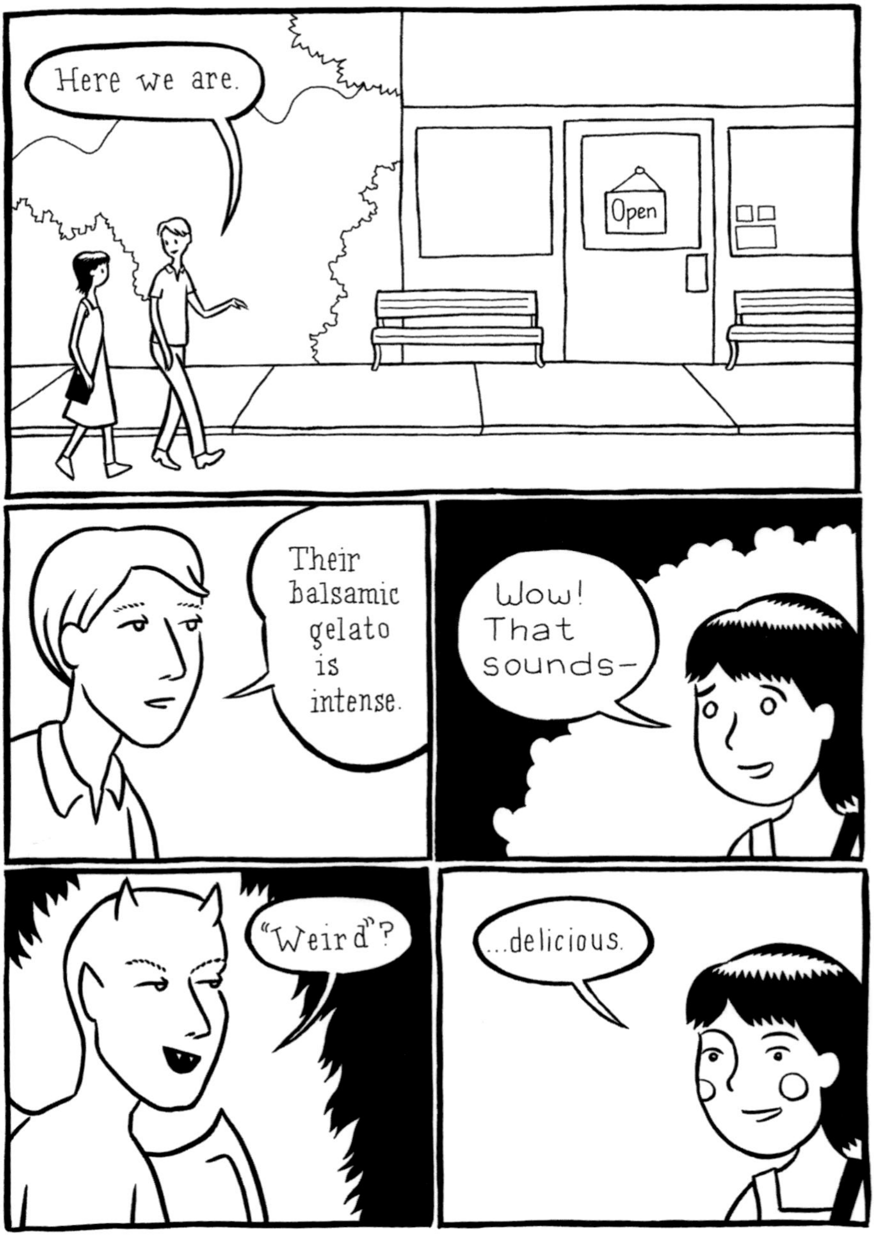
Here we are.
Open
Their balsamic gelato is intense.
Wow! That sounds-
"Weird"?
...delicious.

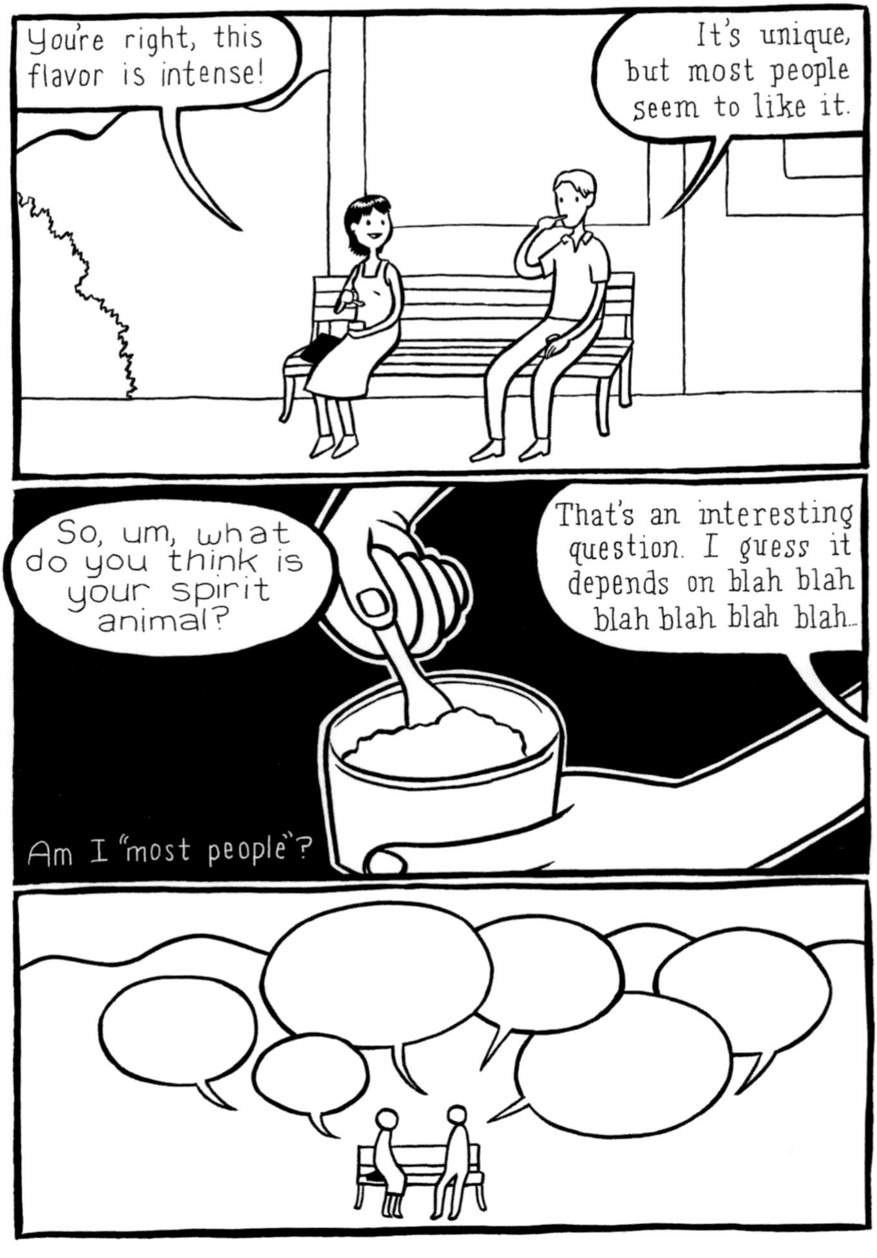
You're right, this flavor is intense!
It's unique, but most people seem to like it.
So, um, what do you think is your spirit animal?
That's an interesting question. I guess it depends on blah blah blah blah blah blah...
Am I "most people"?

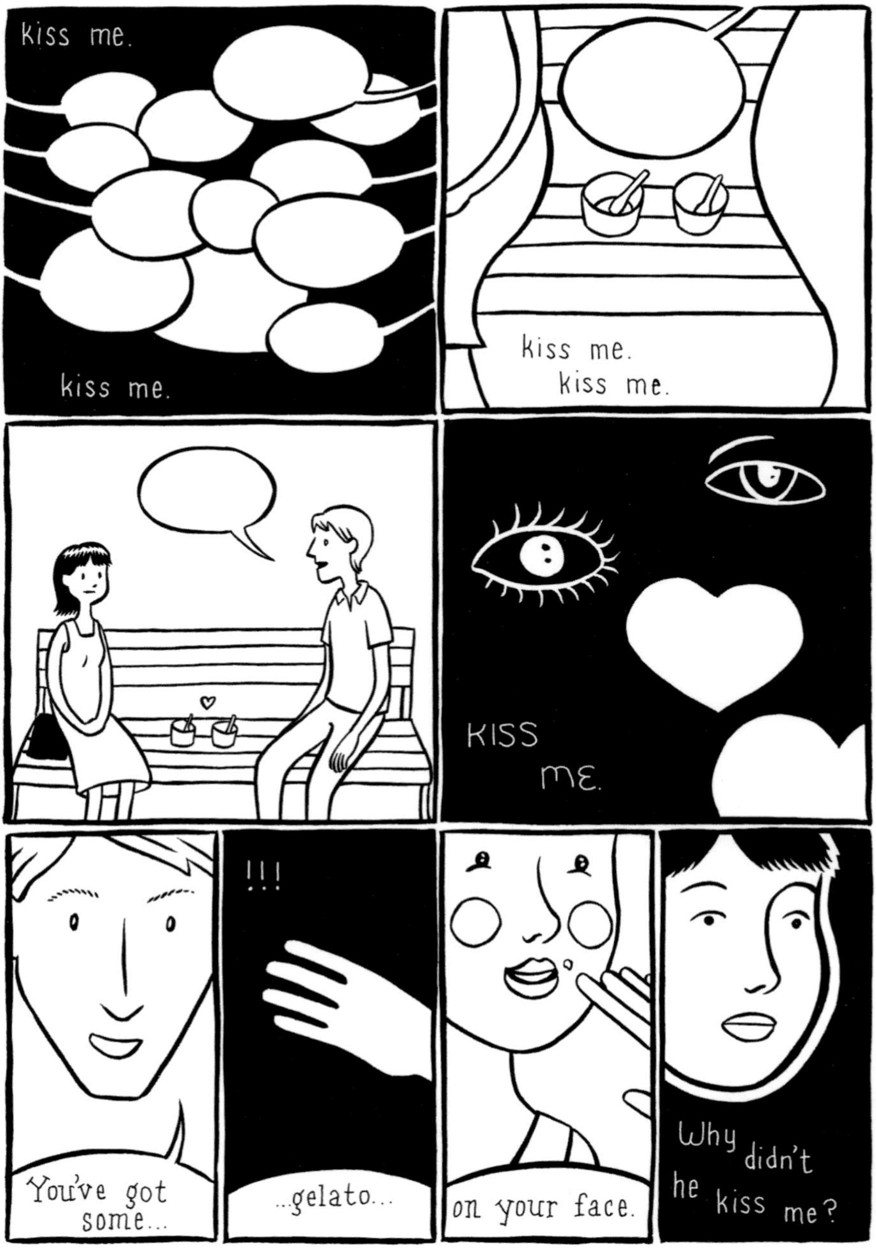
kiss me.
kiss me.
kiss me.
kiss me.
KISS
ME.
You've got some...
!!!
...gelato...
on your face.
Why didn't he kiss me?

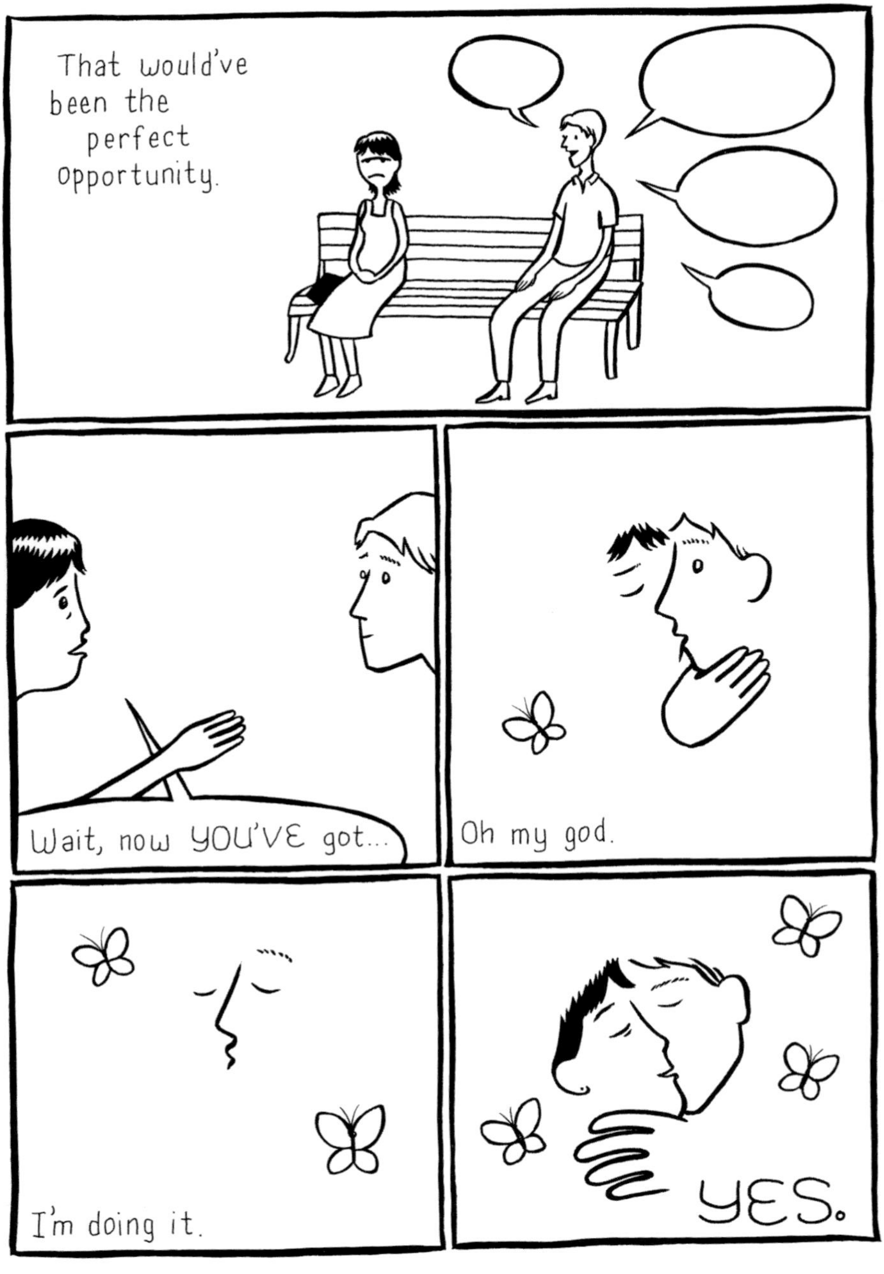
That would've been the perfect opportunity.
Wait, now YOU'VE got...
Oh my god.
I'm doing it.
YES.

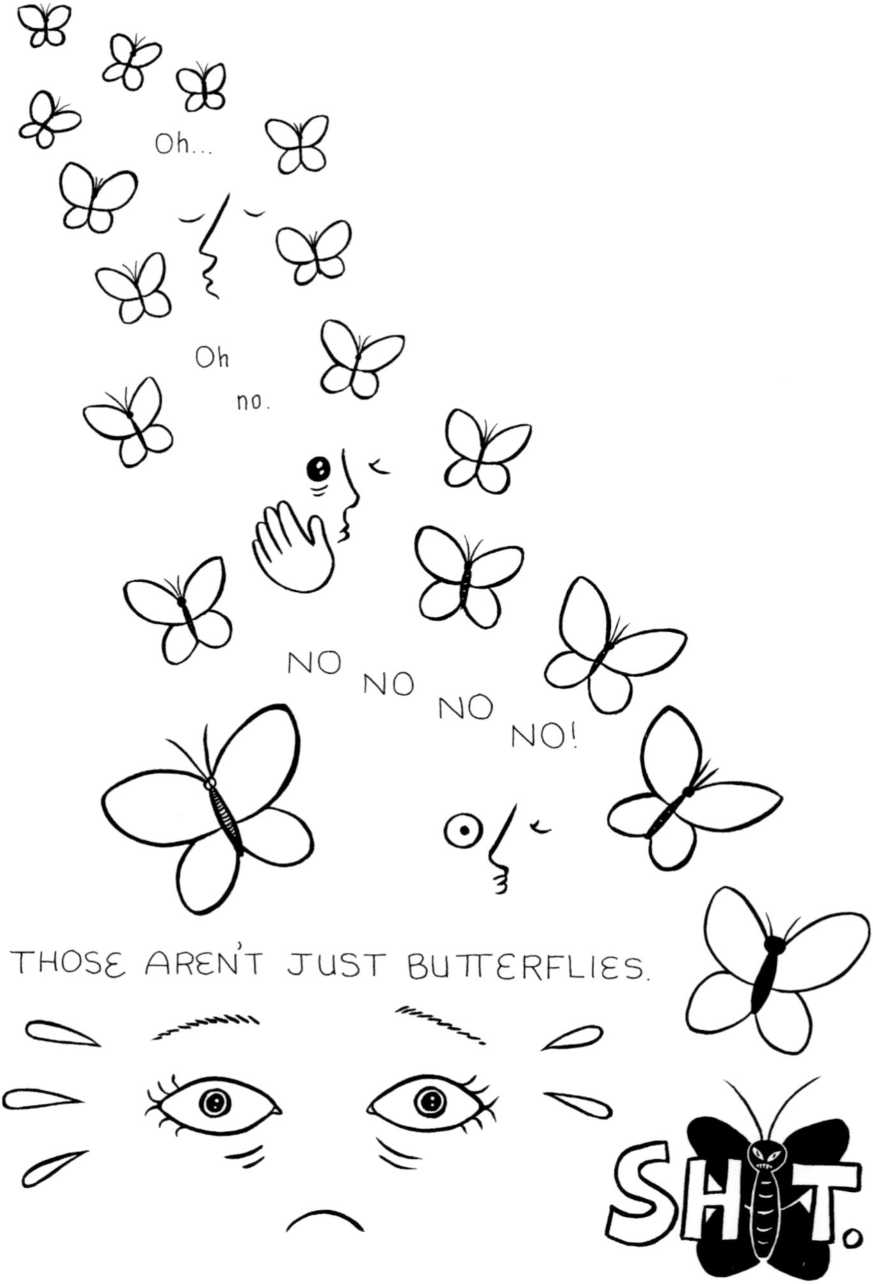

Oh...
Oh
no.
NO
NO
NO
NO!
THOSE AREN'T JUST BUTTERFLIES.
SHIT.

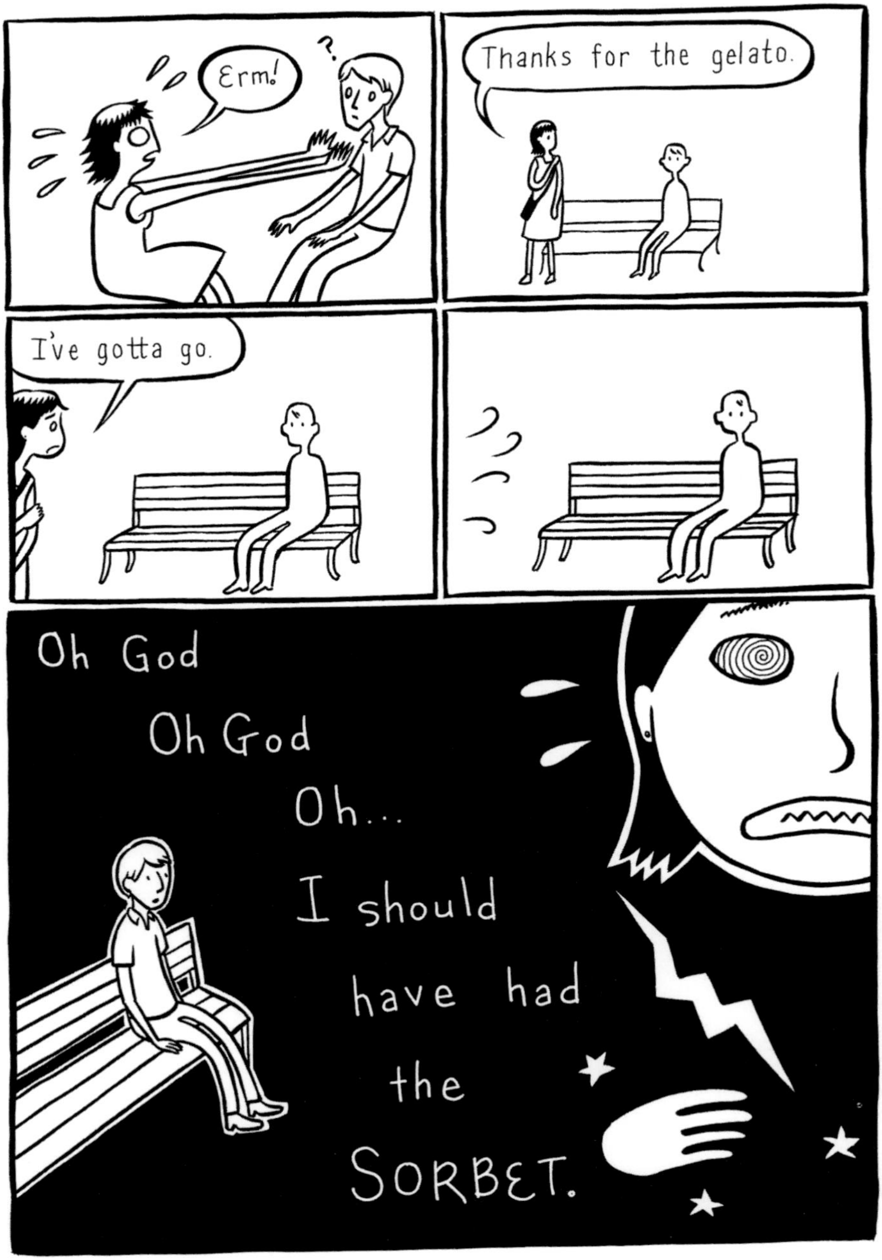
Erm!
?
Thanks for the gelato.
I've gotta go.
Oh God
Oh God
Oh...
I should
have had
the
SORBET.

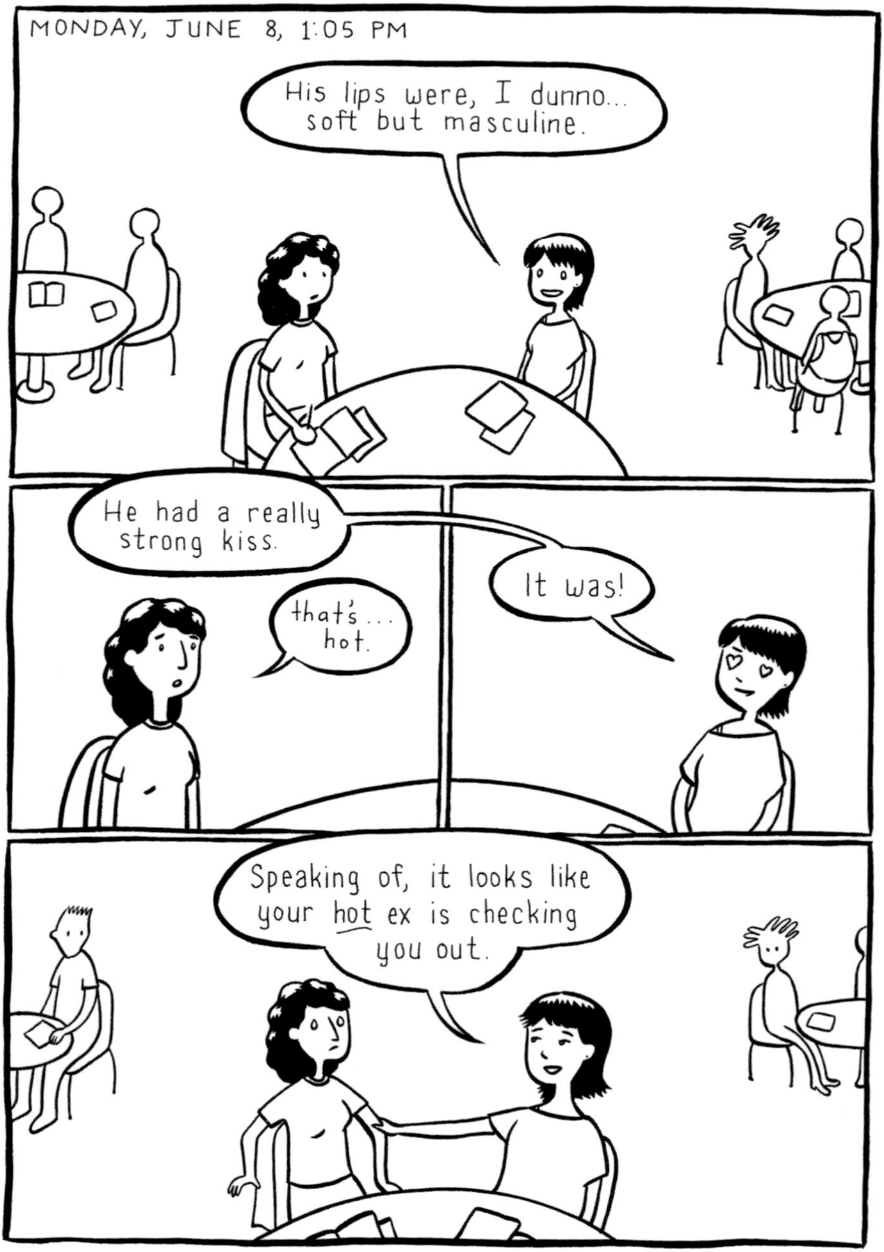
MONDAY, JUNE 8, 1:05 PM
His lips were, I dunno... soft but masculine.
He had a really strong kiss.
that's... hot.
It was!
Speaking of, it looks like your hot ex is checking you out.

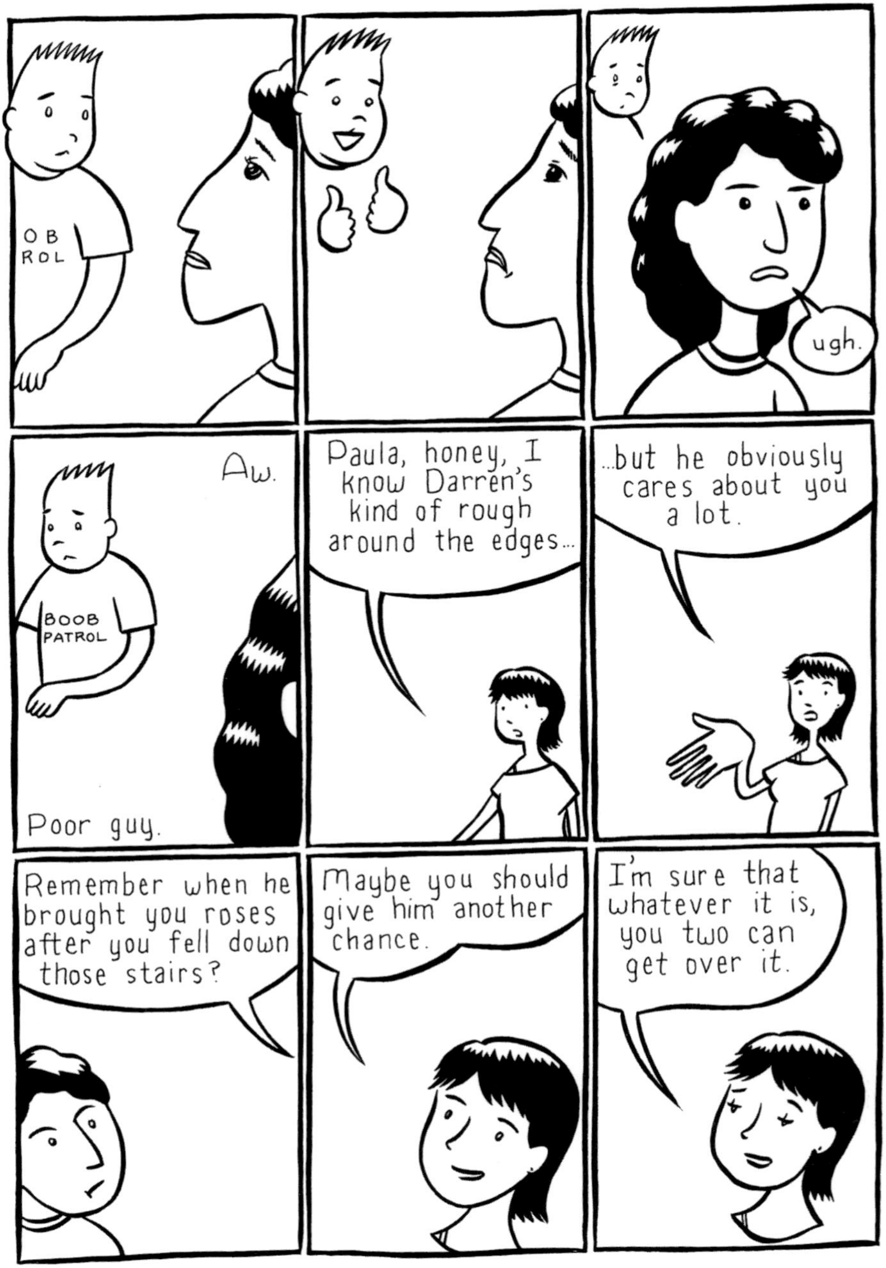
OB
ROL
ugh.
Aw.
BOOB
PATROL
Poor guy.
Paula, honey, I know Darren's kind of rough around the edges...
...but he obviously cares about you a lot.
Remember when he brought you roses after you fell down those stairs?
Maybe you should give him another chance.
I'm sure that whatever it is, you two can get over it.

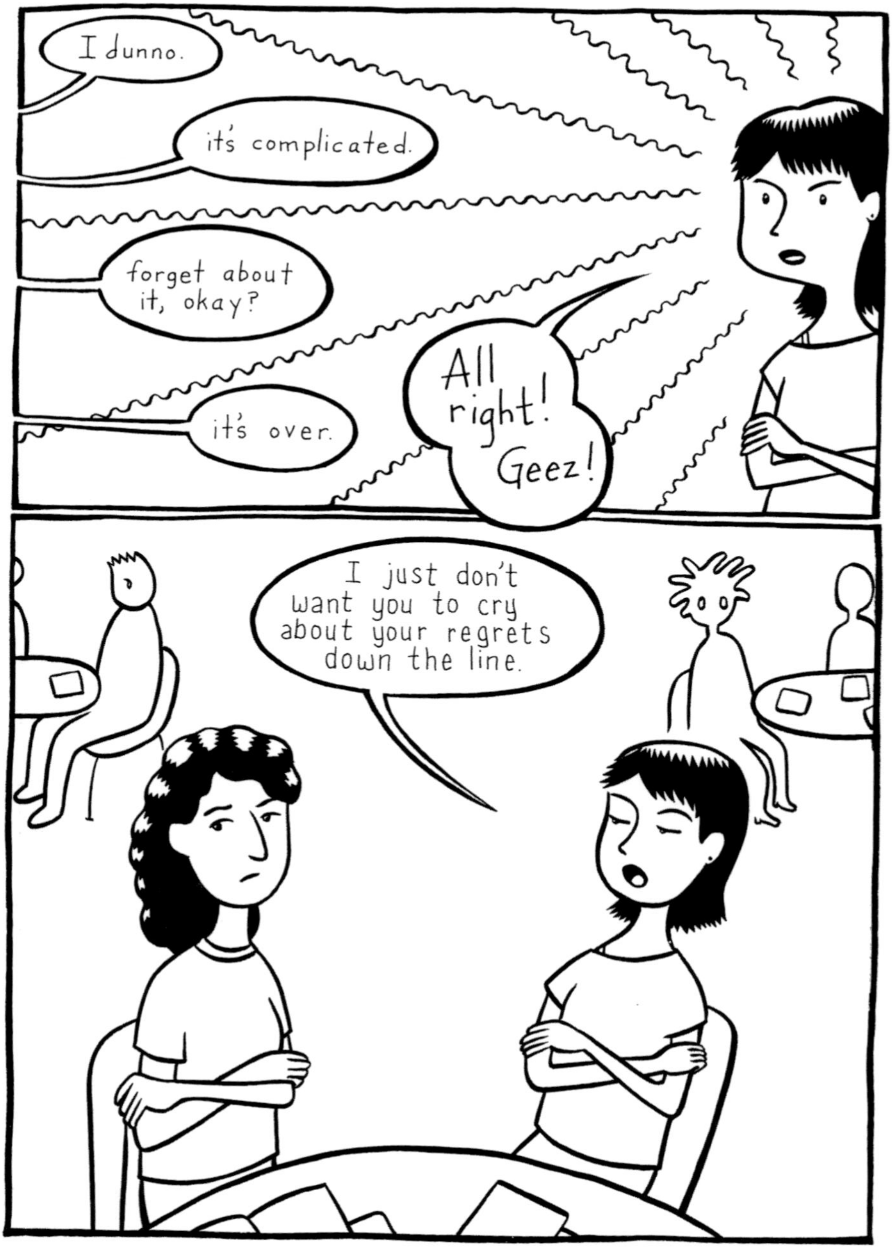
I dunno.
it's complicated.
forget about it, okay?
it's over.
All right! Geez!
I just don't want you to cry about your regrets down the line.

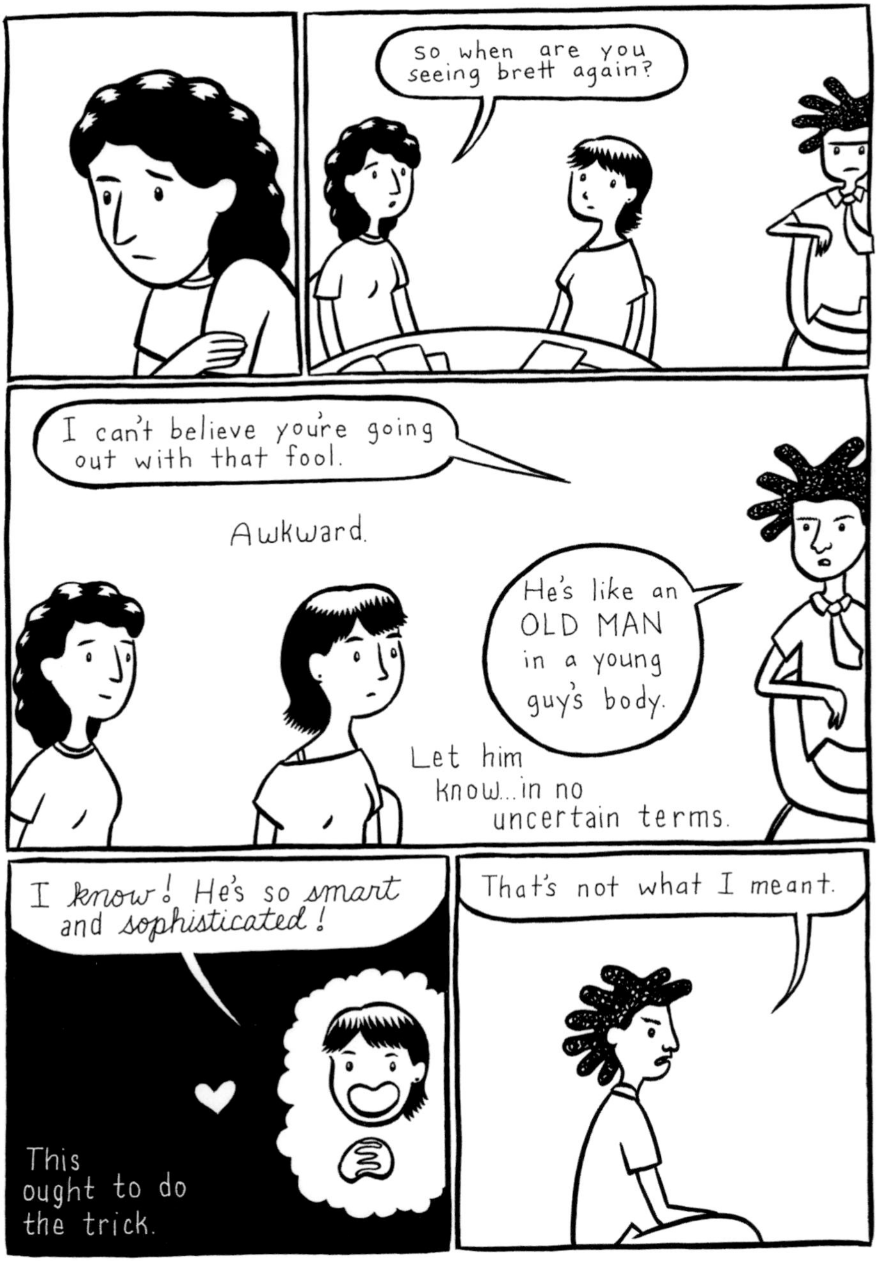
so when are you seeing brett again?
I can't believe you're going out with that fool.
Awkward.
He's like an OLD MAN in a young guy's body.
Let him know...in no uncertain terms.
I know! He's so smart and sophisticated!
This ought to do the trick.
That's not what I meant.

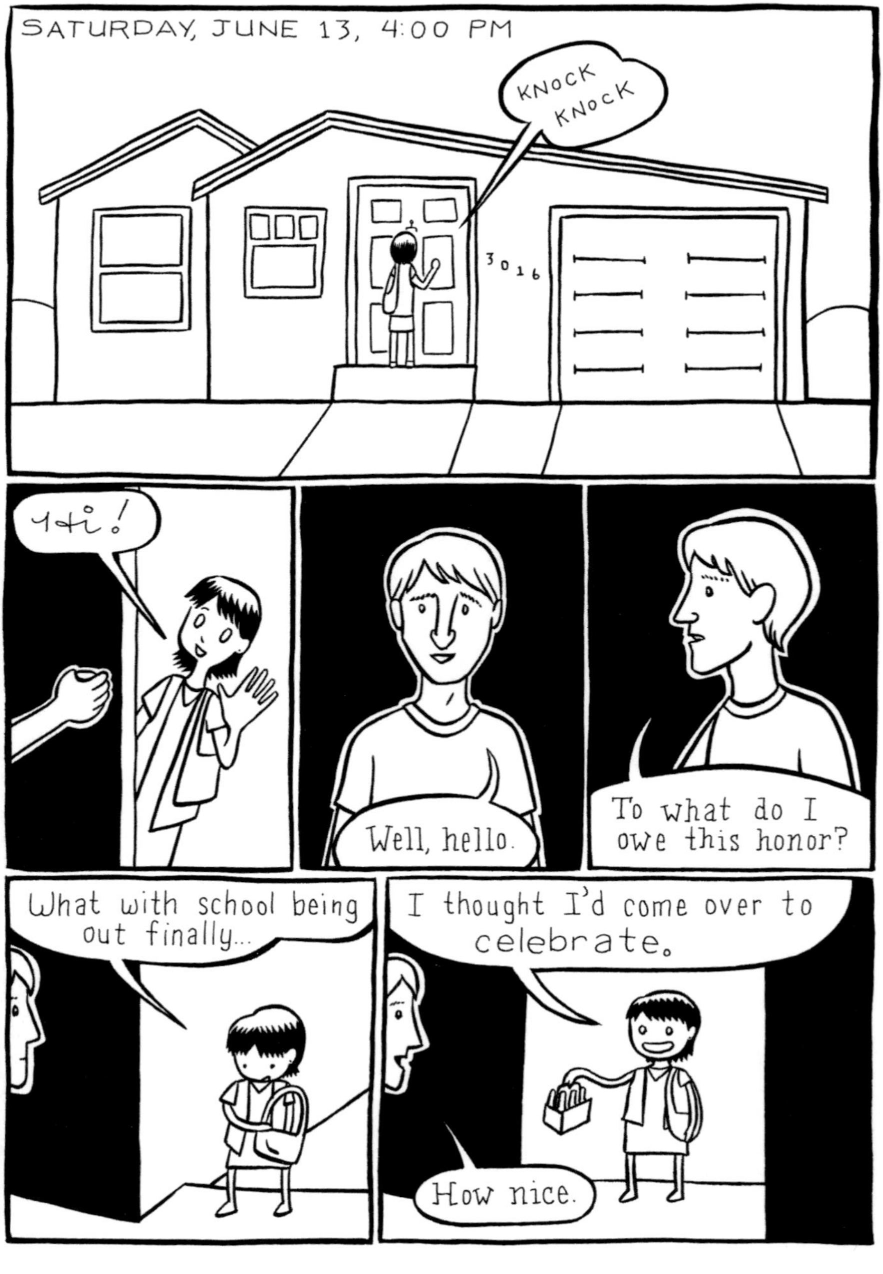
SATURDAY, JUNE 13, 4:00 PM
KNOCK KNOCK
3016
Hi!
Well, hello.
To what do I owe this honor?
What with school being out finally...
I thought I'd come over to celebrate.
How nice.

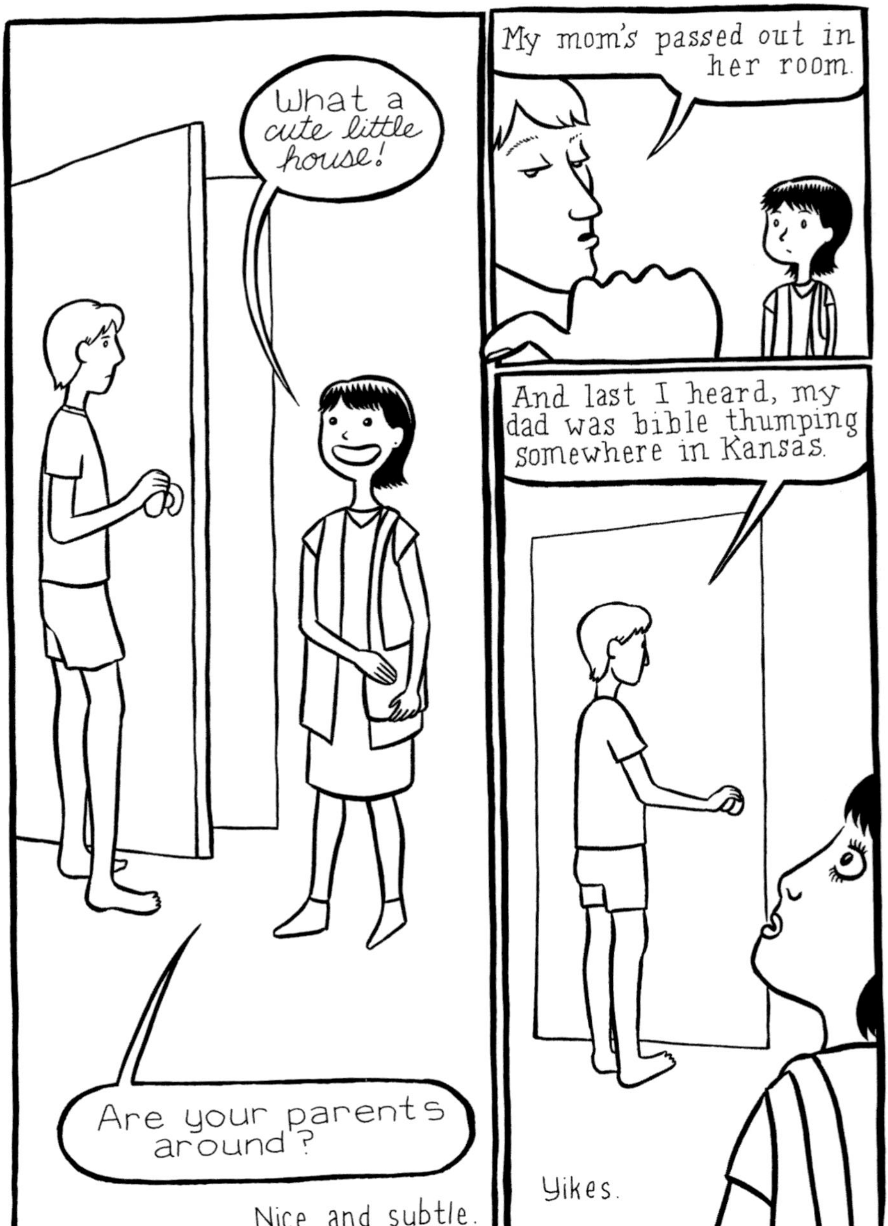
What a cute little house!
Are your parents around?
Nice and subtle.
My mom's passed out in her room.
And last I heard, my dad was bible thumping somewhere in Kansas.
Yikes.

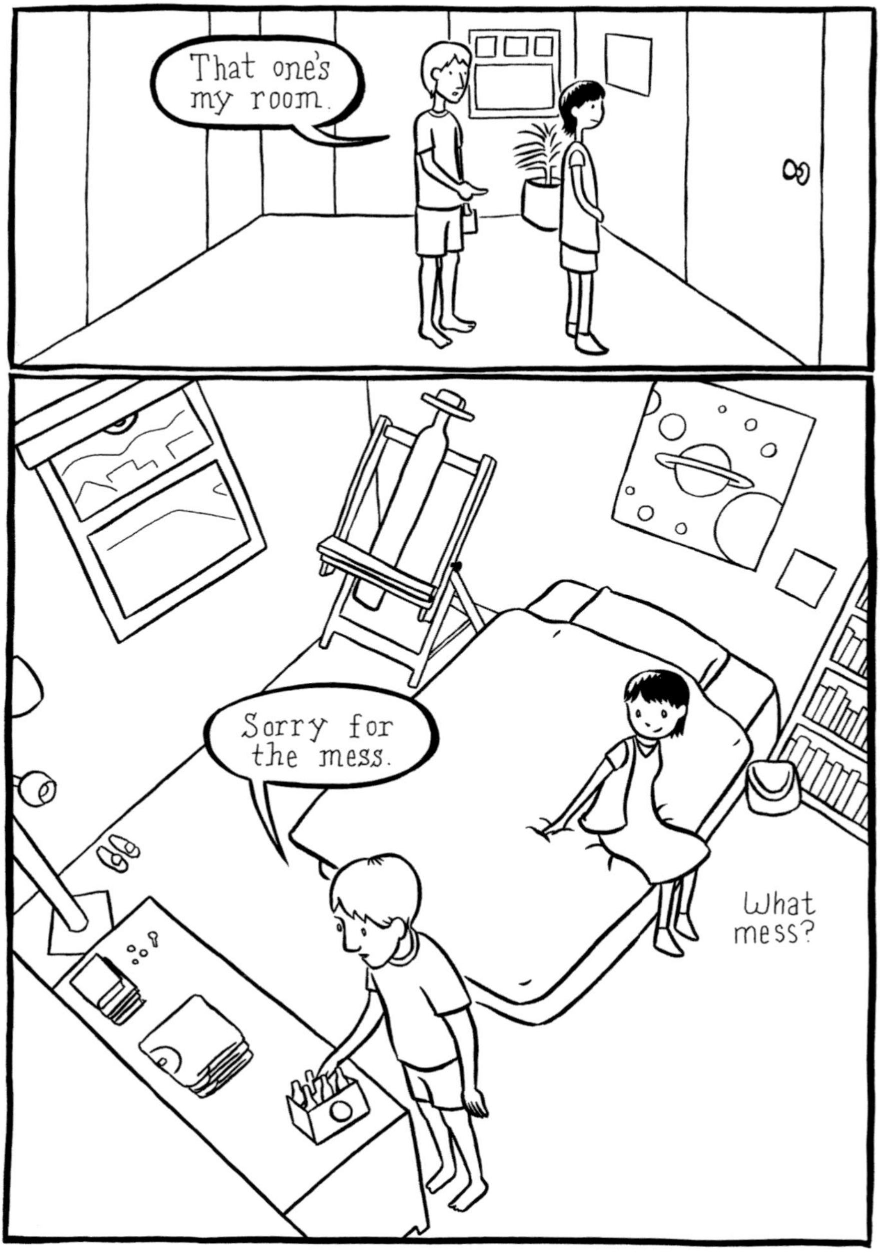
That one's my room.
Sorry for the mess.
What mess?

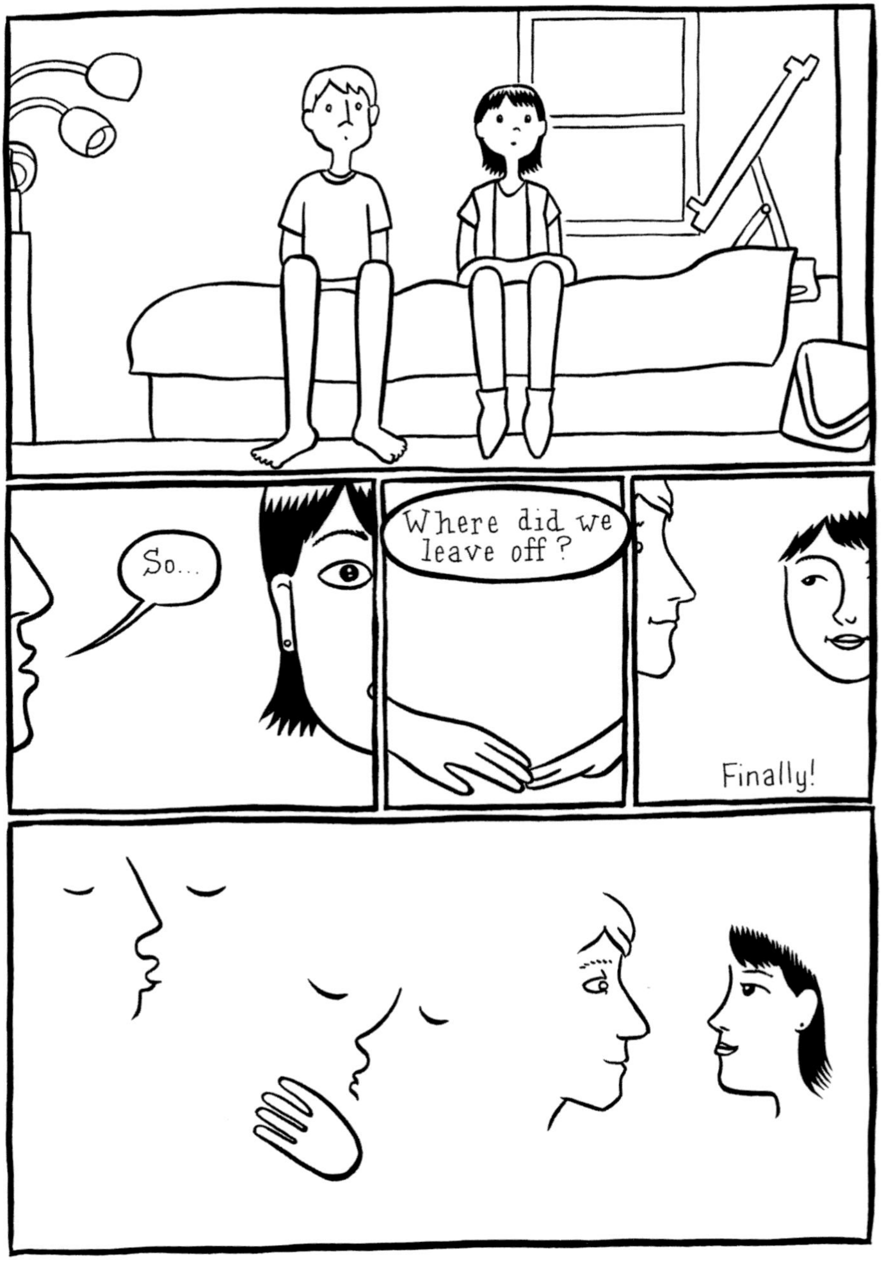
So...
Where did we leave off?
Finally!

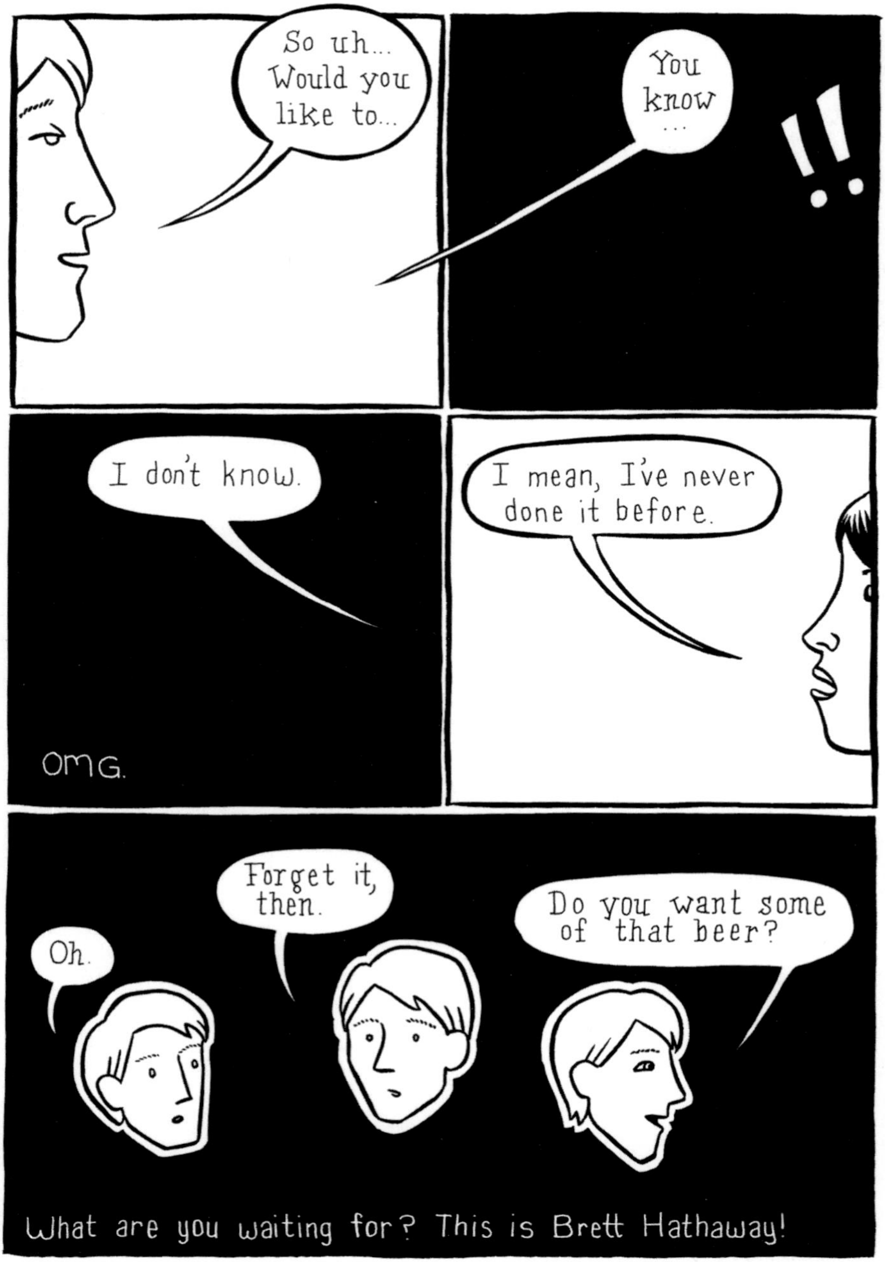
So uh... Would you like to...
You know ...
!!
I don't know.
OMG.
I mean, I've never done it before.
Oh.
Forget it, then.
Do you want some of that beer?
What are you waiting for? This is Brett Hathaway!

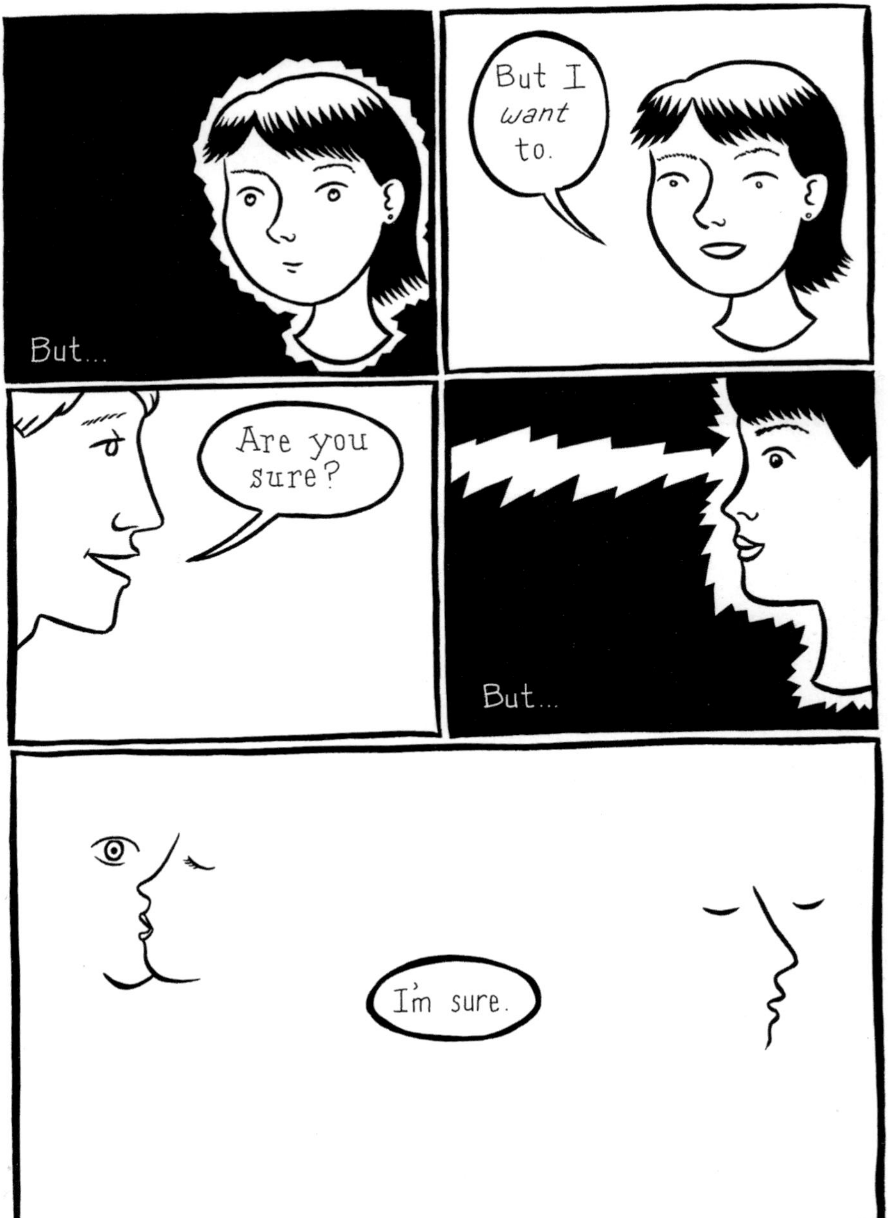
But...
But I *want* to.
Are you sure?
But...
I'm sure.

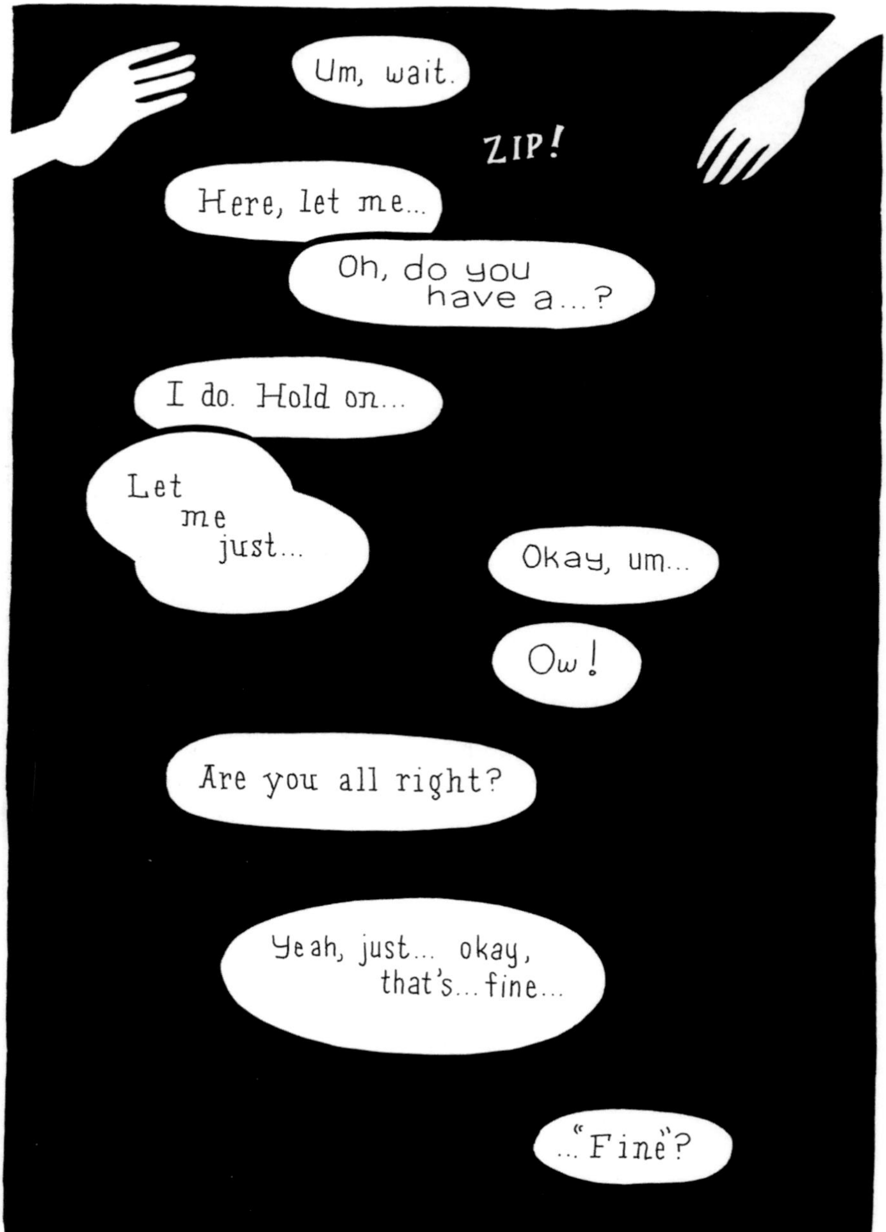
Um, wait.
ZIP!
Here, let me...
Oh, do you have a...?
I do. Hold on...
Let me just...
Okay, um...
Ow!
Are you all right?
Yeah, just... okay, that's... fine...
..."Fine"?

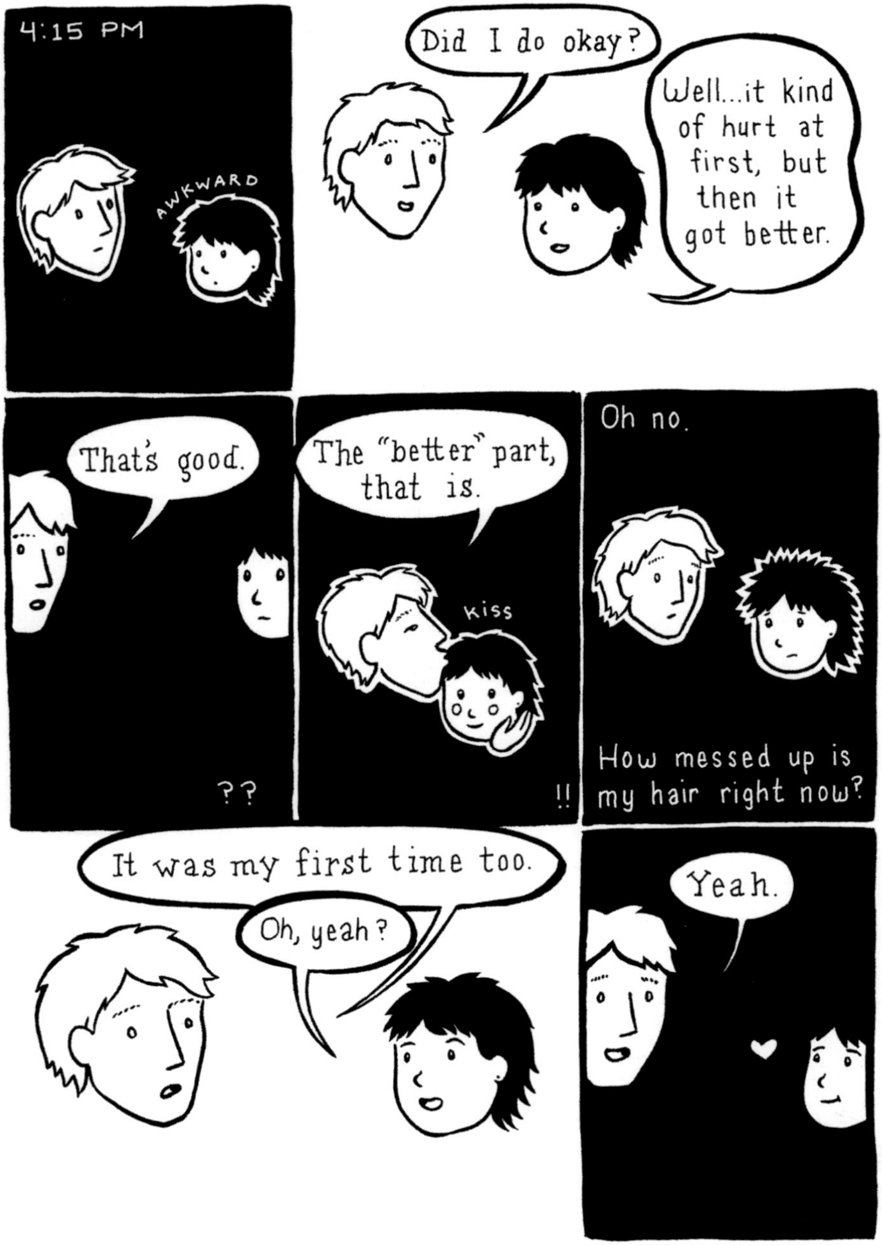
4:15 PM
AWKWARD
Did I do okay?
Well...it kind of hurt at first, but then it got better.
That's good.
??
The "better" part, that is.
KISS
!!
Oh no.
How messed up is my hair right now?
It was my first time too.
Oh, yeah?
Yeah.

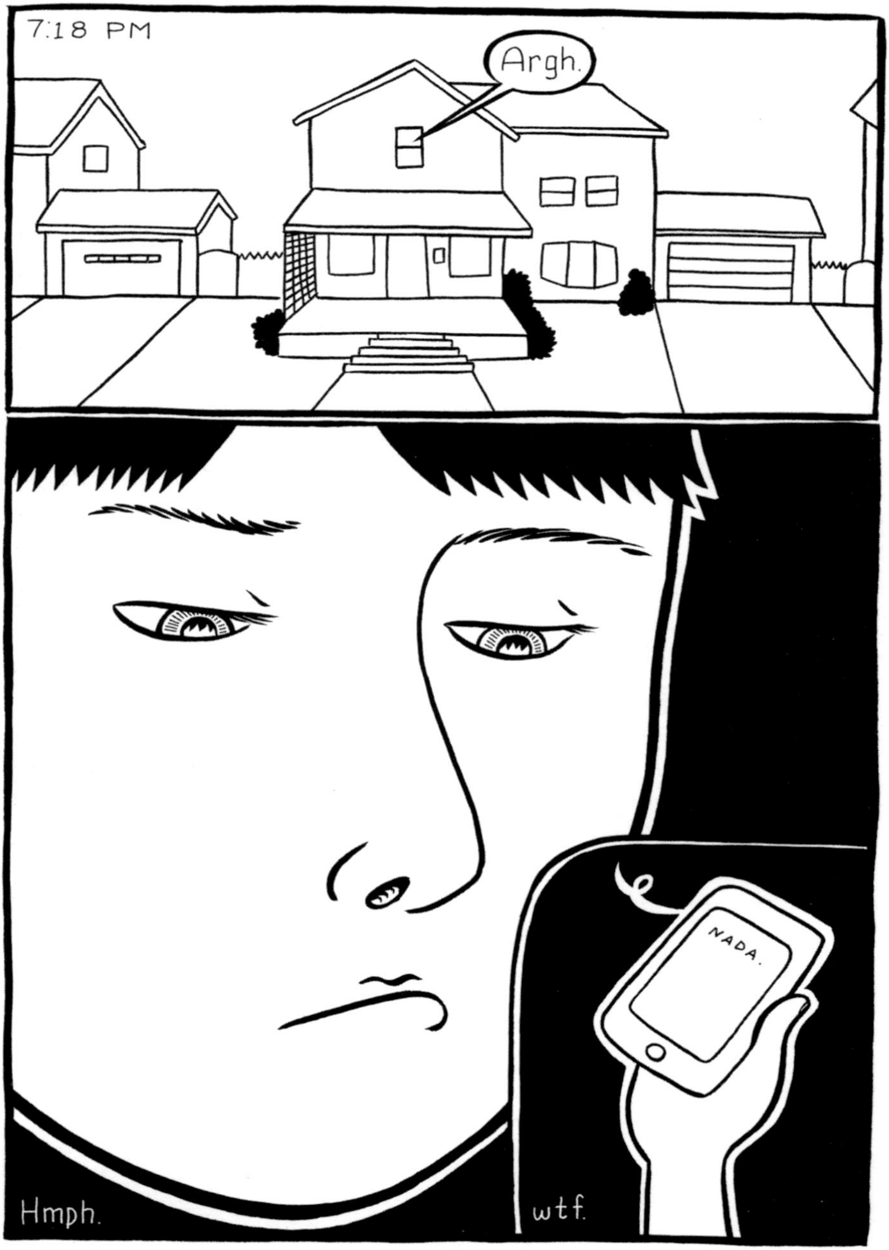
7:18 PM
Argh.
Hmph.
wtf.
NADA.

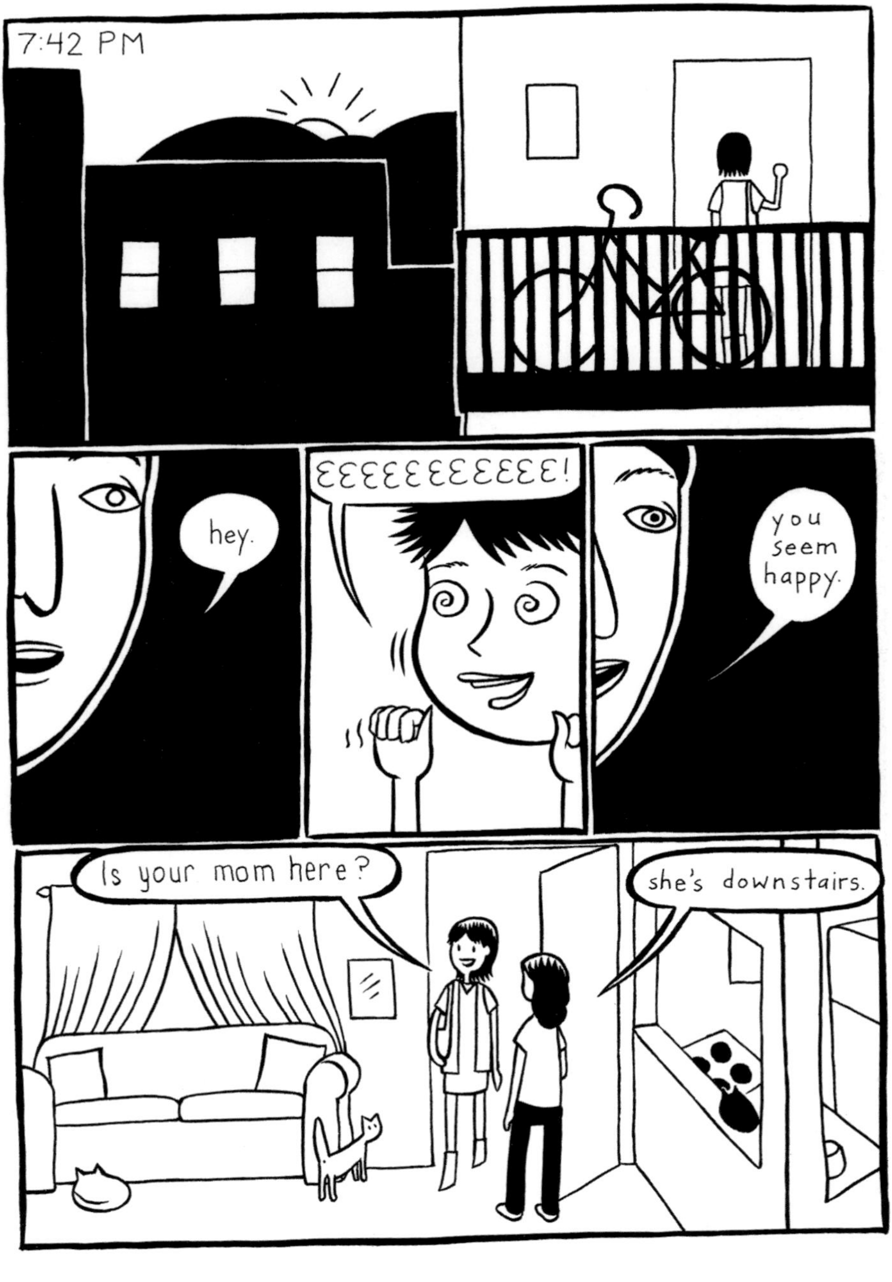
7:42 PM
hey.
EEEEEEEEEEE!
you seem happy.
Is your mom here?
she's downstairs.

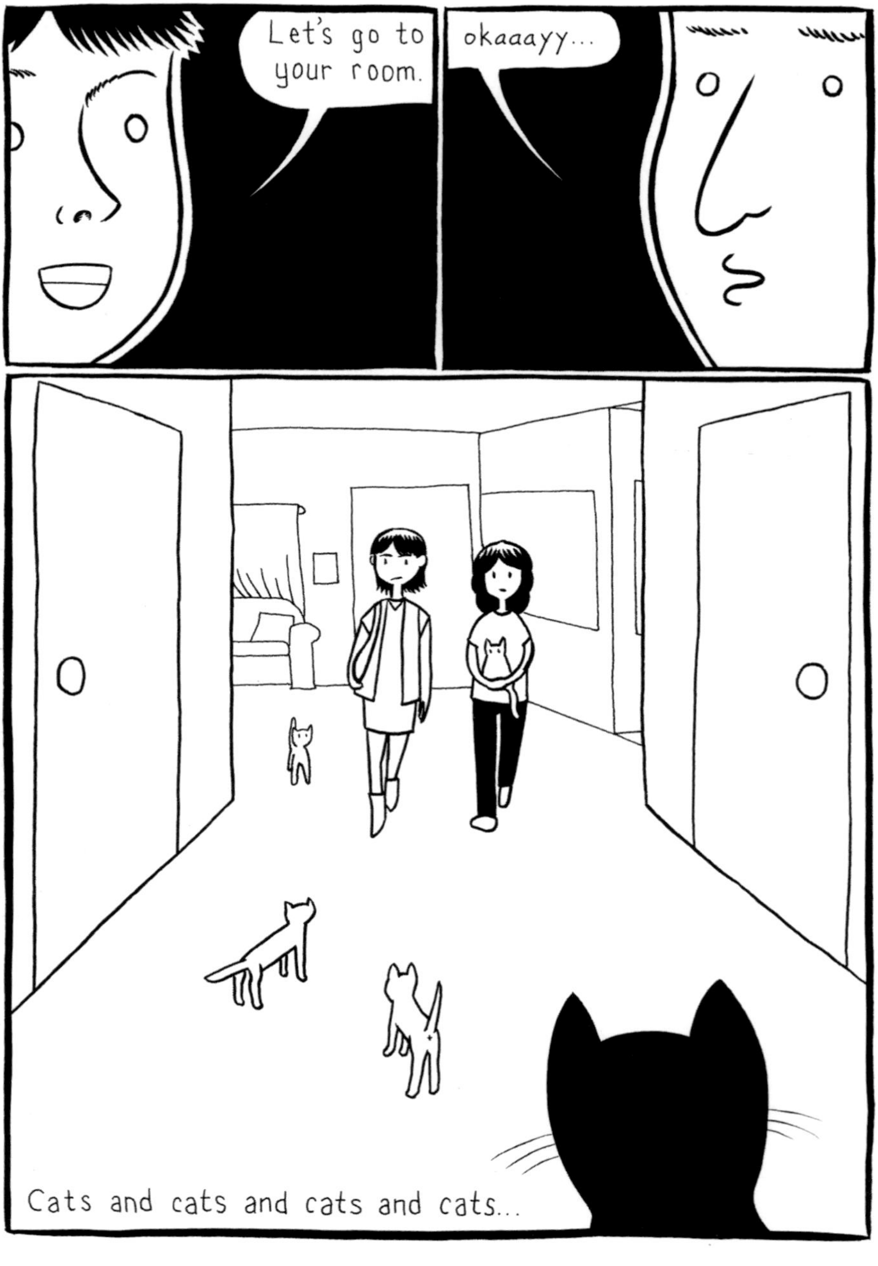
Let's go to your room.
okaaayy...
Cats and cats and cats and cats...

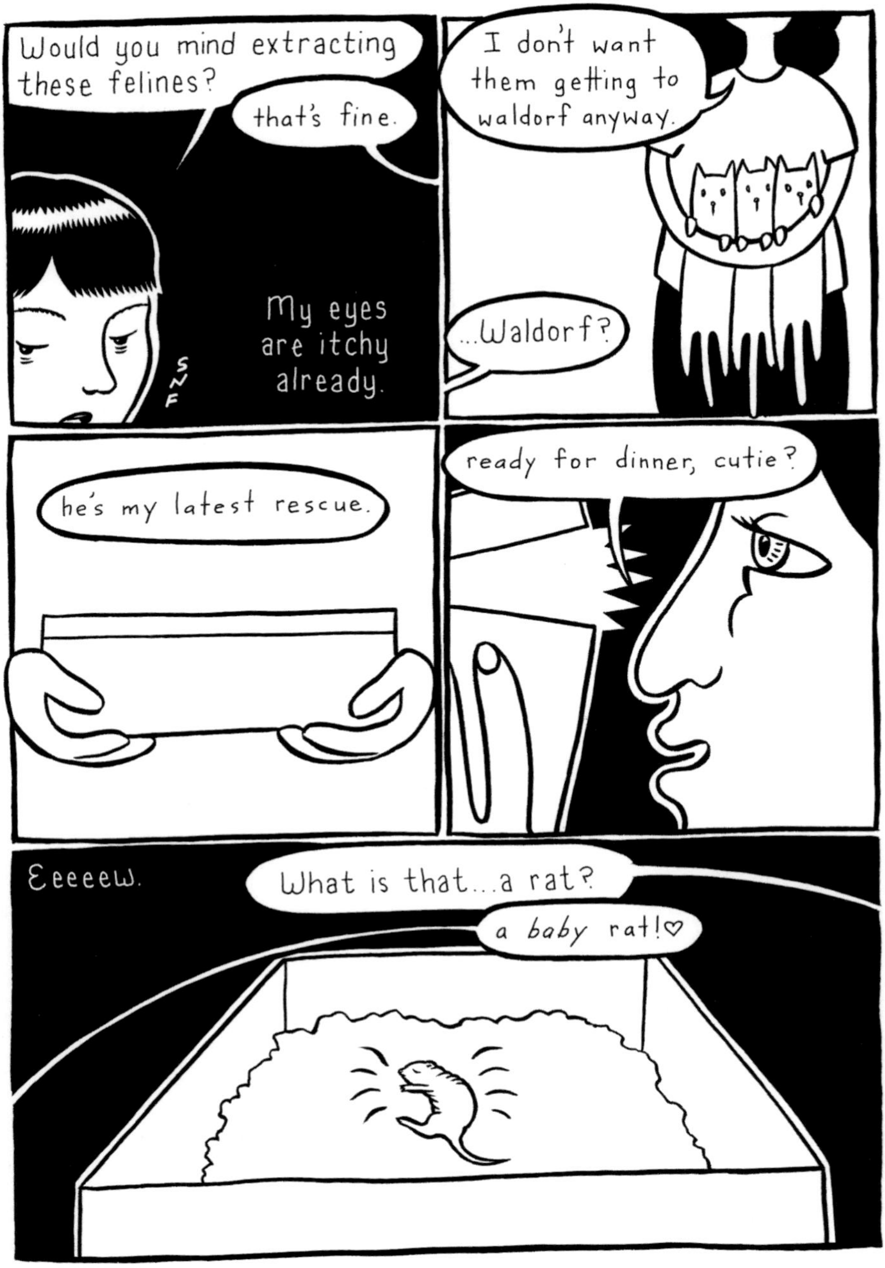
Would you mind extracting these felines?
that's fine.
My eyes are itchy already.
SNF
I don't want them getting to waldorf anyway.
...Waldorf?
he's my latest rescue.
ready for dinner, cutie?
Eeeeew.
What is that...a rat?
a *baby* rat!♡

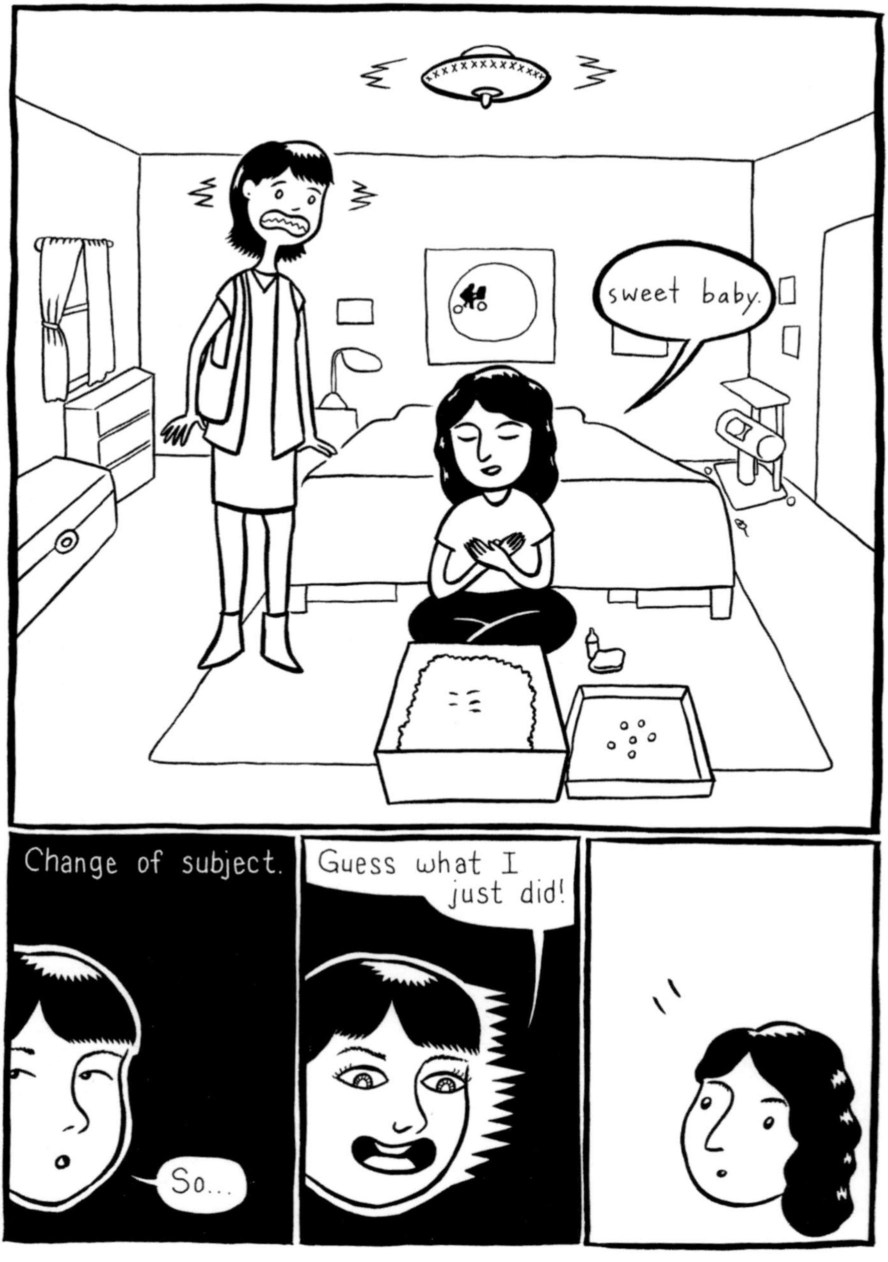
sweet baby.
Change of subject.
So...
Guess what I just did!

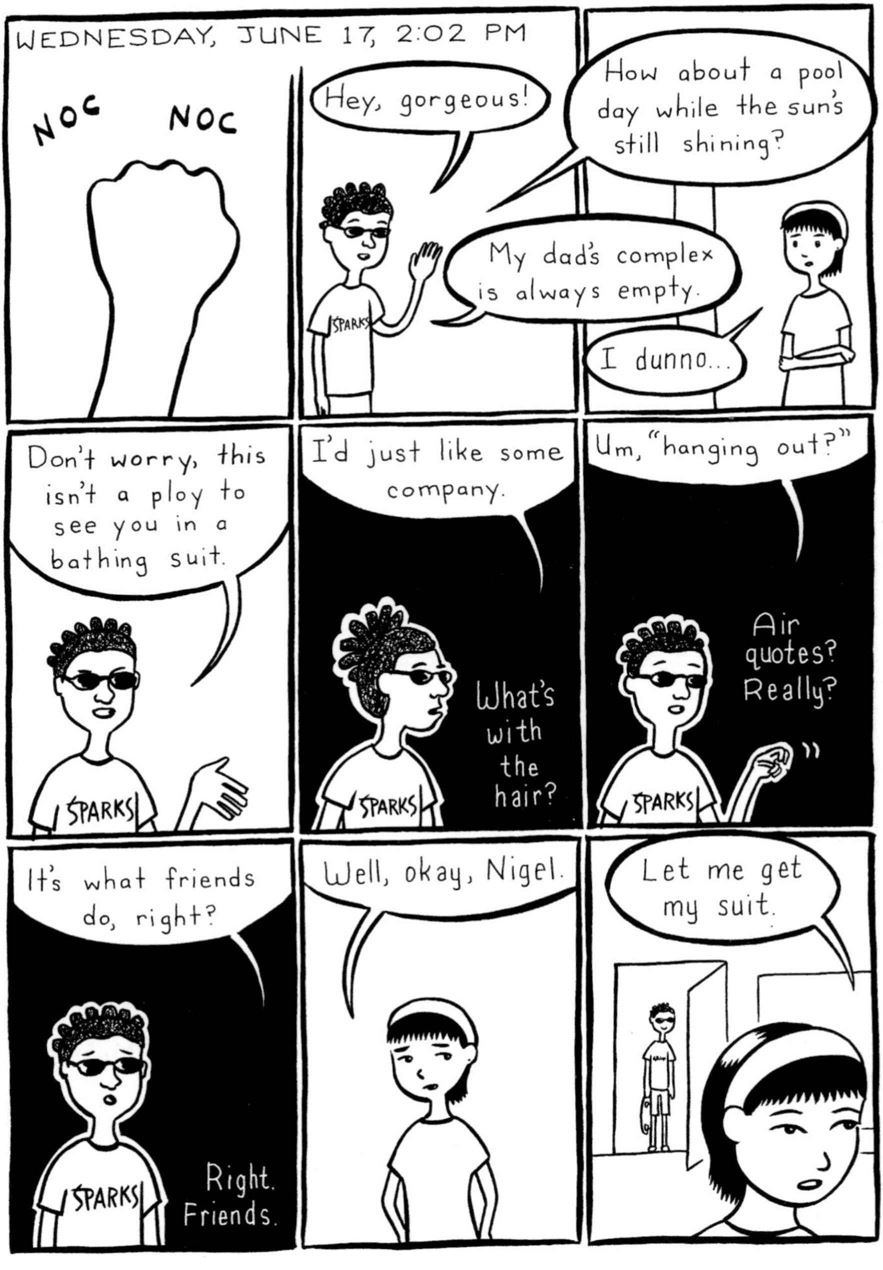
WEDNESDAY, JUNE 17, 2:02 PM
NOC NOC
Hey, gorgeous!
How about a pool day while the sun's still shining?
My dad's complex is always empty.
I dunno...
SPARKS
Don't worry, this isn't a ploy to see you in a bathing suit.
SPARKS
I'd just like some company.
What's with the hair?
SPARKS
Um, "hanging out?"
Air quotes? Really?
SPARKS
It's what friends do, right?
Right. Friends.
SPARKS
Well, okay, Nigel.
Let me get my suit.

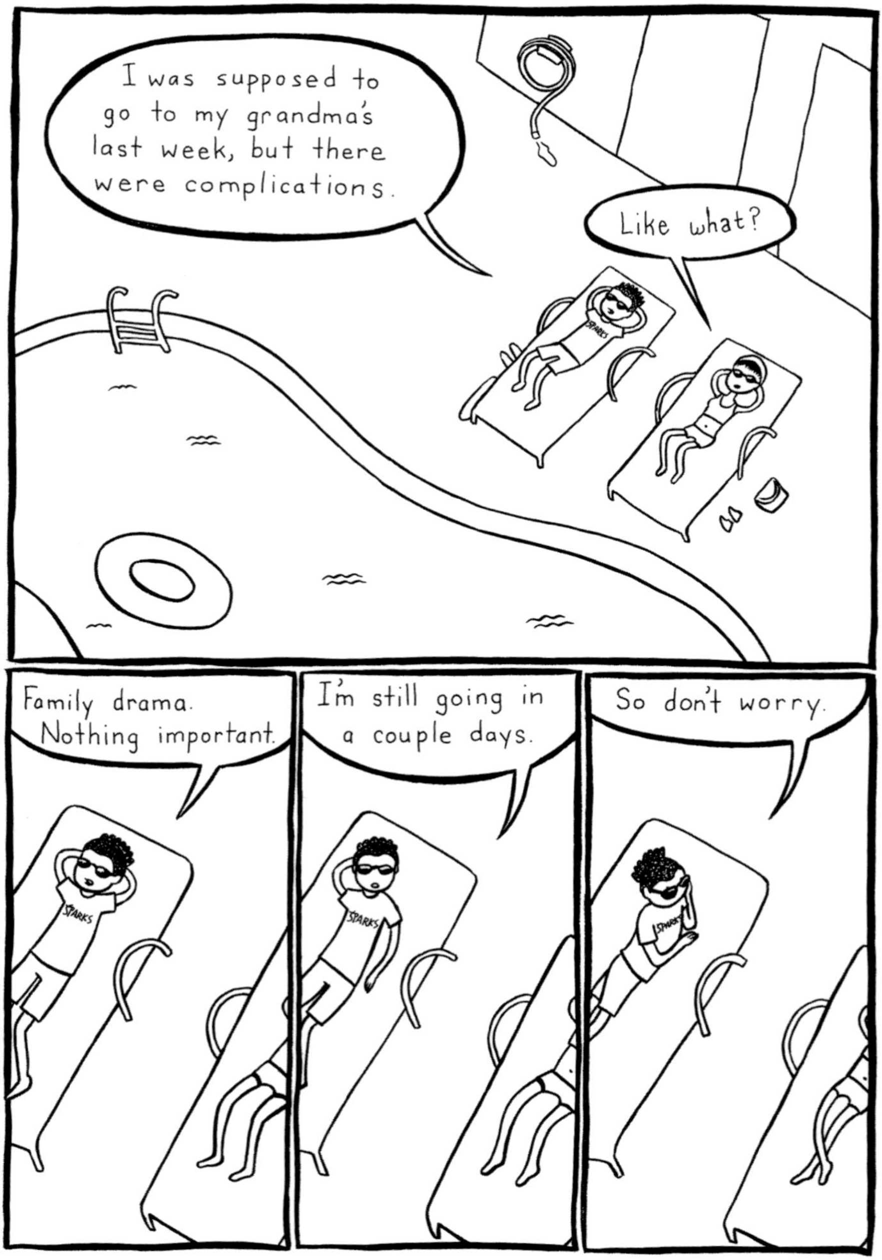
I was supposed to go to my grandma's last week, but there were complications.
Like what?
Family drama. Nothing important.
I'm still going in a couple days.
So don't worry.
SPARKS
SPARKS
SPARKS
SPARKS

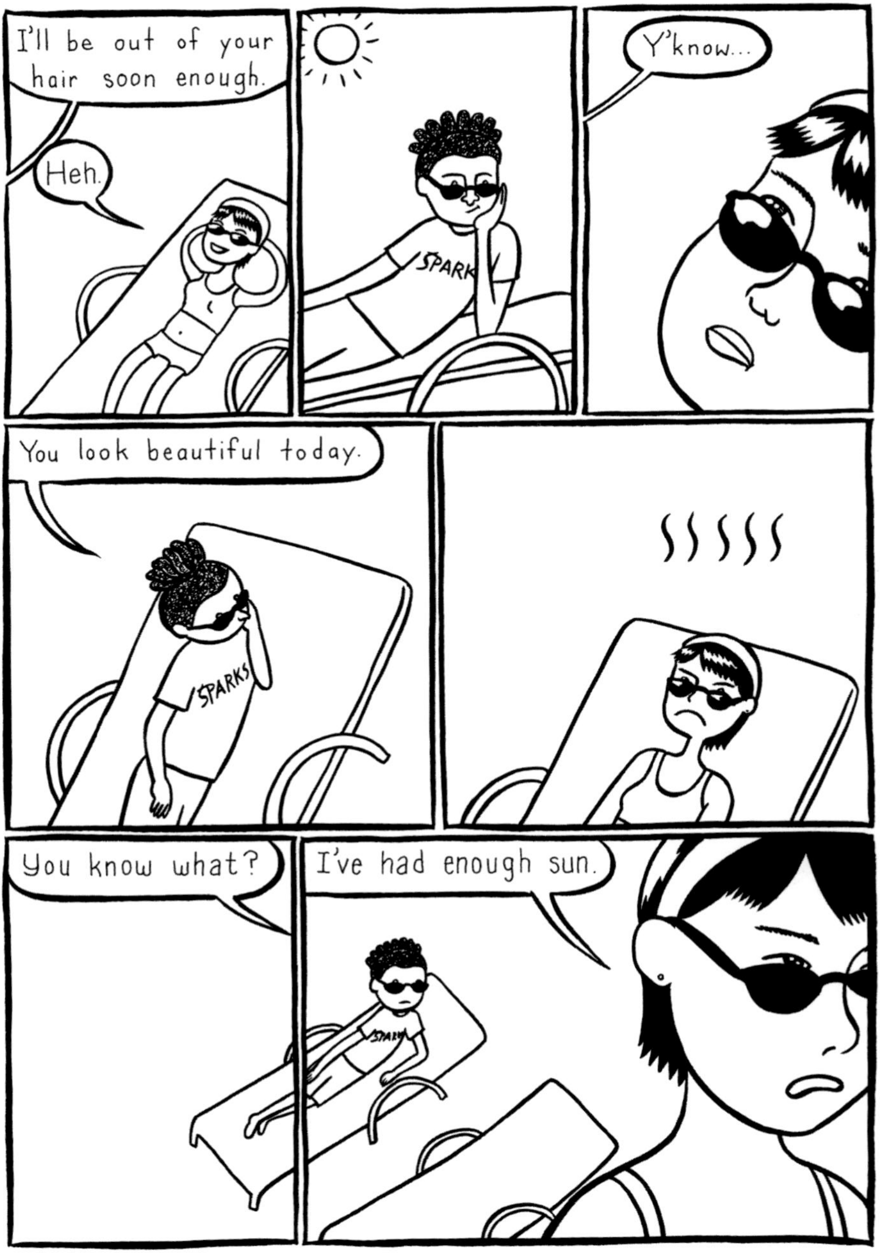
I'll be out of your hair soon enough.
Heh.
Y'know...
SPARKS
You look beautiful today.
SPARKS
You know what?
I've had enough sun.

FRIDAY, JULY 4, 7:03 PM

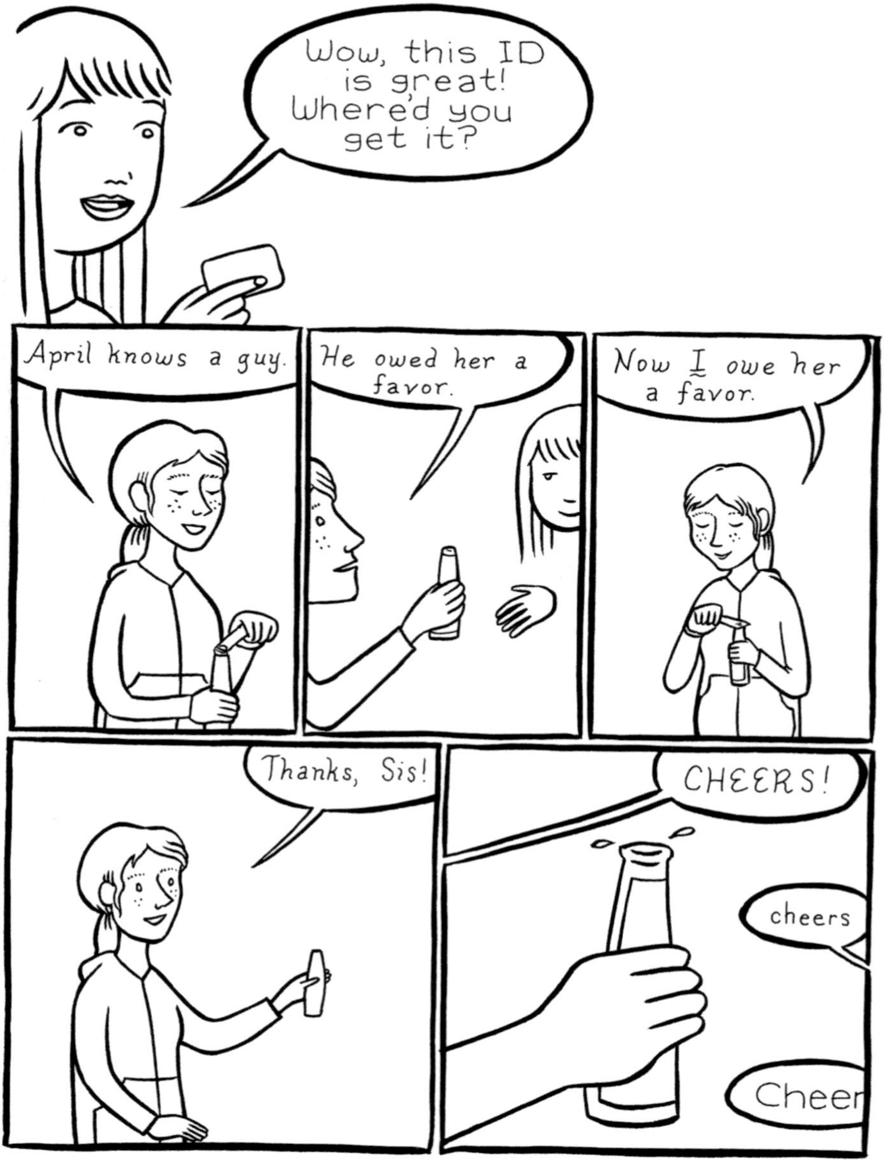
Wow, this ID is great! Where'd you get it?
April knows a guy.
He owed her a favor.
Now I owe her a favor.
Thanks, Sis!
CHEERS!
cheers
Cheer

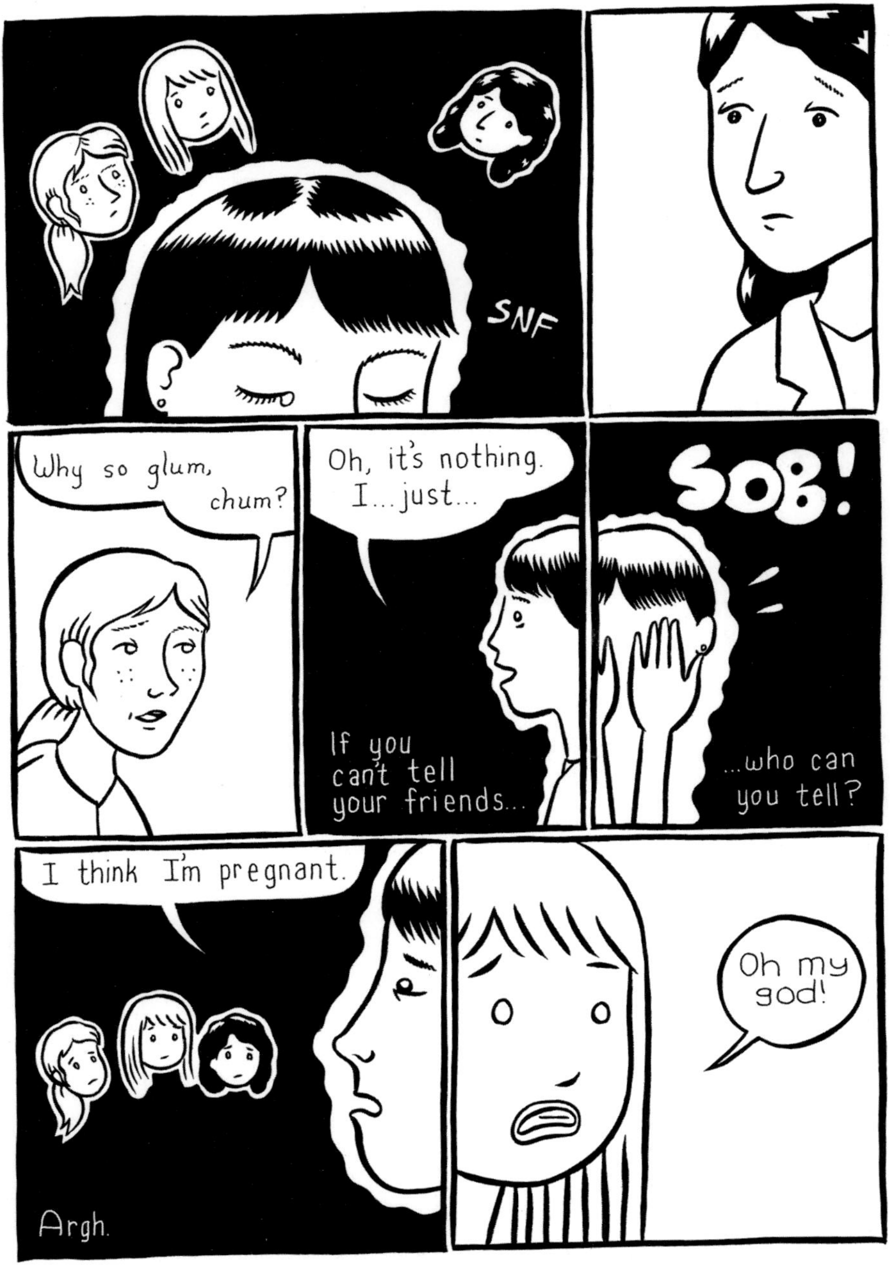
SNF
Why so glum, chum?
Oh, it's nothing. I... just...
If you can't tell your friends...
SOB!
...who can you tell?
I think I'm pregnant.
Argh.
Oh my god!

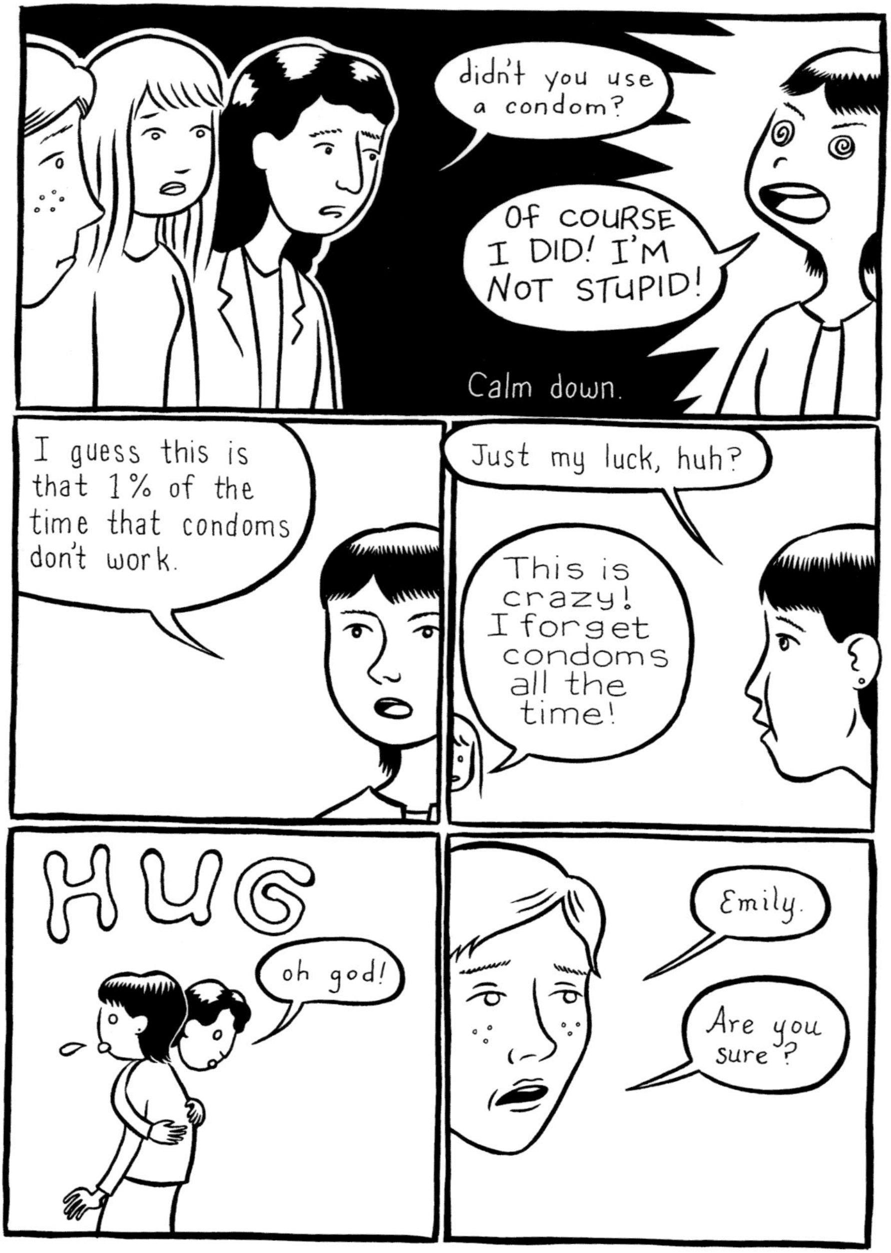
didn't you use a condom?
OF COURSE I DID! I'M NOT STUPID!
Calm down.
I guess this is that 1% of the time that condoms don't work.
Just my luck, huh?
This is crazy! I forget condoms all the time!
HUG
oh god!
Emily.
Are you sure?

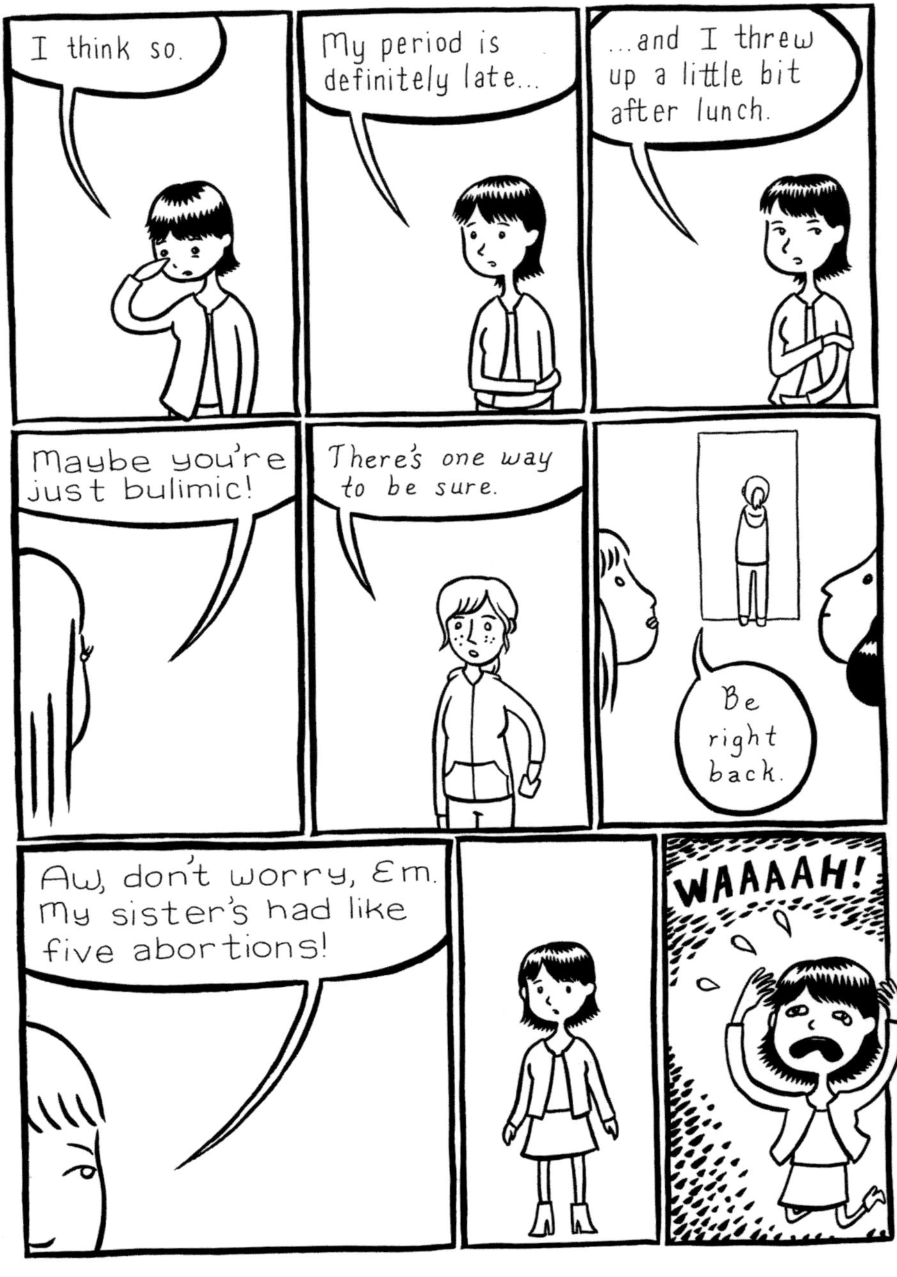
I think so.
My period is definitely late...
...and I threw up a little bit after lunch.
Maybe you're just bulimic!
There's one way to be sure.
Be right back.
Aw, don't worry, Em. My sister's had like five abortions!
WAAAAH!

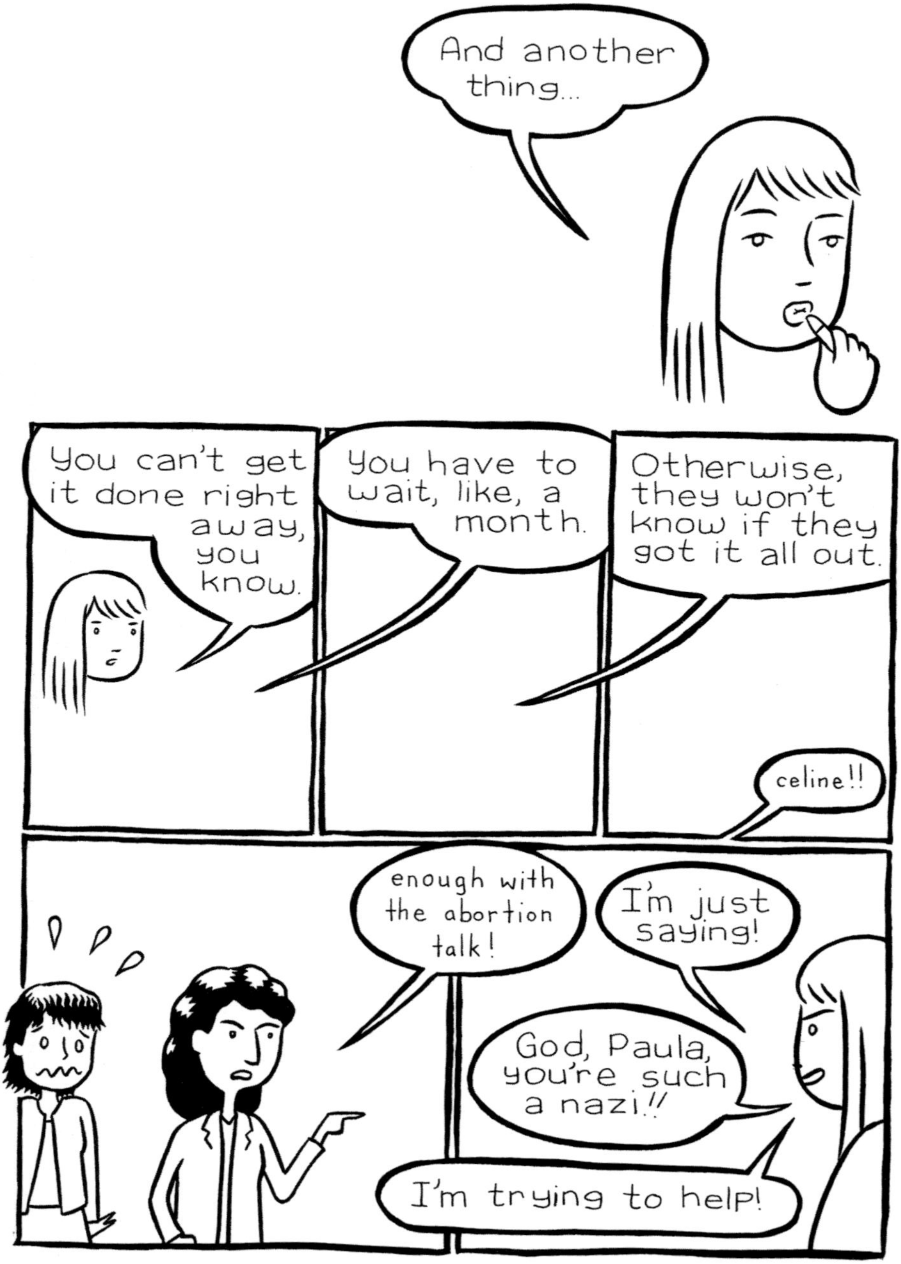
And another thing...
You can't get it done right away, you know.
You have to wait, like, a month.
Otherwise, they won't know if they got it all out.
celine!!
enough with the abortion talk!
I'm just saying!
God, Paula, you're such a nazi!!
I'm trying to help!

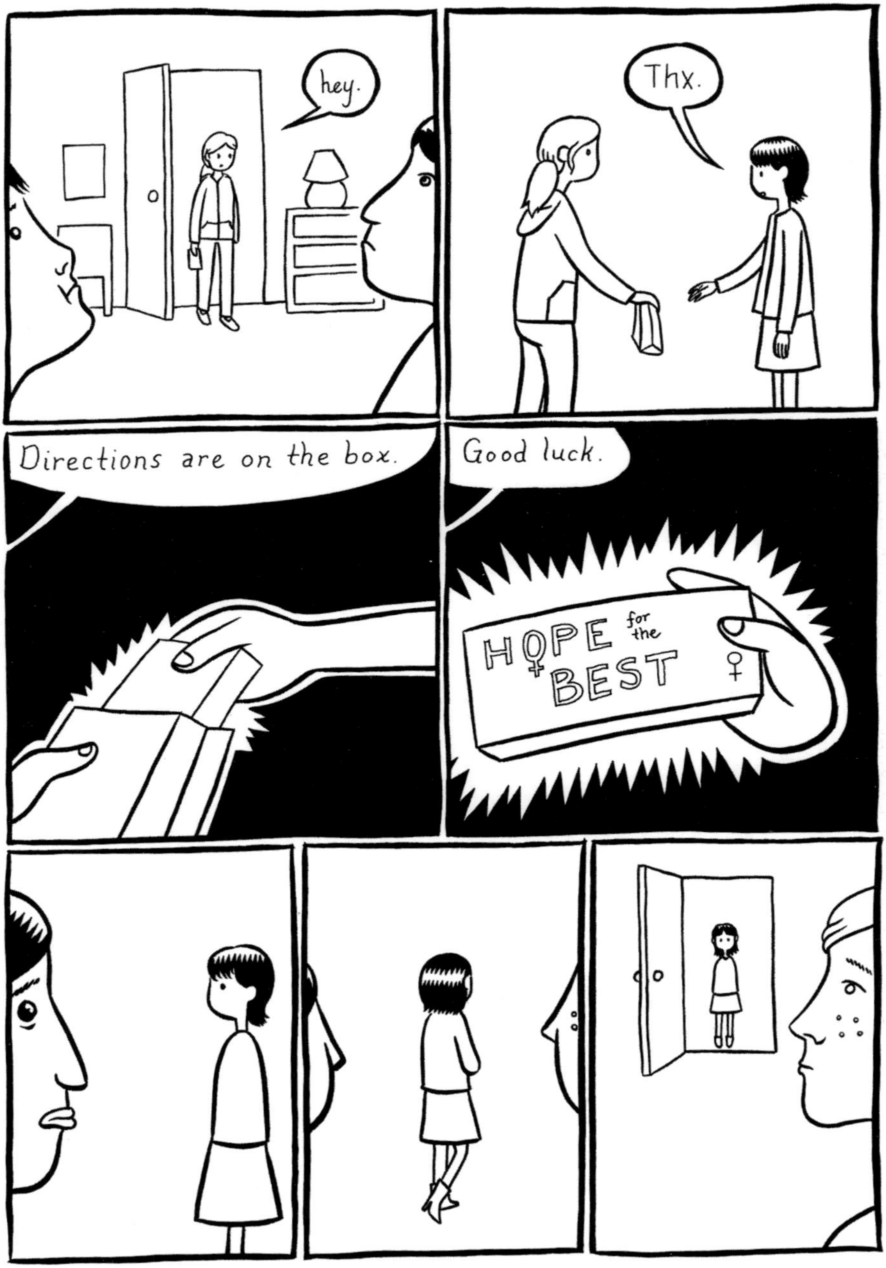
hey.
Thx.
Directions are on the box.
Good luck.
HOPE for the BEST
♀

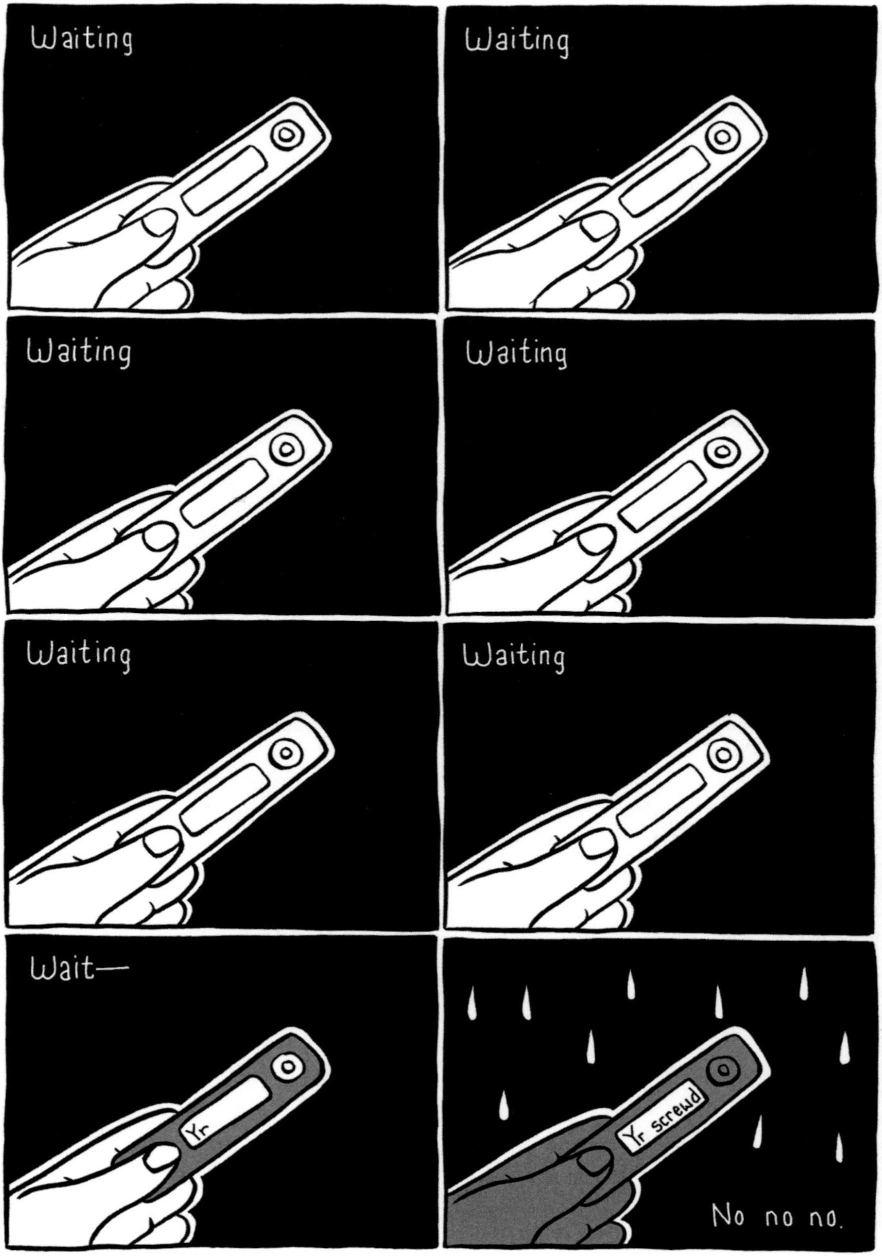
Waiting
Waiting
Waiting
Waiting
Waiting
Waiting
Wait—
Yr
Yr screwd
No no no.

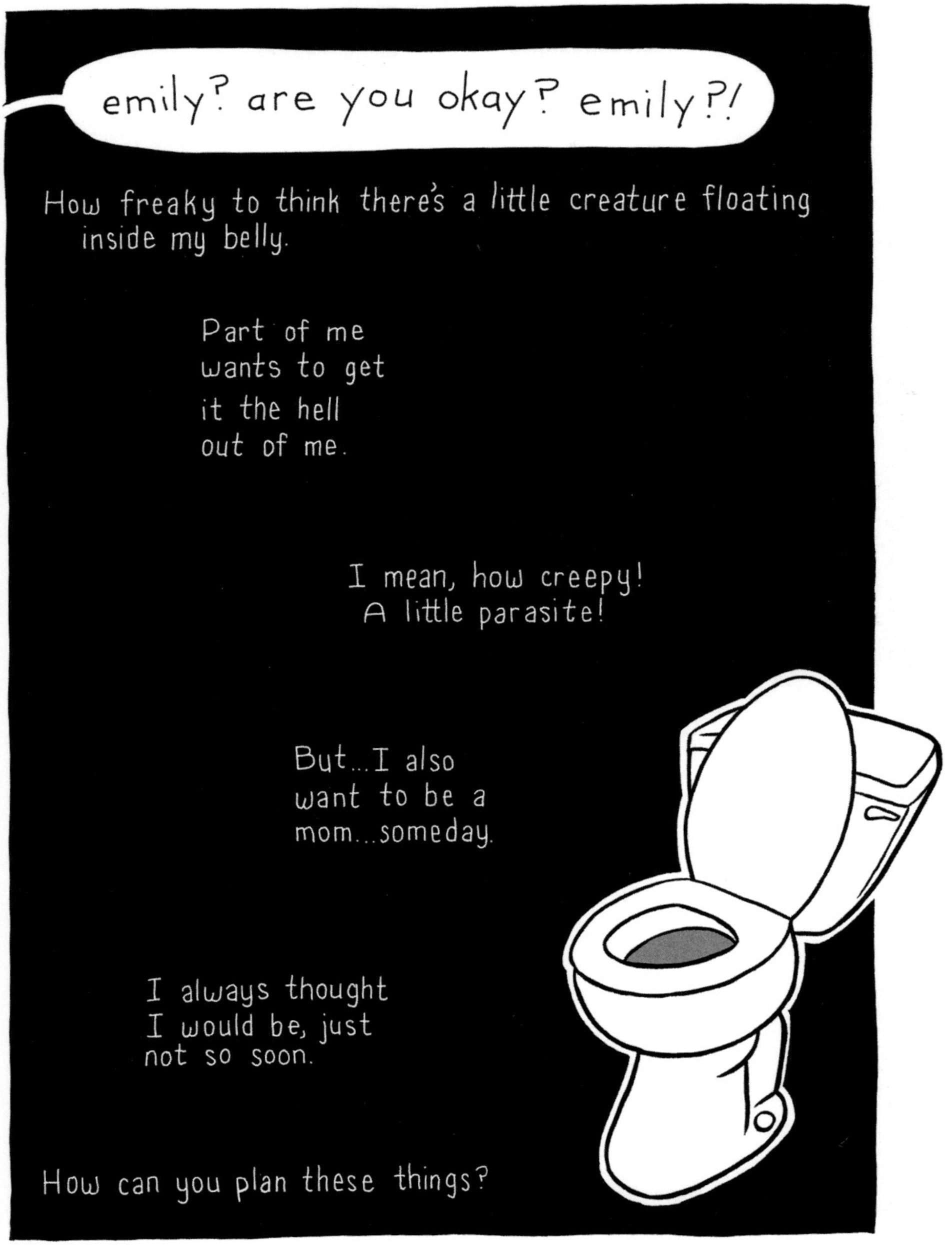
emily? are you okay? emily?!
How freaky to think there's a little creature floating inside my belly.
Part of me wants to get it the hell out of me.
I mean, how creepy! A little parasite!
But...I also want to be a mom...someday.
I always thought I would be, just not so soon.
How can you plan these things?

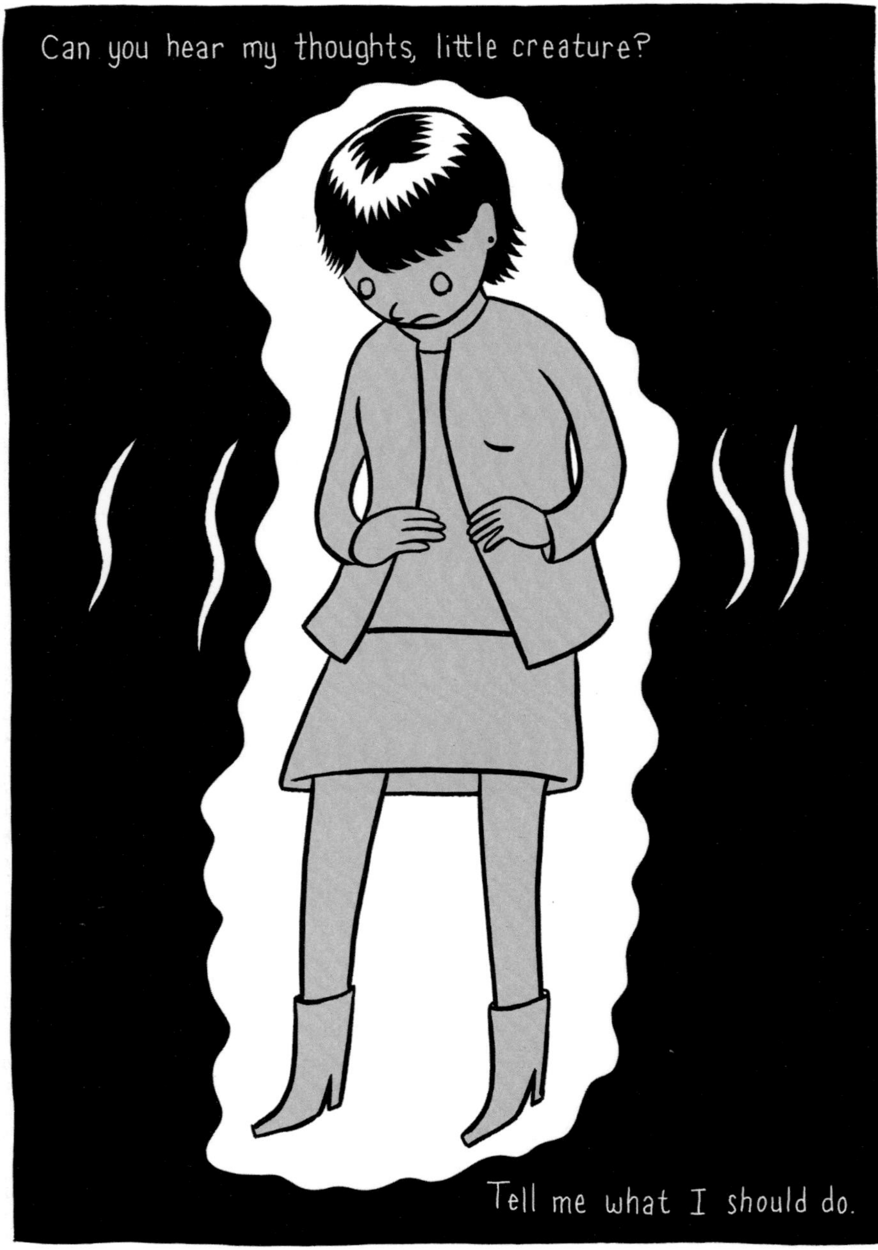
Can you hear my thoughts, little creature?
Tell me what I should do.

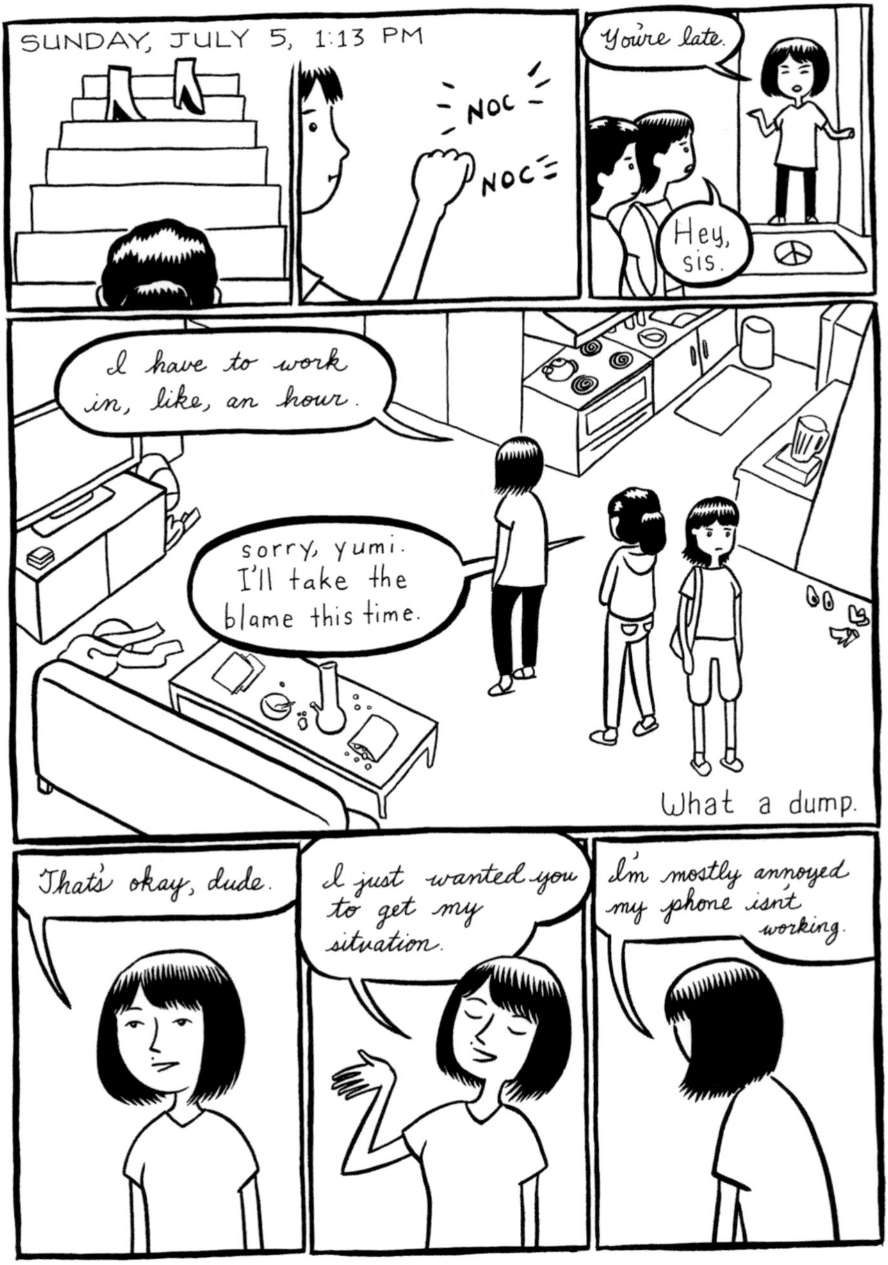
SUNDAY, JULY 5, 1:13 PM
NOC
NOC
You're late.
Hey, sis.
I have to work in, like, an hour.
sorry, yumi. I'll take the blame this time.
What a dump.
That's okay, dude.
I just wanted you to get my situation.
I'm mostly annoyed my phone isn't working.

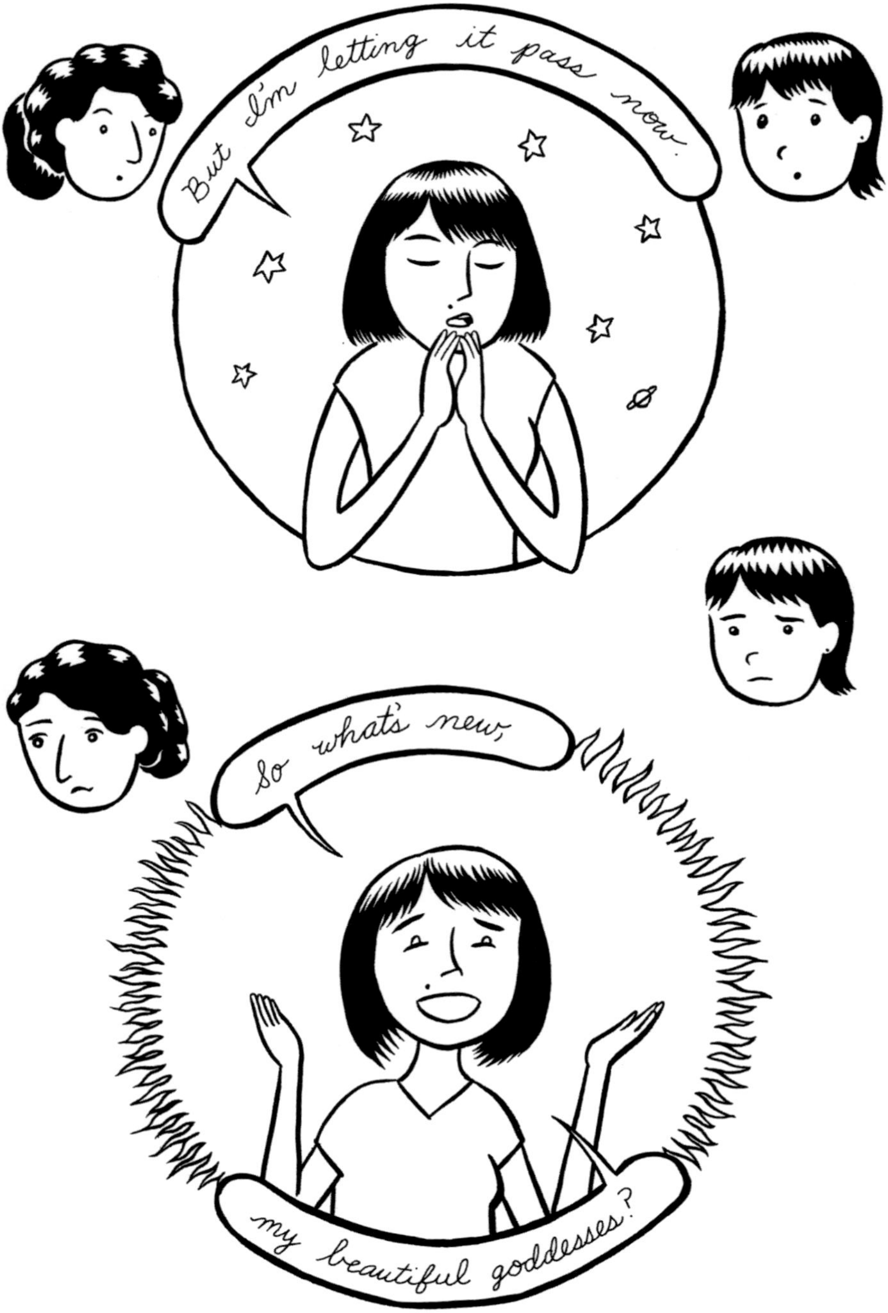
But I'm letting it pass now.
So what's new,
my beautiful goddesses?

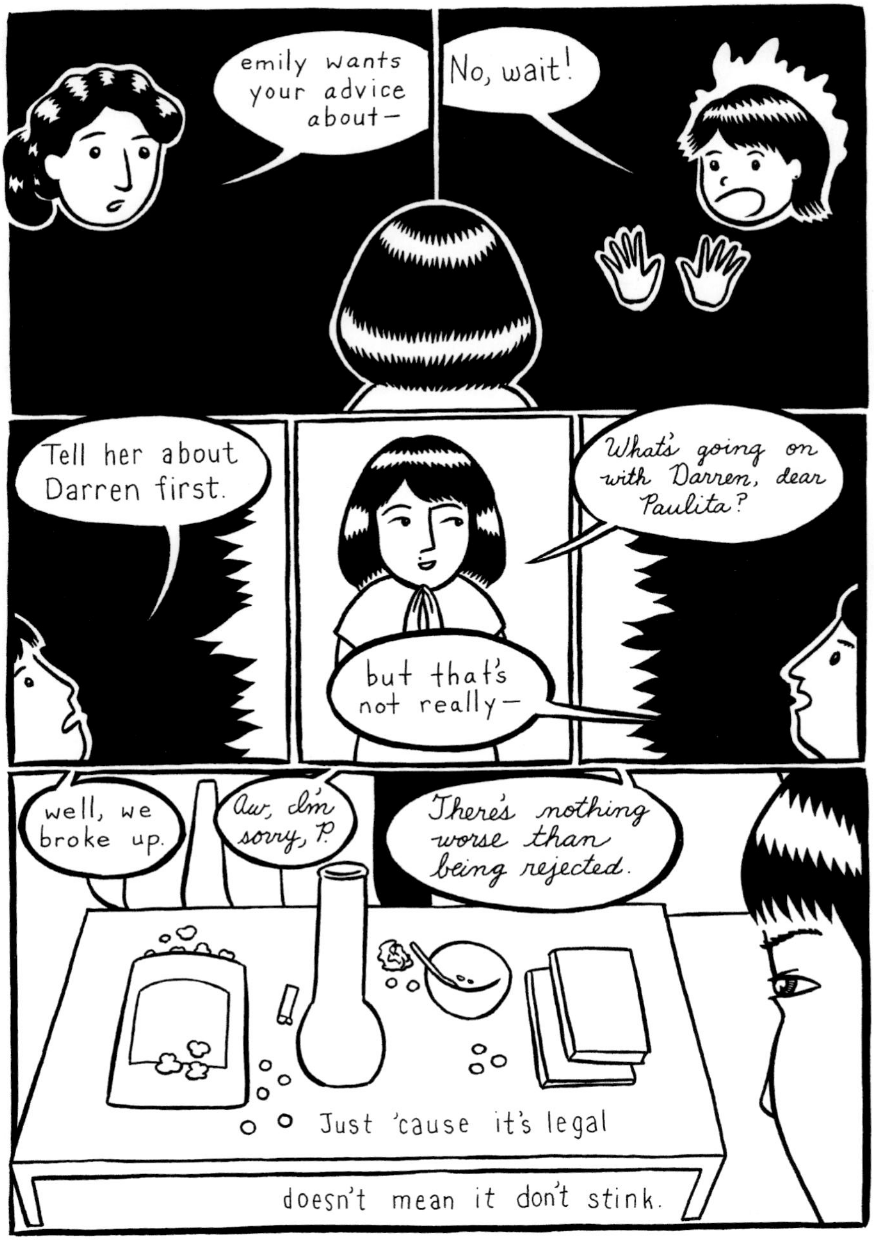
emily wants your advice about—
No, wait!
Tell her about Darren first.
What's going on with Darren, dear Paulita?
but that's not really—
well, we broke up.
Aw, I'm sorry, P.
There's nothing worse than being rejected.
Just 'cause it's legal
doesn't mean it don't stink.

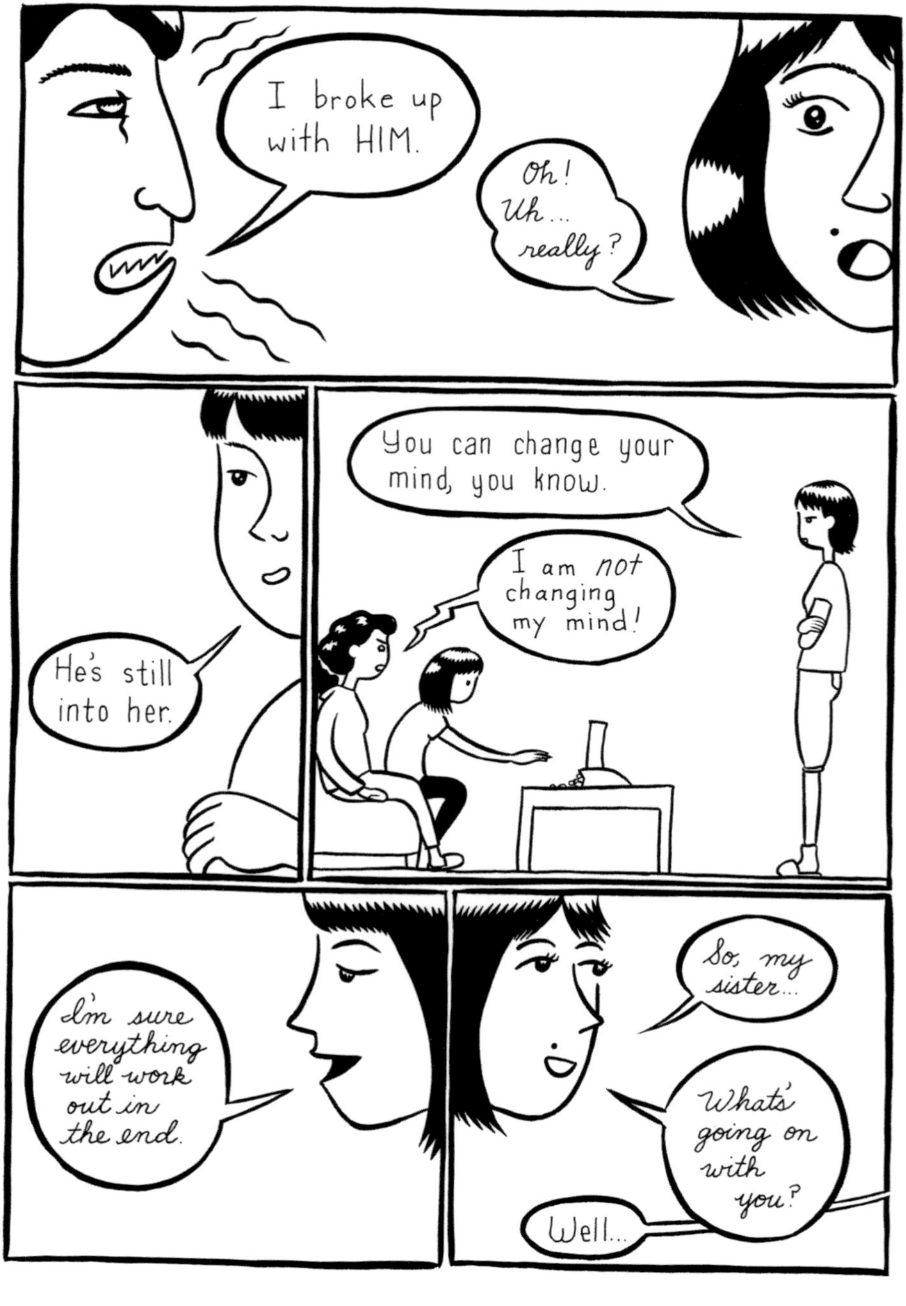
I broke up with HIM.
Oh! Uh... really?
He's still into her.
You can change your mind, you know.
I am *not* changing my mind!
I'm sure everything will work out in the end.
So, my sister...
What's going on with you?
Well...

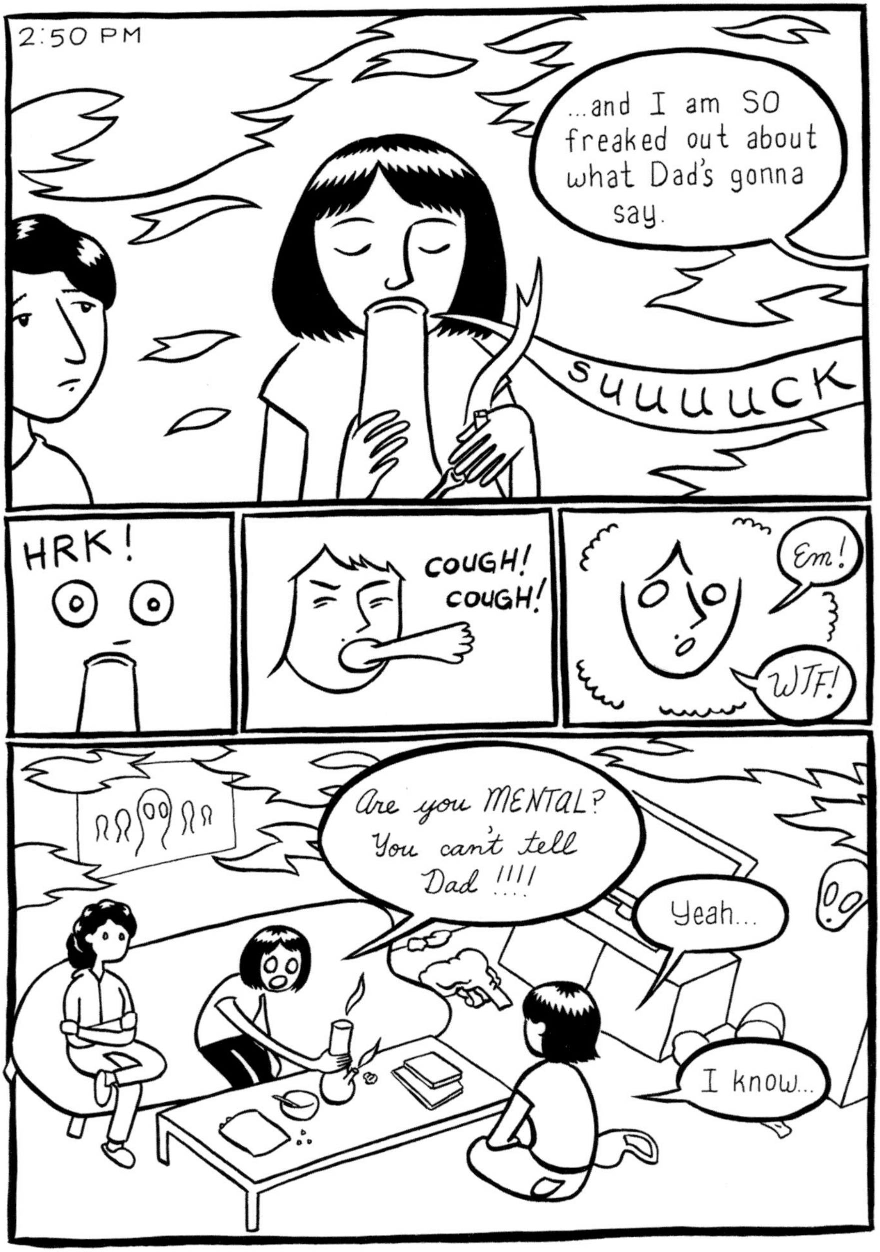
2:50 PM
...and I am SO freaked out about what Dad's gonna say.
SUUUUCK
HRK!
COUGH! COUGH!
Em!
WTF!
Are you MENTAL? You can't tell Dad !!!!
Yeah...
I know...

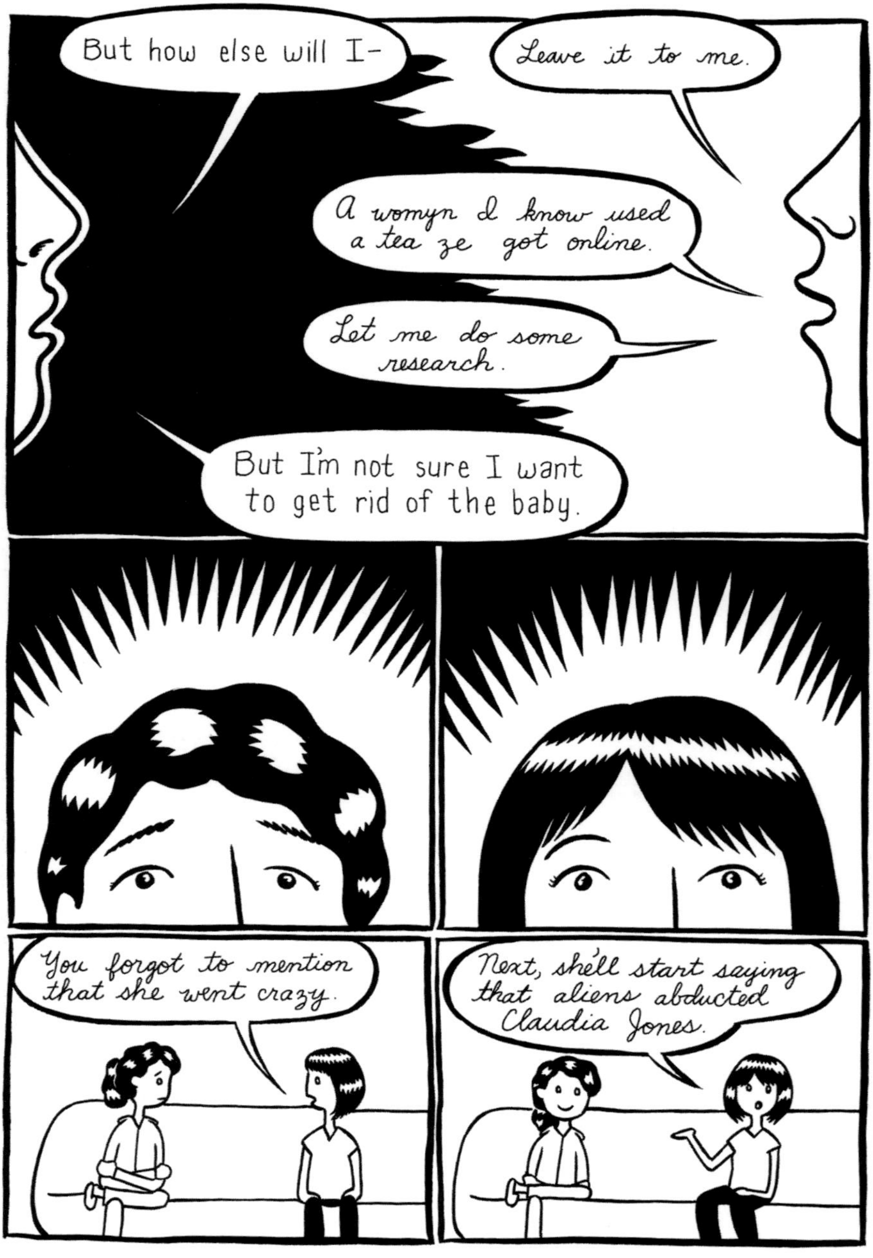

But how else will I-
Leave it to me.
A womyn I know used a tea ze got online.
Let me do some research.
But I'm not sure I want to get rid of the baby.
You forgot to mention that she went crazy.
Next, she'll start saying that aliens abducted Claudia Jones.

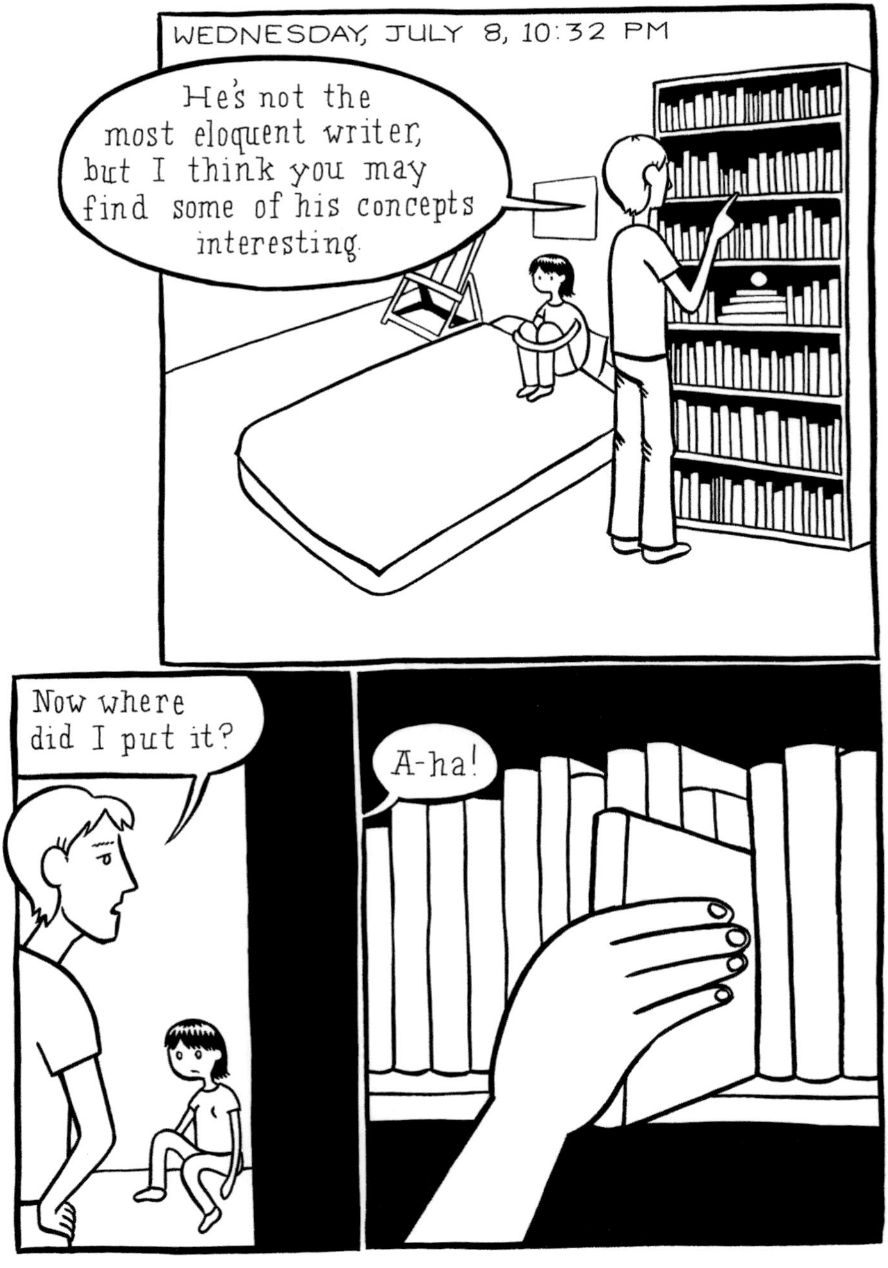
WEDNESDAY, JULY 8, 10:32 PM
He's not the most eloquent writer, but I think you may find some of his concepts interesting.
Now where did I put it?
A-ha!

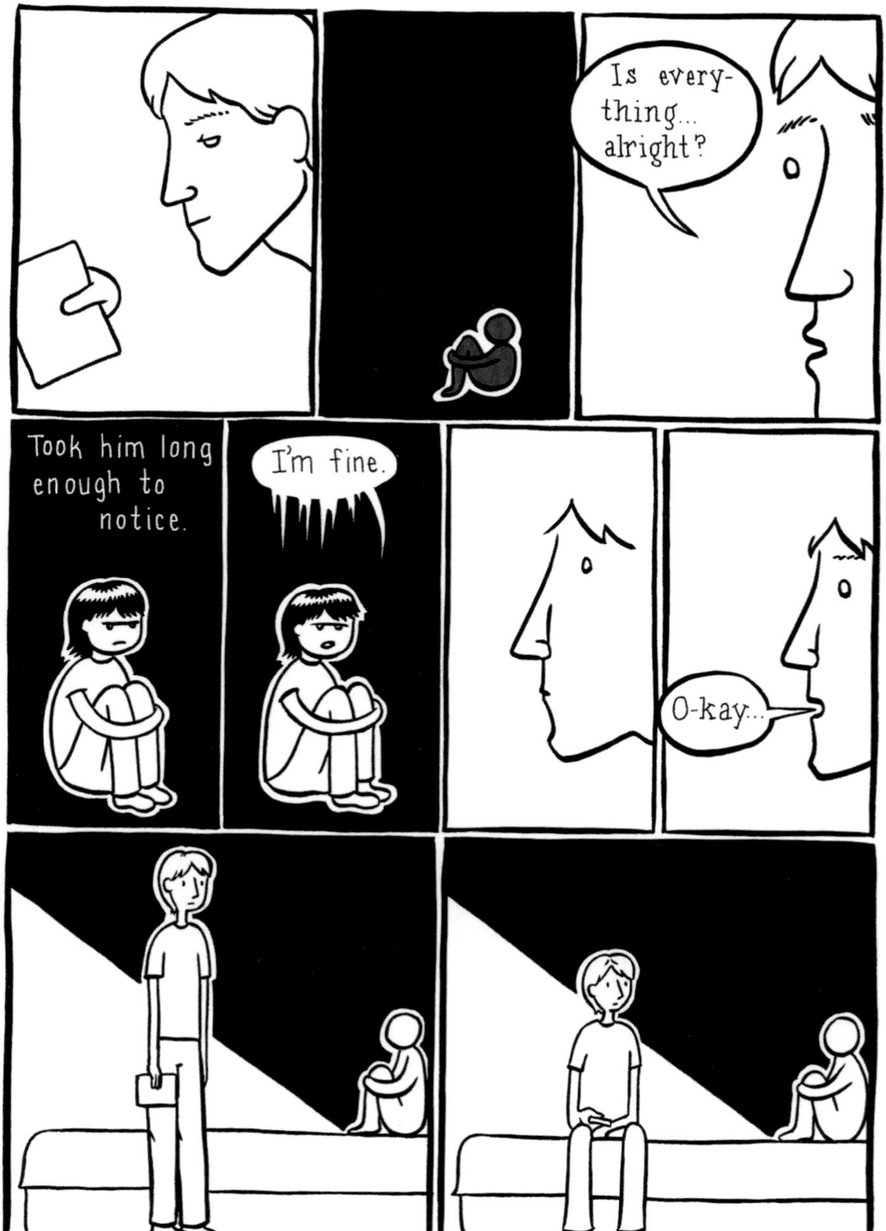
Is every-thing... alright?
Took him long enough to notice.
I'm fine.
O-kay...

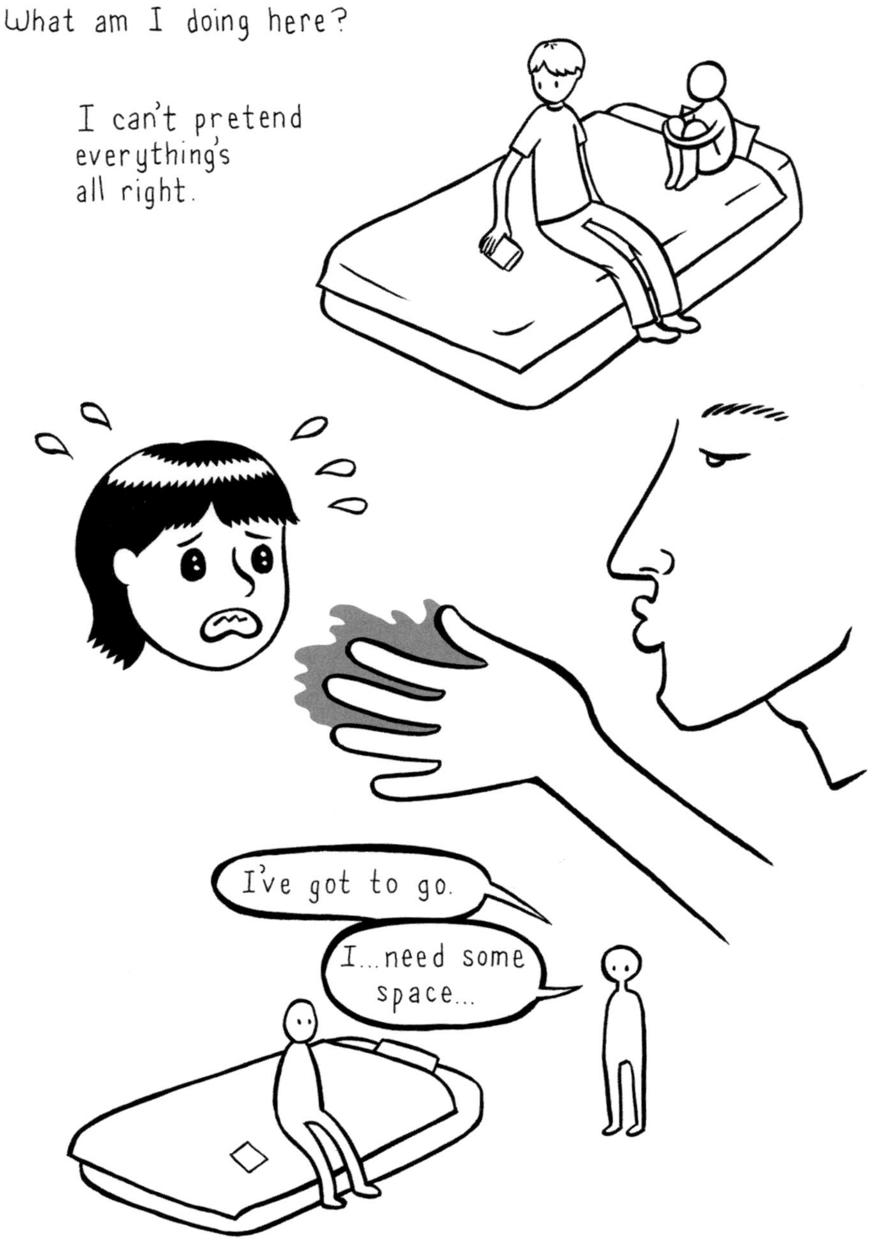
What am I doing here?
I can't pretend everything's all right.
I've got to go.
I... need some space...

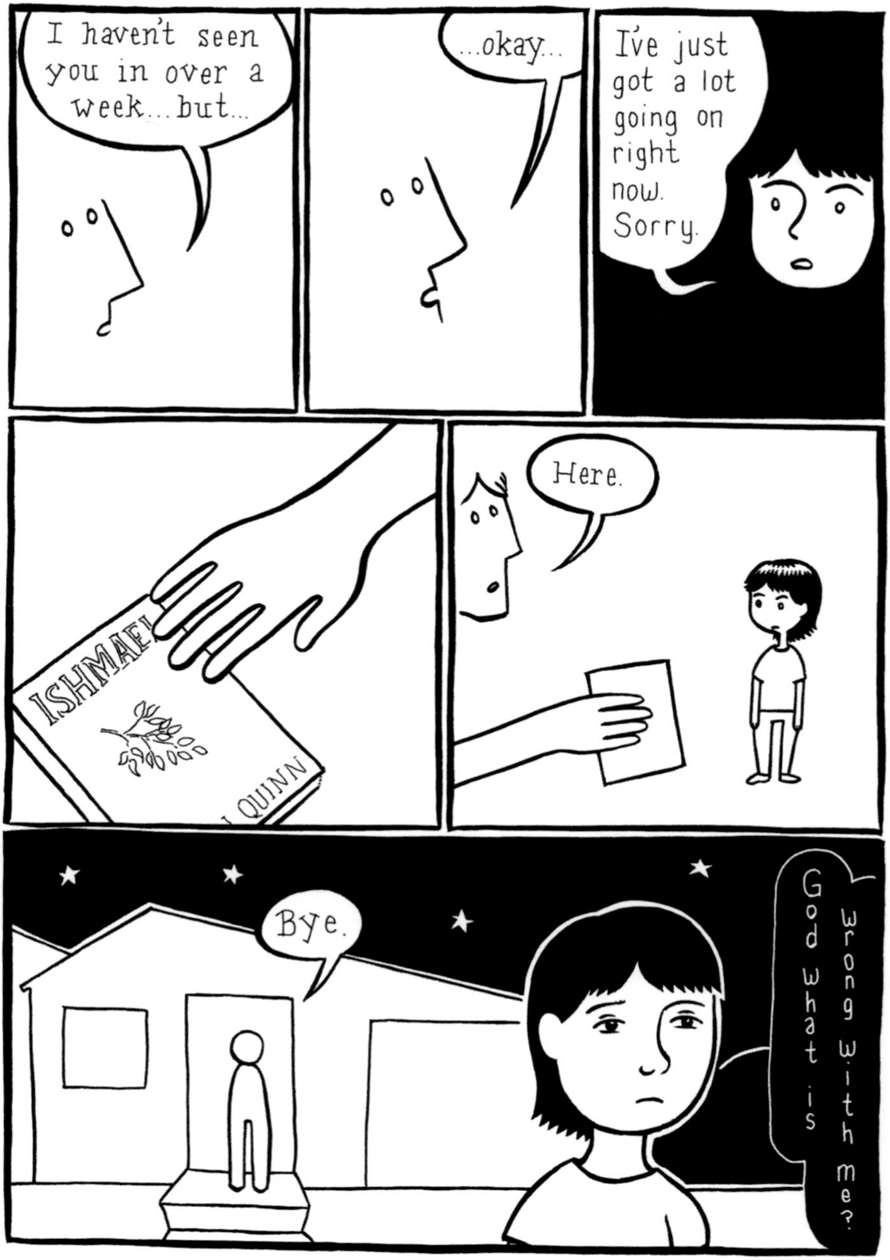
I haven't seen you in over a week... but...
...okay...
I've just got a lot going on right now. Sorry.
ISHMAEL
QUINN
Here.
Bye.
God what is wrong with me?

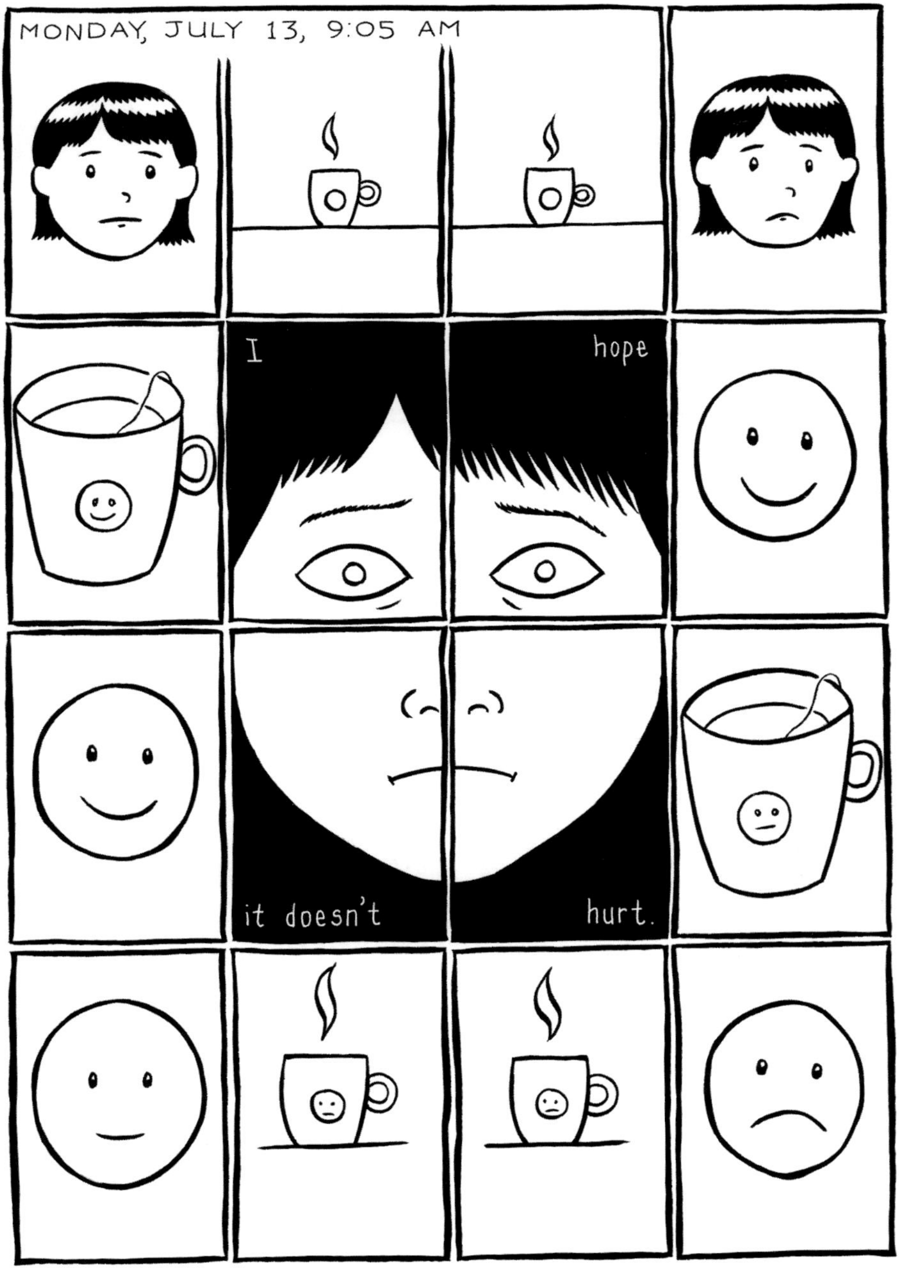
MONDAY, JULY 13, 9:05 AM
I
hope
it doesn't
hurt.

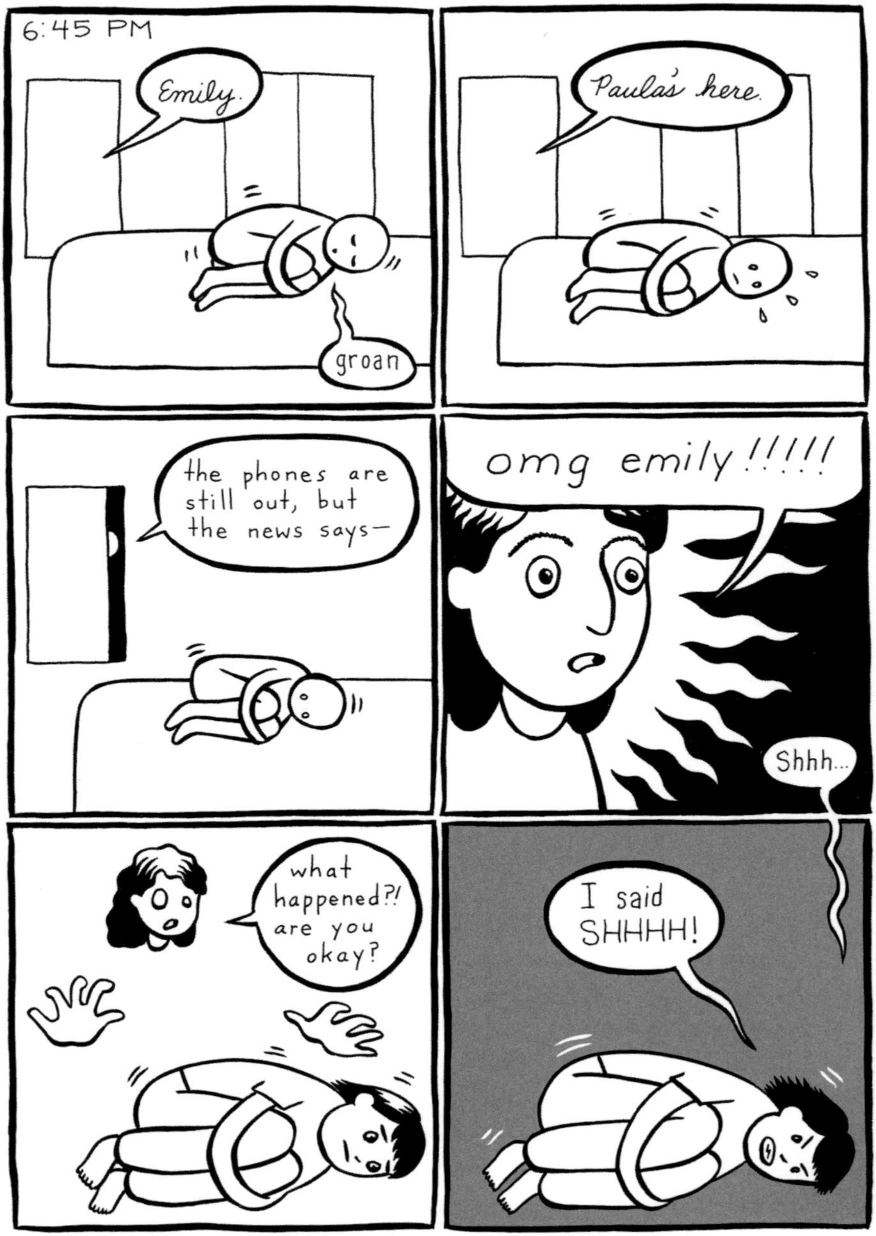
6:45 PM
Emily.
groan
Paula's here.
the phones are still out, but the news says—
omg emily!!!!!
Shhh...
what happened?! are you okay?
I said SHHHH!

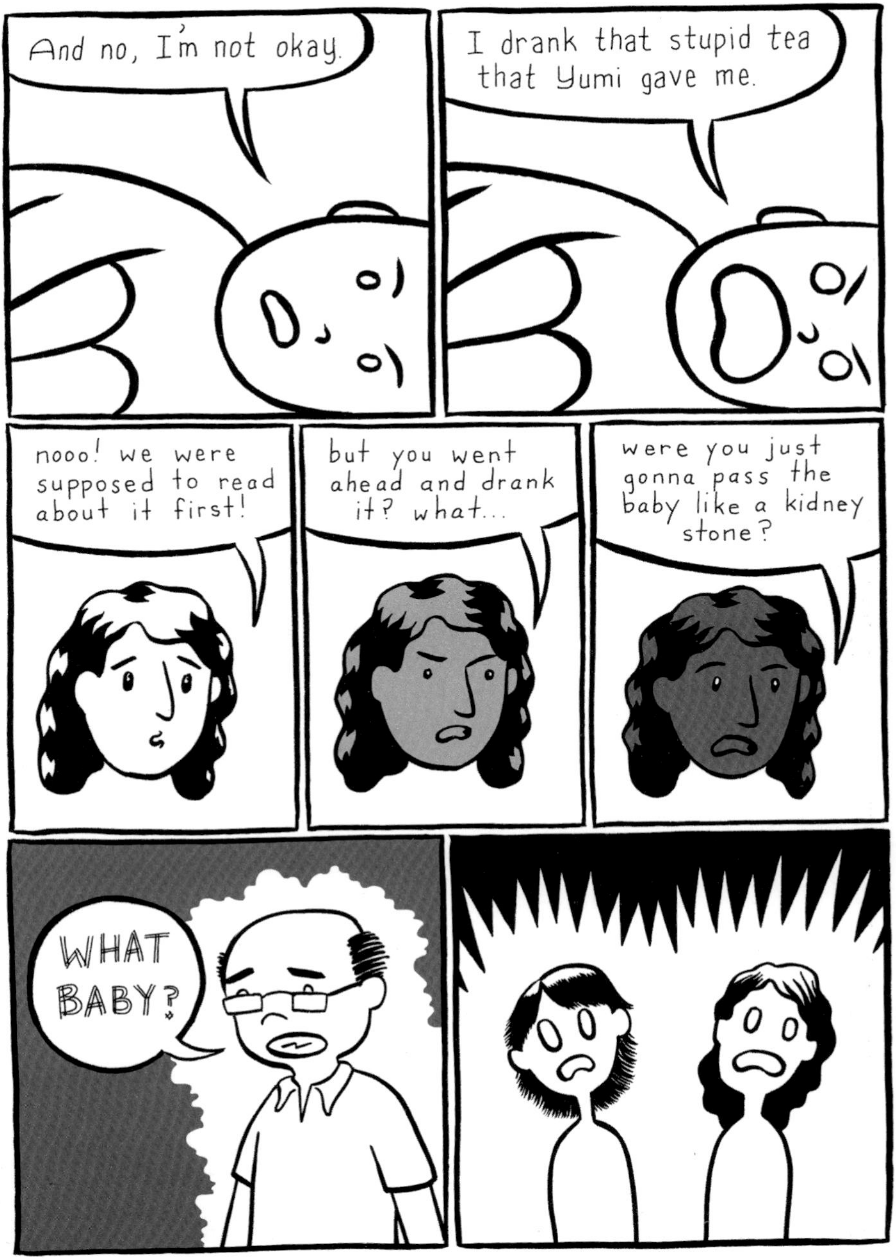
And no, I'm not okay.
I drank that stupid tea that Yumi gave me.
nooo! we were supposed to read about it first!
but you went ahead and drank it? what...
were you just gonna pass the baby like a kidney stone?
WHAT BABY?

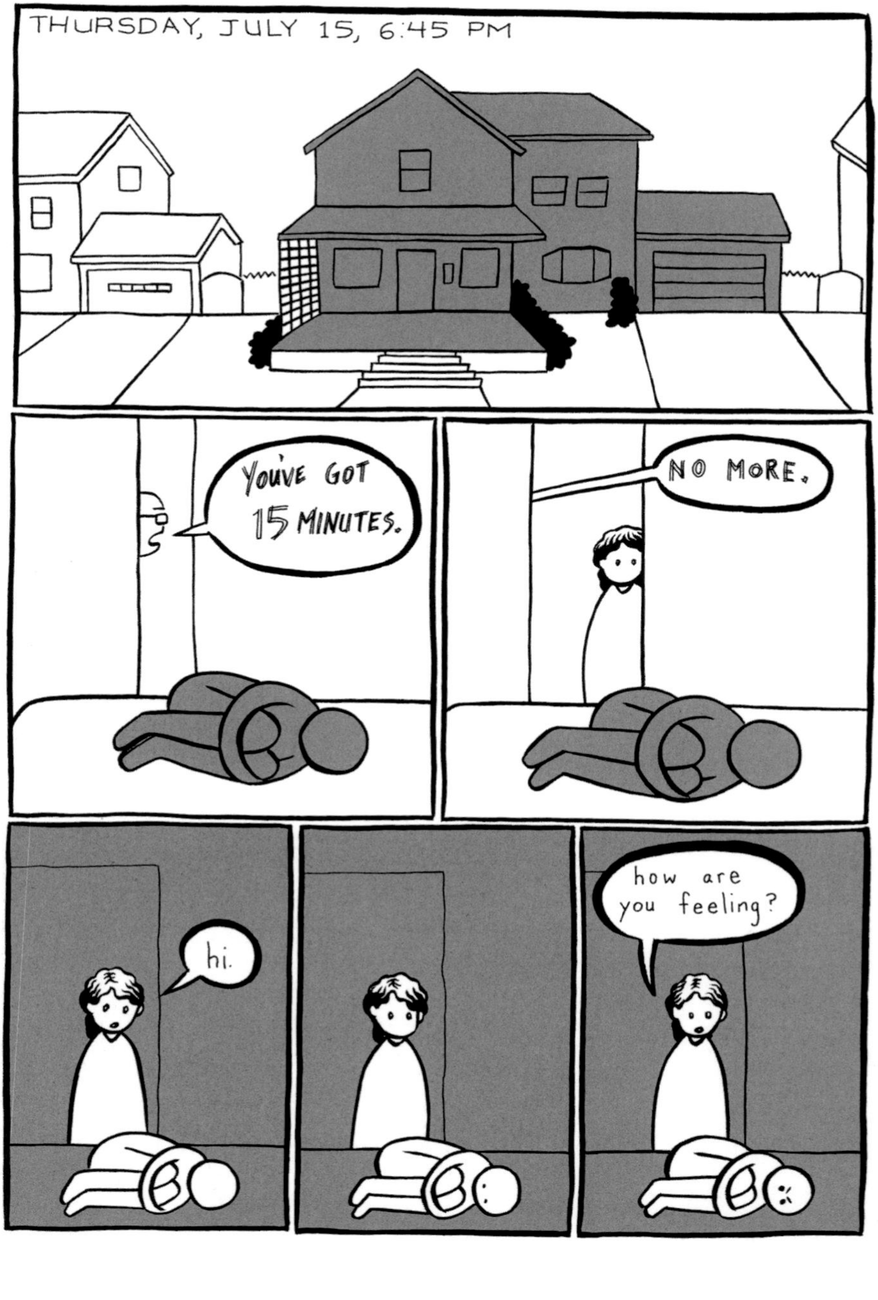
THURSDAY, JULY 15, 6:45 PM
YOU'VE GOT 15 MINUTES.
NO MORE.
hi.
how are you feeling?

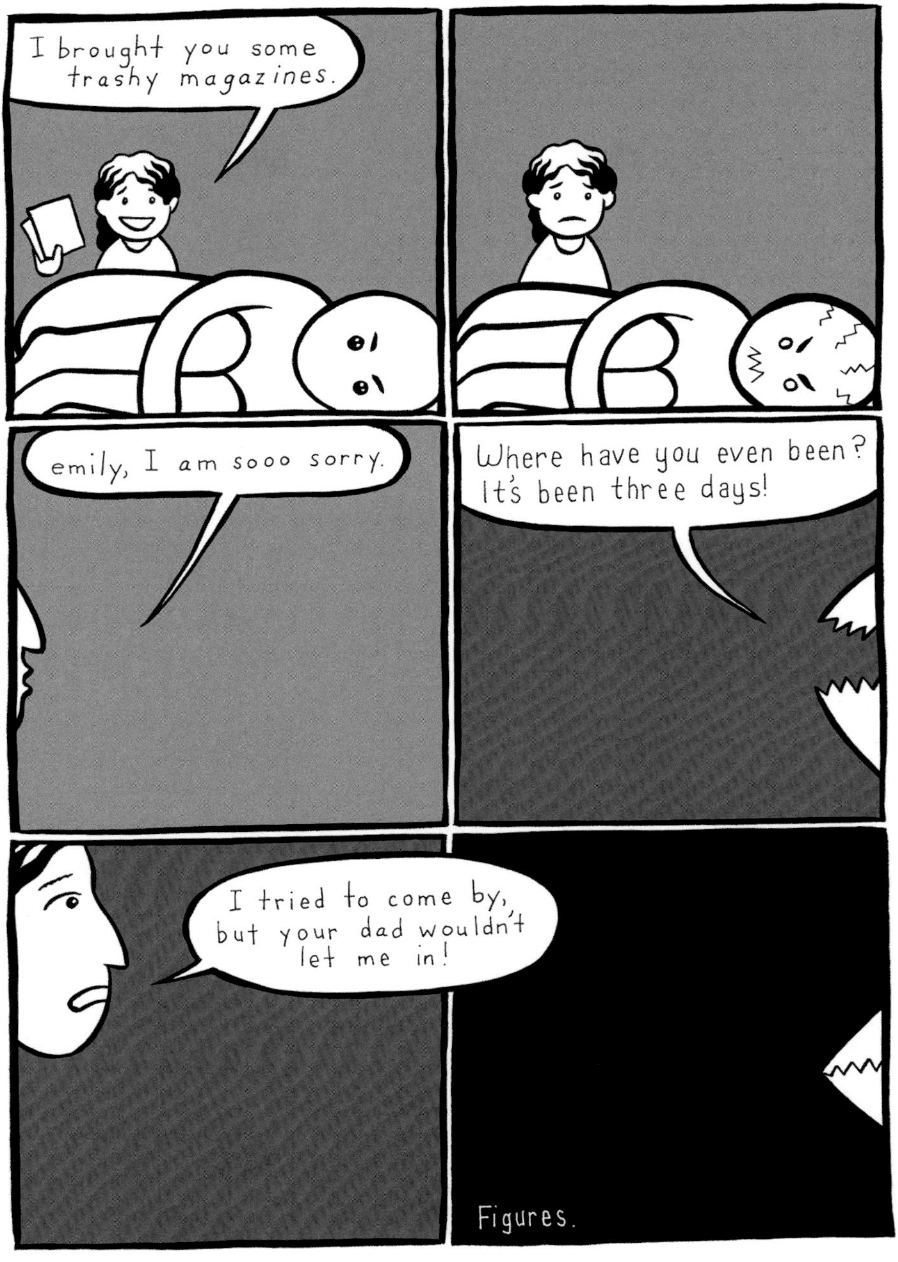
I brought you some trashy magazines.
emily, I am sooo sorry.
Where have you even been? It's been three days!
I tried to come by, but your dad wouldn't let me in!
Figures.

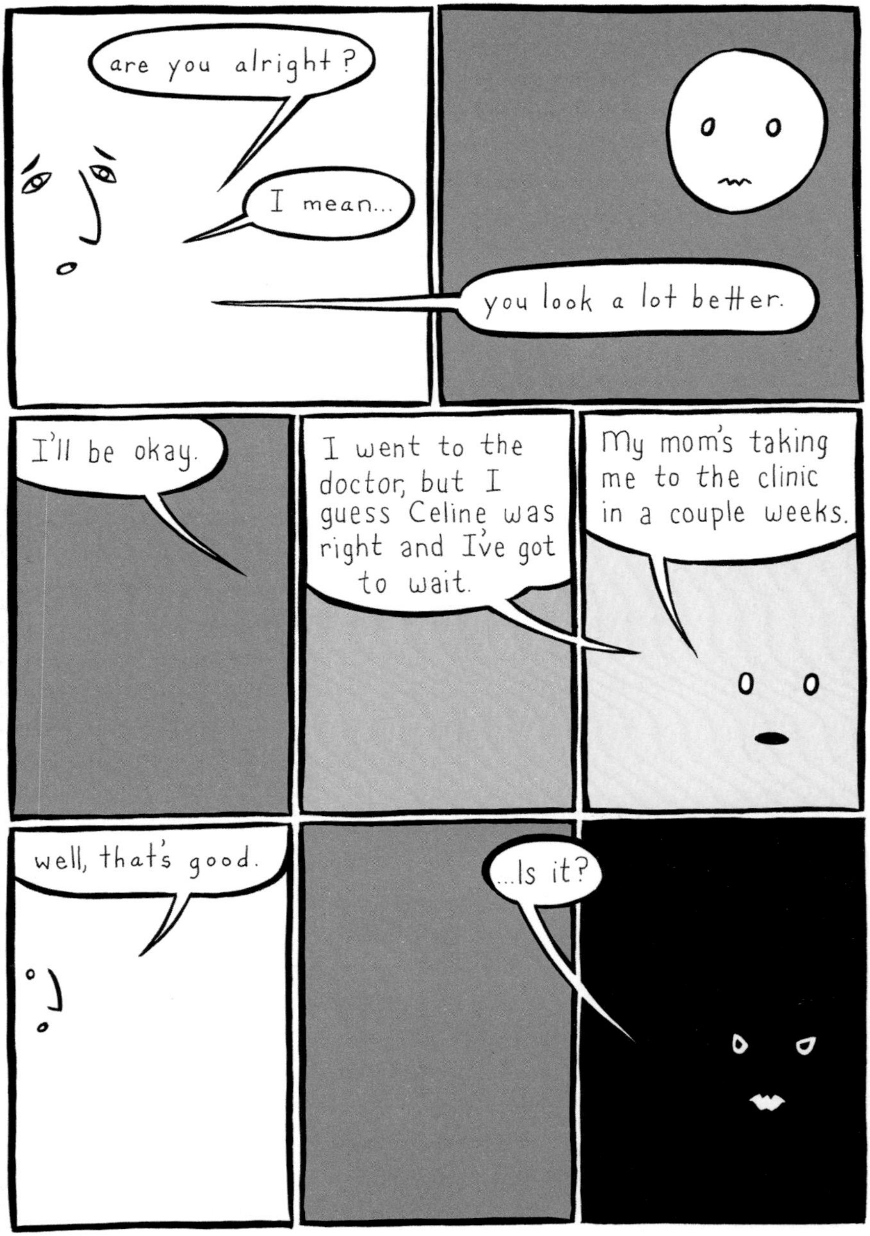
are you alright?
I mean...
you look a lot better.
I'll be okay.
I went to the doctor, but I guess Celine was right and I've got to wait.
My mom's taking me to the clinic in a couple weeks.
well, that's good.
...Is it?

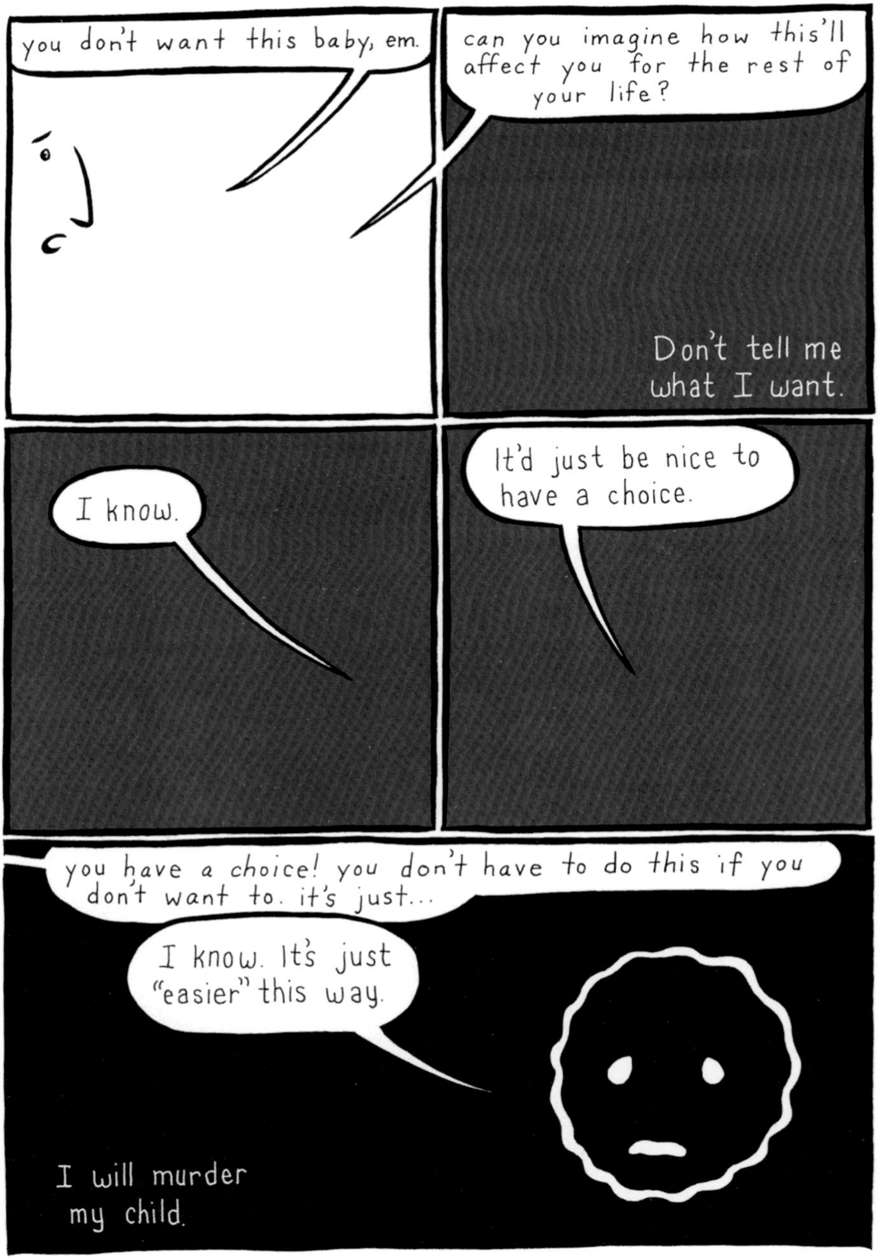
you don't want this baby, em.
can you imagine how this'll affect you for the rest of your life?
Don't tell me what I want.
I know.
It'd just be nice to have a choice.
you have a choice! you don't have to do this if you don't want to. it's just...
I know. It's just "easier" this way.
I will murder my child.

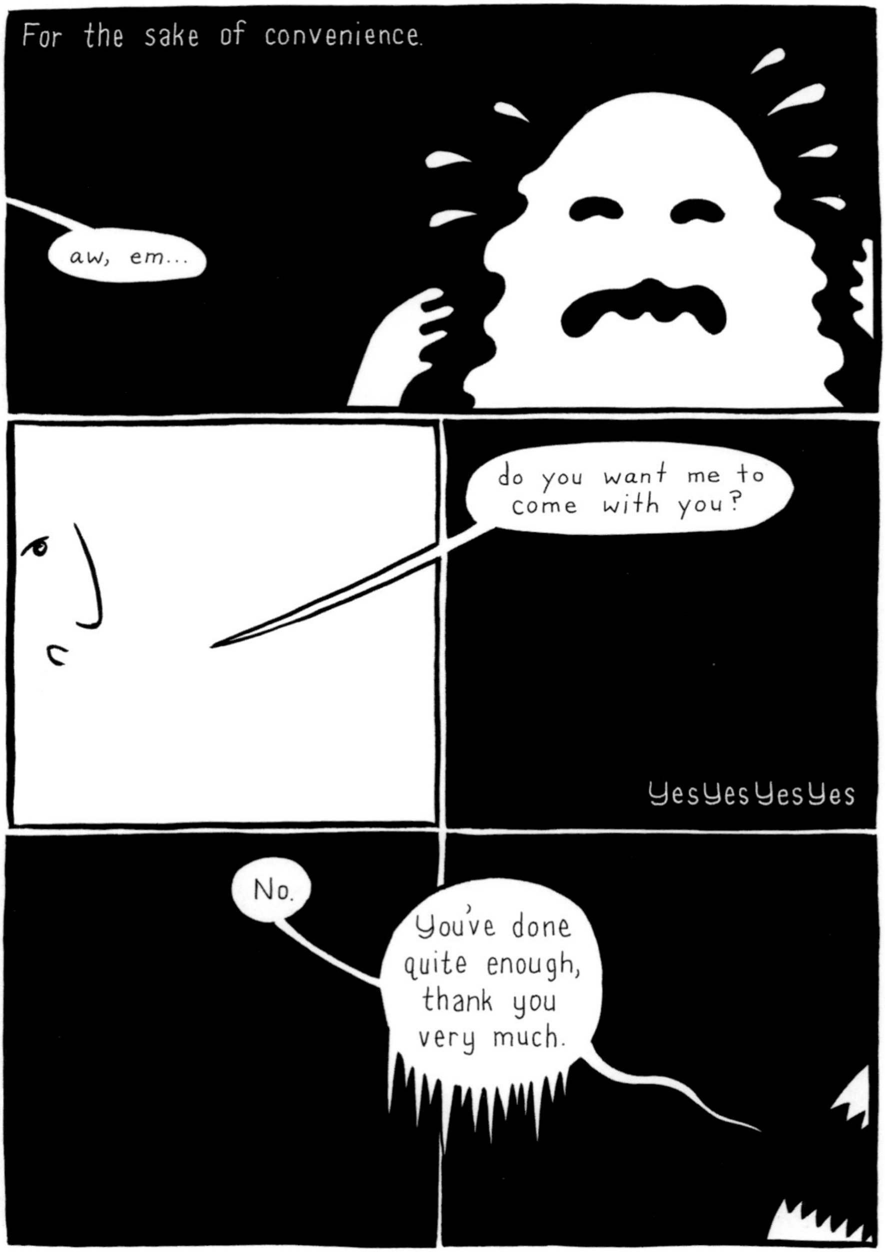
For the sake of convenience.
aw, em...
do you want me to come with you?
YesYesYesYes
No.
You've done quite enough, thank you very much.

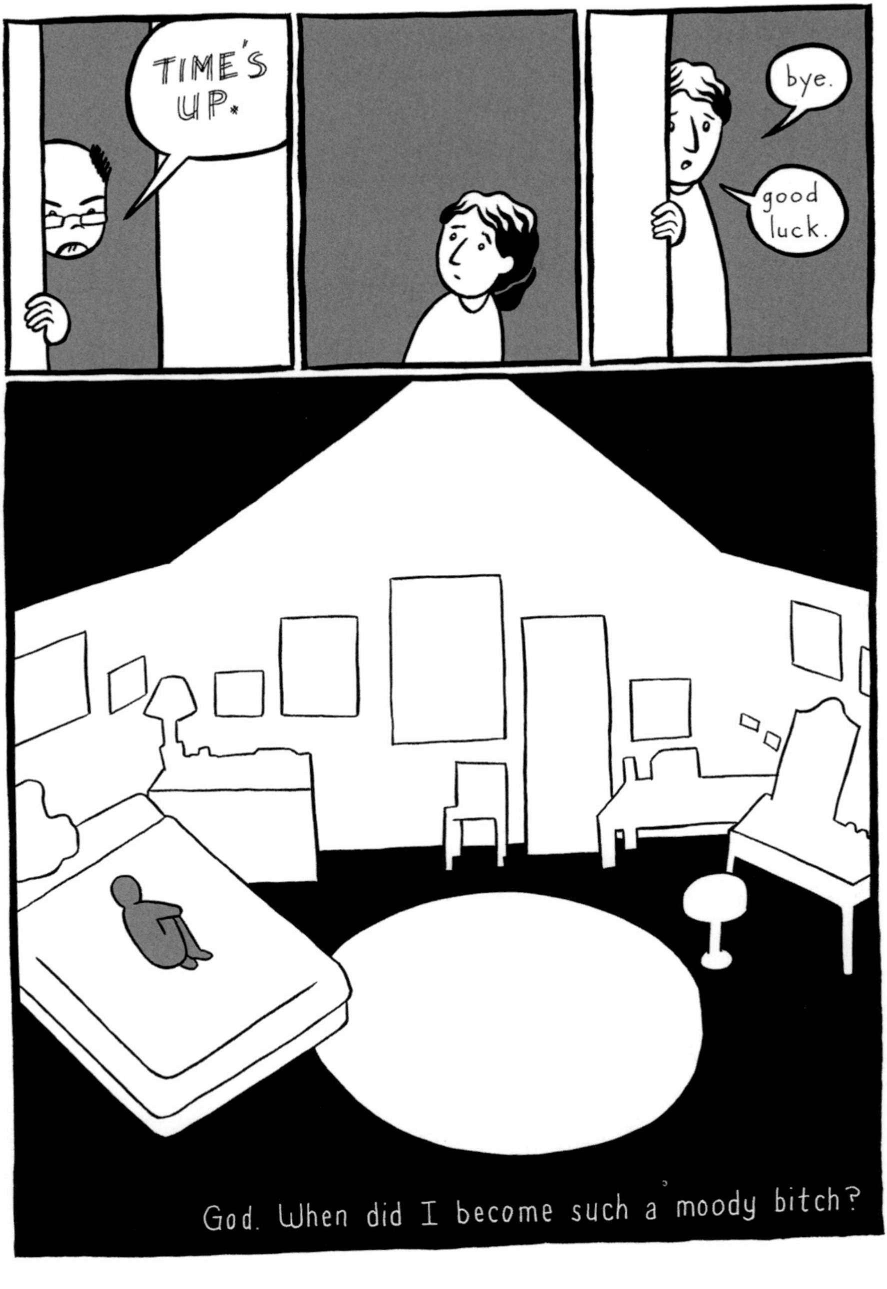
TIME'S UP.
bye.
good luck.
God. When did I become such a moody bitch?

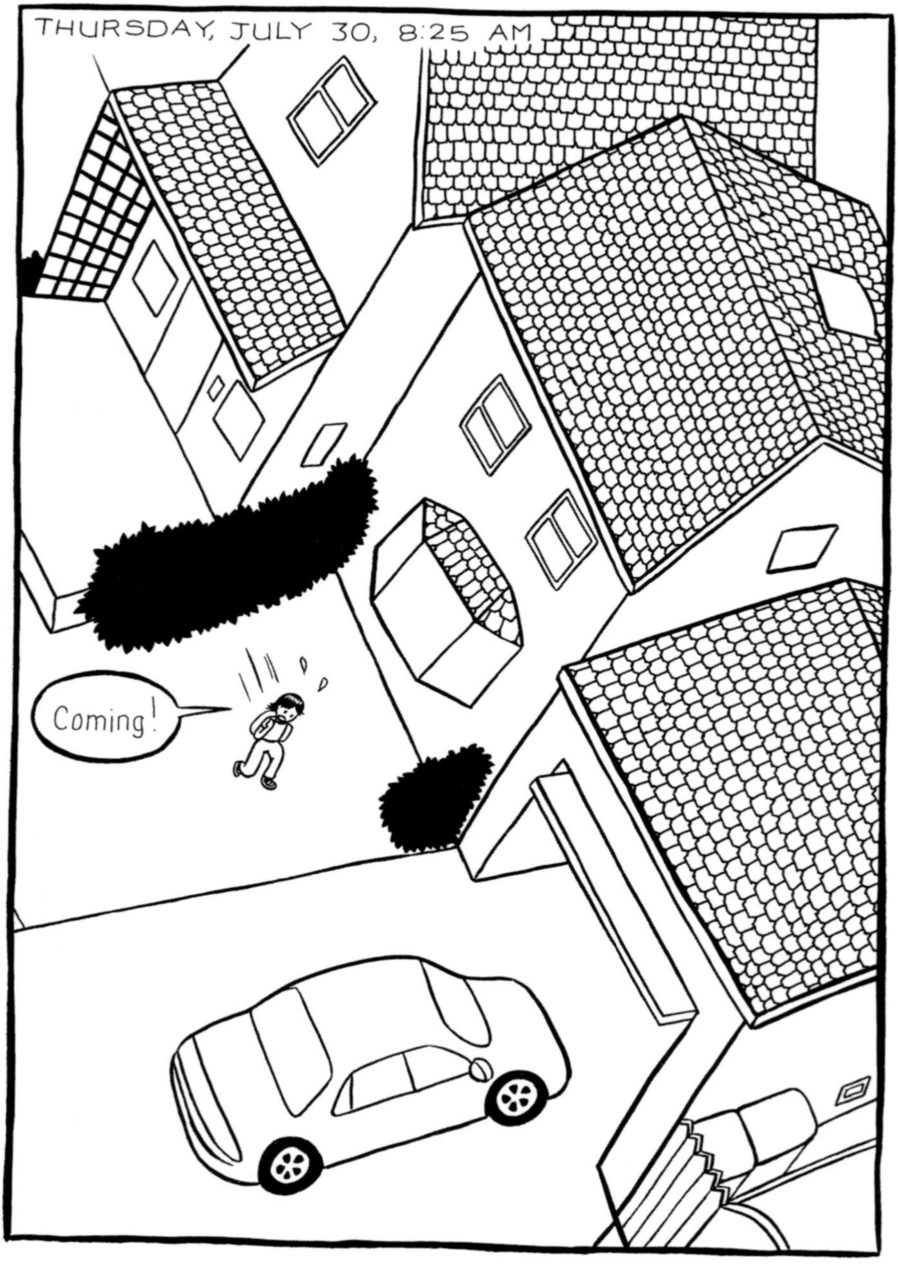
THURSDAY, JULY 30, 8:25 AM
Coming!

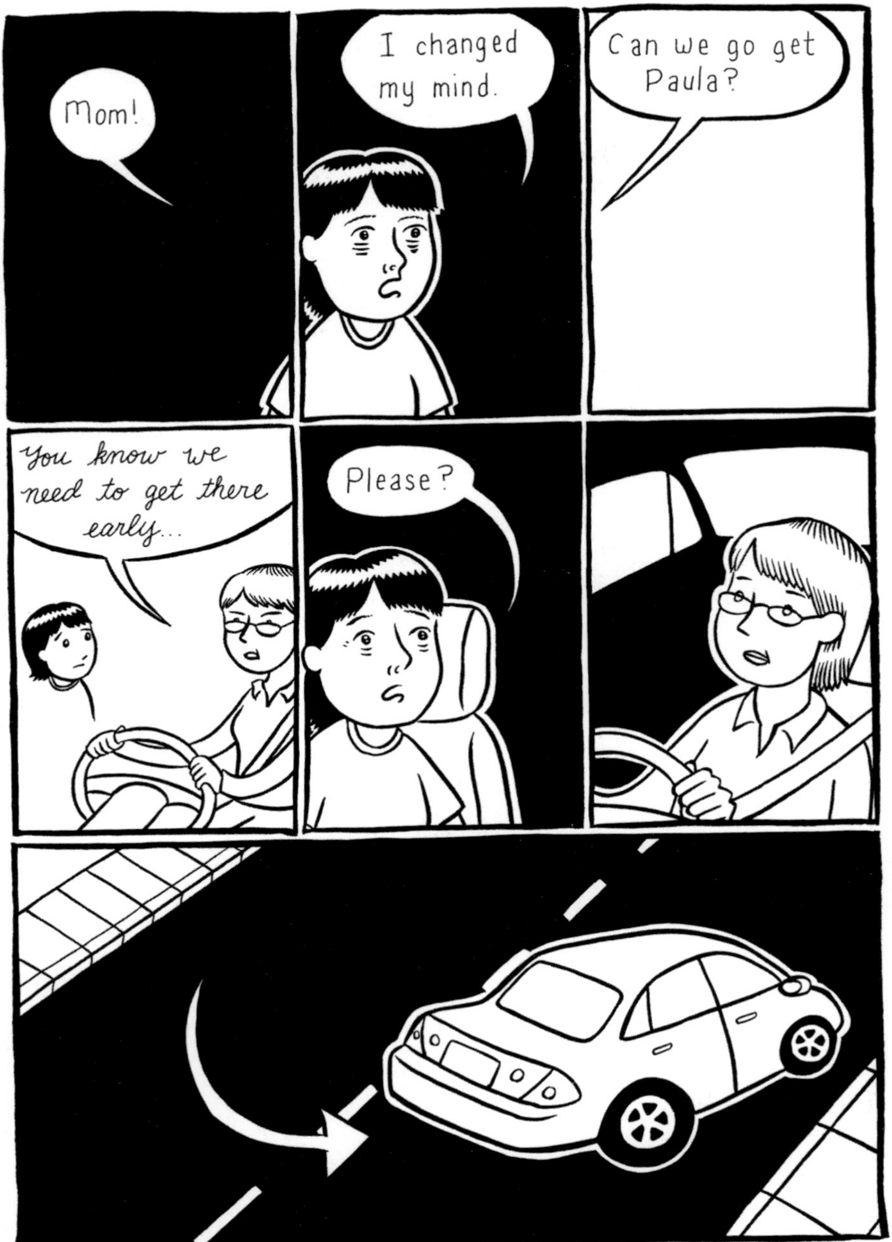

Mom!
I changed my mind.
Can we go get Paula?
You know we need to get there early...
Please?

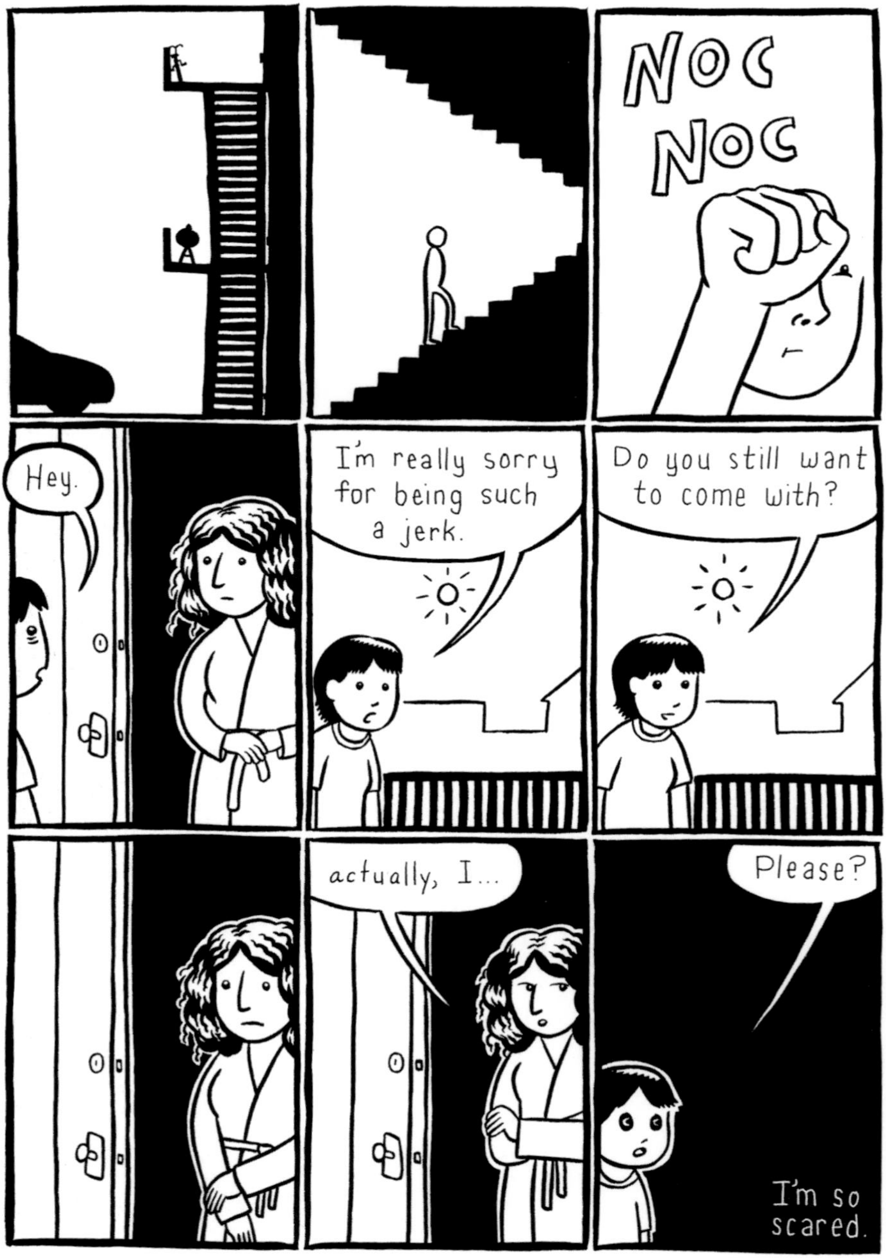
NOC
NOC
Hey.
I'm really sorry for being such a jerk.
Do you still want to come with?
actually, I...
Please?
I'm so scared.

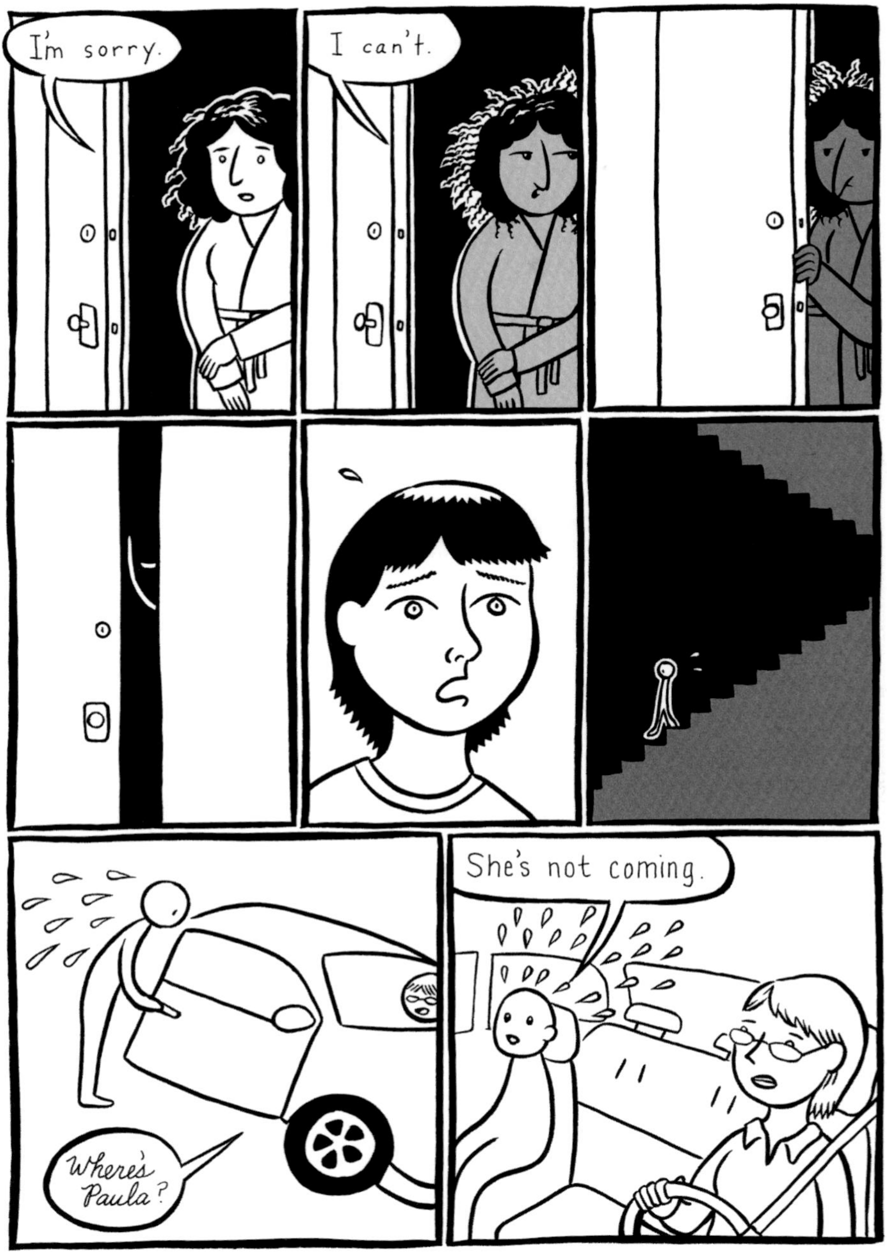
I'm sorry.
I can't.
Where's Paula?
She's not coming.

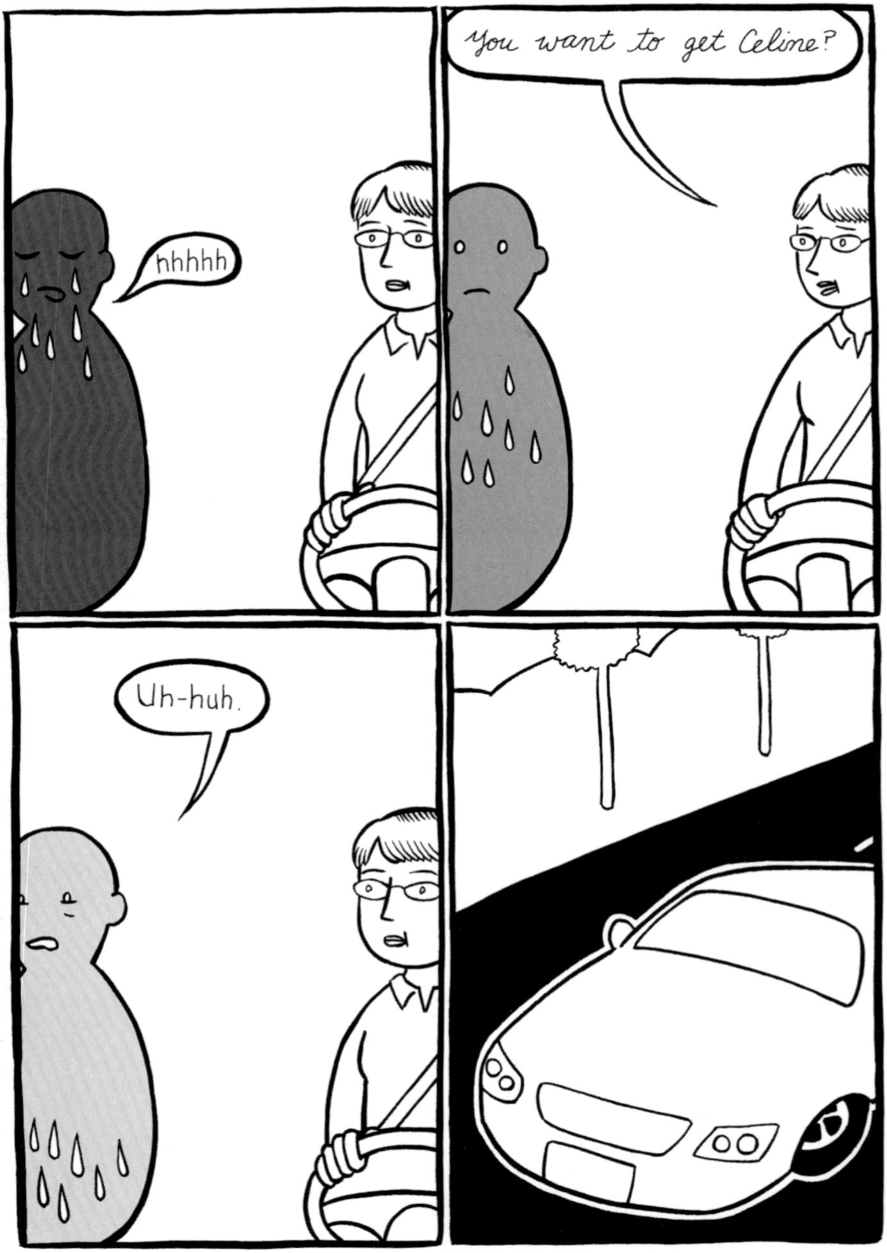
hhhhh
You want to get Celine?
Uh-huh.

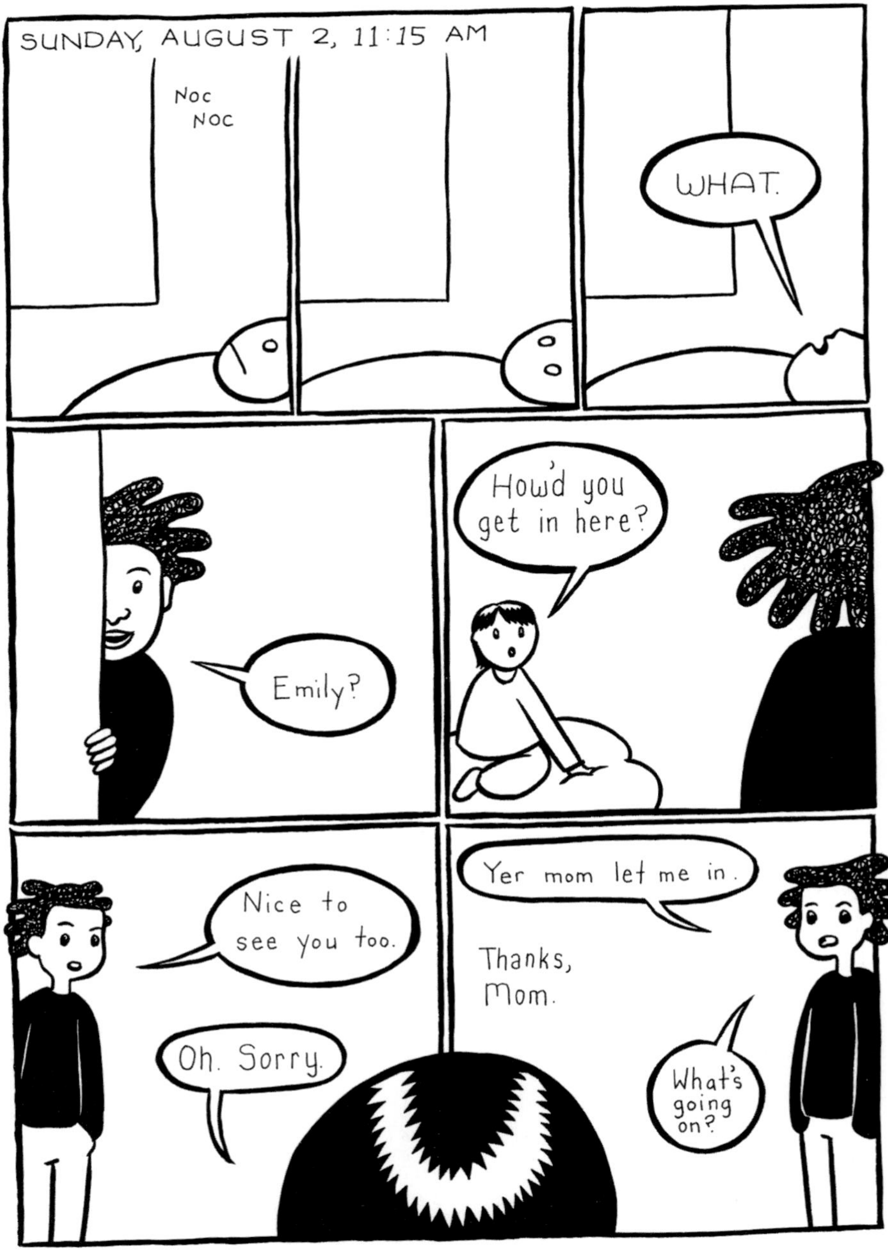
SUNDAY, AUGUST 2, 11:15 AM
Noc
Noc
WHAT.
Emily?
How'd you get in here?
Nice to see you too.
Oh. Sorry.
Yer mom let me in.
Thanks, Mom.
What's going on?

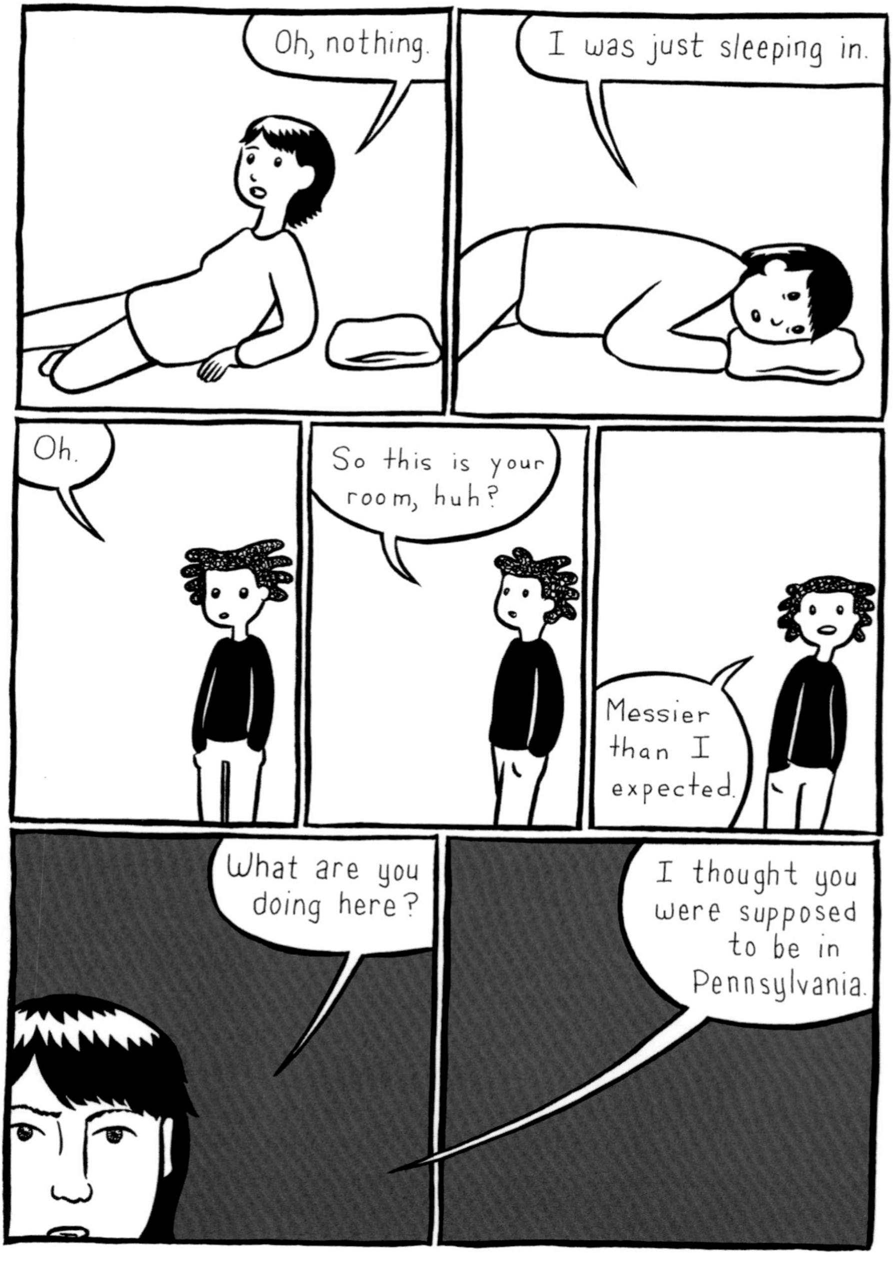
Oh, nothing.
I was just sleeping in.
Oh.
So this is your room, huh?
Messier than I expected.
What are you doing here?
I thought you were supposed to be in Pennsylvania.

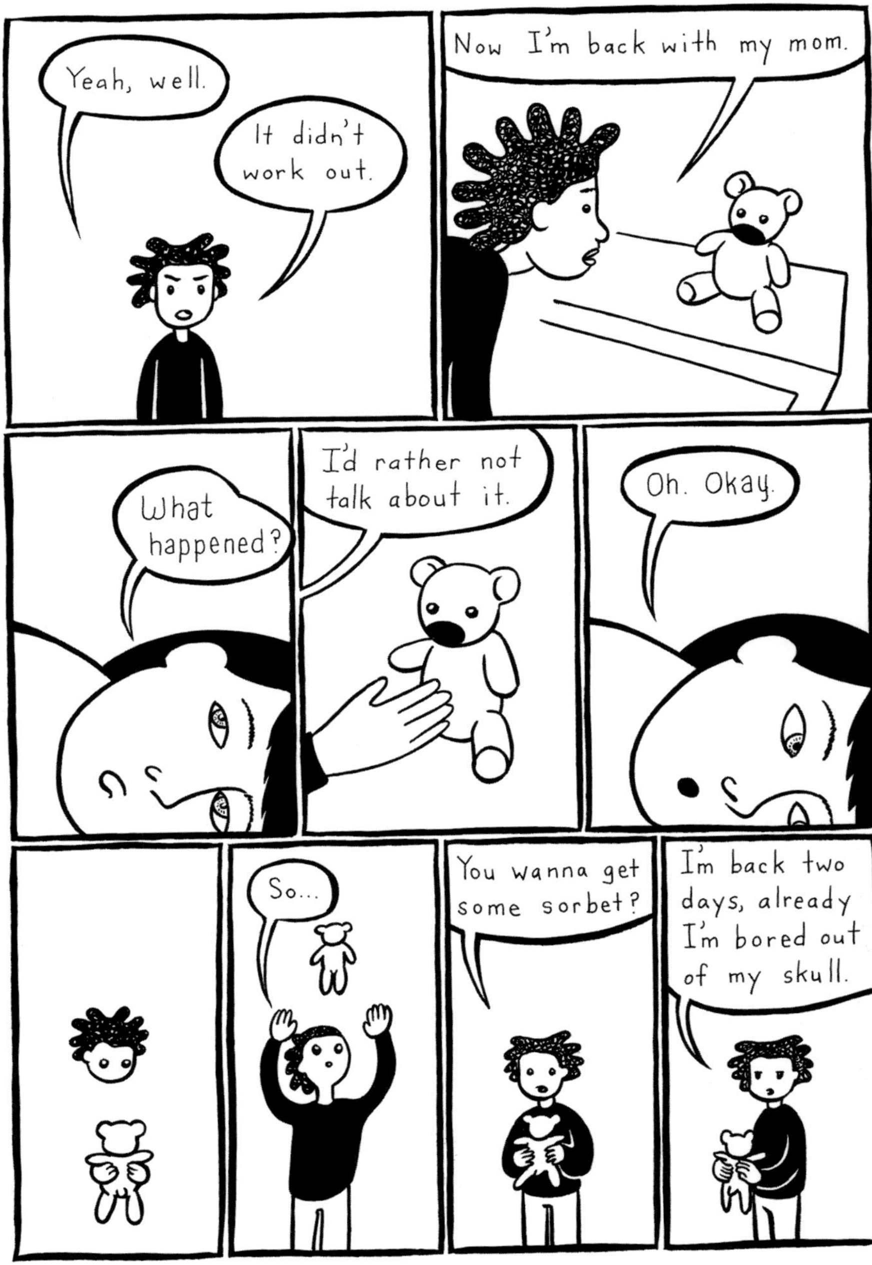
Yeah, well.
It didn't work out.
Now I'm back with my mom.
What happened?
I'd rather not talk about it.
Oh. Okay.
So...
You wanna get some sorbet?
I'm back two days, already I'm bored out of my skull.

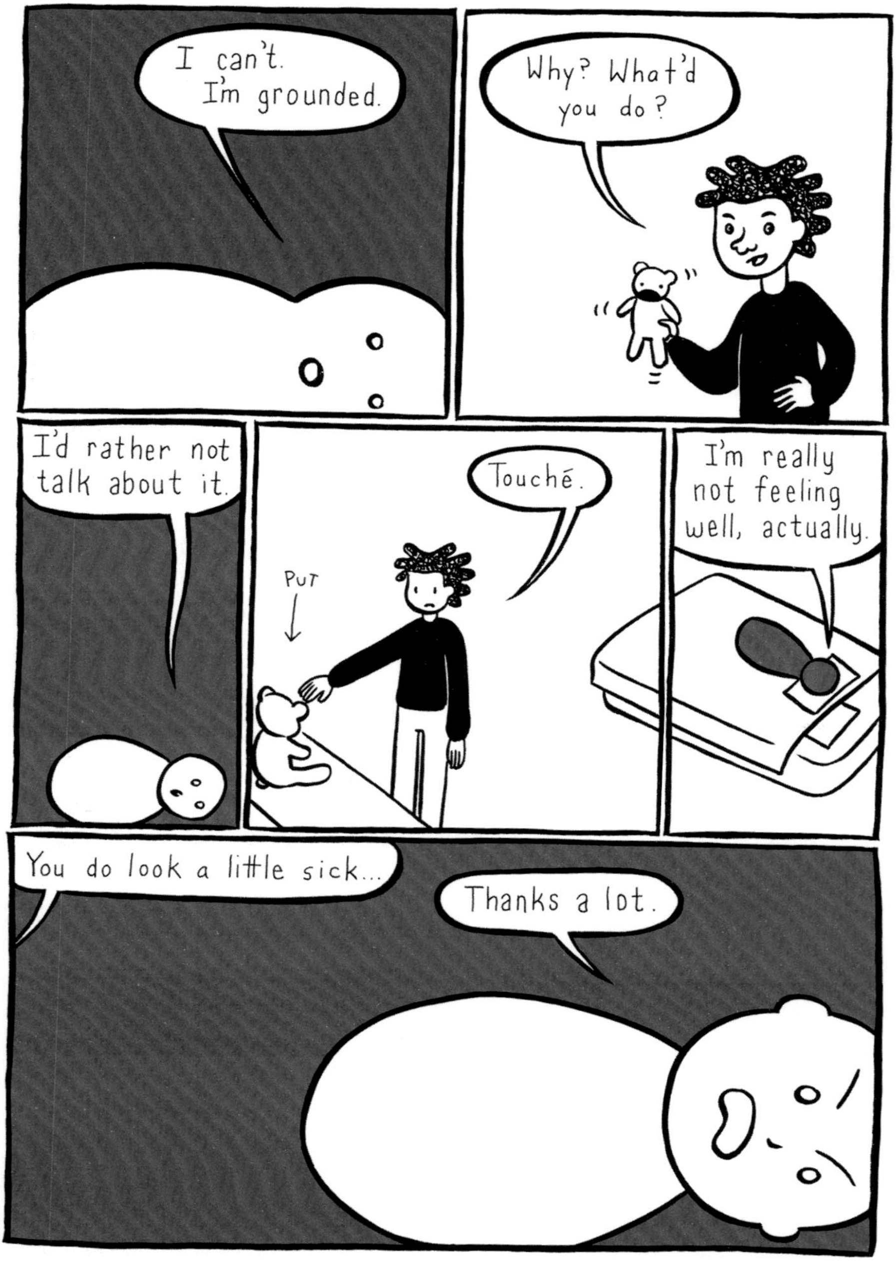
I can't. I'm grounded.
Why? What'd you do?
I'd rather not talk about it.
PUT
Touché.
I'm really not feeling well, actually.
You do look a little sick...
Thanks a lot.

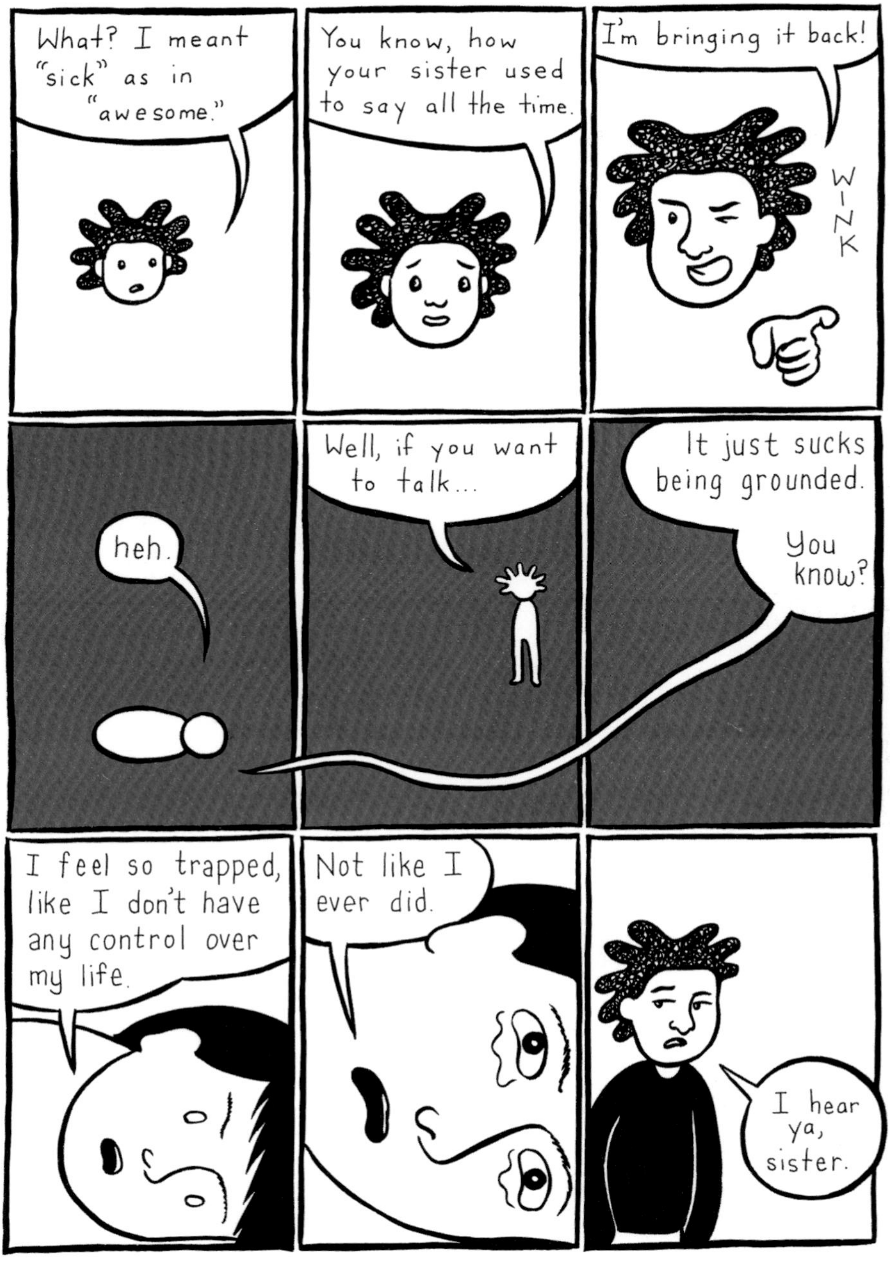

What? I meant "sick" as in "awesome."
You know, how your sister used to say all the time.
I'm bringing it back!
WINK
heh.
Well, if you want to talk...
It just sucks being grounded.
You know?
I feel so trapped, like I don't have any control over my life.
Not like I ever did.
I hear ya, sister.

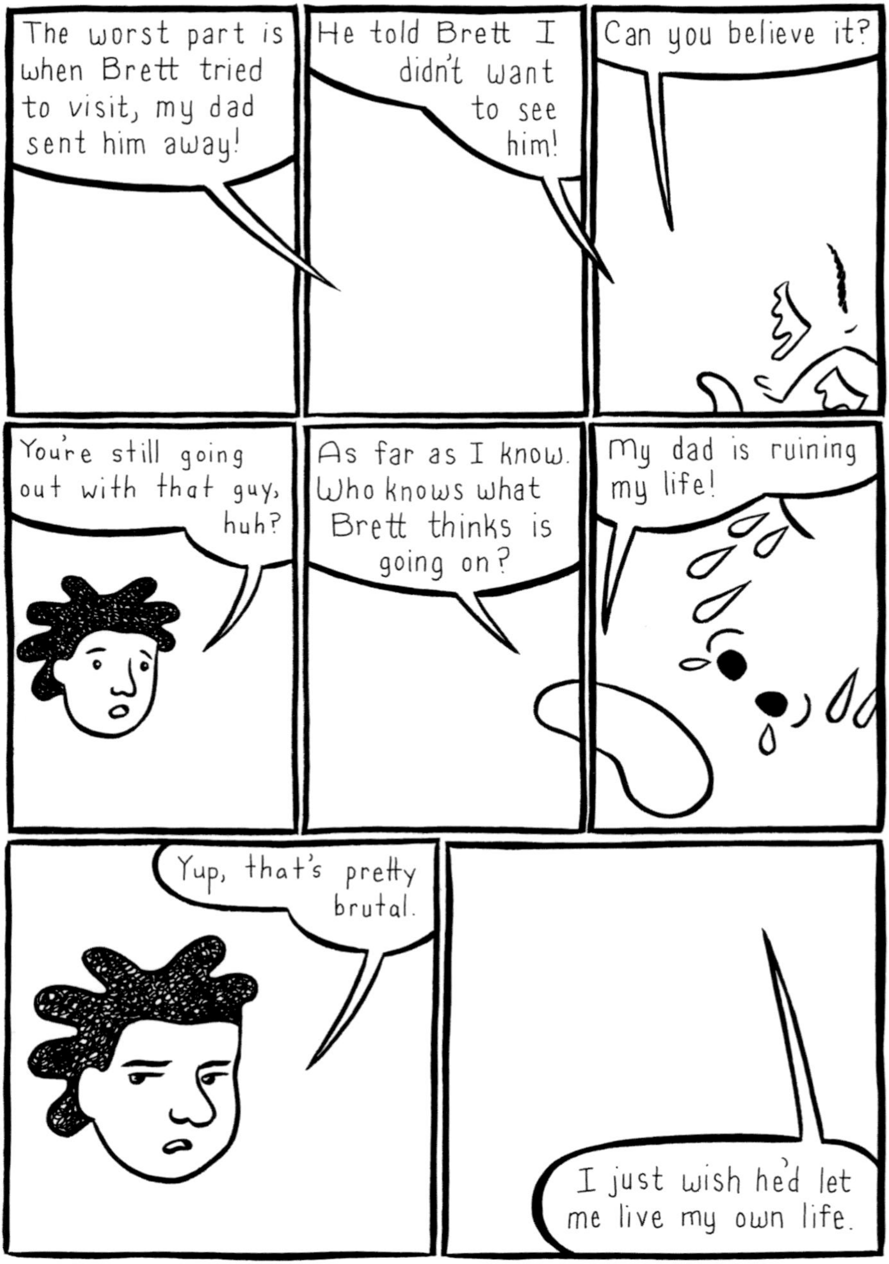

The worst part is when Brett tried to visit, my dad sent him away!
He told Brett I didn't want to see him!
Can you believe it?
You're still going out with that guy, huh?
As far as I know. Who knows what Brett thinks is going on?
My dad is ruining my life!
Yup, that's pretty brutal.
I just wish he'd let me live my own life.

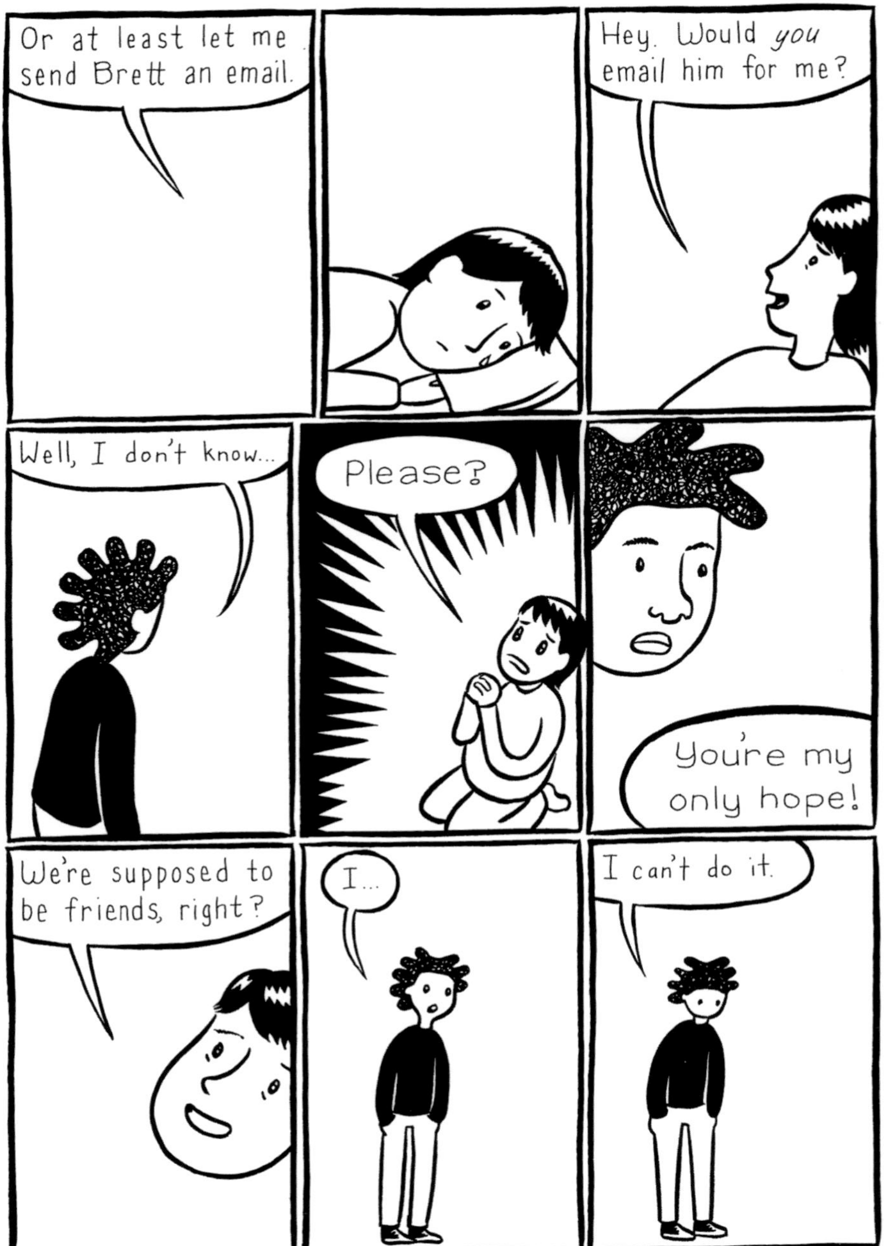
Or at least let me send Brett an email.
Hey. Would *you* email him for me?
Well, I don't know...
Please?
You're my only hope!
We're supposed to be friends, right?
I...
I can't do it.

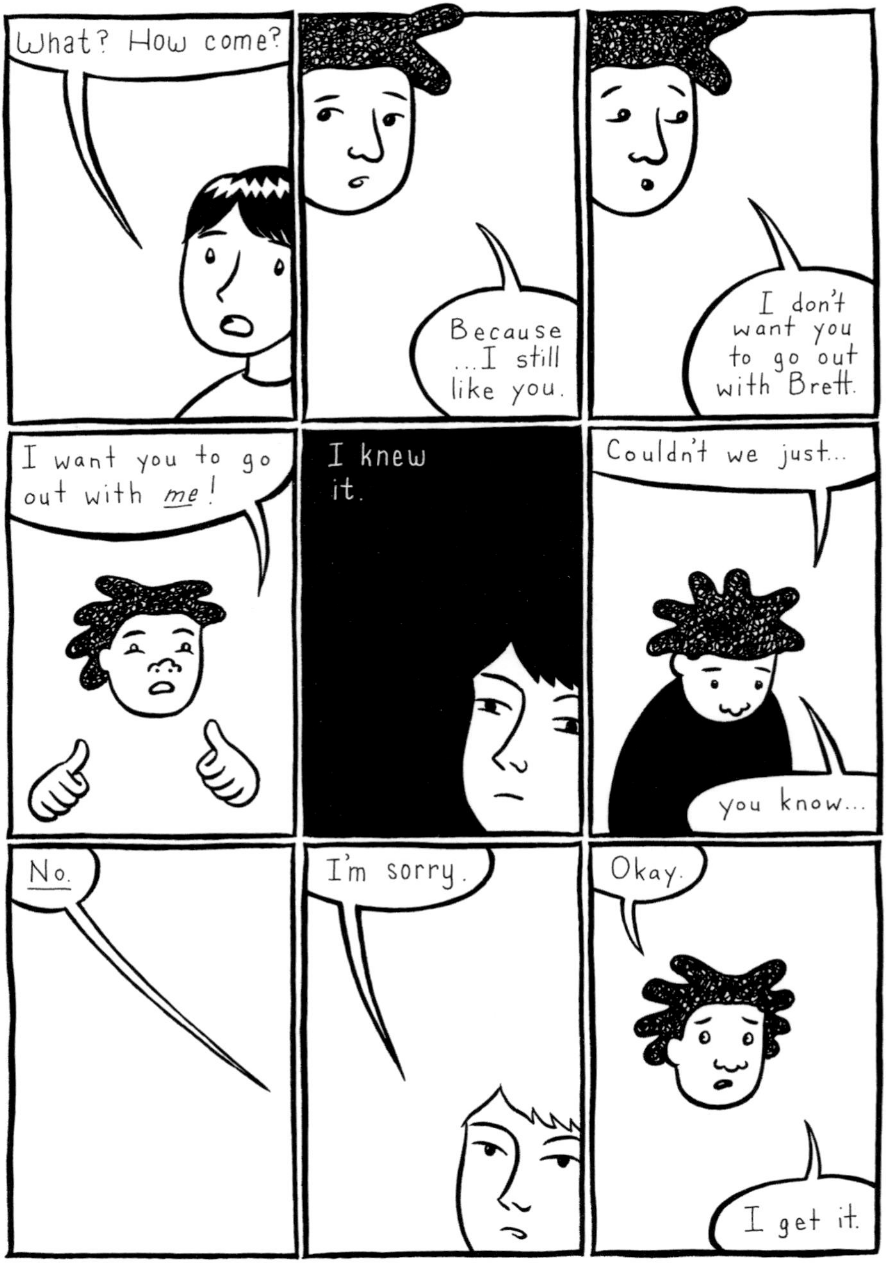
What? How come?
Because ...I still like you.
I don't want you to go out with Brett.
I want you to go out with me!
I knew it.
Couldn't we just...
you know...
No.
I'm sorry.
Okay.
I get it.

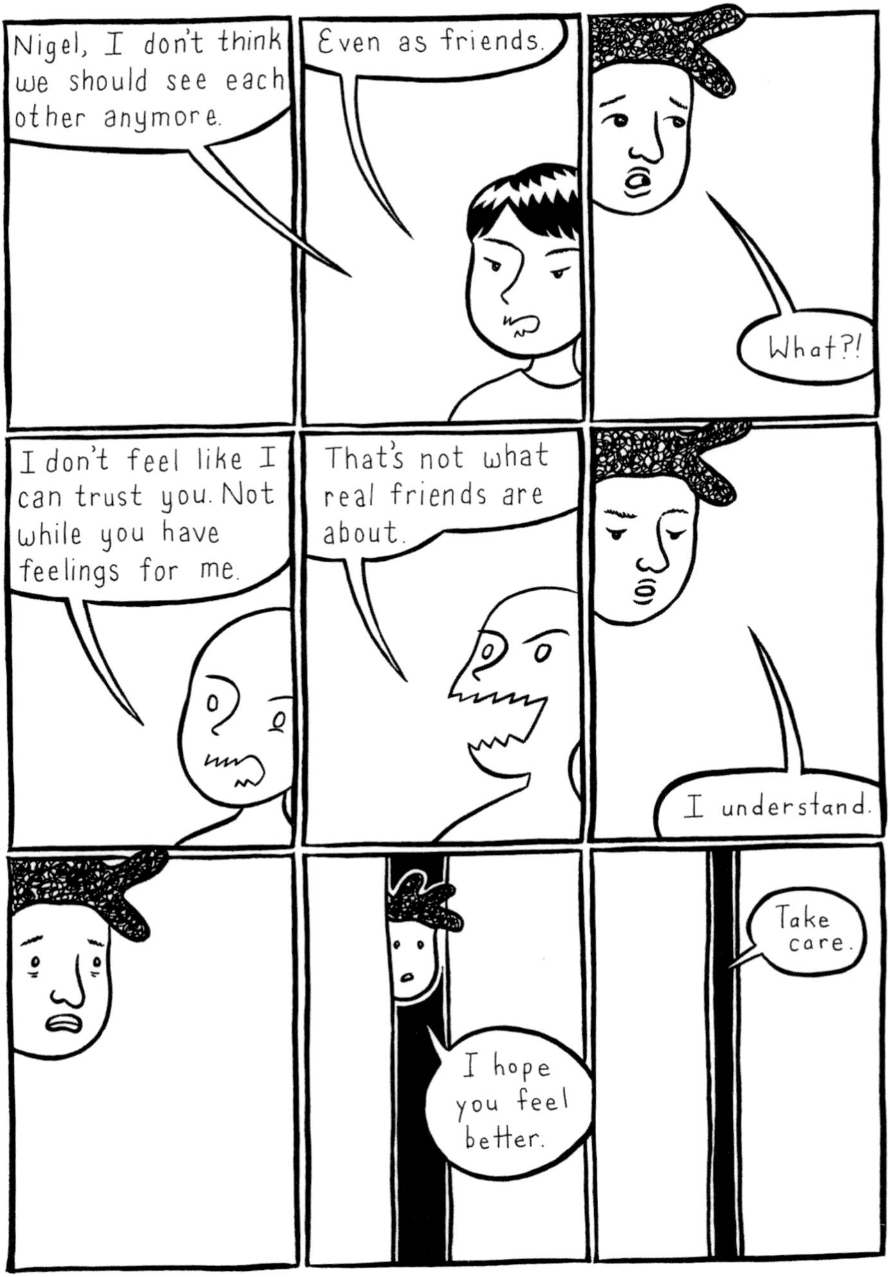
Nigel, I don't think we should see each other anymore.
Even as friends.
What?!
I don't feel like I can trust you. Not while you have feelings for me.
That's not what real friends are about.
I understand.
I hope you feel better.
Take care.

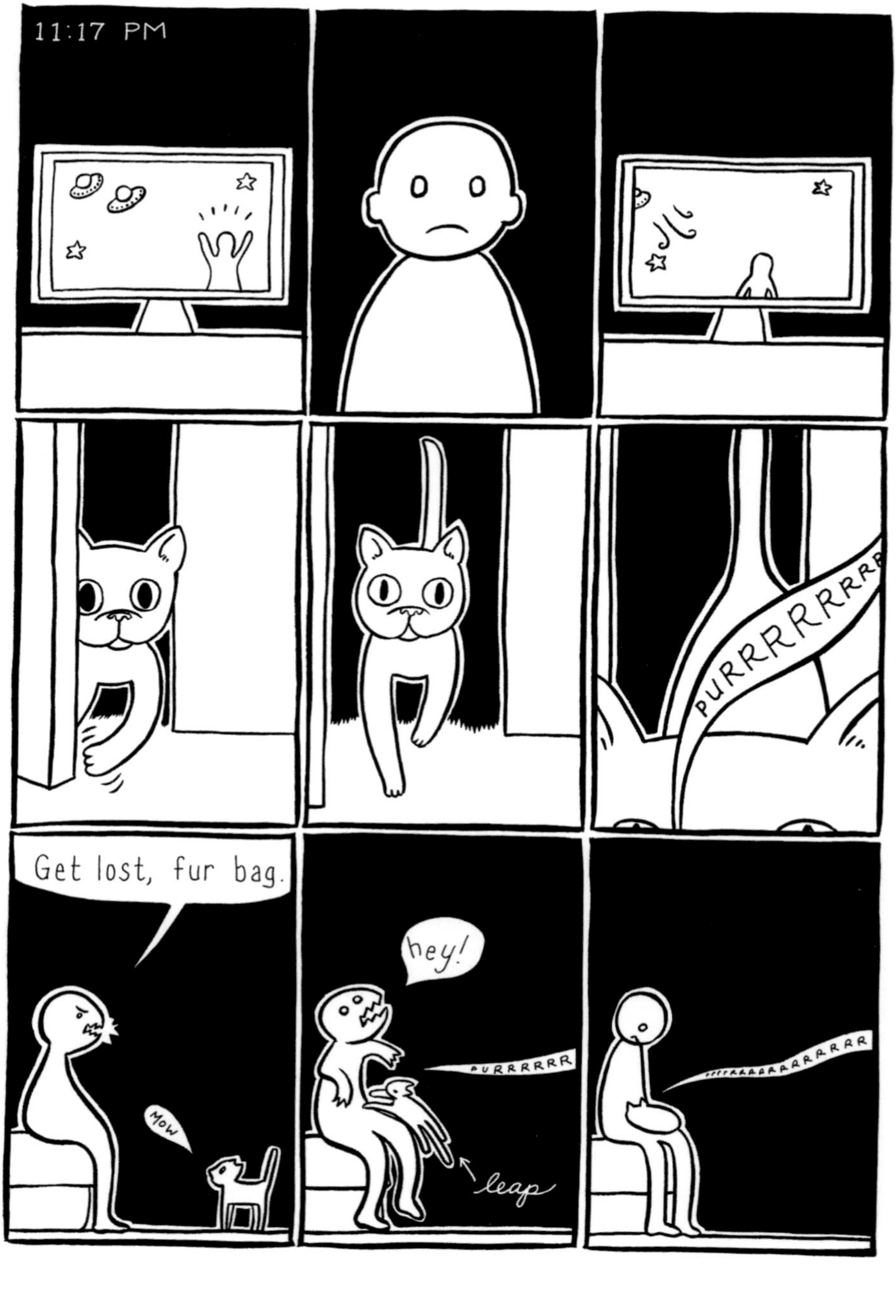
11:17 PM
PURRRRRRRRR
Get lost, fur bag.
MOW
hey!
PURRRRRRR
leap
rrrrRRRRRRRRRRRR

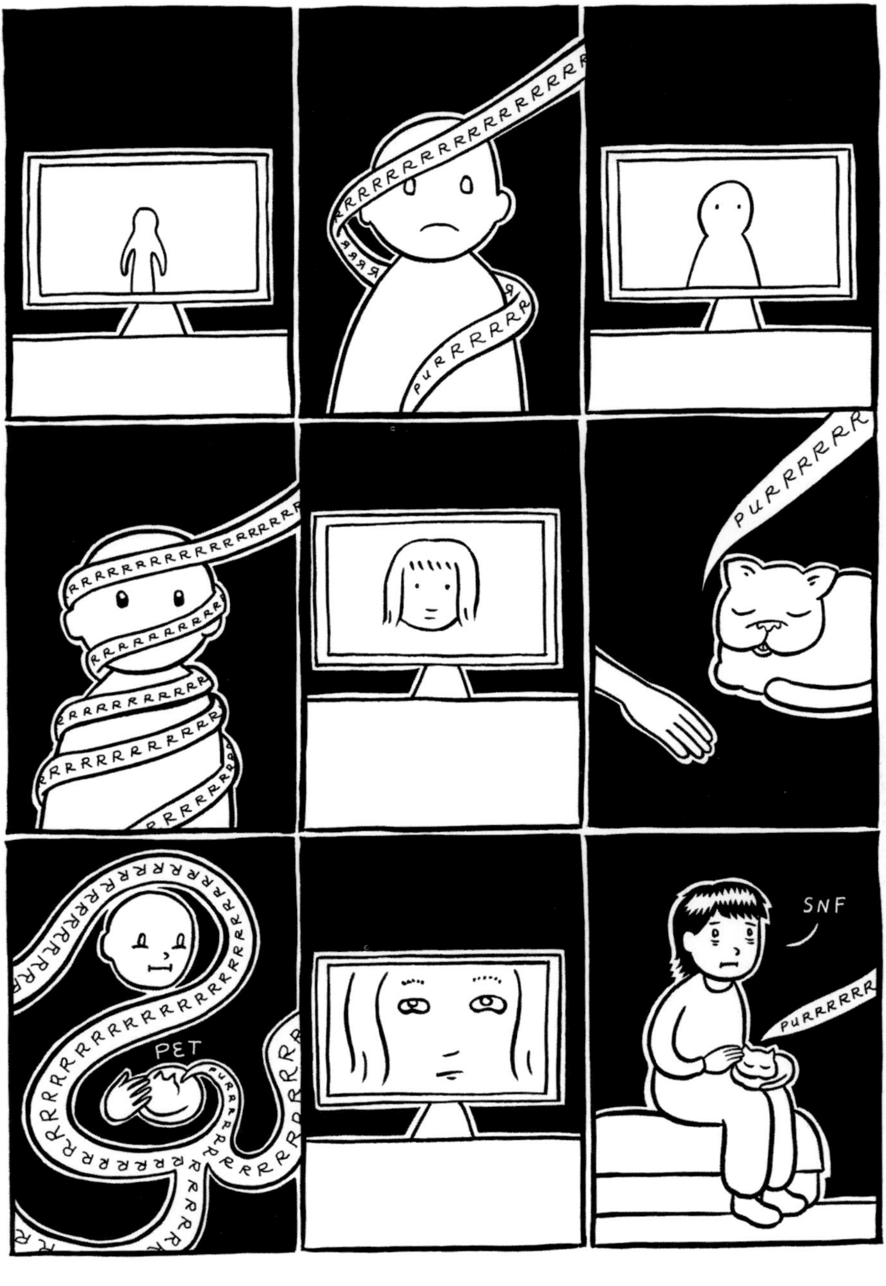
RRRRRRRRRRRRRRRRRRR
PURRRRRR
RRRRRRRRRRRRRRRRRRRR
PURRRRRR
PET
PURRRR
SNF
PURRRRRR

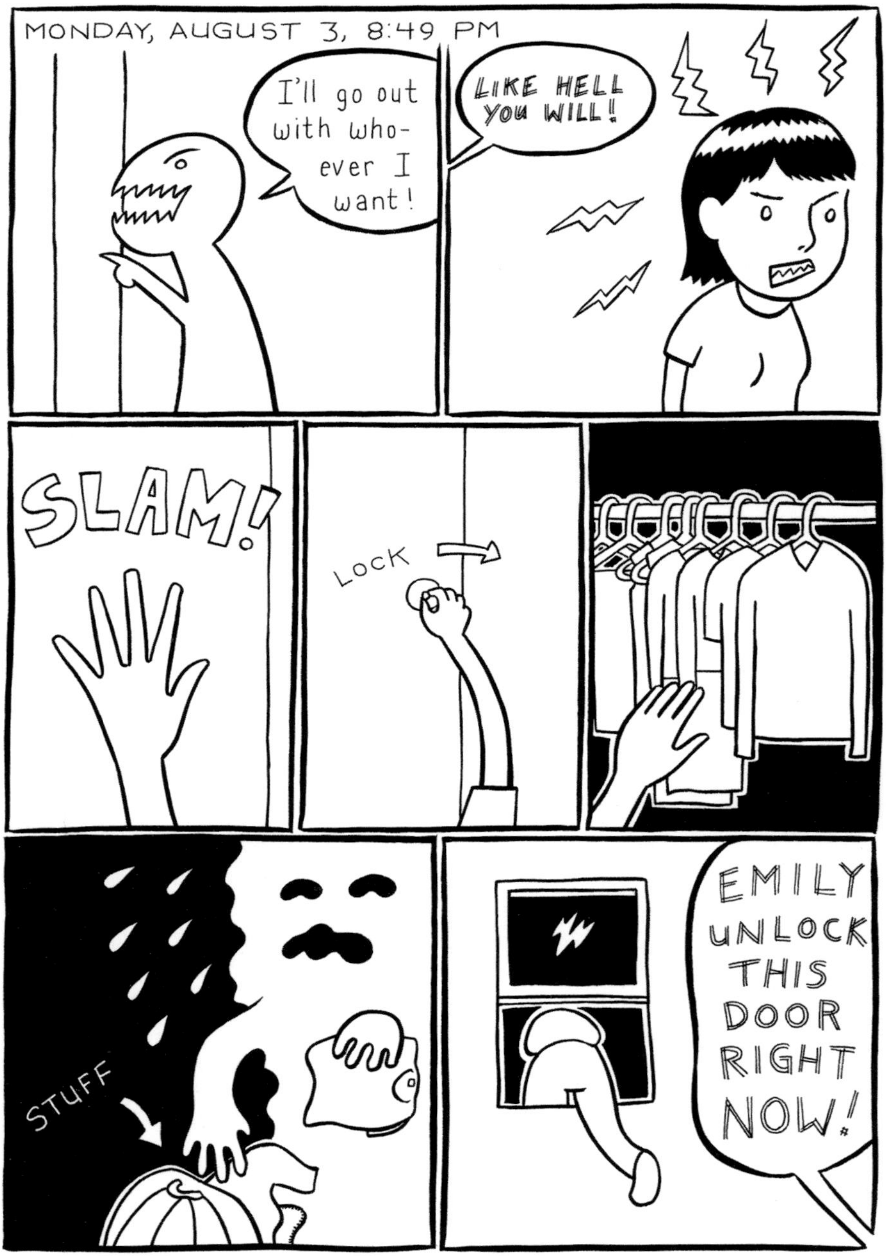
MONDAY, AUGUST 3, 8:49 PM
I'll go out with who-ever I want!
LIKE HELL YOU WILL!
SLAM!
LOCK
STUFF
EMILY UNLOCK THIS DOOR RIGHT NOW!

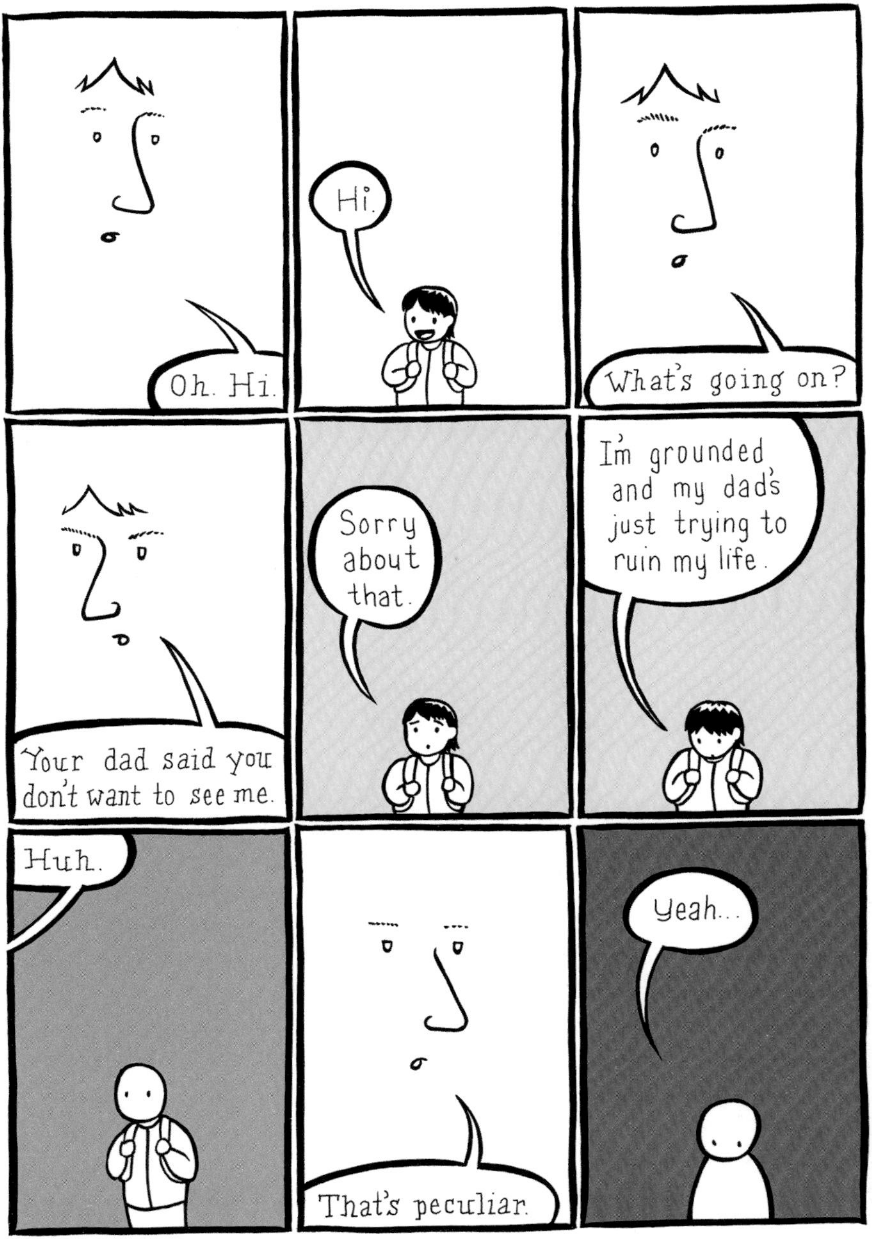
Oh. Hi.
Hi.
What's going on?
Your dad said you don't want to see me.
Sorry about that.
I'm grounded and my dad's just trying to ruin my life.
Huh.
That's peculiar.
Yeah...

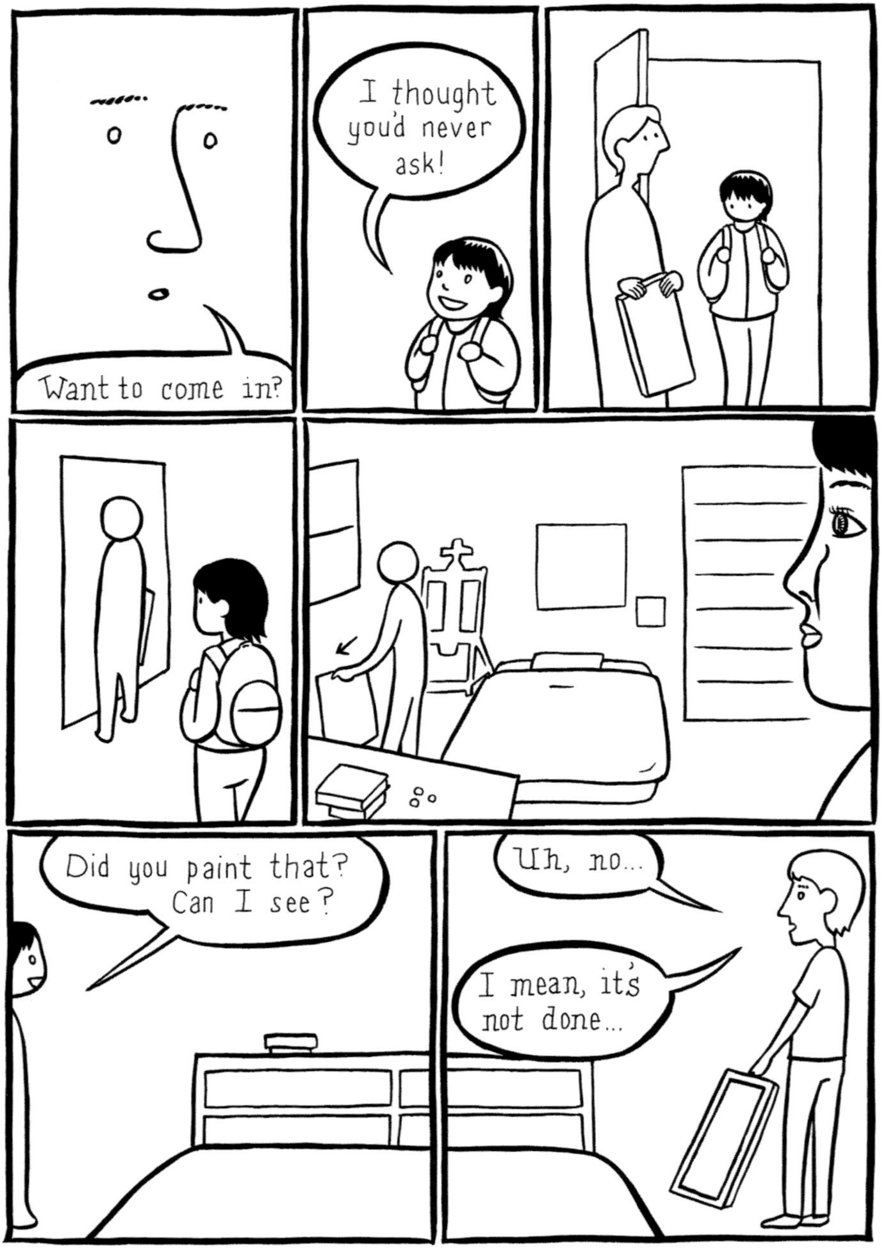
Want to come in?
I thought you'd never ask!
Did you paint that? Can I see?
Uh, no...
I mean, it's not done...

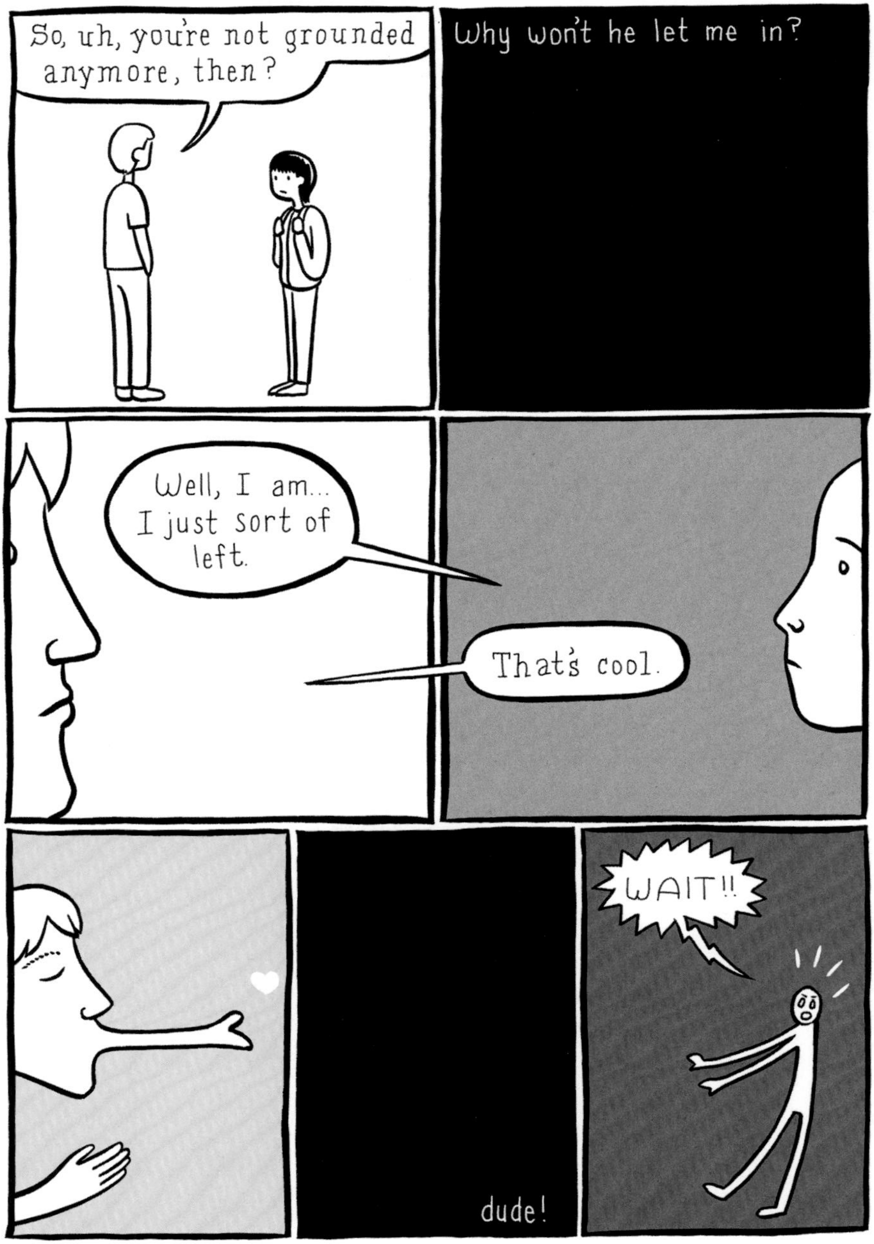
So, uh, you're not grounded anymore, then?
Why won't he let me in?
Well, I am... I just sort of left.
That's cool.
dude!
WAIT!!

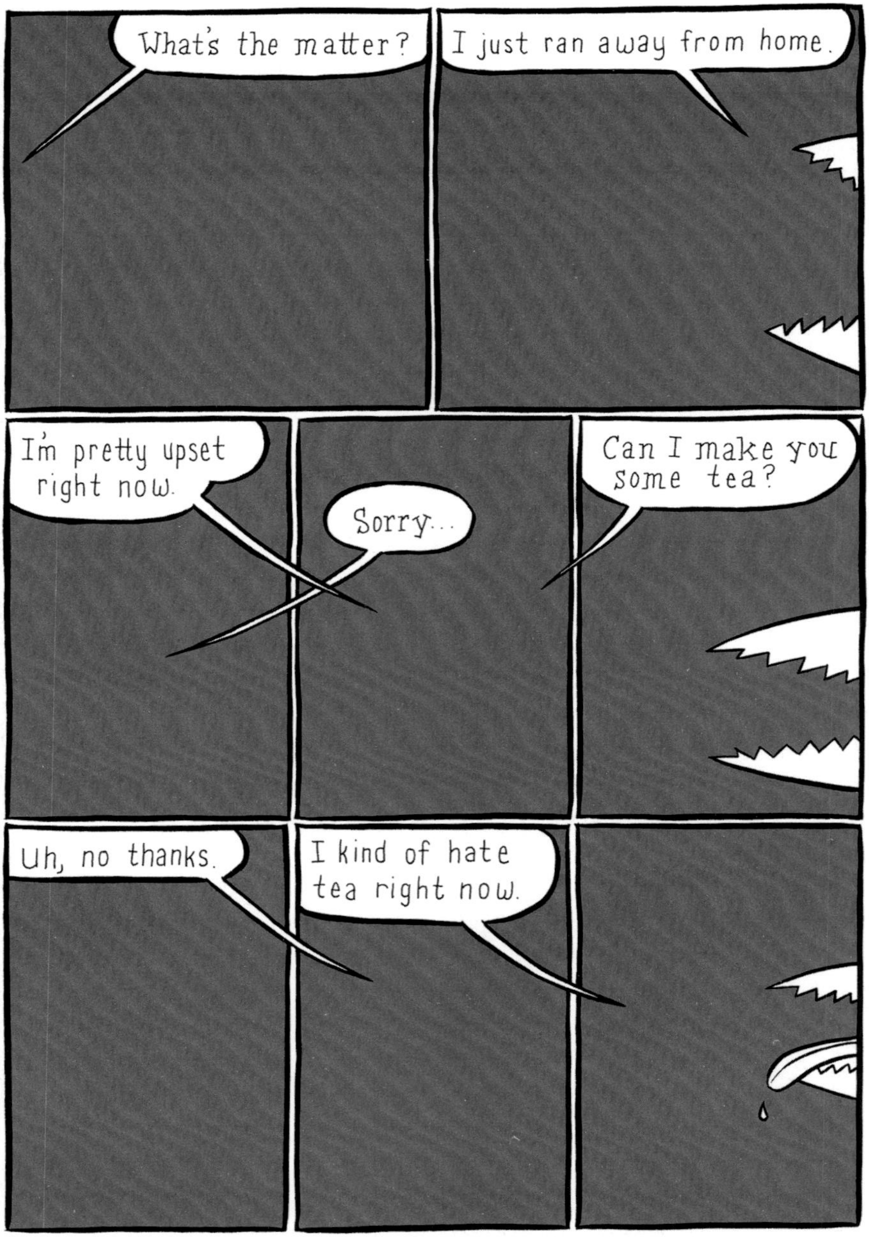
What's the matter?
I just ran away from home.
I'm pretty upset right now.
Sorry...
Can I make you some tea?
Uh, no thanks.
I kind of hate tea right now.

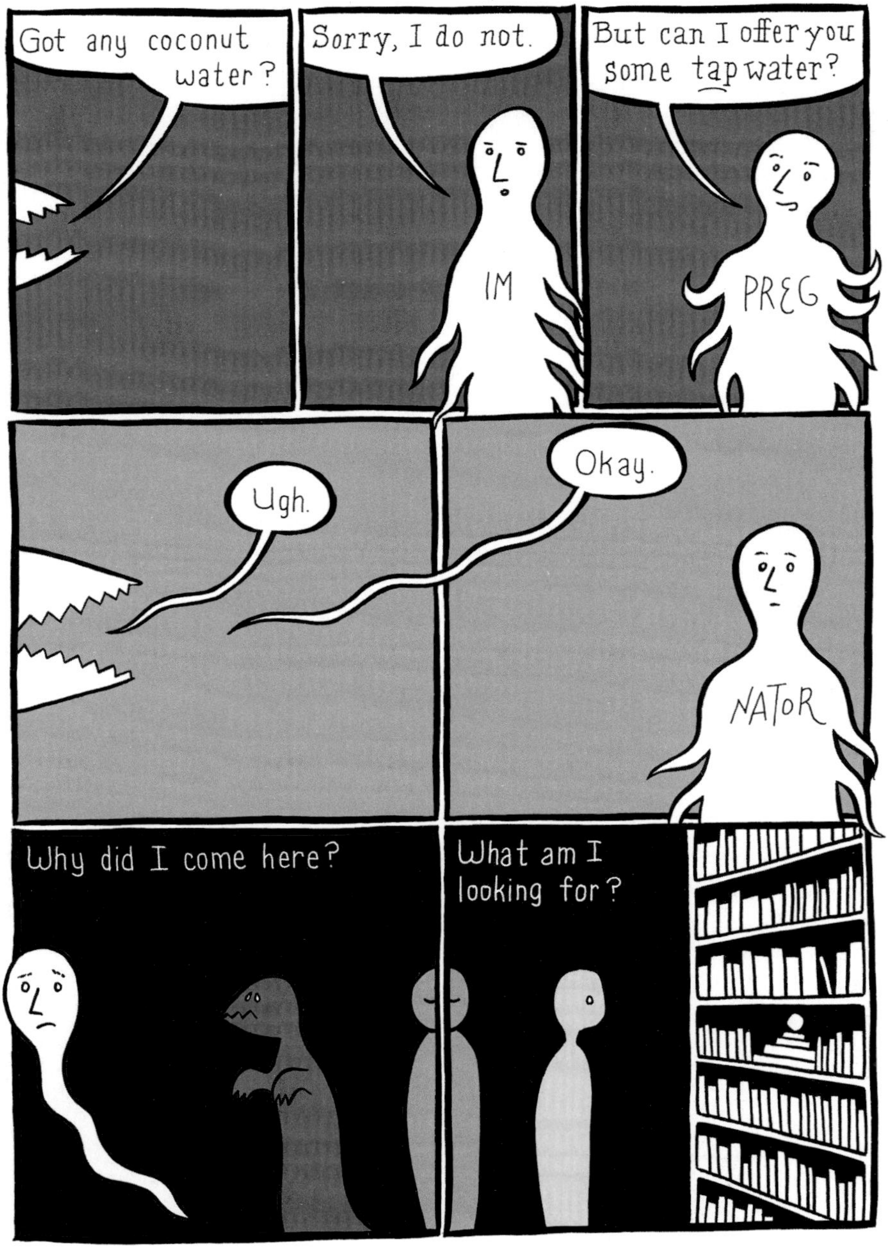
Got any coconut water?
Sorry, I do not.
IM
But can I offer you some tap water?
PREG
Ugh.
Okay.
NATOR
Why did I come here?
What am I looking for?

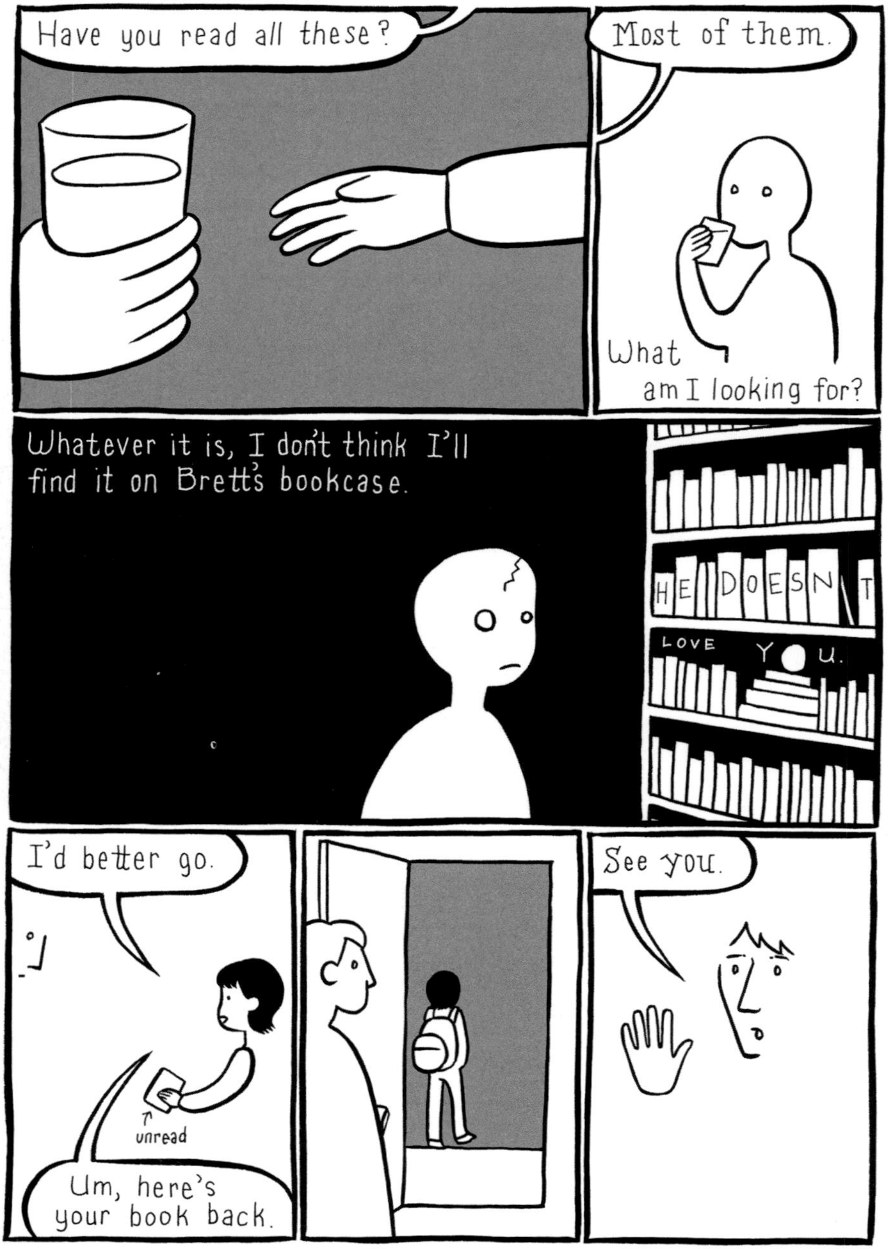
Have you read all these?
Most of them.
What am I looking for?
Whatever it is, I don't think I'll find it on Brett's bookcase.
HE DOESN T
LOVE
Y U.
I'd better go.
unread
Um, here's your book back.
See you.

PART THREE

Brett Hathaway

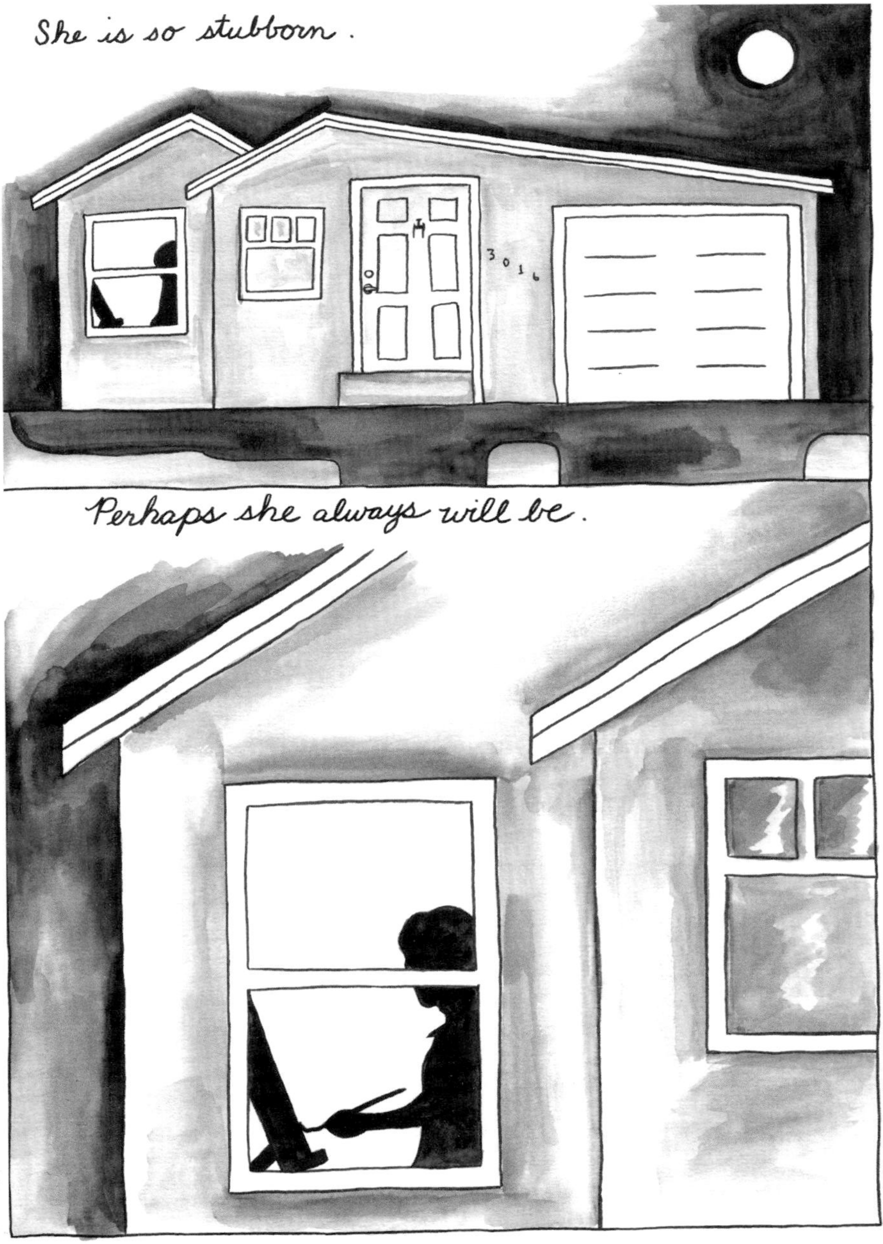
She is so stubborn.
3016
Perhaps she always will be.

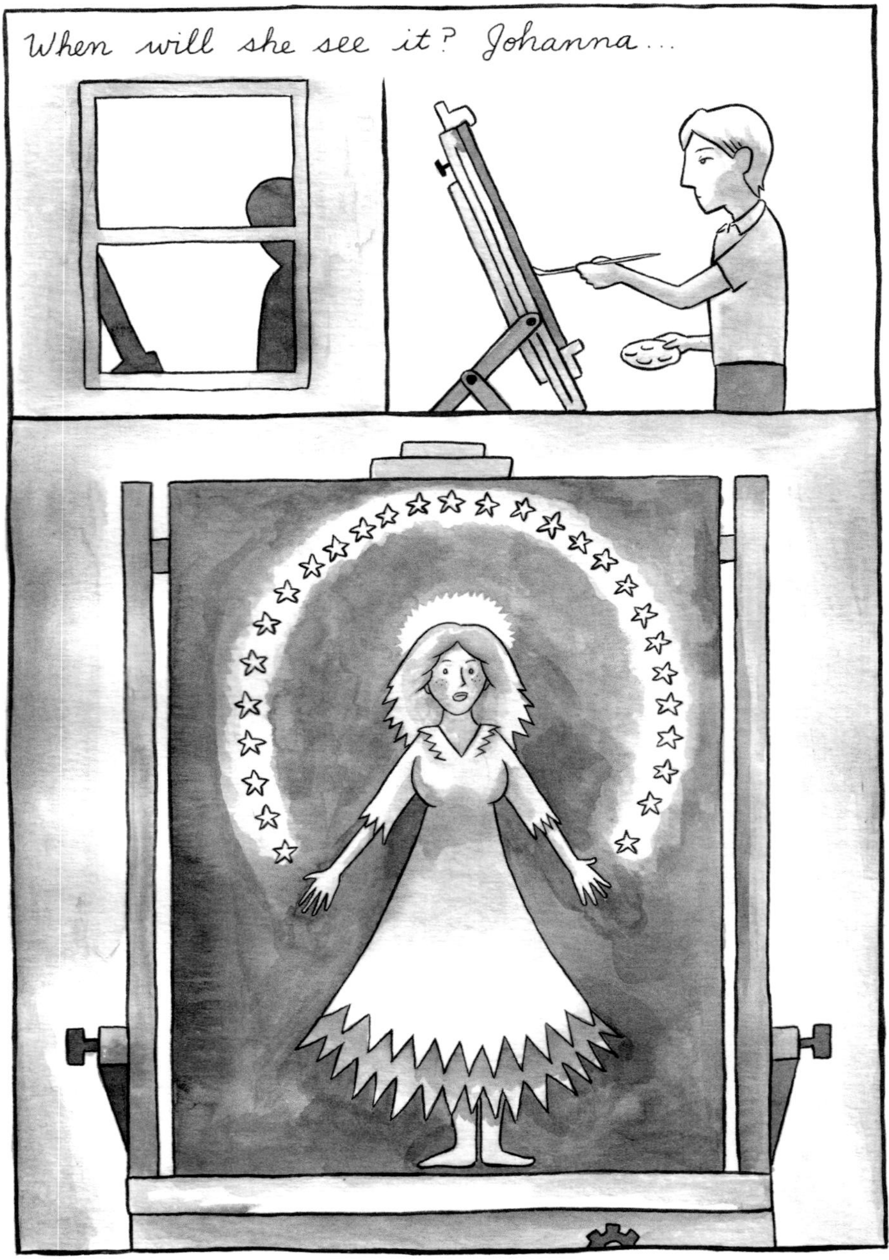
When will she see it? Johanna...

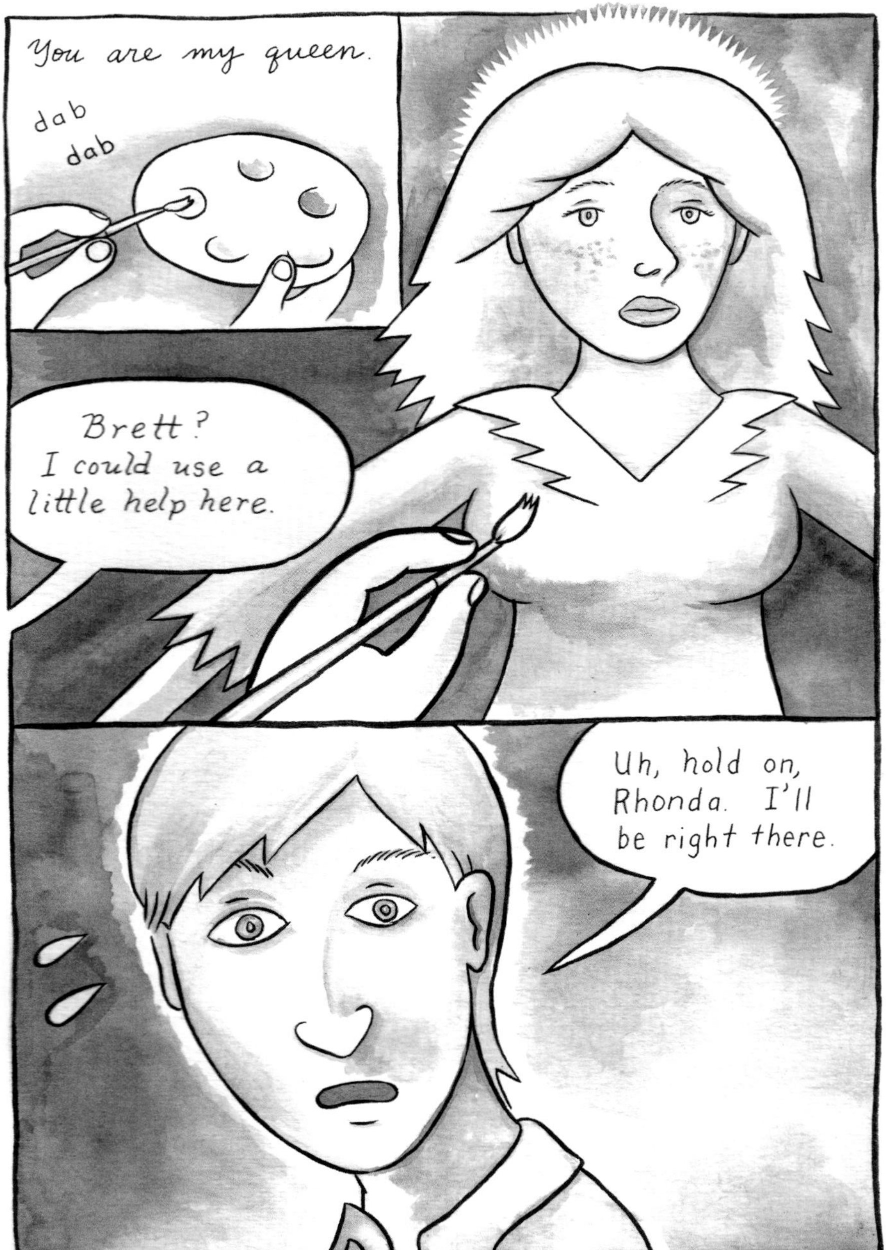
You are my queen.
dab
dab
Brett?
I could use a little help here.
Uh, hold on, Rhonda. I'll be right there.

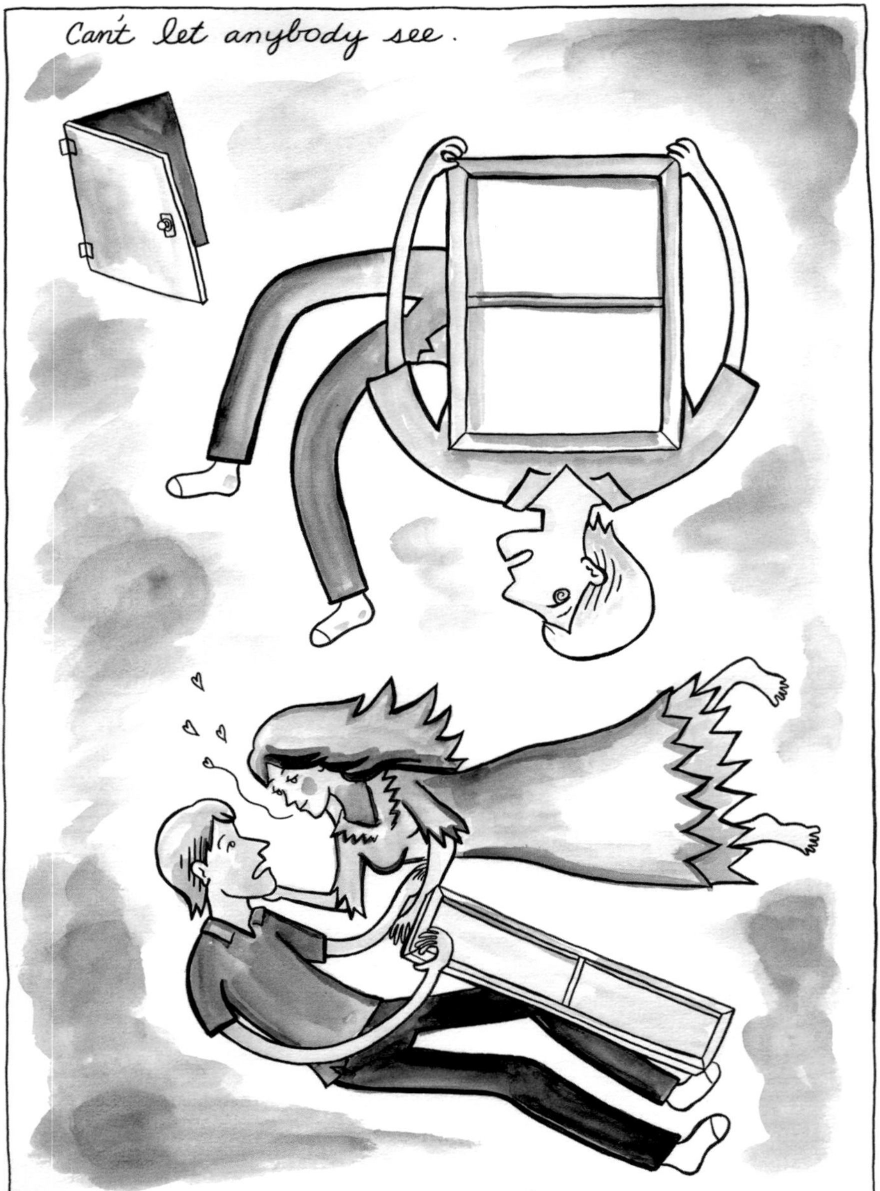
Can't let anybody see.
my big secret.

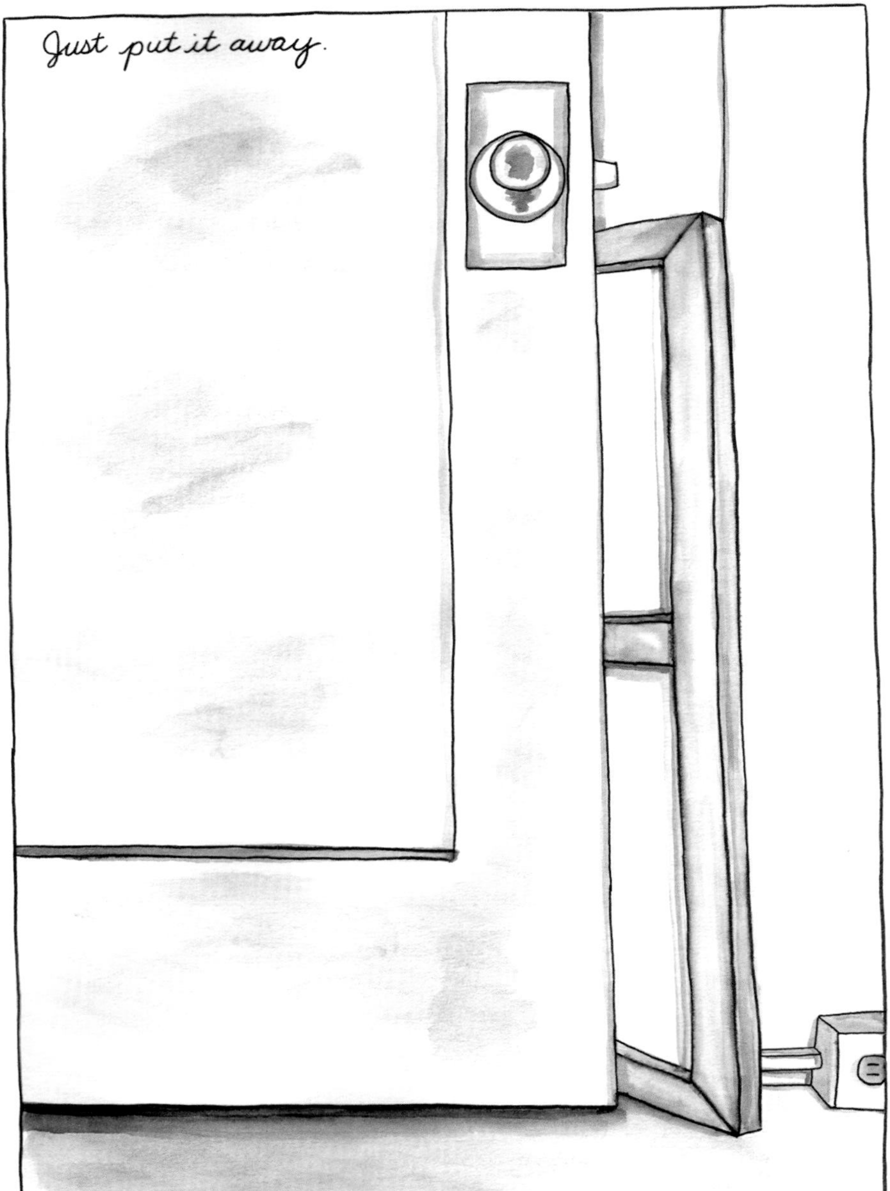
Just put it away.

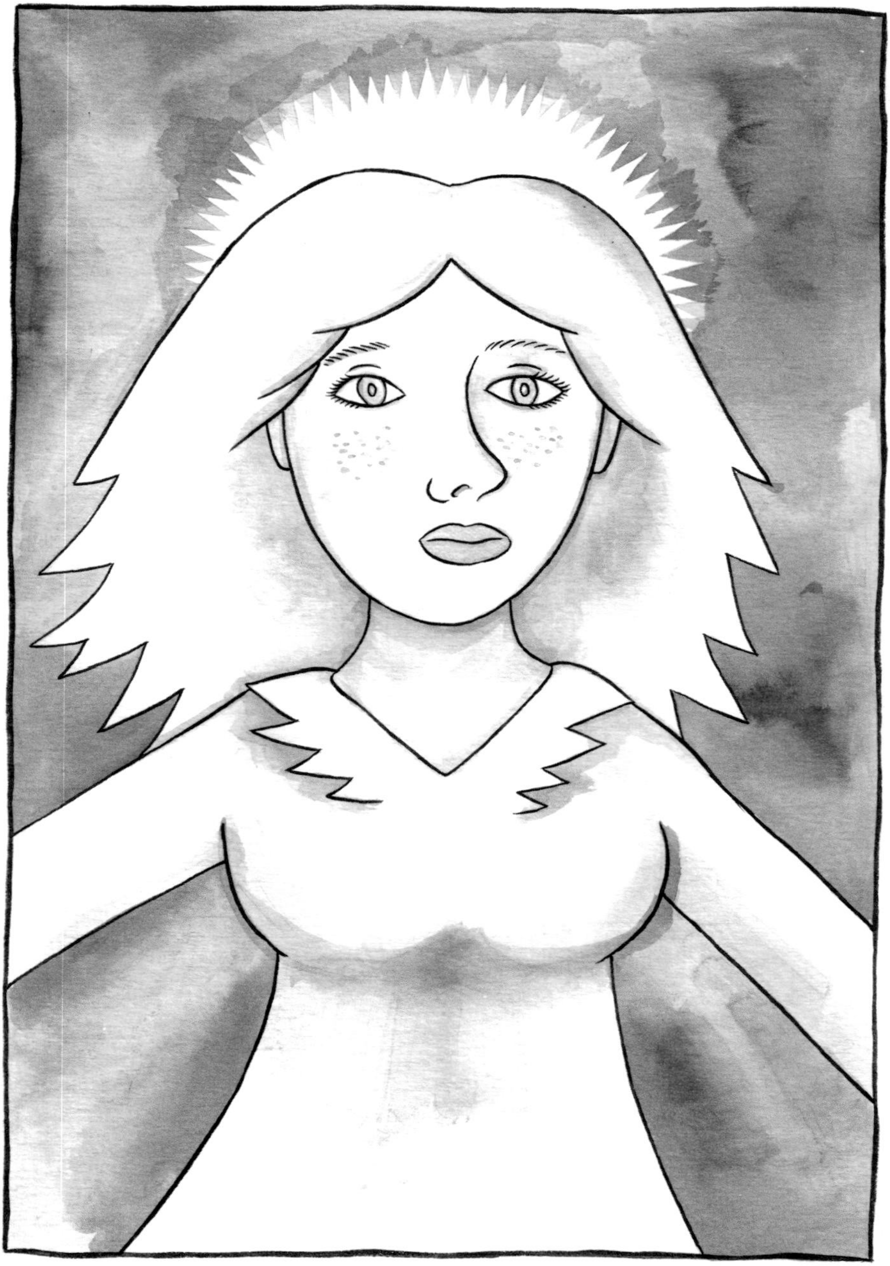

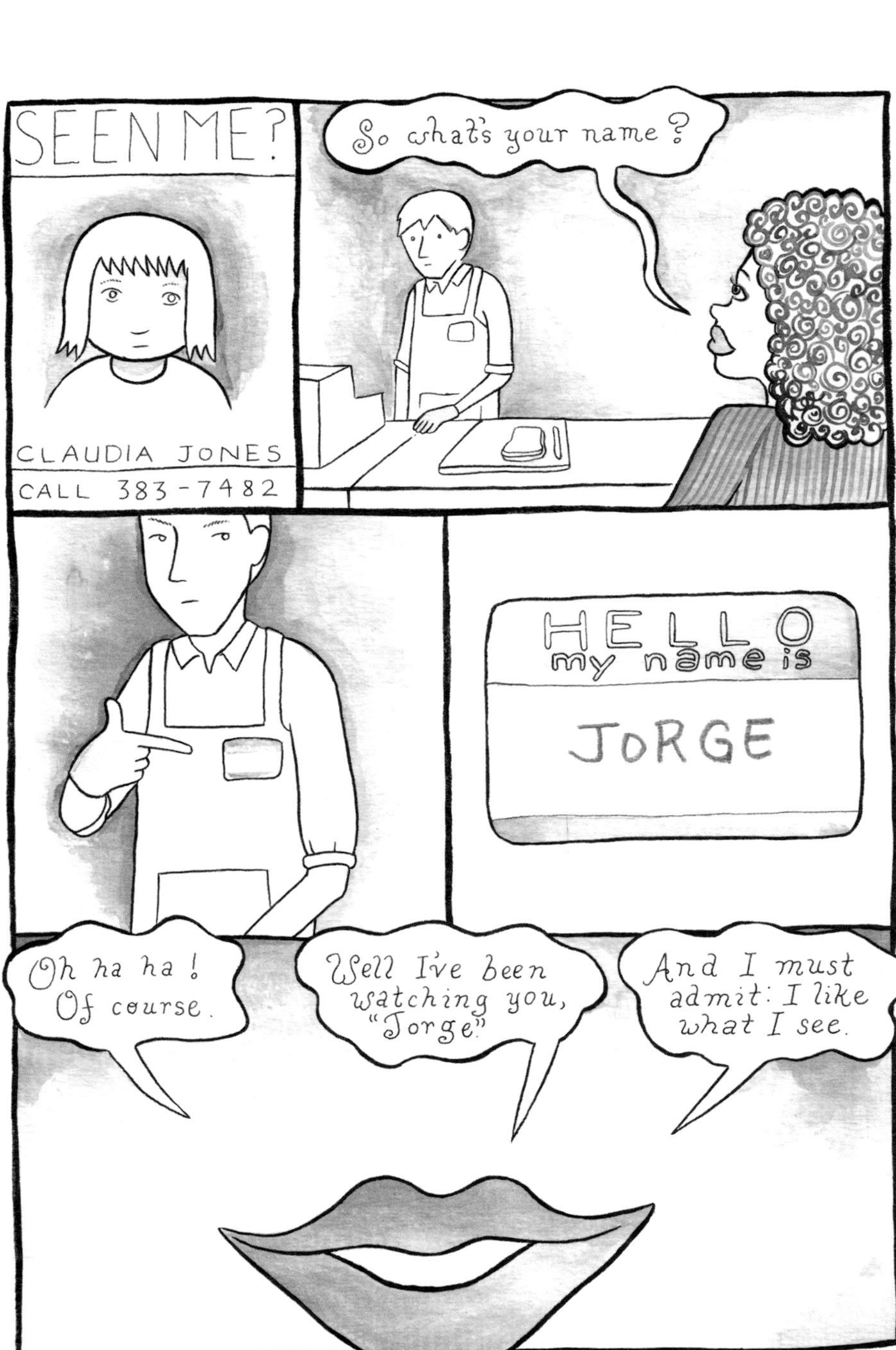
SEEN ME?
CLAUDIA JONES
CALL 383-7482
So what's your name?
HELLO my name is
JORGE
Oh ha ha! Of course.
Well I've been watching you, "Jorge."
And I must admit: I like what I see.

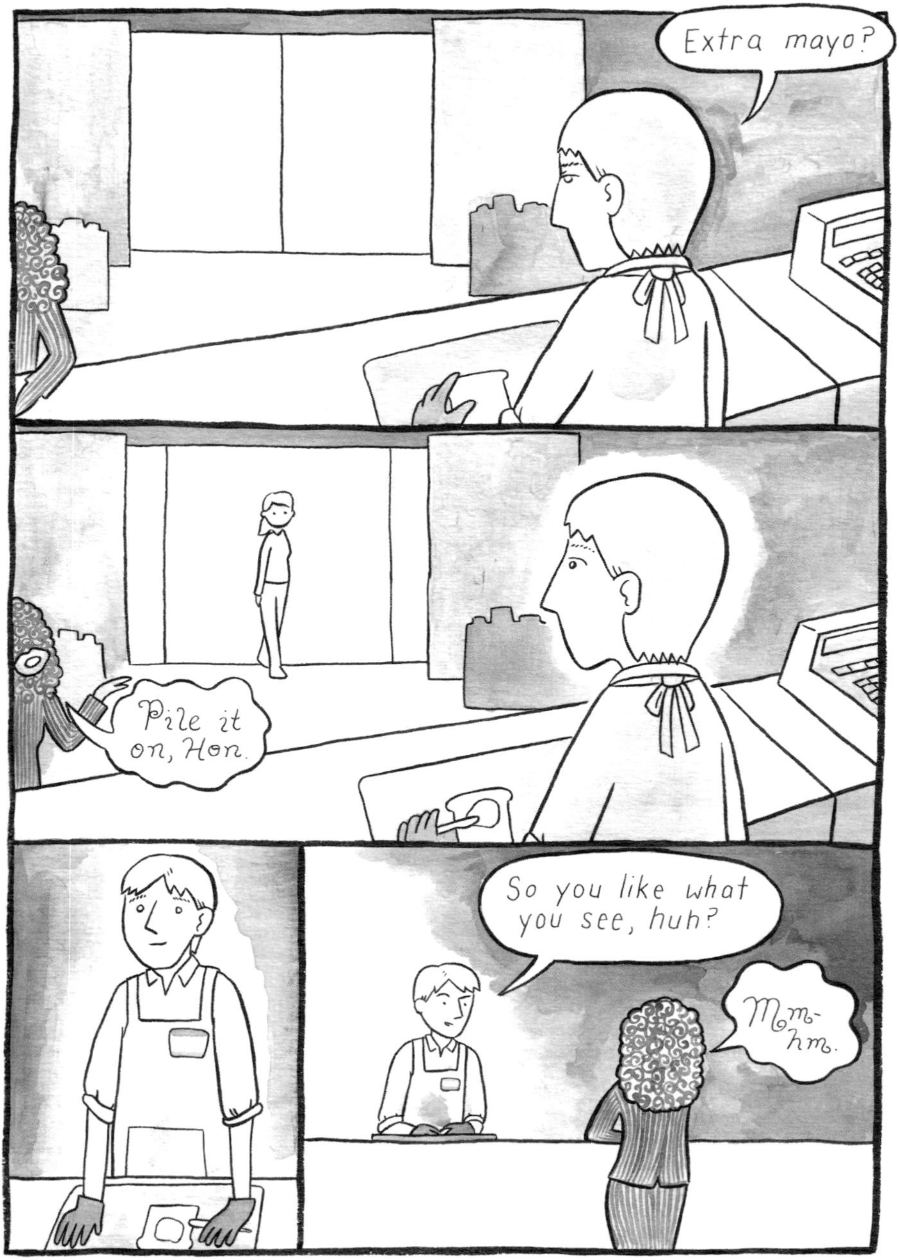
Extra mayo?
Pile it on, Hon.
So you like what you see, huh?
Mm-hm.

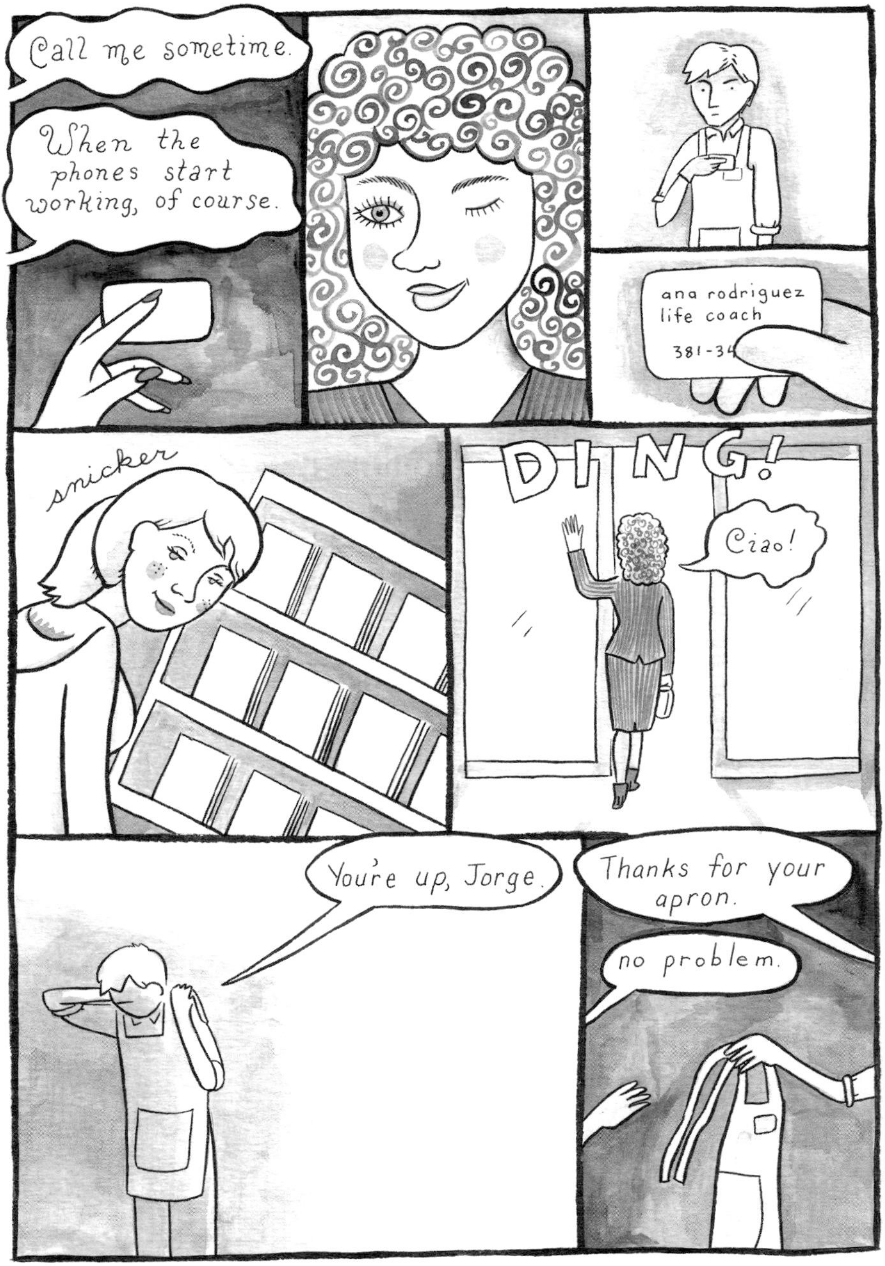
Call me sometime.
When the phones start working, of course.
ana rodriguez
life coach
381-34
snicker
DING!
Ciao!
You're up, Jorge.
Thanks for your apron.
no problem.

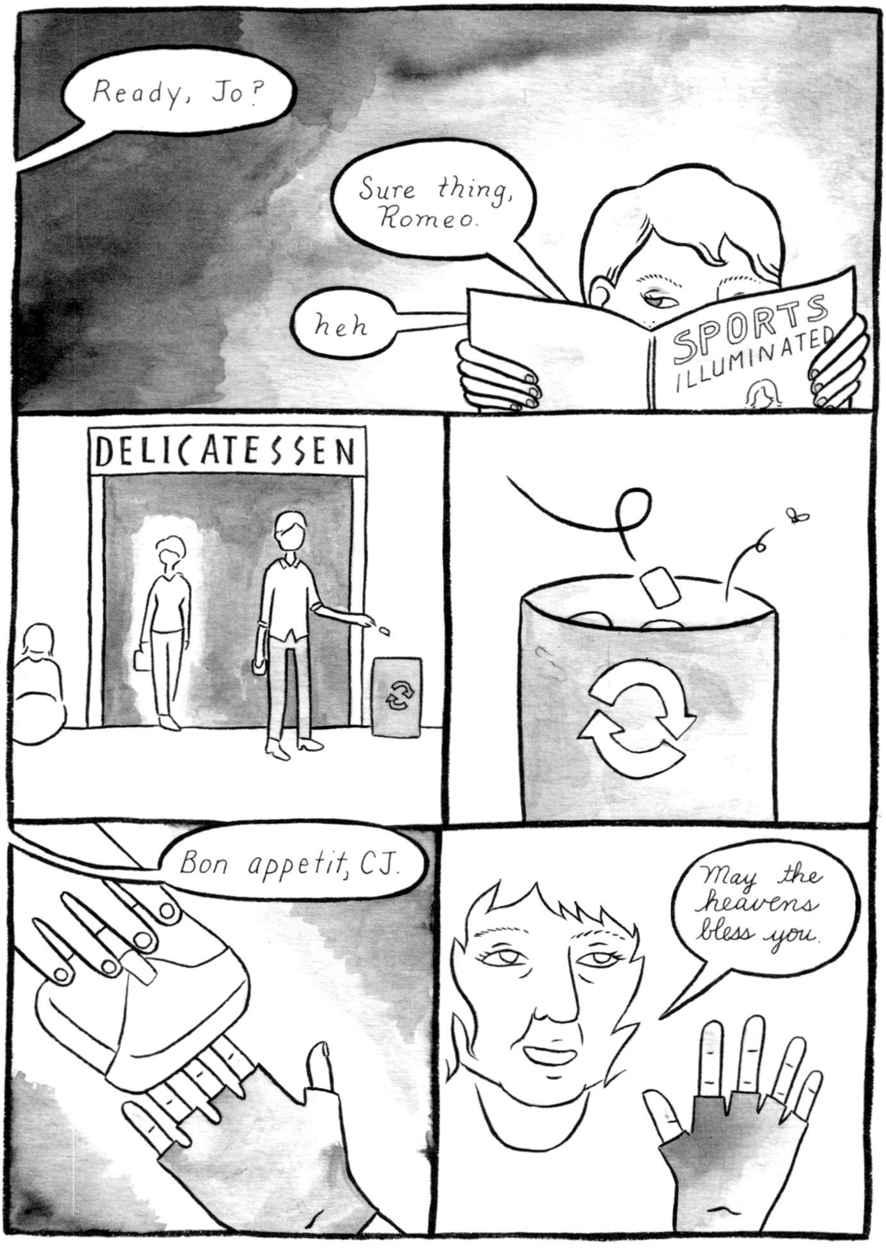
Ready, Jo?
Sure thing, Romeo.
heh
SPORTS ILLUMINATED
DELICATESSEN
Bon appetit, CJ.
May the heavens bless you.

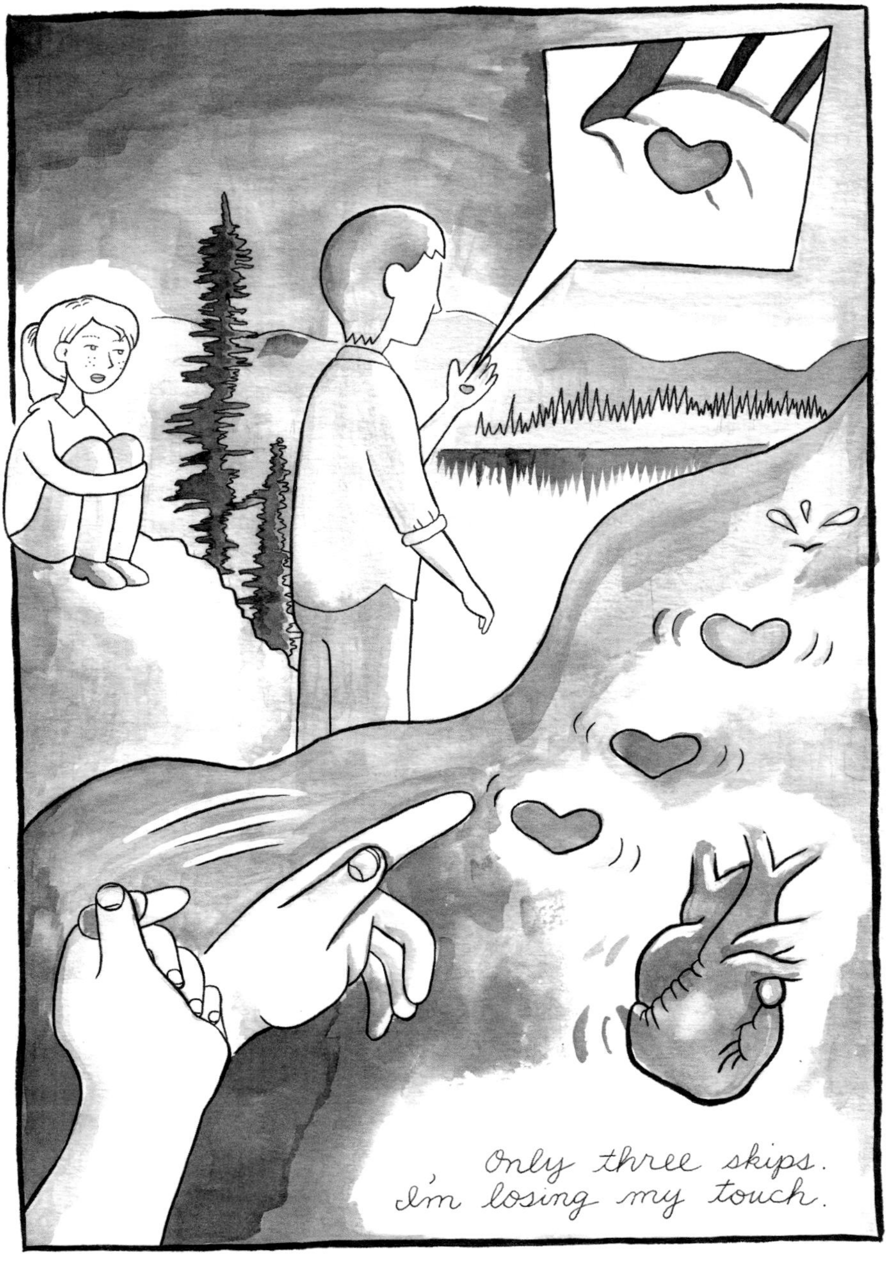
Only three skips.
I'm losing my touch.

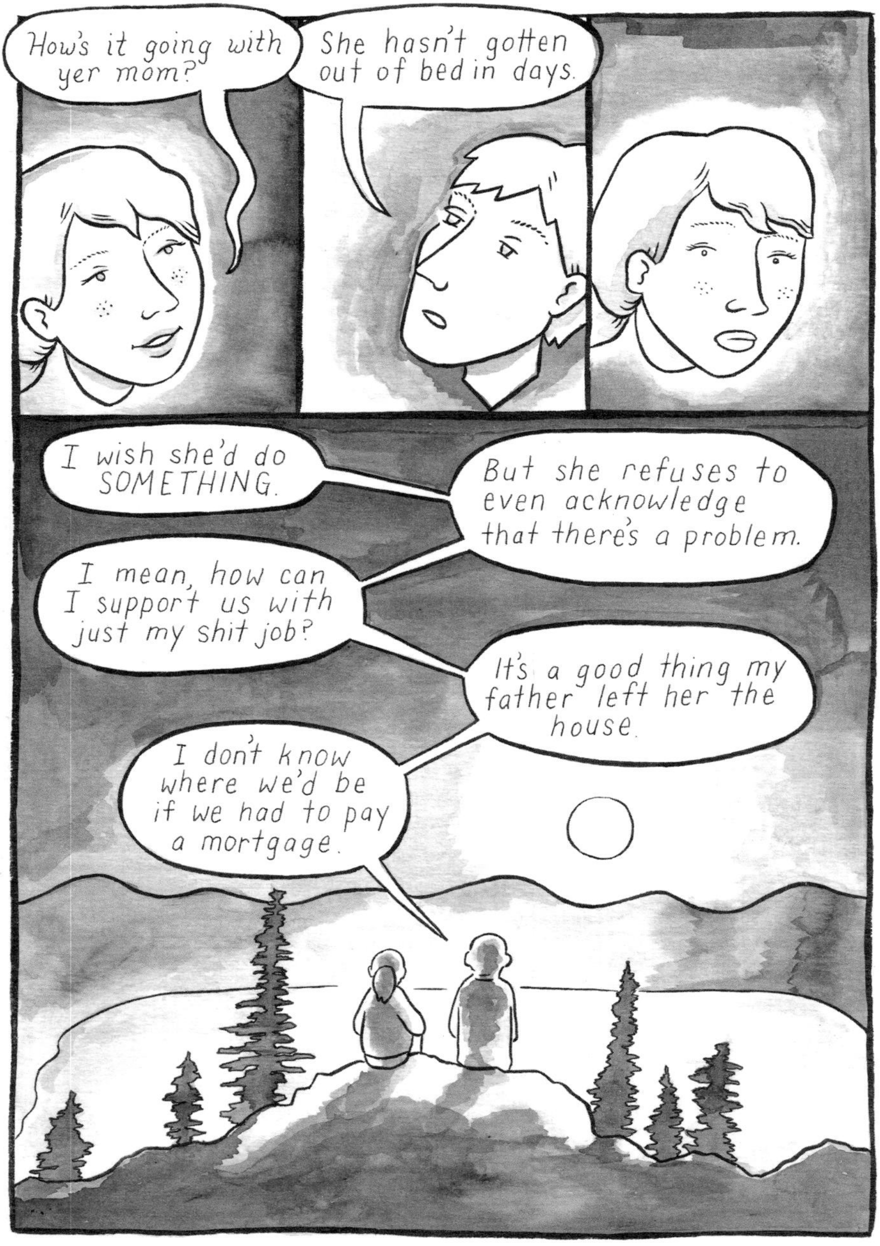
How's it going with yer mom?
She hasn't gotten out of bed in days.
I wish she'd do SOMETHING.
But she refuses to even acknowledge that there's a problem.
I mean, how can I support us with just my shit job?
It's a good thing my father left her the house.
I don't know where we'd be if we had to pay a mortgage.

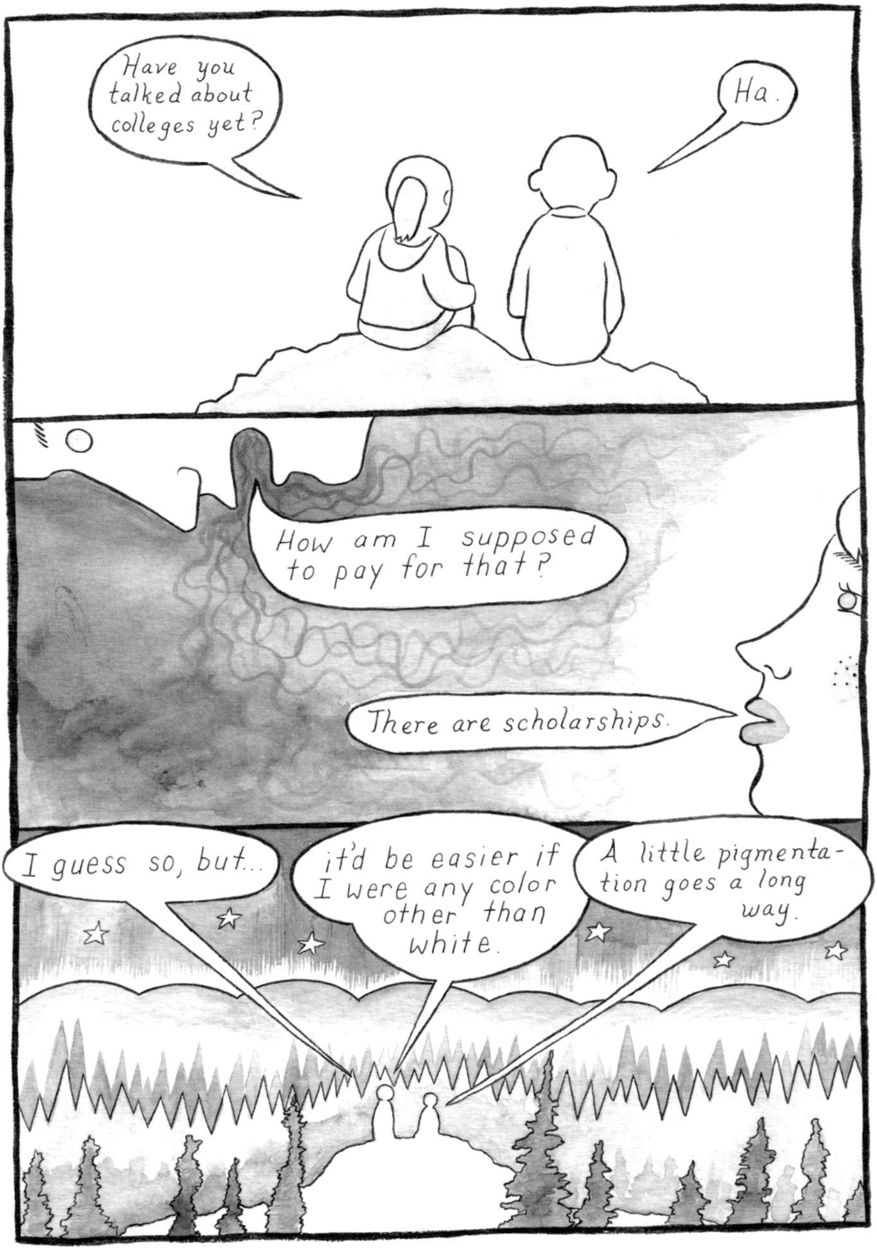
Have you talked about colleges yet?
Ha.
How am I supposed to pay for that?
There are scholarships.
I guess so, but...
it'd be easier if I were any color other than white.
A little pigmentation goes a long way.

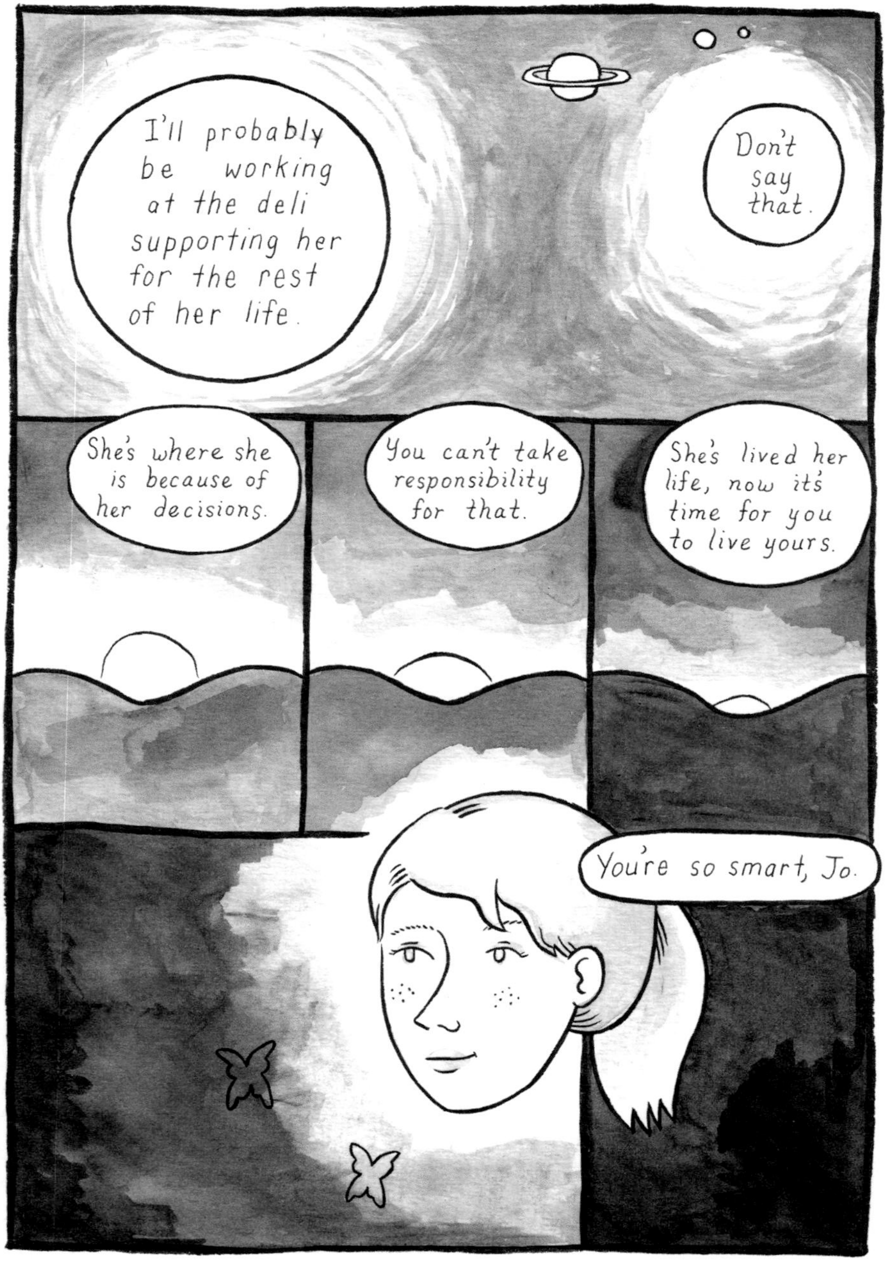
I'll probably be working at the deli supporting her for the rest of her life.
Don't say that.
She's where she is because of her decisions.
You can't take responsibility for that.
She's lived her life, now it's time for you to live yours.
You're so smart, Jo.

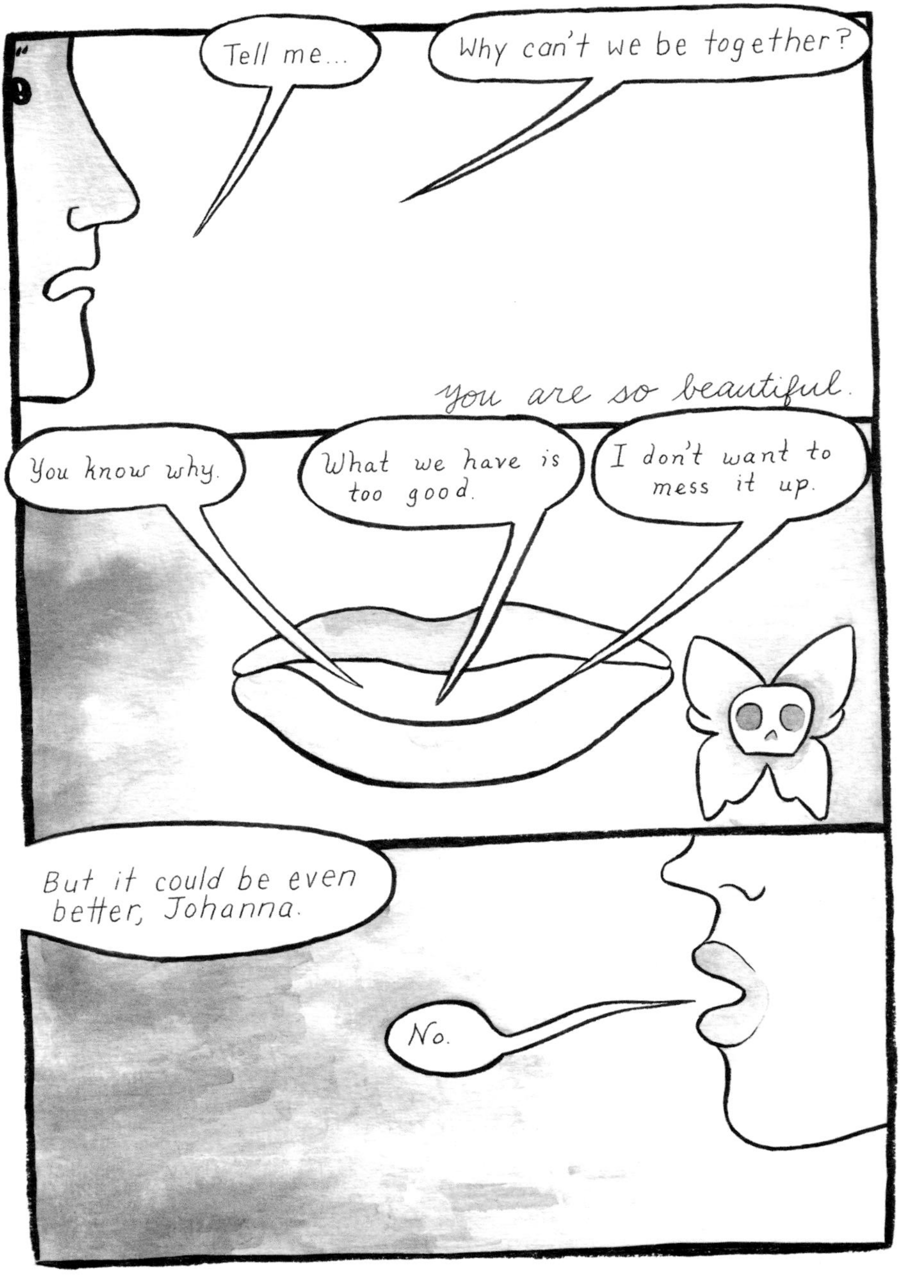
Tell me...
Why can't we be together?
You are so beautiful.
You know why.
What we have is too good.
I don't want to mess it up.
But it could be even better, Johanna.
No.

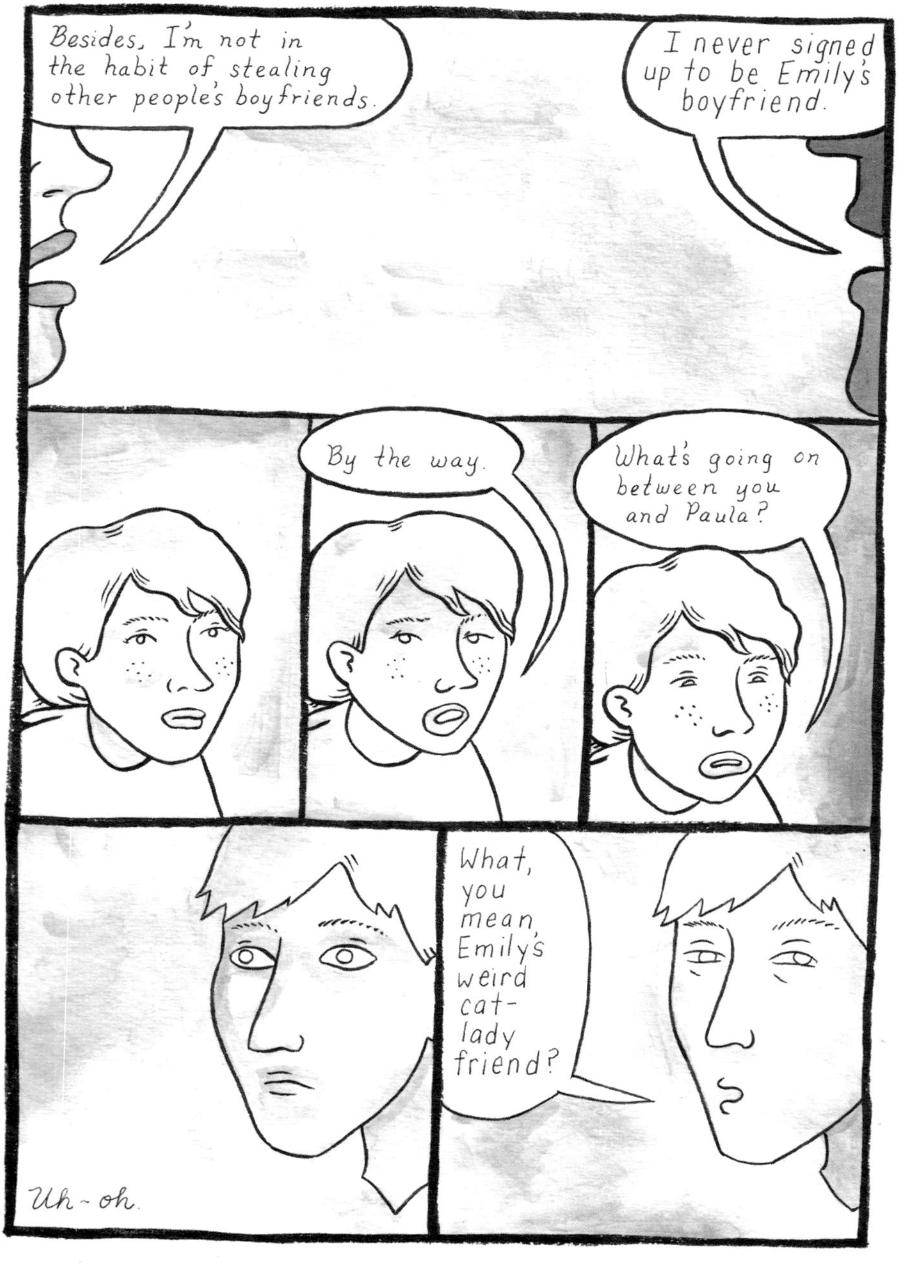
Besides, I'm not in the habit of stealing other people's boyfriends.
I never signed up to be Emily's boyfriend.
By the way.
What's going on between you and Paula?
Uh-oh.
What, you mean, Emily's weird cat-lady friend?

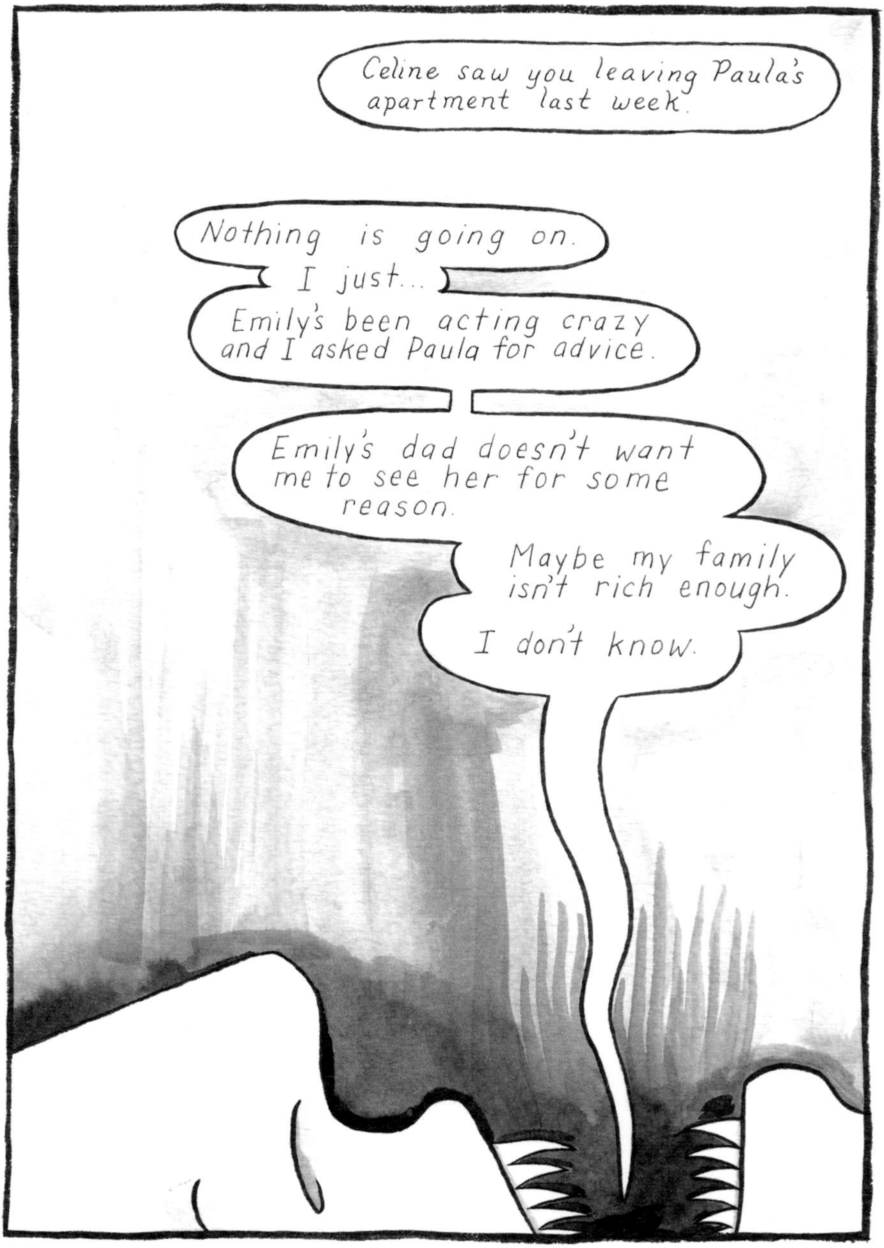
Celine saw you leaving Paula's apartment last week.
Nothing is going on.
I just...
Emily's been acting crazy and I asked Paula for advice.
Emily's dad doesn't want me to see her for some reason.
Maybe my family isn't rich enough.
I don't know.

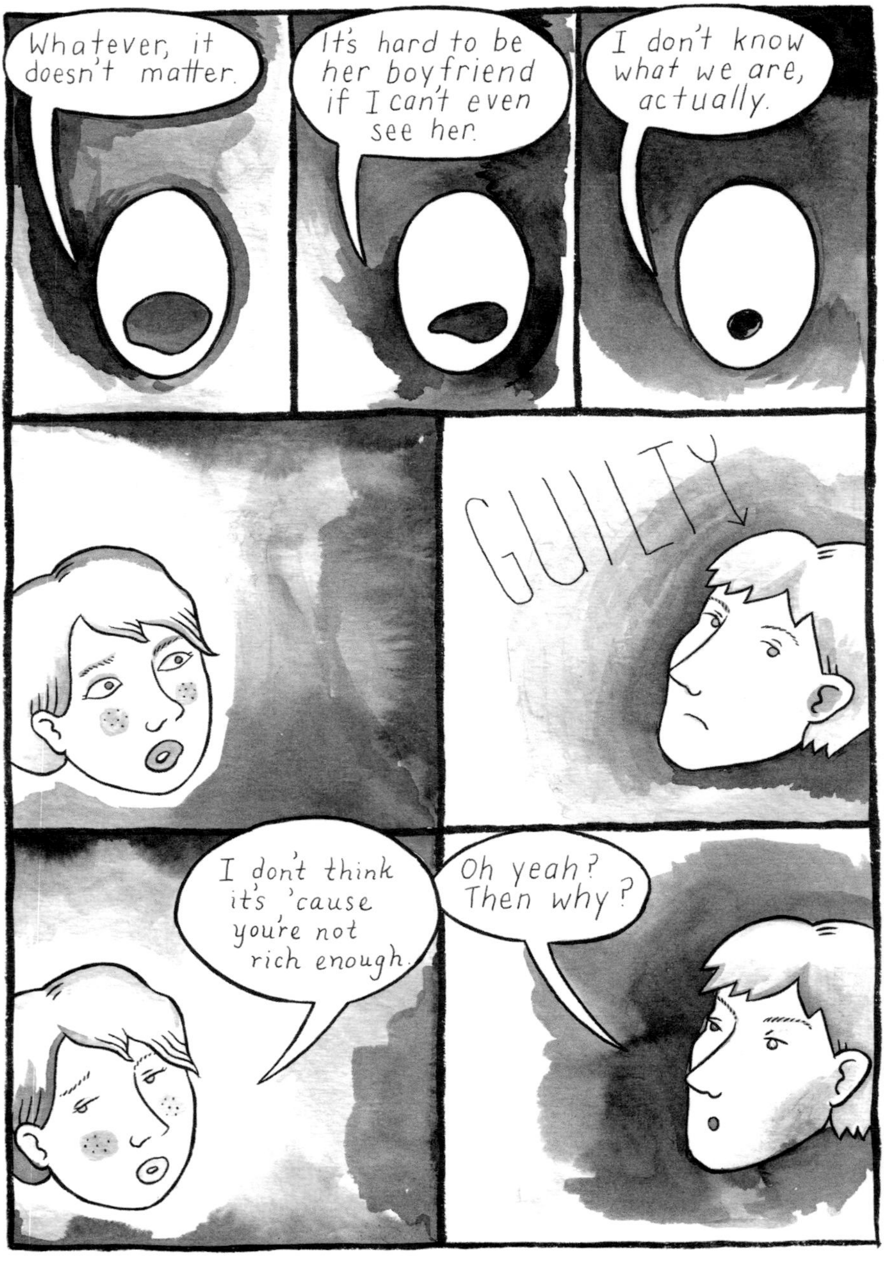
Whatever, it doesn't matter.
It's hard to be her boyfriend if I can't even see her.
I don't know what we are, actually.
GUILTY
I don't think it's 'cause you're not rich enough.
Oh yeah? Then why?

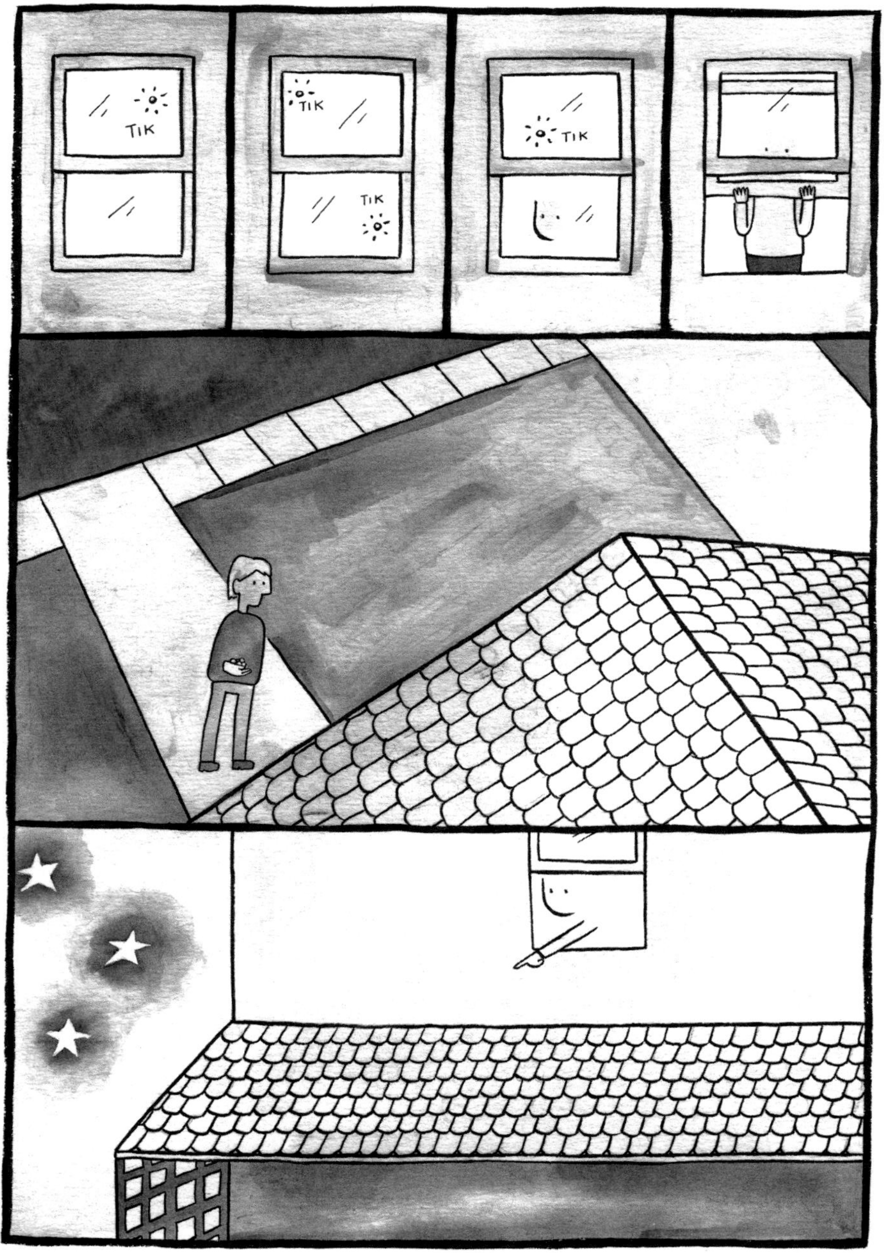
TIK
TIK
TIK
TIK

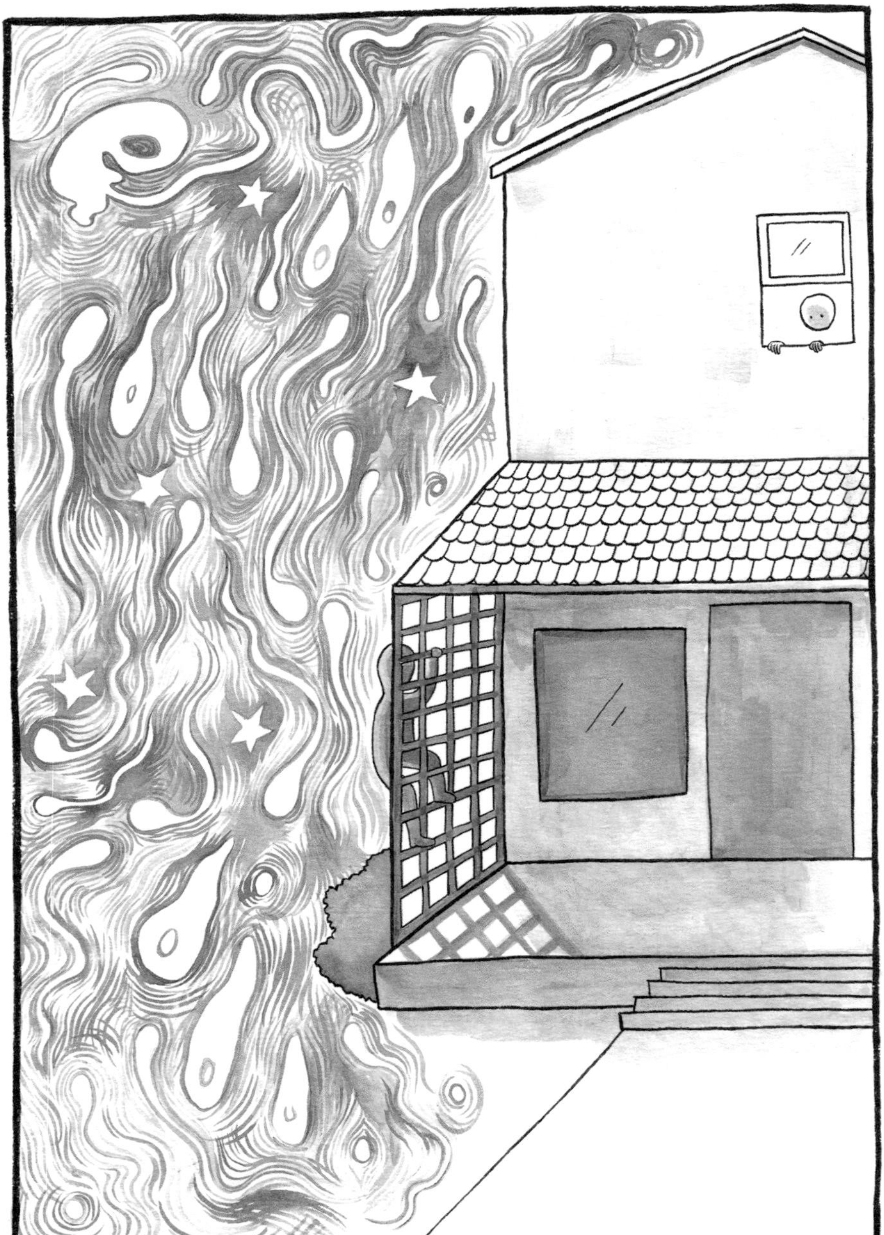

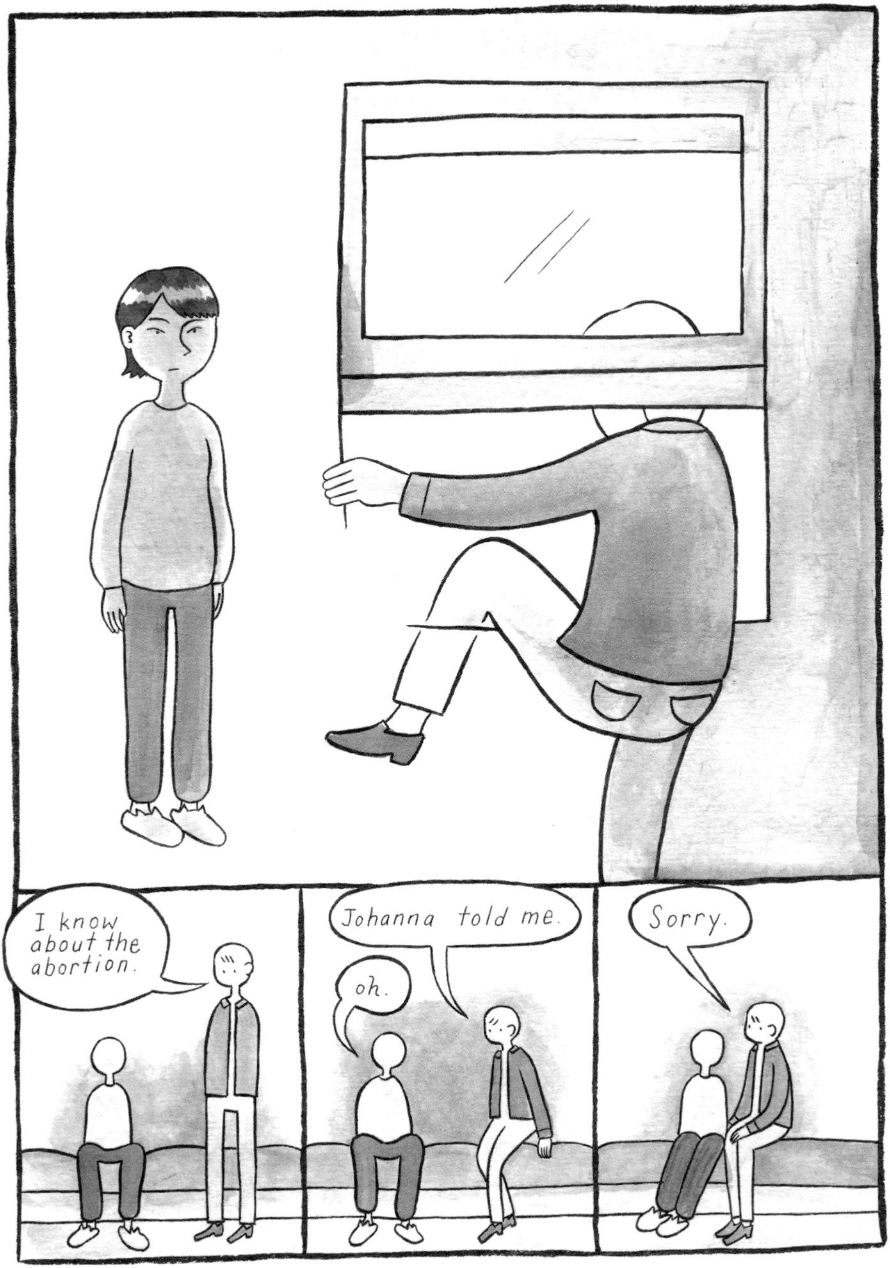
I know about the abortion.
Johanna told me.
oh.
Sorry.

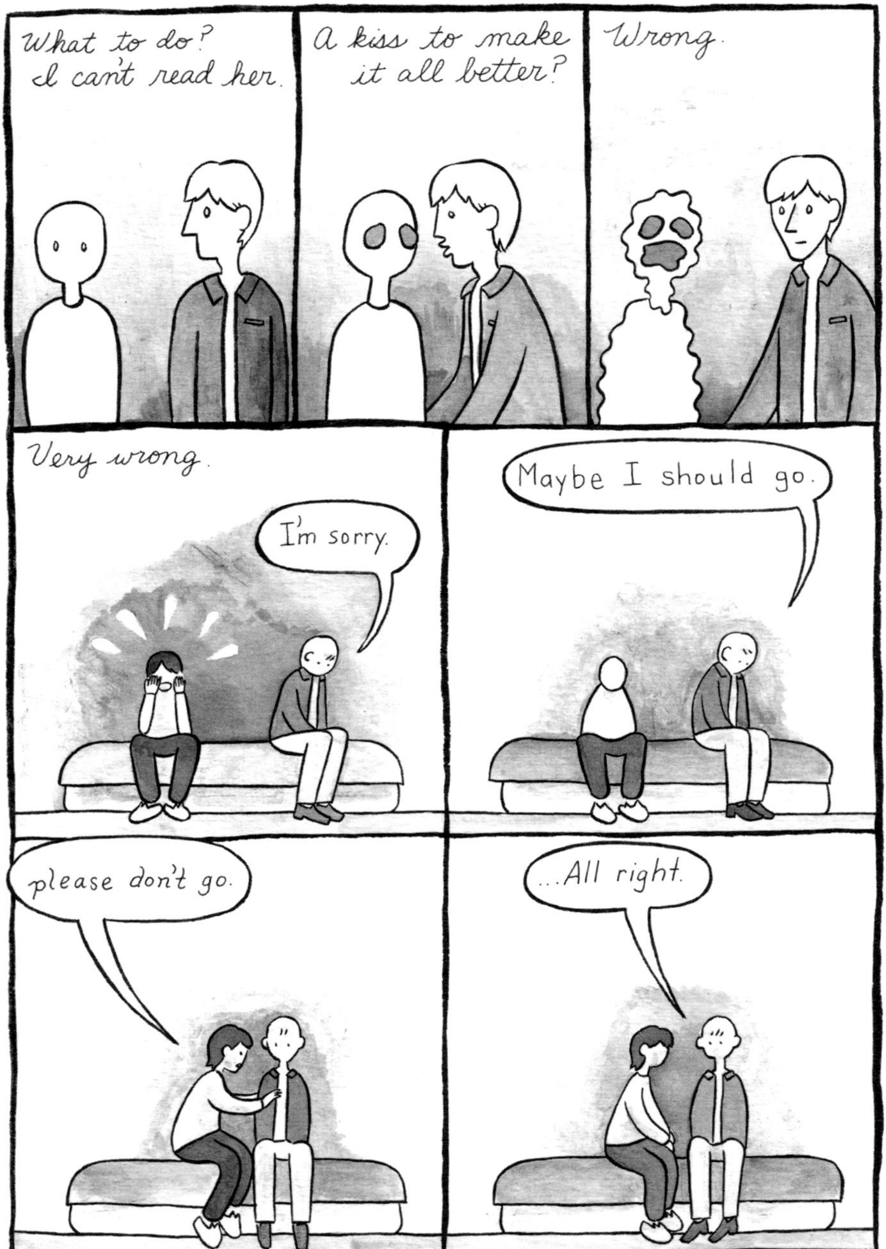
What to do? I can't read her.
A kiss to make it all better?
Wrong.
Very wrong.
I'm sorry.
Maybe I should go.
please don't go.
...All right.

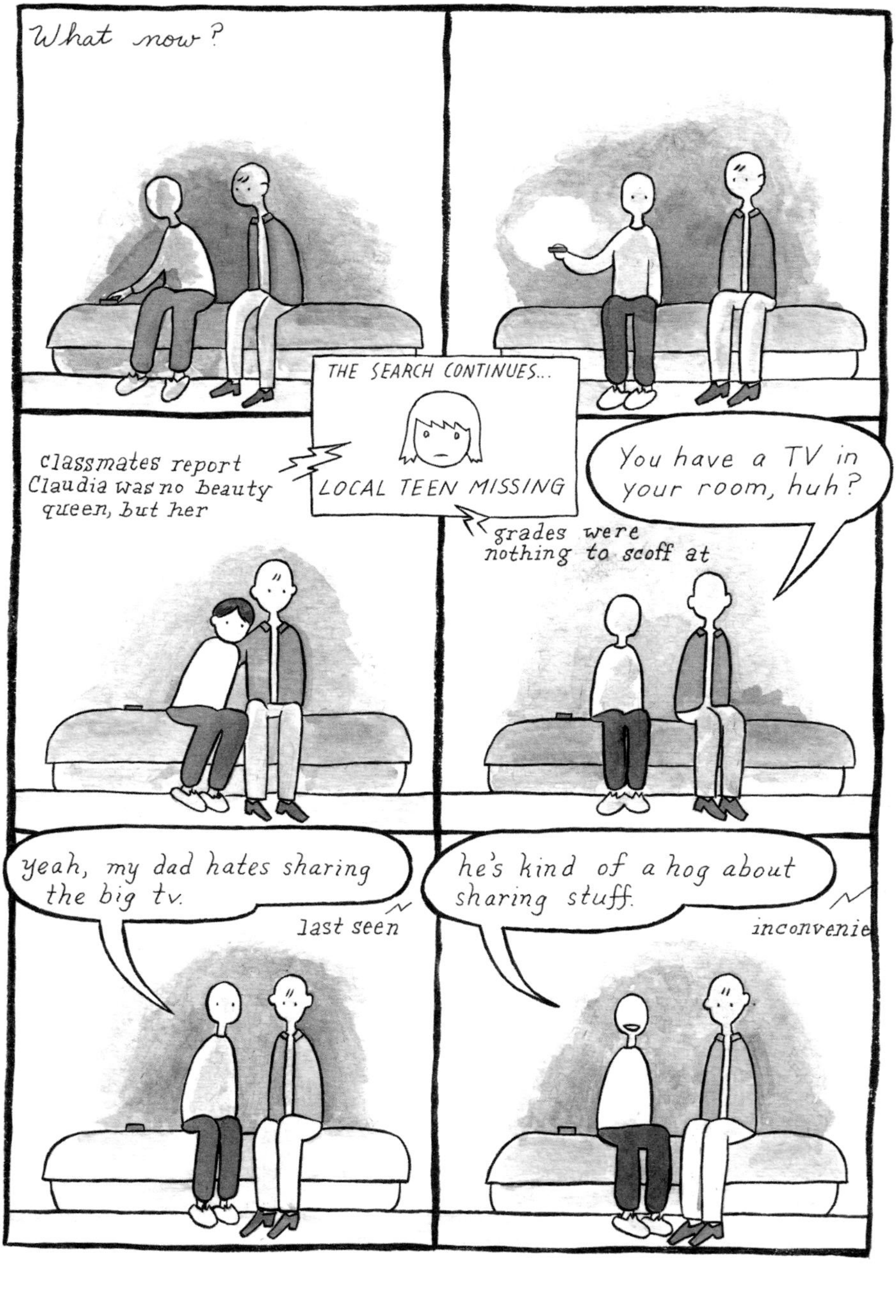
What now?
THE SEARCH CONTINUES...
LOCAL TEEN MISSING
classmates report Claudia was no beauty queen, but her
grades were nothing to scoff at
You have a TV in your room, huh?
yeah, my dad hates sharing the big tv.
last seen
he's kind of a hog about sharing stuff.
inconvenie

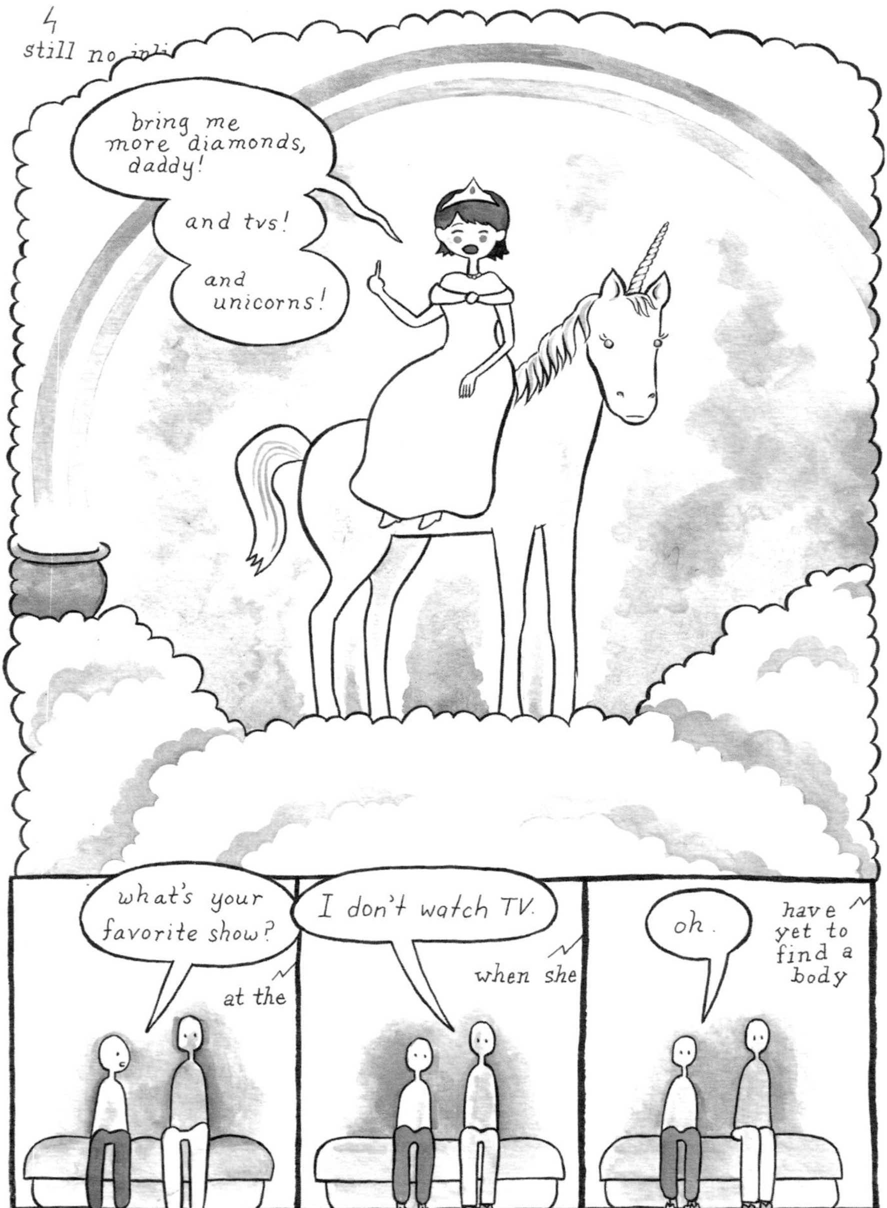
still no
bring me more diamonds, daddy!
and tvs!
and unicorns!
what's your favorite show?
at the
I don't watch TV.
when she
oh.
have yet to find a body

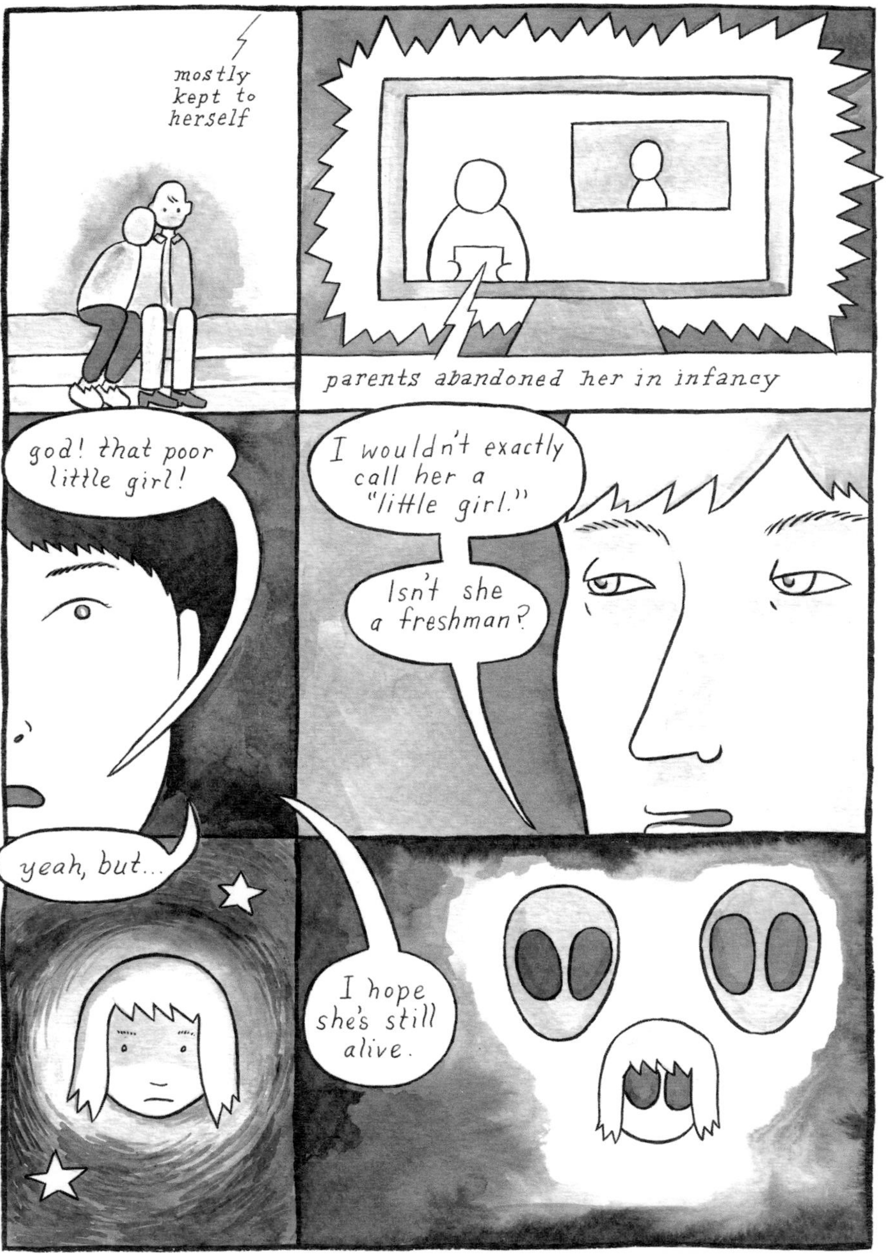
mostly kept to herself
parents abandoned her in infancy
god! that poor little girl!
I wouldn't exactly call her a "little girl."
Isn't she a freshman?
yeah, but...
I hope she's still alive.

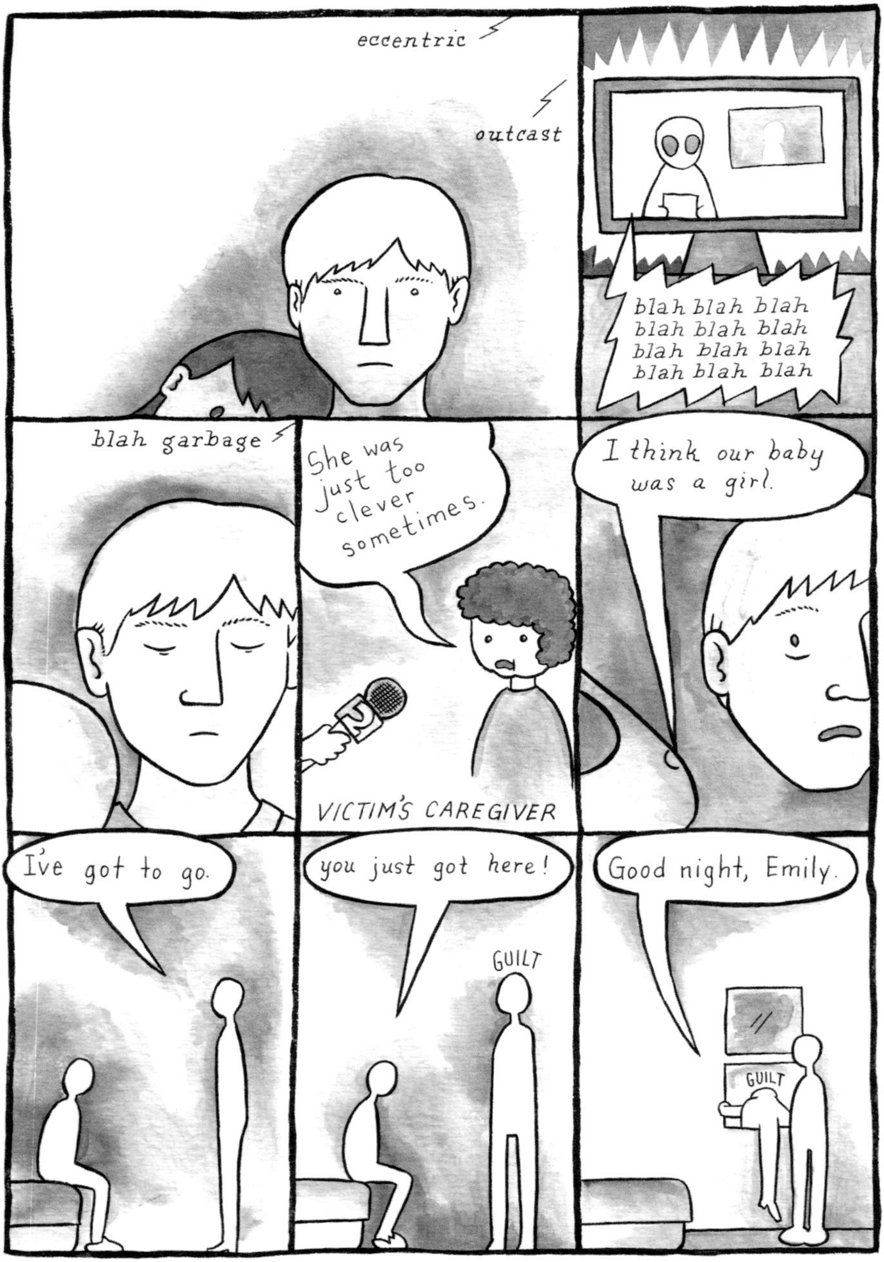
eccentric
outcast
blah blah blah blah blah blah blah blah blah blah blah blah
blah garbage
She was just too clever sometimes.
VICTIM'S CAREGIVER
I think our baby was a girl.
I've got to go.
you just got here!
GUILT
Good night, Emily.
GUILT

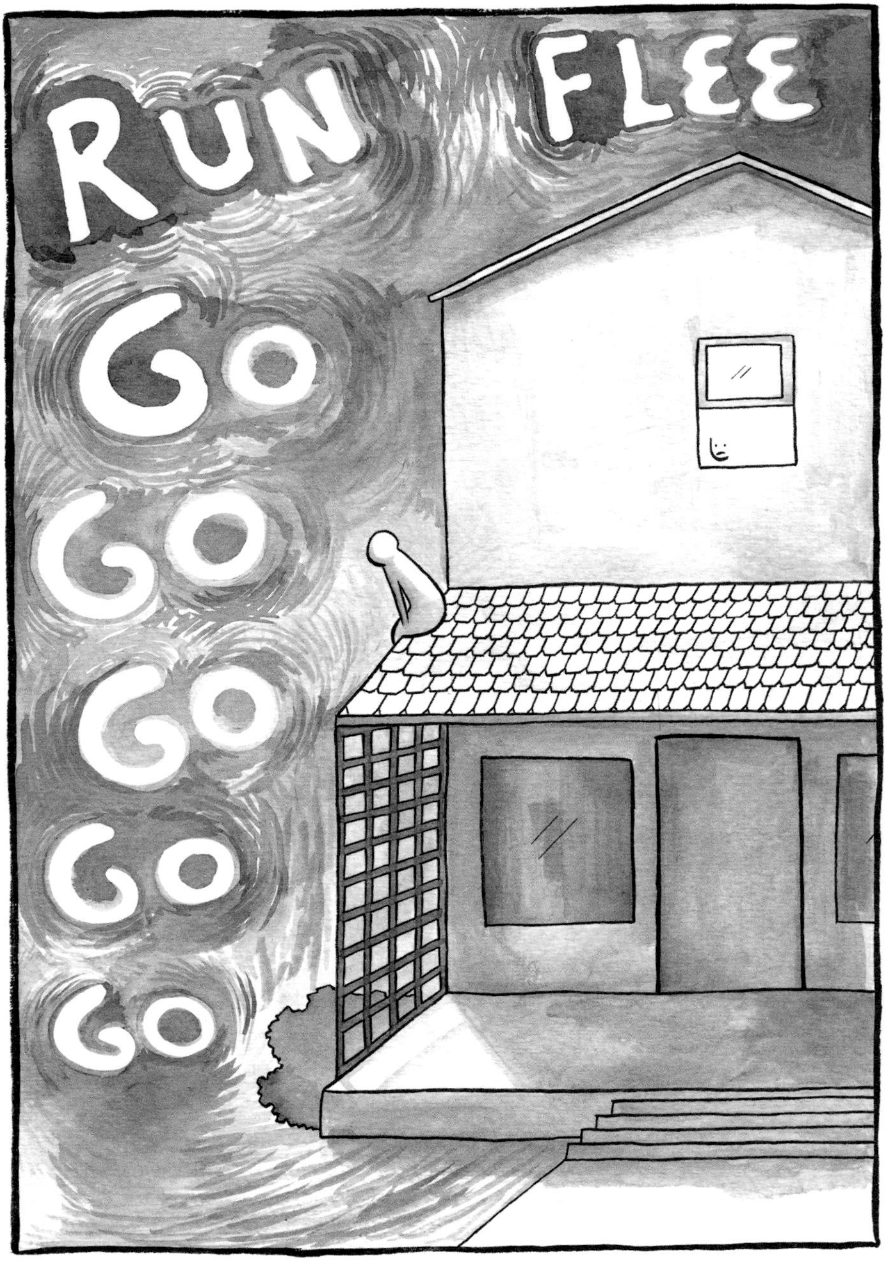
RUN FLEE
GO
GO
GO
GO
GO

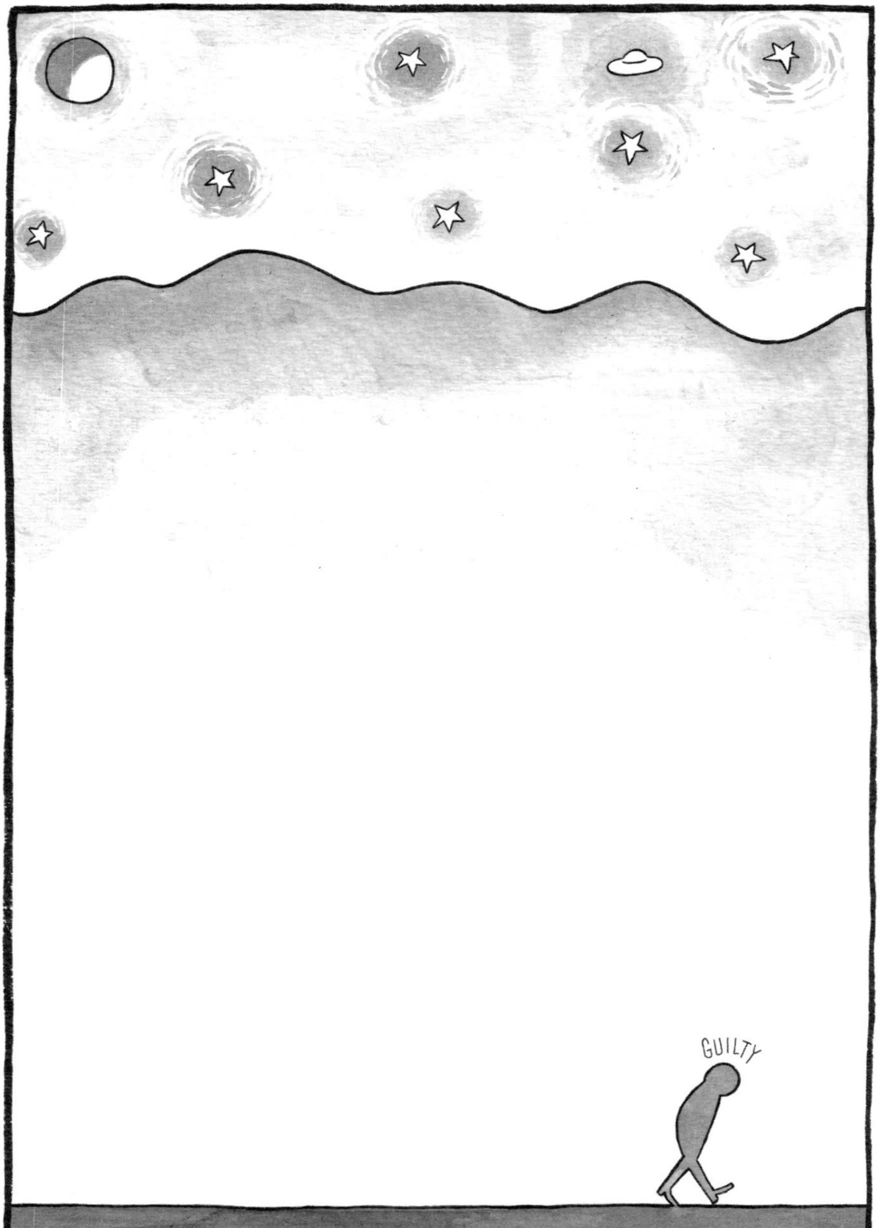
GUILTY

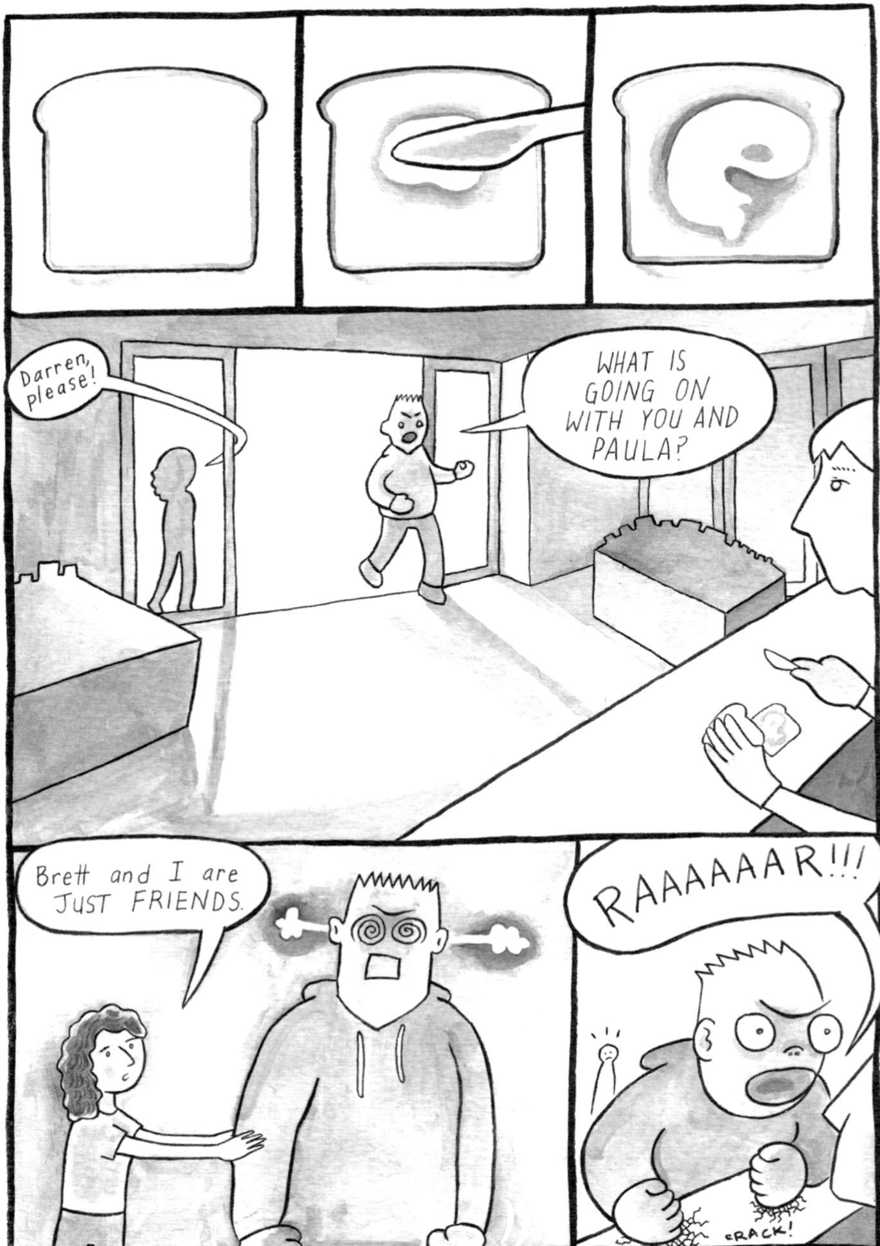
Darren, please!
WHAT IS GOING ON WITH YOU AND PAULA?
Brett and I are JUST FRIENDS.
RAAAAAAR!!!
CRACK!

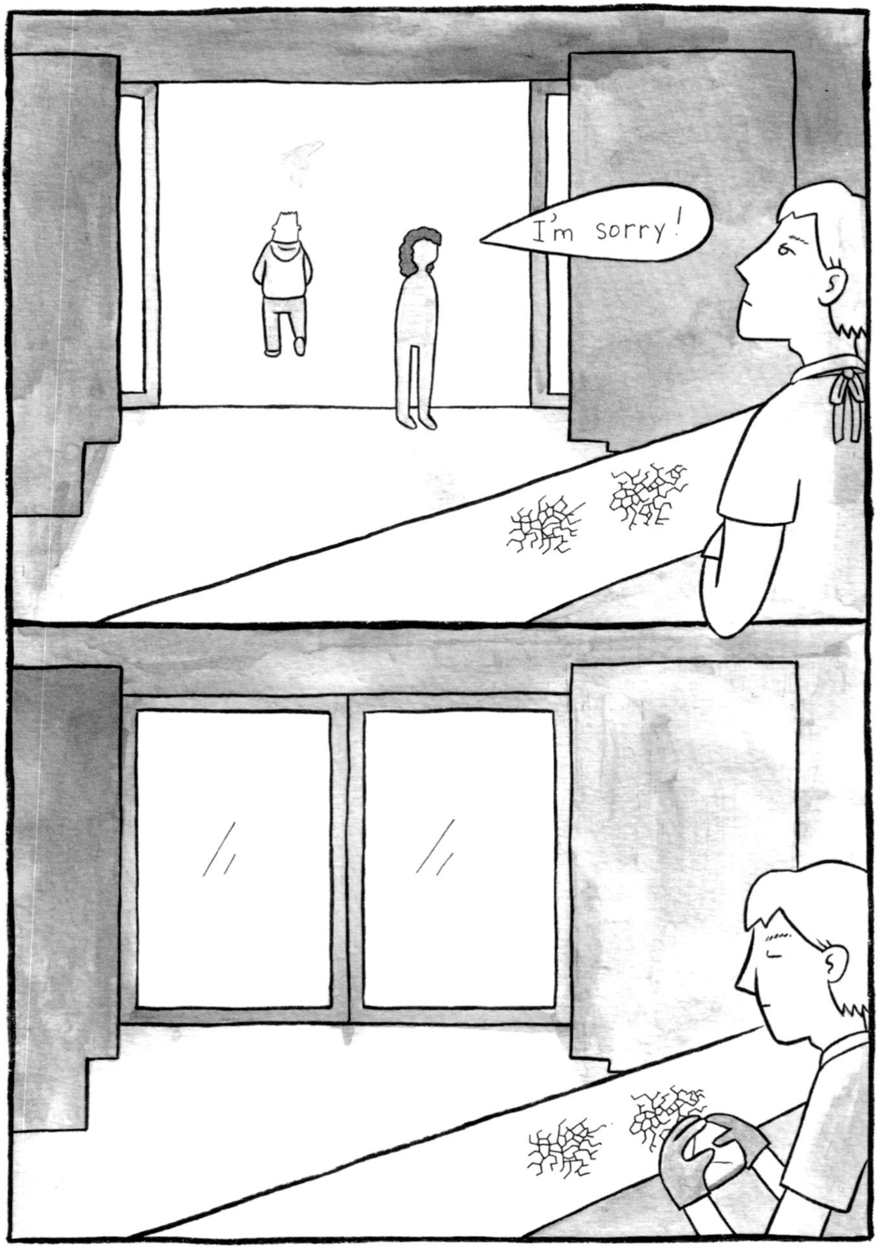
I'm sorry!

PART FOUR

Paula Navarro

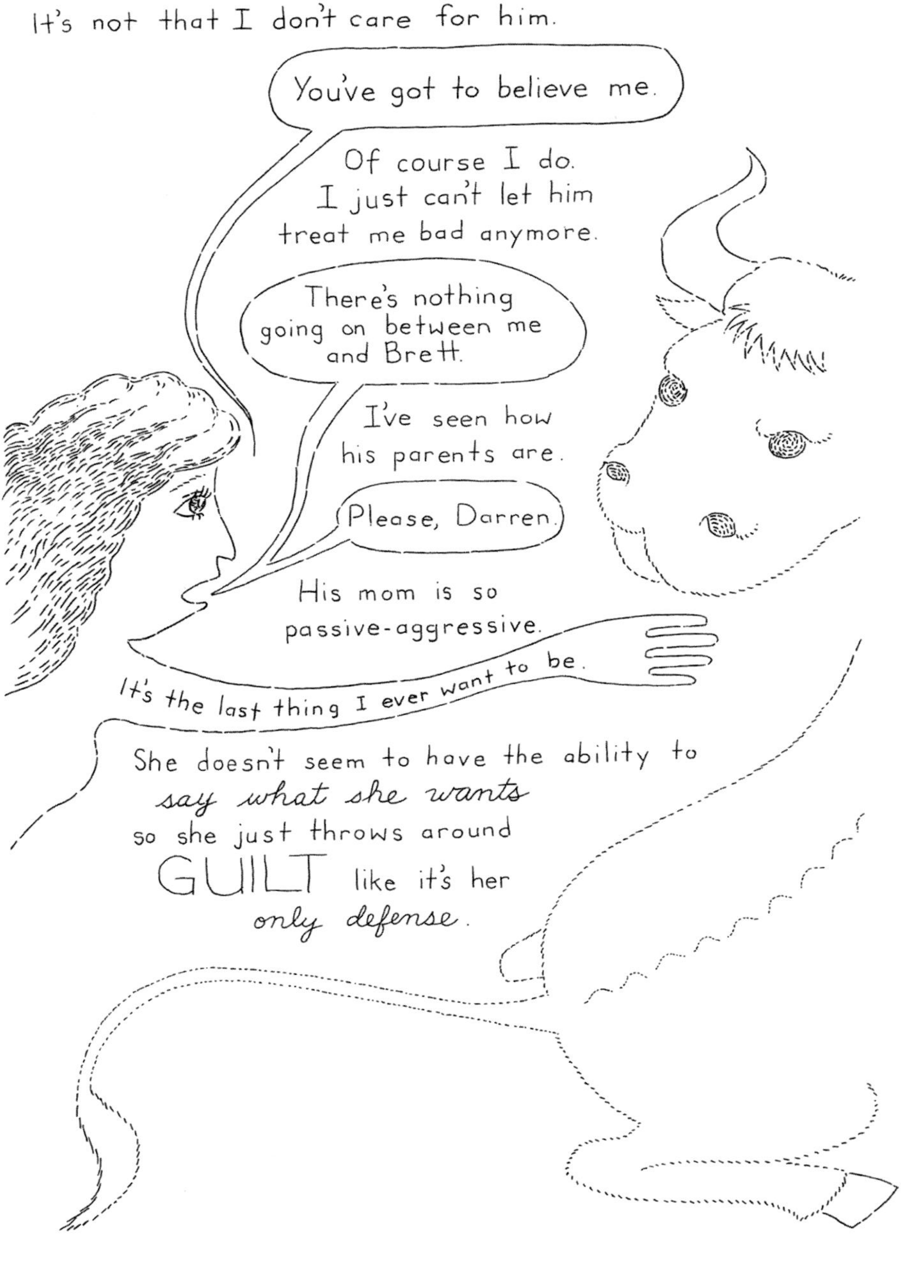
It's not that I don't care for him.
You've got to believe me.
Of course I do. I just can't let him treat me bad anymore.
There's nothing going on between me and Brett.
I've seen how his parents are.
Please, Darren.
His mom is so passive-aggressive.
It's the last thing I ever want to be.
She doesn't seem to have the ability to say what she wants so she just throws around GUILT like it's her only defense.

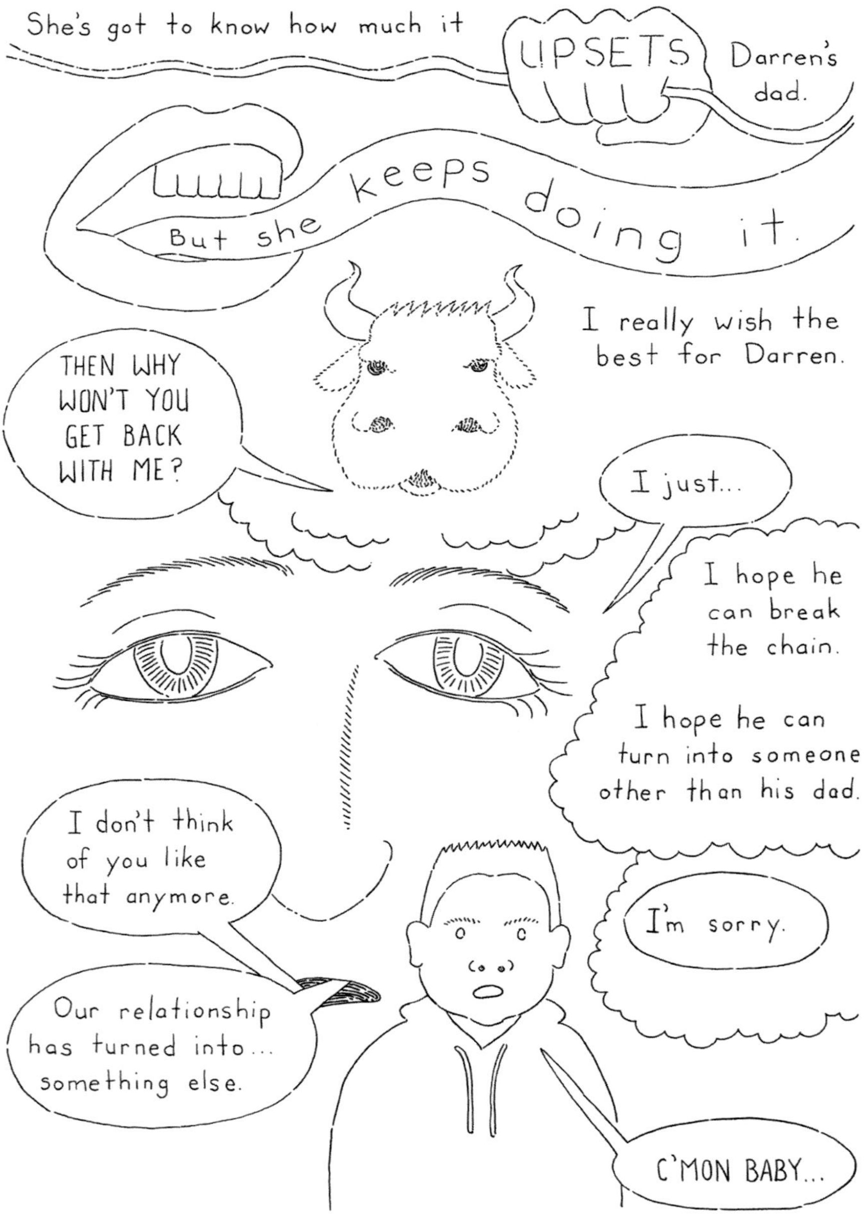

She's got to know how much it UPSETS Darren's dad.
But she keeps doing it.
I really wish the best for Darren.
THEN WHY WON'T YOU GET BACK WITH ME?
I just...
I hope he can break the chain.
I hope he can turn into someone other than his dad.
I don't think of you like that anymore.
I'm sorry.
Our relationship has turned into... something else.
C'MON BABY...

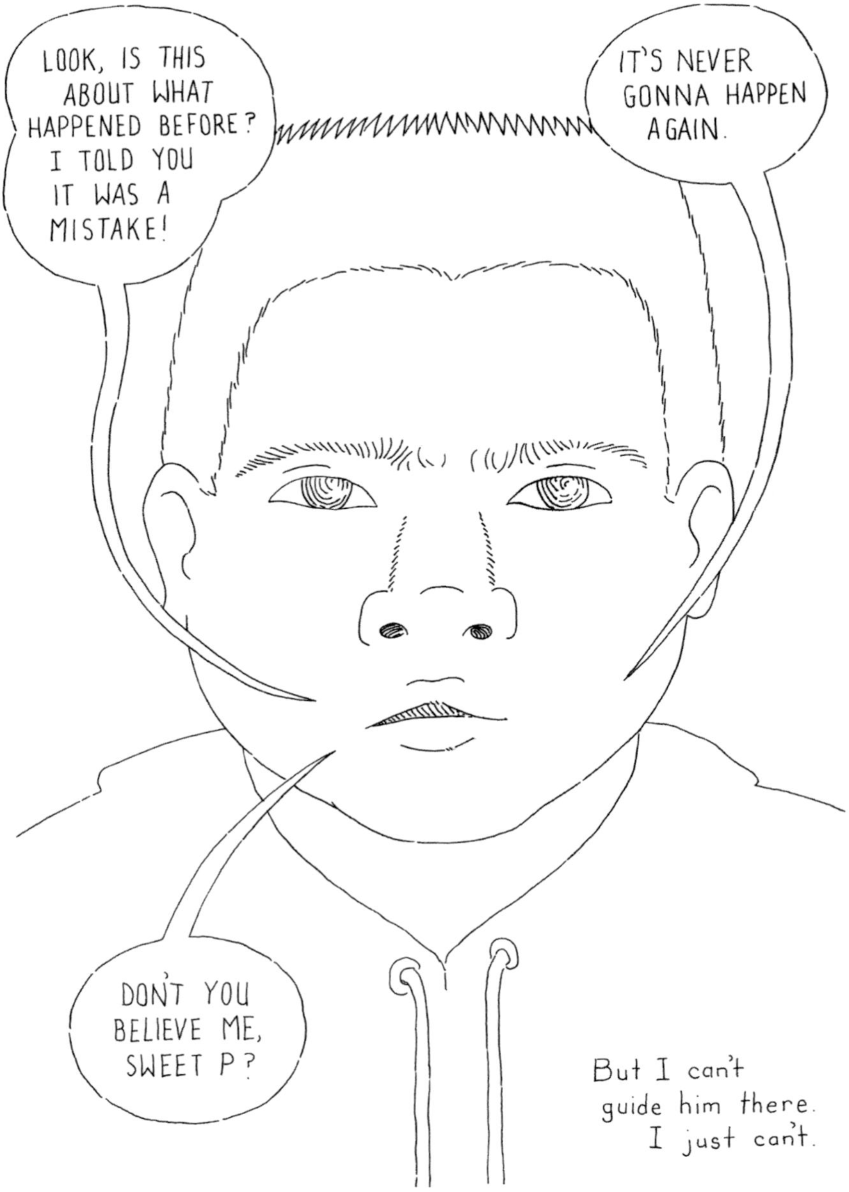
LOOK, IS THIS ABOUT WHAT HAPPENED BEFORE? I TOLD YOU IT WAS A MISTAKE!
IT'S NEVER GONNA HAPPEN AGAIN.
DON'T YOU BELIEVE ME, SWEET P?
But I can't guide him there. I just can't.

If Brett ever found out what Darren did to me, he would *LITERALLY KILL HIM.*

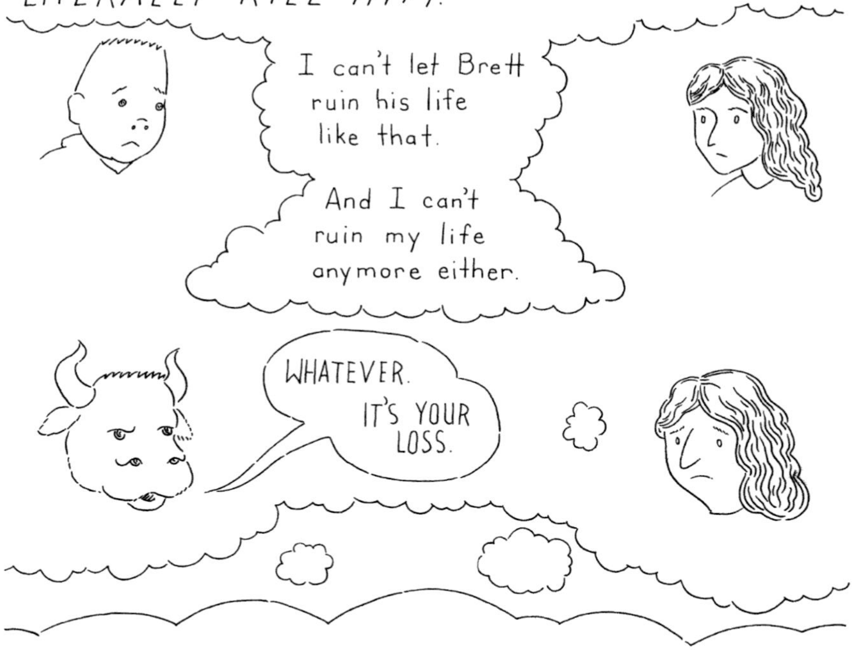

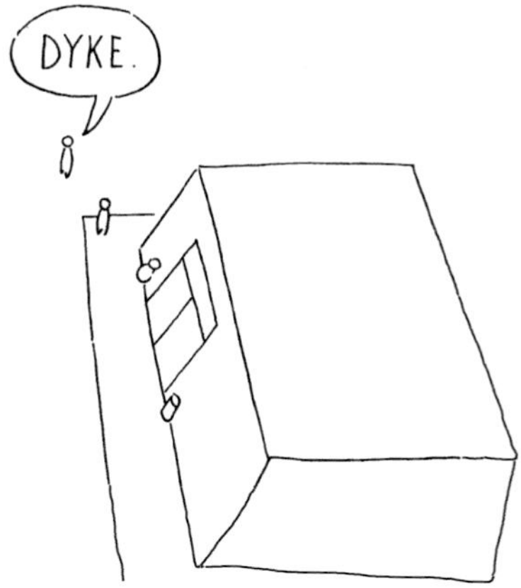

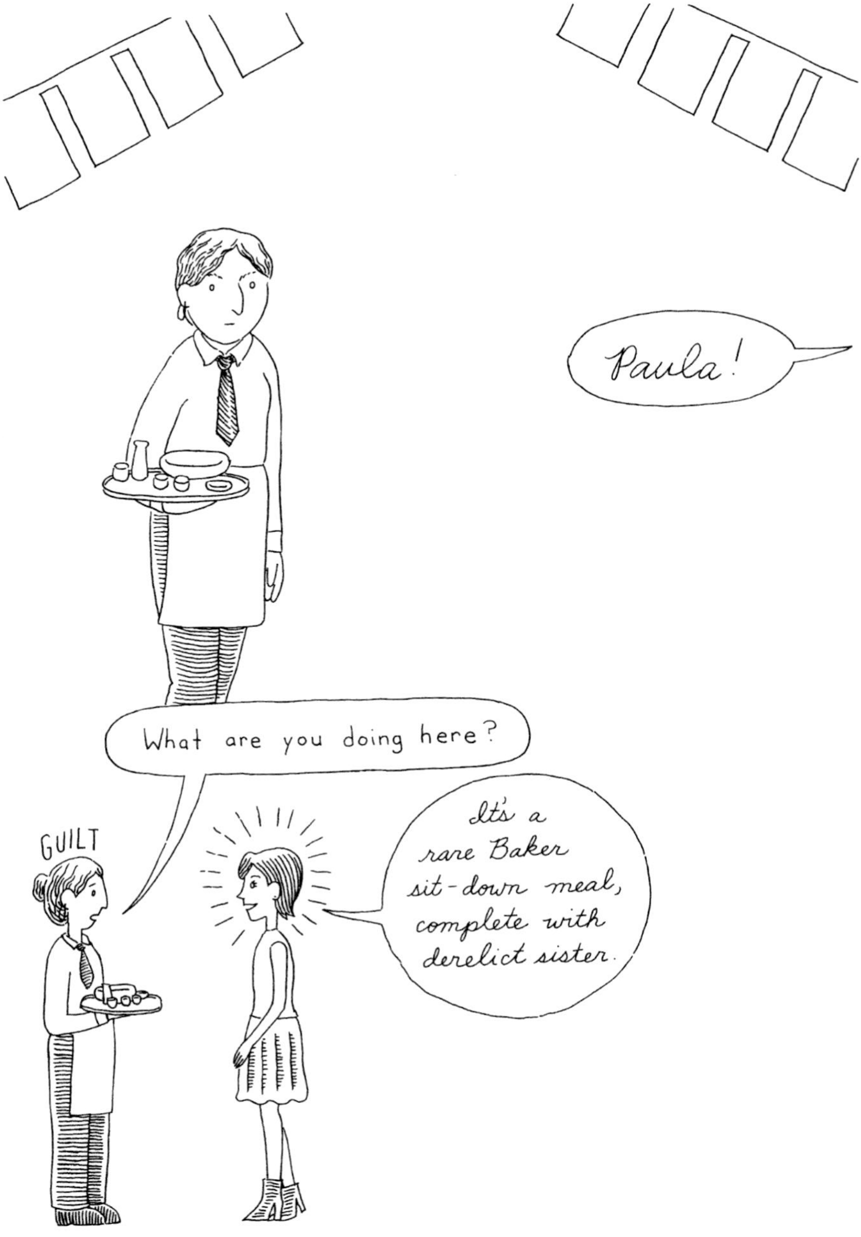
Paula!
What are you doing here?
GUILT
It's a rare Baker sit-down meal, complete with derelict sister.

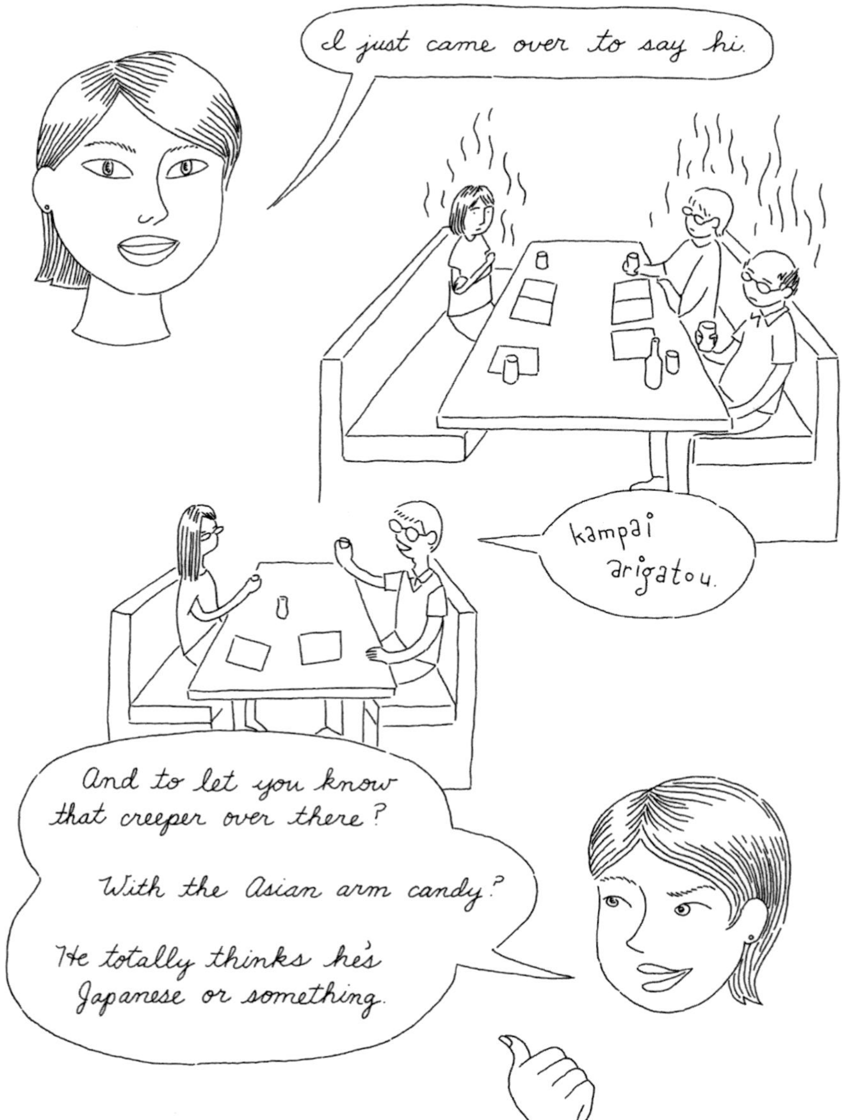
I just came over to say hi.
kampai arigatou.
And to let you know that creeper over there?
With the Asian arm candy?
He totally thinks he's Japanese or something.

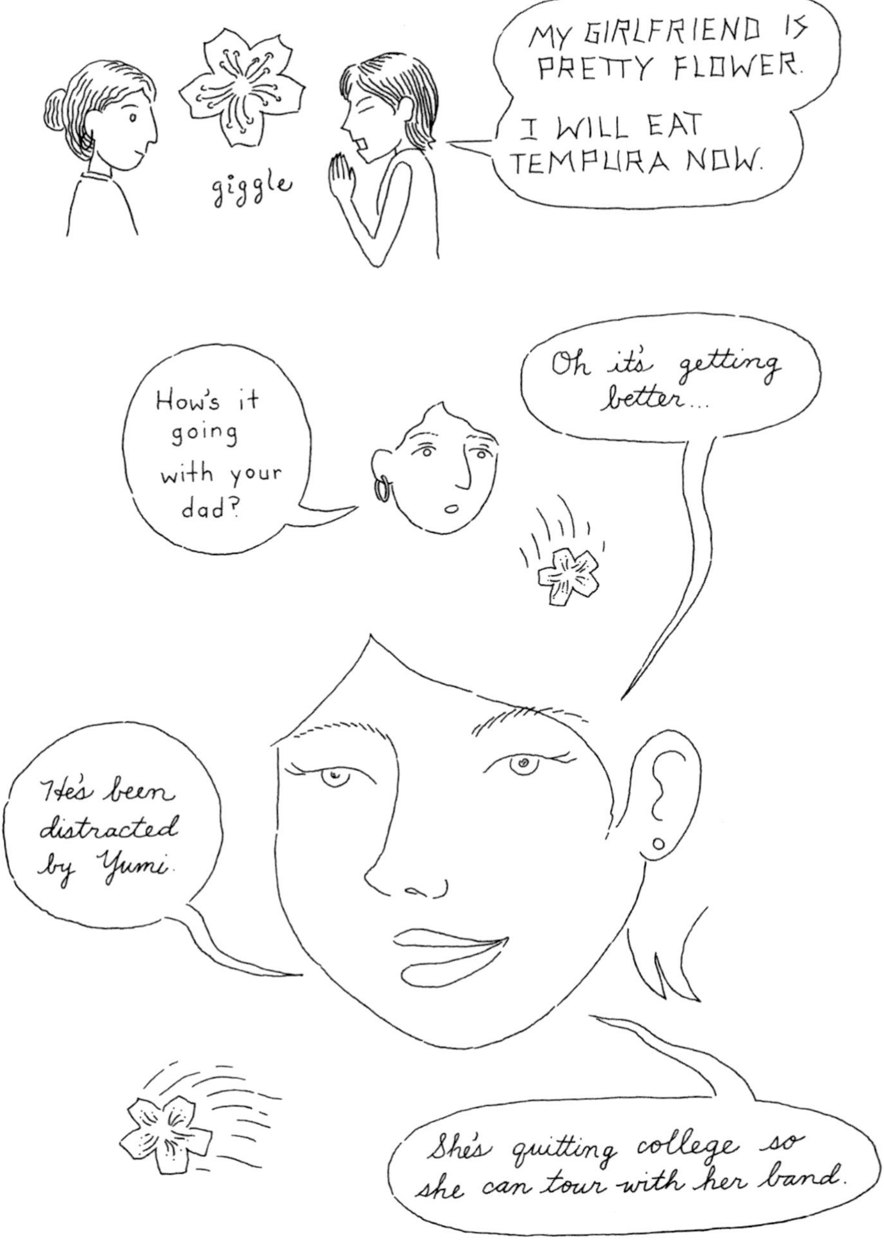
giggle
MY GIRLFRIEND IS PRETTY FLOWER.
I WILL EAT TEMPURA NOW.
How's it going with your dad?
Oh it's getting better...
He's been distracted by Yumi.
She's quitting college so she can tour with her band.

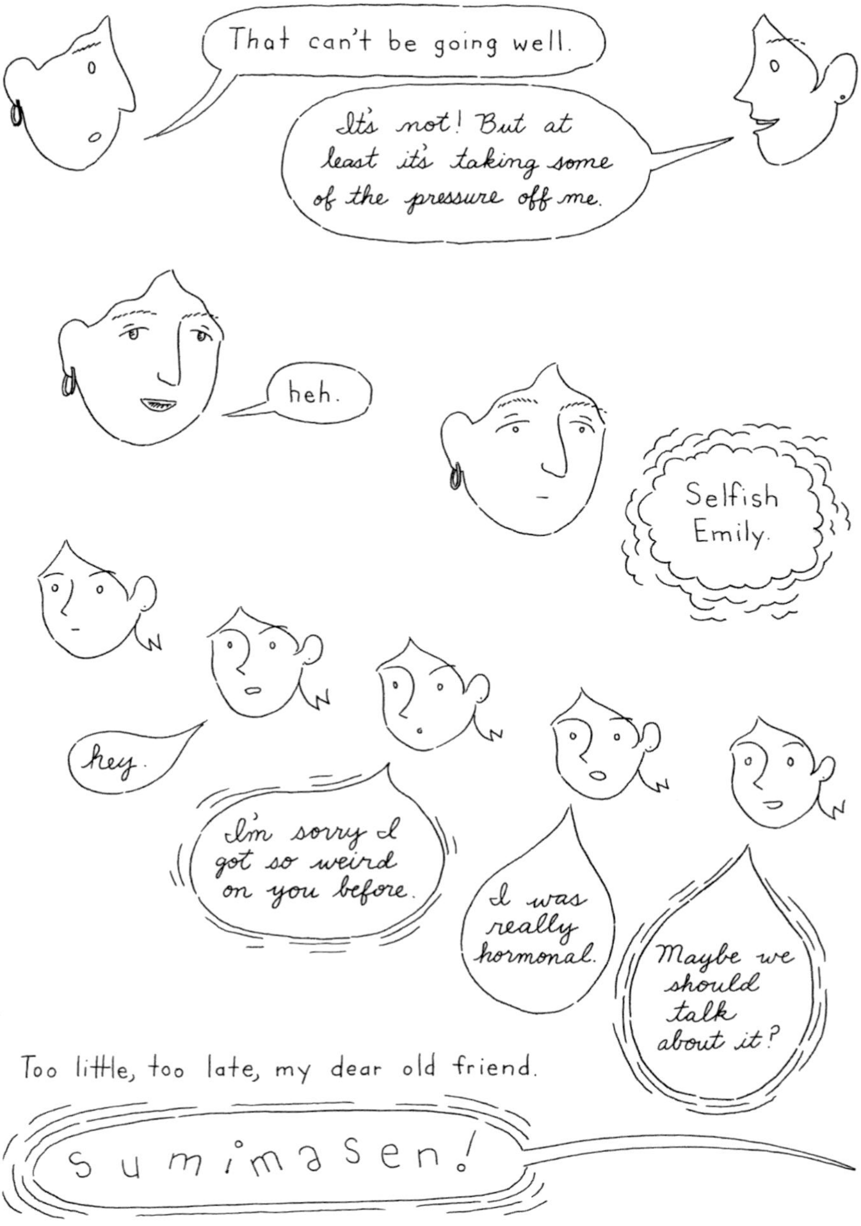
That can't be going well.
It's not! But at least it's taking some of the pressure off me.
heh.
Selfish Emily.
hey.
I'm sorry I got so weird on you before.
I was really hormonal.
Maybe we should talk about it?
Too little, too late, my dear old friend.
sumimasen!

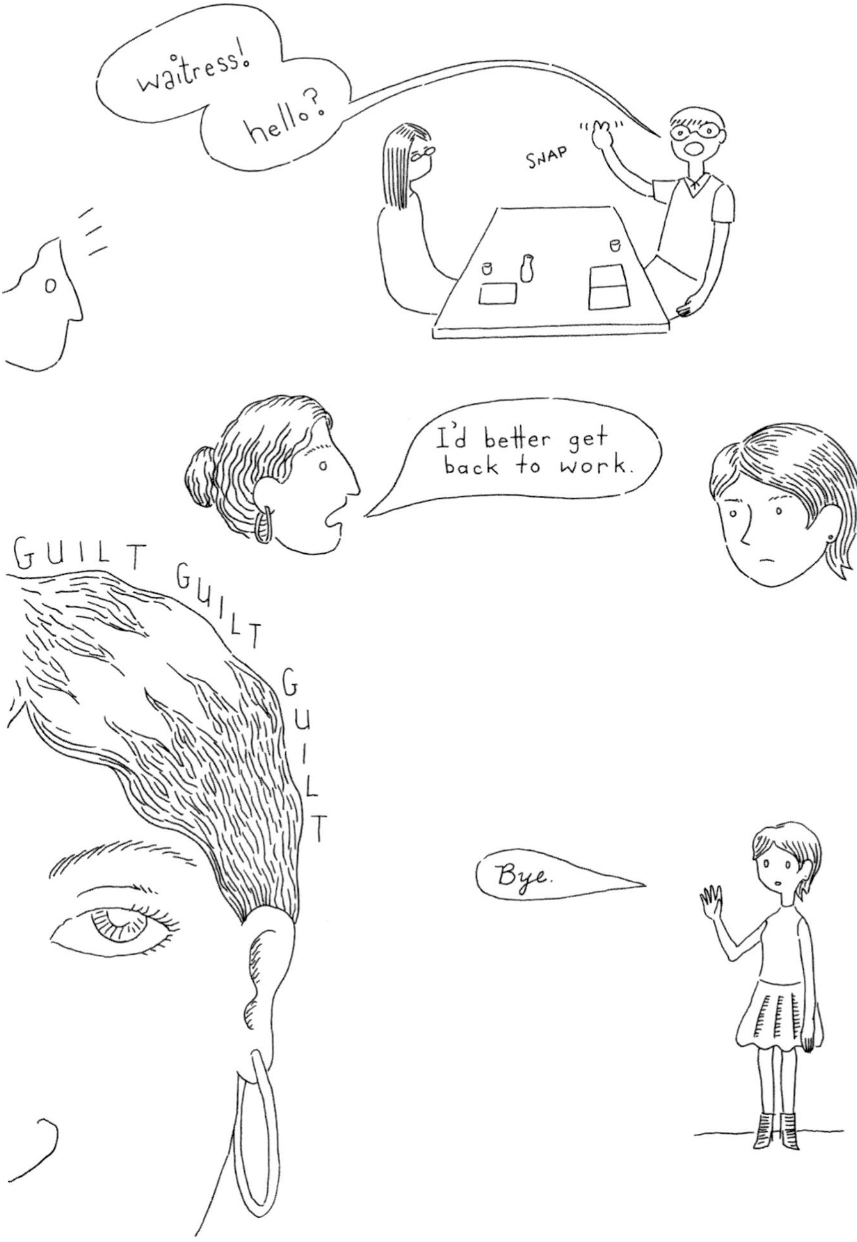
waitress!
hello?
SNAP
I'd better get back to work.
GUILT GUILT GUILT GUILT
Bye.

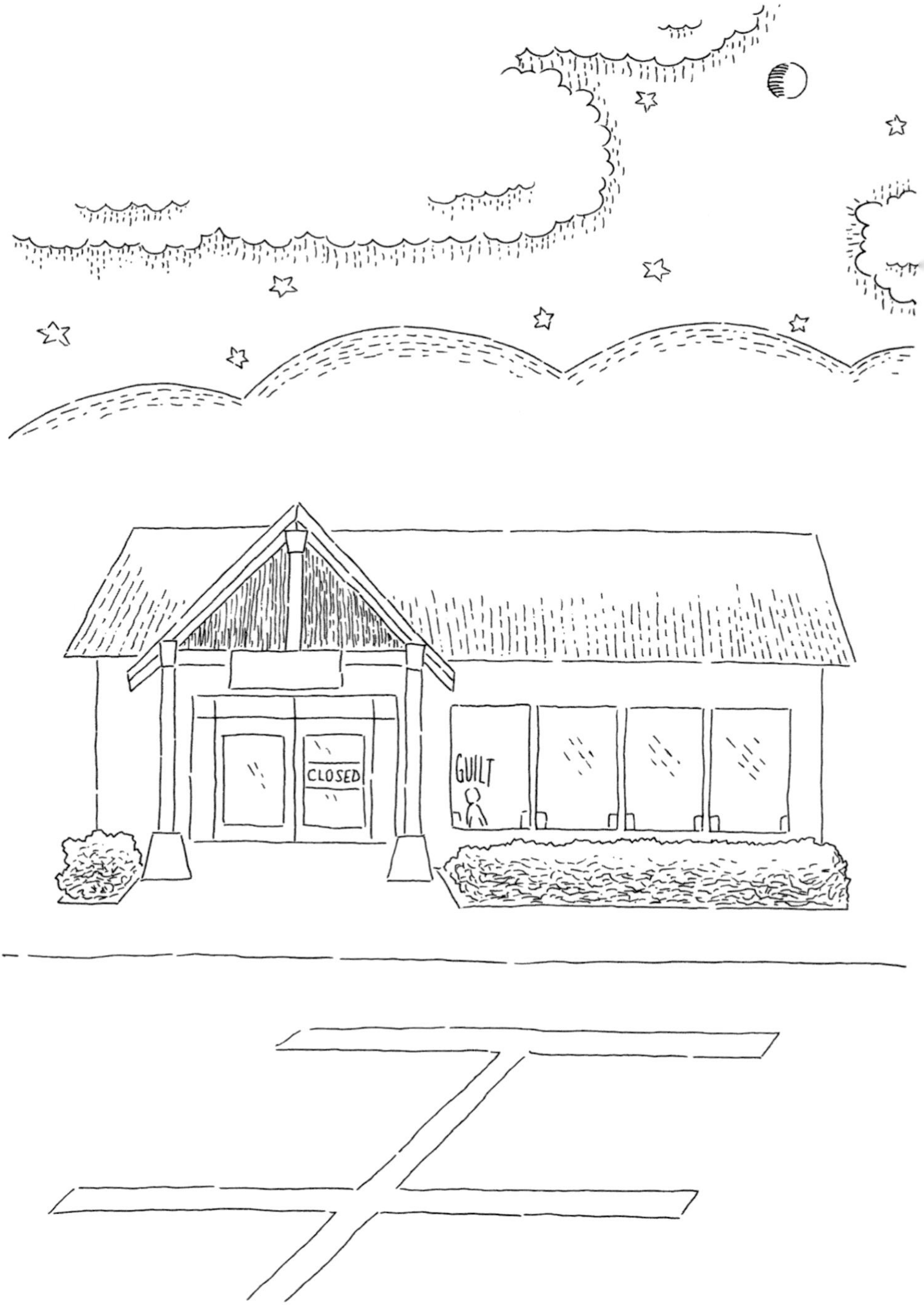
CLOSED
GUILT

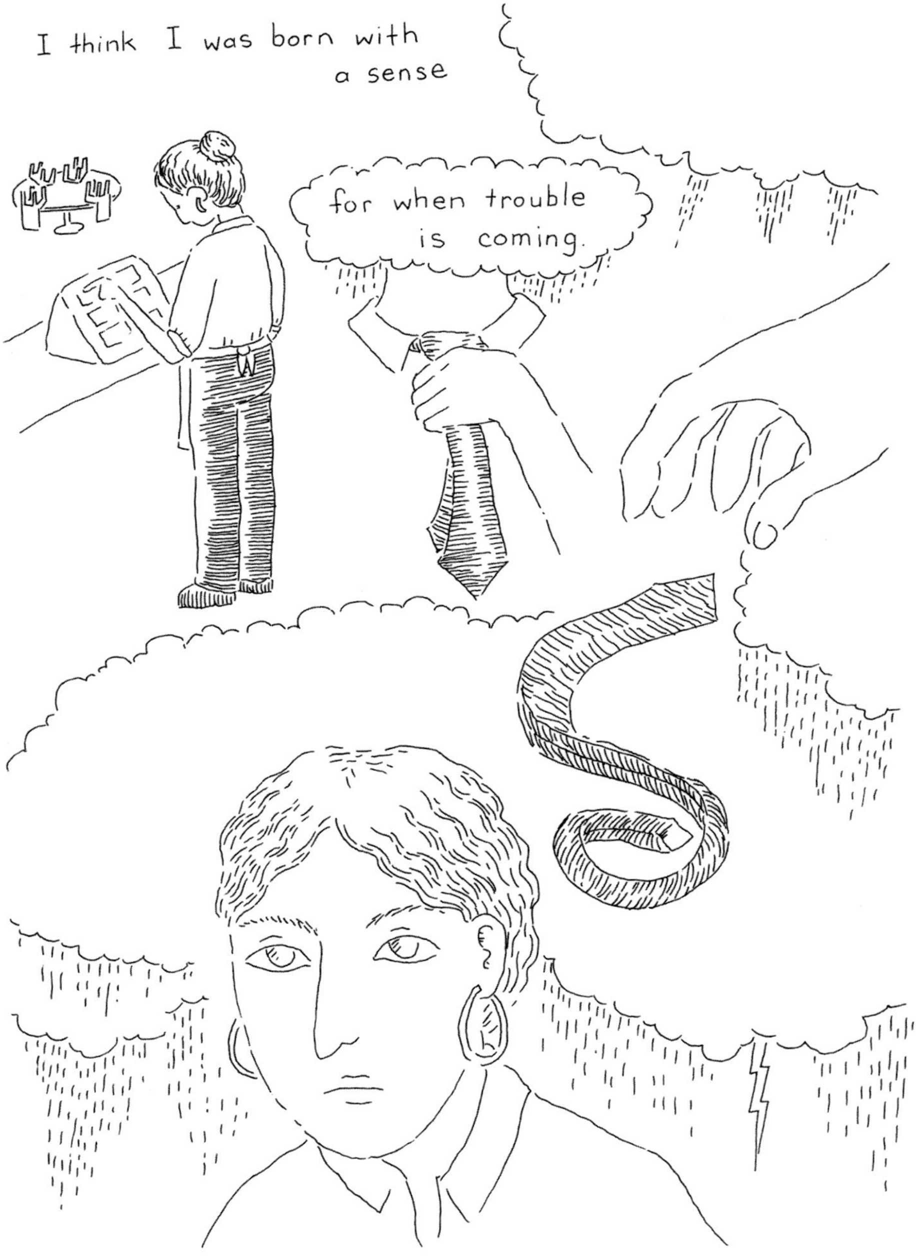
I think I was born with a sense
for when trouble is coming.

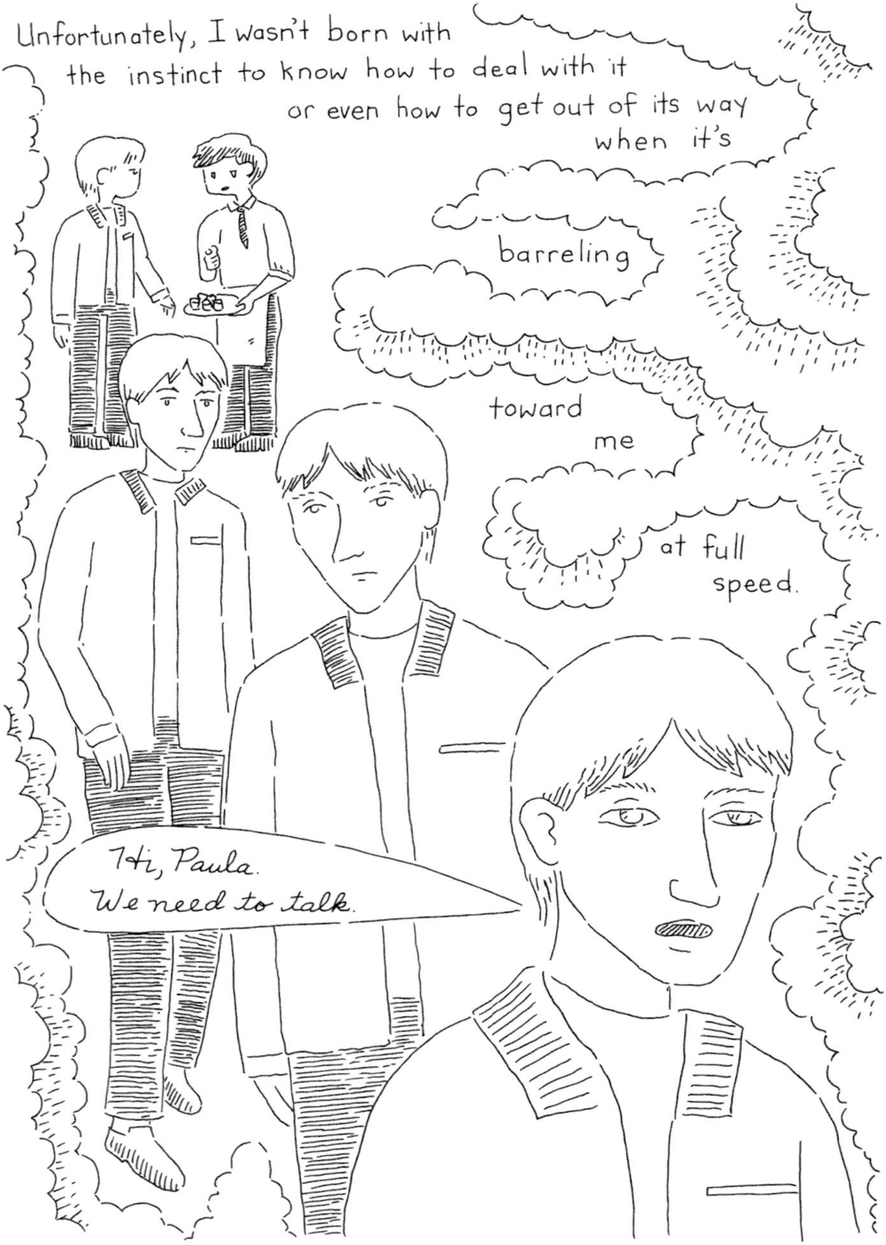
Unfortunately, I wasn't born with the instinct to know how to deal with it or even how to get out of its way when it's
barreling
toward me
at full speed.
Hi, Paula. We need to talk.

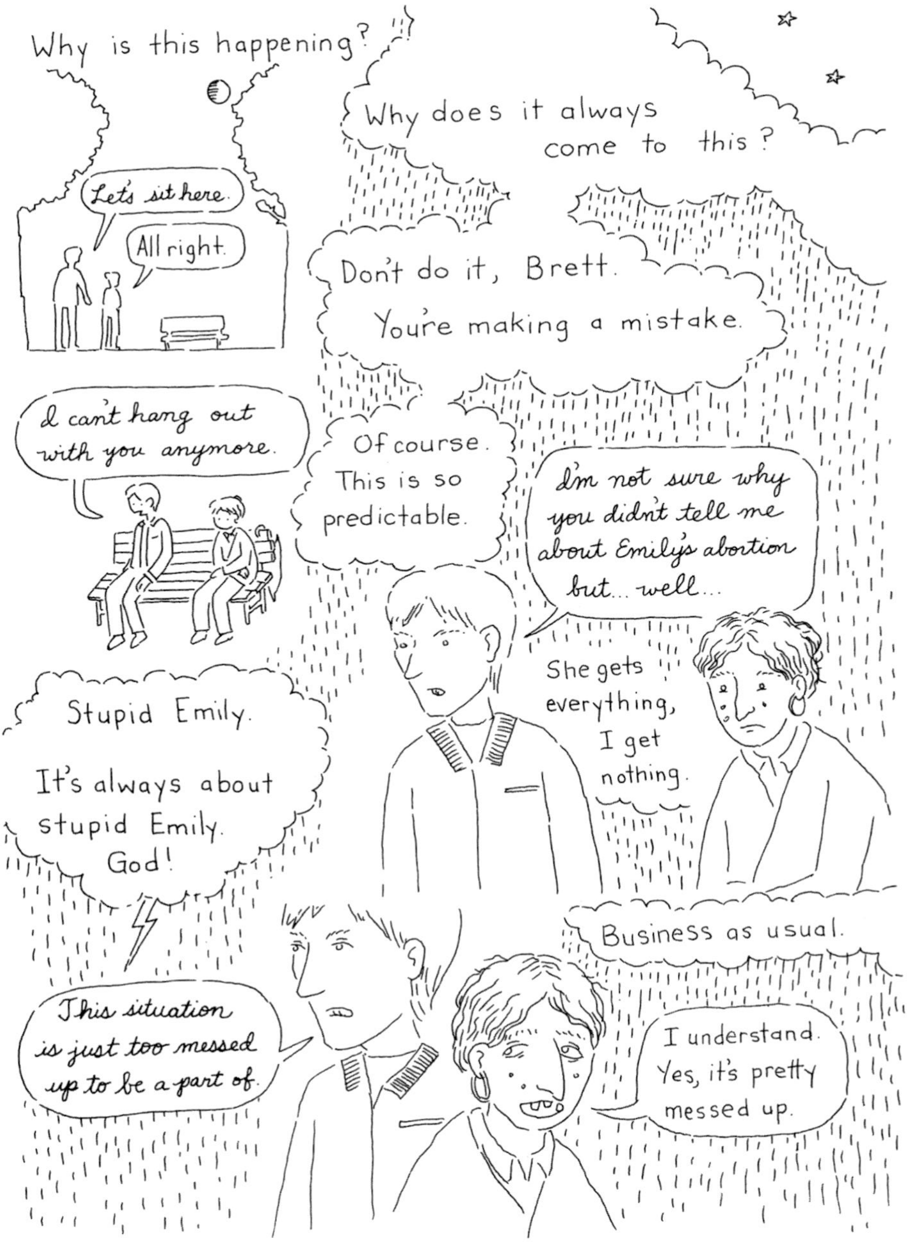

Why is this happening?
Why does it always come to this?
Let's sit here.
All right.
Don't do it, Brett. You're making a mistake.
I can't hang out with you anymore.
Of course. This is so predictable.
I'm not sure why you didn't tell me about Emily's abortion but... well...
Stupid Emily. It's always about stupid Emily. God!
She gets everything, I get nothing.
Business as usual.
This situation is just too messed up to be a part of.
I understand. Yes, it's pretty messed up.

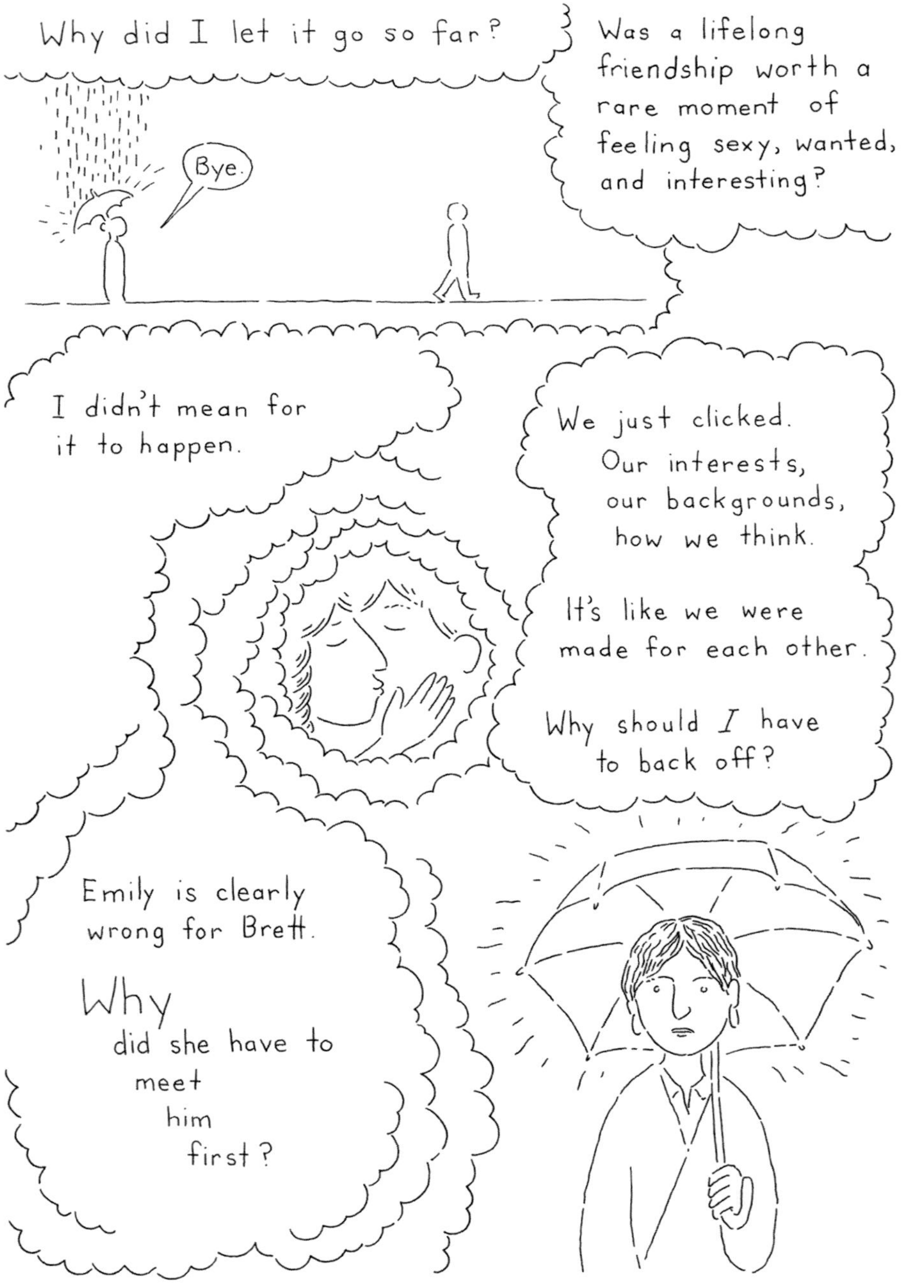
Why did I let it go so far?
Bye.
Was a lifelong friendship worth a rare moment of feeling sexy, wanted, and interesting?
I didn't mean for it to happen.
We just clicked. Our interests, our backgrounds, how we think.
It's like we were made for each other.
Why should *I* have to back off?
Emily is clearly wrong for Brett.
Why did she have to meet him first?

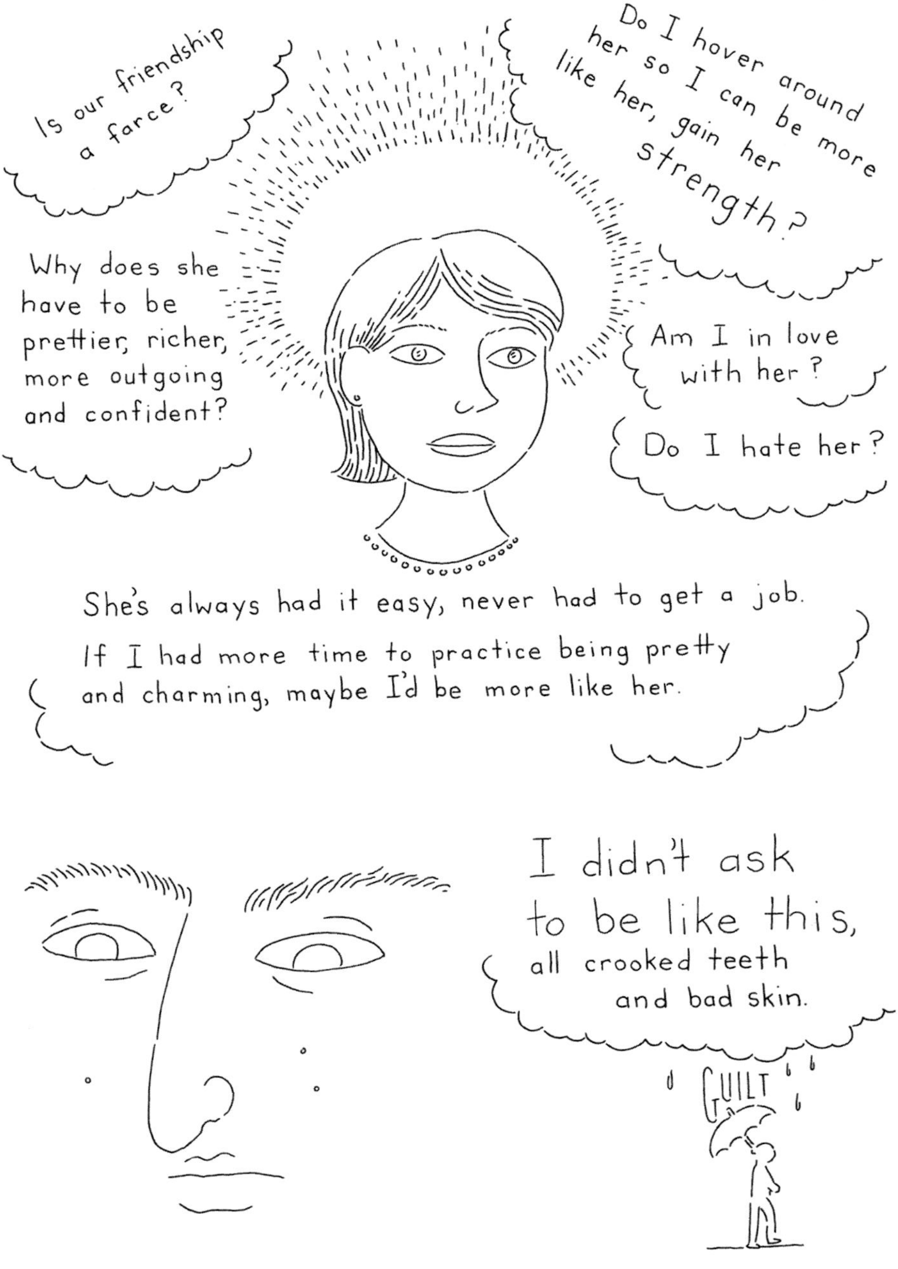
Is our friendship a farce?
Do I hover around her so I can be more like her, gain her strength?
Why does she have to be prettier, richer, more outgoing and confident?
Am I in love with her?
Do I hate her?
She's always had it easy, never had to get a job.
If I had more time to practice being pretty and charming, maybe I'd be more like her.
I didn't ask to be like this, all crooked teeth and bad skin.
GUILT

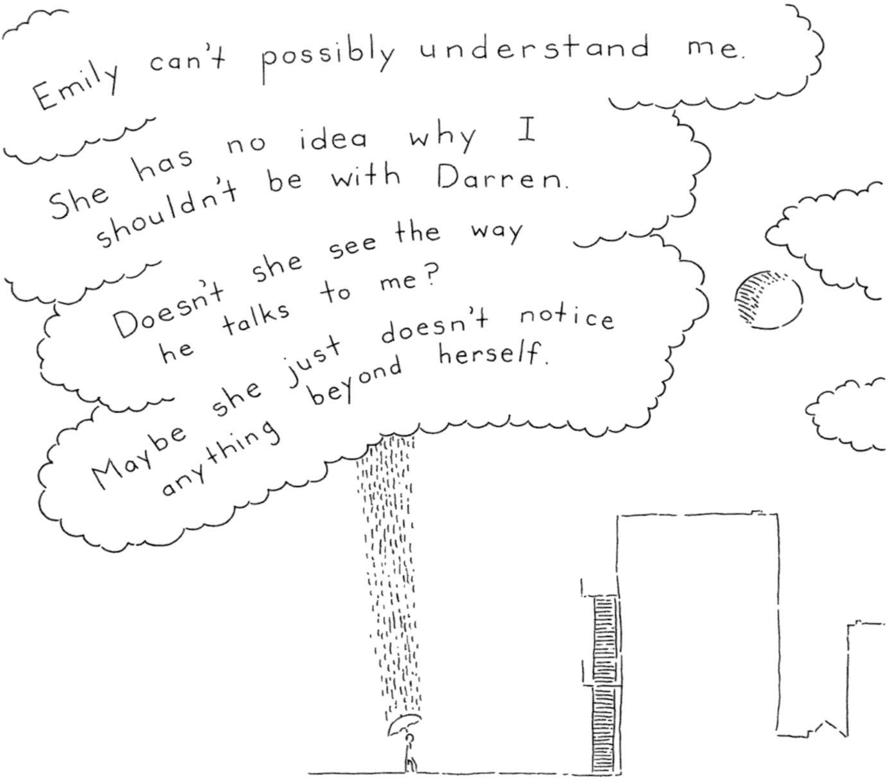
Emily can't possibly understand me.
She has no idea why I shouldn't be with Darren.
Doesn't she see the way he talks to me?
Maybe she just doesn't notice anything beyond herself.

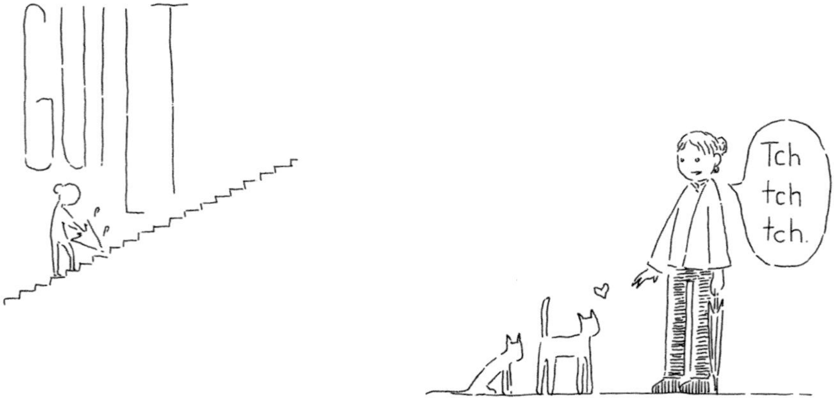
GUILT
Tch tch tch.

How are you doing, little guy?

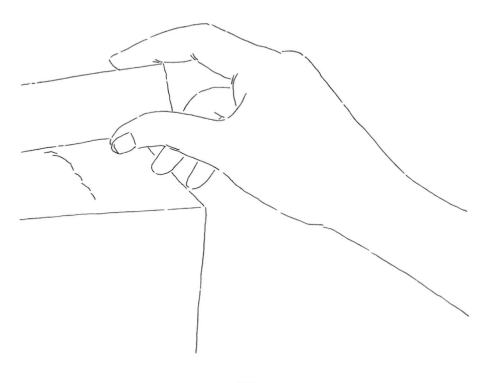

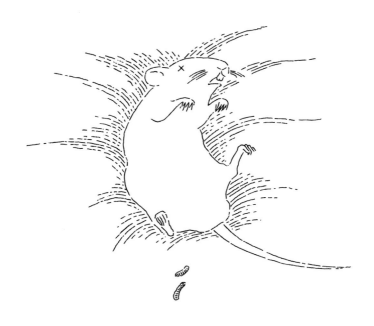

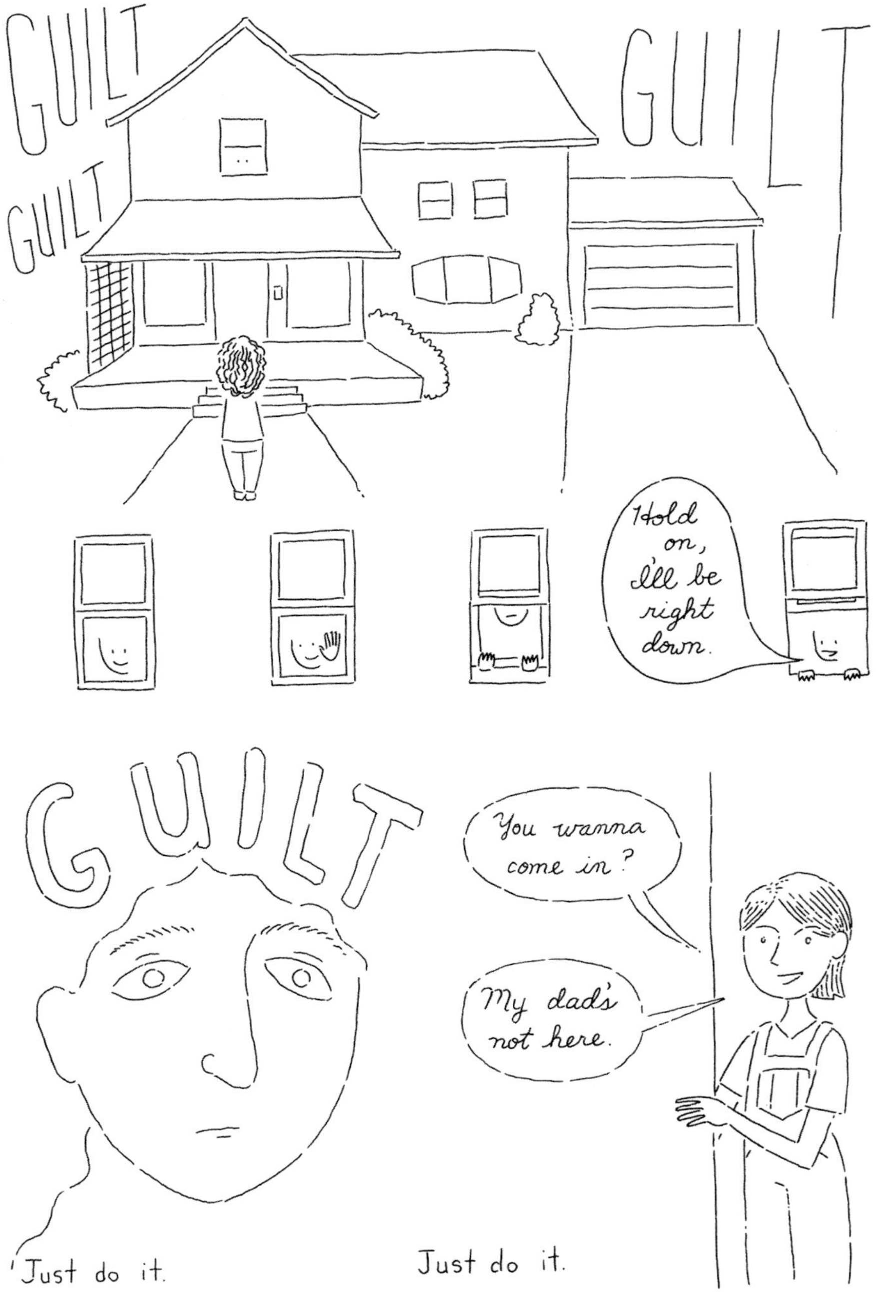
GUILT
GUILT
GUILT
Hold on, I'll be right down.
GUILT
You wanna come in?
My dad's not here.
Just do it.
Just do it.

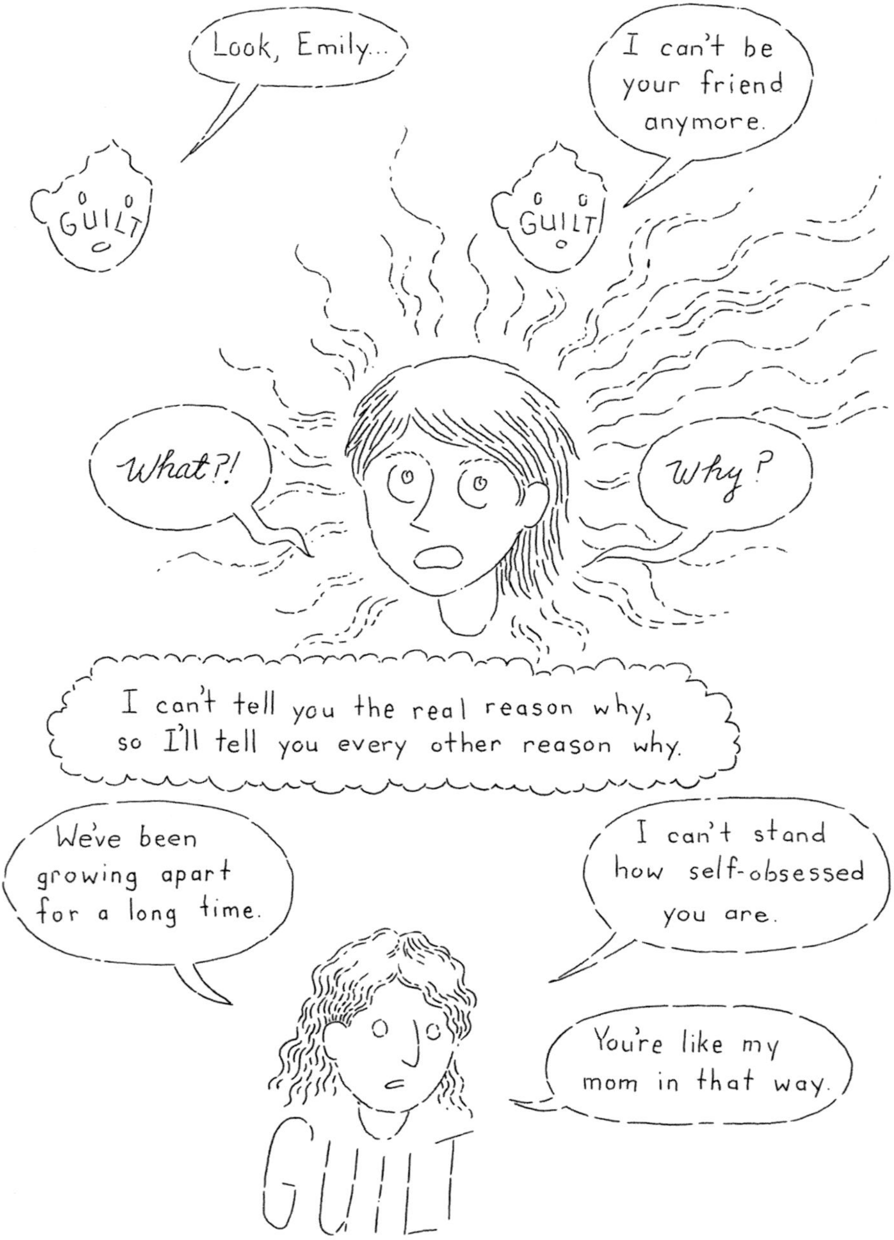
Look, Emily...
GUILT
I can't be your friend anymore.
GUILT
What?!
Why?
I can't tell you the real reason why, so I'll tell you every other reason why.
We've been growing apart for a long time.
I can't stand how self-obsessed you are.
You're like my mom in that way.
GUILT

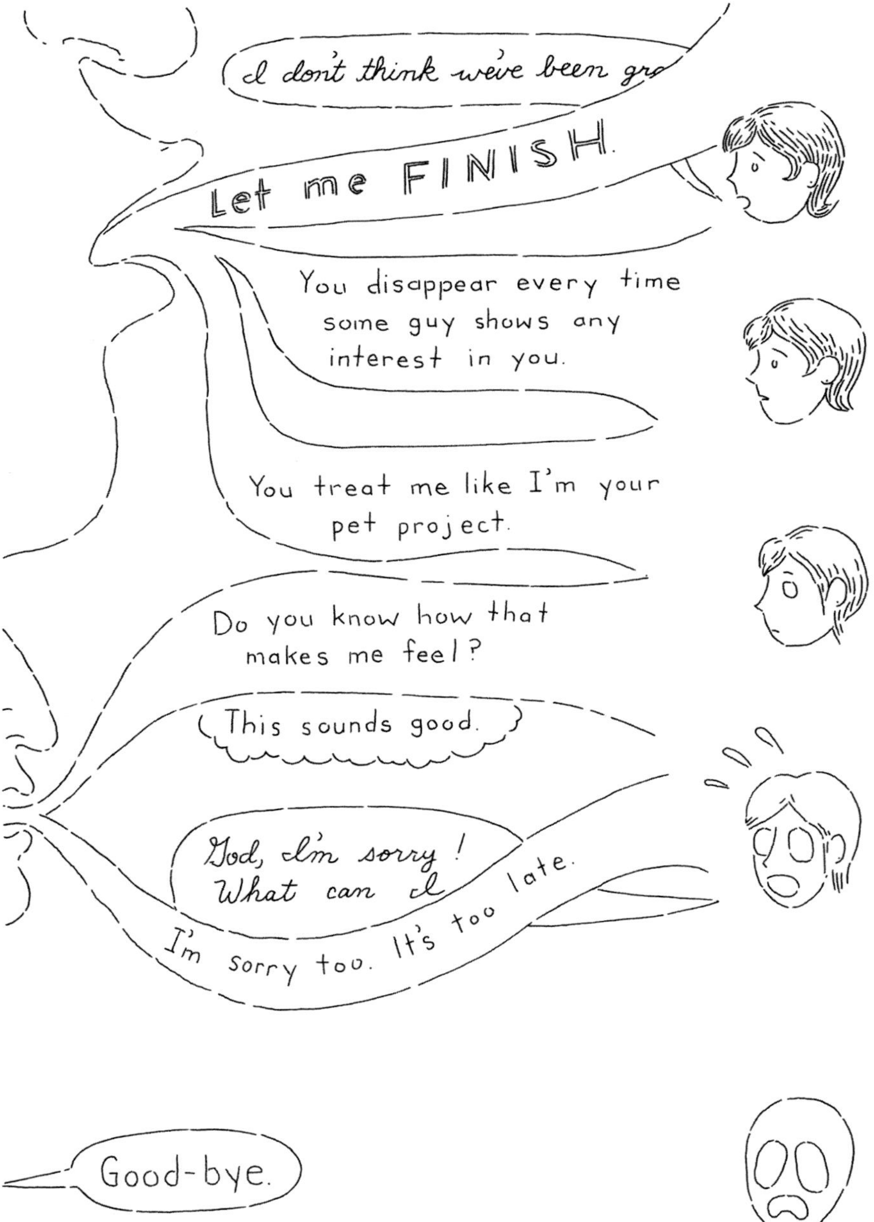
I don't think we've been gr
Let me FINISH.
You disappear every time some guy shows any interest in you.
You treat me like I'm your pet project.
Do you know how that makes me feel?
This sounds good.
God, I'm sorry! What can I
I'm sorry too. It's too late.
Good-bye.

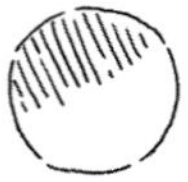

I can't believe it was so simple to cut an integral person from my life.

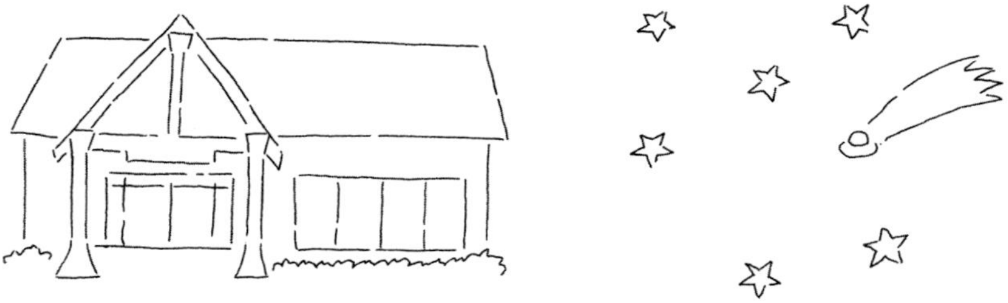

I did it, just like that.

It was the right thing to do, wasn't it?

I can barely look her in the eyes.

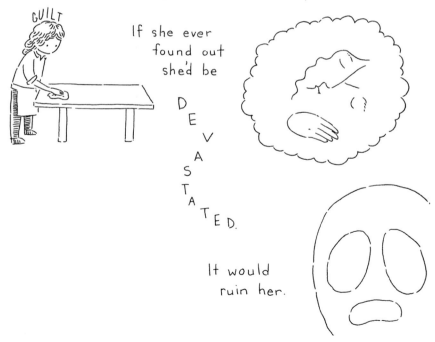

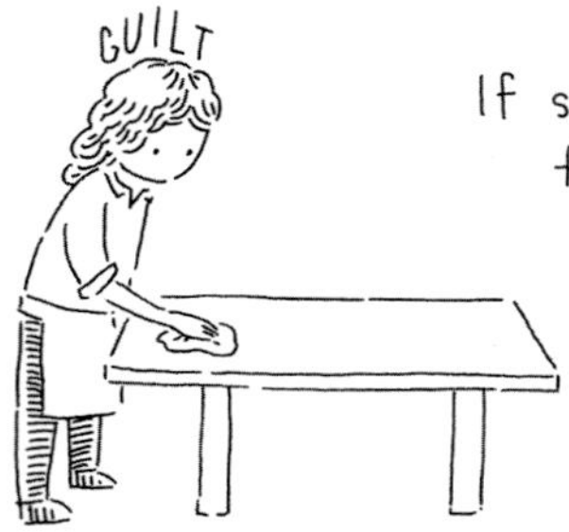
GUILT

If she ever found out she'd be

DEVASTATED.

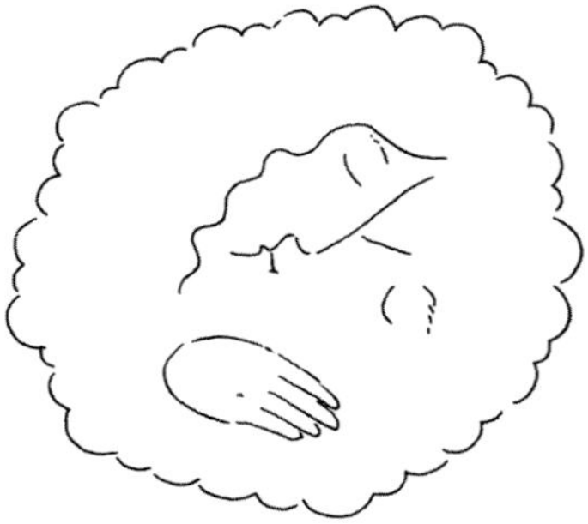

It would ruin her.

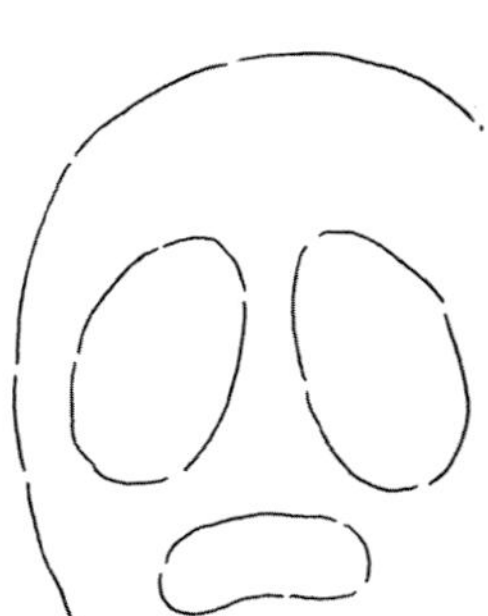

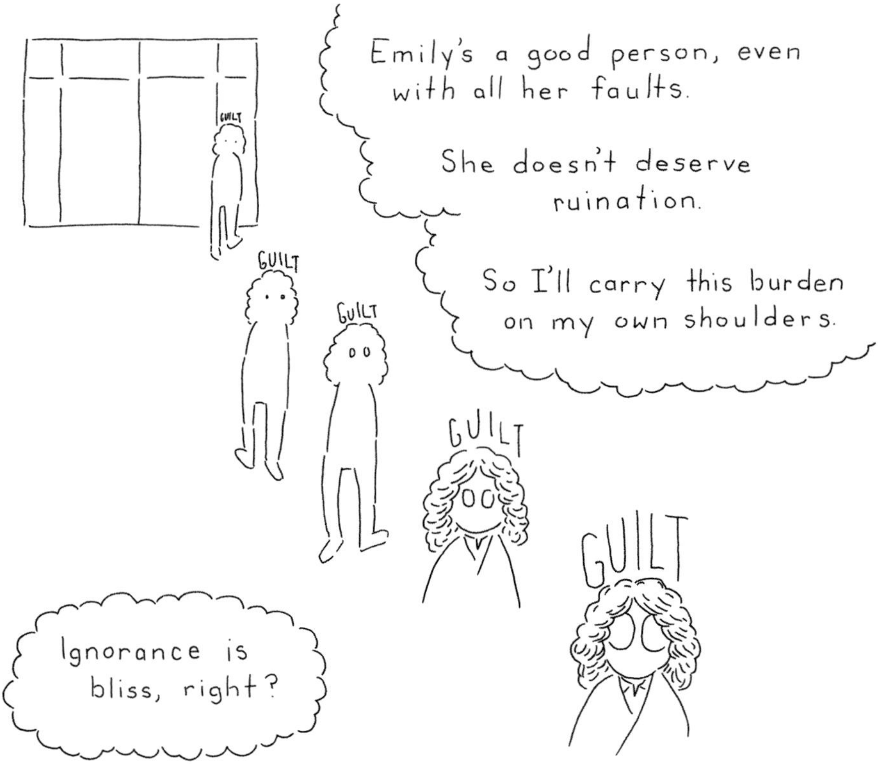
Emily's a good person, even with all her faults.
She doesn't deserve ruination.
So I'll carry this burden on my own shoulders.
GUILT
GUILT
GUILT
GUILT
GUILT
Ignorance is bliss, right?

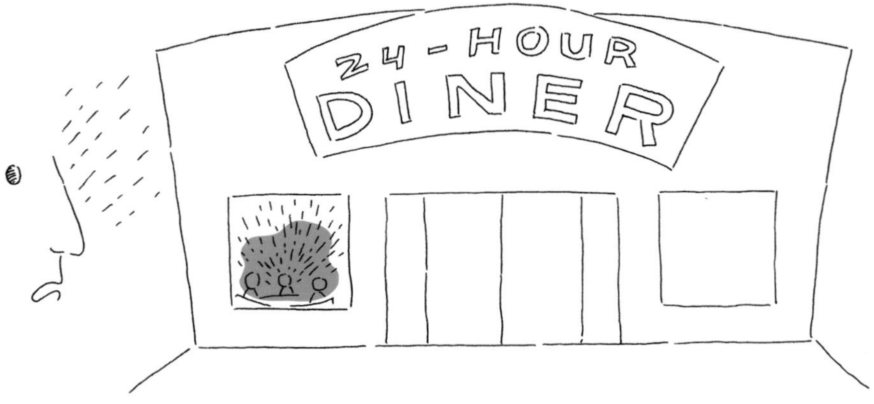
24-HOUR DINER

That girl looks just like...

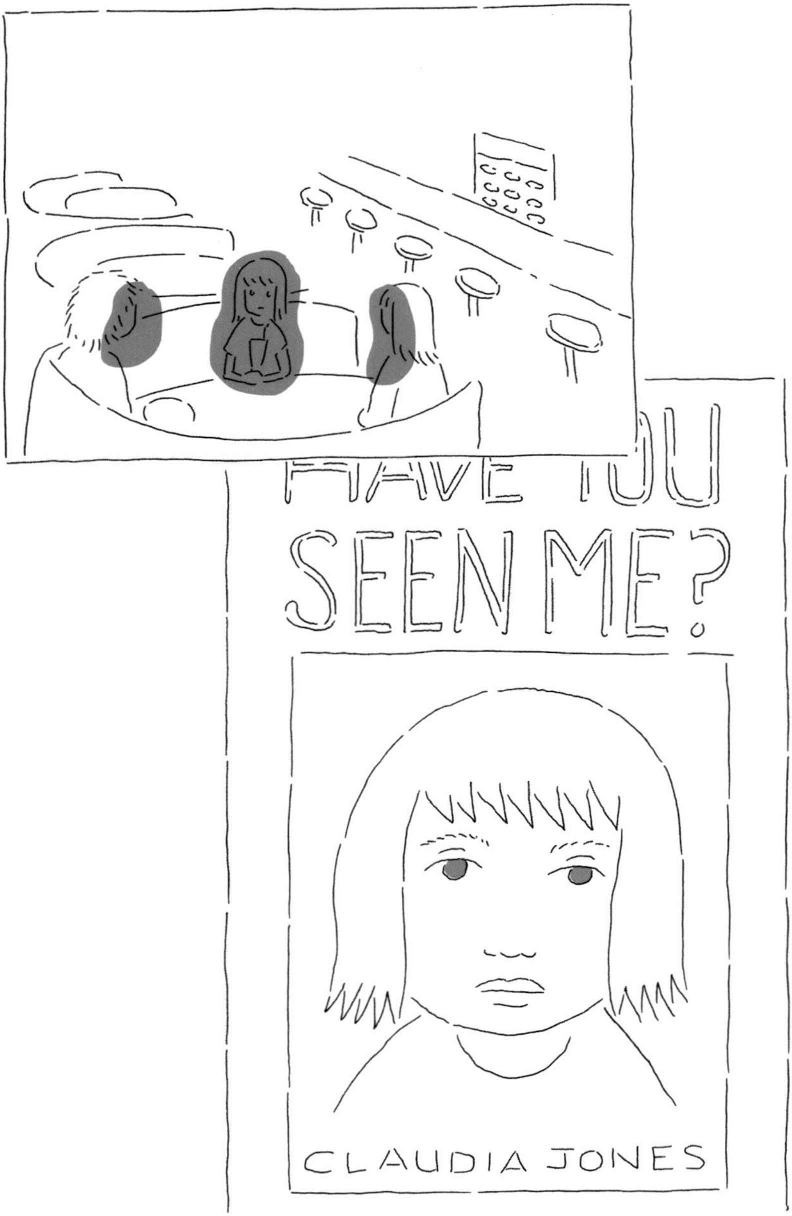
SEEN ME?
CLAUDIA JONES

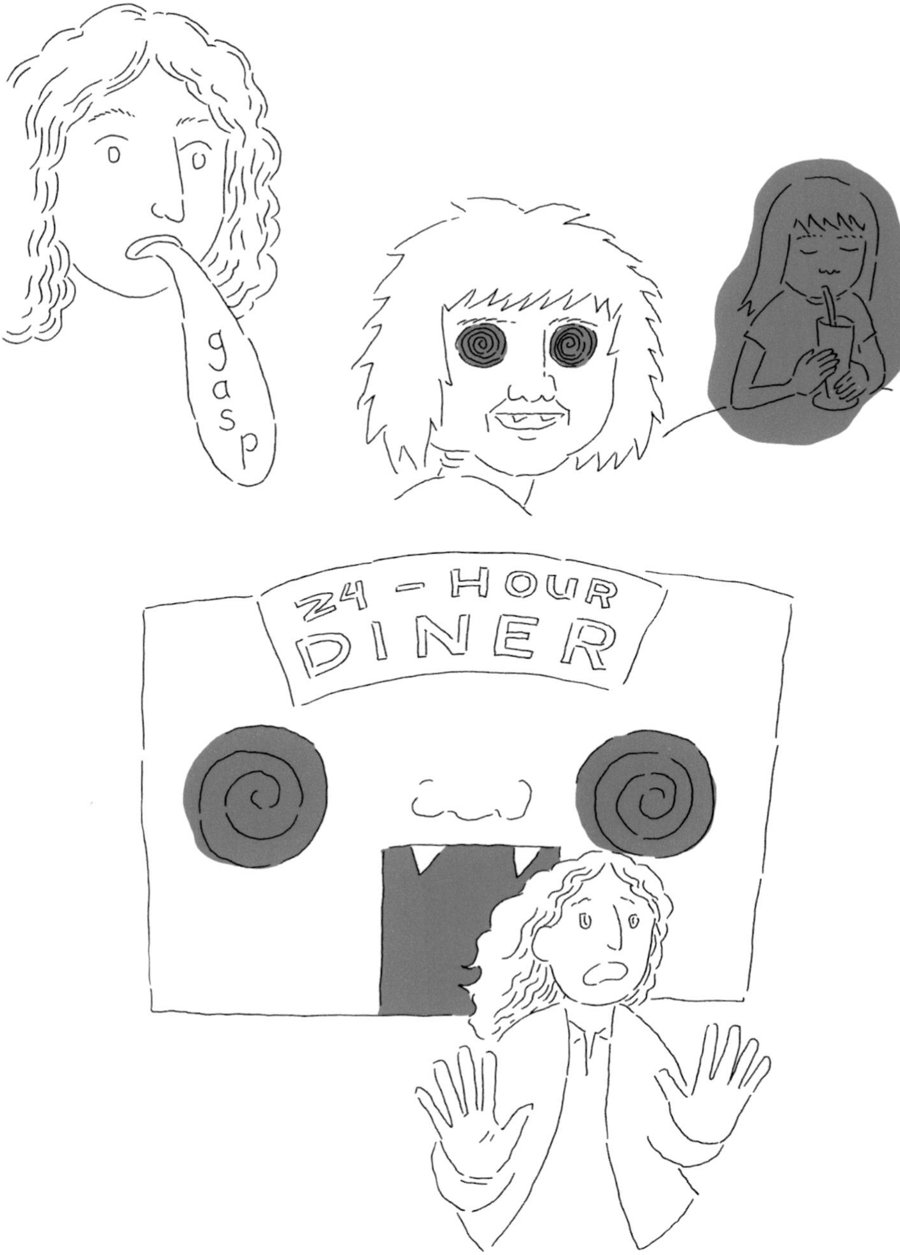
gasp
24-HOUR
DINER

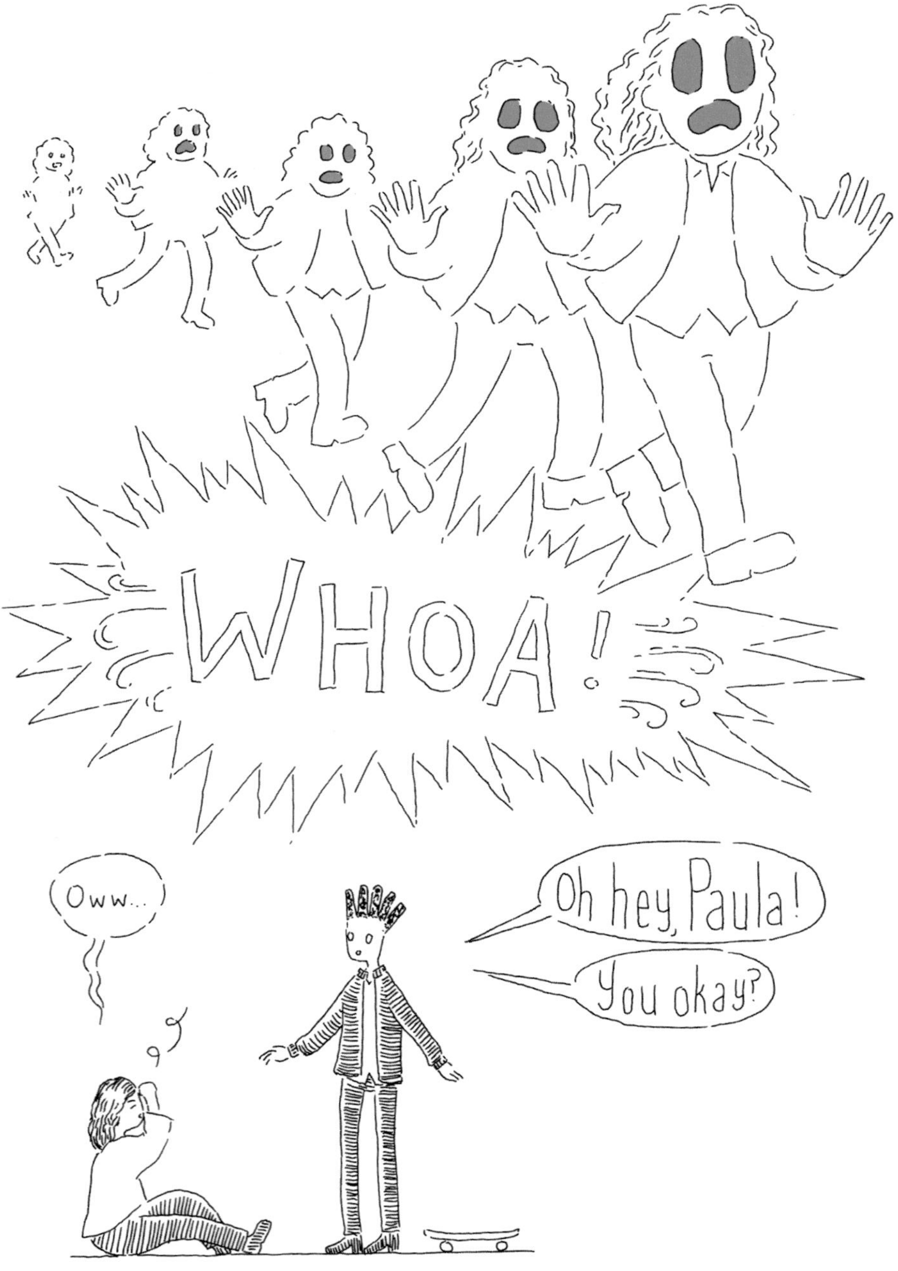
WHOA!
Oww...
Oh hey, Paula!
You okay?

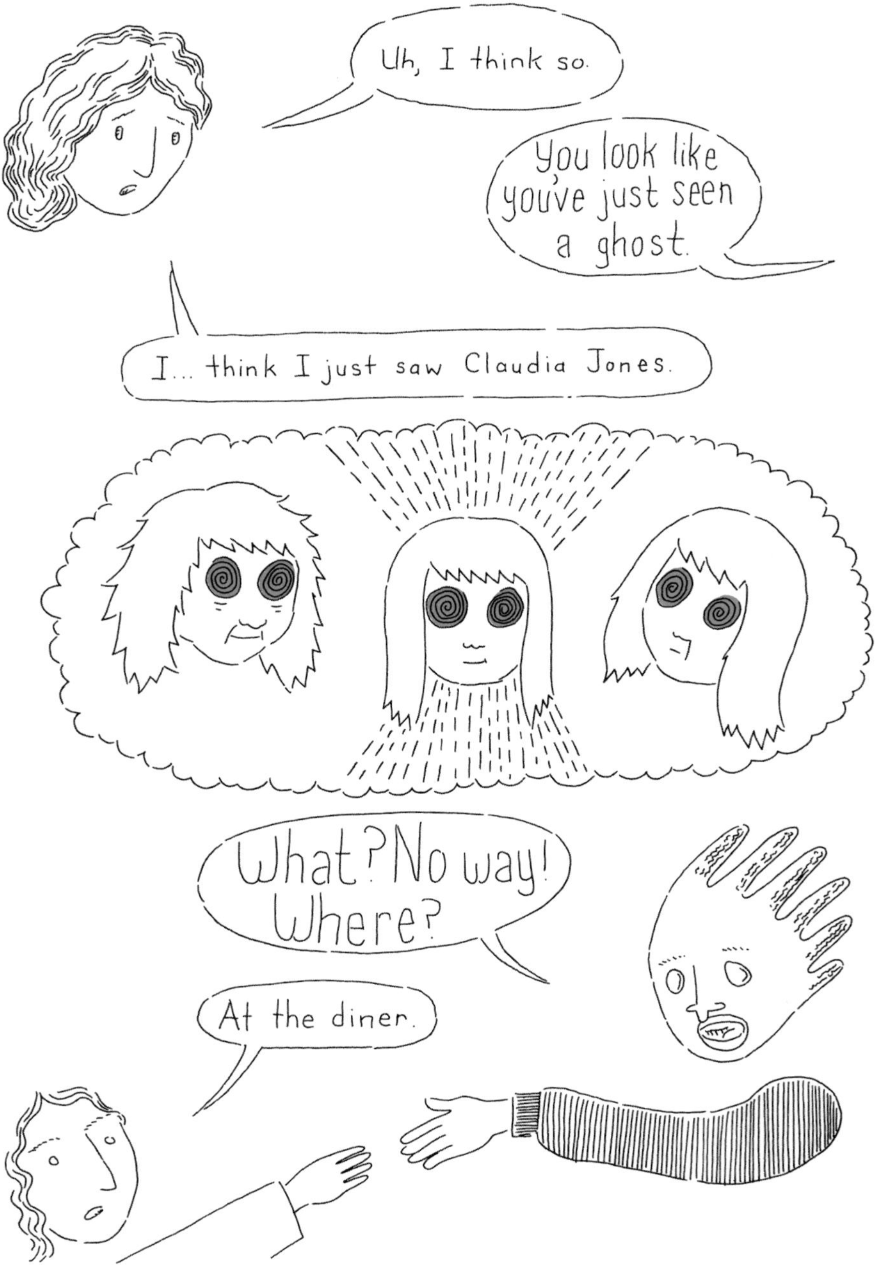
Uh, I think so.
You look like you've just seen a ghost.
I... think I just saw Claudia Jones.
What? No way! Where?
At the diner.

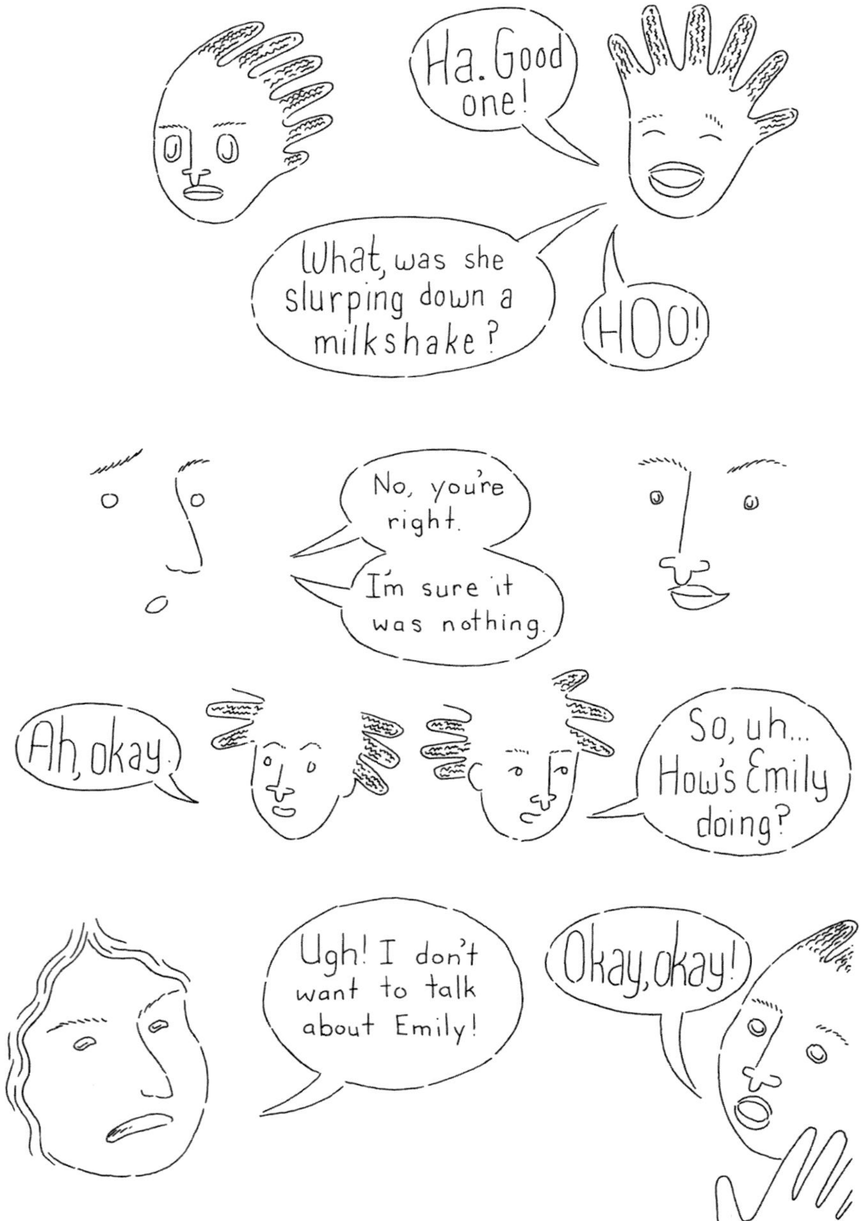
Ha. Good one!
What, was she slurping down a milkshake?
HOO!
No, you're right.
I'm sure it was nothing.
Ah, okay.
So, uh... How's Emily doing?
Ugh! I don't want to talk about Emily!
Okay, okay!

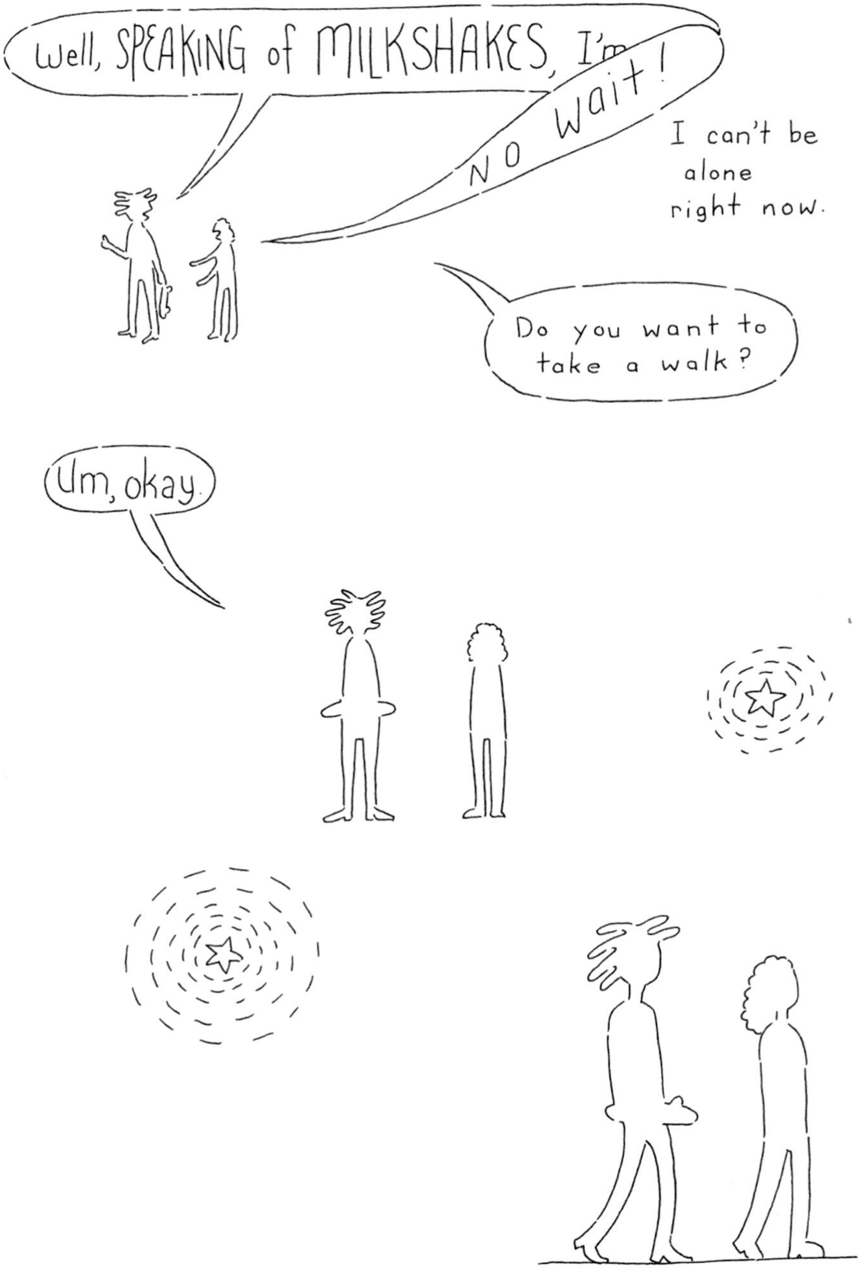
Well, SPEAKING of MILKSHAKES, I'm
NO wait!
I can't be alone right now.
Do you want to take a walk?
Um, okay.

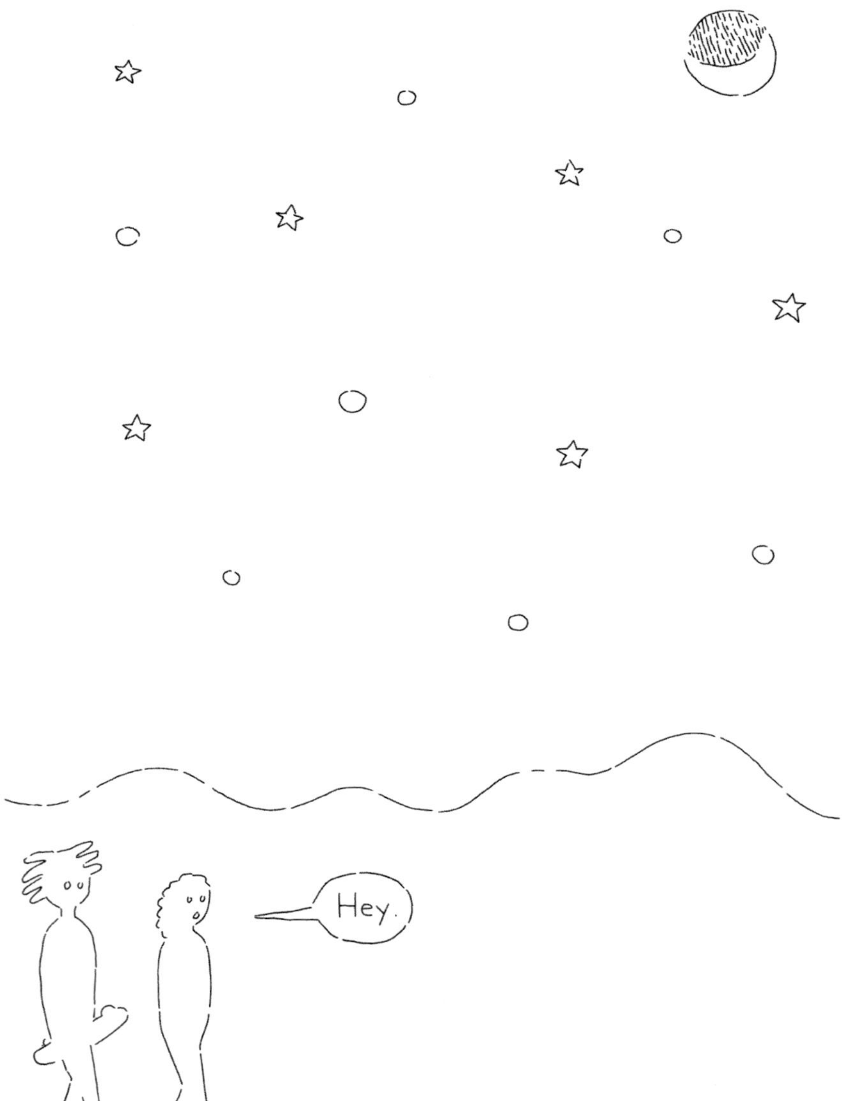
Hey.

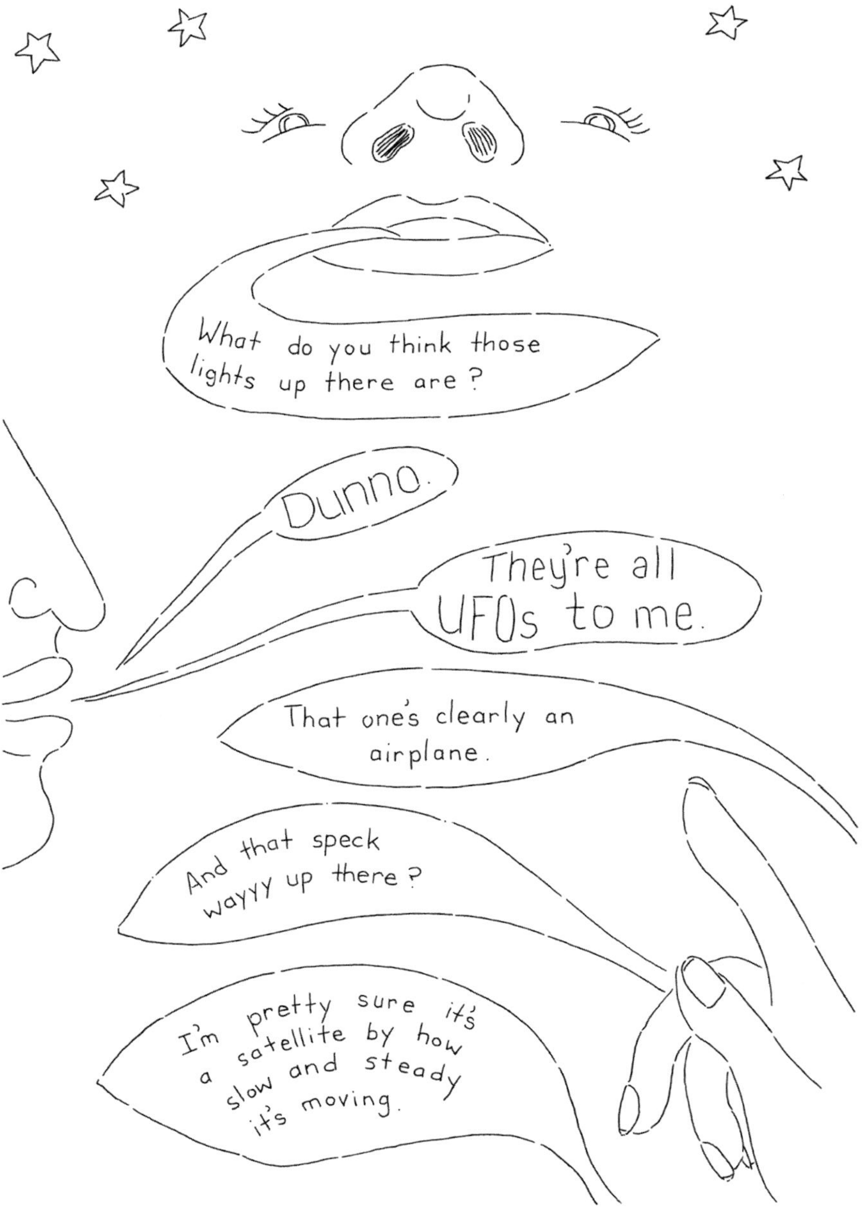
What do you think those lights up there are?
Dunno.
They're all UFOs to me.
That one's clearly an airplane.
And that speck wayyy up there?
I'm pretty sure it's a satellite by how slow and steady it's moving.

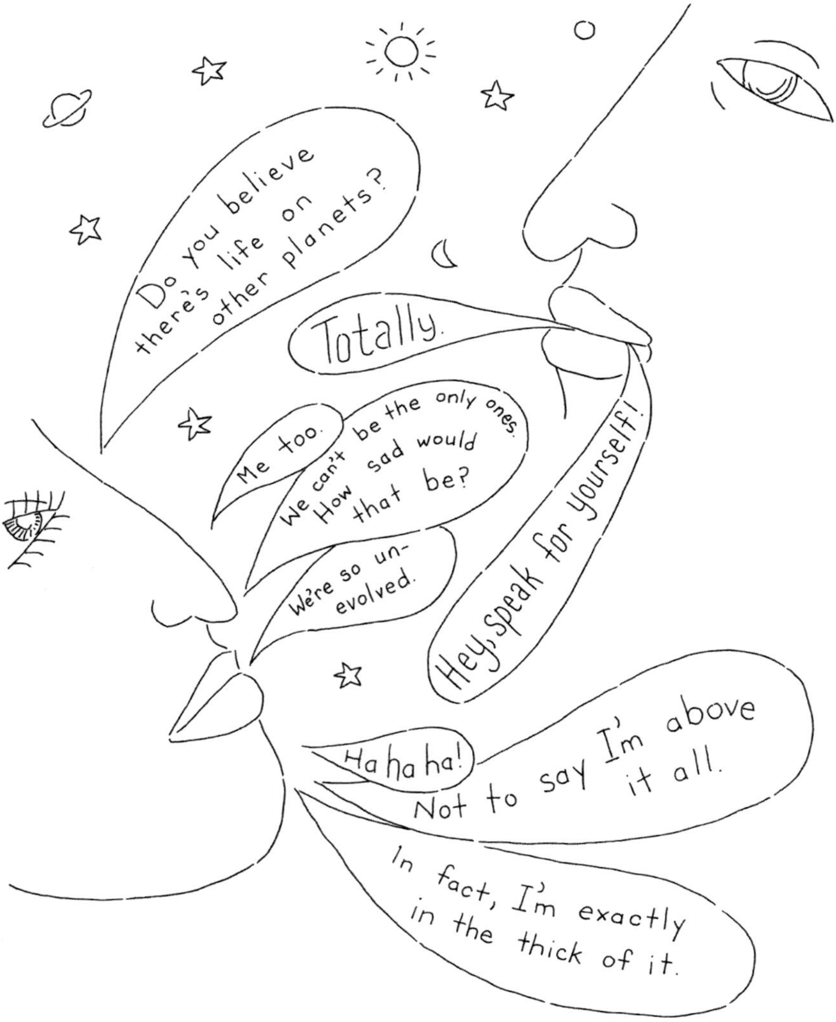
Do you believe there's life on other planets?
Totally.
Me too.
We can't be the only ones. How sad would that be?
We're so un-evolved.
Hey, speak for yourself!
Ha ha ha!
Not to say I'm above it all.
In fact, I'm exactly in the thick of it.

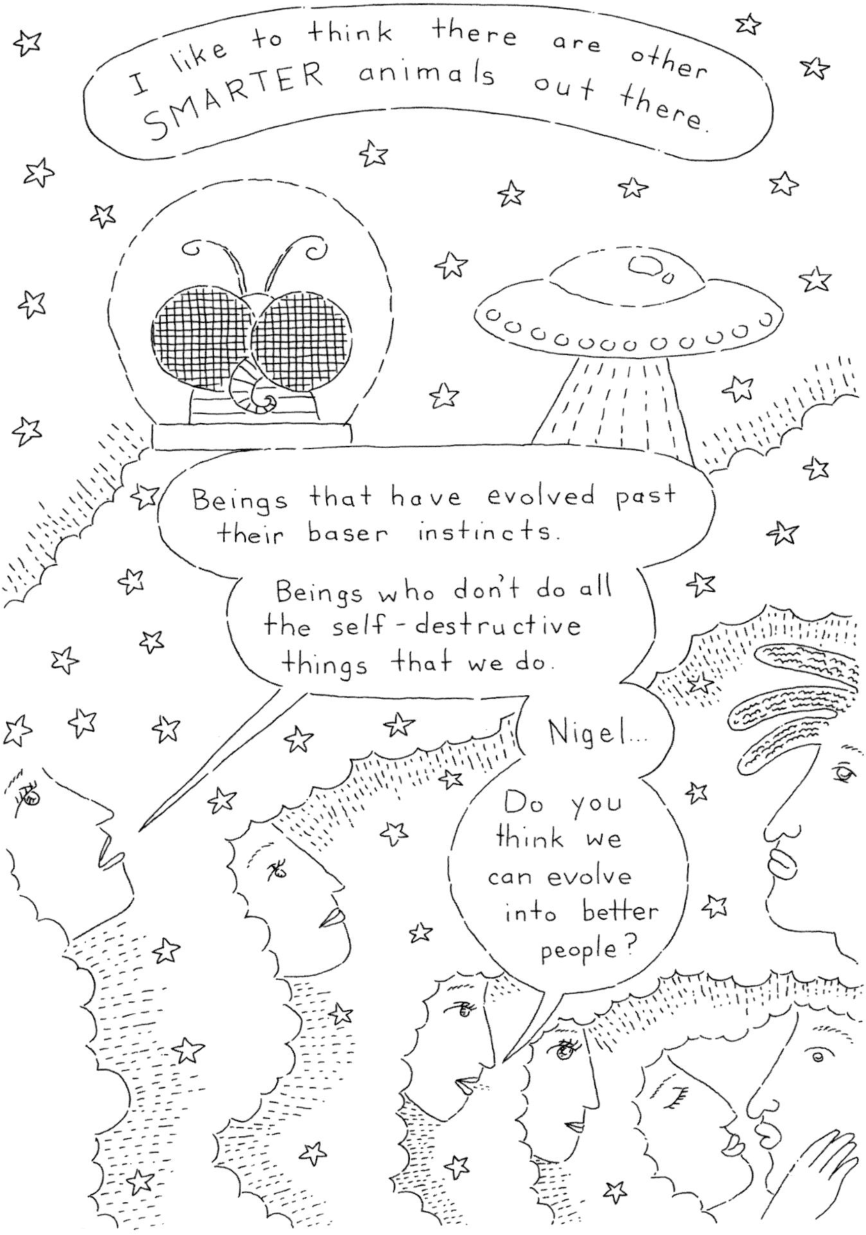
I like to think there are other SMARTER animals out there.
Beings that have evolved past their baser instincts.
Beings who don't do all the self-destructive things that we do.
Nigel...
Do you think we can evolve into better people?

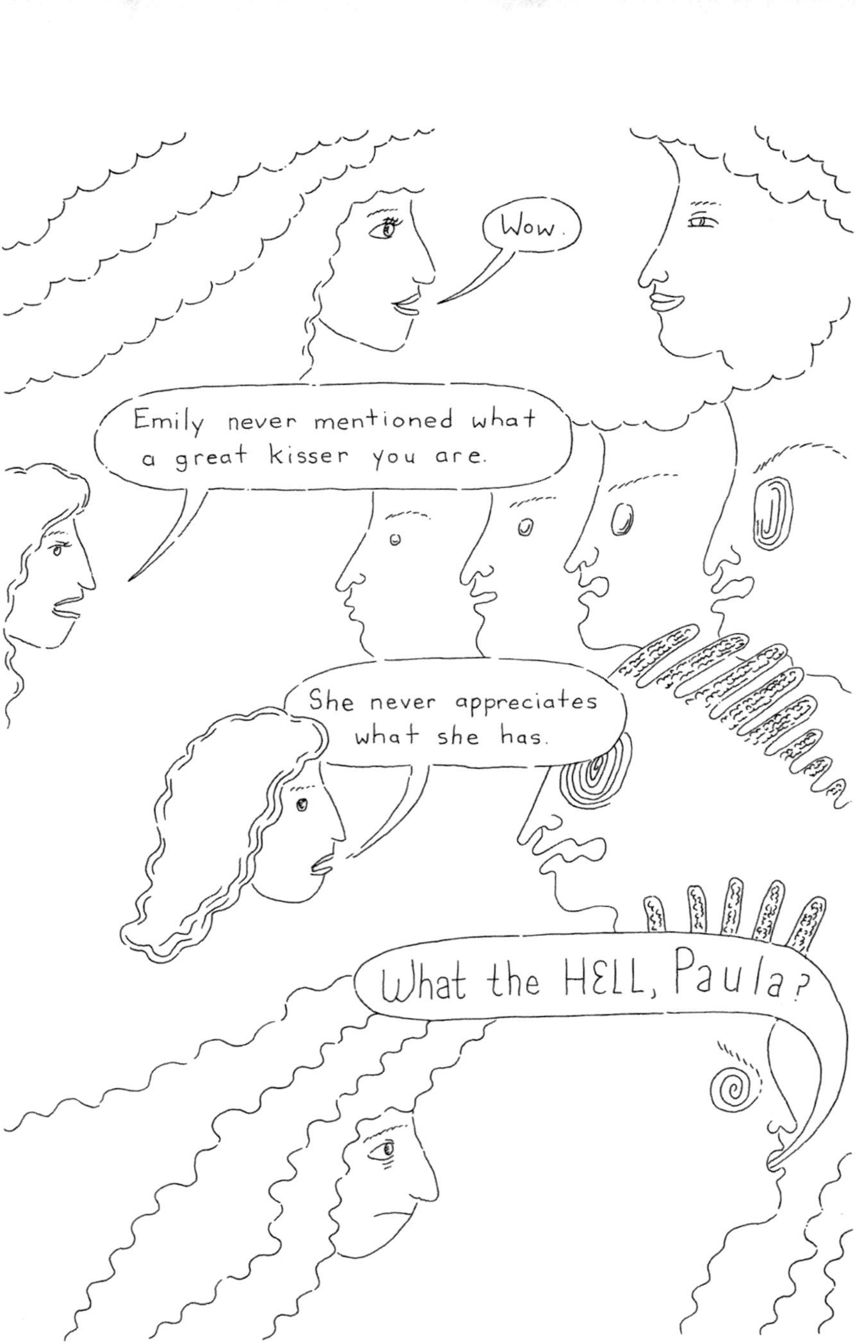
Wow.
Emily never mentioned what a great kisser you are.
She never appreciates what she has.
What the HELL, Paula?

PART FIVE

Nigel Jones

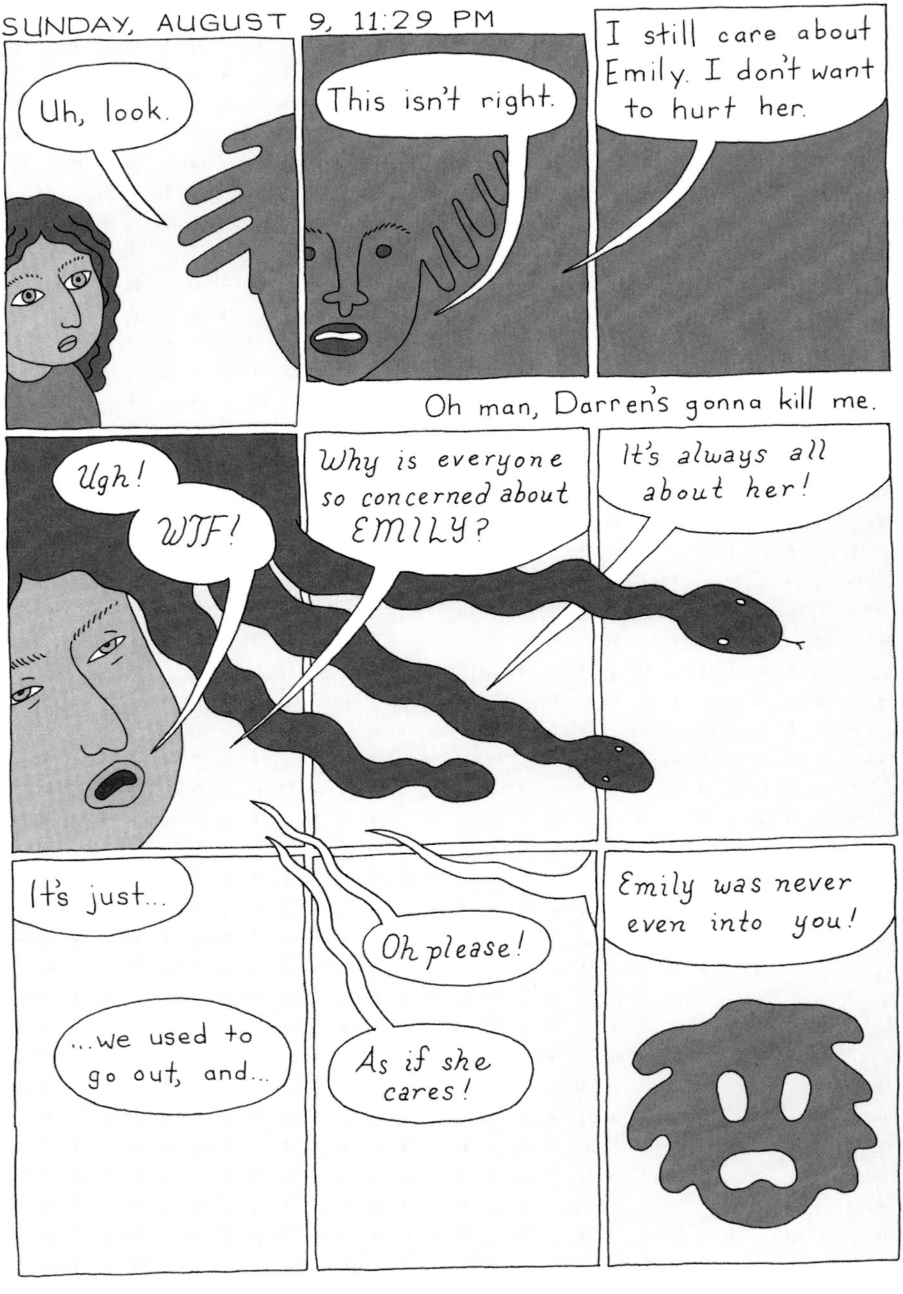
SUNDAY, AUGUST 9, 11:29 PM
Uh, look.
This isn't right.
I still care about Emily. I don't want to hurt her.
Oh man, Darren's gonna kill me.
Ugh!
WTF!
Why is everyone so concerned about EMILY?
It's always all about her!
It's just...
...we used to go out, and...
Oh please!
As if she cares!
Emily was never even into you!

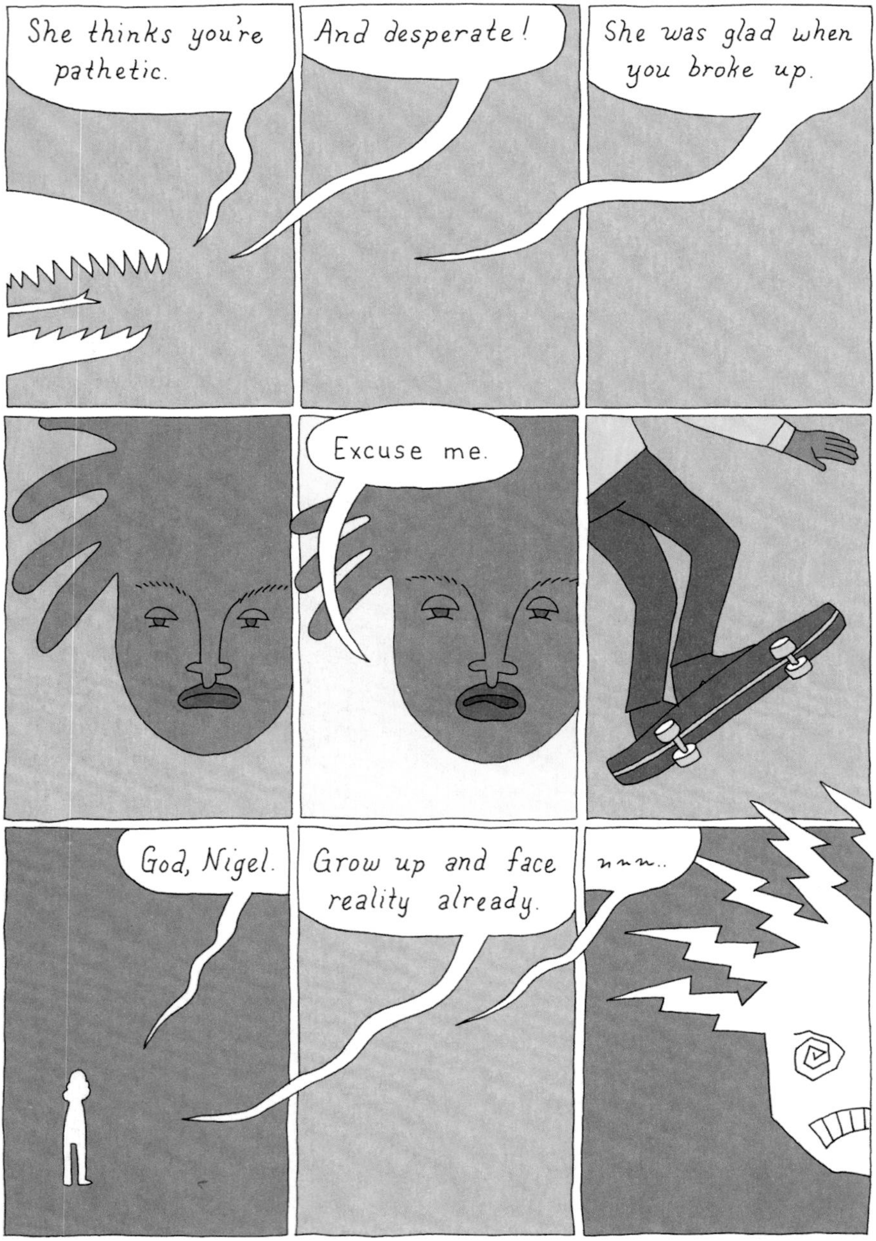
She thinks you're pathetic.
And desperate!
She was glad when you broke up.
Excuse me.
God, Nigel.
Grow up and face reality already.
nnn..

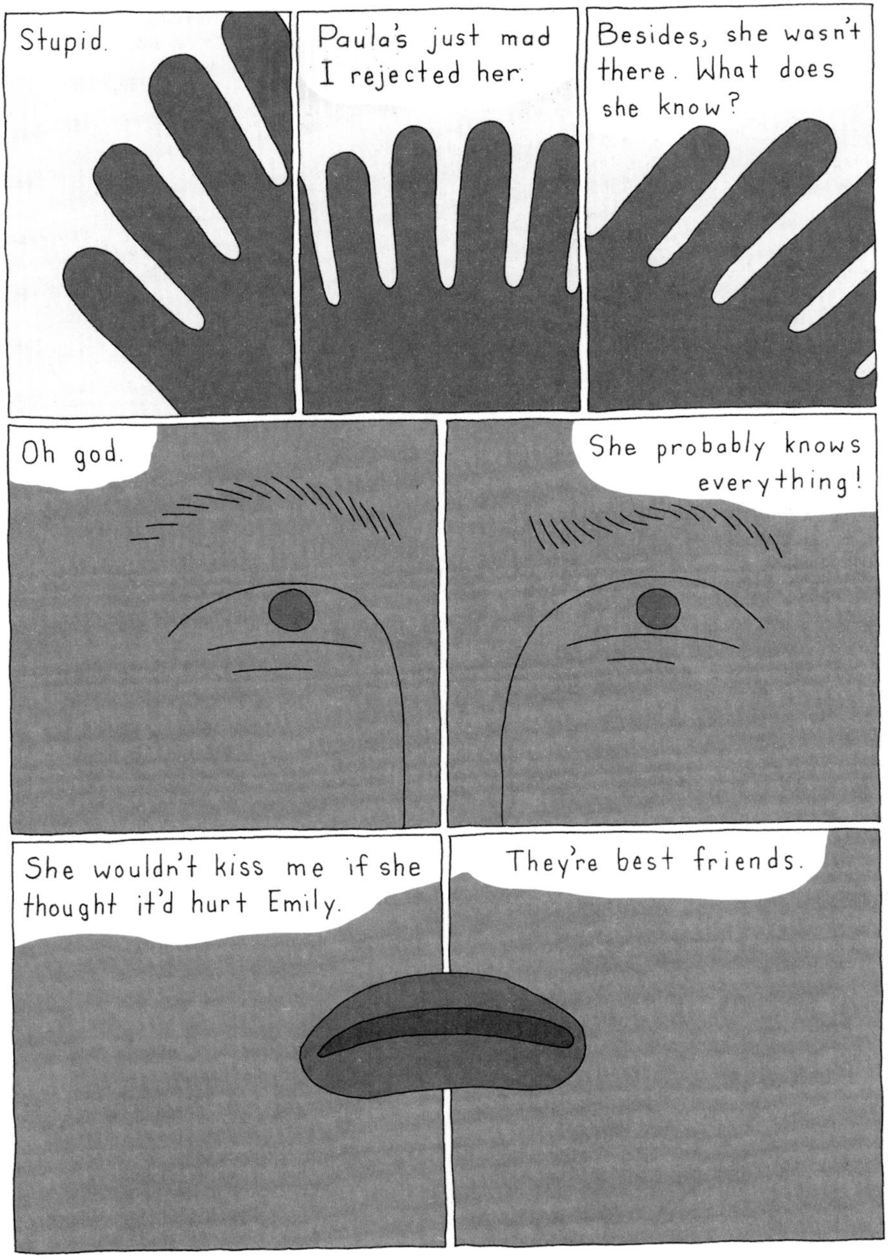
Stupid.
Paula's just mad I rejected her.
Besides, she wasn't there. What does she know?
Oh god.
She probably knows everything!
She wouldn't kiss me if she thought it'd hurt Emily.
They're best friends.

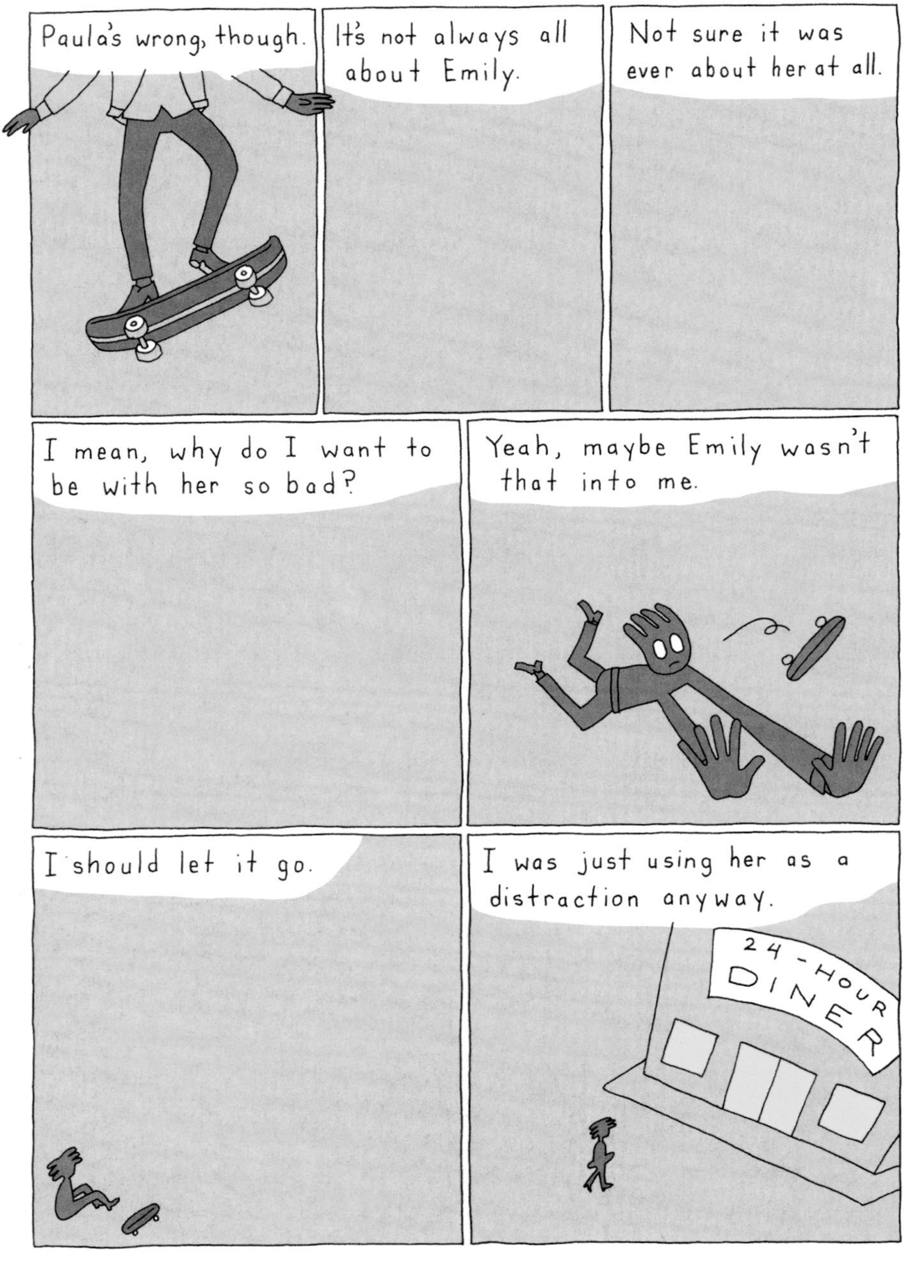

Paula's wrong, though.
It's not always all about Emily.
Not sure it was ever about her at all.
I mean, why do I want to be with her so bad?
Yeah, maybe Emily wasn't that into me.
I should let it go.
I was just using her as a distraction anyway.
24-HOUR DINER

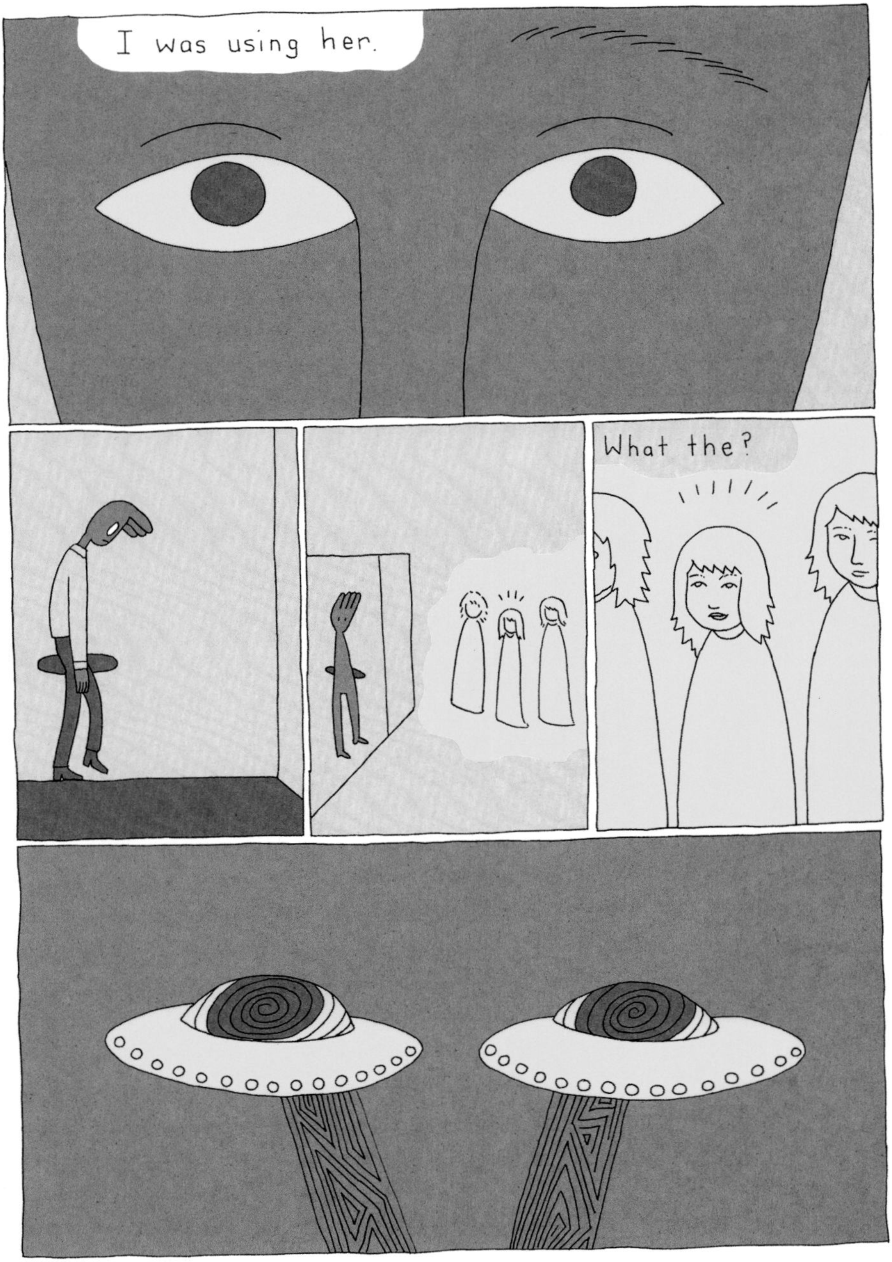
I was using her.
What the?

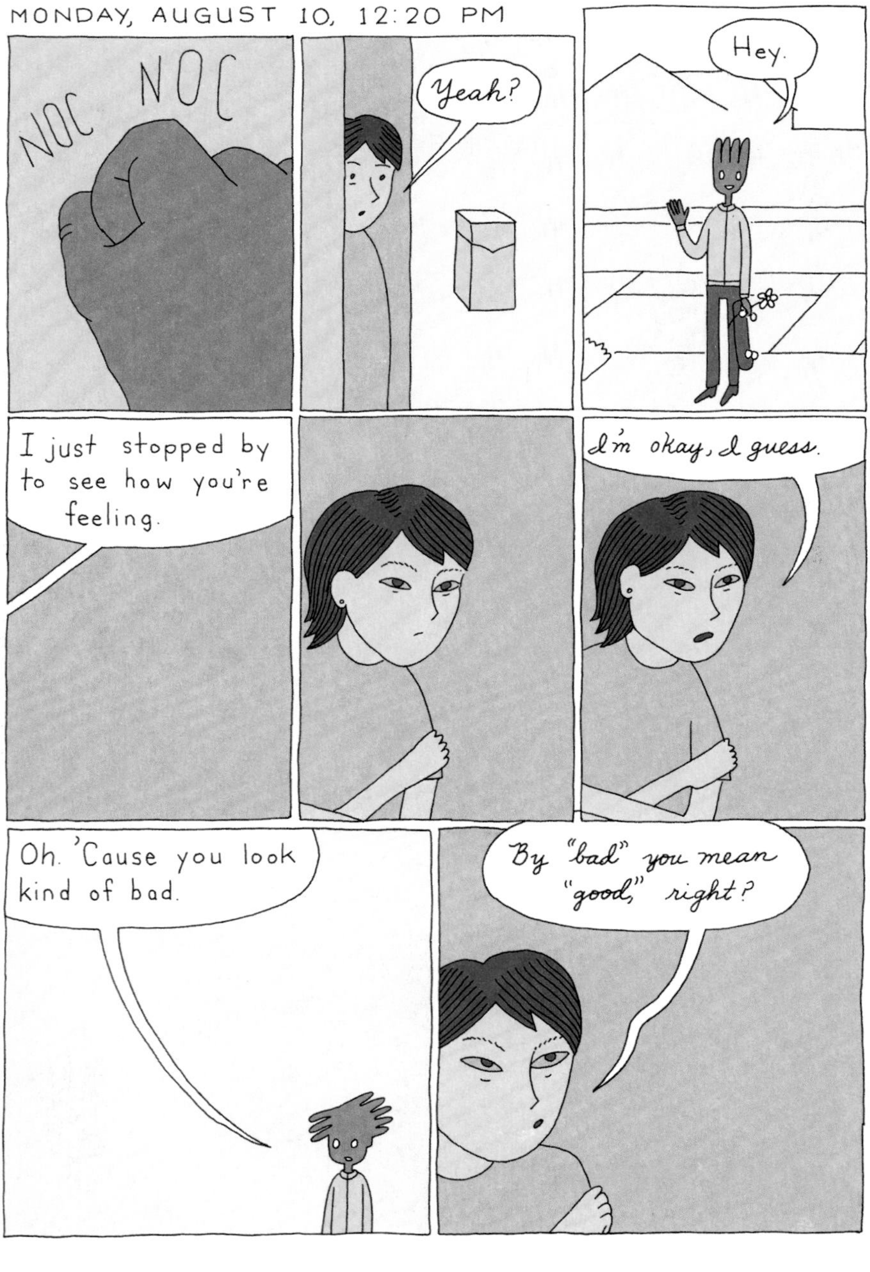
MONDAY, AUGUST 10, 12:20 PM
NOC NOC
Yeah?
Hey.
I just stopped by to see how you're feeling.
I'm okay, I guess.
Oh. 'Cause you look kind of bad.
By "bad" you mean "good," right?

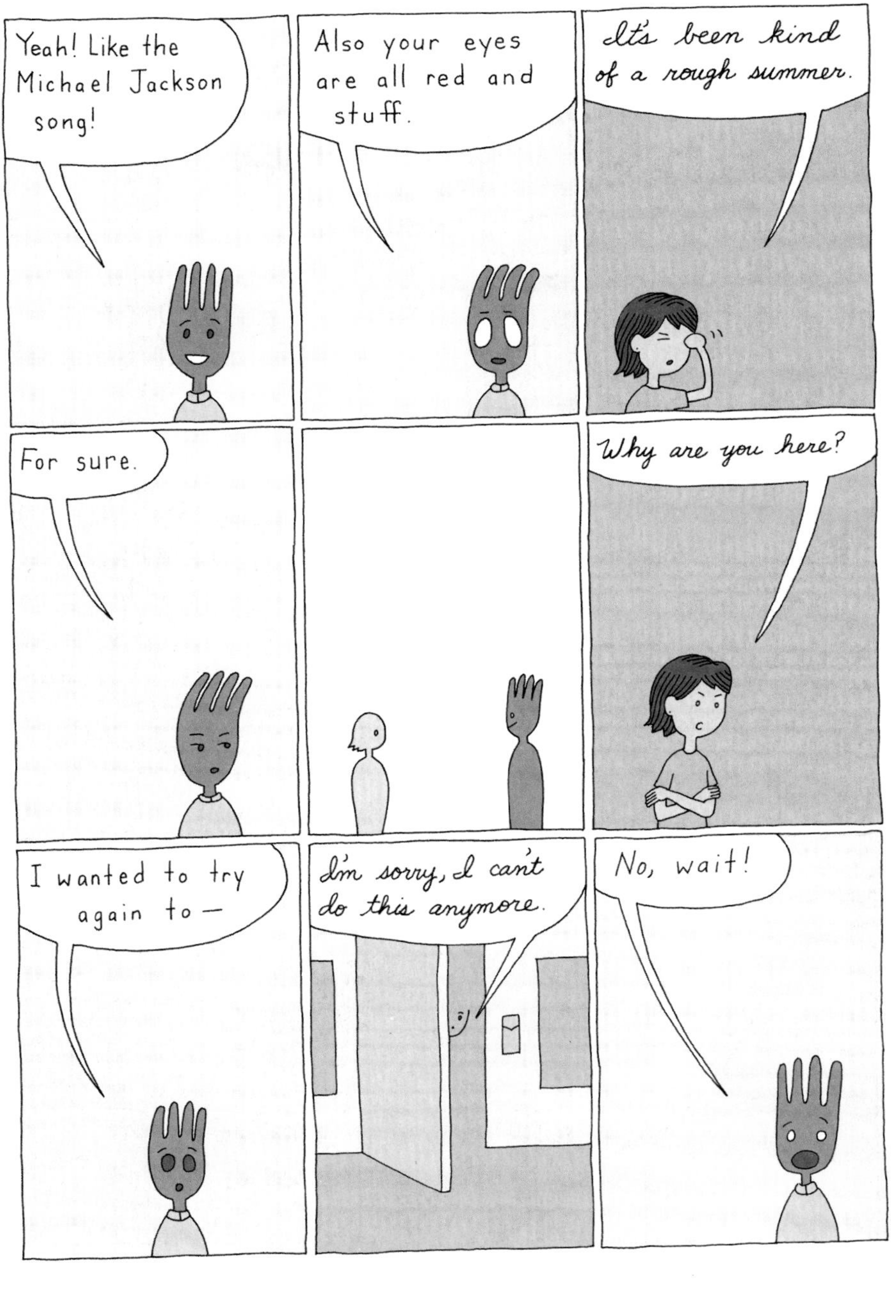
Yeah! Like the Michael Jackson song!
Also your eyes are all red and stuff.
It's been kind of a rough summer.
For sure.
Why are you here?
I wanted to try again to—
I'm sorry, I can't do this anymore.
No, wait!

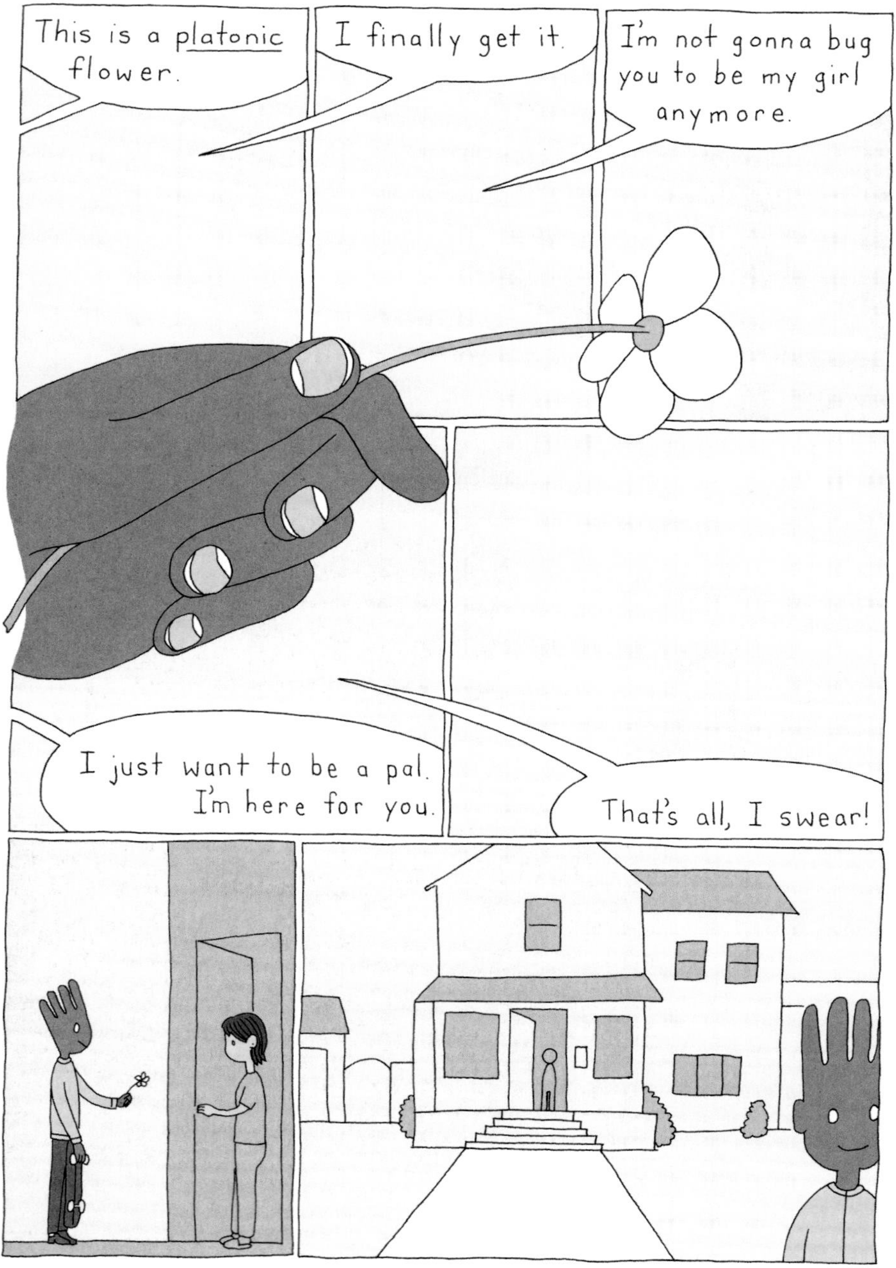
This is a platonic flower.
I finally get it.
I'm not gonna bug you to be my girl anymore.
I just want to be a pal. I'm here for you.
That's all, I swear!

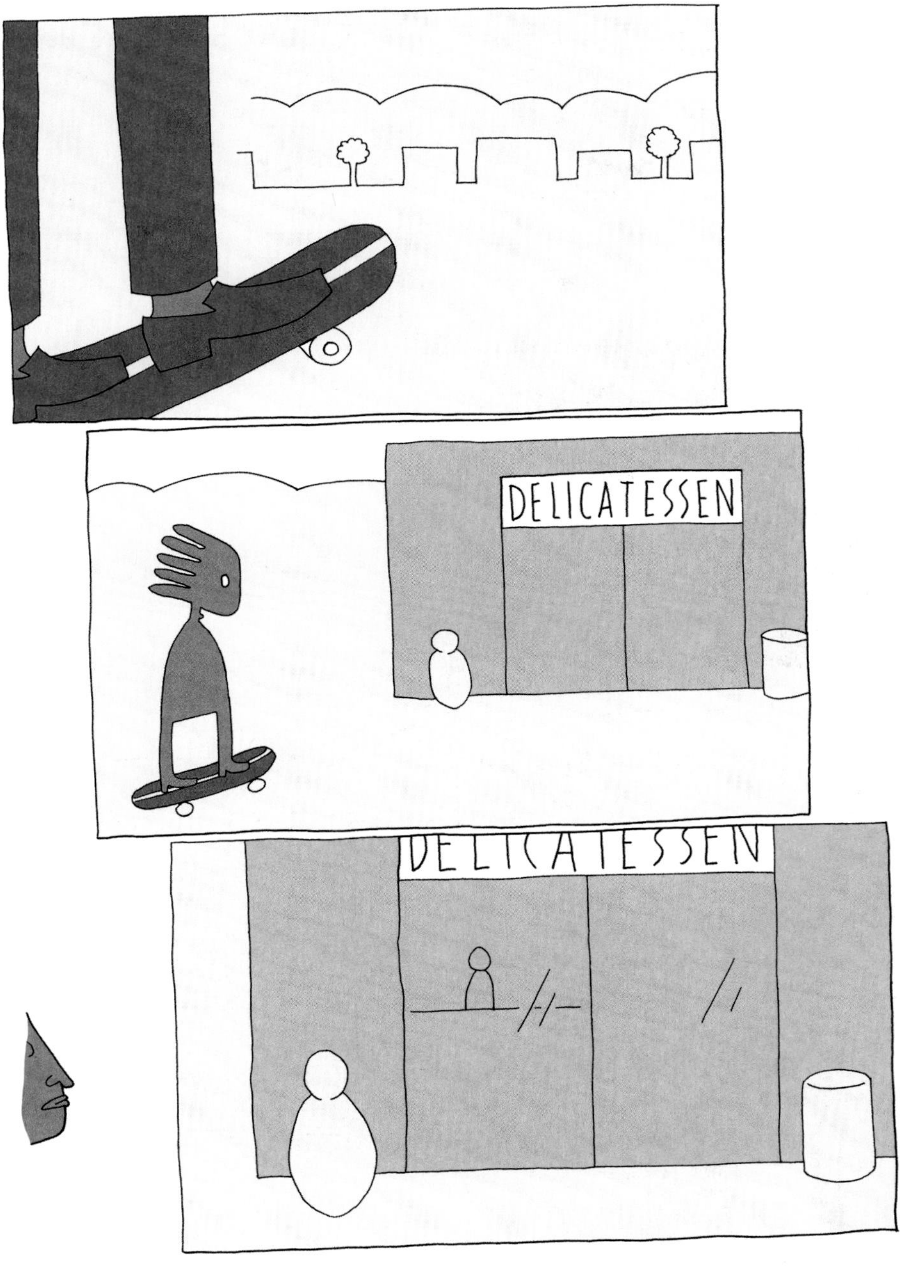
DELICATESSEN
DELICATESSEN

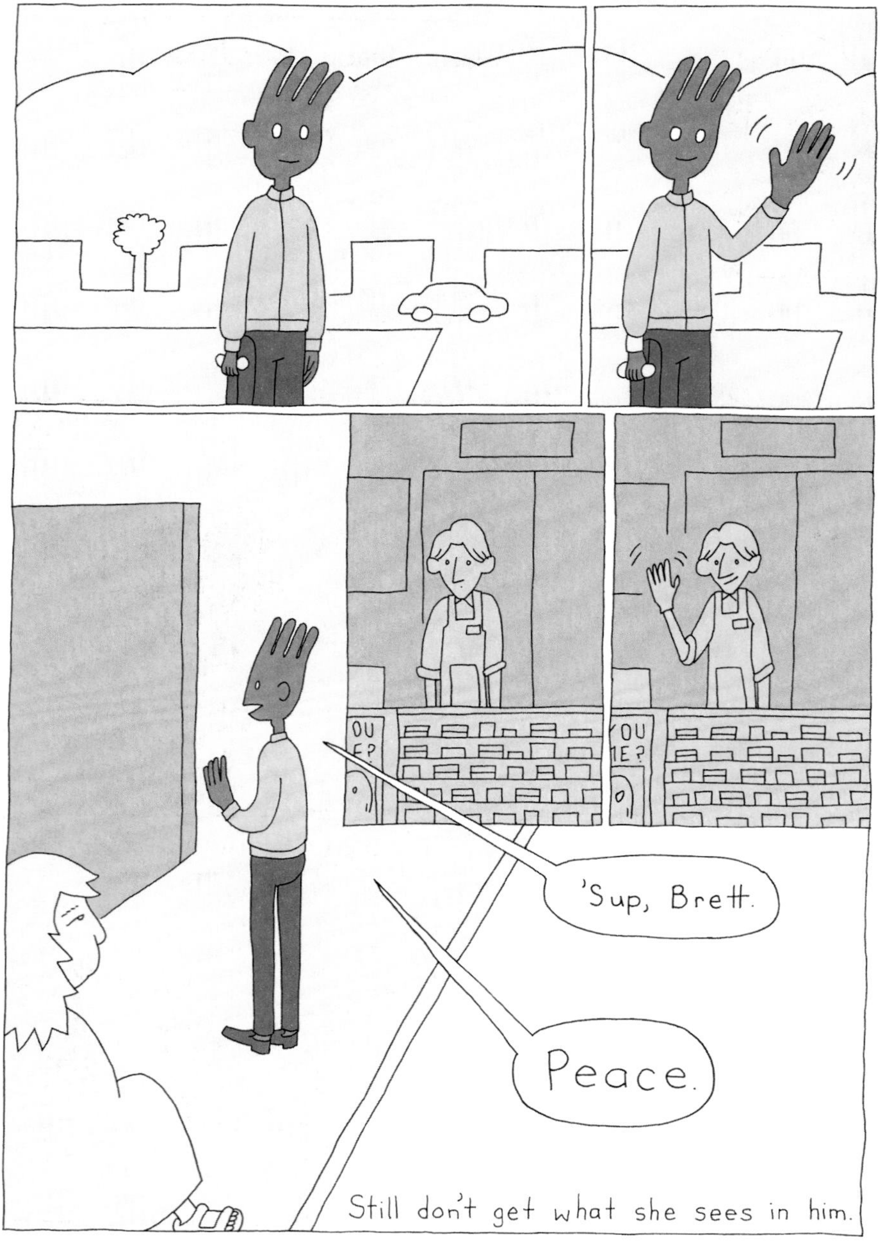

'Sup, Brett.
Peace.
Still don't get what she sees in him.

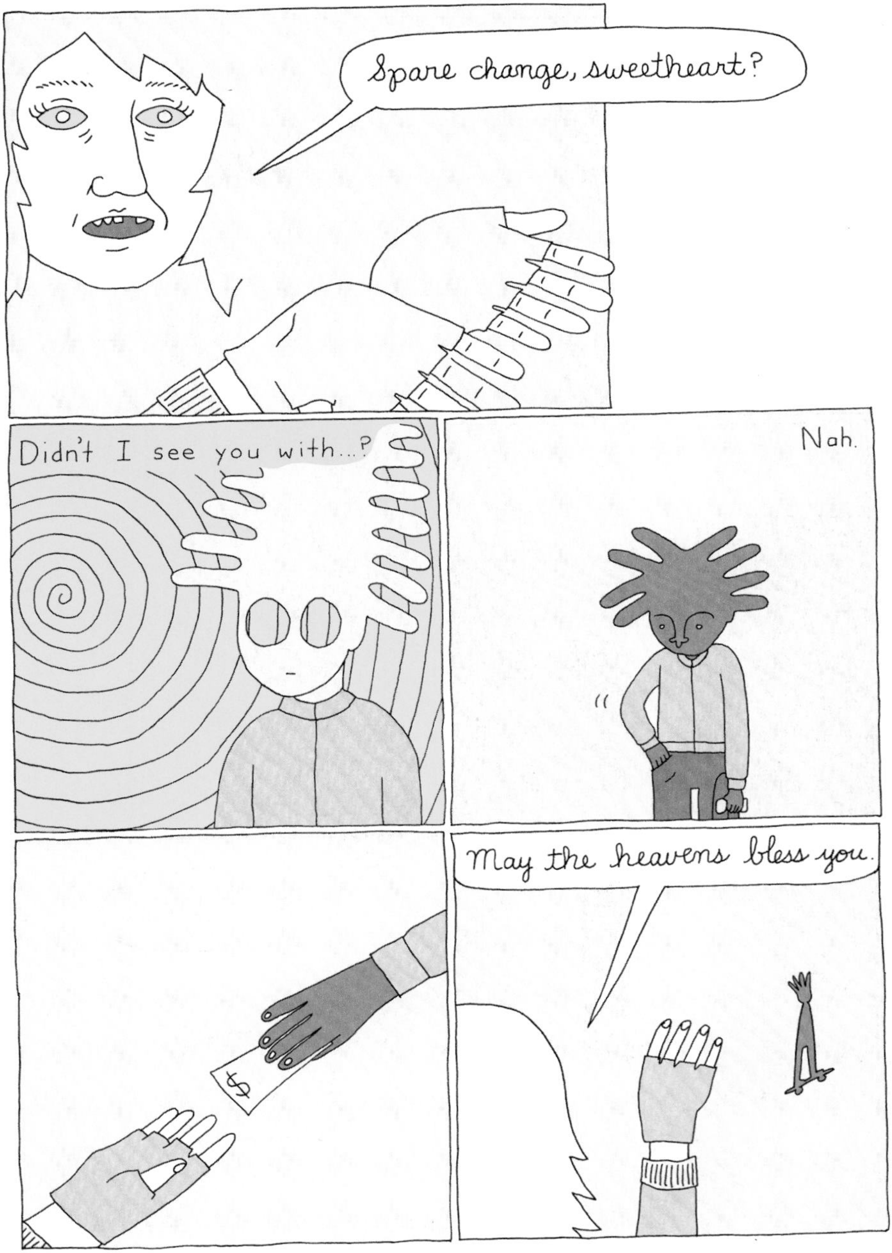
Spare change, sweetheart?
Didn't I see you with...?
Nah.
May the heavens bless you.

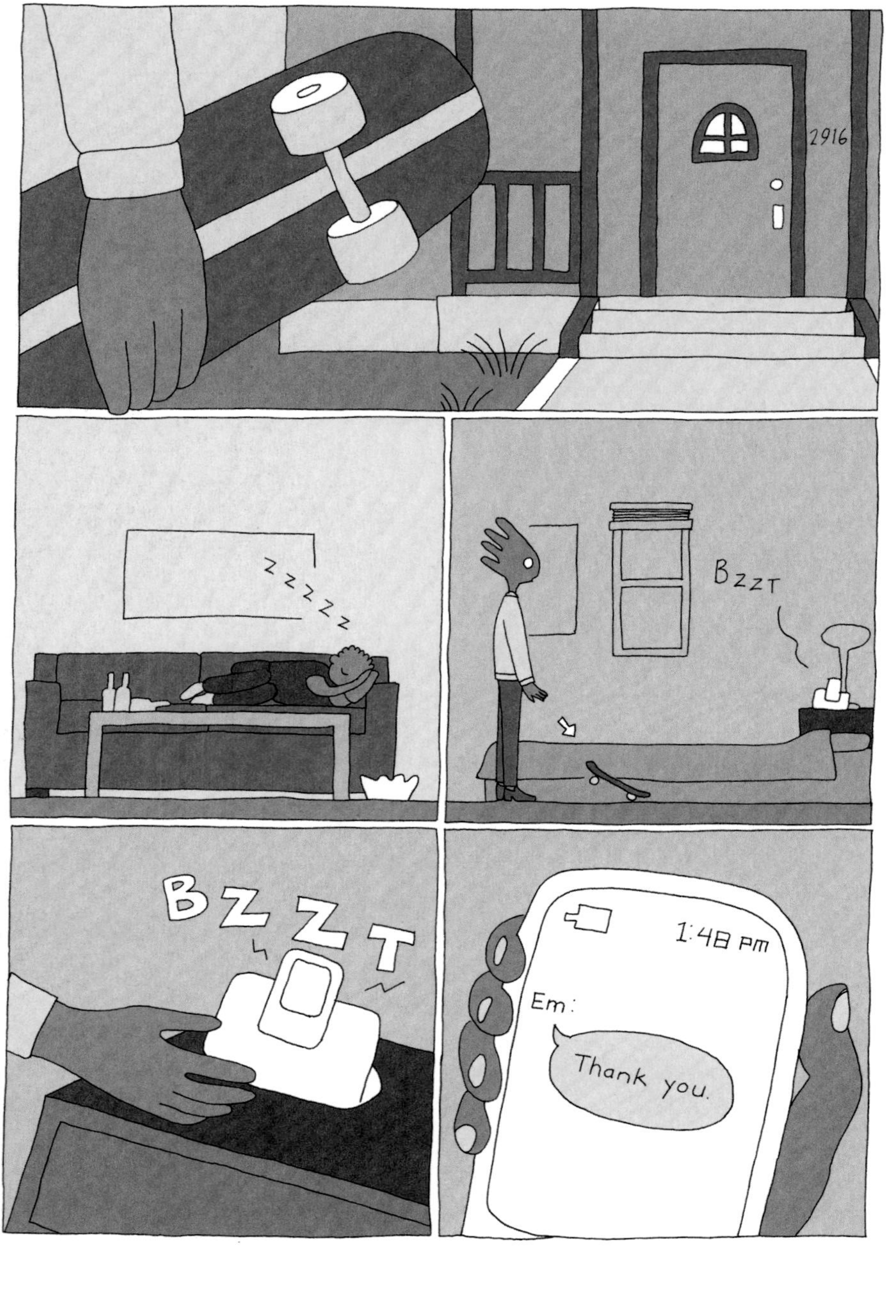
2916
ZZZZZZ
BZZT
BZZT
1:48 PM
Em:
Thank you.

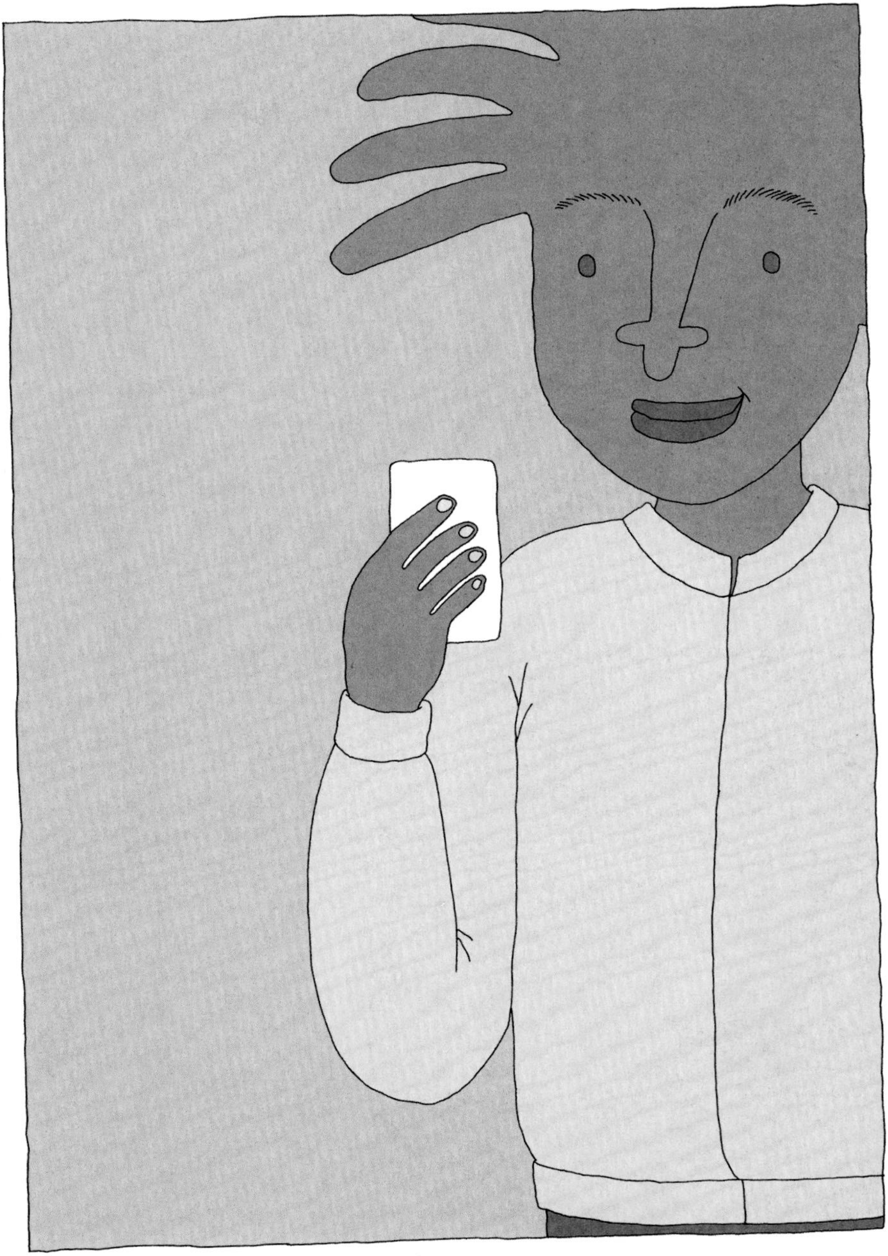

The end...
for now.

ACKNOWLEDGMENTS

Thank you so much to the folks responsible for making this book happen, especially my editor Greg Hunter, my agent Gordon Warnock, and cover designer Lindsey Owens. Big love to my literary and personal cheerleaders Fiona Taylor (whose lovely mountain abode housed me as I put the finishing touches on this book), Lisa Thomson, Rob Kirby, Tom Neely, Craig Thompson, Amelie Sukiennik, Lainie Baker, and Christopher Pappalardo. Thanks to my writing and drawing mates for keeping me from going crazy during my long work days, particularly Yumi Sakugawa, Nicky Sa-Eun Schildkraut, Steph Cha, Amelia Gray, Hope Larson, and Jen Wang. Shout out to my online family, especially the Olds, Her-Moans, and WoC. Most of all, big thanks for the support of my real-life family: Mom and Dad, Sabrina and Greg, Sue Lake, and most of all Gary and the menagerie. I love you all.

ABOUT THE AUTHOR

MariNaomi is the award-winning author and illustrator of four comics memoirs. *Losing the Girl* is her first graphic novel and her first foray into fiction that (possibly) involves alien life-forms. She's also the creator of the Cartoonists of Color and Queer Cartoonists databases. She lives in California with her husband and many cats and dogs. Visit her at marinaomi.com or @marinaomi.

LIFE ON EARTH • BOOK 2

COMING IN 2019

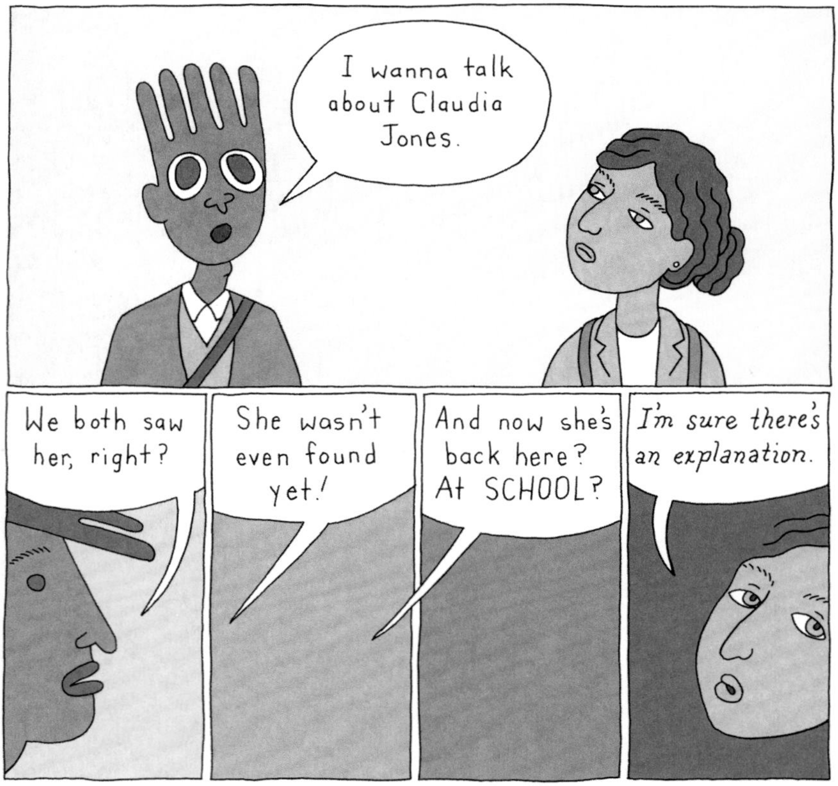

I wanna talk about Claudia Jones.
We both saw her, right?
She wasn't even found yet!
And now she's back here? At SCHOOL?
I'm sure there's an explanation.